MASINISSA: ALLY OF ROME

D1419985

ROB EDMUNDS

Whilst some of the characters in this story were real and influential, and some of the events described are documented, this is a work of fiction drawn from historical sources.

Matador
9 Priory Business Park,
Wistow Road, Kibworth Beauchamp,
Leicestershire. LE8 0RX
Tel: 0116 279 2299
Email: books@troubador.co.uk
Web: www.troubador.co.uk/matador
Twitter: @matadorbooks

ISBN 978 1838594 275

British Library Cataloguing in Publication Data.
A catalogue record for this book is available from the British Library.

Printed and bound in the UK by TJ International, Padstow, Cornwall
Typeset in 11pt Adobe Jenson Pro by Troubador Publishing Ltd, Leicester, UK

Matador is an imprint of Troubador Publishing Ltd

FSC
www.fsc.org
MIX
Paper from responsible sources
FSC® C013056

For the A's

CONTENTS

Historical Context vii

If This is a Man 1
Hercules! Hercules! 18
Returning to Sophonisba 41
Our Elderly Children 56
Teenage Wasteland 72
When an Itch Becomes a Bitch 91
Washed Away 101
Firestarter 122
Finding Their Way Home 146
Pardon and Punish 172
Zama Time 193
The Lies We Tell Ourselves 218

HISTORICAL CONTEXT

Masinissa, the heir to the Numidian kingdom of Massyli, has been fighting as a cavalry commander on the Iberian Peninsula in the service of the Carthaginian Empire for several years. His love for the Carthaginian aristocrat Sophonisba, which had blossomed during his period of exile in Carthage, has remained strong during his absence from North Africa. He is due a period of leave in that city shortly to formalise his engagement to her, as well as to further consolidate his alliance with that empire.

In terms of the present state of the war between Rome and Carthage, the initial Carthaginian successes against the Roman legions have been largely reversed with the arrival in Iberia of the Roman proconsul Publius Cornelius Scipio who has deployed his legions innovatively and successfully. In one of the recent battles, Scipio captured Masinissa's nephew Massiva but the two commanders arranged a clandestine meeting to exchange prisoners, including Massiva. During the exchange, Masinissa and Scipio formed an extremely favourable impression of one another, leading Masinissa to begin to reconsider his present alliance which was already starting to fray with the demoralising strategic picture for the Carthaginian armies.

At this moment in the war, the Carthaginian forces are attempting to reform their military strength in North Africa and in the strategically important and historically allied southern Iberian city of Gades (present day Cadiz.) Hasdrubal Gisco, one of the senior Carthaginian generals and father of Sophonisba, has assigned Masinissa the diversionary task of roaming the hinterland of Iberia with a guerrilla force, mostly composed of Numidian cavalry. During one such action against the Roman occupied fortress of Xativa, a small band led by Masinissa had infiltrated the fortress and retrieved one of the sacred cups of Melqart (Hercules) which had been hidden there. The recovery of the cup is regarded as a significant boost for the morale of the Carthaginian forces, who revere Melqart as one of the senior Phoenician gods. It is also considered to be an appeasement of the god, which may help solicit some form of celestial intervention to reverse the Carthaginian's current battlefield predicament. Masinissa is presently taking a small contingent of his most loyal troops to the temple dedicated to Melqart which is located close to the city of Gades to return the cup to its proper religious location.

IF THIS IS A MAN

Ari looked at Masinissa, a question starting to take shape in his gaze. His tongue was also conspicuously pushing upwards into and around one of his upper canines, giving Masinissa a clear indication that an inquiry of some kind was imminent. The detachment of Numidian cavalry they were leading had been riding for most of the morning and planned to go a little longer before they found a shady glade somewhere in which to pass the hottest part of the day. Maybe they'd take a splash in the Baetis River, which was weaving its serene way nearby for large sections of their journey and whose next intersection wouldn't be too far ahead.

Masinissa, in the novel and temporary position of being the senior commander of the regiments allied to Carthage in Iberia, had made the decision to suspend his guerrilla harassments of the Roman legions and take almost a hundred of his men with him south to Gades and thence to the nearby Temple of Melqart. It was a journey many, if not all, in the party regarded as a sacred obligation as they had in their possession an ancient chalice with depictions of several of the labours of Melqart represented on it. They had recently retrieved the relic from a raid on the Roman occupied citadel of Xativa, which once, years earlier in the war, had been the residence of Hannibal and his wife. It had been consecrated to the Phoenician god and it was imperative that they returned the relic to its place of origin, to both appease the great lord of Tyre as well as propitiate both Him and his priests who were waiting eagerly for its return home. He had entrusted his senior military deputies, his *optio* and *tesserarius* with the bulk of the cavalry in the knowledge that their control of the forces remaining in the Iberian hinterland would be absolute.

He had indulged a little personal preference in the choice of the men he took with him. Naturally, Capuca and Ari, who had both played important roles in their clandestine infiltration of the fortress to rescue the cup, had earned the right to come and would not be rebuffed. His occasionally errant nephew Massiva had to be in the cohort too, as Masinissa would rarely any longer let the impetuous boy leave his side for too long. His other most trusted compatriots Juba Tunic, Soldier Boy and Micipsa also accompanied them. The seven of them formed the vanguard of the group. The Carthaginian officer Hanno, who had been with them on their earlier attack of the Roman fortress, had been recalled by the senior Carthaginian general Hasdrubal Gisco, and he had headed towards Mons Calpe, presumably from there to take a trireme or other galley across the straits back to North Africa.

Of Masinissa's companions, Ari had proven much the most curious and conversational during the journey. It was quite apparent that he keenly felt the honour in the mission in the erectness and solemnity of his bearing whenever he was near to or carrying the cup himself. He was also quite inquisitive to know Masinissa's views and intentions and the question that had been percolating in his head for the last few moments finally bubbled its way into the still fresh morning air. "This is no mundane errand we're making here, is it, sire? Returning the cup to the temple will bring us great favour and blessings from Melqart, more than 1,000 sacrifices and 1 million prayers would achieve, but there is more, isn't there?" He paused and looked at Masinissa with a more questioning gaze, "Do you seek a vision like Hannibal did when he made a pilgrimage there?"

Masinissa was a little surprised by the directness of the enquiry, but he knew Ari had a quiet insight into his nature that others – except for some of the wise, old lags he'd left behind – lacked, and he readily had made Ari his confidant on horseback and in the inn, although discussions in the latter tended to unravel as they both surrendered their lucidity to the wine.

"I'm not sure, I do to an extent, everyone probably would I suppose, we all want something or someone to point us towards the right way to go, but I'm hoping for something more restorative and spiritual I think" Masinissa responded. "This war has stripped me of many of my convictions. My certainties are not as certain as they were. It's like my soul has slipped its anchor. I'm drifting, Ari." He looked at his Libyan adjutant a little imploringly as if the boy had spiritual and moral certitudes to offer and console him with. When none were forthcoming, he added with a forlorn shrug "I, we, just seem to be dancing to the tune of the Carthaginian war machine, day after day, battle after battle. I feel numb. All this killing is stupefying me. I feel like a revenant between the worlds of the living and dead."

Ari merely nodded, perhaps at a loss about how to respond to his commander's despair. Masinissa was grateful for the mute discretion, sensing that Ari, perhaps subconsciously, was offering him a sounding board. The young Libyan was a good listener, and had often allowed Masinissa to nourish and shape his own thoughts into words and sometimes actions.

Shaping them again, Masinissa continued. "I'm getting far too much of this senseless, violent world. Before I started campaigning, when I had time for learning and leisure, I used to be able to project out from myself and understand the world from my own perspective, fit it all in place in ways that conformed with my perception of everything. These days, I can't make any sense of things. I really need a break from it all to try to fix myself a little, and this visit to the temple of Melqart might help. I really hope it will." He paused, thinking a little of his time with his tutors during his adolescent exile in Carthage. He recalled a dusty, ontological conversation he'd had with one of the eastern scholars who he had occasionally been instructed by and shared it with the attentive Ari. "A lot of the Greeks, and other philosophers, will tell you that there's no reality except the one contained within you, and it's a notion that I'm trying to hold onto to keep me sane. I'm still sane, right?" Masinissa quizzed Ari, trying to lighten the tone of the conversation a little.

"Of course, sire," Ari reassured him. "You don't realise how much of an example for us you are. We all have to block this out the best we can, and you have a strength, a moral and spiritual strength, which we all can see. You cope with everything that's thrown at you and that helps us do the same."

"Thanks!" Masinissa replied, with genuine and effusive gratitude. "You know, I was thinking of Metellus earlier, you know that depraved and dissolute Roman legionnaire we encountered at the citadel, and how easy it is to become degraded. So many of the people who have to live the way we do start to degenerate and become corrupted by what they are compelled to see and do. You can forget the man you are, the people you knew and your family. All this violence and destruction stains you. The blood on your hands can also get into your inner being, and your soul can drown in it."

"You know the trick I have," Ari interjected, as he sensed Masinissa was struggling in his explanation, "is to sort of follow that scholarly Greek advice you mentioned but work that inner world like an artist might. I revisit and recreate my memories of better times, often when we're riding like now, patch them up as they fade to keep them close and real. I always remind myself that these things that I am forced to do to survive and keep my brothers alive is not my reality. My reality is the world I have made inside myself, out of the better parts of me: the guidance I had as a child from my precious mother and father, the affections I was shown and the beliefs I have in the gods, in Tanit and Melqart especially. They are not outside me – well, not in ways that I can see – but they are there in my soul."

Masinissa nodded; adversity can be a natural consort to wisdom, and his young friend was an example of that truth. He acknowledged his young confederate's wisdom with a bow and his own condensation of the sentiment. "Yeah, always keep listening to that inner voice, or voices perhaps. Your people are still talking to you. Always find that stillness to hear and remember yourself." He pumped his fist with the renewed strength and conviction his companion's advice had given him.

"Come to terms with destruction too, accept it," Ari digressed. "That's important as well I think. Not destruction in the wanton, evil sense, if you do that you're damned, but in the sense that there may be a something worthwhile to come at the end of all this. Something grander can emerge. Wars do salvage some things, and people can learn. Have some faith in that too. Think of an egg, sire. For the bird to be born, it must destroy its own world. Life is full of those transitions and rebirths."

"I'm not sure about the necessity for destruction, but transitions – yeah, I get that. Maybe that's what I'm looking for." Masinissa pondered, "Rebirth, peace and strength. Let's see what the house of Melqart gives to us."

Ari exhaled dramatically and gave a theatrical nod of agreement.

The riders close by who had heard the conversation were quiet. Soldier Boy, Juba Tunic and Capuca had though been noticeably paying attention, letting the other two express thoughts they, no doubt, broadly shared. They were all strung out and exhausted, and perhaps felt a little less helpless on hearing others articulate similar feelings.

Only Juba Tunic made a comment as he rode up briefly. As his horse nuzzled into Masinissa's mare, Juba leant too, offered a soft pat to Masinissa's broad back and pointed to the sky. "Clouds part," was all he said.

Masinissa gave him a gentle, appreciative smile and returned the pat. Their foray into emotional and intangible territory had made him a little reflective, and he, following Ari's counsel, rode over the remaining gentle slopes towards the river quietly and thought of his other life, contemplating Sophonisba the Carthaginian noblewoman he loved, most of all.

The sun rose higher in the firmament and began to roast them. Both Masinissa and his horse began to sweat, and his thirst grew keener. The others were frequently getting their rags out and drying their necks. Masinissa's wineskin still showed a modest bulge, but his water was all but gone. He'd been a little profligate with it and had showered himself a little liberally earlier. The river was close, though, so there was no harm in it. He saw its first inviting and slightly dazzling shimmer as he reached the summit of the last hill and cried out to the other riders to indicate its proximity.

Relief showed all the way down the column of riders. Even though most of them were North Africans of various clans, the heat of an Iberian midday was best avoided. The men had become accustomed to raids at dawn or even in the darkest part of the night, as had been the case with the recent rescue of Melqart's chalice, and a shady hour by some cool water was a welcome prospect. There was a closer tributary, but it was ignored. As they descended the incline and drew close to the wide, serene river, Masinissa felt a sense of calm at the gently moving water.

His sense of tranquillity was ended however when he saw the state of some of the occupants of a small galley tethered to the shoreline, the only sign of humanity evident along the river's broad banks. A *liburna* of that type was quite a rare sight to Masinissa. He had become used to the desiccated mountains, and the sporadic times he'd spend on ships had mostly been on larger triremes or quinqueremes, most notably crossing between the pillars of Melqart from Mauretania to the Iberian Peninsula. The presence of a Carthaginian naval vessel at this point along the river should have heartened him, and, at first glance, it did present a reassuring picture. However, as he began to gain a clearer impression of the deck of the vessel, a sense of revulsion rose in his throat.

He had heard a lot of stories of the conduct of certain elements within the Carthaginian army. His renown as someone who had a high regard for humane treatment of prisoners meant that he saw abuses of prisoners rarely. His own soldiers knew that any infraction would mean their punishments would be greater. To Masinissa, there was a distinction to be drawn between killing or enslaving an enemy, and degrading and maltreating them for sport or vengeance. There were ambiguous areas – not least below decks on galleys such as this one, where enslaved enemies would be worked ferociously, and the war only stretched the boundaries further – but there was a point at which the treatment of the enemy became vile and without any shred of humanity.

Cramped quarters were inevitable for a captured enemy, but the contorted, emaciated forms he saw on the deck of the *liburna* chilled his being. There were cages in which could be seen angles of flesh and bone that seemed to leave no room for air or breath. The bodies were so closely packed that he couldn't even begin to assess the number of wretches that were confined. If they had been poultry, they would have been treated more kindly. On surveying his own men, their furrowed brows and open mouths suggested that, for all their experiences that had inured them to the most extreme forms of violence, seeing men in such degrading conditions was still upsetting. Masinissa felt a tide of pity and anger rise in him.

"What evil is this?" he asked the air, almost beseeching the negligent heavens for some kind of explanation or, even better, some swift and merciful intercession from one of the gods who must surely share his revulsion at the scene before them.

In reply, and after a short pause for the rumbling echoes of Masinissa's outrage to subside, the quite mortal but reasonably well informed figure of Capuca said quietly, "I think I know what that is. I've heard about something the Carthaginians do that fits with what this looks like."

"Who within their command is authorising treating human beings in this grotesque way?" Masinissa asked, finding it difficult to conceal his rising indignation.

"It's their vengeance, Mas," Capuca replied. There was sorrow and reluctance in his voice, as if sharing his knowledge would be more painful than concealing it. "I don't know for sure how it came about, but most people whom I've heard talk about it say it was started by the Carthaginian general Mago, who was enraged at our losses and some of the actions that he heard the victorious Romans had done, especially to the middle ranks. You know how it goes; it's like the old sense of justice, with an eye for an eye – all that hateful stuff."

"So what does that have to do with those starving, twisted creatures down there?" asked Masinissa, realising quickly that there was an accusatory and aggressive tone in his question that wasn't fair to Capuca.

"It's Mago's twisted revenge, cuz. Those poor men in those cages were commanders under Publius Cornelius Scipio. Some may have served with his father or Gnaeus, but I doubt it. The life expectancy on the wrong side of that boat can't be very long. The common soldiers that we don't kill, we enslave or sometimes enlist have no value, and the most senior ones we have to kill, so Carthage's viciousness falls on these guys." He hesitated and looked hard at Masinissa. "It goes up the river and back down to Ilipa. The Carthaginians take their revenge on the Romans, and then they die or are just thrown overboard. It's sick. Most men who have heard of it are revolted, but those sailors are growing rich."

Masinissa took a moment to absorb what Capuca had told him, and then replied as solemnly as his informer, "Those men are still men, even if they are our enemies, and I am the senior commander of the army that abuses them in the field. I'm not going to have that on my reputation or my conscience. This ends now. Those men will be freed and fed."

"As you command," replied Capuca, and there were nods amongst many of the men he looked at.

Masinissa knew his men well enough to know they fought with honour, and that what they were witnessing on the Baetis would haunt them and needed to be purged. They rode down to the river and spread out along its banks. A hundred or so Numidian, Libyan and Balearic riders ought to have presented a formidable sight, particularly with a stern and agitated Masinissa at their head. The sailors, though, appeared to misunderstand the intentions of the approaching riders. One amongst them, who had been amusing himself by lashing an emaciated boy, seemed to scent a little custom, and grabbed the cowed and petrified adolescent by the hair, crossed the deck, and put one foot firmly on the gunwale of the vessel with the poor boy's head at the level of his raised knee.

Masinissa looked at the former centurion, but his downcast head only indicated his terror and submission. The man with a fistful of Roman hair in his grasp, who appeared to be the captain of the vessel for want of a better term, was evidently not the most perceptive and seemed oblivious to Masinissa's mood. Regarding the Numidian commander as a merchant regards an eager client, the sailor tilted the head of the boy upwards and introduced them both. "I am Balor, Your Excellency, and this is Lucius. I have many others like him, but you have surprised us and the toys are still in their boxes."

Masinissa's revulsion grew more intense at the dehumanising metaphor. The man's appearance added a further layer of distaste. He was as dissipated as a common man could get. His face was jowly and puffy, and his flaccidity extended to all other parts of him. His belly protruded awfully, and there was no hint of definition anywhere aside from a very deliberately manicured beard, which made a futile effort to give the man a jawline. His meticulousness in that part of his appearance may have been demonstrated by the clippers that he'd left splayed on a nearby rope. A final offence to Masinissa was the man's odour. He was rancid, and clearly had not washed himself or his garments in some time.

"I am not here to be entertained by you. You use an honorific so you must realise my senior position," snapped Masinissa.

"I know you not," Balor spat, his demeanour transformed from welcome host to offended-but-wary hostility.

"Well, let me introduce myself then. I am Masinissa of Numidia and I am in charge of the forces of Carthage on this side of the sea. You have the Barcids to the north and south, but right in the middle of it all you've got me… and I don't like what you're doing."

Masinissa could see in Balor's reaction that he knew of him and even recognised that, as far as the Iberian rivers he cruised along was concerned, this might be his temporary suzerain.

However, Balor had a personality that was not intimidated easily – he clearly was not defied by anyone on his barge – and it would take more than Masinissa's displeasure to dislodge him. Slaving makes many people grow to underestimate others, and Balor looked like he possessed a classic example of that trait. His reply was blunt. "I don't care if you don't like what I do. Your status is inferior to the lords who commissioned this vessel. I answer to Mago, Hasdrubal and even Gisco. Your opinion doesn't count, African."

Patience was a virtue that Masinissa esteemed, but, when confronted by a combination of insolence and evil, he was running out of it fast. "Well, last time I saw any of the Barcid clan they pretty much told me I had a blank slate as far as Iberia was concerned. Decorate it with as much blood as you can, they said. I'm sure they wouldn't care too much if I inconvenienced you along the way."

On being backed into a corner, Balor showed no sign of contrition or compromise, and continued his bluff, "I have immunity from the likes of you. What happens on this boat has the full sanction of the Barcids. What do you care, anyway? These are your enemies. They kill and enslave your brothers, the same as we do to them."

"You're right, and their circuses and bloody shows for the masses are full of our fallen, but I've yet to hear of a vessel such as yours weaving its way down the Tiber."

"You're a fool, Numidian!" Balor snorted. "Men have base natures, and men full of hate, loss and fear are the worst. I see the civilised veil slipping here, boy, believe me." He pushed the captive Lucius aside with a sharp elbow, rose with impressive nimbleness for a man of his proportions, pivoted theatrically and drew an imaginary parabola across the whole deck, encompassing the nervous-looking sailors, and those gaunt and ragged Romans who were out of their enclosures. The frozen eyes of the men in cages showed clearly that the gesture held a portent for all.

He addressed Masinissa then as an actor would in a soliloquy. "Are these really men whom you are bothering yourself with? Look at their dirty, scrawny bodies. Is there life there to care about? They have forfeited all their right to peace, safety and comfort by their actions. Let them fight every day for the scraps of bread we toss to them, as if they were birds on a lake. Let them live and die on my whim. Let them lose all the strength and memories they cling on to, remembering the men they were and the lives they lost. Meditate on how they would treat you if the sandal was on the other foot. Their malice would be as great, and your torture as vicious."

"Enough!" Masinissa growled as forcefully as if he were leading a line against *velite* skirmishers in battle. "You make too much of the concept of the enemy. Loyalties and identities are not so rigid as you suppose. How many of our men and theirs desert, for instance? Are you sure you haven't incarcerated a few of our own in those hutches? I don't see any armour or standards. All I see is half-naked, terrified, starving men. They may once have been amongst the most formidable soldiers in the world, perhaps even from the noblest families, but now they are broken. It is enough to strip a man of his weapons, his wealth, his power, and even his liberty and his pride, but there is a point where your humanity must intervene and leave a man with what he has left. The world often turns right around on you, and the gods have a habit of mocking the presumptuous and the wicked. You appear to be well along the path to stoking their ire. It almost makes me wonder if our route has been a little diverted to intercept you. If Melqart himself were here now, he would no doubt tear this ship and its crew to shreds."

"Well, he's not," Balor rebuffed defiantly, with a slightly mocking, rising tone.

"But I am!" said another in a voice full of rancour and loathing.

For a second, Masinissa was surprised. The words were not spoken from amongst his ranks, and the other seaman were steps behind Balor. He had, just as Balor had done, made the complacent error of neglecting the invisible Lucius who, after the initial shock of revealing his condition had subsided, had blended imperceptibly into the background. Perhaps that was a survival skill he had adapted to preserve himself, but he had done it well enough that he had also managed to get his hands on the clippers that had been discarding in the rigging.

So armed, and with barely a pause after his announcement, he very accurately and methodically drove the clippers straight into the eyeball of Balor. It was a short and cruel stab, one that managed to obliterate the eyeball of his tormentor, but one not pressed further into the man's brain. If anything, the motion resembled a hungry man stabbing at meat on a plate. Lucius's appetite for the gelatinous parts of Balor's face was clearly not sated, and he repeated the motion into the other eye so quickly that his victim's reflexes hadn't the time to recoil in agony. By the time his hands had reached his eye sockets, his eyes were useless gore, and he could not see the frenetic delight that had spread across Lucius's face.

The screams of a blinded man are different from those that result from other types of mutilation. Blended in with the notes of pain there is hollow, helpless fear. Identity and existence are tied to perception, and a newly sightless man is more helpless than a newborn infant. Lucius had got even with Balor. The man knew that he would be less enfeebled if Lucius had just cut off his legs. The darkness, even then, was worse than the pain.

In a theatrical sense, it was as if the action reversed the role of the overseer and his victim. Lucius, with his bloody blade and manic grin, by then occupied the centre stage, and his abuser, for all his rowdy agonies, receded.

Balor's men reacted in ways typical of men of their kind, who were not used to resistance or threat. Deprived of the authority of their voluble leader, they simply gawped at the scene in front of them. Their eyes moved from Balor to Lucius and Masinissa. None appeared to feel any solicitude towards Balor, and no one came forward to his aid. If they had weapons, they gripped them tighter. Their instincts appeared to be focussed on self-preservation rather than revenge. Lucius was quite pathetically armed in comparison to some of the *falcatas* that were being held tensely by some of the sailors, but no one made a move in his direction.

The hiatus couldn't hold; outraged cavalry with balanced javelins, scared mariners with drawn blades and cadaverous Romans ready to emulate Lucius with anything they could find, even it was only the few sharp teeth left in their mouths, were poised to throw metal and flesh at each other. Masinissa made a swift calculation. The morality of the crew of this vessel was clearly suspect. If he intervened half-heartedly, any who fled and found an audience would surely excoriate his intervention, and put pressure on Mago and Hasdrubal to discipline the Numidians. Those outcomes were unpredictable, so it was better to either not have a story or remove the witnesses to it. It was time to pick a side. This boat was no place for arbitration at that point. It was let them go or kill them all.

Masinissa turned around to his men and made his choice. "Kill the sailors; spare the Romans," was all he said.

Almost immediately, a dozen javelins arrowed towards the deck, and the majority thudded into some point on their intended targets' anatomies, usually in their midriffs. His dismounting riders then boarded the vessel quickly. The abruptness of the assault gave little opportunity for escape. A few men, rather than face their foes, looked to the water as a temporary refuge, but were thwarted by the slaves on deck, who made their reprisals count by diving on them before they could leap into the waters of the Baetis and try to swim to safety. A few slaves met their deaths that way, but the delays their sacrifices caused meant that the inconvenienced sailors soon followed them.

In all the commotion and killing, Balor lay in his heap, ignored by all except Lucius, who seemed to revel in Balor's every contortion, cry and exclamation of helpless rage. The Numidians were efficient killers, and they were soon looting the bodies. As much as they were propelled into the melee by outrage, their mercenary instincts had no doubt realised that their opponents were likely to have more wealth on them than the average trooper. Their delighted yelps confirmed that supposition to Masinissa quickly. Juba Tunic and Massiva had refrained from the activity, and flanked Masinissa. Juba Tunic showed his merciful side as he yelled to the men stripping the dead, telling them to open the cages. This instruction was soon followed.

The released men were, for the most part, in an even sorrier condition than those already on deck. Many were aided by their compatriots, and some of the less avaricious Numidians took pity on them too. The most obvious sign of their recent contortions were the angle of their necks and heads, as very few of them were able hold themselves vertical properly, and they winced as they tried to move in the direction of their attendants.

"You wonder at the condition of their souls," Juba Tunic whispered. His tone implied a certain respect for those stiff, knobbly forms who were eager for air, water and food, in that order.

"I'm sure their inner beings will improve at the same pace as their exterior ones," Masinissa replied tersely. Despite the nature of their journey, this certainly was not the moment to entertain nebulous spiritual notions. "Find a wagon," he ordered. "Those men aren't floating or walking away from here."

One was found quickly and provisioned, and a number of the spare horses were strapped to it. It was good enough, as far as makeshift transportation went. The Romans were placed on it – some quite tenderly, particularly those with fresh and open wounds from the strikes of the desperate sailors – and a few with sufficient strength were offered horses, and even a few stubbier swords were surrendered.

This aroused a little surprise and suspicion amongst the recently incarcerated men. They were no doubt used to the gruesome spectacles of slaves fighting in the arena against beasts and gladiators, and Masinissa wondered if some of these men, when their fortunes had been reversed, had perhaps indulged in such improvised sport on fresh captives. The hesitation and fear on the faces of a few of the Romans implied as much.

"Don't worry," Masinissa reassured them as they stood or lay in front of him, "I've no intention of inflicting fresh torments upon you. Neither am I going to prolong your servitude, if that is even close to an appropriate term for your recent ordeals. Make your way north-east, find the coast and find your kin, and if you ever come back, vent your rage against the Carthaginians, not the Numidians."

The fact of liberation broke over the Romans like a warm spring rain. Dour expressions softened and tense muscles eased. Several hunched and wept. Lucius, who had been the closest to him throughout the encounter, let his tears run freely. It was an eerie sight to watch as the boy appeared composed. He let out no wails, and his body remained still and free of any convulsions. He didn't even sniff or choke back the tears. He just let them run down his dirty face, making smudgy, little rivers between the corner of his eye and his upper lip.

He made for a very dignified sight as he approached Masinissa, who dismounted in response to the gesture. Lucius held out a firm hand, which Masinissa accepted. His grip was stronger than his liberator had anticipated and it lingered. Lucius pumped his Numidian liberator's hand, as if Masinissa was his bride's father on his wedding day. Gratitude surged between the palms of the two men, and Masinissa gave Lucius an easy, avuncular smile.

"Wipe your eyes," he advised.

But Lucius declined, although he still took the moment to release Masinissa's hand. "It's pointless," he replied. "There will only be others to replace them. Once you turn the tears on, you know..." He let his words fade out. He allowed a thoughtful pause and then resumed, "I am in your debt, and I hope I will be able to repay it one day. I trust to the honourable nature you have demonstrated so far that you will not change your mind when I tell you that I am of the Scipio family, and if I make it back to the Roman lines, I will make the consul aware of my obligation to you."

This admission surprised Masinissa, as such frankness was very brave under the circumstances. His value had certainly risen by the revelation. Lucius had judged him well, however, and he had no intention of going back on his word. There was also an undeniable advantage in shaping some form of alliance within the enemy camp. The tides of war could turn less propitious, and Melqart help him if he were ever caught alive! It seemed to him then that Lucius's handshake had sealed some form of covenant with him, and a sudden feeling of foreboding in Masinissa suggested that, at some core of his being, he thought that the accord would be revisited.

Lucius, as if realising that Masinissa was absorbing the fact that their contract may one day be more equally balanced, gave a short bow and made to take his leave. However, a certain sternness returned to his expression, and he spoke more solemnly, "Sir, you have given me my freedom without my plea, but I have a request to make of you before we leave." In lieu of elaboration, he turned back to the ship, which the Numidians were preparing to scuttle, and gestured towards the one crew member who had, at least in terms of his existence, been spared.

Masinissa thought he understand the boy's request. Balor would not last long in all probability, but disposing of him swiftly was the prudent option for both of them.

"Take your vengeance," Masinissa replied.

This consent was greeted with Lucius's widest smile of the day, although one with more malice in it than pleasure. He returned to the agonised form of Balor, who had braced himself against one of the wooden cages. Much of his blood had caked on his face and hands, and his jaw moved uncontrollably, evidence that his horror and pain had hardly subsided.

On hearing the approaching Lucius, Balor's hands reached up in a defensive-but-curious gesture. It was an odd sight: a cowering figure who also was seeking contact and aid.

Lucius knelt by Balor's side, and simultaneously took his hand and gently whispered to him. "Come," he said as fondly as if he were escorting a virgin to bed.

Balor responded meekly and stood with his former victim's aid. Lucius then led him as attentively as if he was escorting his doddery grandmother to the centre of the ship. There he rested Balor's hand on the frame of one of the cages. Balor's obliterated face turned towards him questioningly, as if his entire adult being had been ripped from him with his eyeballs and he was seeking guidance in every moment. His instincts at least were true, as Lucius appeared to have taken him to the cages for symbolic closure. As Balor was about to phrase a question, Lucius stabbed him for a third time – this time without withdrawing the blade – and left Balor's hand impaled on the wooden frame. As Balor flailed with his free arm, Lucius took another dagger, which he had retrieved from the deck, forced Balor's other hand onto the cage and performed the same act, in a savagely symmetrical reprise of his earlier mutilation.

Balor struggled, but only briefly. The movements only tore open his wounds further, and it would take a man with an incredible tolerance to pain to rip himself free. Balor could only scream and Lucius let him. He let out curses and oaths amidst his howls, but Lucius was finished with him. He disembarked the vessel and returned to his shabby troop. He waved to Masinissa with noticeable exuberance as he led them away towards the refuge of the Roman-occupied coast.

Masinissa watched for a long time as the caravan of his brutalised enemies trekked away. He was vaguely aware of his men hacking into the hull of the ship, and the glugs, sobs and rages of Balor, who would soon be silenced by the waters of the Baetis, but, mostly, he thought of Lucius and what may result from the mercy he had shown him.

HERCULES! HERCULES!

It had taken them only a few more days to reach Gades and the inlet that led to the island where the Temple of Melqart was situated. No news preceded them about the demise of Balor and his deviant crew. If the boat had been heading south towards the city, its presence would hardly have featured in the polite conversations of the inhabitants in any case. The sailors of the Baetis were also quite an irregular bunch and not renowned for their meticulous habits. The boat would have made its way down here at some point, no doubt, but its arrival would not have been anticipated nor particularly welcome. The city had a lively reputation, and the nightlife it offered was famed amongst the troops. It was unlikely that Balor would have found a receptive clientele from the locals. This was not the parched hinterland of the Oretani and Bastetani.

As they approached the city's outskirts, they could see its beauty was quite dazzling, and Masinissa felt himself slacken a little and some of his vigilance slip away as he drew closer to the ocean. Gades was well garrisoned and distant from any Roman presence – even raiders would be at least a hard day's ride away – and so it was natural to place himself at greater ease in its boroughs. The men were in even better spirits. Some were familiar with the taverns and brothels in the city, and were quick to boast about the sport to be had in both. Masinissa had stoked their sense of euphoria even further by promising them a furlough of a couple of days before returning to the mountains or being given an alternative posting. He didn't even insist that all the party escort him down to the beach where they could find small canoes or vessels to take them across to the temple.

His own feelings of exhilaration were also heightened by news from the city. Already, messengers had conveyed his success and its auspices to the citizenry and the Carthaginian detachments who were garrisoned there. His reputation was burgeoning. He had been intercepted on the outskirts of the city by an official group, who had informed him that, as a reward for his retrieval of the cup, he would be given extended leave and he should return to Numidia once his duties had been discharged. They had no need to surrender the cup in the city, but were to go straight to the temple and deliver it to the priest there forthwith.

The populace were not quite so sober and unsentimental, however, and many came out to cheer as Masinissa's party made its way through its avenues. It was clear that the Phoenician city wanted a morale-boosting parade for its Punic heroes. It probably didn't occur to them that they were lionising Numidians. Excitement and hope can blur such distinctions. It was an impromptu affair, however, as the citizens – on hearing the news of Masinissa's arrival – had emptied into the streets and squares, out of curiosity and admiration, to see the cup and its retriever. It was a marked contrast to some of the experiences the group had further north, where the windows and doors only showed grim, uncertain faces, and sometimes even shuttered or curtained entrances. Those towns were no doubt more used to being invaded and plundered.

The merchants and working girls of the town obviously were keen on taking full advantage of the situation, however, and solicited the attention of the cavalry loudly as it made its way through the city. It meant that their ranks were depleted quite rapidly as temptations proved irresistible. The numbers of the party were also swelled temporarily by women mounting up with the men, and directing them to the nearest stables, taverns or private quarters. Some men even turned their mounts around and took off back towards the countryside with their eager new companion bouncing merrily at their rear in a prelude to things to come.

For his part, Masinissa felt an immediate warmth towards the place itself. He had visited several times and found himself to be instantly at ease, far more than had been the case for him in Carthage, Cirta or Tingi. Beyond the throng of the animated crowd, the daily routines of the local people caught his eye. His previous acquaintance had fostered a very favourable impression of them. Their wider reputation was positive, and they were known to be hospitable generally and often quite funny; the Gadeans he had met had been, at least. He liked the beaches too, especially the dunes facing the western ocean, and the food. He was certainly looking forward to the culinary treats the city could offer: peerless seafoods, cheeses and beef. Thankfully, the chefs of Gades were not as enamoured of pigs as some of the inland areas.

There was a distinct languor about the place too, despite the apparent bustle of the foreground. He liked the aimless vibe that the people often exhibited, and he devoured the competing aromas rising from the ubiquitous street stalls and corner tavernas. It was a scene he felt great relief to see: a city virtually at peace and without threat, heedless of the dangers and conflicts swirling to the north and east. Watching men in various states of inebriation stumble in front of him in the daytime plainly showed the imperviousness of the populace to the war. Maybe the fact that their port lay beyond the great inland sea altered their perspective a little? He'd never visited further west of the city, towards Lusitania and the cities of Ossonaba and Olisipo, and he wondered if this tranquillity of spirit was shared by the people of the western tribe.

He loved the wild dances and music of the city too, and the yelps the agile dancers made when they stomped to their songs and swirled their skirts. They were just as uninhibited without wine too, and their pleasures seemed marked by joy, rather than a need for escape or release. He thought of his men seeking out the rowdiest places and revelling with the locals, perhaps well into the night and beyond, he hoped, into a companionable and cosseted morning.

The light of that day, however, was still far from dimmed, and remained particularly crisp and clear, accentuating the lines of the buildings and monuments beautifully. He felt a little sad to not be able to loiter and enjoy the picturesque views, but he felt Melqart calling him. Those amongst the crowd who remained seemed to urge him onwards, as if he was a leading runner in a distance race through and beyond the city towards the temple. As a man on horseback, he felt a little silly in comparing himself in his thoughts to the famous Athenian soldier Pheidippides and his sapping run from Marathon to Athens, but it was the closest analogy he could make for the pilgrimage.

As they departed the furthest end of the city, their numbers had been eroded almost completely. Masinissa had waved most of the men off individually, and had been saluted with lusty cheers and grateful smiles in return. There were no threats between the city and the island, and Masinissa was content to allow the party to reduce as it may. If necessary, he was happy to go the final leg of the journey alone. In truth, he would have been grateful for a few moments of solitude and reflection before he reached the temple.

As it turned out, six other riders rode with him. Capuca and Ari were obvious attendants, and Masinissa was proud that their sense of duty had compelled them to resist the many lures of Gades. Juba Tunic rode alongside him as well, quietly, as if preoccupied with his inner thoughts. Maybe he had some obligations or offerings to make. He had lost as much as anyone in the war, and perhaps he had made promises to Melqart for his survival that he had the opportunity to discharge just then. Regardless, Masinissa appreciated his company and his taciturn mood. Massiva was also included in the group, although it was apparent from his frequently morose glances that he did so more reluctantly than the others and would much prefer to be amongst the revellers back in town. It was revealing to Masinissa that his nephew's discipline held and that his fear of tarnishing his reputation in his uncle's eyes still had a powerful sway over him. He knew the boy, and Massiva's fidelity to him over the famed women of Gades was impressive. He promised to let him off the leash as soon as they had delivered the cup to the priests.

The other two were both young and had joined Masinissa's raiders together in the most recent reinforcement. They had seen about six months of campaigning, and both had distinguished themselves well in that time. They demonstrated good horsemanship and discipline, and had noticeably good range and accuracy with their javelins. In the competitions that were held occasionally, both of them were amongst those who threw the furthest. They were personable characters as well, and Masinissa saw elements of himself in them both, as they too had been emigres in Carthage, and had spent some time with the Greek scholars and in the Carthaginian military academies there. It was apparent that they both idolised Masinissa completely too, to the point of mimicry on occasions. He had even once had to scold one of them jokingly, as it was causing too much amusement. They presented an interesting physical contrast too, in appearance and manner, particularly their striking hair, and this had led the men to coin a nickname for the pair, which had stuck.

The first, Adonibaal, was tall, lean, athletic and quite ascetic in his habits, although warm in his manner. His appearance was untypical for a Numidian, as he had strikingly blond hair, which was almost white at the temples, and a greenish tint to his eyes. The men surmised that his mother must have been a captive from a northern raid or a noble from the east, but he said nothing to confirm or deny either rumour. As his hair was his most distinguishing feature the men had started to call him Straw, which was a moniker that spread quickly.

The other, Batnoam, offered a contrast in stature and hue. He was shorter and burlier, and had become known for his quick wit and mischief. He also had very dark and unruly hair. It lacked the loose waves of the Phoenicians, Greeks and Romans, or the tight curls, which were more typical of Numidians. It was clear that such chaotic strands could only have occured from mixed parentage and that one of them must have been from the deeper deserts or beyond, probably either

Libyan or Toubou. This was confirmed when Batnoam had admitted that he was fluent in the Tebu language. This was of great interest to Masinissa as his own competency in that language was slight at best, and it was always good to have someone who could communicate with a particular tribe, even if that tribe roamed the plains and deserts way to the south of Numidia. It was evident that Batnoam was proud of his hair, and he let it grow wild, so that it formed a messy cloud around his head and across his shoulders. Occasionally, he would tie it up, particularly when riding, and he did so with a rag of Tyrian purple, and it might have been for this affectation, rather than his hair colour, that he had been given the complementary nickname of Berry.

When together, Adonibaal and Batnoam were often hailed as "StrawBerry!" in reference to the fruit that grew in the forest of Gaul, and appeared occasionally on the tables at banquets and even some tavernas. For the most part, Masinissa addressed them formally, but even he sometimes found it hard to resist calling them by their more affectionate names. When Ari had mentioned to him that, "StrawBerry's coming with us too!" he'd chuckled a little to himself.

All of the men had checked the pace of their steeds. In the city, it was necessary to avoid injuring any of the populace in the narrow streets, but, though it was no longer necessary in open country, they had maintained their ambling pace. It was as if they were making a communion with Melqart, and shifting their perspectives prior to entering the holy place. As they gained sight of the island and drew closer to it, Masinissa's sense of spiritual anticipation and feelings of serenity deepened. He even went silently through a few prayers and elegies to himself, in homage and as a greeting to his god. This was a momentous experience, and all seven men felt it. The most conspicuous features of the physical and architectural vision before them were the shallow, calm waters that encircled the island, and the high tower and series of columns that they could spy as the most prominent features of the temple.

He wondered a little how it might compare to the temple dedicated to Melqart at Tyre, which he had read about in the histories of Herodotus of Halicarnassus. He remembered reading a little incredulously that that temple had two enormous pillars at its entrance, one of which was entirely decorated in gold, and the other had attached to it an emerald stone that was so enormous that it would shine brightly at night, even when the moon was at a young or crescent phase. No such grandeur was apparent from the shore, but it was clear that the distant columns had been sculpted carefully and expertly, and that filigrees of gold nestled towards the tops of the columns. Melqart took the modest inlays to be acts of discretion on the parts of the builders and priesthood. Maybe they had reserved their gold reserves for the interior and perhaps even the ornament in his current possession.

They dismounted, found stable hands to quarter their horses, and walked towards the ferry point. In truth, the waters were so shallow and placid, and the tide so favourable that they might even had been able to wade across without too much difficulty, but that would certainly have diminished the style of their entrance. Plans had already been laid for their crossing, however, and several ferrymen waited for them, along with an immaculately white-robed figure, who presumably was the representative of the resident holy order.

The man, who appeared younger and more vigorous than Masinissa had anticipated, advanced towards the party, gave them all a smile and a deferential bow, and introduced himself. "Good day, General," he began, misrepresenting Masinissa's military station a little, "I hope you and your companions are well, and are not too tired by your labours and travel. It is my and our honour to welcome you and receive the sacred cup that you have so heroically liberated. My name is Sikarbaal, and I am at your service"

Masinissa looked at the young man and could discern easily that he was doing his best to rein in his excitement and enthusiasm, and comport himself with the dignity and formality he presumed was expected of the occasion. He was quick to break the spell. "Relax, kid, I'm sure we don't need any more praise. Our heads are as swollen as we want them. We're just relieved and happy to be here. I want to take full advantage of your hospitality, but I don't expect you to be on your best behaviour around us. We're the servants of Melqart, the same as you are, and we're just blessed to have been able to serve him and be protected by his mercy."

Sikarbaal's demeanour eased visibly, and his smile added genuine warmth. He retained a little of his rigidity, but a large portion of his tension blew out of him. Masinissa gave him a pat on the arm and guided them both towards the waiting boats. In reality, they were more like canoes, as they could really only accommodate one oarsman and two passengers in comfort. Nothing grander or more substantial appeared necessary across this body of water. There may have been rare holy days when a larger barge may have been more suitable, but the island was close and the crossing easy, so numerous, quick journeys would probably satisfy even a very large number of pilgrims. They took four of the canoes, and they were divided neatly: Ari and Capuca in one, Juba Tunic and Massiva in another, Adonibaal and Batnoam in a third, and Masinissa, as guest of honour, with Sikarbaal.

Such proximity obviously delighted the young priest, who – after confessing his elation at meeting such a heroic figure and seeing the cup of Melqart once more – dug into his robes and fished out a tightly bound leather wallet that contained pieces of linen and papyri. He offered a clean square to Masinissa and drew out from the small bag he was carrying a pot of ink and a very elegant, possibly silver, stylus. Offering the shiny tool to Masinissa, Sikarbaal made a request. "Sir, would you do me a kindness, and commemorate this moment and your visit, by marking this cloth with your mark and maybe some words of your choosing?"

Masinissa was taken a little aback by his boldness, but agreed to the request, nevertheless. It was quite a novelty to use ink instead of wax and papyrus rather than wood, and the fact that they were in a gently bobbing canoe added another dimension as well. He looked at Sikarbaal and laughed, mostly at how incongruous the moment was in relation to his recent existence. Liberating cherished religious icons and Roman slaves had become more familiar experiences than punting across a tranquil sea with an awestruck novitiate. It put him in a good place. The water that swirled around the oars as they glided through the water with apparent effortlessness reminded him of stirring a spoon in a bowl of milk. There was an idleness and a peace in the play of the paddle in the water. His instincts were to place his fingers in the moving sea around him, and let the ripples of the waves and the disturbances of the boat play on and cool his fingers. His courtesy towards his host checked his impulse. Succumbing to such an idle whim was, at that moment, hard to resist. He had not felt so at ease for a long time. He looked across to the other canoes, and he could see the same torpor resting on his comrades. *Such moments are rare for us,* he thought, *and more precious than wine, women or gold.*

He picked up the stylus, and regarded its simplicity and design as it shot light randomly at him as he turned it. He wondered, *Is it only in moments of tranquillity that our senses and minds allow us to be mesmerised by such trivial shows of nature? To be spellbound by beauty and life should not be a gift so easily stolen back by the gods from their children.*

Surrounded by such ease, Masinissa's mood shifted suddenly out of his control, and his thoughts turned to the horrors behind and ahead of him. He tried to resist and remain in the moment of comfortable lassitude, but he could not. His thoughts turned dark against the azure waters and cerulean sky, and his mind began to dwell impotently on the abruptness of life and death, and the faces of the dead as they changed from being the faces of the living. He had seen that moment many times by then, and he could always recognise the moment when life left its host. When the soul departed, it took away something the living could detect if not understand. He had come to understand that, in all their tragic and brutal ways, dying, killing and surviving were all forms of spiritual emptying. He only could really comprehend the latter two, but the deaths of others always snatched something out of him, even those with whom he had only ever exchanged the occasional ribald comment or barked order. You could never prepare for loss, even on a battlefield when it was such a strong possibility. There was no time to pause in such moments, and afterwards the sense of sudden loss, whilst dissipated a little with exhaustion and shocked senses, hung on like a cauterised stump looking for the useful portion of the limb that had been hacked off.

So many times, he had enjoyed relaxing times with friends and compatriots, who were full of life and cares, only to see their remains the following day, lying like sacks to be disposed of. The enemy dead were even more dehumanised. The vultures of any victorious army cared little for the heaps of flesh they had robbed of existence, and then of dignity and possessions.

With those macabre thoughts occupying him, Masinissa pressed a piece of linen against a shield lying in the hull of the boat, which was the flattest and driest thing he could see, and, wrote with as steady a hand as possible, a line that he thought Sikarbaal might appreciate, and which he felt encapsulated his present mood or, perhaps more accurately, his yearning.

He wrote deliberately, making sure to write each symbol and letter as clearly as he could. Fortunately, both the oarsman and lake-like ocean cooperated with his penmanship. He even took the time to write his message in both the Punic and Greek alphabets, wondering a little to himself whether this was for the sake of some perverse sense of his own importance or out of consideration for a reader who may be boastful enough to share the message with his educated peers. He wondered a little at his own ego too, in that he felt obliged to do more than write a recognisable autograph with an extravagant "M" and perhaps a horse and palm tree underneath as an artistic Numidian flourish.

When he finished, he offered the cloth to Sikarbaal, but in such a way that allowed him to read it aloud, which he felt made the gesture more memorable. As he held the linen open and as the *atramentum* dried on its white threads, Masinissa read out his thoughts in a way that appeared reasonably solemn as well as faintly risible in its unaccustomed theatricalism. "I, Masinissa the Massylian, today return the most holy relic of Melqart to its home on the western edge of civilisation. It is my greatest and most humbling honour. I beseech my celestial lord to grant me favour, protection and guidance in times of war and peace, danger and safety. I ask the same favour for my men, and for the priests who worship and petition you in their prayers and sacrifices."

He let go of the cloth, and Sikarbaal took it, quite delicately and reverently, and put it in his wallet, which he then pressed against himself to shield it better from the light spray that moistened their faces occasionally as the canoe dipped into the waves, which had gained a little height as they drew closer to the island. Masinissa whimsically wondered whether Melqart was acknowledging his gesture and giving him a sign of his approval in the rocking ocean.

The moistness that had begun to glisten around Sikarbaal's eyes, though, was evidently generated internally, and he was clearly very moved by the inclusion of his vocation in Masinissa's comments. He gave Masinissa a smile that didn't break open his lips, and that held a little ruefulness in his cheeks and expression. "You know, it's common for only the old and the young to pay us much attention on a daily basis." he stated, "Those fresh to the world and those who know they will be leaving it soon. Unless it's a holy day or if they need to make a sacrifice, or have suffered a loss and need to reach out to Melqart, we're left alone here most of the day. Your rescue of the cup has generated much excitement and put the gods back into people's lives. It's a funny job being a priest, you know. For the most part, people dismiss you. The common preconception is that if you are not good at anything else, are weak or come from a wealthy family then you become a priest. It is only in times of desperation or obligation that people seek us out, and then, for a brief time, they believe us to be wise and powerful."

Masinissa listened but didn't feel the need to interrupt. Perhaps the priest had found a moment to switch the usual confessional roles and had found an appropriate figure in him. It might be that he was finally surrendering a little to the languor the short, idyllic crossing was inducing in his companions in the other boats.

Sikarbaal noticed his ease and willingness to listen, and continued, with Masinissa's body language signalling to him that the Numidian commander was quite willing for him to monopolise the conversation till they reached the rapidly approaching shore. "You know, it is easy to underestimate the burdens of the priesthood. People think we spend our days singing the praises of our heavenly masters, burning our incense, sacrificing our beasts and making our honey. At a distance, it seems all very uncomplicated and relaxed." He paused and gave another pursed smile. "The flaw in that supposition is the absence of the gods. We have to fill that absence with our faith, and support others in their weakness and doubt. Melqart's legacy is in his deeds and relics, such as the one you carry, but he doesn't pop his head through the clouds every day and tell his faithful servants, 'Good job down there keep it up!' No, our omnipotent creators have provisioned us barely adequately in some respects. Of course, our material needs are met abundantly by the bounties of a rich earth and sea. If a man is strong and works hard, he can take good care of himself and his family by his own labours. But what of his spiritual labours? What are the dividends of his prayers, sacrifices and moral conduct? What is to stop him thinking that all life, especially at this harrowing time, is cruel and meaningless. How do you hold on to belief and resist the nagging sense of futility? I've even seen it in priests. They despair at the silence their calls to heaven are met with. They don't see the signs, the beauty and the miracles of life all around them. They lose their dreams and their visions, and the connection to the other world is cut."

Masinissa held Sikarbaal's gaze throughout his monologue. He was glad he had let the priest speak. It made him turn his mind to ontological matters, which was correct, as the oarsmen had only a few more shallow paddles to make before they made it to the jetty that lay below the watchtower, and perhaps irregular lighthouse, that dominated the closest end of the holy island.

He felt he needed to reply to Sikarbaal. It was if the priest was making an oblique enquiry into his spiritual views, as well as explaining the struggles of the faith and the faithful. "I still have my dreams, and I hold fast to the beliefs that your colleagues imbibed in me in Numidia, in my exile in Carthage and here in Iberia, most often as we are saying our farewells to our fallen brothers. My faith in Melqart, Tanit and Baal Hammon sustains me in my adulthood, as my mother's milk did in my infancy. I don't need the physical presence of Melqart to know he is there and that the gods made us for purposes beyond their own amusement. Our salvation is meant to be hard; as hard as the miracle of our creation. I wish you strength in your struggles, Sikarbaal. I don't underestimate the job you do or the burdens you must carry. As they say, in our darkest times, it is not we who move forwards but it is the gods who carry us, and a portion of the gods is carried by you priests. I do not mind that the gods always show us the edge of the knife and not its hilt. Look at Melqart himself and his trials. We are meant to be tested as he was."

The comment satisfied Sikarbaal. "You are wise as well as brave, my lord. One day you will be a fine king. I pray your people will see you reign for many years."

"I hope so too!" Masinissa replied, although he had spared precious little time thinking of his ascension. It meant thinking about his father's parting, which he couldn't bear.

The noise of oars scraping on rock and the cry of thanks the boatman raised as he caught a tethering rope brought both men back to reality. Masinissa wondered what the man, silent throughout the passage, had made of their discussion. No doubt he was used to people exploring the mysteries of the cosmos, given the waters he ferried, and perhaps the views held little freshness or insight for him. If anyone would have heard it all before about the gods, it may have been him.

The man – and Masinissa felt a little rude for not even asking his name – fastened his mooring line to the nearest bollard, and leant back in the boat to allow his passengers access to the wharf and maybe also to be able to catch them if they lost balance and tilted towards the sea as they clambered out of the boat. It was a needless precaution. Masinissa and Sikarbaal barely checked themselves as they made shore without either of their dignities being compromised by a stumble.

Waiting for them were a number of priests, and even one or two more military-looking figures, but only the apparently most senior of them approached Masinissa's disembarking party.

Masinissa had a few moments to survey his host, who was presumably the high priest of this most important shrine. His dress was simple. He wore a long, white robe that revealed a quite gaunt frame. Masinissa was struck most notably by his shoulders and upper arms. They showed some muscular definition but little obvious power. Maybe the man used to run for exercise. He certainly didn't labour too hard.

There was one obvious adornment that hinted at his rank. He wore a cord around his neck, and attached to this was a wooden figurine that held two small, golden objects in both hands. The figure was carved in impressive detail and was clearly intended to be shown as athletic, in noticeable contrast to its wearer. Little nicks had been made in the figure for a beard, and a high, rounded hat was perched on his head. That alone would have revealed to Masinissa that the object was meant to be a representation of Melqart himself. The golden objects he held in his tiny hands, though they more closely resembled wooden holes, were recognisable associations with the god. In his left mitt he held what looked like the symbol of Tanit, although the lines were such that it could have been an ankh. There wasn't such a great difference anyway in either appearance or meaning. In his other hand, the figure held a slightly out-of-proportion fenestrated axe.

Melqart for sure! Masinissa thought to himself. As he looked back up towards the priest's face, he could see the man's clear delight. Masinissa wondered if, for the priest, it might relate more to excitement at the return of a lost icon rather than meeting a hero of the Iberian campaign.

"Welcome to the island of Melqart, Masinissa," the man greeted him. "Thank you," he added briskly, bowing and clasping his hands together. Turning to the men who ringed Masinissa, he continued, "And thank you all too for braving such perils to bring Melqart's cup home where it belongs. I'm sure such service bodes well for you all in the afterlife."

"It is our honour and duty," Masinissa responded. "May I ask a small favour? May I fulfil this last leg of the journey and take the cup to its altar? May I also ask your name?" he added, almost as an afterthought, as if both men had forgotten the usual protocols.

"Of course you may; it is most fitting that you do should do that. I am Bodashtarte. I have served in the temple here for forty years. As a young acolyte, one of my jobs was to polish and buff the cups daily, and they never failed to mesmerise me in their beauty. I may revert to that station tomorrow and relive the pleasure, now that the two are paired once more."

Masinissa was quite touched by the man's sincerity and his willingness to refer to his humbler youth so readily. He was also struck a little by the incongruity of his name. Someone with a name that reveres Ashtarte in the Temple of Melqart! A reference to a goddess associated with fertility, sexuality and war was also a little unexpected in such a figure as the priest presented.

Bodashtarte stood aside, as did the small congregation around him. The movement gave Masinissa a strong impression that they were forming an honour guard, and he was meant to walk the final distance to the temple and beyond to the altar in a reverent manner.

Back on parade, he thought to himself.

He'd seen triumphs before, and heard how they were in Rome, and felt that maybe this was his in miniature. In any event, he was quite willing to slow his gait, stiffen his back and hold the cup in two hands in front of him in as close an approximation as he could muster to a formal procession. His men read the cues unconsciously and slotted behind him in the same pairs they had formed in the canoes. The rear pair of Adonibaal and Batnoam looked particularly serious. Ari appeared the most light-hearted, and gave him a quick wink of reassurance. He resisted the instinct to do the same, but let enough of a fold form on his lips to give his comical adjutant notice that he appreciated the gesture.

The exterior of the temple was quite striking. The supporting antae were the least impressive and most functional, but the interior columns that framed the entrance were beautifully carved pillars. They were more slender than he imagined they would be. For some reason, he had presumed that a temple dedicated to Melqart would have sturdy Doric features, but these clearly fitted into the more elegant Ionic style.

The entablature was also reminiscent of the classical temples he had seen in drawings. He had always hoped to visit the colossal temples to Athena and Artemis at Athens and Ephesus, respectively, and walking the steps into the Temple of Melqart only whetted his appetite for such an adventure.

When this war ends, I'll go, he promised himself. His fanciful diversion made him think of taking Sophonisba to the Greek states one day, and enjoying the culture and peace. *I deserve that,* he thought, *but it is an excursion predicated on victory and survival, neither of which were assured.*

His slow pace also allowed him to view the frieze in the central section of the entablature. It was populated by very elaborate bas-reliefs that Masinissa quickly identified as depicting scenes from Melqart's labours. The one that struck him the most was a representation of the Amazonomachy and Melqart's ninth labour to retrieve the belt of Hippolyta, queen of the Amazons. The opposing figures were almost entwined, almost suggesting a sexual encounter, rather than a fatal one.

By stepping through the porch, the small band entered the naos, which was the largest chamber in the temple. Masinissa could detect a further door to the rear *adyton,* where the holiest rites were performed and where, no doubt, the reunited cups would be securely kept. On this occasion, however, the consort to his vessel lay waiting on a wide altar that stood before the statue of Melqart, which dominated the centre of the temple.

Masinissa had seen many representations of the great god in so many guises, but the one before him was amongst the most welcoming and hospitable in appearance that he had seen. The head of the statue held a curly crown of hair, although in a style far longer and looser than those depicted in the sculptures he'd seen imported to Carthage from the Seleucid Empire. It would seem that the stone masons of Gades were more relaxed in their styling than those in Antioch and beyond. The figure was tall, but not excessively so. Masinissa's head would have rested just under Melqart's rib joint if he'd approached it. There was no soft pillow below the rib cage, however, as the statue was as athletic as would have been expected, with the god's abdominal muscles sharply defined. The figure did, however, retain a softness in its pose and expression. Melqart's left arm was held at his side, with an open hand of welcome, which would have just about touched Masinissa's shoulder if he was directly in front of it. He quietly vowed to pat it when he placed the cup before it. It may have been a little presumptive, but he'd earned the small indiscretion. He felt that the pose may have been created with precisely that form of contact in mind. Melqart's other arm rose upwards and just touched his head. Masinissa couldn't quite decide whether this was intended as a wave of greeting or a relaxed playing with his hair. He thought it was probably meant to be the former, and the craftsman considered it prudent to keep a stone connection between the limb and the skull at this most tenuous point. The right thumb of the stone god seemed to have been lost amidst his rock mane. Complementing the inviting gesture was an equally amiable expression. Melqart's mouth showed an upward curve that the skill of the artist had even managed to extend to the eyes, which seem to have a slight squint as the imaginary muscles underneath stretched his alabaster cheekbones out. The temperament of the artist was also somewhat in evidence from the attire that the statue wore. Rather than a simple tunic, the figure was depicted in the god's most heroic aspect. A lion skin was draped across his shoulders and chest, with the paws of the beast forming a knot on his chest. The hind paws, legs and tail of the slain beast's skin were also apparent behind, which added greatly to the gallant impression. Masinissa turned to Bodashtarte to murmur his approval.

"Our lord is looking pretty impressive," Bodashtarte beamed. "It's for the priests to be dull. It certainly wouldn't do for Melqart to be anything less than valiant."

"I'm sure that's not the case," Masinissa replied reassuringly, if not particularly convincingly.

Bodashtarte nodded, seemingly both in assent as well as to indicate that a ceremonial moment was due. The surrounding priests bowed their heads, grew quiet and then, in unison, spoke familiar incantations to Melqart. It was rare for Masinissa to be present for these kinds of benedictions, but he felt his spirit move and receive a sense of awe and divinity. For a few moments, Masinissa listened to the priests and their murmured chants.

The prayers of intercession and gratitude were repeated in hypnotic ways, "Melqart *uru* [Melqart is my light]," and "Melqart *hilles* [Melqart has saved]," rang sonorously through the temple, enhanced by the building's excellent acoustics.

Masinissa was not averse to litany, particularly when it involved propitiating his protector god. The priests had given the rite its due solemnity, and he was thankful to them for their prayers. He had expected no less, but, in the moment, it was still touching and humbling. He looked down on the beautiful vessel cupped in his scarred hands and saw the beauty of it, and became even more aware of the contrast between its inviolate perfection and his own vulnerable flesh, with the cicatrices that traced his fingers and arms.

He placed the cup next to its sibling and retreated, taking a sly moment to caress the open palm of the statue. The cold stone felt no different from the wall of the entrance, but he was glad that he had made the connection, and he tried to hold the sensation in his mind and fingertips, as if it was the morning parting stroke to a lover.

There were a few *klinai* loungers in the alcoves of the temple. He surmised that they may be there for contemplation, as there was the possibility of drawing a curtain across to offer seclusion and there were ornate-looking oil lamps giving adequate light. There were also small fires, with hot stones placed neatly on them, presumably for scattering seeds. The smoke of the oracle was most pungent in these recesses, and in one there was even a very drowsy-looking priest.

Masinissa had been told by many of his Greek tutors and friends that, although the custom was long incorporated into the temple rituals and divinations, the use of hemp seeds had originated with the

Scythians. He had read a little of these people, and felt an element of kinship with them, as fellow nomads and renowned masters of mounted warfare. He felt somewhat that the Numidians were almost the southern equivalent of this vast tribe. As he speculated, the lethargic priest idly, but with unerring accuracy, tossed some hemp on the red-hot stones at his feet. They smoked instantly, and the seeds' unique scent soon reached Masinissa's nose. The priest appeared delighted by the vapour and inhaled deeply of it, as if it were the freshest meadow.

Masinissa looked across at Bodashtarte for approval.

The priest waved an open hand in a gesture of blessing and encouragement. "We are not ascetics here. I'm sure Melqart would like you to join him for a while. It's the least reward you deserve. One of the chambers has been prepared. There are dates, blankets and wine. If you need anything else, blow the horn next to the *klinai*, and Sikarbaal will attend you. You may be hungry after your communion, and we will cook fresh meat for you. A goat is being stripped for you now. You may have it all if your appetite desires. You are the most blessed of Melqart; *barek*, Masinissa, *barek*!" Bodashtarte continued, using the Phoenician religious dialect.

It pleased Masinissa, and gave him a greater sense of being in a sacred place and being at one with his divine master.

Bodashtarte repeated the litany, "Melqart *shama* [Melqart has listened]. Melqart *uru* [Melqart is my light]. Melqart *hilles* [Melqart has saved]. *Palti* Melqart [My refuge is Melqart]. *Barek* [Blessed]."

Masinissa looked back towards his men. Some of them appeared to want to linger and prolong the ceremony, whilst others seemed ready to depart. Massiva was twisting his foot a little, as if poised to make a sharp leap towards the porch and Adonibaal seemed more fixated on the ceiling than the altar just then. Only Juba Tunic was passive in his body and appeared to be looking straight at the eyes of Melqart, with an expression that seemed to be both faraway and questing.

Turning to them, Masinissa indicated his intentions. "I will pray now. You can too if you wish."

For a moment, the men were uncertain, as if at the end of a parade they hadn't prepared for.

I'll leave them to it, Masinissa thought as he discharged his sense of responsibility for his hesitant men.

He gave a short wave to Bodashtarte and walked towards the alcove. As he drew the short curtain that gave the space seclusion, he noticed the men drift apart from each other, as if they were the plumose seeds of a plant blown casually or taken by a sharp gust of wind. In any event, they seemed irresolute. A few seemed to mumble words to the priests. Ari made for another alcove, Adonibaal and Batnoam separated slightly and made for the deepest corner, whilst the others dawdled in the general direction of the entrance.

With the curtain drawn, and the little fire and lamp out, the alcove was a tenebrous refuge. It was saved from being austere by the luxurious *klinai* and the treats left on a small table, which Bodashtarte had promised. Masinissa was a little peckish and couldn't resist the dates nor the wine, which was cool on his tongue but warmed him quickly. He suddenly felt a little like his men, not knowing which posture to adopt, or which thoughts or supplications to frame in his mind and on his lips. He settled for a mix of humility and luxury. He knelt at the edge of the *klinai* and murmured the familiar incantations the priests had used, "Melqart *shama.* Melqart *uru.* Melqart *hilles. Barek, barek, barek.*" He added earnest appeals for the safety of his loved ones, as he always did, and then let silence form its cloud around him. He rose in slow and separate motions, and yielded to the temptation of the cosy lounger, but more from a desire for contemplation rather than rest. He was not of the ascetic school, which favoured discomfort as a vehicle to the transcendent. He filled another cup of wine and put his nose deep into the vessel, almost snorting in it before slugging it. He was caught in that moment when the spiritual vies with the sybaritic, and he sought revelation and obliteration almost simultaneously.

He knew he was going to give himself just a brief moment to attempt to be profound or seek enlightenment – a moment of remembering and trying to understand, before the relief of forgetting and inebriated unconsciousness. His thoughts drifted to those he loved and cared for the most, and who had been uppermost in his prayers. Naturally, he thought of his father and of his men, but it was thoughts of Sophonisba and a quiet arcadian retirement with her that nudged out his other thoughts if they lingered too long. He allowed the wine to show him his deepest cravings.

"Maybe you can see me or feel me," he wondered, speculating on the possibility that the temple and Melqart might give Sophonisba access to a spectral version of himself in Carthage. She must know that he would return soon, and they would spend time together, to plan and love and dream all at once.

"How do you see me in your mind, my love?" he asked to the stony cloister, with the wine starting to win the battle over his sobriety. "Do I glow like fire? Do you feel the weight of my body, the affection in my hands and the desire in my loins?" He stroked the material of the *klinai* as a pathetic substitute for her curves. He felt silly reaching out into the emptiness for his lover, but it comforted him a little. It was only the sea between them, and he would cross it again and with ease.

With his thoughts still intact, he wondered about his own worries and stresses, and the oddity that he only really became aware of them when he was given transient relief from them. His anxieties were usually just in the background, like a numbed pain that lingered but could be ignored. He wondered at the gulf between his real life and the one he was conjuring in his cups. Were all these movements, engagements and intrigues leading anywhere other than futility and death? Would he ever know the simplicities of home and family again? The more he dwelt on his condition and the more he drank, the more appalling his situation looked.

"I want to go home; take me home," he whined, slobbering into his pillow.

How distant he was from where he wanted to be. How empty was this life that the fates had given him. Even this triumph was scant compensation. Would Sophonisba even care about the stupid cup? He doubted it somehow. He imagined that she must think of him, but never proudly parading a cup before a priest on a little island a short distance from Gades. He wondered how she might worry about him, and he found some consolation in the fears he imputed on her. Would he return to her recognisable, in spirit more so than in body? After all, if he was changed in body, it was unlikely that he would return at all. The experience of battles and raids, the proximity of death, and the mutilation and destruction of enemies must have piled up on him like sacks on a donkey. *I must be diminished and degraded by it,* he thought.

For all his heroic reputation, he had built nothing of substance through his campaigning. In fact, it was the opposite: he had brought agonies and losses on himself and his companion. It didn't matter if he believed in the cause or alliance he was fighting for. He knew that fervour was a delusion from the beginning. Like everyone else, he was a puppet of circumstance and made his way as best he could. He need not be a fool, though. Life had sweetness and rewards, especially for men like him, and he had a duty to himself to ensure these prizes were his. He must be alert to opportunity and change, as well as danger. The course of the war may have turned, and news of Hannibal seemed to suggest that his momentum was faltering and the Romans were frustrating his strategies increasingly. The recent losses in Iberia only appeared to reaffirm this ebbing of Carthaginian fortunes. "No one rides a lame horse" went the old Massylian saying, and there may come a time when the Barcid nag was no better than meat.

He poured the last of the wine, which still filled his cup to its brim, and sipped it with care. He'd got to the place he wanted to be, and now he would savour the flavour whilst his taste buds still maintained a line of communication with his brain. It was a mercy to hold on to that point in his drunkenness, when his body and worries had faded away, but his senses were still revelling in their stupefaction.

He enjoyed feeling his mind lose its alertness. His breathing slackened and slowed, and his eyelids drooped a few times, indicating a longer closure was imminent. For the last moments of his day, he let his yearning mind frame little portions of Sophonisba's body. His imagination grew erotic as he tried to recreate the softness of her belly, and the lines of her hips and bum as he turned her midriff in his mind, exposing her rear and its peachy promise. His arousal went from half-hearted to rigid, and he beat down on himself with a fury at odds with the torpor of every part of him other than his hand and member. For a moment, just before he ejaculated, he wondered if he was performing a sacrilegious act, but he reassured himself quickly that Melqart was the least prissy of all the pantheon and continued his pleasure to its climax. Moments after his orgasm, he was asleep.

RETURNING TO SOPHONISBA

It was a bright morning, and the prow of the Carthaginian quinquereme was the ideal place to enjoy it. Masinissa felt himself cleansed by the spray, and he looked down at the foam and the waves below him, and occasionally noted a stray dolphin playing ahead of the vessel. In truth, the galley moved slowly in comparison with the cavorting porpoises, but the wind had dropped and it was only the unrelenting toil of the slaves in the three decks below that dragged the hulking ship through the doldrums.

His mood was as light as the zephyr that was doing little to aid the speed of the journey but was doing a great job of vivifying both his body and his spirits. He was a man returning to safety from danger, and, although Carthage would only provide him with a brief interlude between torments, he was heading towards it and not away from it, which allowed all his other cares to evaporate. Furthermore, he was returning for a well-earned and long-coveted prize. He had paid his dues at the tip of the Carthaginian spear in Iberia, and now those labours and destructions would be rewarded. Hasdrubal Gisco, who had afforded himself the same furlough and who was accompanying him on the journey home, had finally assented to Masinissa's claim on his daughter's hand, and their return to North Africa was intended to seal his engagement to Sophonisba. For both men, time away from skirmishing in the hills with the Romans, or tearing at their formations or bastions was like a holiday in paradise, although neither would have been willing to betray that to the other for fear of revealing an otherwise imperceptible weakness.

Their troops, however, had no such circumspection, and the decks of the ships were full of men dozing after a night of drinking and gambling away the gold that looting the northern peninsula had granted them. Fortunes had no doubt been won and lost, and would no doubt change hands again, either by more games or by a knife to the purse or throat. The men were also keen to return to their wives or women. For most, they had heard no word from their partners for a few years, so there were elements of presumption from the more assured, and doubt from those who were less certain of their beloved's fidelity or affection. To a man, though, they were as foaming as the seas they sliced through. Iberia, whilst full of beautiful women, was not a land of opportunity for the libidinous, which was a trait most men acquired when confronted with the prospect of death on most of the days of their lives. Naturally, many women had fallen victim to the soldiers of Carthage, but these would have been pretty exclusively those attached to Roman camps, either wives or comfort women, but, elsewhere, the libidos of the Numidians and Carthaginians were checked by their commanders. Iberia was an allied territory to be wooed and not raped by their resident armies, and the ordinary soldiers knew that very well. All knew the penalties for field indiscipline and, where women were concerned, it could cost you your manhood. The prospect of castration had the effect of neutering even the most lustful.

The African coast was starting to reveal itself, and in the sharp light, Masinissa could just begin to discern its features. The lumpy silhouette of the land mass was breaking into more appealing and familiar shapes. He could see the inviting horseshoe of golden sand, which – whilst not remarkably different from the windy beaches west of Mons Calpe – made him catch his breath a little in the knowledge that his homeland was back in sight. For Masinissa, the sands ahead were not ordinary but an auric belt greeting him on his return to his own kingdom. Who, if anyone, was waiting on the shore was incidental, for that moment, anyway.

He knew Sophonisba waited a few days' ride ahead. For now, it was the land itself that he craved and to which he belonged. The tug of return in his guts hit him again when he started to pick out the green fronds of the palm trees that ringed the high tide of the bay. Seeing them, he reminisced about the times he had held Sophonisba under similar ones in Carthage, enjoying the light shade they had granted them, but that also allowed the breeze and the tree to cast a feathery light over them, as a half-shade that sparkled, and caught the flashes in their eyes and in their smiles every once in a while. *Kissing a beautiful woman under a palm tree on a sunny, windy day is one of the finest pleasures to be had,* Masinissa thought to himself.

The final colour band on the closing horizon were the red hills which marked out the beginning of Africa. On much of the coast – particularly further east towards Carthage – lush, cultivated farmland, orchards, and vineyards announced the fertility of the soil and the skill of the farmer, but, even where there were fertile plains, the mountains lay beyond. In the darker seasons, these often turned white, especially when the Iron Mountains, or Mons Ferratus, were in full and splendid view. The foothills, however, remained stubbornly red and scorched; they were scrubby in places, where the earth triumphed over the rock, but mostly barren. The effect seemed even more striking to the advancing Masinissa, as the sun blasted away at what moisture the night had left. The dark background held more of the heat haze and it shimmered at him, blurring the scene but also flashing off opalescent light like beads of sweat on the brows of exhausted men.

His passivity in the journey also made his senses more acute, and the moment seemed quite serene. The rhythmic lap of waves had always calmed his body whilst sharpening his mind, and the motion of the vessel was having the same effect. Only on the breaking surf, where the white horses pranced merrily, was there a disturbance or an obvious movement in the landscape. As he looked away from the land, the Mediterranean was as blue as its deeper waters would allow, and, when he turned again to the African coastline, the shallow waters lightened to almost harmonise with the cloudless sky. Nothing else moved on the waters. In all the vast expanse of water, the quinquereme ploughed through it alone, a single galley rowed by a doomed crew, but ferrying two of the most important and agile generals in the world.

The fact that the ship was Carthaginian was undisputed, as it paraded its identity with the pride of an imperial vessel. Atop the mainsail was the flag that would be hailed everywhere to the east of Syphax's lands. It was rarely used beyond the navy, but it proudly indicated Carthaginian occupants. It was a tricolour of Tyrian purple, blue and silver, which were the three colours most associated with both Tyre and Carthage. Many murex marine shells had been ground for the purple, and that alone showed the eminence of the travellers.

As the ship was rowed across the placid ocean, which that day could have been convincing as a lake if not for its vastness, its stately beauty would have been obvious to anyone on the shore. It was as wine dark as the hills it was heading towards, with a colour scheme accentuated by the triple-banked scarlet oars that protruded from it and made stiff rhythmic movements on either side of it, making it look, from a bird's-eye view, like nothing more than a giant arthritic centipede. Its sails were let out but draped limply on the thin breezes. The Tyrian purple stain on the enormous cloth added an odd femininity to the massive warship. Its brass bulwarks shone immaculately, without trace of combat or contact. Dipping below and extending beyond where Masinissa stood in the prow was the thick ram, which – whilst currently splitting the seas could clearly do as equally an effective job on Roman galleys. Behind and at the furthest point from him on the aft deck, above the officers' quarters, was a golden representation of Baal Hammon. The god was primarily responsible for fertility in man and nature, but he was also god of the weather, and so a ship with his golden figurine would surely be favoured. A little too much so in Masinissa's opinion at that moment, and no doubt in the opinion of the slaves below decks, who had to labour in compensation for Baal Hammon's current gentler disposition.

A series of noises on the other side of the vessel alerted Masinissa to just how much was being endured below deck. There was scraping, the sound of a lash and yelping screams mingled with pitiable pleas, and then a splash and maybe a faint gurgle or two before the normal rhythm of the boat reasserted itself. *Maybe that poor bastard got lucky and got hit by an oar on the way down,* Masinissa thought to himself. He knew that sometimes Carthaginian captains had sadistic streaks and picked out captives who had no chance of survival on the oars. Probably, the person who was thrown overboard was one of those. Someone older, of a higher rank and thicker girth, who had been lashed raw during the voyage, and was now spent and dragging on the oar. *Over the side with you, patrician; I bet you didn't think you would wind up this way when you were taking grapes from a slave girl's cleavage.*

Although he held a powerful revulsion for that type of Roman, and it was only a presumption of his that the unfortunate slave had been one of that class, Masinissa felt a sudden empathy for the men in the decks below, as much because there were no doubt compatriots of his own enduring similar hells on Roman galleys. It was the worst kind of fate, and, with both sides capturing enemies at a rapid rate, there was little chance of those in chains being viewed as anything more than utterly disposable.

He had only spent the briefest time in that part of the ship. The mingled odours of fear, sweat, blood, urine and faeces was a world away from the fresh sea breezes above. He saw shattered men, open waisted, rowing two to an oar and patrolled relentlessly by warders who would lash blithely at any slave who paused even for a second, cutting deeply into their back or even face. It was not the duty of the warder to be accurate in their lashing, and collateral damage was inflicted to areas beyond the line of the victim's spine. Forearms and biceps seemed to be spared miraculously, however; the men with the bullwhips took care enough to ensure that the sting in those muscles was only being supplied by the oarsman's own efforts. To see weary, bloodied men of all casts – although it would appear on this journey that they were mostly Roman – toiling mechanically beyond exhaustion and the ordinary extremes of endurance, and being reduced merely to fleshy levers was an appalling sight. None would meet his gaze, both from fear of having more stripes cut into their hides but also from a fatigue that bowed heads and gave energy only to their burning limbs.

Masinissa shook his head, shaking out the image a little as he did so, but leaving a little of the pity he felt in his heart. *You have no obligation to the damned,* he thought to himself. *You helped put those men in those manacles by your actions, after all, and they no doubt would relish the opportunity to do the same to you. A man of your stature would be right on the leading oar and the immediate favourite of the Roman lashers.*

Whilst below deck the pulsing, fake vitality of the tortured continued to beat out a stroke, the scene on the foredeck could not be more contrasting. It was a scene of complete languor and listlessness. On the water, you need post no sentries besides the man high in the rigging, scouting for enemy galleys. The men who might threaten you are chained and broken, and would offer no threat even if given the keys to their irons. The previous night's revelries had taken their toll, and most men still slept, and most noisily, whilst those who had drifted back to consciousness had found corners in the shade, and continued to daydream or chat with their fellows. The games of the evening had yet to be resumed in earnest. There were pockets of zealousness from those who had responsibility for the sails and navigation, and the odd pot-boiler who had been charged with breakfast, but the deck was about as energised as the quiescent sea beneath them.

Spying movement in the stern of the ship, Masinissa saw Gisco emerge from the quarters he occupied alone. Masinissa slept on the deck with his men, and he felt no slight in not being offered the same cosseted hospitality as his senior. He liked to maintain a little separation between himself and the Carthaginian general, even if their present journey was intended to unite them as father- and son-in-law. He cast a critical eye over his prospective new in-law, but he was cautious not to stare too blatantly, as no doubt it was towards him that the general was walking. No one aside from the captain would merit any kind of conversation at all. He might simply be taking the air and acquiring his morning sea legs, but Masinissa thought a little exchange before they resumed on horseback was in Gisco's mind.

The ship's deck was long, and it struck Masinissa how differently the officers and men viewed Gisco as he passed them by. As he approached, they feigned being preoccupied and looked at him furtively, if at all. When he had passed, though, many looked directly at him, as if needing to place themselves on wary guard. Clearly, they had learnt that he was someone to avoid. Masinissa surmised that the same ought to apply to himself, but he rarely encountered men who shied away from looking at him directly. Fear and respect were quite different, after all.

As Gisco drew closer, the differences between them appeared even more apparent. Masinissa was far darker and taller than Gisco, and his features blunter and harder. His posture, even when relaxed, was imposing, an advantage accentuated by his physique. Gisco, in comparison, stooped ever so slightly and carried an emerging paunch under his robes, even after the long campaigns they were taking their leave from. There was still a little wire in his limbs and face, though, and there was a keenness and perhaps hints of cruelty in his aquiline features. He had discarded his armour for the journey, and now wore the full regalia of the Punic aristocrat; the long, purple robes of the *suffete* flowed behind him like the waves that trailed behind the galley.

"Good morning, my lord, most exalted son of Canaan," Masinissa hailed, still unsure of what balance to strike between the formal and familiar.

Gisco gave him little opportunity for the latter, and so he relied mostly on the former. "Greetings to you, Masinissa. How is our little cruise affecting your spirits?" he enquired in a jovial tone, which implied that the general had just slept rather well. On many mornings on campaign, Gisco had made scant efforts to disguise the irritability of a short rest.

"Pretty well, in all honesty," Masinissa replied truthfully. "I'm looking forward to sheathing my sword for a while and not having to think about looking into another man's eyes as I stick it into him."

"That's a part of life I would have thought you would have got used to by now," Gisco replied unsympathetically. "Are you not also looking forward to resuming relations with my daughter?"

Naturally, Masinissa was, but he was hesitant regarding the tone he should adopt to reply to such a direct and personal question. After all, this was Sophonisba's father, and the ribald banter he may have used around Capuca, Massiva or Juba Tunic would be a gross indiscretion in front of Gisco. It may even cause him to be thrown overboard, with his importance as a cavalry commander paling beside the rage of an offended father. He was therefore suitably circumspect in his response. "Yes, sir, I am. She is the kindest and most beautiful woman in Baal Hammon's creation, and I have yearned to see her again every moment of our time in Iberia."

"Relax, Masinissa," Gisco interjected. "I'm not going to cut your balls off for lusting after my daughter. I'm not so blind as to not be aware of her attractions. Her charms are both obvious and subtle. I credit you with the sense to recognise her subtler ones as well as the ones the lecherous fools in the street can spy from many paces away.

"Let me caution you, though, or maybe give you some advice. As it's clear that your pity and humanity are intact, and that you have not become inured to killing other men, and the war has yet to calcify your heart, there are certain doorways into your being you should seal. Loving a woman is a heartache when you are not with her, and when you are together there are weaknesses that you should never betray. Keep a separation in yourself, son, or it will consume you. I am ultimately in charge of my daughter's affections, not you, and certainly not her."

Masinissa was not quite prepared for the abruptness in Gisco's manner, and he felt a little reprimanded by his senior. His natural tact, though, held him together in his response. "I understand, sir, and appreciate the advice and reminder." He couldn't quite resist a little insolence though and added, "I've yet to reach the point where I have to sacrifice my decency. I hope we get out of this mess before it comes to that."

"Well, I have no interest in your decency," Gisco scolded. "My need is for a ruthless and able cavalry commander, and don't you ever lose sight of that fact. This mess will be our doom or our triumph. Patch up your sympathies for your fellow men after you have destroyed them and can safely indulge such a whim."

It certainly looked like Gisco was in the mood for a speech or perhaps even a tirade, and he continued with barely a pause, "You know the civilisation we have, certainly the civilisation the Romans have built, has not been constructed on emotions or affections. There is a need for detachment, particularly by a general. How many men did we lose today and how many men did we kill? For me, a man is simply a unit of measurement. It is not a face or a name, just a loss or a gain… pardon my rhyme. We are like merchants of blood; our merchandise, our men, are to be considered only by the profits or losses that they accrue for us."

"But what of loyalty?" Masinissa tried to interject.

"That can be bought in many different ways. You can fight for me or you could fight for Scipio. What difference does it make when you are actually fighting? Only the banners change. You know I observe you, Masinissa, and you are halfway there. You know what to do, and are brave and tactically astute, but you still let your guts and your heart mess with your decisions. We and the Romans are building our civilisations here, and what we both have done is to renounce our instincts. The Greeks have given us their *logikos*, their logic, and that's how we live now. The myths and legends of our forefathers don't win battles and save cities. We do it with our cunning and ingenuities. Don't be emotional. If you trust your guts and act on the promptings of your emotions, you will be a fool. You'll be like those barbaric Gauls whom we convince to man the front of our lines, lashing out at the slightest insult. They last about five minutes in battle, you know, and no one remembers them; they are just a speck on our records, nothing more."

"Yes, sir, I will try," Masinissa replied, conceding wisdom to the older man.

The comment put a wan smile on Gisco's face, but it was momentary and barely lingered long enough for Masinissa to even be aware of it. It flickered out to be replaced by an icy furrow on the old patrician's already forbidding features.

Suddenly, and unexpectedly, his fingers closed upon his subordinate's wrists, and a quick nod to the burly boatswain who had been loitering a little behind Masinissa led the sailor to take hold of them both from behind. For practical purposes, this incapacitated Masinissa even though the sailor chose not to apply too much pressure. Masinissa had just enough awareness of their movements to have been able to react, but, in that same flash, he had recognised the futility of any resistance and chose to be as compliant as possible in allowing matters to unfold. Whatever Gisco had in mind, he would do anyway, so clobbering a few seadogs would only have made matters worse.

"My apologies, Masinissa, but I need a little more from your engagement to my daughter than you were expecting," declared Gisco.

Gisco's gaze left him for a second, allowing Masinissa to observe the sour, pinched profile of the man; the general was squinting as he surveyed the blue horizon and perhaps puckering in readiness for his unsavoury task.

"All right, General, but why the rough stuff? You're not thinking of snipping me are you?" Masinissa's thoughts had viscerally swung to protecting his nether regions, an instinct no doubt abetted by the fact that their intended nest was his captor's daughter's moist centre.

"Not at all, but I intend to mark you – to brand you, if you will – to remind you of where your loyalties lie and to declare your treachery should you ever betray them. It's only fair. I'm giving you something, so it is right that I take something in return," Gisco confirmed.

Masinissa's mind was scrambling for clues as to Gisco's intentions, but with the general's choice of the word "brand", his corporeal awareness became more distinct. He knew of the things to which the patrician sadist was hinting. Men were often marked, most often the most loyal or the most suspicious, either as badges of honour or marks of imperial possession. Masinissa knew which of those categories he was being regarded in. The aloof Carthaginian was clearly bracketing him in with the slaves and mercenaries. *You'll pay for this you bastard,* he thought.

Gisco made everything clear very quickly. "I know how much you revere Melqart and how much the men view you as almost his reincarnation – physically, anyway – but I think you need a little extra support from the mother goddess, and so if she can see her symbol on you, she may favour you as much as Melqart appears to. It can't hurt right? This will, but I'm sure your benedictions to Tanit will receive more favourable responses if she can see how you have suffered for her blessings."

At that point, Gisco drew his sword. Like most senior Carthaginians, his preferred blade was a Greek *xiphos*.

At least the cuts have a chance to be clean and shallow, Masinissa thought morosely. He was at the point that the best consolation he could grant himself was the fact that Gisco had not drawn a *falcata*. That would have surely made a complete mess of whatever part of his body Gisco intended to carve.

"I'm not going to make a portrait on your body. Just a few strokes on your chest that you can easily conceal, and will no doubt mingle and be barely noticeable amongst your other scars. You have almost the colour of a Libyan, so the marks will hardly be lurid as they fade."

Masinissa looked at Gisco and tried to drain his eyes of all emotion, particularly fear, and replied as flatly and curtly as he could, "I am used to trials, sir, and am prepared for them. Proceed."

"Hah! As you wish; you have at least passed the test of defiance." Gisco lowered his eyes from meeting Masinissa's stare and sliced right down the centre of his tunic, exposing his chest, which was the canvas he planned to decorate. "My apologies for ruining your clothing, but I have others for you and you will need a proper bandage to soak this up."

His next motion ripped a scarlet line right across Masinissa's left breast. His reflexes pulled him back into the boatswain, and he pursed his lips, sucked back the pain over them and bit hard on his tongue to keep himself from crying out. Gisco hadn't even considered giving his impending son-in-law a piece of leather or even wood to bite down on. *Take it,* he implored himself. His blood flowed freely, but the pain was manageable. There were far worse places to take a blade, and he knew the next cuts would hurt him no more than the first, or at least the first wound had given him a shorter distance of pain to traverse before it crested or could be endured.

The first triangular shape Gisco cut was done almost before Masinissa's body had absorbed the first shock. The circular head took a little more care and deliberation, and tore at his body at different angles. It was worse, but mostly in the anticipation of the changing direction. Gisco had to change tools to manage the shape also, and used a field knife, which brought him closer in. Masinissa could sense the older man's relish in his work, and he observed Gisco's concentration as intently as he could, even though his chest was jerking involuntarily at every burning cut into him the metal made. Gisco drew the arms of Tanit more deliberately and looked hard at Masinissa whilst doing so, drawing across Masinissa's taut pectoral muscle until the arms were roughly symmetrical. He added a late flourish to represent the open arms of the goddess, but they were relative flicks compared to the gouges and lines that had formed the body and the head.

"There; all done. You are certainly a son of Canaan now too, or a defender is perhaps a more accurate description." Gisco almost beamed with the satisfaction his mutilation of Masinissa's breast had given him.

Masinissa relaxed his arms a little as they were released, but still drew his chest inward, and resisted the temptation to shake and run the pain off. *Yeah, I'll show you my rejection of instincts you piece of shit,* he thought, *I'm not going to go yelping and dancing around this deck for your amusement.* He took the wine that was offered to him by one of the concerned Numidians who had gathered close by, drank a big slug from the clay cup and let a little run into his blood. That would help. He looked at his men and around the deck of the galley.

He'd clearly been the show, and no doubt many were looking to him for a reaction. He recognised that this moment would be memorable and his behaviour could elevate or tarnish his reputation considerably. He fought the anger the pain engendered, and tested his body a little by clenching his fists, thrusting forwards his chest a little and raising his head to the sky. He sensed that the motion opened his wounds a little more, but that the pain had more or less plateaued. *Here goes, then,* he thought, and he executed a wide stretch of his arms, which was a motion that seemed to take Gisco aback somewhat. He stopped short of adding a little yawn, but the effect was as nonchalant as if he'd risen from his pillows in his Carthaginian villa.

"Will someone get me some honey for this, please?" he called out, as if it was just for his bread, not to treat the screaming pain in his breast.

Massiva ran to the quartermaster, and came back with a pot and a brush as quickly as he could. His haste was plain to everyone, as his panting strides were the only sound to be heard on deck. A hush had taken hold of the men, who seemed unsure whether Masinissa's insouciant gesture had fallen the wrong side of insubordination. Aside from the settling breathing of Masinissa's nephew, only the water below and the measured heave and thrust of the oars punctuated the silence.

Gisco seemed to realise quickly that the spectacle he had initiated had somewhat backfired. He had won in the sense of the indelible marks he had made on his junior, but he was the vanquished in the eyes of the watching throng, as his victim stood before him casually defiant. He had hoped for Masinissa's public emasculation and the reinforcement of his authority. Instead, the reverse could be easily identified in the low murmurs of the men and their fixation on Masinissa's bloody chest. They had all seen bravery in the field, but they also all knew that pain of that sort was not so easily camouflaged, and, as eyewitnesses to Masinissa's resolution, they granted him a higher station of respect. His prospective victim had turned the tables on him, and Masinissa had added even more heroic lustre to his standing.

He conceded by declaring to the admiring audience, "Behold our finest; look how he barely notices his own wounds. Were we all so brave, if we all could show such fortitude, we'd be dancing on the Palatine Hill by now, drenched in the booty of the sacking of Rome. Unfortunately, our soldiers, allies and especially our mercenaries are lacking in such spirit. Take heed, men; take the example of Masinissa as your inspiration. Face your trials as he has done today."

As exhortations go, it was effective, despite its insincerity, and the men gave out a lusty cheer, a mixture of relief and genuine admiration.

Emboldened, Gisco felt he needed to add a little bit of gloss to his rhetoric. "In your hearts, I know you understand this already..." He perceptibly raised his voice and urgency as he continued, "But know from me too that it is an inviolable rule of the gods that the world we have belongs, and belongs utterly, to the strong, to the resilient and to the disciplined – to men like Masinissa. Those who would deny or renege on their duties as men, who show weakness or turn from the trials of life will find themselves quickly stripped of all they cherish, be it their homes, their wealth, their possessions, their wives or even their most humble garments. You only need to remain still for a second to hear the lashes and the wails of the men who are manning the oars of this galley to know the fate of the weak."

The reaction to Gisco's bluster by the men on deck was a little more muted than their response to his praise of Masinissa. The soldiers and sailors knew their fates would be quite contrasted, depending on the course of the war, and they let their general's self-evident tirade wash over them.

For Masinissa's part, realising that Gisco's speech was allowing him an opportunity to leave the stage, he let Massiva and Capuca help him to the prow of the ship. The wind had a little more vigour there and it cooled him a little. He would take a little more of the wine shortly and that would numb his pain sufficiently.

Away from the earshot of the patrician, whose rescue act had been performed and who was looking for an exit of his own, Masinissa held the rails of the ship and let them support him. The flow of blood seemed to have been staunched. It was over at that point. A long pause and peremptory turn from the scene in the other direction by Gisco indicated that it was over for him too.

"He blew his trumpet as loudly as he could then, huh?" Masinissa stated to his two kinsmen in a tone that was uncharacteristically sardonic.

"He had to," Capuca replied. "In the end, he turned it into a good tune. You can't trust these bastards can you, Mas?"

"Nah, you're right. He and his kind need us but are afraid of us. These things they do are their attempts to put reins or shackles on us. We're like our horses, though, aren't we? We don't need reins. We just need to believe in our riders, if that is a comparison that is not too demeaning for me!" explained Masinissa.

"It might be, but I understand," Massiva said reassuringly

Masinissa's mood was turning sanguine. He looked over to the southern horizon, criss-crossed his fingers close to his face and blew out a little philosophy. "My view of things is that the bravest man in the universe is the one who forgives first. That is the most powerful virtue and a sign of character. If I accept your injury to me and let it go, then you might do the same for me, but it is the one who swallows his anger first who is the braver man. Gisco was on to something earlier, dismissing our baser instincts. I'm sure if I had done to him what he has done to me, though, he would have me flayed alive. Equally, whilst I make the choice to forgive, I don't forget. I know where I stand in this game, and if the pieces move, so will I. I will take Gisco's life if I need to, but not as my own personal act of vengeance, rather because it preserves me or helps Numidia, my father or you, my brothers."

His cousin and nephew assented quietly, and Masinissa gripped the gunwale and focussed his view keenly ahead to the shadows on the horizon, which were the first hints of his native lands. They would soon find anchor, and, from there, journey through the mountains and vineyards, with the lands becoming progressively more conspicuously fertile and wealthy.

Soon, Sophonisba, he thought to himself. *Your father's knife didn't go so deep as to cut you out of my heart.*

OUR ELDERLY CHILDREN

Reunions and returns are so different from farewells. The emotional streams flow in opposite directions, in inversion with the actual physical movement. At the point of going further away, you feel closer to one another, and when coming closer there is a tendency to feel more distant. However, how far away the separation is in terms of either time or distance becomes moot very quickly. For a soldier and his sweetheart, this can be categorised as out of sight, beyond reach, or dead or abandoned. Nevertheless, emotional distances are more subtly graded, and, in many cases, can be delineated by how faded the memory or hopeless the infatuation or war becomes. There can be species differences between realists and romantics, but the evanescence of love can often be a shared fate. It was an ironic contrast for a man on campaign that he could lose his life instantaneously, but he was probably losing what gave it meaning infinitesimally, not by the minute or second, but dripping away by the season and the year. Beautiful women are always prey to men, and a distant lover could never know when his beloved's heart may be turned, by flattery, boredom or whatever other means of distraction.

The most overt manifestation of this contrast was the sense of intimacy. When leaving – and Masinissa certainly remembered Sophonisba clinging to him desperately when he had departed Carthage, as if she was on a cliff's edge, and he was the only piton between her and oblivion – the sense of closeness was intoxicating. The knowledge of separation stripped them of any reservation or concealment, and they bared their emotions in a little time capsule that they hoped would sustain them for the long absence to come. Their secrets, truths and vulnerabilities were all on the table for the other person. In such situations, it is easy, particularly for the more ingenuous, to enter a delusionary reverie where the imagination and the heart spin out of control and conjure exaggerated versions of those core parts of their being. In other words, the heady nature of departure can trick you into believing in emotions that don't really exist. There is love and there is the fantasy of love, and it's often very hard to tell the difference. It's easy to buy into someone's passion and ardour when you won't have anyone to hold your hand for months or where there is a doubt that, if you are ever fortunate enough to see them again, those parts of your beloved's body will still exist.

Conversely, when the reappearing beau is finally reunited with his partner, he – and this condition certainly afflicted Masinissa – can be beset with questions and doubts. Have I changed? Has she changed? Has the world changed? Was this love a fantasy love? Am I fool? Big questions, but no answers.

Suffused with these tidal anxieties that lapped back and forth over him, as he tried to push them back with logic and memories, it was predictable that he would stumble when he eventually saw Sophonisba again. He had overthought things, which put those thoughts into patterns of behaviour that locked him in and paralysed both his body and his spirit.

He wondered why on earth he would be posing questions to himself such as "Will she still like me?", "Is it going to be OK?" and "Do I smell OK?" For Tanit's sake!

He had been in Carthage for a few days and had sent word to Sophonisba of his presence in the city, but had not rushed to meet her. His first social contact had been with Conon, and it was good to see his old friend again and have his intellect stretched into neglected regions. Conon was much the same. He always seemed a little dishevelled, but always in slightly different ways. It could be his clothes, his hair, his beard, or the state of his villa or horse. The guy always had other things on his mind than the mundanities of appearance.

Regardless of this preference, Sophonisba was on his mind constantly. It wasn't a tease that he had failed to orchestrate a more expeditious rendezvous. He was hauling up buckets of hesitation from a deep well of uncertainty. He needed to rest too, and to soak the war out of his soul and the fatigue from his muscles. He was a much leaner man than the one Sophonisba would be preserving in her mind's eye. He was not gaunt or haggard, or with that haunted or distant gaze you often saw in veterans of the war, but she would notice the change.

Finally, he found the resolve to knock on her door. He had asked about her current movements, and the activities and habits of the household. He wanted to catch her when there were few, or preferably, no others there, aside from the slaves and any gladiator posted on watch. It was mid-morning, not too early that she would be still in bed, and not too late that her uncles and brothers would be around looking for victuals, if they hadn't found a friend, tavern or sport to divert them.

As he prepared to hail the nearest domestic, his self-consciousness started to tingle and his throat tighten. He came close to retching, and the presence of the attendant slave was the only thing that allowed him to hold his composure together. The first and primary focus of this uncharacteristic diffidence and personal recrimination was at his wrists. Half an hour earlier, the gold bracelets he was sporting appeared to be a good idea and ornaments that lent him stature. Just then, all of a sudden, he could see that he was trying too hard, was plainly overdressed for the morning, and, at worst, could be seen as being vain and ostentatious. The puffy grandeur that crowned his hands would draw attention to his every movement and tick. What if he got a little tremor? Would he have to hide his jewellery, or try to sit somewhere and bury the refulgent beacons of his nervousness under his thighs? He didn't even have the camouflage of some kind of cloak. His injudicious clothing choices had included, excepting his glittering cuffs, wearing only a very light and short tunic, with the intention being to beguile Sophonisba with his impressive physique. He should have known better. He did, but his anxiety had made a fool of him. At least it was hot, and, hopefully, Sophonisba would see it for what it was: nothing more than a gauche attempt to impress her.

His tension was stretched as taut as a fishing line that's hooked a whopper when, through the courtyard, he glimpsed Sophonisba striding – well, practically breaking into a trot – towards him. Her smile almost resembled the gasp of a struggling fish as she sucked in and tried to restrain her joy. The obvious euphoria of the approaching tornado ought to have mollified Masinissa, but he stood there stunned, like a hare in front of a chariot. The portents were good, but his thoughts still couldn't free themselves of doubt. The "does she still like me and am I going to dazzle her with my dumb jewellery" questions fizzed in the forefront of his mind when the racing Venus heading his way should have put all his worries to rest. Fortunately for him, she didn't check her pace as she reached him, as that would have made his jitters immeasurably worse, and she hit him with all the force her soft curves could generate.

Masinissa's composure, or what of it there remained, flipped on impact, and his dam broke as he jumbled her body and mouth into his arms and mouth. It was a corporeal overdose. His ardour matched her incandescence, but it was not practised or at ease. It was as rushed and panicked as a young boy cupping his first breast or finding his way down into a region he really ought to be mapping with his mouth.

When his mind caught up with his senses, he became aware of the thumping rhythm of his heartbeat, which was going at a pace, as if he'd sprinted for a few minutes. He made a deep exhalation of tension and carbon dioxide, an expiration which was immediately revealing of his state of mind to Sophonisba, who had credited his fumbles to passionate overexuberance.

She looked at him with her doe eyes, held his arms and pulled back at the same time, at once solicitous and inquisitive. "Ah, my precious love, it's OK; it's OK." She moved her hands to his cheeks and flattened them there. For those moments, it was as if she were pressing hard on a burst artery.

His tension found the door in the middle of his chest and let itself out of his body. When she saw the sag, she went on her tiptoes, brought his face to hers, kissed him and then embraced him. His vigour returned, his arms wound around her with more certainty and possessiveness, and he brought her into him to the point where if it were any further, it would become painful and suffocating.

"Hey, Crusher, you're home," she said, as they unlocked themselves finally, and could see the emotion and happiness on each other's faces.

For the first time, Masinissa looked at her in terms of her physical form, as opposed to their pure reacquaintance of nerves, senses and souls. The feelings of his hands and heart gave way a little to the assessments of his eyes and mind, which viewed her through a slightly different prism. It was not quite judgemental, but it noticed the tiniest changes. He had to resketch the outlines of her to repackage into his memory. In truth, the contours of her body, and the smoothness of her form and face were little altered and intact. Similarly to him, her physique had become marginally more athletic, at least in her arms and calves. The gentle convex line of her tummy, which he had stroked as if it sheltered the first glow of new life, had shaved away and, whilst not concave, pinched slightly inwards when her diaphragm contracted. Fortunately, her fractional weight loss ended its infringement of her femininity right there; her breasts and arse remained full and plump.

Sophonisba said earnestly, "You know I had a thought, one of those dreamy thoughts that are mostly imagination, a totally what-if line of speculation, just me hypothetically musing about my guesses and hopes for the future. I have a lot of empty time on my hands, so I was wondering what if this happened or that happened, that sort of thing. I wandered down the road of our imaginary, interweaving lives, took myself to the places I want them to go, and envisaged what outcomes and people came out of that. OK, basically, I imagined the phantom people who would come from us, the kids we might have together, and their ultimate reflections on us. Our children, if we have any, would sit together one day when we've passed and make their judgements on us. They will share their fond anecdotes, their grief, what they hold on to, and what shreds of us they hold tightest in their memories and hearts. You know, in my mind, I imagined a scene where our elderly children – two girls and a boy, incidentally – talk about us. Our boy, now infirm and weary, will have a little tear in his eye and a gulp when the conversation turns to us. It's hard to throw your mind forwards to beyond your days when your whole existence is considered only by a few old people. In any event, I can't quite imagine their words, but I can see their nods, quivers and downcast eyes. It made me sad. Crazy isn't it? They're people who may never exist, and certainly will not conform to the way I'm conceptualising them, who are less real than dolls. It makes me sad."

"Yes, it will," Masinissa replied, strangely touched. "Our dreams do make us sad sometimes; mine do… for all sorts of reasons. Maybe they're unattainable, or if they are, most of me doesn't really want them. Most of the time, I don't even know what I'm striving towards or what I should really be considering to be important. Would I be a fool now to grab you and as much as a few horses will carry, and head south and lose ourselves somewhere beyond the deserts? I want peace, I want to give my hopes – our hopes – incipient life. Should I care where that is, or what honour or power my name carries? Am I the successor to a country or tribe? Do I want to forge one out of the other? Is that my grand fate or is it to be trampled under a Roman's horse, lamenting my follies and stupidity?"

"Hold on to yourself, my darling. Sometimes we have agency over our own lives, and it's frustrating when we don't, but mostly we don't. You'll pay your dues, somehow there'll be peace, and we can find a better destiny for ourselves. I'm sure it must sound trite, and the pat line you hear from your seniors, your parents and everyone else all the time, but stay the course, hang in there. The world will sort itself out, and if it doesn't, then we can run and hope no one picks up our trail." She put her hands under his arms and around his waist, and laid her head on his chest. "I'm always going to be here," she added.

He put his hand on her nuzzling head, and traced her hair as it curled, twisting it a little between his fingers and letting it loose. Her words and the little preoccupation soothed him. His tone dropped to a soft murmur when he spoke again. "You know, it's hard to come back, and it's harder still to know that, when you've come back, you have to go again. It will be harder than the first time, and no doubt the time after will be harder again. My chances of survival must shorten all the time, as my knowledge of the ways of dying and styles of pain increase. I won't say more of that, to spare you. I will confess that I'm more afraid. That is all."

Masinissa kissed a tendril he loosened, wondering how much Sophonisba would sense it or the passion behind it.

He went on, "The longer I soldier the more I see us veterans as marcescent beings. We wither, we hollow ourselves out, we despair, we suffer, we grieve and, ultimately, we die, but until we do we cling on to the host. We can't take our swords, metaphorically, and cleave ourselves from that which is chewing us to pieces. I guess I must have become one of them. It makes this small portion of another reality so overwhelming."

He looked towards the sun, squinted and rubbed his nose, as to rub his watery eyes would have demonstrated that he was beginning to succumb emotionally. It would have been OK, but he wanted to try to make sense of things and help Sophonisba understand where he was, and he didn't want to tip the balance over, either for himself or for her. "You know, it's an amazing thing for me to simply see you, and to look at you with my own eyes instead of my memory. It's bringing it all back for me. The happy moments we had together. They've been treats that I've preserved for any moments I had to myself. They've been my most precious sanctuary that I eked out to myself, like a starving man portioning his meagre grains during a famine. Now they are cascading back into the centre of my being. It's a flood! You look beautiful – as beautiful as the first day I set eyes on you."

Sophonisba smiled sympathetically and cooed, coalescing her emotional response into equal parts pity and flattery.

"I'm such a fool," Masinissa continued his confessional. "Coming here, my self-consciousness was through the roof, my blood was going and my face was flushed. It was like I was back in school and a thirteen-year-old boy with his first stumbling crush. My heart was battering itself, thumping like a drum. Emotionally, I was beaten raw. Having been through all I have, you'd have thought I'd have more of a clue. I built this reunion up in my mind, you know. My soul and heart are gaspingly empty. I've been like a landed fish flapping for water."

He knew he was floundering but making some sense of himself in the process, and tacked a little towards a third party. "I'll tell you something about someone who got to me once, and made me understand how potent and to be cherished memories of happier times are, and of you most of all, obviously. I knew already, but the guy sorta rammed it home for me. Well, one of the troops – he was a junior *tesserarius,* I think, so he'd been around a bit – was sitting with me around a fire one evening. We were drinking a little, but we were still well to the right side of it, and he turned to me and started talking about mundane stuff. Then he went on about the past, the good past – though the past is always good when you're in the shit – and then he started talking about forgetting. We try to forget a lot of things, but he was telling me about the things he'd forgotten that he wanted to remember. People he knew and things he had done that were slipping away. He talked about half-remembered names and faces. The more he clutched at them, the more they eluded him. He said he could accept this as just a natural waning when it was not all that important, but it made him desperate when it happened to things that he valued the most. He cried then; he told me he had forgotten the colour of his wife's eyes, and it made him feel ashamed and lost. His fading memory had taken away the pegs that held his other reality together, and it felt like his life was flying away from him, like a piece of clothing that flies off a drying line in a storm.

"It was like a loss for him, and I got that. His life had been diminished. His whole world had become achromic with the loss of being able to recall his wife's eyes. To be honest, maybe he never knew, maybe he never bothered to look that intently at her or it was just one of those things he didn't absorb about her. But… but the fact that he didn't know then broke him; it really broke him up. It's… let me explain. For him, and for me, all you have beyond your brutal purpose of finding and killing your enemy is your thoughts and memories. I had all these memories and images of you to keep me going. I didn't need more than that. It was the little dose of nourishment my soul craved. You work it like putty, but so much gets in the way, during all that time you're away, till you can be left with just the idea of someone, with almost no shape or form. That's where this guy had got to. He was fighting to remember his lover, and all he had was the idea of her. He had nothing else to hold on to. I have to fill myself up again with you as much as I can, so that reservoir is full for the next campaign…" He stopped there, and his final words trailed off quietly and perhaps questioningly.

Sophonisba took his hands in hers and squeezed them, as if pumping vigour into his being. "I have to too," she said after a while. "How about you fill me up some now… and work me like putty a little as well," she added as boldly lascivious as she had ever been. She underlined the invitation with a wink. She let go of one hand, tugged at the other and skipped into the villa, leading him bouncily into the bedroom. There were a few pauses for passionate embraces en route, and by the time they'd reached the room he was naked, and she was almost in the same condition, clad in only the most diaphanous undergarments he'd ever seen.

Her hips and arse jiggled invitingly, and Masinissa found himself trying to slow himself down as he was ripe to blow before he had even got her stripped. She was happy to keep the pace slow initially, leaving his tumescence to him after a possessive grab led to him telling her to cool off. After a few minutes, when his composure and seed were reasonably back in check, he descended her, from her pert mounds – where he lingered – on down, with detours to her soft corners and crevices, till he found his way to her softest crevice. He could tell quickly, as he parted her with his nose and then his tongue, that she was as aroused as him.

Her intensity mounted and rolled, and she gave slow-motion mule kicks with her pelvis with his every flick and toss around her sensitivity. He relished her every motion and desire, and lapped and licked voraciously, and her shakes and moans were as pleasurable for him as if they were his own. The beauty of a woman's raptures is that they can be strung out, and peak and crest. For Masinissa, it was a thrill to take control of her pleasure. It was, in some sense, a way of taking possession of her whole being. For those moments, he was satisfying every fibre of her being, and the mark and the memory would be indelible for them both.

She relished his probes, but soon called for him to penetrate her and take possession of her. She was ready, and neither of them knew when, or if, the opportunity would be theirs again. Masinissa slipped off the bed, pulling her hips towards him, turning her over and raising her arse. He kissed her neck and ear, leant away and in, took her haunches and entered her deeply.

She gasped briefly and muttered, "Baby?" which was part question, part anticipation, part revelation.

He caressed her rear, and then fizzed and flicked his flat palm across it. "There's only so much heaven I can see in your eyes, sweetheart!"

She laughed so hard it almost shook him out of her, but he regained purchase and let rip. His stamina held together as well as his libido, and they roiled together, sometimes in sync and sometimes slightly out, Masinissa enjoying setting the tempo and the pace. Eventually, as he tired, he came off his feet and got closer to her, joining her to finish their pleasures more horizontally. He used his arms some more to anchor himself, as well as to roll her on to him, a grind she much appreciated. Fortunately, she was light enough for him to maintain the movement. It took her to the edge quicker and more intensely than anything else he tried, but, boy, did it tire him. Kneeling and lifting hips was fun, but it burnt the biceps as much as it rasped Sophonisba's sex.

Eventually, flat out on top of her, deeply, more softly, but as abruptly as all male orgasms are, he came, and it was the backed-up release of months. He hoped his timing was right, and he decorated well the cleft of Sophonisba's back, leaving a sticky line in the lower furrow of her spine.

They both let their breath and their bodies recover their normal repose, and tucked into one another as stillness and ease returned to them. More than their words and dedications, their embrace indicated their affections and devotion.

Tucked into the crook of his armpit and playing with the fringes of his beard, Sophonisba's limpid eyes started to glisten with the dew of her feelings and satisfaction. "My sweet boy," she whispered "My sweetheart. Was that worth the wait?"

Masinissa looked down at her. Her hair curled around her shoulders and a little of it nestled in her cleavage, which was accentuated beautifully by the angle of her body and ripened as it rested against him. It was a beautiful sight. She had never looked so radiant or more his.

"Of course," he grinned back, and he added a caress to the nearer of her nipples.

"We have to say goodbye soon." Sophonisba spoke a little morosely, and the realisation carried a twin meaning to be applied to the immediate and near present.

The dial was moving on them again. They had transported themselves outside of the confines of their lives and situations, but it was necessarily furtive and clandestine, even if the suspicions of the extent of their previous attachment was widespread, and the gossip focussed explicitly on its physical consummation.

The minutes they had left together then became more important than the seeking of flesh and expression of desire. The thoughts that were in each other's minds, they understood and weighed intuitively, as if the fusion of their bodies had been superseded by the synthesising of their deeper beings. The silence remained as their tender touches gave tacit pledges to each other.

Sophonisba broke their reverie. She asked him for his hand as solemnly as if she were a priest at a ceremony of their union. Masinissa hovered it in front of her vaguely, and she smirked at his hesitance and clasped it between both of her own hands, flattening his palm between hers. She then opened it, stared at it and inspected it as if she were an infant enthralled suddenly, and then placed it on her bosom. Masinissa made to cup her breast, but her hands pressed down on his maintaining the flatness, and depriving it of movement and thrill. It was clear that, for her, this was a gesture, even an oath of some kind, rather than an impatient act of foreplay.

"It's a sad thing that our love must be counted in minutes, and that it can't stretch out and be easy. It's like we have to fill our flask or jug of love in a rush, and not be at our ease, like this, all the time." She smirked a little at the accidental humour of the expression and repeated, "Jug of love!" in a more jocular tone. "You know I can give you tangible things. I can cut my hair. I can give you these robes or a scarf, but you will still have to imagine me. It's a little puzzle piece that has to represent me. It might be a little fanciful, but here's another. I give you my heart. In my mind, that's what I've just done. You covered my heart. If you hold out your hand and open it, imagine my heart there. Clutch it tighter then and you're squeezing me. I'm there. I'm there, OK? Wherever you are, I'm there. Be comforted by these memories, by these devotions and by these moments. Try to let me into your being, like a shaman or a priest may summon a spirit or a deity."

"I will," Masinissa replied. "I've done it already. I've practised it. I go into myself and find you, and it does help me. It really does. The life I live is more dreamlike anyway these days. Travelling, training, seeing people disappear suddenly and being on the precipice of death: it all works to dislodge your anchors. It's all uprooted. The hardest thing is giving up control of your dreams; not in the sense of my imagination, I mean, but my hopes. Your plans, my plans and our plans, they're just hopes, not realities waiting to happen or be made. They're a rung lower on the ladder than that. For the people who stay – the politicians and the tradespeople – tomorrow is more of a certainty. For me, tomorrow may never come. I have to live with being a man in his prime who may not see another day. You can't dwell on it too much, though. All we know of the future is that there will be stars at night and sun in the day."

Sophonisba gave him a consoling rub, and he could see she was thinking of words and expressions to ease him. She offered, "Wish on those stars, baby, and those hopes will come true. Believe in love, in me and in all that our love can bring. A new world is gonna be waiting for you. This will end and we will begin."

"Thanks, darling. Yeah, we will. There's plenty in my dreams to explore," he said, without a trace of intentional vulgarity. "I know nothing is promised and nothing is sure, but you give the unknown a little light, which is something to keep me going down the road I have to travel."

"For me, it's the same," Sophonisba replied with a little emotional flapping gesture, as if she were cooling herself and choking at the same time. "I hope that road isn't too long, else by the time you get back I'll be grey as well as blue!"

Masinissa smiled at the whimsy. "You won't, but I might," he joked in kind.

Sophonisba laughed and held him close, burying him in her musk, and then said, "I think you'd better go now… just in case." Her lambent grace, even extending to their parting, touched Masinissa.

"It's hard!" he said, and this time there was an innuendo mixed in with the anguish of leaving.

She gave him a consolatory grimace and led him quietly outside. There, he crushed her with all his force in a suffocatingly ursine embrace. The act of letting go compelled him to do the opposite and hold her tighter, resisting the inevitable. Finally, as voices familiar to Sophonisba could be discerned in the near distance, he kissed her softly for a final time and held her face for a while, brushing her welling tears away with his thumbs, before making a discreet exit.

*

They would see each other on two other social occasions before he departed again for the frontlines. They were allowed modest contact at both, but were more constrained by the company and the nature of the functions. These were gatherings that were dominated by her extended family and the Punic elite of the city. The more notable of the two served as a form of engagement party, although he was mostly a peripheral figure at a gathering where he ought to have been the feted centrepiece. It was full of posh Carthaginians, and the doyens of the martial, philosophical and scientific communities. It was extremely awkward for Masinissa, particularly as he was – in theory, at least – in the spotlight a little as a prospective suitor. It was a scant consolation that most of the guests worked their way quickly beyond him once the initial formalities were concluded. They were far more interested in others of their own background and caste. It was a case of screw the guy who's keeping this party going, and keeping the Roman wolves from sacking the hell out of the place and enslaving the lot of them.

The ostensible highlight of the get-together was concluded expeditiously. Gisco indicated his public approval of their union, pretty much on the tacit condition that Masinissa and thousands of his subjects continued to throw themselves into the teeth of the Carthaginian cause. Gisco swigged a little wine, clinked cups with Masinissa, and gave him a pretty fake but vigorous slap on his back. Then he was gone, back to his own kind.

Masinissa wondered about the bargain and the attendant future sacrifices attached to it, and it inserted a little guilt and shame into him. It wasn't as if there was any fresh choice in the quid pro quo, though. That part of the deal was well established. He was signed up and had served some pretty hard time already, and it appeared like almost a first instalment in the repayment of a debt. *At least I was accepted and not shunned,* he thought to himself. He wondered at the extent of the acceptance and whether, at heart, it just may be quite perfidious. Hasdrubal Gisco was as big a slimeball as any of the Barcid clan, and it was probably no better than a sham convenience to wed Masinissa to his daughter. Maybe he saw the prospect of strong grandsons. Either way, it wasn't as if the news gave rise to an eruption of goodwill and bonhomie. There were a few limp congratulations, but they were tepid at best.

Mostly, the guests treated him less like a reality than a rumour. There would be a rumour that he fought bravely in such-and-such a place next month. There would be a rumour that he died a gallant death in such-and-such a battle the month after. They were just behaving towards him as they were used to, as hardly anything more substantial than a vapour, even though, for that brief interlude, he was for once actually, almost remarkably, in their company. He'd probably be dead before the end of the year. Why pay any attention to him other than offering a civil-but-grudging nod and a feigned smile?

He struggled to find anyone, other than Sophonisba, to have a genuine conversation with. There was a Greek friend of Conon's who had mysteriously bagged an invitation and who gave him brief social respite. He at least shared a little of Masinissa's dislocation, but he didn't stay around for long.

He muttered a conspiratorial and dismissive, "Yeah, they're all a bunch of deceitful Janus faces," and he was off into the melee, trying to find his promise or hook his mitts on to another susceptible young woman of the nobility.

There were several sweet moments that he could still cherish, and these were the glances that he and Sophonisba shared as they eyed each other, like cheetahs stalking their prey, with a restless pacing that somehow appeared undetected by anyone. Every moment of eye contact was a thrill, and surged life forces into his loins and heart. He revelled in every jolt it gave his soul.

Unlike less-formal banquets or dinners, the party followed a tighter schedule, and there was a tacit expectation to comport oneself in a certain way and leave at a certain time. In reality, this meant a trickle of guests leaving quickly turned to a flood. Masinissa was swept up in the egress, but took advantage of the flurry to get close to Sophonisba for a final time. They managed to intertwine hands, and whisper their final affections and commitments. He managed to softly envelop the edges of her neck en route to her ear. The softness and vulnerability of her throat thrilled him. His training and instincts knew how easy it was to attack the jugular vein, and how quickly the red river of life can spurt out of you from that opened fountain. He strived to retain a stout equanimity in the face of the passion and despair that was flanking it. He sighed, squeezed and fortified himself for the long, lonely, uncertain days ahead.

Sophonisba had one final parting counsel for him. She was momentarily more sage than her fiancé, and she clung to his torso and advised him. "Don't listen to the people who tell you the only thing that matters is victory. The only thing that matters is staying alive." She prodded him forcefully for his assent, which was dilatory. "Huh, huh," she prodded him more urgently.

"Staying alive," he assented, yielding to the prompt a little mournfully.

She gave him one final word, "Be," and packed it with vicarious resolution on his behalf.

He didn't want their final farewell to be marked by his exasperation, and so he left the inappropriate pique in the form of, "Gee, that was obvious," till he was at the edge of the gardens and his last wave to the curvaceous silhouette – which he prayed to Tanit that he would one day be reunited with – had been flapped helplessly.

TEENAGE WASTELAND

Masinissa woke early in the last moments of darkness when the stars were making their farewell. He allowed his thoughts to drift as the horizon started to form, define itself and then explode it's colour into the sky to herald the first freshness of the morning. The pinkish light of the dawn sun and its light cirrus crown would soon be tamed into a more mundane yellow, which would burn away the cloud, and then would become too dazzlingly incandescent to look at, and he would have to find something in his closer field of vision to preoccupy him whilst his thoughts strayed and collided.

On that morning, he seemed particularly alert, which was a sensation he noted as a little singular for his current mood, for the long days he had been back in the Carthaginian ranks had worn him down. He had become accustomed to the drudgery of army life, and a creeping numbness was coating him and inuring him to thoughts beyond the most basic and quotidian.

As the sun gathered strength and emitted more heat than glow, Masinissa found the palm of his hand as an alternative to be engrossed in. He looked at the three curving, not-quite-parallel main tracks that crossed it; they had been there since his first day of life, and not added by accident, assault, or just the coarsening and callusing of time. He cupped his hand inward a little to accentuate the lines, and then tried to measure them and compare their length against a presumed average. He wasn't in the habit of paying too much attention to other people's hands, but he had often heard the common myth about the length of these lines reflecting your personality and prospects. It was a spurious claim in Masinissa's view. Lines on the hand and creases in the face: none of it meant anything. Nevertheless, in his idleness, he could succumb as easily as the next person to a little curiosity and reassurance. He flexed an adductor muscle in that hand to form a little mound and in order to deepen the crevices the lines made.

The first line, the heart line, seemed deeper than he thought normal and about as long as you'd expect. Extracting that profile into his romantic sensibilities, he thought it about right. His middle line, the head line, was shallower and shorter. *That figures,* he thought to himself, *I'm a typical dum dum soldier after all.* The last line, the bottom line and the one that those without a romantic interest in him paid most attention to, was the life line. He squeezed the same little adductor muscle a little more, presumably eking out a few more years on to his allotted time with the elongating effect it had on his life line.

Absorbed in that frivolity, he hadn't noticed the surreptitious approach of Capuca, who must have been intrigued by the hand-pumping action of his commander and may have mistaken it for something a little more embarrassing. By the time he had got close to Masinissa, however, he had figured out the play. "You're going to live a long, long time, sire. A lot longer than me, for sure. I'm on borrowed time already, I'm sure."

Caught out in the inanity, Masinissa had nowhere else to go other than concede exposure gracefully. "Thanks, I hope we both live for a very long time and more of it in peace. At least my hand seems convinced I'm still on track to be a centenarian."

"I'd say that's a sure thing," Capuca agreed. "There's plenty of muscle left on those limbs to have plenty of years of wasting away. Somehow, I can't imagine you with those elderly, skinny, creaky, limping-along legs though. Weird, huh? We can't really picture how we'll look in our old age, just as we forget what we looked like as children. Get someone do a great job of making a sculpture of you. Don't let them short change you in the manhood department either. What is it with those guys anyway? They get paid a fortune, make their subjects as ripped as anything, yet give them all the tiniest appendages. You're leaving it out there in the first place. It's not going to offend if you add a little bit more to make your client feel a little bit better. It's kinda like a little bit of self-promotion for them, right? You're not going to impress the ladies if your sculpture makes you out to be buff but a borderline eunuch."

Masinissa laughed at the crudity. "You know what, Cap? If I am so scandalously anatomically misrepresented in the future, I promise I'll take a mallet and chisel to my bits."

"That's the spirit, chief." Capuca applauded, and then paused in his thoughts, clearly moving from a freewheeling ribaldry to a touchier subject. "Anyway, aside from guessing the length of your days, what else is on your mind? I know you. When you start thinking, you start to get obsessive. There's value in that for sure, but sometimes you dive too deep for those coins. Well, you do for this simple bugger, anyway."

"You have a point. Mostly, I was warming up and enjoying the stillness, but I'm getting disillusioned with all this: this never-ending war, the skirmishes, the battles, the recruitment and the recriminations. Worse, is that it's so obvious now that there's not much left in reserve. I see these kids they're bringing in now. Half of them haven't got even a trace of hair on their face. They're children. That's all we've got now. They've run out of men. It's ominous. The Romans are not going to wait for another generation to grow. Where are the fresh troops coming from?"

"Syphax maybe?" Capuca answered. "He's been biding his time."

"Well, we and Syphax ain't compatible. Are they going to wear us down to the last and then put their leash on his mob instead? I wouldn't be surprised, you know. Whatever happens after the next big show is going to throw things around a bit."

"I think things are starting to rattle already. The complete rout of Hasdrubal at the Metaurus has devastated the Carthaginians. I don't even know what Hannibal and Mago are making of it. Aside from the grief at the loss of their brother, the whole plan has got ripped up.

Hannibal is alone and wandering around Italia now, without much purpose. His army must be more like grazing cattle than a conquering force at this point right now."

The Battle of the Metaurus had quickly become a shameful stain on the reputation of the Carthaginian army and on the viability of their entire campaign, and it was something to be avoided in most conversations, like not staring at the stumps of an amputee. It had brought an end to Hasdrubal Barca. He had marched, without too much trouble, through the lands of the Gauls and into Italia, with the intention of bringing much needed siege equipment and reinforcements to the stagnating army.

There had been quite a lot of apprehension amongst the Romans about having to contend with two of the sons of the Thunderbolt, Hamilcar Barca, within their own territories, and there was initially a little hesitation by the armies of the two despatched consuls, Marcus Livius and Gaius Claudius Nero, to engage with the new marauder on their lands. However, this strategic prevarication ended after the Romans captured the Carthaginian plans that were being conveyed by intercepted messengers Hasdrubal had sent to Hannibal.

Faced with the uniting Roman armies, Hasdrubal had made moves to retreat back to Gaul, where he could re-evaluate his tactics, but the retreat was disorderly, and he was trapped without fortifications along the banks of the Metauro, with many of his Gallic auxiliaries either deserting him or drunk. The retreat turned into a fiasco, and Hasdrubal, seeing the inevitable, chose a brave death and charged into the Roman lines, where he was butchered by his enemies. His heroism counted for nothing to the Roman consuls, however, and Claudius Nero did not grant his corpse any dignity, and instead revelled in chopping off his head and taking it south to throw into Hannibal's camp as a contemptuous token of the Roman triumph. It left Hannibal bereft of his brother and his urgently needed reinforcements, and it left Masinissa and many of his troops wondering at the long-term prospects of their current affiliations.

Capuca's observations articulated a smouldering issue and an emerging reality that Rome's ascendancy was becoming inexorable.

Without any potent threat close to home, Rome would reinforce to the south and take the war into Iberia even more forcefully. The ebb and flow of the war would start turning, and, ultimately, the Carthaginians would have to bend towards their own homeland and their own continent.

"You're right, Cap" Masinissa replied, after dwelling on the geopolitical situation a little too long. "We're all thinking about the fallout at the Metaurus. I'm sure the Romans are thinking, *One down, three to go now*. They've got Hannibal, Gisco and Mago all lined up. In what order they go after them is uncertain. It's all or nothing down here now, I reckon."

"So how long do we stick with this cause, Mas?" Capuca asked. "It's not our fault that things are going the way they are. It's easy enough now to see the flaws in the characters of the men who lead us, and lead us to our deaths they blithely will."

"We'll see. Sometimes the rope is strong enough to hold, and sometimes it's no better than a piece of string that a sharp tug will break. These generals of ours are egotists and bullies, and they surround themselves with sycophants who only exacerbate these defects and shortcomings, but they're no fools and they're no cowards. Hasdrubal's final charge proved that much at least. I don't excuse them, though, and I don't like them. Besides that, they're the ones who are responsible for the mess we're walking towards."

"You're not filling me with much optimism, Mas! I've got to ride with you into another soaking any moment now, you know," Capuca demurred.

"Sorry, Cap. Maybe I was being too honest. Just blowing off. You know when you've reached a point at which you really can't tolerate a situation or a person any longer, and you're about to explode? Well, I feel like that now, but I'm risking all our lives for that person – or people, I should say – and if I betray them, they'll probably crucify the lot of us. We're contending with some serious apex assholes here, and there's no honour or glory in it once you see the path we're marching down."

"It sounds like you're storing up some resentment," Capuca observed, "We all are. When you sacrifice and those losses count for nothing, then it's natural to seethe and rage at the indifference or incompetence of your commanders. We've clung to our hatred of our enemies because they kill us and brutalise us, but are the banners and standards we ride under actually worse? When you've been that committed to a cause, can you flip it right over? I want to. I can't trust my hatred any more, Mas, and it's something I need. Don't get me wrong, I'm a soldier. I need to hate, because if I don't hate, then my pain and hurt will walk right up to my throat, and I'll be gagging on my grief and guilt. I can't deal with that shit. Let me hate somebody. Let me hate Mago and Gisco. They've earned it."

Masinissa absorbed Capuca's words like steam in his pores. They weren't exactly purifying, but they were affecting him more than usual. Few of the men had been so frank with him about their loyalties before, and it was more meaningful in its impact, as – in terms of character – Capuca was usually amongst the more circumspect of his closest friends. If he was saying those things, and expressing those misgivings, how much more would Ari or Massiva, or especially Pun, say on the matter? When do mutinous thoughts become a consensus view? And what do you call it then?

He pondered, "Maybe, maybe. Hannibal may well have shot his bolt, and the artillery pieces that are loaded now belong to the Romans, with their adapted Greek weaponry, their scorpions, ballistas and triggerfishes. The stuff they're bringing down now, on the right terrain, will thump through anything, even elephants. They've come through the worst, they've prevailed and they've shown their toughness. Have you heard of that guy with the metal hand?"

"Marcus Sergius? Yeah, I've heard of that guy," Capuca admitted, a little confused by Masinissa's digression.

"That's one guy I admire," Masinissa clarified. "I can't help myself. He kinda sets the standard, you know. He was captured twice by Hannibal, kept in chains every day for twenty months, he got his hand cut off, and then ordered the physicians and blacksmiths make this weird metal prosthetic for him, so that he can grip his shield in battle. That's the kinda toughness I can respect."

"Yeah, I guess, but you wouldn't want to wipe your arse with that kinda contraption, would you?

"You have a point," Masinissa said with a laugh, straight from his gut. It would be one of the last moments of levity he would enjoy for some time.

*

Shortly after, Pun bore the sobering news that Gisco was to strike a new camp, and prepare to engage with Scipio at a wide plain located at a bend in the Tartessus or Baetis River, a little north of Spela at a place called Ilipa. Troops were mustering to the location from all points in the peninsula, and many more were disembarking at the port of Gades. The Carthaginians were dredging up as many men as they could to participate in what many suspected could be a climactic tussle, certainly as far as the Iberian campaign was concerned.

The mood was sombre when Masinissa gathered his old hands together one more time. Soldiers learnt to trust their instincts, and the body language of those around him suggested many had forebodings. Massiva and Soldier Boy, in particular, made no effort to disguise their pessimism, and their slumped postures, downcast eyes and terse responses evinced an ominous vibe. These were the cramped, condemned feelings of young men who most of the time were not afraid to die, but when it came close couldn't kid themselves. For all their bravery and for all the resolution they had shown, they were finding it hard to look their potential last hours hard in the face.

Masinissa read their despair well, and he gave them the out they craved as well as the best spin on the situation he could. "Guys, I know it's bleak and I know a lot of you want to cut loose, but we still have allies and friends we respect, even amidst the many we don't. Our people and our whole lives are side by side with Carthage. We are tied to it like the lower man on the end of a climbing rope. If we let go, we may fall to our deaths. Is Rome or is Scipio going to catch us as we drop? I don't know."

"They've got us bottled up," Juba Tunic said wearily. "The Carthaginian scouting is slack, and their strategies are tired and laboured, certainly in contrast to the elan Scipio is showing. Look at the situation with Hanno. He comes up to reinforce us and has plenty of silver to recruit from amongst the Celtiberians, yet – the moment he unites with Mago – Scipio sends a detachment under Silanus, and they achieve complete surprise. The Carthaginian dolt and his war chest are captured, and we and Mago have to disperse and cower in the cities. It was a wasted opportunity, and maybe the last good one."

"It was," Masinissa conceded, "but we can't dwell on losses and hypotheticals. The army we're in is still strong and may be even stronger numerically than the numbers Scipio can deploy. Estimates, and I know you don't trust them, place Scipio's numbers at around 45,000 infantry, most of whom we believe will be Iberian allies rather than legionaries, so they will be more unpredictable and definitely weaker. As for us, with Mago's troops, we're looking at fielding about 50,000 infantry, 4,500 cavalry (including us) and, of course, the elephants. There are exactly thirty-two, apparently."

"I don't have much faith in elephants, cuz," Massiva interjected sceptically. They're more of a hindrance if anything. They can be a law unto themselves, and the Romans have learnt how to goad and turn them these days. It's a big plain out there. They could work up a head of steam in any direction."

"That is true, but the chances of them trampling over the Romans is still greater than them rolling over us, however erratic they can be."

"That's reassuring," Massiva replied, a little sardonically.

"OK; come on, I'm not driving these pachyderms. I can only control what I can control. Here's the kicker: I think Gisco is sensing our mood. There are spies everywhere and they'll no doubt be relaying the campfire talk; we may have – or likely already have – worked our way out of the elite inner circle to the periphery, where dying is quickest and surest. Either way, I have new instructions. If things turn badly, split, cut right out, and we'll head for the coast, get on some boats and send word to Scipio. I'm sure Gisco and Mago still think they've got this under control, but if they're loading the dice against us as part of the plan, we're not going to show them any loyalty by being the first on the pyres. We can pick a new fight, or see if Scipio is a man of honour and wasn't just flirting with us."

All the men were looking at him then, but none spoke up to question or object, and all knew the wind was probably about to change direction.

*

Masinissa's qualms about his perception deepened on receiving a fresh set of orders from Mago, who seemed to have usurped the chain of command from Gisco, despite his recent failures and calamities. The orders were simple enough: to lead what was pitched as a daring attack on the Roman camp, apparently to catch them unawares, and to do as much damage as possible before extracting themselves and joining the main force.

It could, of course, be interpreted as a compliment and a show of faith that Masinissa was to be utilised as the most devastating striker in the Carthaginian arsenal, but, at that point, his view was more doubtful. Even given his potency in the field, he believed he could be sacrificed in a ferocious assault that might cripple Scipio as well as devastate his own cavalry. Scipio was a wily commander, and it was dubious to think that he would not have adequate defences against that type of raid. In any event, the attack would be undertaken as expeditiously as possible: get in, get out, rely on the speed of your horses, and torch as much as you can before getting back into the Carthaginian lines.

The mood was sombre as they rode towards the Roman encampment. The light was only just emerging, and, when Masinissa looked around, he struggled to make out the expressions on the faces of his men in the indistinct light. They could see the Roman fires in the distance, but the sentries were still too far away for him to kick his horse and begin the charge. He wanted to savour the moment, to suck up the freshness, to leave the new dawn still and let it glide around him, but there were men to kill and no time for any idle reflections.

Whilst the caliginous gloom concealed them, showing only their bare silhouettes, their entrance was harder to conceal from other senses. The ground was rough and hard, and there were many riders in the column, so they were announcing themselves quite audibly with the hooves and snorts of their steeds, even if the conversations amongst themselves were muted. Flanking their approach to the camp was a low hill with little vegetation. However, as Masinissa observed the line of the hazy mound, his dimmed perception begun to see rising lines that were shaped into elongated heads, which then formed more recognisable shapes as the men mounted on those elongated heads crested the knoll's brow, and, despite the darkness, a Roman cavalry phalanx could be identified. The riders held their line, as did Masinissa and his men, who had discerned the threat almost as quickly as him, and were wondering about their next course of action. Should they confront them, retreat or plough straight into the camp with the likelihood that they would then be surrounded and slaughtered?

This pause was exactly what the Roman attackers must have wanted, as the equine outlines were joined quickly by clusters of little podiums. The impression of a range of harmless, emerging lecterns was entirely misleading. They were a trick of the angle, and they were really being confronted with an array of loaded ballistae, which – following a quick calculation – they were just within range of. They must have been smaller *scorpios*, but there were about a hundred of them being wheeled into target range. They were a particularly accurate weapon, and they were a threat even in that light and at that distance. *Charge it,* Masinissa thought, *We'll give their bolt throwers the same view of us as I have of them. They will only get the one volley off in that case, anyway.*

He gave the order and unsheathed his *falcata*, and, as he did so, the barrage rained down on them. The artillery men knew what they were doing. They had taken aim at the largest targets, and about half of the bolts thudded into the shoulders and withers of the Numidian horses, some of which also impaled their rider's legs. A few others held to higher trajectories, and some of these took out men in their chests, with a force that propelled them right off the back of their mounts. It didn't really matter where they took it. If the triggerfish got you in the middle, you were skewered and done. Adonibaal was one of those, and he took one flush in the ribcage. It looked quite heroic, but it was far from that, as his hands gripped the bolt instinctively and he fell backwards.

Let's hope the fall breaks his neck, Masinissa thought piteously.

As they tore up the hill in unison, he realised that this form of attack was not the most familiar to the Numidians. The accuracy and distance of their javelin attacks, for which they were renowned, would be quite negated against a mounted, onrushing foe. Still, he could count on his men to get at least two lances off before the melee erupted when the two charges collided and mangled each other. With a thumping heart, wide-eyed, and every muscle and nerve pumping, he hurled a pair of his own. His pulsating body didn't diminish his precision in the least, and he had taken two Romans off their horses before he was within striking distance of their *gladii*. They were as good as dead in the stampede. That was the lesson to apply just then. Cling on for dear life; fall, and hooves would trample you into mush in seconds.

He found his usual lieutenants in his peripheral vision. Even in the tumult, he sensed Capuca, Ari and Massiva were close, and he was just being outpaced by Soldier Boy and Batnoam, whose rage was shimmering over his taut body, and being released in vengeful curses and shouts, which Masinissa could just hear above the commotion.

As they rode into the enemy, any faint hope that they were as callow as some of the units were known to be was dispelled. There was no flinch in the swipes and no terror in the eyes when glances were caught between focussing on the lunges of the blades. Motions were automatic, swift and practised, and men fell steadily: some in parts, some in screams and some in both. There were no manoeuvres, feints or parries. You just had to rely on your reflexes and your eyes, and trust to Melqart. Cavalry warfare was usually less sustained than infantry tussles, based on the sheer speed of those engaged in the slaughter. You can be through one and into the next much quicker; one lucky whirl might open up a few adversaries. Trying to figure out the tide of the conflict was difficult, but – as his horse found its footing harder as it trod on more and more of the slain – it became evident to Masinissa that things were tipping against him and that they were slowly being outnumbered. Whilst there was vigour in his arms and in his horse, he shouted the order to yield to those who could hear him and – with Ari and Capuca flanking him – he rode into and through the guts of the fight to bellow the order to flee, although not to safety, merely to the temporary haven of Mago's lines.

One of his men, Izem – aka Zee or, even more familiarly, Zeeboy – was just ahead of him, screaming at him whilst flailing in all directions at the muzzles of horses and swords of men. There were very few Numidians left in that pocket of the battle, and Zee was beset on all sides and was seconds from going under. Masinissa spurred on his horse and aimed right at Zee in a desperate attempt to save one life from amongst the many he couldn't bring out of the fight. The most he could possibly rescue at that point was one. One life, that was all, but every one was precious. He scooped Zee up, and Zee launched himself onto the back of the steed with so much force that it almost yanked Masinissa off it. Cap and Ari had done the same with others, who were clinging on, and they burst out with their three charmed passengers.

As Masinissa rode through the lines, he caught glimpses and saw the expressions on the faces of his men; some of those who caught his gaze had been brought to the ground. We all know we are going to die, but those men knew they were going to die in the next few moments, and their anguish couldn't be masked by their rage and desperation. *Where is the meaning in the end they are about to meet? Where was the hand to hold, the compassion and the care? It is no way to die, but most of us die that way,* Masinissa thought sorrowfully.

When they broke free, Masinissa knew they would not be hunted down. They had left enough breathing souls to preoccupy the Romans for a little while longer, and any pursuit would be doomed unless it was backed up by a heavy concentration of Scipio's forces. It wasn't going to happen, and the men knew they had eluded death for another day. The intensity of the reprieve was sharper than normal. Death was always close at hand for them, and they all knew how precarious their existences were, but seeing your friends cut down next to you was a brutal reminder of how arbitrary that connection to mortality could be and how precious every breath was.

As they pulled up in Mago's camp, Zee rebounded from his terror and smothered his grief in euphoric yells. He had been delivered, and Masinissa was the angel who had snatched him from the maws of death. As they alighted from the horse that had brought them out of the maelstrom, Zee jumped onto Masinissa, as if he were diving across a precipice; embraced him with all his strength; and thumped him hard repeatedly in his back, in a hug that reaffirmed life and conveyed gratitude at the same time.

"If I ever loved you before, sire, I love you more now!" Zee exclaimed. "I owe you, man. I should be being squelched in that muddy, bloody ooze right now, with my life knocked out or stabbed out, but I got out and that's on you; that's all you – all on your mercy. It may have been random, and it may just have been my lucky day, but I still owe you the biggest debt. I'm your arm now, your sword. I'll dive in the way of anything that's in your way or coming for you. Count on me like an extra life. My time came, and I wasn't taken. My bonus is your time."

Masinissa was a little abashed by Zee's effusiveness, but he accepted the oath with good grace. He could always use that sort of commitment. The reprieved soldier was known to him and had a good reputation anyway, but he knew he could count on Zee unquestioningly now, however dreadful the circumstances.

As it was, the circumstances were pretty dreadful. The tally of the dead was grave. Ever punctilious, Pun was quick with the accounting. They'd lost about 500 men at a rough estimate, including some of their close retinue in the form of Izalcas and Micipsa. Batnoam, who had torn into the Romans with the zeal of a man who had just lost a brother, had miraculously survived. However, he was bleeding from a few wounds that were being washed and tied, and was screaming with the twin agonies of loss and pain, although the latter was the one that was making him writhe and contort at that precise moment. His jerks were strong, though, and Masinissa felt sure he'd be upright on horseback by the next call.

Needless to say, Mago was a callous son of a bitch. "Be ready tomorrow," was about all he was willing to say. There was no word of commiseration, just a sneer of disappointment.

The dismissal grated on all who heard it, and many curses were muttered once the scornful aristocrat had returned to his own battalions. Their bodies and souls were mostly in various states of numbness of shock, however, and the daze was too great for them to spend much time lingering on how they were perceived or appreciated.

For his part, Masinissa knew no peace that night, preoccupying himself with how capably he had been snared and how appalling was the price of Scipio's accomplished ambuscade.

*

The next days followed rigid patterns, as the opposing generals sent their armies onto the battlefield in the formations that corresponded with their standard tactics. It was a tedious parade, with the respective armies marching out in their allocated lines only to troop off again once the generals had decided that they had neutralised each other or failed to perceive an advantage. Maybe they both simply enjoyed the ostentatiousness of riding along vast lines of men whom they were happy to send to their deaths at a capricious whim. The Carthaginians would lead out first, and Scipio would follow, observing the same pattern each day, with the legions in the centre and the Iberian auxiliaries on the wings.

After a few days of this jockeying, Scipio broke with the convention. He sent his light *velite* troops against the edges of the Carthaginian lines at dawn, and advanced behind them, drawing right up to the main body of the Carthaginian forces. As he approached, it was evident that he had inverted his tactics and the deployment of his troops. That time, his legions were placed on the flanks, with the Iberians holding the middle ground.

The disposition of the forces surprised and spooked Mago, who rushed his army onto the battlefield without any provisions, and with many attendant rumblings from mouth and stomach as if there was a gentleman's agreement in place that the armies would only start slaughtering one another after a hearty breakfast. Mago and Gisco appeared to see no reason to amend their own formations in reaction to Scipio's innovation, and placed their forces as per convention, with the elite African brigades in the middle and their own Iberian allies on the flanks. Even if they had wanted to, the haste of the assault had been too rapid and the enemy was by then too near for them to make any substantial alterations to their plans.

During the initial phase of the battle, the main bodies of both armies were withheld, with the skirmishing light troops serving up almost a prelude or first act to the more violent central phase to come. It may also have been a deliberate tactic on Scipio's part to accentuate the hunger of the ravenous Carthaginians by keeping the main fight till later in the day. As these lighter troops were finally recalled through spaces created between the mandibles to position themselves behind the legions on the flanks, Scipio's main advance began with his wings. These were dominated by the stronger legions and cavalry units, making quicker inroads against Mago's Iberians. The curve of the battle by then formed a concave line, which threatened the collapse of the Carthaginian middle.

Masinissa, who had been holding his ground, could see the encroaching disaster, and realised the only possibility of averting it was if he could repel and turn the Roman flanks. Gisco knew it too and sent urgent word to him to do just that. He was to advance behind the elephant division, and rupture and slowly encircle the Roman cavalry.

He gave the order with as much conviction as he could, but he could see in the vacillating body language of his men that they could perceive an outcome no better than the one that they had recently extricated themselves from. The loyalty that he commanded and the esteem in which he was held meant that there was no dissent, only a grim resolve to ride into the teeth of another storm, but one that was likely to sweep them away with it this time. Zee, making an early return on his promise, rode as close to Masinissa as he could without putting an elbow or sword edge into him, whilst Capuca and Ari fell in as his usual outriders.

They had barely encountered any enemy troops when the roars and trumpets of the elephants started to sound more distressed than intimidating, and they started to baulk, break and turn. There was nothing as effective in checking a charge as a herd of elephants whirling back on itself, and the chaos of their manic attempts to evade more javelins goring their bellies devastated Masinissa's thrust. Some of the cavalry were crushed, and many of the horses bolted for the open ground with their riders not able to control their flight.

Despite the chaos, the Romans were managing to orchestrate some direction to the turned elephants, and were goading and manoeuvring them as deftly as they could towards the Carthaginian centre. The claw was starting to grip, and it soon became evident that the Carthaginians were attempting to withdraw. At first, they seemed to manage this with more discipline than they had at any point so far that day, but, with Scipio pressing hard, the Carthaginian line started to crumble. Their annihilation looked inevitable.

However, the gods must have favoured them, and they were spared a massacre by the direct intervention of the heavens. Masinissa had noted the darkening clouds throughout the morning, viewing them as a baleful portent. When the skies did open and started to dump a monsoon deluge on them, every drop of rain seemed to Masinissa like a substitute for a drop of Carthaginian and Numidian blood that the tempest spared. The storm was disruptive enough for the Carthaginians to make good their retreat and find the temporary refuge of their camp.

As darkness fell and the rain lashed the soaked men, morale evaporated. Inevitably, there would be a more concerted attack by the Romans in the morning and their ability to resist it was dubious. The more resolute were setting to improve the defences in the forlorn hope that improved barricades would keep the enemy at bay. Masinissa regarded this exercise as the futile delusion that it was. As the hours of darkness continued, it was clear that – even in the indistinct and misty gloom – men were deserting in very large numbers. The Iberians, for all their ferocious reputation, were slipping away and making for their mountains and villages, leaving the Carthaginians to their fate. Hasdrubal retained enough of his wits to see that making a stand with the forces he retained would be a suicidal endeavour, and towards the end of the night mimicked the Iberians and gave the order to flee.

For their part, the Numidians were clearly restive and – as they observed the draining away of the fighting strength of their allies, as the desertions went from a trickle to a flood – they too were clearly in the mood to try to escape. Some, mainly Pun and Tigerman, retained their equanimity, as might be expected given their rank and standing, but many were more agitated. When Hasdrubal gave the order for his men to make their escape and spurn a final stand against Scipio, there was no point in staying any longer. There was nothing to be gained from hesitating or dwelling on their options any longer. Only one option remained and that was to run, but in the other direction from their erstwhile Iberian allies.

Massiva was dripping with trepidation when he grabbed Masinissa by his tunic and practically screamed into his face, "We've gotta go, Mas; we've gotta go now."

As the words drilled into him, Masinissa broke out of his post-battle lassitude, and regained some of his vitality and decisiveness. He realised he had let his thoughts meander, and he had lost the exigency of the moment and the need for him to focus on the survival of both him and the men who counted on him.

When Massiva was done with his alarm call, Ari gave a more phlegmatic analysis. "Seev is right. It's done; this is over. We've gotta find some boats. We should make for Mons Calpe and get on whatever we can find. Then get over to Mons Abyla or Tingi, and regroup. I don't know where Mago or Gisco are going, but we need to get home, speak to your dad and get word to Scipio. Do what we have to do."

Masinissa looked at him and at the expectant, apprehensive faces clustering around him. "OK, let's get outta here. Heaven knows where we're headed now, but this noose is cut."

Pun then reaffirmed the point in his booming baritone, which reached all of the men, and even many of the Carthaginians, who were packing urgently and who gave them some rebukes and contemptuous looks when they heard the mutinous words. "Boys, we don't fight for ideals; we don't fight for Carthage; we don't fight for Gisco, Mago or Hannibal; we fight for Massyli, for Numidia and each other. Let's go home."

The men didn't have to hear another word or be urged any further. They mounted up and raced away like young men who wanted to die old.

Unlike the Carthaginians, who were composed mostly of infantry, and presented a more important as well as a slower and more propitious target, they made a fairly simple getaway. Whilst they learnt later that both Gisco (who headed to Syphax's territories, presumably to recruit him) and Mago (who fled to the Balearics) had both eluded Scipio. Most of the men who remained loyal to the Carthaginian cause that night, apparently around 6,000 men, had been caught by Scipio at a nearby mountain peak. Starved of water and without any prospect of evading their pursuers, they fought briefly and then capitulated, and were taken into captivity.

Masinissa was not to know that then, though, as he raced towards the sea, unaware of the fact that he was not the most tempting morsel left on the table and was perhaps being deliberately spared by Scipio, who knew very well of his equivocal loyalties.

They rode hard south-east, and, by the following evening, they could see the inimitable silhouette of Mons Calpe. Abandoning most of the horses, they commandeered every fishing vessel in the harbour, as well as those in neighbouring towns up the coast, set off and reached

Mons Abyla by the following day. They had reached Africa, but this was no refuge and no home.

Looking back towards the northern peninsula, Masinissa wondered if he would ever cross those straits again.

WHEN AN ITCH BECOMES A BITCH

The last of the boats were dragged out of the waves by the hauls of the men on the shore, though a few were left to drift carelessly, and find their own way to dry land or bob out a little into the straits to perhaps be the object of curiosity or sport for amused dolphins. The men aboard them had simply jumped clear into the surf, heedless of the mooring of their vessel. Masinissa pulled himself up, shook himself down and took stock. It was hard to appraise dispassionately the level of catastrophe that had befallen the Punic forces, but no doubt all who had survived recognised that the defeat was going to be defining and decisive, at least on the peninsula.

They had reached the sea at the wide, windy bay close to Mons Calpe. The relentless howl of the gale – which seemed to have no discernible direction, but chewed up the waves and kicked up white horses everywhere in the sea – struck the exact notes of discord and chaos to match their mood and situation. "Live to fight another day" had been the glib phrase on everyone's lips on the journey to the coast, although the concomitant questions of "Who for?" and "Where?" remained unspoken, but were doubtless sawing away in the minds of all the vanquished soldiers of the vanquished army.

The crossing, once enough boats had been acquired from resentful fisherman, had taken most of the next day and night. Masinissa spent the hours of darkness looking at the receding fires of the abandoned shore; then the vast panoply of the cosmos, which was always more awe-inspiring when on the water; followed finally by the beckoning light of fresh African fires, although there were not too many of them to be seen in the sparsely populated coastline of the Mauri between Tingi and Russadir.

At least they would have some breakfast and fill their ravenous bellies when they hit the sands of their native continent. There was enough of an ocean behind them to be heedless of pursuit, although the presence of elements of the Roman fleet could not be dismissed entirely.

Before embarking, they had raided, as cordially as they could manage, a number of farms. Masinissa paused at the thought of it, realising that they had reached the point of destitution where they were pillaging their own allies. There was nothing for it, though, and there was at least a degree of negotiation and exchange. They had preserved some decency in their desperation. The wary farmers had accepted a little gold and even a few *falcatas* from the weary troopers, who thought they might need them if the Romans were in a vengeful spirit when they passed their way. It probably would only make matters immeasurably worse, though, if they were to start brandishing them under the noses of legionaries. Then they had loaded onto the horses' rumps a few crates of chickens, which squawked like crazy until Capuca had enough of their caterwauling and pulled them over to break their necks. They also had eggs, olives and some fresh loaves, and it was more than enough for the small fleeing party to gorge themselves on and satiate their hunger when they reached the other side. A few nibbled the supplies during the crossing, but not many had the constitution of sailors, and the restive swells of the Great Western Sea – or the Syrian Sea, as some of the more old-fashioned Carthaginians insisted on calling it, even though that part of its shoreline was weeks sailing to the east – did little to help the Numidians' appetite. As queasy stomachs settled back on land, the men harvested as much driftwood as they needed, lit their own fires in the dunes, and burrowed in for some restorative cooking and maybe a little sleep when their bellies were full.

Masinissa slept briefly, but he returned to consciousness as the light of the morning was just beginning to rise – soft and misty in the sky, and sparkling on the ocean. The silhouette of the southern pillar of Melqart, Mons Abila, rose at the edge of the horizon, as a beacon of familiarity. It was possible to make out its dome-like contours, but, in the dawn light and at the distance they were, it appeared to have a little blurring fur around its edges. The vision would have been one of incongruous tranquillity but for the moans of the injured, for whom every jolt on the journey had yielded a yelp or a groan, and for whom the mercy of being on land provided only a partial mitigation of their sufferings.

Most of the men huddled in their normal groups with the addition of a few orphans from platoons the recent battle had decimated, who were looking to find new attachments like abandoned cubs looking for new surrogate mothers. Masinissa didn't look for company, though, and gave the others a tacit rebuff by turning his back on them, and leaving his feet in the water and his gaze towards the ocean. After a while – as Masinissa's breathing fell into time with the lapping waves, and he started losing himself in the rhythmic ebb and flow of the tide – Capuca took it upon himself to tap him on his shoulder. Masinissa turned, shocked by the interruption but still sucked into his reverie, and barely noticed his friend as he swept the beach and beyond with his gaze. When he did hold Capuca in his vision, it was as a shape rather than a being, as if his daydreaming had robbed him temporarily of any sense of fraternity.

Capuca grimaced at his friend's blank expression. "Shake it off, Mas. Moment to moment. The present is what matters, and right now, in this present, no one is trying to kill us."

Masinissa looked up and back at his solicitous friend, wanting to console him and, at the same time, scold him for interrupting his thoughts and melancholy. "Let's sit," was the compromise he came to.

Capuca gave a wan smile at the suggestion and sat on the ground a little gingerly, rolling a little onto his side, most likely to protect a wound he was not yet inured to. As Capuca let the wet sands of the beach coat his fingers, he looked out and over the breaking waves, almost mirroring Masinissa's earlier trance. "You know, Mas, I love to be reminded of my younger self. The ghost of my youth still traces around the edges of my being, mourning my maturity and my march away from him. We can just about recognise each other and can just about find room in ourselves to share corners of our soul, spectrally anyway. We seem to reunite in moments like this when my senses become awakened and acute. When I sense the fresh sting of a salt breeze, for instance, it invigorates my soul, and takes me back to the times when I was new and relishing these sensations for the first time. I may have been naive, complacent and probably a little conceited, but I can still see a little of the world through that boy's eyes, and I savour the precious, occasional moments when I can."

He paused, perhaps in deference to the lost boy inside him and then continued, "The last few days have put us all, maybe you most of all, in our little cocoons, or perhaps coffins is a better analogy. The latest versions of ourselves have died with many of our brothers, or are in their last throes. We're not going to emerge like butterflies, all light and delicate, but we have to break into our new selves or cast off our old skins, you know. Today's a new world, and we are new people. Be grateful for the reprieve. Many of our boys are being thrown on pyres or flung down the furthest, darkest corners of the mines, if they haven't bled out. They won't be getting paid with bread, wine and soap either, if they ever see daylight again."

"No, they won't, poor bastards," Masinissa replied. He dug his fingers into the moist granules as Capuca had done, and looked at his hands with their fresh grainy layer as if he had soaked his hands in their blood and the stain was attaching itself to him in silicon. "We should have sat further up the beach. I don't want to make shapes with this stuff. I'm not a child." The subtext that was evident to the both of them was that, there, the sand and maybe his guilt, might just glide off elegantly. He made a little gulp, as if his oesophagus was doing its part to announce their impending metamorphosis, because a horn or a drum was not available.

He went on, "There's no going back, is there? We have to have fresh colours now, fresh hopes and new enemies, often from amongst old friends. You know you can hesitate, tinker around a decision and not really see the truth you need to see, but then – when you finally decide on a new course, and steer away from something or towards something else – it can be suddenly so much clearer. All that you held on to seems stupid. What was I thinking? Dumping this Carthaginian yoke is like finally tiring of the girl that you knew you should have left months ago. Let's get these wheels in motion. We need to formalise our new betrothal."

Capuca looked at him a little quizzically. "I didn't know we were getting married to Scipio. How dreamy!" He placed his hands, with their backs upwards, in a v shape on his gaunt cheeks, and batted his eyelids coquettishly.

The sight brought a gut laugh out of Masinissa, and he fell in line.

"Let's hope our new guy treats us a little more respectfully, huh?" Capuca winked a playful approval, realising that he'd accomplished his intention: Masinissa was free of his clouds.

*

Fresh metaphorical storms were to roll in quickly, though, as if the turmoil were a long season or a lingering curse. Word was sent and communicated, initially to Junius Silanus, who accepted and negotiated the Massylian defection, and Masinissa got word quickly from Scipio himself that the offer originally made was still intact and that, after years of hostility, they were now in league.

Masinissa, a little remissly as it turned out, thought his new alliance would flourish quickly. He would tour the country and the mountains, be greeted as the returning hero, and muster and train till Scipio crossed the sea and they could establish a plan of attack against Carthage, be it on negotiated terms or on the battlefield. He was not to be so fortunate.

The first storm to drench him was no zephyr either, and it kicked his legs from under him and choked his heart, leaving him with the wailing anguish of a helpless mother who had just seen their child trampled under horses. Such sights, whilst not familiar, were not unknown to Masinissa, and he knew the empty howl and the inability to escape his own body or to change the world back to how it was a moment earlier. In the same way as the pitiful, grieving women could often only be stopped in their manic bobs and gyrations by being hauled to the ground and smothered, it took four men to restrain him and stop him wrecking his knuckles on the earth when he heard the news that his father had died.

It was no consolation that his passing had been peaceful, and that he had blessed Masinissa with his love and inheritance in his final moments. He had not been there. He had not been with him as he left the earth. He had not told him of his love for him in his final hours, or tried to comfort and shelter him, and give him what strength he could in his embraces and words. Maybe they would have done little more for Gala, and his presence might not have meant much more than his absence to the frail man, but it hurt Masinissa to the core, as if it were the worst dereliction he could commit. Maybe Gala would have shared some piercing wisdom or imparted a final comment to him that might help Masinissa make more sense of the universe, or that he could always hold on to as an expression of who they were and what value was perpetuated in their relationship, even after death.

Worse still, he was not afforded any space to grieve, and neither were his rights of succession nor his accomplishments honoured. As his men recovered and they made languid progress east, a tawdry series of squabbles erupted in the Massylian court that seemed mystifying to Masinissa when he received episodic word of it, as it was ridiculous for him to regard anyone other than himself as the rightful heir. Firstly, in some kind of senescent putsch, Gala's elderly brother Oezalces ascended to the throne. The thrill of primacy was evidently too much for the old man, and he died swiftly before being able to savour any of the pleasures of his dominion, although most of these had already drifted out of his grasp given his age and senility.

Having snubbed Masinissa so shockingly, there was little else for it than for the court, which by then seemed to be beholden to a faction devoutly antipathetic to Masinissa, to appoint yet another pretender in Oezalces's eldest son Capussa. Sensing weakness and an aristocratic order that was illegitimate and in turmoil, the new king was challenged by another who had tenuous claims as heir, a noble called Mazaetullus. Despite his equally fraudulent assertion to the crown, the tribal imbroglio was such that he gathered enough support to emerge victorious from a brief conflict that resulted in the death in battle or execution – Masinissa was not close enough to the scene to be fully confident of which – of Capussa. Clearly, Mazaetullus had a greater appreciation for court intrigue and tribal politics, and took the prudent approach of placing Lacumazes, Capussa's younger brother, on the throne as the ostensible monarch. The plausibility of his authority was absurd, even from Masinissa's distant vantage point, and it was clear that Mazaetullus had installed himself as regent whilst minimising the possibility of further reprisals or infighting. The fratricidal genie was out of the bottle, and, to plug it back in, Mazaetullus made a show of reconciliation with the installation of Lacumazes. The brisk corruption of his father's throne appalled Masinissa, and he inveighed against the stupidity and ingratitude of his in-laws constantly, most often to Ari and Capuca, who were usually the more patient and forbearing of his potential counsellors.

Fresh intrigues and entanglements were not confined to the Massyli, and equally personal switches and inversions were quick to sprout in the neighbouring kingdoms. Perhaps it was foolish of Masinissa to overlook the consequences he had himself precipitated, but Hasdrubal acted swiftly to replace his Numidian ally with the most suitable and obvious alternative. Syphax had always been opportunistic, and he was seduced easily by Hasdrubal's invitation to become his new ally. Masinissa speculated that he had grown as disenchanted with his Roman confederates as Masinissa had of his Carthaginian ones. Perhaps they both resembled one another, being fatigued by war and the vacuous promises that had only brought stalemate and death. Maybe he had created a vacuum that had to be filled by a desperate Carthage, which had to find a replacement for him in Africa or else be in such a hopeless predicament that it would have to turn to Libyans, Garamantes or even Troglodytae.

The messages from the other parts of Numidia and from further afield were delivered haphazardly at first. He had to move around the countryside constantly and be elusive to his many enemies, and that meant news initially reached him inconsistently and often had been superseded by events. Usually, the young runners bringing the latest news were known to him or at least to some in the camp, or carried some seal associated with Gala or him, although there were occasionally times when neither he nor Pun nor Juba Tunic felt they could trust them, and suspected they may have been emissaries from Syphax or Gisco, trying to lure him into traps or demoralise his forces further.

As they plotted out their future communication channels with loyal sources in Cirta and the Massylian heartlands, more robust arrangements were made, whereby they could relay and receive news more dependably, as well as securing the news's authenticity via passwords. How invulnerable the codes they adopted were going to be was uncertain. Couriers could be intercepted and tortured, and then their arrangements would be ruined or at least jeopardised. Quickly, however, Masinissa found his network of local sources of information growing and concatenating at an exponential rate, as if all of Massyli were supporting him covertly, which he felt sure they were, even if they had to do so using maximum discretion and secrecy. News began flooding in to him from myriad sources, as if he were the local hair stylist and the recipient of all the gossip around. He had to be somewhat cautious, but the eyes and mouths of the people were clearly loyal to him despite the dominance that Syphax was exerting on the country.

Nevertheless, it was rare that the envoys reached him without going through gatekeepers, invariably his *optio*. Masinissa was increasingly of the view that Pun was becoming more avuncular towards him, as if the older he got, the more he required his protection and guidance. A pattern developed whereby routine messages were ushered to him unmolested, but news of a sensitive or damaging nature was delivered by Pun in a form that he felt Masinissa would find more palatable. It infuriated Masinissa a little, but he indulged his old friend in his protective urge.

The news he had locked out of possibility and failed to anticipate was the disclosure that Syphax had not only usurped him as the fiancé of Sophonisba but had married her with the full blessing of the Carthaginian nobility, effectively sealing an alliance that may otherwise have vacillated and collapsed. Syphax was now bonded to Carthage. The extent to which Sophonisba was, by extension, tied to him was a question that Masinissa strongly resisted dwelling upon.

Pun, when he had told him, in as assuasive a manner as possible, tried to emphasise the transience and insincerity of the union, but he couldn't erase the leaden fact of it for all his obfuscations. Whilst the loss of his father had filled Masinissa with despair, impotent rage and regret, the loss of his beloved to another, and to his rival in every other sense, felt like a humiliation and a torment at the same time. His imagination, which had invented fantastical but hollow moments with Sophonisba, had sustained him for years and had filled this dreamland out into an ersatz life of domestic happiness, highlighted by energetic lovemaking and populated with their many faceless, imaginary children. These idle reveries had been his major solace, other than the wine he could take when safety and supply allowed, and which took all his tensions and preoccupations away. Those dreams had been violated by another protagonist, his sworn enemy. His hazy fantasies were now vivid nightmares that could only be dispelled by military victory. He realised that he must exhort Scipio to total war and decisive victory without terms or compromises, or else this compact would not be undone. His future had become a trophy of Syphax. He realised that Sophonisba would be compelled by patriotic duty and no doubt a certain amount of duress to keep the alliance sweet, and he had to draw another veil across his imagination when he allowed his thoughts to stray into those lurid precincts.

It was a useless evasion, though, and no better than a child sticking their fingers in their ears, closing their eyes and chanting a denial. His suppressions were as gossamery as foam, and rarely provided a barrier for his worries for long. The next hours, days and months would grind hard into his hopes and dreams. It took all his convictions and faith in himself, in Sophonisba, in the Massyli, and in the Roman Army and Scipio to preserve his own feelings and his beliefs in his future with Sophonisba. "Love will find a way" was the aphorism that all threatened lovers clung to, wasn't it? How naive he was to believe that love was the property of lovers. He should have known that his betrothal was bound to be revoked when he switched his own allegiance. His only comfort was a steadfast faith in the Roman military and their tactical superiority, and he reassured himself that the Carthaginian capitulation could only be just a matter of time.

He knew enduring that time would not be so easy. In some ways, though, it allowed him a greater sense of personal heroism akin to the legends and stories he had read as a child. Those chivalrous notions were such nonsense, but even the most jaded could be fools for them. He would rescue Sophonisba and ride off into the sunset. There was only the small matter of evading Syphax, and then, in tandem with Scipio's apparently dawdling invasion force, devise and implement a campaign to destroy him and the formidable allied power of Carthage.

"There's nothing to it," he blustered nonchalantly under his breath in the comical, self-assured manner of those fictitious, superficial heroes he was fancifully associating himself with. He had another vision to succour him, as foolish as his original "let's make a house together" distraction.

He wandered away, looking for a wineskin, as the self-delusion required a little wine at this time of the evening when honesty and reality had a habit of intruding. Once one had been found, as he cracked it open and squeezed out a long slug, he sighed. "The lies we tell," he whispered.

The clouds had regathered.

WASHED AWAY

"Pain is weakness leaving the body! Take it, revel in it and know that you are forged stronger by it."

Masinissa listened to Tigerman's exhortations to the men and felt weary. This drum had been banged for years, and the platitude, and others like it, were tired and no longer had the vivifying spirit left in them to give a boost or any kind of edge or sharpness. There was a point, and they were long past it, where the drill sergeant went from fearsome to being trite and a little comical. The act would always work on the new grunts and fresh faces, but the veteran guys regarded it with a passivity that glided straight off them, as background noise bordering on the derisory. They wouldn't buy the transposition of reality. Pain puts weakness into the body, contorts it and limits it. It was pretty certain that none of the men being yelled at would feel any stronger for it when they had taken a *gladius* slash to their body, and tried to stay aboard their mount as they yelped and their nerves shot agonising pulses to the brain that excluded all other parts of their bodies temporarily from sensation.

Maybe I am being harsh and a little too cynical, Masinissa thought to himself.

Tigerman and Pun, to a lesser extent, were never going to rework their material. They weren't playwrights, poets or philosophers who would spark out new lines spontaneously. They just growled deeper, glared more sternly and hoped the act would stick. At least Tigerman received no quip or rebuke. The bark meant well, and there was always the bite, which still was not to be trifled with.

As for their numbers and condition, they were in increasingly lamentable shape. Their numbers had atrophied as desertions, be they clandestine or overtly sanctioned, withered their force. Masinissa didn't resent or prohibit his newer recruits from leaving, but he did demand a resumption of the call to arms at any reversion of fortune, which Masinissa, despite their plight, remained confident about. In fact, he'd come to regard their situation as the elusive prey of Syphax as a stalling manoeuvre, essentially a feint whilst they waited for Scipio to bring his forces over, and for his own dispersed troops to conduct their own hearts-and-minds propaganda on their own population, who were being terrorised by Syphax and despaired of Mazaetullus. The latter being widely reviled, even though he held the purse strings of the treasury and had the upper hand throughout eastern Numidia. Masinissa was increasingly of the view that the mutable boundaries of the Massyli and Masaesyli were being turned into an anachronism by the war, and there was only the ultimate prospect of unity at the end of the fighting. The factions and tribes must coalesce or be vanquished, and, in truth, it would have to be a bit of both.

Over a number of weeks that stretched into months and new seasons, Masinissa and his soldiers had led Syphax and some of the outlier units of Hasdrubal Gisco's army along the coastal trails of North Africa. They had skirted Saldae and Hippo Regius, but, fearing a pincer movement, didn't continue the trail further east towards Carthage. Instead, they had headed south towards the mountains. Cirta – congenitally loyal to the memory of Gala and seduced by his heir, both by achievement and character – was still a danger, as it had been garrisoned by Syphax, much to the rancour of the Massylian residents. The closer to the mountains they travelled, the more they were welcomed and the more effusive was the welcome and succour they received. At Theveste, they even managed to convene an impromptu tribal meeting, at which their resolve to reconstitute and retaliate, once the immediate threats had subsided or could be met on more equal terms, was resoundingly agreed. The roaring of his name, and that of his father and his incipient nation moved him deeply, and gave all a fillip to their ebbing vigour.

Their war had developed two threads: one immediate and pressing, and one promised and more remote. The latter was contingent on the arrival of Scipio, and the guile Masinissa could employ to evade Syphax in the interim. Auspiciously, many of the riders who still accompanied him were veterans of the campaigns in Iberia when they had harassed the Romans from the mountains, raiding the towns, the plains and the coasts incessantly. This time, he had fewer men and he was dispersing most of them for the time when they could unite with the Roman expeditionary forces. It meant he would be a more ineffective raider but a more elusive one. Stalling for time was a greater priority than degrading his enemy, particularly as the enemy was composed in large part of fellow Numidians who had made – in Masinissa's mind – misguided or simply expedient choices, which could be reversed at a later date when the balance of power shifted. The terrain was also more familiar to most of them, but that advantage was negated by the fact that it was equally so for Syphax, if not more so.

As they rode further south into the sparser plateau that separated the fertile coast from the desert, Masinissa was confronted with a dilemma. Where should he lead the enemy? In which direction could they sustain themselves and launch attacks? And if they were caught, which location would grant them the best chance of a miraculous escape? He chose as his consiglieri on the matter the quite disparate pair, both in physique and disposition, of Ari and Pun. The contrast between the lithe, equable and comical Ari, and the more dour and pessimistic hulk of Pun was striking. Their appearances aside, Masinissa chose them as consultants as they possessed between them the most intimate knowledge of the lands they might venture into. Ari was well acquainted with the desert and the dune seas of the grand erg, as well as the nomads, Troglodytae, Libyans and deeper Africans who traversed those empty wastelands. Pun, on the other hand, was an expert regarding the long string of mountains that stretched westwards and traced marginally southwards. He knew all of its diversity of terrain, wildlife and climate intimately, and if anyone could pick a route for an ambush or an evacuation, it was him. He was also familiar with all the dialects and cultural foibles of the isolated communities and villages, and assured Masinissa that he knew all of the many canyons and ravines, and could pick the best routes through the passes and along the spines.

"What's your call, Mas?" he asked. "Baked golds and reds, or greens, greys and whites?" Pun was referring, as subtly as his rough manner could manage, to the colours of the landscapes to the south and west.

"What's yours?" Masinissa probed, throwing the question back.

Pun teased and flicked his index finger and thumb together, as if about to beat out a rhythm. "It depends. The south may be safer from Syphax, but we may die in other ways. There's no water, and if Ari goes, how many others can navigate the dunes? Along the Atlas belt, there are plenty of places to hide too. There are forests of pine, oak and cedar; lakes and rivers; and, with that, plenty of grazers. There are sheep and stags to take, the leopards will not bother us, and we may even be able to round up a few elephants, although their numbers are declining. Their misfortune is to be too valuable for war." He clicked his thumb a little harder. "It's also a sweeter place to die," he added forlornly.

Masinissa nodded. "There is that. I'd rather not burn at the end of my time in this world. It sets the wrong tone for the next!" he added, stretching for a little levity. "What do you think, Ar?" he asked, turning to the desert native.

As Pun had revealed his hesitancy with his flicking, Ari rode his tongue under the grooves of his upper molars, as if a solution to their crisis lay in caressing his teeth. His face, when it lost the appearance of pinched stress and his tongue settled back to its regular position, showed a clear irresolution. "I'm drawn south, obviously. That's where my sanctuary and my spirit is. I will leave no traces there, and if I am beyond our enemies, over the horizon, I'm free. I'm used to it though and I'm not sure if the others will move at the pace we need to. We'd need camels as well, if we go deep. You can't stay in the desert as easily as you can in the mountains either."

"Another thing you need to consider," Pun interjected, "is the propaganda that can be made of you heading into the desert. You'll be leaving your ancestral tribal lands. That means something. If you move into the mountains, you are still in the fight, so to speak. You're still carrying your force on Numidian soil, and still proving yourself true to your father and our cause. You're still recruiting and still defiant. The wolf in the hills."

Tigerman, who was lurking in the background, gave a little howl to lend a little lupine presence to the reference, albeit a hopelessly faux one.

"Tigerman, man! You need to work on your calls. If we get separated, that will only call Syphax's men on to you," Masinissa scolded.

Tigerman smirked. "Don't worry, Mas; I do a great owl and my elephant is pretty decent too."

Masinissa grinned back at the unexpected frivolity. "Stick to the owl; if your enemies hear a trumpeting elephant out here, even a convincing one, and they don't see it, they'll be on you quicker than if you gave that crummy wolf bleat."

Besides the obvious advantages of heading into the mountains, Masinissa saw a favourable augur in the fact that the mountains were not the Aures or the Tell, but the Atlas. He turned a little scholarly and asked, "Do you guys know the legend of Atlas? Why the western range is called by that name?"

Ari shrugged, and Tigerman gave no response, as if his intrusion into the conversation was exclusively to parade his creature calls.

Pun said diffidently, "Well, I've heard of Atlas; he's one of the Greek gods, right?"

Masinissa explained, "He was, or is, depending on your point of view. I like this story; it's short, but it kinda fits with us and with me. Back in the old days of the gods – the Greek ones, anyway, not the Phoenician ones – Atlas and his brother Menoetius fought against the Olympians on the side of the Titans. When the Titans were defeated, most were incarcerated in Tartarus, which is a place of punishment for the damned, but Zeus, the victorious Greek god, gave Atlas a special punishment, forcing him to stand at the furthest edge of the earth and hold up the sky on his shoulders for all eternity. Anyway, this is where it gets interesting for me. In one of his twelve labours, Melqart was tasked with retrieving some of the golden apples that grew in Hera's garden; don't ask, just go with the story. Anyway, these gardens were tended by the daughters of Atlas – the Hesperides – and guarded by the fierce dragon Ladon. Melqart, ever rational, proposed to Atlas that he would hold up the sky temporarily whilst Atlas popped over to the garden to pick some of the apples. Naturally, Atlas agreed to the request. He saw an opportunity to relieve himself of the eternal burden of the sky, and, on his return, suggested deviously that he was willing to deliver the apples himself, as this would mean that, implicitly, Melqart had taken on the burden purposely, and was thus compelled to do so forever or until he, in turn, was relieved of it by another volunteer. Melqart wasn't so easily fooled, though, and tricked Atlas by asking him to hold the sky for a few moments whilst he rearranged his cloak to pad his shoulders. When he did so, Melqart grabbed the apples and ran. There is a more equitable version of the legend where Melqart builds the two pillars of Melqart to take the burden of the sky and liberate them both, but, to be honest, I prefer the more likely of the two stories. Clearly, the pillars of Melqart are doing little more than being pillars, whilst it's reassuring to think that Atlas is still out there doing his job of protecting us all from the sky from falling on our heads."

Unsure of the rather dubious claim, Ari gave him a little sardonic head twist, which was rewarded with a flamboyant wink, confirming that Masinissa's faith in the credentials of this particular component of Melqart's legend was not entirely certain or as strong as his convictions in his regard usually were.

Pun, not known for either his tact or gullibility, rolled his eyes at the conclusion of the story. "Well, Mas, if it makes you feel good, that's all that counts. More importantly, what's the plan?"

Masinissa's mind had already been made up. Responding to the question, he spliced his fingers together and flipped his palms open in a gesture of resigned settlement of the matter. "It's not really a debate any longer. You're kinda confirming my instincts on this. We work ourselves around the ranges, raid where we can, keep supporting and urging our people, and wait for the right moment. And keep one step ahead of Syphax as well, of course."

*

When the message was conveyed to the group, it was met with relief. It gave quite a few the justification to take the opportunity to return to their villages. This was not the moment for full-scale engagements or battles. They could melt way, and so long as there was a reasonable company still giving Syphax something to chase that would be sufficient until the Romans arrived and they could mobilise properly again.

That was the theory, at least, and it worked for a while. Masinissa retained a modest raiding party and rode south-west, descending into and out of the passes of the Atlas to attack small platoons and brigades affiliated with both Syphax and Mazaetullus. In many cases, these didn't even flare into armed conflicts, but turned into quite civil discussions and expressions of fealty. Whether genuinely or duplicitously, many of the smaller units professed loyalty to Masinissa and his cause, and complained bitterly of their conscription into rival armies. These conversations heartened Masinissa greatly. The attachments of many men to his adversaries were loose and easily frayed, and his own heroism was only burnished in contrast with their specious claims and poor character.

Juba Tunic summed these encounters up most succinctly when he ventured the view that, "The sandal's not really on the other foot, is it?"

Nevertheless, the open country was ceded to Syphax, and both he and the Carthaginians knew that if Masinissa's head was delivered and his defeat confirmed, the complexion of the war would be altered radically. Scipio may even lose his resolution to attack the Carthaginians on their own shores and instead focus on ridding Hannibal from his own. Inevitably, therefore, in both his own and Carthage's interests, Syphax's pursuit was relentless.

Masinissa surmised that it must also be deeply personal. He had the freedom to annex his lands, at least on the surface, but he must be having much more trouble subduing his new bride. Sophonisba may have become a pawn in a power game – sealing the alliance between Hasdrubal Gisco, Carthage and the Masaesyli – but she was still his woman, and that was more than a fanciful, optimistic claim. He knew she wouldn't yield any romantic ground to a vulgarian like Syphax, and she would surely be highly resistant to any of his amorous advances if he was foolish enough to launch any. She was recalcitrant enough in her play, so, in her hatred, she would be as obstinate as stone. Syphax, if he had any amatory interest in Sophonisba, would only loathe Masinissa even more than he already did, with the knowledge that his rival had tight possession of her heart. For Syphax to even begin to try to excise him from there, he would have to kill him and then at least take away the strength of character that hope was giving her. Whether her resistance would wither after that was moot. Masinissa felt that her character and emotions would present her with only one alternative at that point: to take her own life and join him in the next.

Syphax's riders and scouts quickly proved as fast and adept as his own, whose trails – as much as they concealed them in riverbeds and forests – always seemed to be picked up. Masinissa's fighting force also, in their periodic raids, exposed their bearings and position. Neither were they able to fully camouflage their daily necessities and ablutions. They had to sleep and eat in the open, and their kills and their fires were not hard for a skilled tracker to spot.

Syphax's riders were also improving in their tracking. Every time they recovered the trail, they held on to it for longer, to the point where it would take many days for Masinissa's brigade to lose them in the folds of the hills. If Syphax could stay within a certain range, there was a good chance that he could hold on to the Massylian tail, and wear them down as they climbed up and down the precipitous slopes of the Atlas.

That prospect looked like it had arrived. Masinissa's most recent raid had taken place more than ten days ago and it had turned out frustratingly, in hindsight, to be a fruitless one. It involved another conversation with errant henchmen who promised a swift return to Masinissa's side. Maybe they were simply bait as, when they rode away, Syphax's division emerged quickly from out of the nearby treeline. There were many hundreds of men on fresh-looking mounts. It was all Masinissa and his companions could do to put some measure of distance between them, with hard riding that took its toll on men and beasts. Several of the men were impaled by accurate spears, but there was no chance of turning to assess the extent of injury or mortality. Death was at their backs and riding almost as quickly as them. Hours later, they had enough space to pause and breathe, but it was the briefest of cessations, as, despite their initial spurt, Syphax was clearly not deterred. This time Masinissa's scent was in his nose.

Syphax's persistence was apparent by how frequently, in the next days and hours, Masinissa would spy his forces over ridge lines and escarpments. His soldiers would detect them in the far distance, howl their delight and hurl themselves down the mountain crests, with the slopes aiding their speed and giving their chase a sense of heightened impetus. It was visibly enervating for the men to see this vigorous pursuit, and consequently have to haul themselves back onto their horses and higher into the mountains.

Their horses too were gradually being worn down. Many were looking haggard and sinewy, and others turned lame, meaning that they were sent quickly into the next pot, and their rider given a rear seat on one of their sturdier kin.

They were also finding that they were having to take what sleep they could on their mounts, as their stalkers seemed never to rest, and the distance between them each day was being narrowed. It was hard, given the terrain, to be completely certain of how fast they were being caught, but the shapes of their enemy were becoming more than just distant, blurry outlines. The inevitability of them being caught loomed large in Masinissa's deliberations. He turned to Pun for answers.

Fortunately, Pun had one. The outline of it was as ingenious as the details were alarming, with the chances of death or multiple injuries almost on a par with what they might expect if captured. As for any other alternatives, there were none, other than to turn and meet their ends against a larger foe on fresher horses. In truth, there was something quite alluring and heroic about the proposal. Pun's idea was initially to detach a few outriders to ride to the nearest town, which he estimated was only a few hours away, and include in the party men who knew the terrain as well as him, and tell them to rustle, buy or beg as many horses as they could and meet him at the Bitches' Bottom.

When Pun first referred to this location, Masinissa was a little bewildered. "What are you on about bitches for? Save those thoughts for safer times. We're the ones about to get violated right now!" His uncharacteristic confusion was quickly allayed, however.

"The Bitches is the name of a series of cascades near here, and the Bitches' Bottom is the local slang for the base of the waterfall," Pun explained imperturbably. "They are kinda legendary. The bravest men – for dares, for gold and sometimes even for a woman – have ridden the Bitches. You're gonna need a lot of luck and your reflexes better be sharp to keep your head out of the rocks. Try to fall well, pick a line if you can, and pad yourself with whatever you have. I've known maybe seven guys to have gone down them: two died before they reached the bottom, and two others didn't survive much longer due to their injuries. I'm one of the three to survive them intact, by the way, with a few contusions and a broken wrist. I was lucky. All you can do is put yourself in the hands of the water and Baal Hammon. You can launch and bounce, but, once you're in the torrent, just brace and pray. Keep your eyes open, though!"

*

The falls took another two days to reach, by which time Syphax was within an hour or two of them and closing at an alarming rate. The acoustics of the valleys boomed the curses and promises of the chasers up to Masinissa and his riders, and they reverberated around the cols as if the mountains were reinforcing the threats maliciously. It was pointless to respond to them. This wasn't a chase game for children, but something much grimmer. En route and as they ascended to the snow line, the men started to improvise protective layers from what they could forage. There was precious little that could cushion a fall. Mostly, it was tearing up their clothing, and lashing them round their joints, and if they were not lucky enough to own a helmet, their heads, and if they were not lucky enough to own a shield, their arses. On Pun's advice, many put splints around their wrists. The first thing to go would be that joint, and, at least with the splint, you could still put force into the ground, and hold or push as best you could. They all wrapped their hands in as much leather as they could find, and many broke their lances and lashed them to their legs. It was more likely they would pop their knees than their pelvis, and they prepared themselves accordingly.

The final part of the climb was particularly craggy and sapped the horses of their last reserves, until they reached the shoulder where erosion seemed to have returned in earnest and passage was smoother. When they reached the top, their collective foreboding increased. The waters roared – part boom, part mischievous gurgle – as if underneath the incessant, noisy charge of element over element was some kind of nymph or sprite laughing at their fate. The boulders on the riverbed they walked over were slippery, and affirmed to them that they had barely any grip when horizontal. When they tipped themselves ninety degrees downwards, their vertical holds over even smoother surfaces would be risible.

Poignantly, when they had dismounted, Juba Tunic brought them all together in a circle, and they held hands and said three quick prayers to Baal Hammon, Tanit and Melqart. There were about two dozen of them left, and they all embraced one another. They knew their lives were about to enter a lottery, and their chance of survival was perhaps only modestly better than one in two, if that. A question was raised about the horses. It was typical of the Numidians to have them in the forefront of their thoughts, even at the point of their imminent demise.

"Leave them," Masinissa declared. "If Syphax takes them now, let him. They deserve life after saving ours. Only a few will ever be as good as they were, anyway. Let's hope they're let loose, and we can find them again when the world is changed."

The final preparations were almost ludicrous. Those who could, which was most of them in truth, secured their shields to their backs and rears in the hope that they would somehow be able to slide to the base of the falls riding their concave metal shells. They then took the last of their javelins and waddled, moving like ducks but looking like turtles, to the ridge line Syphax and his men were climbing. As they drew within range, they unleashed them with as much venom as condemned men could manage. Their trajectories arced beautifully against the sun and the spray, and they glided gracefully into the heads and bodies of the horses and men below them. A rough count of the four or five volleys they got off suggested that they had maimed or killed about forty of their pursuers. They all kept their swords. If Syphax was dumb enough to follow them over the cataract, they would need them to butcher the dazed. Besides, their scabbards were another extra layer of padding that may prove invaluable. Masinissa and Capuca both considerately gave theirs to Batnoam, who was one of the unfortunate ones to not have a shield, and he lashed them both gratefully to his rear cheeks. Masinissa made a ridiculous mental note to himself to make a comparison of the effectiveness of the respective kit. Would it be better to butt skate down the Bitches or take the shield toboggan down them? In the end, they were able to improvise about five scabbard skaters, so everyone had some measure of protection.

They decided to go over one at a time for a number of reasons. Firstly, it spared them smashing into each other or disrupting any attempt at steering a way down a chute. Secondly, it would give those behind a sense of where there might be hidden ledges or points that they should avoid, or where they might slow themselves down without inflicting too much damage on themselves. Thirdly, it allowed them all to honour each other and give each other courage. When it was each person's turn, their name would be chanted loudly enough to be heard above the cacophony of the falls. There was affection and fraternity in the chants. They were never closer as a group than at that moment as they stood on the boulders on the edge of the torrent.

Soldier Boy made a comment that caused general bafflement, as most were unsure if he was being serious or a little droll. He wondered if it might be a good idea to face inwards into the rocks and try to climb down that way.

Masinissa took it as simply an expression of his naivety. "Mate, if you tried that, I think the water would drag you down, and the rock will take your chin and probably your face before you tried to make your first hold."

Soldier Boy gave him a sheepish grin. "OK, shield and arse to the wall it is, Mas; I like this face!" His smile grew a little broader.

Realising that the ones who followed would have the greatest advantage, albeit a marginal one by being able to witness the fates of the others, as far as the obscuring curtain of water would permit anyway, Masinissa made the honourable decision to go over the top first.

The men quietened when he made the call, and then chanted sonorously in unison the four syllables of his name: "Ma-sa-nees-ah."

Pun cupped his hand over his ear to be able to funnel his words into Masinissa's head and speak to him in something just below a shout. "Mas, have you ever wondered if you've passed the point where you've lived most of your life? When most of your story has already been written?"

Masinissa turned his shoulder into his friend, and curved his own hands into an oval between his mouth and Pun's ear. "Given the way we've lived, I think we've all thought that. Most of our time has gone, even for the young and the lucky. I think it's the case for all of us."

Pun smiled and grabbed Masinissa vehemently around the face, so that his little finger nestled behind his ear and his thumbs rested on the dimples at the corners of his mouth. "Except for you, Mas; except for you. You are protected by the gods. They and us will all have to wait for you on the other side, and we will."

Masinissa returned the facial embrace and gave his *optio* the gentlest of headbutts.

He then turned to the water and appraised the line of best descent uncertainly. He vaulted a few of the boulders to obtain a position that he felt was more auspicious, nearly tipping himself over in the process. He looked down and the delicate misting of the spray gave him its own siren call: a false promise of the brutal impacts that would jar his bones and maybe break them in the next instant. He looked down again, then up, as if in the hope that a stray hand from the heavens would pinch his cloak and carry him, serene and unscathed, to the Bitches' Bottom. Any divinities observing his plight predictably ignored the wordless plea.

Masinissa aimed for the nearest of the cascading ledges, and eased himself into the maelstrom. He inched out, feeling his way along the edge until the slippery solidity gave way to air and water, and he pushed or hopped himself out further with a spring of his trailing leg, which was still affixed to the earth. He fell as vertically as he could, his senses overwhelmed by the deluge he had entered. Time compressed and accelerated, and he knew his actions had to be exact. Wait for a split second and then tuck was what he had committed himself to doing as he leapt.

He knew the ledge would rush up to him that quickly, and there was no value in trying to look for the stone protrusion. He needed to count the time it would take a stone to get there, and tense and close. He ticked the second off, tucked his legs in and got a portion of the shield underneath him, praying that the inevitable momentum slide would not whiplash his head too fiercely into the rockface. He bent his head in as far as he could to minimise the prospect, and he imagined himself to be something like a giant armoured hedgehog rolling into itself to repel predators. The fanciful comparison was hammered from him immediately, as the pulsating impact of the rock jabbed upwards into and through him, shaking his organs and his head, which, despite his preparedness, snapped back into the crag. His brace and his helmet mitigated most of the force of the blow, and, fortunately, he didn't lose either alertness or consciousness.

His lower back and neck seemed OK, and his ankles were saved by his shield and splints. He had barely a moment to regain composure as the impact only checked and did not stop his descent. He tried to slow himself as much as he could and spread his arms across the ledge till the water took him again. Then he pushed against it hard to clear the lip, and he momentarily moved horizontally before the grand alliance of gravity and water resumed his ferocious downward propulsion. He took a gulp of air as his face fleetingly cleared most of the cataract, counted one, sucked in, went taut and smacked into the unyielding bluff of the second of the Bitches. It was the same again. His body shook, trying to absorb the enormous jolt that it had tried to anticipate but couldn't really.

Another blow to the back of his head jarred him again, and he felt a blinking wooziness that he shook off as he slid off the second shelf. He exhaled, easing the tension and rigidity in his body briefly, before stretching out to knife his feet mercifully into the welcoming pool at the bottom. His velocity submerged him deeply, but he had taken another lungful just as he sensed contact with the water. His shield, which had saved his spine on two hard landings, switched from being his saviour to being a major encumbrance. It restricted his legs and weighed him down. He gave a flashing consideration to taking his knife to it and freeing his legs, but his upward stroke – though it tightened his chest – was strong enough for him to rise, even with his burden, and break the surface before his lungs started to riot and force his mouth open. He swam breaststroke to get himself to the edge of the lake, thrusting upwards with every movement to compensate for the weight across his lower back. Once ashore, he cut the shield from him; removed his helmet, plus all the padding and splints that restrained him; and dived back in to see the waters splash at uneven interludes with the falling bodies of his comrades.

They had decided to give each of themselves a few minutes before taking their turn over the Bitches, and insisting on that length of interval seemed to be even more prudent from the perspective of the water. It certainly granted Masinissa sufficient time to follow the plummeting men and help them to the safety of the shore. He plunged repeatedly into the water with all the alacrity of a spaniel. The forms he brought back, though, were in various states of consciousness and distress. Some, who couldn't help themselves, he couldn't raise alone, and if they had life left in them, were drowned. As others who were also strong swimmers made unimpaired landings, they were able to help him, and to dredge the river and bring a few of the lifeless to land. Their efforts were rewarded as a few of them spluttered blood, bile and tears of gratitude as their chests were pummelled and their lives struck back into them.

Massiva, Capuca and Bilam – whose name everyone abbreviated affectionately to Billy – were the strongest swimmers amongst the early survivors, and they lent their efforts to the underwater rescue. Ari, knowing only the desert through his youth, was a helpless flapper in the water, and was consigned to resuscitation and bandaging duties once he had waded out.

As the last of them was retrieved from the depths, Masinissa collapsed his sodden, aching frame to the earth, and splayed his limbs to stretch out the tautness of his muscles and feel the exact points of pain in his body. He winced a little, but lay there, numbed in body and spirit, until he saw Ari's imploring features above him.

Ari was loose on specifics and strong on general entreaties, offering his hand and urging Masinissa back to his feet with a questioning, "Sire, will you command us?"

Masinissa rose and found his way over to the dazed and injured, most with scrapes and many with breaks. Fingers, lower legs and collar bones seemed to be the skeletal parts of the anatomy to have snapped most frequently. As far as the more fundamental accounting went, there were two broad categories of survivors, and their numbers were exactly even. There were seven walking wounding, and another seven "hobblers", or guys who would need a stretcher, litter or crutches for some time in the future. Aside from Masinissa himself, the really lucky seven comprised of Ari, Massiva, Capuca, Billy, Soldier Boy and Pun, although Pun's indomitableness probably masked the fact that he probably ought to have been considered in the latter category. Firmly in the latter category was his own trusty adjutant Tigerman, who had broken an ankle and several ribs, and needed a long stitch in his midriff that might suggest undiagnosed internal injuries. How many of the not-so-lucky seven would survive was uncertain, but they all looked like they had a chance. How effective they may be as soldiers or cavalrymen in the future, and how long their convalesce might take were also very open questions but ones Masinissa didn't regard as relevant at that moment.

He looked to the crest of the falls and, although the angle was acute, he could see the shapes of many men looking down on them as if they were the subject of a performance in an amphitheatre. He was struck by their passivity and immobility. As their pursuers and adversaries, he expected to see agitation in their ranks, yelled imprecations of all sorts, violent gesticulations of swords and spears, but instead the men above simply watched, as if at a wake, almost in a respectful or awestruck ring of silent honour. None appeared to be willing to follow them or to have been given that probably fatal instruction.

Masinissa thought he would present them with a target, realising that any projectile hurled from the top of the falls had no chance of accuracy and would only be a gift to his own depleted arsenal. He walked towards a point closest to them, where he was most visible and, he hoped, most audible. As someone usually lacking a flair for the melodramatic, he walked with the composure and deliberation of a seasoned and confident gladiator. This was his stage, and he already owned the outcome.

He spread his arms wide in a gesture of welcome and unrequited embrace, and shouted to them with the most resonant tone he could manage, "*Numidians… brothers… I am your true king. Follow me from this day, as I am your leader. Follow me, and I will guide our nation and our tribes to peace and prosperity. We should not fight for others or amongst ourselves any longer. I have proven my worth, in the north and here today. I stand unbowed and unbroken. I have earned the right to lead now, and I will. Have faith in me, believe in me and follow me!*" With that he unsheathed his sword, and raised it in a salute and, perhaps quixotically, as a command.

Unsurprisingly, none returned the gesture, as to do so would no doubt result in Syphax's henchmen pitching them straight over the Bitches, but Masinissa sensed in their wavering forms and downcast looks that there was irresolution percolating in their minds and admiration for him seeping into them. Those fresh perceptions might allow him to claim many of them to his cause in time. Syphax could probably sense it too, as it appeared that he and the men who must have been his *optio* and *tesserarius* started to pull them back, physically and through orders that, even from that far away, sounded a little hysterical and manic.

Masinissa had made a well-intentioned and sincere appeal to their notions of bravery and honour, but it had also been an old-fashioned stare down, and it looked as if he may have won on both counts. As the last of the men receded behind the apex line of the horizontal water, he did receive a solitary retort to his own sword salute as Syphax did take some measure of aim, as the last man in view, and hurled a javelin at him. It's force and direction went pathetically awry, and it got lost in the veil of the falls, appearing to any observer as nothing better than a pathetic rebuke that was no more hostile than if he had tossed a piece of bread at a duck.

On cue and fortuitously, as if they had been tardy, then Syphax may have regained their trail, the men despatched to rustle some transportation arrived with a dozen horses. The number suggested that they perhaps had been rather pessimistic about their chances of defying the cataract as a full complement. All three were relatively new recruits and had not yet campaigned in foreign lands; they were young men who understood the world they had by then entered more from stories than from harrowing and disillusioning experiences. All three brimmed with vigour, and were athletic youths who bounced on their toes and could run all day for the pleasure of it. As with all young men of their ilk, they had not as yet fully become part of the troop. They were still not scrubbed of their innocence. There was something precious in the vestigial childishness of their ways, which was quite endearing but also kept them apart from the others. Masinissa conjectured that things would not be so easy and carefree for them soon. Their elan was often well received, but at other times it was inappropriate, jarring and a sign of their otherness to the grizzled veterans they had come to rescue, whose movements, thoughts and memories were far more painful and polluted.

The callow little crew had been given a nickname by the others. All their names began with the letter H – Hiempsal, Hiarbas and Herba – so it was an easy shorthand to refer to them collectively as Triple H. Masinissa approached the most senior of the three, Hiempsal, who reminded Masinissa a little of himself as a youth; the boy was eager and deferential, but with a keenness of perception that revealed a quick intelligence and an insightful character.

"Thank you Hiempsal, I was right to trust you. I hope you compensated those you could or those who are not currently our antagonists anyway," Masinissa declared.

Hiempsal grinned. "Of course, sire," he replied with an exaggerated bow, which left Masinissa wondering whether or not there was some discretion applied to his response.

He did have faith in the three, though. They had hung on with them to the last when they could easily have abandoned them. It was a palpable confirmation of their character and loyalty. To have completed their errand so conscientiously and punctually also showed to Masinissa that they had as much faith in him as he had in them. He patted Hiempsal on his shoulder, and the young man's youthful power was conspicuous, as the rubbed deltoid was as firm as stone, yielding nothing to the affectionate grip.

Masinissa stated, "We still have a little time to say our goodbyes. I'm not sure if any of you were close to or got to know any of the guys we've lost, but now is that moment. I'm not going to leave their bodies here to be interfered with. Syphax will want to vent his rage, but it won't be on our dead."

The three took their cue and went to find brothers in arms who had not survived the leap over the falls. They understood implicitly what to do and, with as much respect as it was possible to manifest in the act of dragging a corpse, heaved their fallen comrades solemnly to the water's edge. All the men who could wade out further took the bodies of their brothers gently by the backs of their necks, giving them a little artificial buoyancy and glided them out into the deeper water. Their tombstones would be the shields that they left attached to them, which would spare their bloated bodies the indignity of being exposed to the light again. These large bucklers, which the survivors had ridden to safety, would keep them submerged until the fishes and their own decay stripped them down to their collagen frames.

After offering words of thanks and blessings for the next world, they let the deceased be immersed. Masinissa held Juba Tunic, the closest of the unfortunate to him, poignantly and lingeringly for the last time, took the hand that was underneath his back away first, laid it over his brow and smoothed his wet scalp back. Masinissa's tears added some of his own water to the pool, and he hunched into himself trying to squeeze out the spasms in his chest and regain some control of his quivering frame. Memories of Juba Tunic – his words, his expressions and his affections – showered him. He held on to an image of an embrace they had shared after Ilipa in the euphoria and camaraderie of salvation. He let go of the hand that held him above the surface.

He said, "Let the gods breathe life back into you, brother," and to the heavens he entreated the same to those who could work that miracle.

Masinissa inhaled slowly, held the aspiration as if it were a thought or part of his farewell, and then blew out gently, as if putting wind into a tiny sailboat that held Juba Tunic's essence. He scratched the top of a finger; let the same movement happen again, only for his grieve to trap it in a choked gulp; and waved his arm above the water, indicating that this parting must now end. In the most fleeting of moments, the lifeless forms were gone.

They left the water, continued preparing the horses and began to mount up. He looked at the men who straddled their horses or secured the injured onto them as gingerly as possible before mounting alongside them, and saw that their sadness was preoccupying them, as his was consuming him. The adrenaline of flight and deliverance had waned, the urgency of the former and the intoxication of the later had drained out of them, and they let their silences cocoon them and allow their thoughts to roam. Once they set off, they rode with introspection and pain, both physical and existential, looking for the bolthole that Pun had told them would suit their purpose. There would be no raiding for a while. His men would heal, they would wait for Scipio, and he would show himself to the tribes and the elders, and make the most of the propaganda of the falls. No doubt many of Syphax's brigade would spread the word as briskly and effectively as he would.

Pun himself, in his laconic way, gave his own premonition, which put a little ease and hope into Masinissa's mood. "You don't have to make your reputation at home any more. Word travels. Watch your legend grow." He nodded like his horse, with a sag and a reflexive jolt and reiterated the optimistic conviction, "Watch your legend grow."

FIRESTARTER

As Masinissa and his remaining companions recuperated and waited for news of Scipio's invasion, they found themselves, despite being ostensibly more fugitives by then than an army in the field, paradoxically more at liberty to move around as news of their survival spread and acquired the tint of a miracle. The fact of their survival in itself was impressive, but, undoubtedly, there must have been the odd embellishment in the retelling that made their actions out to be even more spectacular than they were. Sanctuary and safety were easy and quick to find. Any waverers or anyone who might have been inclined to betray them only had to be informed of the fact of their survival, and the indisputable truth of their favour by the gods, for them to offer a fulsome and reliable hospitality.

They moved as heroes and liberators in waiting through the Massylian towns and settlements, hid and recruited amongst the people, and Masinissa learnt at first hand much more about the everyday struggles and grievances of the communities he presumed to lead and command. As he spoke to people and listened, he felt a deeper attachment beginning to form. He met older people whose sons had left them to join the war and who had been killed or enslaved – they preferred to imagine the former – and he listened to their heartbreak and admired their endurance. They had somehow still kept a light in their being, at least in the company of others. Their memories were keeping them alive, it seemed. The past was their only future. He felt he was regaining some of his softness, and that a truer empathy was infiltrating the hard carapace of the weary and emotionally exhausted soldier he had long ago become.

A light of another kind returned to him too. News of his exploits and presence in Numidia was spreading to all parts of Africa, and could no more be suppressed than a true religion. Thus his erstwhile friend and mentor Conon found his way to the camp, expressing a desire to see him, and to stay and offer his services as well as he could. Masinissa took the reunion for what it was, a wonderful surprise, but also as an indicator of the subtler trajectories of the war. For all their fellowship, why would Conon seek out a hopeless renegade, unless he felt that the tides of war were turning in Masinissa's favour.

He had to leave Carthage surreptitiously, and he had brought with him a number of other Greek scholars and artisans, fearful of the rising oppressions, potential military conscription and the ominous threat of invasion, which all feared by then, apart from the still-assertive Carthaginian fleet. They had acquired an escort once clear of the city's sentries, and Masinissa thanked and paid these men generously. Conon's group, whilst hopeless in a military sense, provided knowledge and skills that he lacked and that would certainly be beneficial in any incipient state that he might carve out from the wreckage of the conflict. For that moment, the philosophers would have to lend a hand with the more practical physicians and tend to the wounded as they arrived.

When this was proposed to Conon, as they found themselves following their familiar pattern, sitting together with a *petteia* board and some cups of wine, the scholar demurred. "Ah, Mas. I know I'm not going to be able to throw a javelin or wield a *falcata* with much power, and I'm clearly not the most rugged or sturdy, but I can ride with the best of them, and you can be assured I can ride out of harm's way quicker than most. Use me as an advisor or messenger, and don't assume responsibility for my life. Make my status clear, and I'm sure no one will resent me from not riding hard into the lines. Maybe I can balance out the voices who are going to be clamouring for your attention and who may be looking to take advantage of you. I don't see you as a useful hammer or an open purse, if you know what I mean." He leant over and took one of Masinissa's *petteia* "dogs", which he then flicked towards his opponent's chest in a playful taunt.

Masinissa opened his mouth and wiggled his jaw in an obvious physical expression of his hesitation. When the ramus wobbling started to bother him, he scratched the hair at his temples as if pulling a decision out of his brain. "OK, you know I love your company, so you're playing on my affections a little bit, but stay out of the way of the tough stuff, and carry as many bandages and splints as you can carry. You're my advisor and tutor, but you're also a nurse now too!"

Conon beamed at the assignment and took another of Masinissa's dogs, tossing the fresh catch with as much exuberance as the first one. Masinissa smiled too, warmed by the decision as well as the company. Conon would be useful to the troops as a mentor and a carer for the injured, but also would be a wise counsel and true friend to him. As his newly restored companion focussed on the board and perhaps reflected a little on the substantial step into a more hostile world he had taken, Masinissa took a moment to appraise his constitution. This was done partially in the detached way of a general inspecting the condition of his soldiers and partially too, in a comparative way, from a sudden and absurdly pressing curiosity, assessing which one of them had suffered more conspicuously from the ravages of time and circumstance.

In truth, Masinissa concluded it to be an honourable draw. In physical terms, Masinissa had a clear edge. His injuries and battlefield scars had been relatively minor, and the relentless abrasions of living in the field and training to kill had made his body even tougher and more vital. His military instincts concluded that such robustness was the solitary criteria for corporeal judgement. In contrast, Conon's physical state had lapsed further. His shoulders curved more conspicuously and the line of his tummy traced an equally more noticeable crescent. They were such a contrast. Masinissa made a point to start training

Conon as and when time permitted. He suppressed a little internal mirth at the mental image it conjured.

Where Conon regained parity was in his features, which remained smooth and unblemished, faintly holding on to traces of his pristine youth. He must have spent much of the last few years indoors, Masinissa surmised as he was in possession of far too fair a complexion for a resident of an African city. Masinissa's features were the polar opposite, being scorched by the sun. He had been brushed smooth in a harsher way, which had erased his adolescent blemishes but etched wrinkles around the corner of his eyes and in the other creases of his face; these were far deeper and more noticeable than Conon's. He didn't quite have the complexion of an old crone, but he wasn't all that fresh-faced either. His observation drifted into a greater concentration in the game, and the conversation lapsed in its final throes as Masinissa's stone dogs started to be outnumbered and isolated. He tried to distract Conon, whose final triumph loomed, but his adversary was conscious of the ruse and batted him away.

Conon suggested, "You know, silence is one of the great arts of conversation, Mas, and it seems we have become masters of it in our absence from one another."

Masinissa laughed and conceded the game extravagantly, upending the board to the mild surprise of the exultant Greek. "I think I'm going to introduce you to some interesting people in the next days and months, Con. There's one thing to remember, OK? Let them win or let them think they're winning. Always play the deferential junior, OK? Obviously impress them, but not to the point of embarrassing them, particularly intellectually. You'd probably struggle to do that with Scipio in any case. He's a pretty sharp guy; well, that's probably nothing you're not already aware of."

Conon gave the self-consciously reverent bow of a slave and winked. "I know my place, Mas, and I won't reveal my hand or pop anyone's ego. It'll be a thrill to even hover in the background of such exalted company."

*

Conon did not have to wait too long to apply the tact that Masinissa had insisted upon. Scipio had moved down the spine of Italy, and managed to acquire en route the province of Sicily and its garrison, with the latitude to act in any way that he believed was in Rome's interest. For a man like Scipio, that was a very loose remit with a very specific outcome. Augmenting the already quite considerable garrison that was already there, Scipio's burgeoning popularity meant many volunteers flocked to his cause; as many as 7,000 enlisted as volunteers. His final invasion force comprised around 20,000 infantry and a cavalry contingent of about a tenth of that, which was a paucity of horsemen that made his alliance with Masinissa all the more imperative. He had also reinvigorated the core of his army: the two Cannae legions, or the fifth and sixth legions as they were otherwise known. The old and the injured had been released from service, and had been replaced by younger, abler men to make a formidable nucleus to his army.

The first intimation of the mustering invasion fleet came in a series of pirate raids along the North African coastline by elements of the Roman fleet. Scipio had outfitted thirty warships and placed them under the command of the capable Gaius Laelius who was Scipio's trusted senior *legatus*. The raids sent most of the Carthaginian and Masaesylian troops to their fortified towns and cities, and freed Masinissa up to venture to the coastline, where he was able to rendezvous and discuss their plans with Laelius. It also allowed Masinissa the opportunity to vent a few of his frustrations.

Despite his best intentions of upbraiding Scipio's second for delaying – in his view, at least – the invasion and effectively leaving him to manage on his renegade wits in Numidia, Masinissa took an immediate liking to Laelius. The Roman possessed an almost preternatural calmness and mild manner that Masinissa found quite infectious, in so far as someone's ability to ease your tensions can be regarded as virulent. Laelius had the air of a man who had always chosen the most difficult challenge and had thrived on it rather than been shattered by it. He was also a man who appeared to be very open and keen to learn as much as he could. He showed a distinct curiosity about Masinissa, an attentiveness that was quite the opposite of what Masinissa had been accustomed to when he had sported Carthaginian colours, and had needed to endure the bombast and haughtiness of Gisco and the Barcids.

His features were notable too, as they gave him the appearance of a slightly exaggerated version of a typical Roman. His nose in particular drew Masinissa's attention. He had the typical aquiline hook, but his was quite bulbous, which gave an odd dual impression of potency and decadence. It looked as if, and Masinissa repressed a giggle at the thought, Laelius was sporting a slug on his face, or as if he had poked a couple of holes on the extremities of a fat mollusc and stuck it on his face. He knew that the Romans were really keen on the medical uses of leeches, which had been prescribed by the Greek physicians Hippocrates and Herophilos, but this was going too far. A slight smirk tweaked his lips at the frivolity.

Laelius, obviously oblivious to the stray thought that had crossed Masinissa's mind, smiled back unsuspectingly. It was an auspicious misunderstanding. Over food and a little wine, they talked freely and long into the night, as the fires of the new allies lit up the shoreline, the lapping waves gave their thoughts an acuity, and their mood a mellowness. They were able to spend a few days formulating and exchanging views about the next phase of the campaign, and, importantly, their men were able to mingle, and establish a connection and the first glimmers of trust. Masinissa's brigades had a fearsome reputation in Roman camps and being able to placate these lingering tensions would be useful when the two groups would have to watch each other's backs.

In his last moments on the African shore before resuming his marauding, and filling up his hull with more booty and unwary Carthaginians, the singularly diplomatic Laelius further soothed his new ally and encouraged him in his stoicism. He had been quick to realise that Masinissa was no goon and had received an education broadly analogous to his own. His reassurances seemed always to return to encouraging Masinissa to persevere.

Aware of Masinissa's fondness for Greek scholarship and also conscious of Conon being within earshot, Laelius quoted Aristotle as he watched his men load the last of the supplies onto the quinqueremes. "Whenever I feel my mood is becoming restless or impetuous – which is rare for me these days, admittedly – I remember a comment of Aristotle. Do you know the one I mean? 'Patience is bitter, but its fruit is sweet.'"

Masinissa was a bit hazy on the quote, but it had a vague familiarity to it so he must have read it somewhere. "Let's hope you're right. The taste in our mouths is certainly quite sour at the moment."

Conon gave a restrained smile at his friend's admission, and Laelius simply nodded, having the grace to acknowledge the trials the Massylians had endured, if not the words to express the appropriate consolation.

The Greek, with his philosophical inclinations, couldn't resist his own interpretation of the point. "Rivers know there is no hurry to get to the sea. The water will get there eventually."

Masinissa's brows crumpled a little at the slightly trite analogy. "OK, Con, but say someone sticks a few boulders in it and dams it all up."

Before Conon could formulate a response, Laelius interjected, "Well, it just means that when you kick those boulders out of the way, the rush of water is all the more powerful. Trust me; the longer we can prepare, the stronger we'll be. There's nothing for it other than for you to wait for Scipio. Sit tight and stay put; he's almost ready. He's got to get his greener troops up to the necessary levels, as not many of his men are veterans of Baecula and Ilipa now, and the garrison troops in Sicily are used to a completely different type of warfare. We need to get them out of their siege mentality, if you know what I mean." He gestured a slowly downward tracing index finger theatrically punctuating the comment and giving time for the loaded remark to sink home. He needn't have gone to the trouble, as Masinissa immediately recognised the intentional pun. He mirrored the action with his own; the act of doing so indicated the extent of familiarity the two had already reached in that he could mildly mock the Roman's movement.

"Just be as quick as you can, OK?" Laelius smiled and put his index finger to more good use, spinning it in the air and whistling in the mode of a magician conjuring up a miracle. "I'll be back before you know it, and it'll be a sight to see."

*

Laelius's promise was only proved partially accurate, at least to Masinissa, who was measuring the commitment in terms of weeks rather than months. He hadn't considered the intrigues of the senate or the indispensable logistics of feeding thousands of men on another continent, and the accompanying delays those issues might cause. When the invasion fleet finally did sail into view it was, as forecast, a magnificent sight. There were around 400 transport vessels accompanied by a relatively modest escort of forty warships. Masinissa was a little perturbed by the paucity of warships when he saw them, but they had reached their destination unmolested and that was all that counted as far as he was concerned.

Masinissa had been lucky with the interception of the fleet, as Laelius had been somewhat vague, offering him two potential landing points. He had initially proposed that the fleet would find a harbour east of Carthage, in one of the sheltered, shallow bays of Emporia. Masinissa demurred at this suggestion, as it meant exposure to the Carthaginian fleet if he took the coastal route, and a highly circuitous trek if he took a long, southerly loop around Carthage. The alternative was much more feasible. To the north-west of Carthage was the promontory of Cap Farina, which was often referred to as the promontory of the beautiful one. It was indeed an idyllic spot and an incongruously peaceful one for an invading army to land. Masinissa had brought his forces there, which were swelling with his own returning cohorts as well as fresh volunteers encouraged by the imminence of the Roman invasion, a few days before Scipio's ships arrived.

It was a peaceful interlude of sports, swimming and feasting on the bountiful harvest of the shallow waters. To Masinissa's eyes, the sea at Cap Farina was the most turquoise he had ever seen, a colour accented by the widespread splotches of viridescent algae that had found hosts in the pebbles close to the shoreline. A short way out to sea was a rock formation that drew attention; it almost resembled a trireme, with its ram facing out to the north as if it was a solitary Carthaginian defender. In truth, its shape was such that, like certain cumulus clouds, it could be compared to a wide variety of objects. Over the few idle days he waited, as well as its similitude to a naval vessel, Masinissa noted its resemblance to both the pompous hat of a magistrate or *suffete*, and some kind of elegantly constructed napkin that a creatively minded slave might have added as a flourish to a particularly important banquet.

The initial landing was a scene of turmoil and excitement, but the introductions and pleasantries had to be suspended almost before they started, as a squadron of Carthaginian cavalry arrived on the scene and made a woefully inadequate attempt to repel the Roman trespassers. Perhaps they had misjudged the disembarkation point, or had only meant to stalk the Romans and spy on their numbers and equipment. It may well even have been a well-intentioned attempt to protect the local population and allow to escape those who hadn't already taken the opportunity to flee to Utica or Carthage.

Regardless of the intention, the outcome was a brutal failure. Masinissa sent his fresh and presumably unexpectedly large contingent to attack the rear of the charging Carthaginians, and the Romans exited and organised themselves off the boats efficiently. The hapless Carthaginian forces were caught on the horns. A few pacier riders broke out of the melee quickly, but those who didn't spot their doom early, which was the majority of them, were slaughtered with minimal casualties to either the Romans or Masinissa's forces.

Pun, who had led the first wave of Massyli into the unwary

Carthaginian unit, gave his usual pithy appraisal as he rejoined the senior observers who had stayed at the top of the ridge overlooking the bay. "Well, so much for the reconnaissance fellas."

It brought a fraternal cheer from those around him, and he was clapped and plied with titbits and liquor as he dismounted.

The Romans were not in as leisurely a mood as the Numidians, however, and, as they lolled in the shade of the pines, Masinissa observed the Romans as they dispersed inland.

As the day progressed, and throughout the following night and morning, in small parties, the fruits of their raids were dragged – some still screaming, and others already acquiring the wisdom not to do so – back onto the boats, which looked as if they would return to Sicily bulging with unwilling human cargo.

As the vessels hauled their anchors, and fresh, piteous slaves rowed them out of the shallows, Masinissa watched a group of riders leave the beachhead and ascend the ridge to come towards them. He ordered his men to form an honour guard along the track, and – with the many who had flocked to his standard in recent days, as their allegiances need not be concealed any longer – they represented an impressive number. Reflecting on his recent travails in the mountains and at the Bitches, he could barely credit the success of his most recent, mostly clandestine muster, as 1,000 riders on either side of the pathway saluted Scipio's approach with raised javelins, each of which almost touched the tip of the javelin of the rider opposite. Masinissa couldn't fault the impromptu choreography of the scene. He wondered who had come up with the idea of the spear canopy. He suspected Capuca, who had quite an eye for the theatrical.

The final troopers flanking the arrival of what had turned into a cavalcade, as Scipio paid attention to some of the individuals within the salute, were two of the younger men: Bilem, who was revelling in the cachet of being one of the survivors of the falls, and his friend Izem, who had reunited with them a few weeks after their deliverance. Billy and Zee, as they were more affectionately known, couldn't have been better chosen to terminate the line of lances. Their excitement and pride swelled in them, and when Scipio pointedly took time to exchange words with them both, they stumbled over their words and clumsy greetings in ways that were clearly endearing to the Roman consul. Young boys of the desert were not supposed to practise their Latin with one of the most senior leaders of Rome. The benevolent side of Scipio's character was also evident when, spontaneously, he asked for and took a *gladius* from one of his aids, and handed it to Billy as a gift, with a few flourishes to show the best way to use the weapon. Billy, hardly in need of the coaching, took it, beaming with unrestrained delight as if he were a child and his kindly father had just given him a carved wooden facsimile of the sword.

When Scipio dismounted and gave Masinissa the warm embrace of familiars rather than expedient recent allies, Masinissa felt a surge of relief pass through him. The promise had become a reality, and he could see a light showing the way out of his dark times, a means to navigate himself back to his father's throne and his lover's arms. He could see that there was evidently a glow in Scipio's features as well, and one not exclusively formed as a result of exposure to the winds and rays of a sea crossing. Scipio was thrilled. He looked like a man in his moment. The preparations were over and he could put his schemes into action.

Masinissa felt the meeting was a little reminiscent of his times with Indibilis and Mandonius. There was an easy and instant kinship, a recognition of worth, and deeper affinities between men who could still balance codes of honour and brutality. Scipio spoke to him as an equal, both intellectually and militarily, and it was a courtesy that he appreciated. Their location at the crest of a ridge, which allowed them to soak up the full beauty of the breathtaking panorama of the bay, helped immeasurably with their mood and ease; nothing could really beat distant, lapping waves across an azure crescent when it came to mellowing tensions.

As Scipio looked out towards the ocean and allowed the fresh sea breezes to cool him, Masinissa regarded his profile. Perhaps the sea crossing had done him good or perhaps his succession of victories had been a boon to his health, but he showed a much more youthful aspect than he had in their previous encounter. Masinissa scratched for the recollection, doubting the veracity of his memory, but – like Conon – Scipio seemed to be making a good effort at resisting the ravages of time. Even his jawline – the first place on one's face to show softness, puffiness or the first bumps of future jowls – seemed to jut proud and even from his ear to his chin.

Masinissa wondered at what remark to use to break the consul's spell, and he opted for a mild reproof: "You know you needn't have done that. Billy's got a pretty good sword already." It was said amiably enough and didn't jar with Scipio in the least.

"I know, but there's a symbolism attached to it, isn't there?" Scipio replied, turning towards him slowly, still holding on to the reverie of the view for as long as he could. "It wasn't just the boy. Everyone else could see the gesture and, hopefully, the meaning behind it. It's like the baton being passed in a race. We're a team now, and we'll each take a turn with the sword. Besides, I like to reward valour when I see it, and that boy showed guts. The same goes for you too." He paused and added, "Sorry I'm late, by the way."

Masinissa laughed at the casualness of the apology, wondering a little about what portion of it was frivolity and what part genuine. "Your Eminence, for your arrival, I can wait till my beard is as white as the moon."

Scipio's quick smirk indicated that Masinissa had struck the right note in trying to mirror his playfulness.

Masinissa continued, "Anyway, your mere arrival is in itself atonement for any delay. I'm sure it can't have been easy getting that many bodies across the great sea. I'm grateful to you." He cupped his hands across his chest and gave Scipio a deferential bow. "I know you have your own war, but you have allowed me to fight mine as I should have fought it all along. I and these men of mine will do our damnedest in both causes."

Responding to the promise, Scipio revealed a little of his philosophical temperament. "You know, gratitude is a virtue I prize very highly when it is sincerely felt and expressed. It is the seed for so many other principled behaviours. If I can see someone's appreciation, I can see their honour. If I can see that someone lacks it, then I start to worry. I lose trust and faith in that person. You..." He clapped Masinissa fervently on his ample biceps. "You, I can trust," and he added a little humorous addendum, "despite the fact that you have just earned a certain reputation for treachery."

Masinissa felt a little humbled by the assurance. "We all make mistakes, but only a fool persists in their folly once they see it. I'm pretty sure I've done the right thing. You use a harsh word. Maybe you could call it treachery if I were betraying a just or noble cause. I wasn't helping to preserve anything of value or honour. You know, I see a lot of faces in my dreams – old friends lost forever – and I can't look those ghosts in the eye. When someone under your command suffers an appalling death, and they're hammered or slashed to pulp you have to rationalise the decision you made that resulted in that outcome, and when you throw that justification away and lose the reason you've given yourself for it, guilt comes a calling. All I can do now is keep as many as I can of my own intact and give them freedom and a secure nation – or the promise of it, anyway, to their sons and daughters."

Scipio narrowed his gaze. "You will earn your country, Prince Masinissa, but turning a territory into a free nation is not an easy endeavour."

The Numidian nodded but couldn't resist reminding the consul of his recent ordeals. "It's gonna be no harder than staying alive has been."

The acerbic tone was accepted by Scipio, who was a man indulgent of a certain type of frankness from a certain type of person, even when it steered close to insubordination.

The two men then reverted, with their adjutants and *optios*, to more practical considerations, and began more earnestly to devise plans to neutralise and conquer their enemies.

*

Their machinations were not allowed to go unhindered for very long, however. Before the claws the Romans had dug into African soil could knead the ground and settle further, the Carthaginians sent another cavalry probe towards them. This one was, ostensibly, more threatening and a little bit more personal from Masinissa's perspective. It was a contingent of about 4,000 men, mostly fellow Numidians, but also incorporated a smattering of Carthaginian citizens. It was commanded by Hanno Gisco, the son of Hasdrubal and the brother of Sophonisba. Masinissa surmised that the command had been entrusted to Hanno deliberately in order to try to test or soften his inchoate loyalties. He may not be able to fix the breach he had made in any event, but could he attack the brother of the woman he loved, whom he had known in very cordial situations, someone he had drunk with, made vacuous oaths with and regarded as a future in-law, for Tanit's sake? He was going to have to. Would Hanno's presence in the enemy's ranks force him to waver or to weaken? Or, in the event that he prevailed, would Sophonisba view his actions as a form of fratricide, which might twist her ardour into rancour? He tried to bury the potential ramifications.

Scipio, unsuspecting of Masinissa's paramour or her brother, had no such compunctions to worry him and, if anything, was dismissive of what he viewed as Hanno's timid approach. The Carthaginian's initial foray had brought him no closer than fifteen miles from Scipio's camp, and he appeared to have taken temporary refuge in the city of Salaeca. Scipio derided such a manoeuvre as feeble and practically contemptible, scoffing at the notion of confining a cavalry division to the arcades of a city when they should be roaming the country gaining strength in the open.

His orders to Masinissa were simple and familiar. The consul referred facetiously to the tactic to be deployed as a "chase me" gambit, and, a little uncharacteristically, gave a coquettish flick of his head as he gave the order, to remind Masinissa to make sure the tease was alluring enough to make the enemy come after him. The gesture was intended to be light-hearted, but it did little to allay Masinissa's misgivings. Regardless, he had used the tactic previously in Iberia and trusted in its efficacy. He could bat his eyelashes almost within touching distance of Hanno's troops and knew he could get clear, at least over the short distance between them and the ambush being set by the Romans. There was something a little bit demeaning about being bait rather than brawn, but he fancied he could be back and through the Roman line with barely a scratch on his men to show for their theatrics.

Hanno proved himself to be as innocent and impetuous in the arts of war as Scipio had anticipated, and Masinissa, who had ridden to Salaeca with half of his riders, offered a very enticing morsel to his erstwhile in-law, who rode hard out of the city with his full complement.

"So much for our kinship," Masinissa rasped as he turned from the pursuers and galloped as fast as his horse could be goaded towards the concealed Roman lines.

A few miles from the coast, where Hanno still must have presumably felt secure from the Roman invaders, Scipio's infantry erupted out of the pine forest that had hidden them well, and their initial fusillade of ballista and javelin cut down hundreds. The shock was so abrupt that the charge of the chasers dissipated into nothing as Hanno's callow leadership fumbled at an exit strategy. Not much of one was left to him, as the remaining Massylian cavalry – led ably by Pun and Capuca – flanked him, ensuring Hanno's charge was funnelled either straight into its ruination or spat right back in the direction it came in panicked retreat. As Masinissa banked around and split his forces to bolster and reinforce the pincer, he could see how well trained Scipio's legions were. They cut up Hanno's men as if they were sheaves of wheat under farmers' scythes. Before they had the wit to run, a quarter of Hanno's men were dead or within a hoof's trample of it. Of the remaining 3,000 or so, two-thirds were chopped in a wretched flight towards the sanctuary of Carthaginian lines. They rode a long way past Salaeca before Scipio called time on their gory pursuit, which – given the inability of the fleeing riders to put up even the most token resistance – had turned into more of a hunt. Hanno's remnant seemed to Masinissa more like harmless moving targets rather than rivals to life.

As for Hanno himself, unbeknownst to Masinissa, he had fallen early but not fatally, and, due to having clear insignias to show his station, he had been captured, dragged to the rear of the battle behind Roman lines and interrogated before those insignias and everything else he had been was stripped from him. He might as well have perished on the battlefield for all he would be known about or cared for subsequently.

As an exhausted Masinissa returned to the congenial campfire kitchens of Cap Farina, he rode close to the improvised jetties where the latest galleys to arrive were being filled with the few hundred captives taken in the engagement. Their horses, arms and armour remained ashore, ready to be assigned to the eager Massyli. As Masinissa stared at the line of vanquished men who had lost all their rights in the world, he suppressed a choke of pity for them. He always found it difficult to detach himself from the misery of defeat. It was only the grace of Baal Hammon, Tanit and Melqart that preserved him from the same fate. His eye and his compassion were drawn to the hunched backs of the men, where spreading already were the angry, seeping, crimson lines of the lash, which was in a hurry to condemn them to a new category of wretchedness.

The scene was on the edges of his vision's clarity, but he felt sure he could see the familiar profile of Hanno towards the front of the group, leading his men in their abjection as he had in their euphoria. It stalled him. Should he ride over to them and try to plead with the Romans to release Hanno into his custody, or would that expose a humane weakness of his to them and outrage the normal mores of the battlefield? The fond memories he retained of Hanno overcame his reservations quickly, and he spurred his horse towards the ships. He rode against the line of both Massylian cavalry and Roman infantry to the surprise of both. All were ready to fill their stomachs and carouse into and through the night. As he was about to pass a line of senior Romans led by Gaius Laelius, the legate himself rode across his line, obstructing him, and forcing him to turn and stop.

Laelius held the mane of his beast to confirm that there was a purpose to the interception. "Where are you going?" he asked Masinissa blandly but pointedly.

There was nothing for it other than candour, and Masinissa told his ally, whom he was becoming fond of, the truth. "I know one of those men well. I want to claim him."

Laelius did not seem surprised by the admission, as it was the only plausible explanation to hand. "I'm afraid you can't do that. It's too late and those men ain't your kind in any case; the way we see your kind anyway. Obviously, for the Numidians who aren't entrenched in Syphax's cause, you can make them the offer of swearing an oath to you and jumping horses, but the Carthaginians – and all those men are of that stamp – are spoils. They're property now. What happens to them now is no concern of yours. I am sorry. It's just how it is. You know it is." He put a little softness and condolence into the last of his words in an attempt to take the edge off the savageness of the reality.

Masinissa knew Hanno's chances of salvation were gone at that point. There was no prospect for any slyness or misunderstanding on his part that might extricate him. Forcing the issue would be futile. The Roman mariners and overseers would simply ignore him. He would just be viewed simply as another kind of fodder to them. He gave Laelius a resigned nod. He was unsure of the nature of his own emotions, but there was a hint of mourning in it.

"Come," Laelius cajoled "let's have a drink. In the grand scheme of things, this was a good day for us."

Masinissa gave his assent, but knew it would be a few cups into the evening and a long way towards insensibility before he could let the image in his mind fade. The picture was made even more vivid as, when he turned his mount alongside Laelius, he caught sight of Hanno. This time Masinissa saw his full face, and the plea in his expression was easily discernible, as if he had recognised Masinissa too and was inferring that the nature of the exchange might have a bearing on his fate. As their gaze held for a few awkward moments, Masinissa felt a tremor or paralysis grip him, as the condemned Hanno combined his desperation and hatred in his leer, burning through Masinissa with both emotions.

Pathetically, Masinissa made to raise his arm to wave as if it was an ordinary farewell and then realised the offence inherent in such a gesture. Poor guy was about to endure plenty of those. He lowered his gaze and turned towards Laelius, not realising that Hanno's stare was also curtailed at the same moment with a vicious blow from the pommel of a sword, which nearly collapsed him to the ground and would have done so but for the fetters that shackled him to another misfortunate soul. They would not be the last to suffer the same journey over the coming days, as the boats and manacles plied a profitable course back and forth between Carthage and Sicily, whilst the Romans – with their usual zeal – ravaged the coast for plunder and useful life.

*

Despite the depredations and successes in the field, both Scipio and Masinissa estimated that they were still significantly outnumbered by the combined armies of Hasdrubal Gisco and Syphax, particularly in terms of their cavalry, which was an assumption largely confirmed by their scouts and skirmishers. Their hunch was proved to be accurate soon enough. Gisco and Syphax grew bolder, as their own scouts had presumably assessed their numerical advantage just as well as Masinissa's had done, and pitched their camps about a mile apart from each other a mere seven or so miles from the Romans' main base, which had now moved to Utica to besiege that city.

Masinissa observed, a little wryly, the clear distinction in the construction of the two camps. It almost reminded him of a comical folk tale from his youth involving some unfortunate anthropomorphic swine. Whilst the Masaesylian camp was casually and flimsily assembled, using reeds for the most part as building material, the Carthaginians made efforts to create much more permanent and sturdier structures, no doubt feeling that they would better keep the elements and the Roman wolves at bay. The slackness of Syphax's camp was further evidenced by the fact that many of his soldiers found themselves bivouacking outside the ramparts.

Despite the perfunctory establishment of his camp, on the diplomatic front, Syphax deployed greater initiative and guile, responding to Scipio's tentative and insincere overtures with an offer of his own that he would be willing to act as a mediator between Scipio and the Carthaginians. The essence of this would be a quid pro quo that if the Romans would leave Africa, then Hannibal, in turn, would leave Italy. However, Scipio's curiosity was no more than a ruse, as it would benefit him little – certainly not in relation to his personal ambitions and political standing – to agree a truce on equal terms, and he used the opportunity of the diplomatic communication to infiltrate his opponent's camps for the purpose of reconnaissance. Masinissa had informed him that a plan could be devised to trap and immolate large numbers of the enemy, and that possibility piqued the consul's interest considerably.

Within his delegation to Syphax, Scipio included some of his most able centurions disguised as slaves, with the instruction to map the camp in detail, paying particular attention to the exit routes. After assuring himself that the camp was highly combustible and would become an inferno if precisely torched, Scipio and Masinissa assembled their senior commanders and outlined a plan of attack that they hoped would take the enemy by surprise, as it would be an unexpected night-time onslaught. Furthermore, the activity around Utica would be increased as a diversionary tactic, and was also to ensure that the garrison there were unable to retaliate once the assault had begun. Such a reprisal was dubious in any case, as the time difference between a forced march from Utica to the Roman lines and the life expectancy of a burning man was pretty enormous.

The attack would split the Roman forces evenly. Laelius would join Masinissa in an attack against Syphax. The logic of this being that they might require the greater mobility that Masinissa's cavalry could offer in the event that the Masaesylian could get his troops to the horses and outside of the stables before they were engulfed by the fires set. The other group, composing more of the veteran Roman legions, would be commanded by Scipio and attack Hasdrubal's camp.

On the day of the planned attack, Masinissa felt invigorated as they rode towards the hostile camp. The plan, as they had devised it, had more of the hallmarks of a game – perhaps some kind of grizzly variation of *petteia* – than a conventional military engagement. He saw the genius of the trap, and so did his men, who shared his euphoria. Conon was a little nauseated by the notion of setting fire to human beings, and Ari confessed a milder revulsion for the same thing, but the others saw it simply as cunning and an action that would establish an efficient killing field where risks to themselves were meaningfully reduced.

Syphax's camp, for all its inadequacy, had a number of routes out, and Masinissa ensured all these were closed in his preparations. He placed his finest throwers and most robust swordsmen at these points. These were largely composed of his veteran soldiers, who were unlikely to be distracted from their purpose by screaming fireballs heading towards them. As they set themselves at all the points of egress, Soldier Boy made a comparison with splaying and pinning an octopus's tentacles to describe their preparations. He used the commonly used Iberian word *pulpo*, which seemed a little like an inadvertent metaphor to Masinissa, as the unsuspecting Syphax was surely about to get *pulpoed*.

His preparations were meticulous and unusually cold-blooded. He was used to engagements in which they barely announced themselves, and then were dependent on his wits and reactions to prevail. This one had more of the feel of a tailor, sewing up the holes in a garment diligently, making sure every stitch was in place and tied in. From whichever direction Syphax's troops might try to break out, they would be cut down. Every route was sealed.

His calculations then turned to the time the men who would infiltrate the camp would need to get in and out, and to, as simultaneously as possible, ignite their targets. The camp may have been quite slovenly made, but it was compact and congested, and, as soon as the fires caught, they would spread and combine with the others quickly. Masinissa judged that unfamiliar riders approaching the camp from different points might be suspicious, but idle men finding their way in the dark was less so. Those would have to turn on their heels quickly, though, and rely on their pace and elusiveness to get out to the edges. They were all given a safe word for passage, so that they would not be hacked down as they ran back into whichever pocket of the ambush they found their way to. He wasn't sure which of the jokers had come up with it, but they'd decided on calling out "Bitches", which was a grim and implicitly vengeful reference.

The group of runners was composed of many of the younger, speedier men. They'd even managed an impromptu competition as part of their preparations. There'd been a number of race heats and even the allocation of medals as if it were a legitimate Olympiad. The podium places went to Hiempsal, Zee and one of the Troglodytae, who won in the end with some ease. Masinissa found his name a little tricky to pronounce, but settled on Feecza as the closest approximation to the guttural sound the runner emitted when he shook his hand. They seemed to be developing a habit of recruiting the occasional Troglodytae who'd strayed north out of the desert. They were usually pretty hopeless with either horse or javelin, but were perfectly suited to being messengers and to anything involving running of any kind. Ari seemed particularly fond of them, and retained a rudimentary grasp of the clicks, whoops and calls that appeared to represent their form of language. Feecza was a blur as a runner, with a fluid stride that didn't seem to vary once he had reached optimum speed.

As it transpired, he was as swift when the pressure came on as when it was just for sport. He was the first to return from lighting up his hut and was barely out of breath. He did cause a little amusement though by his call. It started with a few barely recognisable, "Beechy beechies!" before he gave up and pleaded with the men staying their swords, declaring, "Me Feecza! Me Feecza!" It was fortunate that his victory in the preparatory sprint race had made him something of a celebrity amongst the Massyli, so they let him through with a few cheers. The other runners were not far behind, and then the night started to glow and crackle.

Masinissa suspected that a large portion of the Masaesyli didn't get far from their blankets, as the huts went up ridiculously quickly, and the camp was ablaze and streaked with wagging, orange tails in minutes. The blood-curdling screams were mostly drowned out by the sizzles of the fire, but Masinissa could make out the highest-pitched ones as the searing heat stabbed into nerves and wiped away epidermal layers as if they were fresh dustings of snow on a rock. Most of the men who ran out of the inferno, however, were untouched by the fire or had used wet blankets to shroud themselves, but that was the extent of their good fortune as there were enough of the other kind to illuminate everyone. Few were armed and fewer still gave much of a challenge to the waiting ambushers.

It appeared that Scipio's attack on Hasdrubal's camp was just as devastating, if not more so. Even as the fire started to ebb to smouldering chars in Syphax's camp, where wood and bone by then so resembled one another they were mostly distinguishable by silhouette rather than form, the one a mile away still raged, stoked by the better fuel that Hasdrubal had thoughtfully supplied. Inevitably, though, despite the completeness of the surprise and the extirpating rage of the fire, there were survivors, and it seemed that a fair proportion of them had been cavalry. They were hardly enough to launch a counter-offensive, but the commanders had enough time to at least rally enough men to storm one of the exit points, which they had managed to do in both camps, extracting the two senior figures – both Gisco and Syphax – as a bonus.

As the victors returned to their camps, received the testimonies of the soldiers and were able to clear the camps of their seared enemies – usually by burning them more thoroughly and collectively – a clearer picture of the extent of their victory emerged. Scipio was exultant and sought out Masinissa for praise. Scipio congregated everyone who had participated in the attack between the two consumed bastions, and encouraged the Numidians and Romans to mingle with one another. He broke out many amphorae of wine, some of which appeared to be quite vintage by the artwork depicted on them, and allowed the men to revel in their triumph and erase as much of the more horrific aspects of it as they could in their cups.

There were other pleasures to enjoy too, as scores of pliant bodies – slaves, and the usual camp followers and comfort women – swarmed to the scene, as well as the mercantile chancers, who must have seen a treasure trove like this as a rare opportunity and hoovered much of it up at bargain prices as the soldiers had pillaged far more than they could carry. Masinissa felt a curl of revulsion towards the merchants and their detached, stolid exploitation of death. To him, their trading felt more sordid than the act of taking the valuables from the bodies themselves. Their neutrality and their blithe indifference to the outcome of the battle, so long as there were plenty of bodies to pluck, made him feel that they were little better than carrion chasers – birds with bloody faces, all instinct and primal urges and nothing else. He fingered the buckle his father had given him, wondering if one day one of these grubby merchants would have it for a pittance and care less for its provenance, owner or meaning. It would just be a shiny thing that would turn a profit.

Before the revelry commenced in earnest, although field discipline became pretty frayed when the wine started flowing, Scipio counted out the extent of the victory in terms everyone could understand. He gave the estimates of the original composition of the two enemy armies, and an informed guess of how many of them had survived with their skin on and chains off. The accountants of the vanquished had calculated that Gisco had managed to flee with about 500 cavalry and maybe 2,000 other troops, whilst Syphax's remnant probably included even fewer men. The joint Carthaginian and Masaesylian offensive was stymied before it had even made its first overture of battle. To the exultant cheers of the combined and carousing forces, Scipio hauled Masinissa up to the makeshift little platform from which he was proclaiming, and grabbed his arm and raised it to the sky. It was akin to an athlete rejoicing with his admirers in tingles of adrenaline, validation and consummation, but it was an excitement with more seismic import.

"Your king," Scipio announced in an almost formal anointing of Masinissa's claim. "The king of Numidia, my friend, Rome's friend and the man with the plan!" He winked at Masinissa in such an explicit way that even the men at the furthest edges of the field would notice the affectionate gesture.

Masinissa understood the significance of the moment – both in terms of the morale of the troops and his own nationalistic ambitions – and eked out the cheers for as long as he could, incorporating a few comical encores en route to finally taking his leave of the adulation. Scipio helped him down, although this only entailed Scipio gripping his hand whilst he vaulted to the ground. Both sensed the strength of the other in the brace.

FINDING THEIR WAY HOME

True to his vague promise to himself, in the brief interlude that followed the inferno of his enemies and the resumption of further attacks upon them, Masinissa found a little time to train Conon. Rather futilely, he focussed his initial efforts at military conditioning of his friend's offensive skills. The Greek proved himself both willing and hopeless, particularly with the javelin. He followed Masinissa's instructions conscientiously in terms of appropriate exercises for improving the right muscles and levers, and did his best to emulate his tutor's technique, but made only fractional improvements in his range and accuracy. By the time he might be able to unleash a spear that might connect with a foe with some spite, said foe would probably be close enough to take a swipe at him with his *gladius*.

Endearingly, Conon remained quite sanguine about his own inadequacies. "You know I practise all the time to get this rubbish, Mas," he offered as guilelessly and honest as a child.

"I know," Masinissa erupted. "I've seen you. You apply yourself with all the rigour of a Spartan and all the improvements of a jellyfish!"

Conon winced comically. "That's not harsh. I do throw more like a girl than a soldier."

Masinissa laughed at the comparison, but looked to commiserate with his friend too. "Well, it's not like I'd ever be so dumb as to throw you into the vanguard of a charge or even the tail end of one. I think we'd be better off just practising evasion. We should improve your reflexes and arm strength, enough to parry a few blows until the cavalry, probably literally, show up."

Conon dimpled happily at the change of focus. "Let me dodge, Mas; I've been pretty good at that figuratively for quite some time. You could say I've made a career out of it! I might take to literal bobbing and weaving just as effortlessly."

The assertion quickly proved to have some legitimacy. Whilst Conon was poor at striking, he was elusive, surprisingly agile and adept at deflecting blows, which slid down his sword and dissipated their force into the earth. Masinissa, for all his usual enjoyment of duelling, grew as frustrated as a taunted bull by the time Capuca and Pun interrupted their exercises.

"What's happening, boys? Have Cap and I disturbed a feud in progress?" Pun asked roguishly. "Is this one to the death or merely first blood?" He added a little more drollness to his dollop of playfulness.

"It's always first blood between friends, Pun; you know that," Masinissa replied.

Noticing Masinissa's momentary distraction by his *optio*, Conon seized the opportunity to conclude their training with a little lunge towards Masinissa's inattentive flesh, hoping to slice a little red line opportunistically, which would end their match. Masinissa, however, was not as preoccupied as he may have appeared, and parried and turned the attack easily, spinning behind and over Conon in the process, disarming and embarrassing him.

"Stick to keeping your enemy off you, Con. Don't get too ambitious. You're more easily unbalanced and exposed if you reach in," He gave his friend a little push to underscore the point.

It was hard for Conon to preserve much dignity in his stumble, but, as he regained his footing, he gave Masinissa a little salute acknowledging the advice. "OK, big guy, I'll stick to blocking from now on. I don't know what possessed me then, to be honest."

"Your balls decided to crash the party," Capuca interposed. "Make sure those guys don't confuse their urges and surges. It's easy to get a rush when you have a weapon in your hand, and I don't mean the weapon they're attached to, by the way!"

Conon laughed and his slight self-consciousness eased. "You got it, Cap. I'll save my impetuous thrusts for softer targets."

"Make sure they're naked, amply proportioned and ready for some fun too!" Masinissa added, and he kneaded the academic in his trapezius muscles, feeling a little unfamiliar rigidity between the Greek's neck and deltoid. "You're getting stronger, buddy." he complimented as he noticed the improvement. "There's hope for you yet."

"There may be hope for Hasdrubal too," Pun abruptly and soberly remarked, pulling the four men back to their wider predicaments.

Masinissa, quick to notice the seriousness of his friend's tone, gestured him closer and switched his own more frivolous gears to something more earnest. "Oh Pun, I had a feeling this wasn't going to be a social call, or an invitation for some food and wine. Lay it out so we can play it out." Immediately feeling a little silly by the asininity of his choice of phrasing, his journey from idle play to grave occupation accelerated from the gradual to the immediate in a flash of awkwardness.

Pun – never one to be too judgemental, especially of casual form – brushed it off. "OK, well, to lay it out, we've got developments. Hasdrubal has a few more *petteia* dogs up his tunic, and he's dropping them on us quicker than we thought he would be able to."

Masinissa, perhaps wary of bunging another ludicrous phrase into the conversation, indicated with an open and imperative flick of his fingers that Pun should expand on the details.

With a slight heave, suggesting an extended monologue and perhaps a slight irritation at his commander's brusqueness, his *optio* continued, "Well, our networks of informants – some via the Romans, they pay more after all – have supplied us with news of significant Carthaginian reinforcements and a consolidation rather than a weakening of our enemy's strength. Naturally, the general population of Carthage are in full-blown panic, imploring the Punic senate to immediately recall Hannibal, and sue for some kind of orderly and tolerable settlement. The senators and *suffetes* seem implacable in their course, however, and have moved to reinforce and strengthen. Their envoys have convinced Syphax to remain steadfast, and, recently, he has been highly active around the city of Abba, recruiting and press-ganging as many as he can, probably draining a chunk of the Carthaginian exchequer in the process. Whilst he may be picking up a bunch of novices who he's probably trying to drill into something functional as we speak, Hasdrubal's efforts to bolster his divisions have been more productive in terms of veteran soldiers who know how to drive into and hold a line."

This naturally piqued Masinissa's interest. "OK, so where has Hasdrubal magicked fresh troops from now?"

Pun gave him an oblique glance and furrowed his brow, a little disconcerted by Masinissa's need for clarification on the source. "Where else, Mas? There ain't much for them south or north but Trogs and Romans. Looks like they've managed to still hold on to a few of their alliances in the west. Perhaps Rome's control of the Iberian Peninsula is not as robust as Scipio might have assumed, since the Carthaginians were expelled. They've mustered over 4,000 Celtiberians from assorted tribes apparently. I'm not sure if any of what's left of Indibilis's and Mandonius's men have been persuaded. Those poor buggers have fought for all the causes going over the last few years."

Masinissa shrugged. "Who knows? Those guys just couldn't stick to anything, could they? They always had to fight someone. Anyway, those kinds of numbers suggest that Lentulus isn't quite as fearsome and capable as Scipio."

"Ah, for sure," Pun agreed readily. "We're lucky that we're riding with the main man these days. As for the Celtiberians, they're getting a bit of a propaganda push out in the hills. We're dubious about their true numbers, but their prowess in the field seems legitimate from the observations we've received. Then again, riding and throwing ain't the same game when someone else is trying to put you off your stroke by ramming their lance hard into your innards."

"You know what, Pun?" Masinissa interposed. "I bet you we either know or have fought with quite a number of those guys in the past. If they're any good, they'd have ridden with us in Iberia. It won't be easy putting our swords into them, but they won't be any more ferocious or capable than us. Let's move. Cap, fetch horses and send word to break camp. Scipio will know all this already, and you know he's going to be impatient to ride. I know he likes to intrigue at times, but he's decisive when he needs to be, and he won't want these fresh units to settle or build up any further."

*

Masinissa's estimation of Scipio's reaction proved accurate, as when they rode into his camp, it had been struck, and the wagons and horses were fully loaded. There was barely any time for pleasantries or even the briefest of machinations. They would have to improvise something on the journey. Fortunately, they were all pretty well seasoned, whilst their adversaries – despite the arrival of the Celtiberian auxiliaries – would include more than a smattering of callow fighters, who, they surmised, would be unlikely to hold their positions under any kind of concerted pressure.

Scipio was a little cryptic about the situation. He smiled enigmatically at Masinissa as they led their men south-west towards the great plains. This was where Syphax was heading – with what Masinissa thought seemed to be more alacrity than a man in his position ought to have – to join Hasdrubal in an assembly that rough estimates indicated would reach about 30,000, which was a substantial but perhaps a little misleading figure. Masinissa wondered how many of those men would be real soldiers.

"Do you we need to be as impetuous as our enemies?" was the cautious query Masinissa put to Scipio as he set a brisk pace into the hills.

"Ah, Masinissa," the consul replied, "I know you've often been on the back foot, particularly in more recent times, but when your instincts and your knowledge give you positive indicators, don't hesitate – not in warfare. Always seize those moments and opportunities, as they can and probably will multiply. I'm looking for the rampant chaos of a collapsing army now. This is a tipping point. Knock this one over, and the Carthaginians will have to settle or recall Hannibal, and probably both if they have any sense."

Masinissa nodded, reassured, and the two – with the inclusion of Laelius as a necessary participant in such matters – spent the next hour or so outlining a rough deployment, although neither he nor the two Romans felt the need at this stage to broach anything innovative or unusual. Wheeling his mount back towards his own men, he felt buoyed by his own surging optimism, which was mirrored by those he met throughout the line, Massyli and Roman alike.

The Panglossian spirit endured throughout the long days on the march, and, unusually, songs became frequent and of all styles – patriotic, licentious and comical – and even new ones were devised. It was funny for Masinissa to see men who had been dour and grim-faced just months ago busting out their baritones and working on their harmonies in light-hearted but unlubricated revelries. Since when did war become so carefree?

When they rolled over the final hills and onto the great plains, Masinissa surveyed them more like he was at the top tier of an amphitheatre. *The great plains are an apt description,* Masinissa thought. He rode down into them from the dusty, green slopes where the shrubs were denser than normal but without much evidence of cultivation until you reached the shallow inclines on the edge of the plain where there were some neatly tended lines of olives and grapes. There was little shelter beyond the few low buildings and squat, cloudy trees that held to the fringes of the hills.

The plains themselves were parched and dry; the only interest being the modest variations in the browns of the mostly smooth dirt and the lighter, chalky lines of worn trails, which intersected haphazardly in ragged, drunken curves and corrections across it. This was clearly not conforming to Roman design principles.

If they were to ultimately triumph here, Masinissa wondered somewhat whether the Romans may take umbrage at these careless semi-desert bridleways and construct more linear paths as a gift of their victory. *Maybe "gift" is a misnomer,* Masinissa corrected himself, *as it would no doubt be the freshly conquered and enslaved on whose backs such a marvel of engineering would be built.*

Maybe it was a fancy in any event. Roads had to go places after all, and the powdery flatland before him was of no use to cultivators; the rarest wet season might coax something out of it before it was roasted or devoured by stray goats, but, in truth, from a productive point of view there was little to separate it from the more arenaceous lands to the south of the gentle, triangular hills in the distance.

The ornament in the middle distance that broke the sun-bleached aridity was the snorting and glistening ranks of Hasdrubal's and Syphax's hastily assembled army; its standards were chaotically but proudly raised across the battlefield, causing Masinissa to squint as the sun sparked random little white suns off the metal. Masinissa's first appraisal of their numbers hinted at a slightly larger force than their own, but this bare fact didn't cause him nor Scipio any anxiety. They arrayed their forces as impressively as they could about four miles from Hasdrubal's camp. Then, as insouciantly as an army in the field could, pitched their tents and fires, cooked and rested, heedless of any threat that may be posed by the Carthaginians, who – it was presumed – would be somewhat daunted and hesitant in the face of a wily and recently victorious foe.

Let them second guess our roast chickens and snores as battlefield ruses, Masinissa smirked to himself.

*

The unhurried tone continued for the next few days, as both armies marched onto the plains, but remained at a tantalising distance from each other. Masinissa sent units of his cavalry into skirmishes, but casualties on both sides were negligible. Whilst indifferent to the delay, he doubted that the procrastination would do anyone any good other than the mercy that those soon to die would be graced with a few more sunsets to savour. In truth, these type of dawdling battle preparations always made him feel a little sentimental, and he would become greedy for the merest sensation or become lost in a memory long neglected. It was the same for everyone. If there had been women in the camp, they would have done brisk business. If anything sharpened licentious appetites, it was the prospect of personal termination. In this war, as with all others, many had begun their journey to life courtesy of someone who would lose theirs brutally on the next morning.

By the fourth day, the flirtation lost its charm, and the armies marched closer as a prelude to their liquid intimacy. Before they formed into position, Masinissa rode up to Scipio for any last instructions or pow wow. The consul cut a proud and confident figure. He was resplendent in the full fig of his office, with a brilliant burnished and inlaid *lorica segmentata* protecting his shoulders and chest, and the vital organs beneath them. His equally impressive and thick-looking *cingulum* dangled beyond his loins in solid, metal reassurance, promising the same for his vulnerable manhood. As the broad and bolted strips of ferrous metal swayed with his movements, it caught the eye with its polished iridescence. However, it was quite inappropriate to be absorbed by the most senior Roman's midriff, or even spare that portion of Scipio's body a passing glance, and he left the dance of bright light and new metal to their own devices, and returned his attention to the general's face.

Rather than dwelling in the final moments before the assault on the immediate strategic imperatives, Scipio's thoughts appeared to have vaulted beyond the imminent battle to its spoils. "Are you familiar with Roman law, Masinissa?" he probed.

A little nonplussed by the digression, Masinissa shrugged and offered a terse, "Not especially."

Scipio noted his ally's surprise with a little tilt of satisfaction. "Well, in that case, I'll take the very rare pleasure of informing you. There is a category of property law known as *bona adventitia*. Unlike inheritance laws, this law relates to all property that is acquired by someone through their own efforts or from sources other than their father. In the present circumstances, all the lands you currently lay claim to have been inherited from your father. Today, your labours will bring new conquests, most from Syphax but, depending on other matters to follow, maybe some from Carthage too. Victory will carve new borders that Rome will acknowledge as the *bona adventitia* of a new and unified Numidian kingdom."

Masinissa was surprised by the formality of the comment, and a little by its generosity. Scipio was clearly in no mind to annexe the lands of his rival and was willing for Masinissa to strengthen his own at Syphax's expense. There was obviously more than fraternity at play, and, in truth, any gains would be contingent in the short term on the assurances and muscle of Rome. As the embodiment of that state, Scipio must have concluded that a part vassal, part buffer in the form of an emboldened, unified Numidia would be highly advantageous. *Canny fellow!* Masinissa thought.

Out loud, he replied, "My lord, I am grateful for you consenting to the establishment of a more natural boundary for our people, but aren't we being a little presumptuous? We could lose our lives as well as our lands in the next hours."

Scipio looked at him with a soft, paternal conviction in his expression, as if he was guiding a strong-but-unsure infant up his first flight of stairs. "We won't fall in this one. Defeat is Carthage's habit now."

Masinissa smiled at the confidence and benevolence of Scipio, and put the depth and sincerity of his gratitude into a simple thank you. It was all that was needed. They understood each other.

"Go form your line, comrade," Scipio ordered in the softest murmur that this type of command could ever be uttered.

Summarily dismissed, Masinissa rode back into his cavalry line, and as he did so he could see that Pun had followed the preliminary arrangements and taken the Massylian riders out to the left flank of the formation. The legions were already prepared in the centre in their usual gradation of *hastati*, *principes* and *triarii*, with their own *alae* on their edges. Laelius and the Roman cavalry had deployed to the right. Prudently, Hasdrubal had put his new Celtiberian troops in his centre, with the remnants of his infantry and cavalry on his right flank. Mirroring Masinissa, Syphax took the left flank.

"Nice job, Pun," Masinissa commended briskly as soon as he had reached his *optio*.

"Thanks, boss," came the effusive reply. "It looks like you've had some good news already. Did someone add a nipple to the breast you've been suckling?"

Masinissa grinned, but he let his teeth alone confirm the boon.

It was sufficient for Pun, who gave him a jovial slap. "*Milky time!*" he bellowed riotously to any in earshot.

They did not have to wait long for the signal, and their fidgeting had barely begun when, practically in unison, the two flanks led by Masinissa and Laelius charged as the trumpeter closest to the Roman command pushed a stream of air through his horn, and made the long and high-pitched note to propel them forwards. It would soon sire many human-generated equivalents as sturdier, sharper metals joined the chorus.

It became quickly evident that Scipio's faith in their advantage and superiority had not been misplaced. The initial volley of their javelins as they got into range was accurate, well timed and devastating, and was met with a feeble riposte. The Carthaginian cavalry line had practically buckled before it had tasted the appetisers on the swords of Masinissa's men.

"*There's already a tear in this sail!*" Massiva whooped imaginatively, within his earshot, and he had a point.

They poured through a breach that earlier defeats had ripped open. To Masinissa – as he rode his beast, and felt the surge of adrenaline that was coursing through his body and flailing sword arm – it was as if the tipping point in the battle, which usually took many dead to reach, had happened the moment the horn had sounded. The enemies he drove his horse at invariably were pointing their own charges towards open country rather than at him, which made separating them from their rides or their existences almost physically effortless, albeit that they would remain actions that carried the same psychological and spiritual price as more even duels. Masinissa launched his *falcata* into his opponents with the almost metronomic regularity of a chef chopping vegetables on his board, and cleaved skulls and shoulders in a rhythmic mutilation, rarely striking the check of a Carthaginian sword.

As his senses occasionally spied intervals of safety, he could cast glances between the combatants in the melee at the further corners of the battlefield. Although, at first, this was difficult, given the flatness of the terrain, the bodies thinned out rapidly to reveal that the fortunes of battle were being replicated everywhere else. Laelius's flank was also quickly turning into a rout, and the then exposed Punic and Numidian infantry were either being run through or attempting to find some kind of egress from the killing field. No doubt a fair number, given the dearth of options, would resort to playing dead. The masquerade stood little chance of success, and they would join the real dead soon enough, unless their acting skills extended to begging hard for mercy and enslavement.

The only resistance, as may have been expected, came from the Celtiberian middle, which was being rapidly isolated and encircled. Even from his vantage point, where the exact condition of the enemy's resolve was difficult to ascertain, Masinissa's gut told him that those men would die hard and honourably. The Roman legions working into their lines would have the toughest job.

The next Roman manoeuvre denoted Scipio's scorn for the enemy, and his certainty that the Punic flanks had been ruined and posed no further danger. In a stratagem that Masinissa realised was becoming a favourite of Scipio, the Roman general ordered his deeper lines of *principes* and *triarii* to march out from behind the *hastati* line and bear down on the flanks of the Celtiberians, creating a three-sided formation that would turn slowly into a vice for the hapless mercenaries.

Masinissa regarded the move as if it were the action of a shepherd herding his flock into a pen. The only exit left open was the rear, into which he sent groups of riders to harass and effectively close that figurative gate. Even though their fate was sealed, the Celtiberians fought to the last, and Masinissa found himself unable to suppress emotions of pity and respect when his role in the battle became more spectator than participant. The Celtiberian sacrifice, whilst virtually total, did occupy the entire Roman infantry for several hours, which allowed significant elements of both the Punic and Masaesylian armies to flee ignominiously.

As mopping-up operations began – which was a euphemistic description for some very grizzly and sordid business, despite the discipline and restraint Masinissa tried to inculcate into his troops – the exultant Massylian troops were eager to ride after their tribal adversaries, who were now showing their dust trails on the edges of the plains, and were ripe for extermination or conversion. After a brief consultation with Scipio – during which the restiveness of his men, who had taken little of the battlefield spoils, became more pronounced – Masinissa set off in pursuit.

*

Fortuitously, it was agreed that the operation against the Masaesyli would still be composed of a joint Roman and Massylian force. Scipio would continue to rampage close to Carthage and Utica, but Masinissa – abetted by the legions and cavalry commanded by Laelius – could go claim a kingdom and eliminate his rival decisively. This necessitated a certain compromise, as Laelius's legionaries contained a substantial number of foot soldiers who would slow their pace. In truth, more sedate progress wouldn't harm them as, at a certain point, Syphax inevitably would have to turn and face them, or at least try to hole up in some city or bastion where he might make a stand with whatever fresh loyalists he could gather to his ranks. The numbers of fast riders and scouts Masinissa had at his disposal by then also meant that he could relay them ahead to spy on the enemy and gain regular updates about their whereabouts; the consequence of this was that the prospect of Syphax eluding him in the wilder terrains would be small.

Syphax took a while to find a spot for a last stand, and he rode deep into his heartlands before stopping and trying to put his remnant into some kind of antagonistic order. Masinissa and Laelius took a full fifteen days to catch up with him, albeit in the rather leisurely style that defined their tracking of the newly fugitive Masaesylian king. They trotted after him with the padding, indifferent deliberations of a pride of lionesses appearing to have scant interest in the object of their stomach's desire. This occasion was not a time for a frantic bolt after the enemy, as if they were cheetahs after a gazelle. They were the apex predator now and had earned the right to dawdle.

Over those days, Masinissa felt his own hopes return to him – both in the revived ardour of his loins, which swelled fitfully as his thoughts drifted towards a probable reacquaintance with Sophonisba, as well as in resuscitated ambitions for the future of his country and crown, which seemed far closer to a positive change than for many years. His mind strayed complacently beyond defeating Syphax to what such a demolition of his beloved's husband might personally mean. The world and what he craved within it would be his again. His dreams could stop being discarnate and dispossessed, and become substantial once more in the sultry form of Sophonisba. He speculated a little anxiously at the extent to which Scipio and Rome may regard Sophonisba as an exotic piece of their triumph; her beauty would no doubt make for a spectacular humiliation on some cart or courtyard in Rome. However, as with his lands, he hoped that Scipio would be indulgent and allow his efforts their just rewards. For all the alliance that she had become associated with and probably helped to consolidate, Masinissa could not place her as an adversary of Rome, just a helpless trophy bride held captive against her will. A nagging doubt that started to fester at the margins of his instincts, however, was that – for all his generosity – Scipio might not regard her in quite such unimpeachable terms as he did.

As news spread from the animated scouts that Syphax had turned and resigned himself to a showdown, the impetuousness of the chase reasserted itself, and Masinissa yielded to the fervour, knowing that they were now so close that Laelius would not be too far behind. It was as if the years of training and experience of orderly battles had evaporated, and the wild horsemen of the mountains and the desert found their innate style of combat in their rush to confront one another and resolve their enmities in a style that was not, in this last act, beholden to the methods of their Roman and Carthaginian suzerains. It was a haste, however, that Masinissa quickly realised was a miscalculation, as Syphax's horsemen were as numerous as his own and just as predisposed to wilder engagements. Thankfully, the disciplined strength of Laelius's legionaries strode in tight formation to their rear. Masinissa ordered his riders to jettison their messy stampede, an instruction that was quite hard to convey initially in the disorderly melee, and regroup in and around the line the Romans were establishing. In tandem, they pressed Syphax's horse, who possessed no such infantry counterpart, and gained the rapid ascendancy that a more modern method of combat ought to expect. The diminished morale of the mostly young and raw Masaesylian forces was then exposed in all its uncertainty and dejection, as the initial boost given them by the first skirmishes proved as ephemeral as more common youthful urges.

It was then that Syphax proved himself in a valiant gesture that was as brave as it was hopeless. With the resolve of his men collapsing, he tried to rally them in a charge at the Massylian cavalry, perhaps in the deluded hope that his own example might turn the tide. As he rode towards them, casting not a glance behind him, it became clear that his cohorts possessed none of his resolve and were showing their capitulation in abstaining from joining his foray. A few of the more willing ones started to follow, but, as the mass of riders pulled their steeds to a stop, they showed quickly how little of their leaders indomitable spirit they had by slacking, turning their horses and trotting shamefully back to their fellows. As Syphax rode close enough to distinguish the Massylian's features, it seemed as if he recognised Masinissa and shifted his horse's gallop to aim straight for him.

Almost simultaneously and without prompting, three of the most loyal and dependable of Masinissa's own retinue kicked their horses into motion and hurtled into the empty ground to intercept the raging, abandoned king. Masinissa could have predicted who had decided not to give Syphax the opportunity to attack him. Ari, Capuca and Soldier Boy rode straight for Syphax and, as if sensing that those three's usual places on Masinissa's flanks needed filling, Billy and Zee moved subtly closer to him, almost to the consternation of Pun, who was nudged a little in the process.

It was Ari – utilising his sling with his usual unerring precision, despite being on a cavorting horse – who brought Syphax's stallion down. Whether it stunned the animal or killed it was moot, the significant fact being that Syphax was dumped unceremoniously onto the ground before he had a chance to fling his javelin or draw his sword. The three riders surrounded him, kicking up a small cloud of dust in the process. Coated a little in it and dabbing at some blood from his mouth – Masinissa speculated that Syphax may have bitten into his tongue as he hit the dirt – the abrupt change of elevation and the point of three spears in close proximity to his head immediately contracted Syphax's vigour and reduced him to a pathetic captive before he had even surrendered. In reality, there was no such formality to the process. He could have scrambled to draw a weapon, but the delinquent limb would have been pinned, sliced or trodden on before it could manage anything hostile. Instead, broken, he merely raised his arms in abjection, and had his weapons and pride cut from him by the dismounting riders.

As Masinissa rode up to Syphax, a number of competing feelings percolated through him. There was a hint of grudging admiration for his action, a visceral and bitter hatred towards his tribal rival, and a deeper resentment towards a man who had the audacity to take Sophonisba as his wife. Uncertainties about the extent of their intimacy also assailed him and just the thought of that scrubbed all traces of mercy from him. *It's him or me,* was the thought that was uppermost in his mind. As he pulled up his horse and regarded Syphax, who stood erect and looking back at him impassively, he gave a passing thought to the fact of their similarity. Their physiques and appearance were so close that they could have been mistaken for cousins or even siblings, but – as with many inter-ethnic animosities – it is often the ones that you are nearest to in physical or cultural terms that you reserve the greatest hostility towards.

"You think this is your moment, don't you?" Syphax spat at him. "You need to get down from your horse, bend your knee, and accept that I am the king here and that everything here is mine first. Then, whatever I flick from my table or scratch out of my beard, you can claim." This was making an oblique and intolerable hint about his relationship with Sophonisba, in whatever dubious form that took.

"Do I now?" Masinissa scornfully responded.

Still proud and maybe even a little dismissive of the extent of his plight, Syphax reaffirmed his futile demand with a caustic, "Yes."

This could have precipitated a slightly petty and childish dialogue of assertion and denial, but it was interrupted by the sudden and enraged figure of Pun. Normally unflappable and calm under the most fraught conditions, Syphax's pride in captivity had spun Pun into a spasm of anger. He dismounted from his horse, landing his considerable bulk two footed, not far from the Masaesylian, and strode towards Syphax, pumping his hands into balls as if he intended to strike him. Syphax may have assumed the same, as he raised his arms in a gesture of both defence and defiance. He had misread Pun's target, as the burly *optio* swung his foot right into Syphax's groin, and then – as the king collapsed – he reprised the move with a longer strike to the jaw that his earlier one had brought into easier range. Not content with the forceful reminder of his new standing, Pun reiterated the point by hitching his tunic, bringing out his member and hosing the king with the contents of his bladder.

As the honey-coloured stream struck and flattened his hair in a steady gush, Syphax's own hands tensed, but the reason for his muscular contraction was quite distinct. Whilst Pun's flex just pulsed rage through his body, Syphax's in comparison tried to help him brace against the shame the little, yellow torrent was bringing him, as if he was a teenage girl who'd had her first taste of the other liquid that came from that pipe, and the news had just been shared amongst her prissier and delightedly appalled girlfriends. The tension in his hands, shoulder and jaw aside, Syphax made no effort to resist, even when Pun brought himself closer and shook the final drops right across his face, as if he were chastising him with the hilt of his sword. Syphax endured, cast his eyes down in dejection, and, as best he could, brought his despair and humiliation into himself.

Pun gave him another forceful kick to the nose, which must have altered the cartilage and noble profile somewhat, and gave a little deferential look towards Masinissa to concede control of the situation, and to show that his rage had abated, and that he was waiting for further instruction or signal.

Masinissa's hatred for Syphax – although locked in his heart – wasn't clearly articulated at that point, and he showed his loathing in the tightness of his eyelids, which had narrowed into slits of enmity, and in two abrupt, jerky gestures that he gave to Pun as an answer to his unspoken request. He placed his fist in his mouth and then made a tug with his forearm, as if pulling on an imaginary rope. Pun smiled in response and barked the order, which Hiempsal and Hiarbas satisfied quickly.

With barely a demur, Syphax found himself with a very tight gag and an equally restrictive collar, which attached itself to a long processional chain as if he had become an animal on a leash. Unlike the typical creatures such harnesses were attached to, such as a cheetah or a hunting dog, Syphax had neither dignity nor the prospect, at least figuratively, of being released from his choker.

With Syphax subdued and his army scattered, there was nothing to prevent Masinissa and Laelius from riding to Cirta to recapture and reclaim it. Such a conquest would have just as much symbolic resonance to the people as the chained captive, who would be dragged a fair portion of the way to the contested capital – till his exhaustion dropped him, and he rubbed his face and chest in the tearing stones of the earth – and he would be lashed roughly and pitilessly to an available camel for the rest of the way.

*

On the short journey to Cirta, Masinissa found himself dwelling on the contrary feelings of hatred and love, embodied in the corporeal forms of the vanquished lump on the dromedary and his former consort with whom he was soon to be reunited, Sophonisba, who was about to be liberated as the most precious prize in the occupied city. In truth, he didn't balance the two for long, and the latter quickly came to hold sway, finding a welcome host in his exultant and expectant mood. Neither Laelius nor Pun seemed alarmed by his carefree demeanour or the unpreparedness of their approach to the city. Similarly, his other close confidants – such as Massiva, Capuca and Ari – who could be relied upon normally to raise even the most trivial doubts or issues, left him to his bliss. It seemed that, to a man, they felt they were not riding into another battle or skirmish, but were simply returning home.

Their feelings of returning to a place of their own, despite their long exile, was validated quickly as, once the bloodied and broken usurper was shown to the city's gates in all his emasculation, the city immediately shed its tenuous link to its erstwhile overlord, and welcomed Masinissa and his men as the liberators they were. Down every avenue and at every vantage point they were cheered and festooned with garlands and gifts of all descriptions. There were lavish embraces and hearty welcomes, as if the population was exhaling a collective sigh of relief. Inevitably, there would be a number who had consorted with Syphax recently, but these, no doubt, would be showing a greater reserve until their more effusive neighbours pointed out their perfidy. Then they would be asked to account for their actions, and if offered a pardon of sorts, amend their error by swearing a fresh allegiance.

Masinissa, however, was not in a frame of mind to consider either the immediate enthusiasms of the people or the rehabilitation of the errant. He gave irritated nods to the embraces and encomiums he received, and tried to jostle through the throng as quickly as he could. He was in a hurry to find Sophonisba, whom he presumed may still be taking refuge in the royal villa. It seemed prudent. Her relationship with Syphax was open to speculation, and it would only take a quick knife to extract the ultimate reprisal on the easiest target. He gave word to Pun and Capuca to ensure that, should any of his men find Sophonisba before he did, they should protect her with their lives.

The order proved unnecessary as Sophonisba had acted in the way Masinissa had supposed and had waited patiently for him at her opulent residence. Whilst it was a judicious decision, to her eager sweetheart it seemed that part of her behaviour had been influenced by her coquettishness, which made the idea of her bounding down the road to him completely out of character. As he found his way to the steps of her residence and the servants who eagerly encouraged him up them, Masinissa thought of the games the two of them used to play in the Byrsa. He wondered whether they would be as unmolested if they tried to roam this city as freely as they had in Carthage. He doubted it. Carthage was a new enemy and Masaesyli an inveterate one, and those associations would taint Sophonisba now for all the efforts Masinissa might make to cleanse her of them. That kind of purification would take a while. *It will probably take an heir!* he speculated.

He felt the air tighten at his throat as he reached the outer doorway. The steps had been short and shallow, and his shortness of breath had nothing to do with his mild exertions. He inhaled shallowly and snorted slowly in an effort to regain composure. He even smoothed his growing and tousled hair, a sure sign of his sudden and choking self-consciousness. As he looked at the probable last veil between him and his reunion with Sophonisba – a diaphanous curtain so thin that if the fabric had been cut to wear, it would have been intolerably revealing in all but the most dissolute company – he wondered at the condition of the woman behind it. They were both changed. He knew that. He could trace and forgive the physical changes, but could he map her interior ones and still navigate his way to her heart? Was that even the same? Are our finer feelings as inviolable as we dare hope, or would such preservation of our most meaningful affections just be the follies of youth and innocence? He hesitated, touching the edges of the material barrier gently, as if he were a timorous virgin attempting to glide his hand over his first feminine curve. Wild doubts rushed at him, and he fought himself to keep at bay the creeping thoughts about any profanations Syphax might have imagined or inflicted upon her.

This is the first moment in a new chapter, he tried to think positively to himself. *We can restore ourselves, cleanse what we need to, and let our wounds heal and fade. It will be OK.*

As he wrestled with himself, the middle of the curtain parted, and Sophonisba revealed herself to him once more, starting a little unromantically with her midriff; he hadn't expected the first sight of their reunion to be of her tummy. As she parted the screen quietly, more of her was revealed, radiating her intact beauty to her extremities in a smooth exposure till the smile in her eyes welcomed him with moist relief. There was a delicious moment, more inhalation than hesitation, where the two lovers looked at each other, saw emotion and belief rather than flesh and blood, and read each other and the truth of themselves – which they realised had survived as easily as if they had opened a reading exercise for a child, and seen simple descriptions of colours, shapes and numbers.

Masinissa let the words that he had prepared and revised in his mind over days, weeks and years retreat behind the lucid silence that bisected their first sight and first touch, and let Sophonisba's soft expression draw him into her. Their touch had more clarity than their words could, and he held her, at first like a blind man holding an ornament, rolling his fingers gradually and meaningfully around her, and letting them find their furthest anchors around her shoulders and waist. Finding her delicately in his embrace, he let the faint, exquisite contact linger, as if he needed to take a moment to sense and process the reality of their union and the pillowed femininity of her body. Satisfied, he pulled her tighter, forming his limbs into cords around her that brought their torsos and their heat together. It was a mutual arousal without urgency, and one that only accentuated rather than accelerated their ardour.

Her arms held him just as fiercely, and communicated with his body just as intelligibly, her digging tautness needing to assert the reality of his presence and push their closeness into his epidermis. Their urgency, as if in the throes of an even closer passion, was slow to subside, with each knowing that they were surer in the communications of their bodies than their words, and, besides, each needed the reminder and comfort of the other's familiar contours. It was Sophonisba who loosened their contact to begin a more precise communication, putting her hands to his face and patting them all around it as if fussing the family dog. Masinissa looked at her with exactly that animal's style of canine pleasure and docility.

"I don't have to imagine you now," she murmured, with the assurance of possession, but the slight artifice of a certainty she couldn't put all her force into. She stroked his hair back from his temple, cupping his skull as if he were a newborn. "I don't know how it will be now," she stated, yielding to the doubts Masinissa's embrace could not dispel. "I can sense that we are the same with each other – you are you, and I am me – but the world and where we fit in it are not the same. I have been less and less a free woman, my condition as the wife of your enemy makes that obvious, and I don't think your rescue – if that's what it is – will change that." She looked at him imploringly. "Am I yours? This was never my choice."

She let her hands drop and her eyes nearly followed, but Masinissa wouldn't allow her to collapse into dejection and tilted her chin upwards, holding her throat in a choke grip that slid into a caress, which brought his thumb around to her earlobe and the jewellery that dangled seductively from it.

He waved in the air, and the discreet attendants took their cue and receded. Sophonisba also took hers from his gesture, and led him to the softest room, the gentleness of her grip and the space being a counterpoint to the firmness that was sprouting in him. At the point where she was about to bump into an ornate triclinium, which would serve as a creative additional brace for their overdue play, she turned, squeezed his hand and then released her grip as she saw the smile, full of anticipation and possession, that Masinissa gave her.

He sensed his own urgency in his breathing and in his manhood, with the energy cresting, packing his loins with the juices that swelled his member with agreeable-but-impatient force and attention. He allowed himself a little haste, which he knew he would soon need to check, and tore at his own clothes. Sophonisba gave him a quizzical smirk as if her expectation was the reverse, and it would be she who would have her garments shredded and her nakedness exposed. Instead – in the seconds it took for him to unbuckle leather and metal, hoist his tunic over his head, and throw it beyond the edge of the unsullied triclinium – it was he who stood before her in his full rawness, his extra limb taut and stout, with its proud curve aiming at her like a broken lower branch of a tree in a northern winter. Stripped of his robes and his weapons, he was no less impressive a sight, and he gave a narcissistic, peacock flex to the muscles that remained fully under his control.

She paused for a moment to regard his battle-lacerated physique, full of criss-cross cicatrices – some barely noticeable and some like massive and monochrome caterpillars, which were the ragged, slug-like silhouettes of slices from larger blades that had cut wide gashes that had been agonising to sew. Then she moistened at the eye and mouth, and, slowly – easing but not subduing his ardour – kissed the scars around his shoulders and chest, nuzzling them with her nose and then giving the balm of her lips to the long-knitted gashes. For both, it was more symbolic than passionate, and allowed his member to become accustomed to its fullest range and pride.

She slipped out of her white-but-not-virginal robe, which bunched around her ankles in such a way that she had to step closer to him with nubile elegance. Masinissa closed his eyes momentarily, as her unadorned beauty soaked his senses. He inhaled her scents, bowed his head into her throat to find the sharpest notes, and nuzzled into her neck. Then, with his free hand that left her hips to glide down her back, traced the sliding feminine furrow of her lumbar spine till he could spread his fingers across her hips and arse, and enjoy the spreading curve of her gender till he could bring his middle and index fingers around to the fuzzy line that marked the short path to her interior.

After taking a moment to touch his fingertips to his tongue, he found the handle to her gate.

She gasped and squirmed, and he found that her body and arms gripped him with a familiar fever and intensity. They played with each other's mouths and sex at a rising pace, each enjoying the reacquaintance with the erotic thrill of the other, before Sophonisba could exclude him from within her no longer. She, almost in a penetrative form of foreplay, wanted him inside her whilst he still had both his feet on the ground. She was still light and lissome in her own physique, and she hauled herself urgently up him treating his shoulders as if they were the edges of a ridge she needed to clamber over. Once set, she hitched her face above his, giving him the delight of her breasts to tease whilst they spread their hips and thighs to find their fusion.

Using her limbs, and the grip her thighs and calves had formed around his back, she rocked herself in harmony with Masinissa's hands, which had found firmer grips on her arse and were giving her the shelf upon which she was rolling herself deeper over his pole. As her pleasure mounted, she pulled her throat and breasts away from Masinissa, allowing him to settle his eyes and then his mouth around them at his leisure. His strength and passion held the rhythm for some time as she fell on him in ecstatic yelps and heaves, till he needed the support of the raised edge of the triclinium. Whilst her pants were still composed exclusively of rapture, his heart was beating as much with exertion as fervour, and, in his first of many changes of position, he dumped her without ceremony or warning onto the couch. She squealed at the suddenness and roughness of the separation, but placed her body quickly into a familiar posture, the rear of her thighs offering him an obtuse angle of soft ingress. She raised her rear invitingly, wiggling it a little until Masinissa could ease himself back into her and they could resume their union.

As he forced her underneath him, he enjoyed the yelps as he surprised her with the occasional, accurate flicking finger to her sequestered bubble, and flat, stinging slaps of his palm across her haunches. Her abandonment smothered him, and he realised that his pacing couldn't be maintained and he could not stem his own flow any longer; he released it in spasmodic thrusts that gushed out his love in viscous relief. Knowing his dam was breaking, she reached behind and held his hand in a sweet, slightly incongruous and innocent clutch, offering him the permission to pour himself into her with all his backed-up, glutinous adoration.

Exhausted, they found a shared, comfortable space on the ample triclinium, knotted in looser ways, entwined silently in each other's arms in a transient but just as intimate a moment, and savouring a different closeness in the easy, lingering interlude between their chapters of lovemaking.

When they resumed, Masinissa's body had lost the insistence of its own satisfaction, and he enjoyed pleasuring Sophonisba until she collapsed, worn and satisfied, as evening drew its cloak around them, and gave them a shivering excuse to stay wrapped in one another, and drift out of delirium and into dream.

*

Morning left them unmolested as no one, either from Sophonisba's entourage or Masinissa's retinue or the sun itself, which stayed coyly behind its dawn cirrostratus, had the gall to disturb their overdue moment.

Masinissa watched Sophonisba rediscover the movements of her own body and retake conscious possession of them as she woke, her eyes fluttering open eagerly as if in a hurry to confirm the reality of her solidifying reverie. As he did so, he felt a peace he had never known. This was a sense of belonging and connection that was even deeper than his memories of their previous moments and his own fervid recreations of her in his long, lonely nights, when he saw her eyes implore him through the flickering licks of the waning fires and her body in the shapes of the fuller clouds as they moved, and he and the gods conspired to trick his eyes into conjuring shapes of alluring, Rubenesque wooliness out of the wisps.

He kissed her lightly on the cheek and welcomed her to the day with a simple, "Good morning." His words may have been trite to other couples, but, for him and for her, the occasion was fresh, new and redolent of a romantic optimism that filled their hearts if not their senses.

She returned the simple wish with a mirrored softness and affection, which conveyed both her ruffled semi-consciousness and her purring contentment.

Masinissa felt a different urge come over him then. The sensual exigency of the previous day and night had receded, cooled and been replaced by another need; this was a need for another type of synthesis, one more occupied with identity and legality than sexuality. His status as her partner, as her man, was known to them and was inviolable, but – to the world – she lay in his arms as another man's wife, and that situation was intolerable. Of course, given recent events, Sophonisba could easily just renounce her vows to Syphax, if she had ever made them. Masinissa didn't really need or care for an answer to that question, for even if she had expressed such a commitment, it would have been insincere and spoken under duress. So, as he thought about their union, he let his thoughts race as his eyes played the dazed counterpart to his ruminations by guiding his index finger casually around the areola of her left breast as it poked invitingly outside the line of her sheet. He decided to pop the question that he had long framed in fun, but asked with solemnity this time, and without any contingencies or dependencies other than his own free will.

"Will you marry me?" he asked, trying to lend the moment some formality, but rather failing as a post-coital bed was far too easy a setting for any buttoned-up protocols.

She looked at him without surprise and let the request invade her slowly. He'd asked the question before, as a gesture of intention in a world of fantasy, but – right then – there were no obstacles or impediments, no alliances to seal, or geopolitical situations to defer to or wait to resolve. There was still a war, but, for the precious moment they occupied, that was distant. All she needed to give was a simple yes or no as an infinity of sweethearts before and after them had done, and would do exactly as succinctly.

His mischievous paramour was not going to be make it so simple, however, and instead hit him with the complication, "But what about Syphax?"

As Masinissa bridled in instantaneous injury and confusion, she rushed to allay him and correct herself, cupping his jawline delicately and bringing him onto her soft lips, which murmured, "Of course I will, darling," before opening her lips and allowing them to graze, then cushion his, and continue confirming her agreement with the proposal with eager, generous and grateful licks of love.

PARDON AND PUNISH

For as much as Masinissa craved to prolong his time in their own private idyll – enjoying the peaceful delights of promises kept, futures plotted, and souls and bodies weaving together in easy frolics and wilder frenzies – they couldn't break the temporarily imperceptible but otherwise rigidly implacable demands of the world outside the villa where they sheltered. They had only one more peaceful morning before their interruptions turned into more compelling demands. In a forlorn attempt at making his intrusion into the lovers' quarters appear uncontrived and independent of coercion by utilising the pretext of bringing them some dates and wine, Conon paid them a visit and laced his initial conversation with inconsequential small talk before he informed them clumsily that the view outside was that a couple of days of isolation was considered to be quite enough time to become reacquainted. This was a perception most acutely held by Laelius, who had heard of Masinissa's distraction and had sent a disapproving missive to Scipio's camp regarding it. Besides the Roman's irritation, Pun too was becoming increasingly annoyed by Masinissa's absence, and – not unlike a jilted lover – was at that time kicking his heels outside the villa, cursing and fulminating at the pebbles on the pathway, repressing his instincts to barge in and insist upon Masinissa's return to military duties.

Masinissa whistled a mute resignation at the news of his ally's and the *optio's* impatience with him, but rather than sending immediate word to them that he would resume his duties forthwith he said flatly, "Get Pun in here. I need a favour from him… and one from you too. You are qualified to perform ceremonies right?"

Conon squinted at him uncertainly and went to fetch the burly sergeant. When they returned, Masinissa surprised them by informing them that they would perform the necessary roles in an impromptu marriage service. He wasn't expecting much of them, and he would have a proper, far grander ceremony when time and warfare permitted, but for now a brief rite would be adequate.

Showing herself as disdainful as she could be of the rudimentary style and form of their imminent nuptials, whilst not wanting to put too much of a dampener on Masinissa's good intentions, Sophonisba gathered her closest handmaidens and retired to prepare herself for the moment she had dreamed about for much of her life but had conceived of being in a much more resplendent and well-attended venue.

"You ain't gonna rush me now, darling." She winked at Masinissa as she left the three men to an uncertain wait.

"That sounds a little ominous. I've got a feeling we may be here for quite some time," Conon commented as she briskly left them to their inevitably more perfunctory efforts at dressing for the occasion.

It proved a percipient observation as, aside from a light polishing and donning of armour, the men contented themselves with their everyday clothes and style. Despite their differences, and only quite rare and haphazard interactions, Conon and Pun were very at ease with one another, and their conversation flowed, mostly along more abstruse tributaries where Conon excelled and Pun was surprisingly curious. As with his admiration for Masinissa, Conon esteemed Pun for the fortitude and strength he possessed, and the humanity and morality he preserved, despite the most grievous and continual challenges to his qualities of decency and bravery. For Pun, Conon represented a different and mostly alien type of discipline, perception and knowledge and he avidly asked questions of the scholar as Sophonisba prepared herself at her leisure.

The preoccupation of the pair with swirling, inextricable threads of philosophy, politics, astrology and medicine suited Masinissa, as he wanted to honour the moment quietly as a personal landmark – perhaps his most important one, despite its spontaneity. It wasn't that he wished to savour his last drops of bachelorhood before putting his being into a lifelong bond, but more that he wanted to reflect on his past and his future, his emotions and commitments, and evaluate himself as a man, a man now ready and fortunate to be with the woman he adored. He thought of Sophonisba's ordeals, her loneliness and her helplessness, and he felt a swell of sorrow and admiration for her. She had endured in ways as gruelling and tormenting as any he had emerged through, and her preservation of her essences was as laudable, if not more so, as his own struggles to retain the core of who he was. He was sure that she had maintained more of her finer qualities than he had managed to. Someday soon, this woman and this condition would be familiar, and her company routine, but not that day. It was unique and special, and it was his duty to mark it with his full attention and imbue it with its proper meaning, to honour the couple they were and the closer partners they would still grow to be.

His idealism warmed him, and he poured himself a cup of wine and another two, which he passed to Pun and Conon. They paused in their discussion, and both seemed a little guilty about their neglect of the groom and seemed willing to widen their circle into a more inclusive symposium. Masinissa braced himself for some kind of toast or roast, but it was then that Sophonisba decided with the fanfare of a very dulcet lyre to make her entrance. Her time away had been well spent, and she had dressed herself with a deceptive-but-well-ornamented simplicity. Her robe had two lower layers, one of which drew a short and seductive cut less than a third of the way down her thigh.

The modesty for the ceremony, though, was retained by a gauzy overlay, which reached to her ankles and hitched over the gold anklets that she wore, which tinkled their charms around her graceful movements. Her middle was wrapped reasonably tightly; this accentuated both her hips and her breasts, which were crushed together in mesmeric curves that all three men, one greedily and the other two furtively, found it hard not to dwell on. Her shoulders and upper arms were bare, but she demonstrated her regal stature by the modest train that dropped from the back of her neck, almost to the floor, and was lifted and carried by two of her servants, who wore garlands in their hair and silver at their wrists. This may have been to accent Sophonisba's own jewellery, as on her arms she wore magnificently inlaid gold cuffs. She had put some colour around her eyes and on her lips, and wore a broad tiara in gold filigree, which bunched her hair above her brow and allowed it to fall in Medusa-like tresses over her shoulders.

It was just a short distance between the betrothed, but Sophonisba, to the accompaniment of the lyre, danced across it with light, sensuous steps that beguiled Masinissa and gave him a memory for eternity, as her exquisiteness tricked everyone around her into a slower, but more acutely observant, awareness. She stopped beside him and regarded her beau passively, whose heart fluttered suddenly and raced conspicuously, her features as quiescent as a mountain lake in summer.

As she sensed his tension, she broke her matrimonial repose. "I can't do this by myself. Which one of you fools is giving me away and which one knows the words?"

"I know the words," Conon admitted sheepishly, almost raising his hand as if to answer the question of a teacher.

"I'm the designated other fool," Pun added, with a little more hesitation than was usual for him.

He offered her his hand, and she went slightly beyond it and took her grip on the anterior part of his forearm. It may well have been the smoothest part of his entire body, but the contrast in that connection of flesh was enormous. Pun turned and patted her hand reassuringly, exposing the even rougher, hairier side of the complementary limb, with its nicks and furrows of muscle and wounds, and ragged, blade-cut ridges as wide as Sophonisba's index finger.

Their familiarity with the scene as witnesses to the days of others meant that they quickly fell into their roles and positions, as if ceremonial osmosis turned their movements automatic. Masinissa wondered at the routineness and banality of the occasion, as he moved alongside Pun, who shielded Sophonisba from him for the moment.

He consoled himself with the view that it was just this familiarity and commonness that gave the moment its value. It was a necessary, obligatory duty, without which his feelings, both sentimental and legal, would be diminished in the eyes of others. He thought of how cuckolded he felt when he heard of Syphax's marriage to Sophonisba, however counterfeit and expedient it may in reality have been. The same repeated words, although exchanged between genuine lovers this time, would finally efface that lingering shame.

Conon spoke the words he needed to say, exhorting the couple to fidelity and devotion, and reminding them of the sincerity such a commitment as they were now making insisted upon.

As his friend spoke, Masinissa blended both a solemn attention and agreement with something more astral, as a part of him swam into his past and visited all the other moments of import he had experienced: deaths, near deaths, unions, partings, revelations and epiphanies. He choked at the thought of his father, and he looked behind him as if looking for some manifestation or apparition that could suggest his father's presence or blessing.

When it came to the betrothed making their declarations, Sophonisba turned almost coy with her assent. Looking down at her and seeing the depth of emotion in her eyes, Masinissa listened to the familiar timbre of her voice, and picked out extra hints of joy and sincerity in her vow. She smiled and pumped his hand in hers as if they were runners crossing a finishing line together at an Olympiad.

He turned to Conon and gave his own proclamation in the unnecessarily terse form that the tradition maintained, then leant into Sophonisba when the formality had been articulated and whispered, "Forevermore," in her ear to give his devotion its most extreme parameters.

She smirked in gratification and amusement, and elbowed him jovially in his ribs. For a moment, they were lost in each other, folding the moment into a special shared space in their memories and hearts.

Ever the alert warrior though, Masinissa, even in his rapture, could not completely detach himself from his peripheral attentiveness and, out of the corner of his eye, caught the vacillation of the ad hoc official he had hastily appointed. Perhaps it was the fact that Conon was unfamiliar with such moments and unaccustomed to witnessing the rare spectacle of a loving couple in their most defining moment, and perhaps time was taking its normal linear course for him, but he seemed suddenly lost and almost impatient with the couple's apparent love trance. His restlessness sparked Masinissa into action and, as the uncomfortable functionary was about to conclude matters by ushering the newlyweds together, the new husband interposed before he got too far into stating the obvious.

"I'll take it from here, Con, thanks," he offered, and he placed his hands around Sophonisba's waist, and lifted her off the ground and into his arms. If it had been a wrestling tussle, he may have been able to throw her right over his shoulders, but his new wife took her cue and wrapped her arms around him, clutching his face as if her arms were the levers of a nutcracker and his head the nut in the vice, and planted an enthusiastic kiss on his lips, as if they were alone and on the brink of a feverish, urgent intimacy. As they broke apart, ceremony and passion satisfied, Pun nudged his commander tactfully, not wishing to make a direct reference to the more mundane but essential duties that sought to truncate the joyous occasion. Masinissa gave Pun a quick glance and nodded his willingness to accompany him back to the other world, which still held dominion over him, despite his fleeting sanctuary from it in Sophonisba's embraces.

He felt a little trapped, as if the previous days had wrapped him in a cohesive tangle with his new bride, which he couldn't blithely disengage from. It was not as if Pun was going to tug more obviously at his tunic either, to make the hint more evident. They were not children in the elation of imminent play, with one grabbing the other to drag the pair of them excitedly from home to field to the euphoria of innocent thrills. Sophonisba saw his irresolution with the insight of an older rather than a younger wife, and offered an indulgent and perceptive squeeze, which he understood as her acceptance of his exit.

"It's OK. You need to go. We will be with each other again soon enough. We've sort of inverted our honeymoon and wedding haven't we? We're so unconventional," she stated.

Masinissa, thankful for her jest, extended his reluctance and agreement. "We have, haven't we? I promise to resume all this..." and he waved his arms around without too much definition, "as soon as I can."

Sophonisba feigned a scold, declaring, "Be sure you do young man," and ticking a pair of fingers under his nose and cupping her hip with her other hand for comic emphasis. "You need to keep these fires burning from now on, you know. I'm not going to be kicking around cold embers any longer. Don't stray too far or stay away too long."

In response, Masinissa gave her a final embrace, not needing to offer a response to the instruction beyond a soft, lingering cuddle. Tugged and torn between love and war, and paralysed slightly by being presented with the dichotomy, he released her slowly. Before she was willing to do the same, she laced her hands around his neck, both to reassure and to focus him on her for a final moment.

"Don't be afraid, my love. Don't be afraid," she urged.

Not certain whether she meant this as a general exhortation or one that applied more specifically to their new condition, any fresh vulnerability her softness had recently interpolated into him, or the usual dread of combat a soldier has to suppress, he agreed quietly, putting a soft murmur into his voice that expressed both regret and devotion, as well as an indeterminate resolution. When he turned, he didn't look back towards her till he was at the door. He felt a little ashamed of his brusque sweep out of the room until, like a victim of Medusa, he turned at the door to wave goodbye and caught her hastily brushing moisture from her tear ducts, leaving a slight sheen across the edges of her face and giving her otherwise barely distinguishable zygomatic bones a noticeable gloss. She gave him a sheepish wave and a glug of a laugh as she swallowed her emotions and let him go with a smile.

Once outside, he was joined quickly by Pun; a wave by and to Conon indicated that the scholar would catch up with him later, with

Masinissa's next appointment having no need of Conon's more esoteric abilities.

"At long last, eh?" Pun ribbed. "That union took the long way around, didn't it? How are you feeling? Still in shock?"

Masinissa shook his adamant head. "Oh no. I've known I've wanted to marry that girl from the moment I set eyes on her. I was shocked when another man did it before me, but I've lived this day in my head for years, so, no, I'm not in shock. This is the for-all-time one, not a fancy or something of no consequence. It's solid, you know."

"Good," Pun replied with a rambunctious thump to Masinissa's shoulder. "Well, if getting married isn't going to throw you off your stroke, maybe I can find something that will."

Masinissa eyed his *optio* suspiciously. "Oh Melqart, you've got something up your tunic, you old dog."

Realising his exposure and not minding in the least, Pun grinned. "It's about time we put the old band back together, don't you think?" Without giving Masinissa an interval to conjecture about the hint, he continued in his allusive vein, "You know we've been missing something, someone, for a while now..." adding a little nudging hint with an almost immediate, "beginning with T, for both name and position."

Masinissa eyes lit up as the clue proved sufficient. "You've made it obvious now, haven't you? Where are you hiding my *tesserarius*?"

Pun made no answer, but, with the theatrical manner of a mage revealing his trick, he gestured forwards, adding a smart bow for good measure. No doubt if he had been wearing a helmet, he would have doffed that too. As if his two old mentors and occasional martinets had some kind of intuitive understanding, Tigerman took his cue and emerged around the corner of the nearest building. He carried a cane and bore a pronounced, wincing limp, but one that it was clear he had learnt to accommodate, and he was finally free from the yelping ligamental refusals of the earlier phases of his recovery.

He could bear his own weight, and a restored vigour was evident in the contours of his shoulders and the prominent arteries of his forearms. He'd clearly been carrying a few stones around lately, and may have been in the sea a little. Those bulges of muscle were enough for Masinissa to conclude that, once back on horseback and free from the impediments of the ground, Tigerman would have recovered much of his old range in his javelin and would have the power to use his sword again at close quarters. His features showed a little of his struggles and weariness, though. His cheeks were pinched with the gaunt look strong men get when they're not strong any longer, his eyes sat deeper in the hollowed bowls of their sockets, there were silver flecks at his temples, and, around his chin, his beard was practically white, having been stripped of the dark pigment of his more vernal days.

There was a trace of self-conscious inhibition in the uncharacteristic diffidence of his approach too, as if his slightly contorted gait had undermined him a little with his peers, and Masinissa, in a hurry to dispel any awkwardness, put a little haste into his steps and ebullience in his greeting. He wrapped the man renowned for his flinty dourness in a fraternal bear hug, where he was able to sense both the reverting physical power of the recovering convalescent, as well as the quick and thankful easing of his tensions.

"We've missed you, Tee. Things were just falling apart around here without you," confirmed Masinissa.

Tigerman snorted dubiously, but smiled with the familiarity and compliment. "As if" he scoffed, but with a little fluff under his wings, as if the mild commendation had got through to his flagging ego.

"I swear," Masinissa continued, veering a little too close to the melodramatic, "you're like our very own Rhadamanthus. The guys know you're fair and have integrity, but they all know too that you won't tolerate any slackness, failure or any kind of breach of discipline, and they certainly don't want to cross you. It's not like Pun has gone soft or anything, or Capuca for that matter, but you are the one who makes people think twice; you know what I mean. There are a few petty thieves waiting to learn the hard way about the rigour of your discipline."

"Well, I may have lost a little bit off my sprints, but I'm sure my scourges will still add a few crimson stripes when the offences warrant them," Tigerman replied more pungently than was usual for him.

The comment was a little grim, but Masinissa still gave him an amiable, "That's the spirit," as an endorsement to his most capable and enthusiastic ramrod.

The reunion would not have the opportunity to continue any longer however in the light-hearted and casual manner it had embarked as Ari arrived with news that the enemy soldiers and their associates, who they had weeded out and corralled, really should be addressed, and as many as they could reasonably trust should be re-enlisted in their own cause. It seemed a perfect first task for the returning Tigerman, for whom a pleasantly meandering conversation with his senior commander may have become a little uncomfortable after a while.

Masinissa remembered a line Tigerman had said once, which was as succinct as any about the nature of their relationship: "*You tell me what to do, and I'll tell the others what not to do.*" Simple, insightful and sometimes a little chillingly cold-blooded, that was Tigerman. It was a good time to have him back.

Pun, perhaps recognising that two burly drill sergeants at one event may have been excessive, and with the veteran percipience of a man who could always see what another man needed – be it a boost, a beating or anything in between – made some plausible excuses and let Tigerman take Masinissa's flank in his stead.

"What have you really got planned?" Masinissa enquired. "Don't you want to see your latest greenhorns?"

Pun scoffed at the flagrant inaccuracy. "Mas, if there's one amongst those men in that pen who hasn't already killed their share, the drinks are on me later. Besides, after what I did for you today, you owe me a little furlough. If I strike it lucky, you might even have to come looking for me the way I had to come fetch you today. I'm already married, though, by the way, so I won't fling any surprise demands in your direction if you do. Well, probably not."

Masinissa laughed. "I know you bailed me out, but you made Conon do your bidding earlier, you cheeky bugger. I'm hardly likely to forget the details and sequences of my wedding day, now am I? You get going. Go crazy. By the time you get back, you need to get your arse-kicking face back on."

Pun winked and gave a slow, smirky nod, which revealed that there were playful, perhaps even salacious intentions rumbling in his mind. Then he left the others in pursuit of his objectives.

As Pun strode away to whatever recreation he could find to suit him, Masinissa quipped to the remaining two, "This is some wedding party I'm having. All my guests have already made their excuses and left."

*

The amphitheatre was full of men as Masinissa rode in with Ari and an almost robust Tigerman. There was something quite affecting to Masinissa about seeing the grizzled veteran back at his side, as if they were back in the old days and once more starting out to go to Iberia together. Tigerman had been a mentor and a barking, stentorian authority back then, who, with Pun, gave his command much greater discipline and a resolve that it otherwise would lack. Seeing the old guy once more engendered quite a paradoxical feeling in Masinissa. The correct impulse may have been to feel his *tesserarius's* weariness, and the aches and breaks that he carried and endured, but, instead, Masinissa felt his company was a zestful and invigorating tonic, as if they were back in the morning of their lives again, and the war was an adventure, and not an endless round of pain and grief.

Tigerman must have sensed a little of his nostalgia and fraternity, as when Masinissa turned to look at him directly, he gave him a vigorous fist pump and goaded his mount a little, expressing both his vigour and delight at his own reinstatement in the ranks. Tigerman had been an exceptional and tenacious *harpastum* player, and there was a sporting exhilaration in his glee, as if he had made the winning steal at a particularly important tournament. Masinissa's digression continued as the thought swirled. Maybe when the war was over or when it was nearly done, he and Scipio or, if the consul was preoccupied, he and

Laelius could organise a *harpastum* tournament. Teams from Numidia and Rome could compete with each other and start to savour the miracle of peace by running with the balls of their unsullied youth. He fancied that the Romans might win at *harpastum*, it was often incorporated as part of the exercises for many of the legionaries after all, but the Numidians could gain a little revenge if they expanded the tournament to include horse racing and javelin throwing. The Romans would be hopeless in comparison in those events.

He snapped himself back to the present, as the amphitheatre was currently not a venue for play, entertainment or even the grim combats of the gladiators but rather a place of improvised internment for the mixture of Numidians, Libyans, Iberians, Carthaginians and Troglodytae who had found themselves without allies or justifications in Cirta and in the skirmishes in its outskirts. They were about to be presented with the narrow options such men were fortunate, if not necessarily grateful, to receive. In truth, not many of the Carthaginians had got as far as the dusty bowl, and were either so despised or so inveterately opposed to the Roman and Massylian cause that their status as enemy combatants could not be reversed. Hence, they were carted into slavery or despatched by the mobs who found them, who saw no value in commodifying their lives and took more satisfaction in vengeance than slave trading.

As he observed the ragged men – many of whom had betrayed their tribal loyalties and him personally – rise grudgingly and, in many cases, painfully as he entered the arena, he suppressed a surge of anger towards them and tried to switch his perspective to theirs. These were only men, after all, who had known war too long and whose actions had many motives, but the strongest amongst them was their own survival. Their decisions then and their decisions now would have a seam of pragmatism running right to the core of their beings. At their lowest, men were like packs of beasts, who would prey on the weak – like he himself was about to do – or do anything to preserve themselves, as he suspected most of his woebegone audience were about to realise. They could always be turned, like horses or sheep. He had the better offer for them. He had dignity and salvation in his gift, and could rescue them from the bonds of slavery or the lotteries of the arena. They were only meat now, and all the men he was addressing knew it, and he was going to offer them the chance to be men again.

Ari – who was the least authoritative of the three and feeling somewhat disconcerted, as if he was going to have to step up and make the offer to the desperate – rode close to Masinissa both from an ingrained instinct that compelled him to ride tighter in the face of an enemy, even a subdued one, as well as to allay the fanciful worry that he may be deputised as a public speaker.

"You got this, Mas?" he enquired gingerly.

"Of course," Masinissa assured him, "this is as straightforward as it comes. All these men want now is a sword in their hands and not at their throats. How much they appreciate the mercy is not really relevant. They will swear to Baal Hammon and Tanit, and that will hold most of them; they're all going into the first line of the next fight, anyway, and will have to earn their way into the back rows. Saying that, though, I'm not sure how many more large legions or divisions we'll be facing now. Carthage has only one more move to make, if they still want to fight. If I were them, I would make terms and bring Hannibal home as part of the deal. He'll be coming anyway, but he might think he's still the man; you know what I mean. Hannibal against Scipio. Those are two big reputations opposing each other. I wonder if either has the will to resist joining battle with the other. For all Scipio's virtues, he shares the same flaw as Hannibal."

Ari furrowed his brow in a quizzical uncertainty.

"His ego is bigger than his heart," Masinissa clarified, rather pleased with his description of the two generals' shared fallibility, even if it was likely to continue to endanger the lives of the three of them and everyone who rode with them.

The amphitheatre was ringed by Massylian riders, with another inner ring of legionnaires surrounding the vanquished, so there was no risk of harm, and they could treat the venue as theatrically as if they were performing in a play by Euripides or Sophocles, or perhaps a comedy of Philemon. Feeling himself to be a little unconvincing as a thespian if not an orator, Masinissa announced himself as ostentatiously as he could manage with the aid of his mount. He rode hard at the edge of the line of captives, flanked by Tigerman and Ari, and then continued right in front of them, with all the pace and power that his equine partner could propel from its haunches, forcing many to lurch backwards. Showing the earthbound men the power of an able cavalryman served the purpose he intended. He drew his sword for further effect and swept it across them, in a curiously ambivalent gesture that contained both threat and redemption.

Drawing his steed to a stop before the centre of the detained and uncertain men, he began to address them with the assurance of a tyrant. He boomed, solemn and sonorous, at all the questioning faces before him, "I am going to give you a choice now, but know you have no real choice and know too that you have no will of your own. You swear fealty to me; to a new, united Numidia; to Baal Hammon; to Tanit; and to Melqart; and you seal that pact – that commitment – with any freedom you still imagine you possess. I will not make you a slave, but do not be under the misapprehension that you retain any shred of liberty. You are directed and commanded solely by me and my lieutenants, by these men…" He gestured to Tigerman and Ari. "And men like them. They know what's best for you better than you do now. Nothing comes from you now, not even your thoughts. I give you those." He paused, waiting for the murmurs or rumbles of dissent, but none came.

He continued, "You know a nation – and you and us, the Masaesyli and Massyli, have the opportunity to become a proper one now – unified by mutual commitment and forgiveness, can be hammered into any kind of shape, and can reconcile itself to any kind of condition or constitution, be it for good or evil. Do not think that even those of you who followed every word or decision of Syphax zealously and fanatically cannot avow the same fanatical devotion to me. In time, you may – and I think you will – find me a much more just and congenial leader. We have been two tribes and one people for too long. We will be stronger together now, maybe not an empire like the Romans, the Carthaginians, the Ptolemys, the Seleucids or even the distant, eastern kingdom we barely know of – Shalishuka and his Mauryan Empire – but we will be strong, sovereign and not a vassal to be harvested for fighting men at the whim of our suzerains."

He fell quiet, and, in the lull, appraised the men before him and saw something restored in many of them. Their postures were straighter, and their expressions had lost a little of their suppressed hostility. They were listening, and many, perhaps, were starting subconsciously to tie the first knots of loyalty to him.

Impressed with his start, he ventured further out into metaphysics of identity, trying to loosen the knots that Syphax or the Masaesylian tribe may still have tethered around their beings. "You know knowledge is a dangerous thing because a lot of what we can take to be knowledge is nothing of the sort. There are facts and truths and science and nature, and we trick ourselves that other things, the beliefs that others force upon us, are as real as the sky above us or the earth below. For instance, you knew that Syphax was an invincible leader, the true king of Numidia and the only sane person to follow, and I was his despised, illegitimate rival. He told you this, and you told it to each other. All you were confirming were your beliefs and illusions, nothing more. Am I any different by telling you the same thing and summoning you to fight for my cause? No, in this I am the same as him, but the truths of identity can be temporary and tenuous, and it can take great strength to retain them and consolidate them into more than air. I have proven my strength. However twisted the tales of my victories and my survival have been portrayed, I have that quality and I have others besides. Cast aside your old selves and swear allegiance to me now. This is a new day; this is a new truth. Believe in it. We are one now; together we will go into battle and we will come back home again."

Sensitive to the moment, Masinissa noted the pulse that the last comment put in the chests of some of the men listening to him and repeated it with even more deliberation and conviction. "We will go to battle and we will come back home."

He turned to Tigerman and gestured to him to unfurl the standard of Gala, with the horse and the palm tree, the symbols of a unified Numidia. Perhaps he had gone too far in his rhetoric, or reached out into vaguer areas when he should have kept to the usual script of fear and bombast, but he felt positive about his oratory. He knew his army had just grown in power, and that these fresh auxiliaries were accomplished horsemen who knew the country and who would, in reality, find turning on Carthage just as simple a matter as he had.

The oaths took time, and, predictably, there were some who were still resistant. There were only a few of those, however, and even fewer when the first of the recalcitrants found themselves dragged away by boorish legionaries who would admit them into a new reality that would show them quickly the folly of their obstinate loyalties. The process became a little tedious, as each man took his turn to bend his knee, kiss the flag and state the prepared oath. However, as the mass induction continued, the tensions appeared to ease slowly, as the worst of the forcible enlisting was over, and the process became gradually less formal. Food and wine were brought, and that assuaged hostilities further. Conversations were started and the divisions between the guarded and guarding became more blurred, to the point where Ari dismounted and joined in with the mix of reconciliation and alfresco dining.

He seemed to have the facility to locate amusing or singular company, and returned to them quickly with a young Masaesylian who appeared to have digested Masinissa's exhortations without too much metaphysical reflux. The newcomer bore a measure of resemblance to Ari and the two seemed to have established a quick and easy rapport. The heat of the day and the wine swooshing down their oesophagi were also helping with their general bonhomie. It was clear that Ari was invigorated by how readily the Masaesylian had befriended him and, so it seemed, their cause. He bounced in between the horses of Tigerman and Masinissa with all of the effervescence of a child reaching up to his parent to swing him between their arms.

Ari declared, "Sire, you have won them over. They understand. They know they are the lucky ones, and they will honour your mercy. They are good soldiers, as good as us and the same as us." He looked back towards his former enemies as they reclassified themselves into confederates via conversation and inebriation; it was a glance that seemed to underline his conviction further. "Nothing can stop us now, Mas, nothing; we've never been so strong."

Masinissa smiled at his verve. "Who's your new friend?"

The answer came promptly and unexpectedly from the object of the enquiry, who must have felt that formality had receded sufficiently for him to introduce himself. "My name's Do-it Boy." and he repeated the name with a speedy and compacted emphasis on the first two syllables as if the first part of his moniker was a challenge to an adversary to attempt a first strike.

Masinissa laughed but Tigerman, more familiar with giving and receiving sobriquets, laughed harder and responded to the eccentric introduction with the obvious question, "You're going to be easy to remember! How did you end up with a nickname like that?"

Do-it Boy clapped his hands, hinting with the gesture at a comical anecdote that emerged as nothing more than a banal statement of the obvious. "Because everything I get told to do, I do." he answered. The bluntness and obviousness of his answer only appeared to ingratiate him further with the *tesserarius*.

"Well, I tell a lot of people what to do and them doing it don't make them any kinda special," Tigerman reproved but in a way that exposed a lot of a relatively recently acquired indulgent quality. "And the first thing you can do is help me off this horse and get me some of that grape juice."

Do-it Boy obliged and helped Tigerman hit the ground with a softer landing than he might have managed if unaided, though his healing bones still gave a mild yelp that his mouth stoically refused to serenade. Instead, he was about to repeat the command, but Do-it Boy released his cradling grip promptly, gave a brisk salute and ran towards the nearest amphora, keen to confirm the appositeness of his name as well as perhaps sneaking a swig or two for himself.

"You know," Masinissa observed wryly, "I think if you keep that kid around, you're never going to give an order that won't be obeyed."

Tigerman grinned. "We'll see. You know I have to give some pretty nasty orders sometimes."

Masinissa dipped his chin in an empathetic acknowledgement. "Yeah, you're not the only one." The war had added layers of savagery with each passing year, and Masinissa suspected that Do-it Boy and most of his cohorts had perpetrated, or at least observed, some pretty nasty stuff in their time, so it was pleasing to witness a very recent enemy fulfil such a mundane order with obvious keenness and an apparent lack of bitterness.

"You know there's hope for us yet, Tee. Look at that boy. He's taking this all completely in his stride. He's like a horse who knows the kicks and grips of its rider, but little else. It doesn't really matter who's giving him directions, just so long as he has some. He's inured to everything but the knowledge of his place in the world and the associated duty to do exactly what he's told by whoever is in charge. Maybe we, as a people, just have a knack of getting by. We're more practical than the Romans, whose arrogance would, I'm sure, nurture resentment and sedition if they were in these Masaesylians' places and had to bend to another's will."

Tigerman looked at him benevolently. "Maybe, Mas. I'm a little more sceptical by nature. We're going to have to see how well these new recruits hold to their vows. I'm pretty sure I'm going to be seeing a fair few more of them than you in the days ahead."

Masinissa wondered a little at Tigerman's cynicism, but conceded inwardly that he was probably going to be proven right in his supposition.

*

Fortuitously, for Masinissa, Tigerman, Ari, Do-it Boy and all the others, old and new, in the freshly branded national army, there followed a hiatus in the hostilities that allowed Masinissa to absorb many surrendering remnants of Syphax's forces and fuse them reasonably amicably into his own divisions. It appeared as if the war was moving into a different, more conciliatory phase. The appeasers in Carthage were becoming more vociferous, headed by the most senior members of the Punic senate, the Gerousia, who following the defeat of their armies on the Plains and the annihilation of Syphax sent a delegation to Scipio seeking a treaty and armistice.

The terms Scipio demanded were quite onerous, but initially appeared to be acceptable to the Carthaginians, perhaps as it allowed them some breathing space to stall for time. The consul insisted that all prisoners, runaways and deserters be repatriated; the Carthaginian forces must leave Italy, Cisalpine Gaul and Iberia; and they must abandon their claims to the islands of the Mare Nostrum, and surrender most of their naval fleet. They were also ordered to supply enormous amounts of grain to, effectively and humiliatingly, help feed the Roman army in the field. A Carthaginian delegation was sent to Rome for the ratification of the agreement, but, whilst there, began to renege on the terms and seek modifications to it, and so were, for their temerity and lack of good faith, expelled.

Nevertheless, the truce of sorts persisted throughout the winter. Scipio's supply lines from Sicily and Sardinia were maintained, and, most significantly, Hannibal and his grand army returned home. As soon as the inimitable and revered general came ashore, the public mood in Carthage became more emboldened. If he could humiliate the Romans in their own lands, logic suggested that he would be even more ruinous to their ambitions on his native soil. It was a presumption that garnered rapid and eager support amongst the populace, who were still conceited and complacent enough to seek a military solution to the incursion that was starting to appear more like some form of occupation.

Spring rolled around, and Masinissa's forces were now in fine fettle, as were Scipio's, who – despite the pause – continued to drill for imminent battle. Their collective preparedness in regard to the strategic probabilities proved well founded, as Carthaginian restraint collapsed when news reached the city of a large Roman convoy, of approximately 200 transport ships filled with supplies from Sicily, being blown off course with many of them becoming stranded. The oared vessels were able to row westwards under their own power into areas under Roman occupation, but those without manual propulsion abandoned their vessels and allowed them to drift towards Carthage. They proved too tempting a prize for the city to ignore, and may have appeared to them almost like some kind of gift or tribute rather than a mishap of weather. When he heard the news, Masinissa speculated that it might have been somewhat engineered as it possessed all the hallmarks of a ruse. It seemed too transparent a lure and one that even the most impetuous of fishes ought to leave dangle in the water. Nevertheless, Hasdrubal led fifty of his warships to claim them and tow them, in cavalier triumph, back to Carthage.

When Masinissa mentioned it to Pun, his *optio* tempered his derision and scepticism by offering a more pragmatic or desperate interpretation of the capture. "They're probably running low on food; that city is swollen with refugees now, and their grain stores must be running out."

Whether it was renewed bellicosity, encroaching famine or some kind of hybrid truculence of the starving, Carthage defied Scipio's insistence that their supplies be returned, or else they would jeopardise or annul the fragile armistice. The consul sent a quinquereme with three of his senior negotiators aboard to the Punic senate to express how seriously he regarded the violation, but the Carthaginians added insult to injury by mobbing his emissaries, who barely escaped the city and who were subsequently intercepted and attacked by Carthaginian triremes as they tried to make it back to safe harbour. They managed to do so only by the capable handling of the Roman captain, who dexterously manoeuvred his ship clear of the Punic rams, and the veteran mariners aboard, who successfully repelled the attempts of the Carthaginians to board.

Enraged, Scipio sent word to Masinissa that the offensives should be renewed, and with even more zeal and brutality than previously.

The opportunity for leniency, even for those cities or towns that surrendered voluntarily, had been lost. Any continuation of the tentative negotiations was abandoned, and the scene was set for the final confrontation between Hannibal and Scipio, and their oscillating allies. The long war and the many battles that had erupted spasmodically on two continents over the fifteen years since the Roman disaster at Lake Trasimene was racing to a final, decisive denouement, which would leave either one empire ruined or the other braced for a fresh invasion. The situation was beyond any civil mediation of redrawn borders and uncomfortable coexistences. Empires are monopolies of power, and Rome and Carthage were just too close to tolerate an overlord or upstart. One would prevail. It was in the hands and minds of Scipio and Hannibal to determine which.

Of the other hands that would make a difference, Masinissa sensed and believed his would be the most vital. He had prevailed in battles and trials, and knew as much as anyone how to lead a cavalry force and destroy, in skirmish or set piece, any foe. He was a little doubtful, however, that, in the event of Roman success, that his part would be commemorated in the correct proportion. He was esteemed, and, no doubt, Scipio would convey on him all the kudos that his bravery, acumen and sacrifices merited, but it was improbable that he would elevate him to anything other than a subsidiary role when the honours and credits were allocated.

ZAMA TIME

As had become a convention in the passing of orders and information, Capuca seemed to be always the first to know. Masinissa surmised that the messengers probably had made common knowledge amongst themselves the fact that he had a tendency to tip them, and the fact that they would invariably seek him out first to cash in on his largesse whenever they reached camp gave credence to that speculation. In addition, he had a more amiable and deferential relationship with Laelius, so, in the event that fresh news was exchanged directly between the senior commanders rather than via envoys, the two would often have the initial exchange before either Scipio or Masinissa was approached.

Masinissa could always gauge the importance of the news by the first words that Capuca spoke. This insight was gained not from the urgency or substance of the comments but rather from how his first words revealed the extent of Capuca's recent exertions. If it was something significant, Capuca wouldn't dawdle but would rush to Masinissa's tent. His heaving respiration as he greeted Masinissa suggested that the most recent news had been important enough for him to run.

"Take a breath, Cap," Masinissa enjoined his gasping lieutenant. "Get your composure back. I'm sure the Carthaginians are far enough away that a few seconds rest won't cost us anything."

Capuca nodded and took a stabilising infusion of air, which he released in a drawn-out pout of exhalation. It did the trick, as his heart settled back quickly into its usual inconspicuous thump. "Well, it's coming, Mas; more to the point, Hannibal's coming. His forces have been putting their final preparations together at Hadrumentum, but the entreaties of the Carthaginian nobility seem to have hastened his plans. It looks like he's found enough cavalry as well. We would have wiped out his weak flanks, but the last renegade elements of Syphax's divisions have reformed under his cousin Tychaeus's command and come to Hannibal's aid. He now has, from the estimates of the Roman spies, who saw them whooping into his camp, about 2,000 local riders and they're the meanest that Syphax had. We're better and more numerous than them, but they'll cause problems. Anyway, they're all on the move heading west, and we have to bring ourselves to Scipio's camp before they get there. Hannibal needs to see what Scipio can boast in terms of cavalry. We'd better break camp and get there before the Carthaginians do. Scipio has it in his head that he needs to parade the whole show, you know, and we're the plumage on this peacock."

Masinissa had sensed from Capuca's wheezy ingress that the time had come, but he had listened placidly as the details of the message were conveyed. "Thanks, Cap," he replied "Let's move on out then. It shouldn't take us long. Get the fighting men moving and let the others find their own way. I'm sure Scipio will have enough provisions to keep us fed and watered until they catch up. Tell Pun, Tigerman and Massiva to form their cohorts, and instruct Ari, Billy and Zee to meet me at the horses. They'll be my close retinue on this march. You tag along too."

Capuca clicked his fingers with alacrity and, as speedily as he had entered, he left to execute Masinissa's directives.

*

In a coincidence that seemed propitious and that Scipio turned quickly to his propaganda advantage, the first wave of Massylian cavalry, headed by Masinissa in untypically burnished and coruscating armour, rode into the Roman camp just at the moment when a group of somewhat astounded captured Carthaginian spies were being shown around every corner of it. No doubt this was with the only conceivable intention of allowing them to fully appraise the military strength and morale of Scipio's legions, which were, in both respects, quite obviously brimming with irrepressible vigour and confidence. The shock of seeing such an impressive and eager foe could only have been magnified by witnessing the haughty trots of the long line of 4,000 Numidian riders. Though some were decades into war and some relatively callow, with their proud bearing and javelins held in vertical salute to their genial Roman allies, they looked collectively as daunting an adversary as the Carthaginians could have ever observed. Traipsing behind the cavalry – and mostly seen only as a low, dusty, boisterous cloud in the near distance – came 6,000 or so infantry, composed of a mixture of troops under Masinissa's and Laelius's commands. They would be another dispiriting note to be included in the Carthaginian spies report to Hannibal, which would need a great deal of creative deception to appear in the least way positive or encouraging for the returning general.

The futility of any attempt to make light of the strength of Scipio's alliance and the acceptance of its threatening reality seemed obvious from the short interval between the spies returning to the Carthaginian camp and Hannibal sending an emissary to seek a parlay with Scipio. The conclusion that everyone in Scipio's camp who was blessed with even a moderate level of intuition regarding military diplomacy could and did make was that Hannibal had received, from his point of view, a rather bleak portrait of the strength of his enemies' forces, and that the insight given by the review had made it imperative for him to seek some form of truce or settlement that would preserve his armies from destruction from the combined Roman and Numidian forces.

Scipio's reaction to the cordially expressed but desperate act was ecstatic, and he agreed unhesitatingly to a meeting. The practicalities were settled upon quickly. The two generals would advance towards each other, with Scipio making a fresh camp near to the city of Naraggara, whilst Hannibal would halt on a small hill about four miles away. The two would then meet alone on open ground. Scipio, however, felt such an arrangement was rather too similar to the ancient fighting tradition of respective armies sending out their champions to settle their disputes on their behalf.

"This isn't *The Iliad*, for Jupiter's sake," he exclaimed. "Who are we? Hector, Achilles or Ajax?" With that outburst, he insisted to the messenger that he would be accompanied by a pair of other commanders. That one of his sidekicks was going to be Masinissa may well have played a part in his decision to demur on meeting Hannibal alone. The wink he offered Masinissa on informing him of the decision suggested that there may be some sport in meeting erstwhile allies and unbeknownst in-laws if, as was probable, Hasdrubal Gisco was in Hannibal's group.

Masinissa winced inwardly at the prospect as he had yet to inform Scipio of his nuptials and Gisco was certainly not privy to the event where Pun had deputised for the Carthaginian general more than adequately.

*

When the meeting took place, there was only one slight surprise in either of the threesomes. Accompanying Scipio were the obvious duo of Masinissa and Laelius, whilst flanking Hannibal were the familiar, if a little more gaunt than Masinissa remembered, Gisco and a swarthy, innominate figure whom Masinissa assumed to be Tychaeus, for want of any other indication to the contrary. He was evidently Numidian and, by process of elimination, he would be the only one left of any prominence from his tribe to be invited to such a party. Whilst Hannibal had the deference and courtesy to nod respectfully to each of his enemies before speaking, the other two did nothing. Tychaeus surveyed the three with the detachment of a killer, rather than the gaze of a statesman, whilst Gisco had eyes only for Masinissa, and narrowed his eyes into discs that radiated his hatred as forcefully as if he had leapt from his horse and attempted to strangle Masinissa. In response, Masinissa did little other than to roll his tongue against his cheek in lieu of a shrug and switched his entire attention to Hannibal.

He had heard descriptions of the renowned general many times, both in terms of his appearance and his bearing, and he did not disappoint in the flesh. There was something intangibly charismatic in his gaze, and his repose on horseback was striking and defied the immense stress of the moment. It was as if no threat could touch him, not even the imminent assault of Scipio's eager legions. His time on the Italian peninsula had added a few northern – mostly Etruscan, Masinissa surmised – adornments to his tunic and to his helmet especially, which resembled that of a Roman senator parading for merely ceremonial purposes. The cheek pieces or *bucculae*, which you might expect to see from a man about to face an enemy, were missing; they had either been removed or, more probably, not even added, as they would detract from the baroque swirls that flowed like short tresses over the golden *casque*. The visor, too, was short and equally ornate, providing no protection for his forehead. For a man so familiar with being exposed to danger, it seemed a complacent look. Masinissa wondered if there might be a more protective lid being held by a retainer somewhere in the ranks, which he could switch into in the event that his diplomacy failed.

As the pause stretched less comfortably, the general began his pitch. His initial foray was conciliatory and confessional. "It was I who first began this war against the Roman people, and, though I seemed so often to have victory in my grasp, fate has willed it that I should also be the first to seek peace. I come of my own free will, and I am glad that it is you from whom I seek it; there is no one I would rather ask it of. I am glad, too, that it will not be the least of your many achievements; that it was you that Hannibal surrendered to, who had claimed so many victories over Rome's other generals, and that it was you who brought an end to a war made famous by your countrymen's defeats before my own."

Masinissa wondered if the reference to his previous victories might have been a hubristic miscalculation.

This was an error Hannibal seemed to compound as he continued with a personal reference that could have been misconstrued by Scipio as being a jibe. "This is indeed one of Fortuna's richest jokes that I first took up arms when your father was consul. I fought against him first of all Rome's generals, and now, without my arms, I am here to seek peace terms from his son."

Masinissa felt suddenly that Hannibal had revealed a little subtlety in his choice of helmet with the pointed remark about his lack of arms. The choice of such an ill-suited helmet made much more sense when accompanied by a profession of weakness. Masinissa gave Scipio a darting glance to see how he was receiving the petition so far, and his expression and his arms being planted firmly on his thighs suggested that he was probably as obdurate as stone in his resolve to defeat the man who was doing his best to douse his vengeful fire.

Hannibal was likely drawing the same impression, and he doggedly resumed his attempts at rapprochement. "It would have been better if the gods had given our ancestors a different attitude of mind, a willingness to be content with what they had: Rome with Italy, and Carthage with Africa. For you, Sicily and Sardinia are a barely adequate reward for the loss of so many fleets, armies and outstanding generals. But, sadly, though we may regret the past, we cannot change it. We fought to capture what belonged to others; now we fight to defend what is our own. Our war was fought in Italy as well as Africa; yours in Africa as well as Italy. You saw the arms and standards of a Punic army at your gates and beneath the walls of Rome; we now hear the roar of a Roman camp from the walls of Carthage. The luck has turned and Fortuna is on your side – something we feared greatly and you desired above all else. But the issue we must now decide upon is peace, and, for both of us, peace is the greatest prize of all. Whatever we decide upon, our two states will ratify. All we now need is quiet and sensible discussions."

The Carthaginian general sighed, perhaps at the futility of his own optimism, and turned reflective. "As for myself, time sees me now as an old man returning home to the native land he left whilst still a boy. Success and failure have long since taught me that philosophy is a better guide to action than any reliance upon Fortuna. You are young, and luck has always been on your side. This, I fear, will make you too aggressive when what we need is quiet diplomacy. The man who has never been deceived by Fortuna rarely thinks carefully about the uncertainties of mortal destiny.

"You stand today where I once stood at Lake Trasimene and Cannae. Almost before you reached military age, you held supreme command. Whatever risks you took, however bold, Fortuna never let you down. You avenged your father's and your uncle's deaths, and, in so doing, from your family's calamities, like battle honours, you won a glorious renown for courage and filial devotion. Iberia was lost; you won it back by driving out four Carthaginian armies. They made you consul, when others lacked the guts to fight for Italy; but you went further, and sailed out to Africa. There you slaughtered two armies, captured and fired two camps, took our most powerful ruler Syphax prisoner, and seized innumerable cities in his kingdom and our empire. And, now, finally, you have dragged me out of Italy after sixteen years of stubborn occupation of that land.

"To men of action, victory can often seem a greater prize than peace. I too was once a man of action indifferent to practical decisions; once upon a time, Fortuna smiled on me too. But if, when all goes well, the gods would only give us the blessing of good sense, we would bear in mind not only what has already happened but also what may happen in the future. Forget everything else; I am proof enough of how Fortuna changes. Not so long ago, I pitched my camp between the River Anio and Rome. You saw me preparing to attack and about to scale the battlements of Rome. Look at me now. I am bereaved of two brothers, heroes both and famous generals; standing before the walls of my beleaguered country; and pleading with you to spare my city the ordeals with which I once threatened yours.

"The more Fortuna smiles upon you, the less she should be trusted. You are basking in success; we are in the depths. Peace is yours to give, and the rewards will bring you many blessings; peace is ours to beg for, and for us there are no honourable rewards – we beg because we must. The certainty of peace is a better thing by far than a victory you can only hope for. Peace is yours to give; victory rests in the hands of the gods. Do not leave so many years of glorious success to depend on the lottery of a single hour. Compare your own strength with the power of Fortuna and the chance of battle, which we share. For both of us, swords will be drawn, and men's lives lost; nowhere less certainly than in battle does victory come in answer to our hopes.

"If you prove victorious, you will add far less to the glory you can already claim by making peace than you will lose if for you the outcome is defeat. All the glory that you have and hope for, Fortuna can turn away in a single hour. If you make peace, Publius Cornelius, yours is the world and everything that's in it; if not, then you must take whatever Fortuna may grant. There are not many examples of courage linked to success. Remember Marcus Atilius Regulus, who once stood here victorious on Carthaginian soil. My ancestors sued for peace, which he refused. He rode his luck to the limits and failed to rein it in; it galloped away from him. The higher you rise, the further you fall – and his fall was truly terrible. The one who grants peace has the right to dictate the terms, not the one who seeks it. But perhaps we Carthaginians deserve to propose some penalties for ourselves. We are willing to concede that all the territories for which we went to war belong to you: Sicily, Sardinia, Iberia and all the Mediterranean islands lying between Italy and Africa. Since that is how the gods have ordained it, we are content to be confined within the boundaries of Africa and to see you as an imperial power ruling over foreign kingdoms by land and sea.

"I cannot deny that Carthage's good faith must be suspect, because we lacked sincerity in seeking peace and patience in waiting for it when offered. With the integrity of any peace agreement, much depends on those who seek it. I understand, Scipio, that your senators turned down our overtures of peace, in part because our envoys lacked sufficient status. But now it is I, Hannibal, who asks for peace. I would not ask for it unless I felt it was to our advantage, and that is why I shall defend the peace that I have asked for. I was responsible for that war, and, as long as heaven was on my side, I worked to see that none of my people regretted my decision. In the same way, I shall now work with all my might to see that none regret the peace that I have gained for them."

Hannibal gave Scipio a smile that expressed a certain assured expectation that the olive branch he was extending, as eloquently as he could manage, would be taken, and that the enmities and scores that Scipio had stored up and waited to settle in a victorious bloodbath would be released like doves into the air. Masinissa knew better, and – deep under the general's confident carapace and flimsy helmet – he suspected that Hannibal knew it too. Hannibal was good at bluffing, though, Masinissa conceded. Hannibal knew how to face down a bull.

The particular ungelded bovine in question leant forwards in his saddle, shook his head barely perceptibly and gave an abrupt snort, which, in itself, would have served more than adequately as a rejection of Hannibal's proposal, and began what everyone then knew would be an unalloyed repudiation of Hannibal's carefully scripted peace. "I am very well aware, Hannibal, that it was the hopes raised by your return that led the Carthaginians to breach the terms of the armistice and wreck any hopes of future peace. You have been very frank about it, whilst contriving to leave out of your current proposals anything in the terms of the original agreement that was not already in our possession.

"You want your fellow citizens to recognise what a huge burden you are lifting from their shoulders, but I too must strive to make sure that they make no profit from their treachery by excluding any of those previous conditions from the terms of any settlement on which we may agree today. You are actually asking to profit from your treachery, even though you do not deserve to retain even the original conditions. Our ancestors did not start the war in Sicily; we did not start the war in Iberia. In Sicily, it was our allies, the Mamertines, who were under threat; in Iberia, it was the sack of Saguntum that drove us to take up arms in two just and holy wars. You have acknowledged, and the gods are witnesses to the truth of what you say, that you are the aggressors. Justice and the laws of heaven gave us victory in Sicily, they have given us victory in the recent war, and they will do so again if we fight here.

"As for myself, I am all too aware of human weakness, and there is no need to lecture me on the power of Fortuna; I know very well that all our deeds are subject to 1,000 strokes of luck. If you had come to me to ask for peace of your own free will before you abandoned Italy, embarked your army and withdrew to Africa, and if I had rejected your proposals out of hand, I would be all too willing to admit that my conduct was high-handed and unfair. But now I have no such inhibitions when we are here in Africa on the eve of battle, and I have dragged you protesting and against your will to these negotiations.

"Therefore, if you have anything you wish to add to the peace conditions previously proposed, as compensation perhaps for the losses to our ships and their supplies which you destroyed during the armistice, and for the violence done to our ambassadors, then I will have something to take back to our authorities, But if that is too much for you, prepare for war, since peace you clearly find intolerable."

Hannibal looked at him wearily, like a man who knew it was going to rain felt the first drop of water on his cheek. He covered his mouth and said something quietly to Gisco, who patted his sword menacingly and spat where he was looking, right at Masinissa, before whirling his horse back in the direction of his own condemned forces. His tenuously held restraining bolt had clearly been sprung. If they lost the battle that was now ineludible, Masinissa vowed to not leave his bones at Gisco's mercy.

*

Once the meeting was over, as the three trotted back to their own expectant lines, Scipio was manifestly elated by his own rebuttal of any terms and the proximity of a battle that would define his long campaigns.

Masinissa raised a quizzical but mordantly framed question, "May I ask you something, Consul? I don't wish to be insubordinate, but you had Hannibal by the balls then. You could have pushed him to make significant concessions. I know your renown has been forged on the battlefield, but I do remember you saying once that you didn't believe that winning one hundred battles was the acme of skill. Rather, you said that to subdue the enemy without fighting is the acme of skill. You could have tickled Hannibal's tummy just then. He was rolling over ready to purr, yet we have to turn around, suit up and risk our lives again. Wouldn't terms be acceptable now?"

Scipio rolled his head and then scratched the back of his neck in the style of a man who knew the reasoning in the comment but still needed to resist it. "Yeah, I can't exactly disagree with my own words, but those are ones I framed in more rational moments when I was looking to impress people with my wit and logic. I'm not looking to show off now. I'm seeking vengeance. I've had a long time to let that cool, and to let the grief, shock and agony of losing a beloved father and uncle distil into its oozing, primordial essence. This is not about my personal glory. This is right back to basics. I owe a debt to my dead. This has lived in the pit of my guts for years. Besides, as far as risking my neck goes, I've got a good feeling!"

Laelius gave a ready murmur of assent that broke into a heartier endorsement. "That goes for me too, Mas. We've lost too much to allow the men who took so many of our own from us to scuttle back to their comforts and forget about all the blood they washed off."

Listening to the two senior Roman generals reveal their baser urges took Masinissa a little by surprise, but it wasn't as if he was trying to dissuade them. Quite the reverse. Projecting forwards, it was plain that Numidia and Carthage would, as antagonistic neighbours, have an inverse power relationship. The weaker the one was, the stronger the other would become. Masinissa had a vested geopolitical interest in bringing Hannibal and Carthage right down onto its knees.

Masinissa responded, "Sounds like you're ready. Do I inform the troops that there won't be any false dances this time and we're flying right into them?"

Scipio nodded. "Tomorrow. No messing around. Get 'em ready!"

Masinissa found his ally's zeal infectious, and he made his horse rear and whirl around in premature triumph, as he gave them a frisky departing salute and galloped off to find his *optio*.

*

True to his fervid assertion, Scipio marched out onto the battlefield the next morning with the solitary intention of ending the long war that day with the total ruination of Hannibal's veteran army. That he was so bold and self-assured was, to Masinissa's mind, a direct testimony to the faith and confidence the Roman had in him. Hannibal's infantry was grizzled and capable, and it outnumbered Scipio's army almost two to one. Scouting estimates put Carthage's foot soldiers, of all stripes, at around 50,000 men, a number that dwarfed the figure Scipio could field. Capuca had gone to the trouble of having the Roman camp appraised, and the rough tally he had come to was 23,000 foot and 1,500 horse. Despite their evident quality and discipline, that made Masinissa's cavalry the decisive force in the deployment, the equivalent to a mounted legion, and one that Masinissa was sure had all the necessary resolution and ferocity to turn whichever flank Scipio felt was the more suitable target for his singular Massylian commander.

Ari was the first to make sport of the distended importance of the nearly local cavalry when Masinissa asked him, with counterfeit casualness, how he expected the battle to unfold. "We'll just let this two versus one mismatch play out, shall we? There's no pressure on us. Just watch the show. The Romans will surely take a pair of Carthaginians in each hand and fling them around like rag dolls. There's no pressure on us. Nuh-uh! We might as well just follow the river down to Ammaedara, do a little fishing and come back when there's nothing left but a carpet of fat maggots."

Masinissa smiled at Ari's gruesome version of levity, thinking that such a lack of seriousness from someone who would know better than to act so blasé if he felt that this was his last day intact and free was a very good indicator of his soldiers' morale.

Word came quickly from Scipio about how he wished to array his forces, and, as Masinissa had suspected, his cavalry would protect Scipio's right flank and Laelius would bring his Italian horse across to cover the left. As Masinissa observed the infantry lines assemble, he saw that they were forming into lines that anticipated an immediate rush from the bludgeon of Hannibal's still-sizeable elephant brigade. Scipio had formed his legions conventionally with his *alae* in their triple battle lines of *triplex acies*, but, rather than positioning the *maniples* of his line of *principes* to cover the intervals between the *maniples* of his *hastati*, Scipio instead had instructed his *principes* to line up behind the *hastati*, with the third line of *triarii* quickly following suit. By doing so, it established a series of clear lanes, which would run right through to the Roman rear. Camouflaging this ruse, Scipio ordered *velites* to occupy the gaps and give the appearance that the Roman battle order was quite orthodox.

Looking towards the enemy lines as they formed their own muster, Masinissa saw the standards of Syphax and the Masaesyli opposing him. Inwardly, he felt it fitting that this confrontation, if it was to be the last of the war, would pit Numidian directly against Numidian from the beginning. In front of him was all that was left to oppose him in the internecine tribal conflict that had blighted the continent for so many years, and been the subject of abuse and exploitation by the imperial allies who formed the centres of both battle configurations that day. All the willing arms that could be scraped from the furthest outposts of Numidia, and all the unsettled grudges or full-grown vengeful orphans that could be plied with a little wine and strapped to a sword were here. Masinissa didn't think much of it. It was a remnant. He'd smashed it when it was in its full majesty. Just then, it was not much better than a lame dog ignorant of the merciful stone that was about to collapse it's skull into oblivion.

At the very front of Hannibal's lines, his elephants stood magnificently but bearing many deep gouges and cicatrices that blended forgivingly in their saggy, tough skin. Masinissa wondered a little how many of these had crossed the Alpine passes long ago and had somehow managed to be subdued enough to be shepherded into the large-sterned transport vessels to return for their final call to arms. Poor creatures, they seemed too docile and placid to be put to such martial purposes. There were perhaps as many as eighty of them, most with turrets and all with elaborate headdresses. *What good will frilly tassels be to the beasts,* Masinissa wondered, *other than to tickle the top portion of their unique proboscises. Perhaps it will make them rear their snouts more to ease the itch, which would make the metal tusk swords that many of them wore much better aligned to spear the Roman heads they would be soon be goaded towards.*

Engrossed in his pre-battle observations, Masinissa took to analysing the weaponry, dress, features and pigmentations of the three lines of infantry before him. It was difficult to fully appraise the rear lines, but he needed only the slightest visual cues to identify the origins of the enemy. It appeared that the front rank was substantially composed of the residue of Mago's army. There were a lot of fierce-looking Gauls and Ligurians, and slingers from the Balearic Islands, who would do their best work when the lines were still at a reasonable distance apart. It would certainly benefit the Roman *hastati* line to make their advance brisk once they were in range of their stones, presupposing that the initial elephant charge had been adequately diverted beforehand.

The Carthaginian second line was composed of far-more-local African forces. There was evidently quite a large number of Libyans amongst them, many looking not unlike Ari when Masinissa had first met him in his desert ambush. If his trusted deputy was anything to go by, they would likely be courageous and accurate. Of course, that may be paying them too great a compliment. There couldn't be that many who shared the same degree of skill and valour as his own Libyan auxiliary. There was also, more revealingly, a large number of Carthaginian citizens amongst this line. They were a rare sight in formations and, in such numbers, unprecedented. It betrayed the extent of Carthage's plight that such men had to leave the safety of their city to face an enemy they must have thought complacently that they would never see. The Romans might as well have been minotaurs or gorgons for as much of a tangible, personal threat they had previously posed these men but right then, as their hitherto vague enemies reached the edge of the Punic sanctuary, they must appear as terrifying to the Carthaginians as the stories of those legendary monsters would have been to impressionable Greek children.

The final line, which was easier to discern as it had been withdrawn a few hundred yards behind the forbidding Libyans and feeble Carthaginians, was comprised of Hannibal's veteran brigades. They were startling in both appearance and number. There must have been nearly 20,000 of them, and they would have accounted collectively for many more times that number in Roman lives in their long campaigns throughout the Italian peninsula. Seeing them, Masinissa realised that there would only be the most meagre prospect of Scipio's infantry having their measure in an even contest. Fortunately for the Roman general, the Numidian horsemen would tilt the battle towards him if they made it past their antagonistic kinsmen. Without scrutinising them too closely, it was apparent that Hannibal's finest was as cosmopolitan and diverse a collective as was ever likely to be bound together in arms. It was as if all the slaves and gladiators of Rome had absconded en masse and were seeking their retribution. No doubt many in that line had emerged from those forms of bondage after being liberated by the Carthaginians. That must have been the most effective method of recruitment for Hannibal in the whole war. Tear down the fences in any gladiatorial school and you will find plenty of able swordsmen with vengeful intentions. Evidence of their previous engagements was also clear in their armour and weaponry. Even at a distance, the provenance of most of their kit was obviously Roman. Over the years, there must have been plenty of such superior equipment to share around as spoils. They were probably a little more dented and cratered than their facsimiles on the opposite side of the field, but they would no doubt serve their purpose just as well.

Adopting a strategic overview, Masinissa could tell that Hannibal, being conscious of his army's inadequacies on its flanks, had dispensed with any aspiration to envelop the Roman centre, as he had done to such effect in his devastating triumphs at Trebia and Cannae, and instead was intent on driving his infantry lines behind the vanguard of his elephants right into the guts of the Roman formations, and was hoping that his cavalry could delay or divert their counterparts.

As both armies formed up, the discipline in both deployments held, notwithstanding a few skirmishes between Tychaeus's horsemen and Masinissa's own riders. In all probability, there was some impetuous and personal score settling at work there, which Masinissa didn't care to restrain. The usual speeches and exhortations followed, but Masinissa kept his short, merely urging his men to believe in him, themselves, Tanit and Baal Hammon. They had heard his lines enough times that he was unlikely to inspire them any more if he ventured into less familiar incitements. He ended, though, with a novelty, pumping his sword towards the heavens and bellowing, "Numidia," looking to arouse and inflame his soldier's sense of shared unity. It was their kingdom not their tribe, that they were fighting for then, and that fact was not lost on any of them as the thundering echo surged back towards him.

Satisfied that the men's blood was coursing in a more rapid flow, he indicated to his senior commanders, Pun and Tigerman, to peel themselves into a form of trident formation with him, with Masinissa's corp in the centre, and his *optio* and *tesserarius* flanking with their own brigades. In all probability, any sense of division between them would blur swiftly, but at least the soldiers would have some form of initial focal point in their section of the charge, assuming none of the three succumbed to an early javelin or fortunate *falcata*. As the trumpets were about to sound, his most trusted and reliable lieutenants rode in tighter ready to protect their king from such presumptuous weaponry. Masinissa felt both a sense of comforting reassurance as well as a suspicion of finality – that this would be their last battle, the termination point of all that destruction, and the last rage of the thrashing beast of the endless war before it fell, and its cessation would be evident in the last pitiful, shuddery flutter of its diaphragm as either Scipio or Hannibal lay spent on the battlefield. One way or another, there would be a corpse of an army in a few hours. Capuca and Ari rode closest to Masinissa, with Billy and Zee protecting their seniors' left arms, and Massiva fell in just behind, as if loitering in the event that the Numidian kingdom might need an imminent heir.

The two armies, as if in synchronisation, put the single, long note of their collective orchestra of horns to the eerie battlefield in a harmony that started forcefully but ended almost poignantly. This was an impression that few could appreciate, as the final susurration of the buglers' lungs was lost in the screams, curses and thunder of hooves that the sound precipitated. The elephants in particular were startled by the commotion, suggesting that many of them were actually recent recruits, just like many of the Masaesyli opposing them and the Carthaginians in the weak-looking middle ranks, and, as far as pachyderms can be described as such, were rather callow and skittish. In any event, their charge, such as it was, was a chaotic muddle. Ari, in tandem with many of the nearby riders reared his mount in delight as they observed a significant portion of the recreant mammoths turn and stampede right into Tychaeus's cavalry. Perhaps they sensed this was the easiest route to survival but Masinissa couldn't have hoped for a better battlefield boon as he thanked Melqart for the elephant's detour, raised his javelin and kicked his horse towards the stumpy tails of the panicked beasts, who, from his fresh angle, looked faintly comical in their laboured, wobbly gaits. No doubt the Masaesyli, quite unprepared for the manifestation of an array of tusk bayonets coming at them from short, unavoidable range, were not seeing quite the same charm in the hulks' hurried deportment.

By the time Masinissa's cavalry had crossed the short distance that separated the armies, racing to a blurry gallop as they reached the enemy, the elephants had passed through and beyond them, wreaking havoc in their wake. The Masaesyli must have taken the elephants charge in numb shock, as no fallen mammoth checked the Numidian cavalry's charge. There were, however, many broken horses and bucked-off riders who were far easier to vault or crush. The whooping, ecstatic wave of Masinissa's cavalry hit their opponents, whose resistance was nominal and they were routed so quickly that Masinissa, as he urged the bulk of his riders after the staggering survivors of the consecutive charges of elephant and Massylians, was able to observe Scipio's *velites* bravely agitating those elephants that had shown more stolidity when the clarions had been sounded. Once the Carthaginian's unreliable trump card was dropped, a coordinated shower of javelins, thrown with unerring accuracy by the Roman *velites*. Some of these men were trampled or gored for their temerity, but most were able to retreat behind the embraces of the formed-up *maniples* of the second heavier *hastati* line. The integrity of this line was barely dented as the lanes that Scipio had astutely interposed in his formations worked as well as the Roman consul could have dared hope, and most of the elephants were funnelled into irrelevance towards the rear of the Roman line, losing most of their steerers en route and stuttering to an impotent halt, where they were later either shepherded into new service or put out of their misery.

Masinissa could see that, to a lesser extent, some of the misfortune that had befallen Tychaeus's wing had also assailed the Carthaginian's other flank a little later, as the more resilient elephants got rocked by the *velite* spears. Those elephants that didn't find their way through the gaps laid for them baulked and spun for another exit, and chose the misfortunate Carthaginian cavalry on the far side of the battlefield as the thoroughfare for their evacuation. The resistance of that flank proved just as feeble, as Laelius, emulating Masinissa's example, charged with just as much relish as his ally into the dazed enemy line, destroying what remained of the belligerent and putting the remainder to flight.

Similarly, following Masinissa's tactical example, Laelius despatched the largest portion of his troops in pursuit of the fleeing enemy to obviate any chance of a surprise rally from the Carthaginian flanks, with the same instructions not to let the pursuit extend too long and return to engage the rear of Hannibal's army once the lines of the two armies' infantry were locked together.

Masinissa, who had moved beyond the battle physically but remained within its sensory radius, became grimly mindful of the change in the rattles of battle. The cacophony of tons of terrified, gigantic quadrupeds, by then destroyed or run off, was replaced by the stormy blusters and threats of both sets of infantry as they marched loudly to their possible deaths, announcing to the gods and their antagonists that they would go out of this world as raucously as most of them had arrived.

In an attempt to drown out the threats of their enemies, the Romans began an intimidating ploy as they advanced that raised the acoustic levels even higher; they banged their swords and javelins against the bosses of their shields, which was a tactic that was half-heartedly mimicked by the Carthaginians, who mostly preferred to continue raining down their polyglot threats through the relentless metallic thumps. Momentarily detached, Masinissa thought the actions fringed on the puerile and silly, but reasserted the context of the moment quickly. When your face is seconds away from the muscular thrusts of another man's angry blade, you're going to start yelling something. Masinissa had screamed his own throat ragged many a time in similar circumstances. In truth, he had done precisely that only a few minutes earlier.

Both lines sped up as they drew closer and, almost in a mutual abstention from a preliminary projectile engagement, saved their javelins for spearing rather than throwing. There were many veterans from Mago's brigades in the Carthaginian first rank, and they fought with all the skill and enthusiasm that association implied. They held their ground well, and the Roman *hastati* line was made to pay dearly for their slow-but-inexorable advance through them. Regarding them, Masinissa dwelt on the differences in measurement and structure between the cavalry and infantry. A step forward for the interlocked legionnaires was a tangible gain for them, but a paltry advantage for someone more accustomed, as he was, to the far less coherent attacks of mounted charges, which could break through whole battalions in minutes in a powerful rush.

The bravery and pertinacity of the veteran Ligurians and Gauls, amongst others, in the first Carthaginian line was contrasted with its obverse in the second line, as many of the men wedged into that line showed no inclination to join the fight, and seemed to treat their confederates as a barrier protecting them, albeit a collapsing one, rather than interwoven pieces in the same cause. As the inexorable tide of the Roman assault pressed Hannibal's front rank, many exhausted men tried to retreat behind the fresher troops behind them, but were deprived their exit as catastrophic infighting erupted. The confusion and lack of coordination in the Carthaginian brigades contrasted with the smoothness of the Romans, who, as their first wave tired or were too injured to do anything more, were able to withdraw and fresh soldiers from the *principe* line were brought forward to engage the enemy, injecting vigour and momentum back into their attack.

The Carthaginian retreat was only briefly tardy, and their demise soon accelerated as the Romans rammed them back towards their veteran divisions. As the final denouement of the battle seemed to approach, Masinissa began to feel a little impatient as this was surely the moment for his and Laelius's cavalry to return and pounce on the rear of Hannibal's strongest units. Although the resistance of those elite fighters would undoubtedly be the most resolute, victory seemed only a matter of time, as the numerical advantage Hannibal may have enjoyed was rapidly being eroded. Many of his men had taken serious, paralysing wounds to their legs, and their stumbles and crawls – some were even fully prostate as they crawled along clawing at the earth, looking more like they were attempting to get under it rather than across it – back to any point of safety were checked quickly, and their lives extinguished with swords through their backs or across their throats. Many lives were ended in even more ignoble fashion, as their heads were stamped on and their necks broken with barely a downward glance from their executioners at the obliterated lives that had seemed so significant and cherishable hours earlier.

How quickly we are nothing, Masinissa thought to himself. *How easily we strip others of their humanity.*

As he grew restless for Pun, Ari and the others to emerge back from the horizon, Masinissa found himself observing a point in the battle where he could admire the antipodal but complementary talents of his Roman counterpart. In all the tumult of broken lines and a battlefield scattered with fallen and dying men, Scipio ordered his trumpets to sound in a cue for his fraying legions to reform. To perform such a complex manoeuvre in the heat of a battle that was abutting its critical, wildest phase was a remarkable feat of discipline and one that Masinissa doubted any other army could have managed so adeptly. This time, however, the formation became cruder. Rather than forming into successive lines, Scipio ordered his *hastati* into the centre and placed the *principes* and *triarii* on either side, forming a single broad line resembling the shape and tactical style of a *hoplite* phalanx. Masinissa speculated a little about Scipio's motivation for such a ploy. There would be no tricks and no feints at the end, just an uncomplicated, defiant march straight into your adversary.

Maybe the Roman's calculations and forecasts were more accurate than his own, as – just as the second round of horns was propelling the long string of men back into the tussle, and almost in harmony – the two pursuing cavalries of Pun and Laelius rode back into view. Distance was an easy commodity to overestimate in an enthusiastic cohort of riders, and it was only a few brief minutes between seeing the dust trails and standards of his own men emerge back into the plain, and Capuca and Ari arriving – grinning and agitated – before him. They barely broke stride; the blood of men and horses simmered into an exigency that sucked up Masinissa and his waiting entourage, like a stick in a shore break, and spun them into a charge at the vulnerable rear of Hannibal's finest.

It was in that moment that Masinissa sensed a little of his own personal significance. He was experienced and perceptive enough to recognise the delusions of ego and pride, but, perhaps for the first time, he sensed the import of himself and his hands on the clay of the world. He was playing a part in shaping the future. With each man he and his kinsmen tore the life from, an altered world would be closer to inception or, perhaps more accurately, ascension, certainly on this continent but also on the northern one, which would become much more enduringly secure with the demise of its only rival and claimant to a bipolar world. The hegemony of Rome would be sure, and the tectonic impact of that on every living being west of the Ptolemaic and Seleucid Empires, south of the Scythian and Sarmatian tribes, and north of the nomadic, formless shifts of the Garamantes finding life in their sands, would be felt hard and deep, right down to the merest details of everyday lives and understandings.

Perhaps noticing a little loss of focus in his commander's gallop, Tigerman, as observant as he was often impertinent, whacked his commander and presumptive shaper of the future out of his Ozymandian daydream, by applying the broad side of his *gladius* to his back, and yelled over the thud of hooves, "*Game face, Mas. Game face!*"

Appreciating the wisecrack and restoration to the present, Masinissa kicked his horse hard, roared his loudest and most incoherent exhortation, and let his javelin fly at a semi-distant Carthaginian trooper, who heretofore must have thought it was his lucky day to find himself so deep in the reserve of the Carthaginian formation. Once all those in the charge had flung their spears, in almost choreographed metallic rainbows, and exhausted that part of their arsenal, Masinissa ordered a shift in the attack. It would be harder to drive through such seasoned troops, and if they did, they would reach a point where they found the hinges of the battle and be unable to distinguish between friend and foe, and end up fighting both. To avoid such folly, the attack turned oblique and they strafed the most exposed troops with their blades, only to wheel at the termination of the line, switch their blades to their other hands and attack again, trampling as they went the misfortunates whom they had previously sliced on their forehand and dropped to the ground to await an even more savage blow from the hooves of their horses.

Between his cavalry and Scipio's legions, they compressed Hannibal's troops tighter and tighter for a number of hours. For all the advantages of the pincer they held his forces in, the men against them were worthy foes and used all their skills to prolong their lives a little longer, adding to their existences a few final painful and pointless extra minutes. For their part, the legions engaged in a diametrically opposite way to Masinissa's raking bursts. The Romans fought in brutal hand-to-hand dances, which were full of spite and vengeance. The Carthaginian line finally degraded into a pocket, at which point Scipio ordered a pause. Masinissa wondered if it was a lenience or a final humiliation to allow the last of Hannibal's men, feted for their heroism and many triumphs, to take a moment to suck on their ignominy and make the desperate Hobson's choice of slavery or suicide. Exhausted yet proud, many took the option of the latter, but still more saw more value in a freedomless life than a liberated death and surrendered.

As they tossed down their weapons and standards, and sat morosely – ready to be stripped, beaten and chained – Masinissa, sagging a little himself on his horse, more in relief than fatigue, felt his pulse slow and his attentiveness to the moment sharpen. He had known from the instant he and Laelius had obliterated Hannibal's flanks that victory was assured, but his own survival and that of so many of his men had been far from guaranteed. The adrenaline of battle had given him the vigour and vitality to lead and slay without pause or compunction, a surge that was as quick to now ebb as it was initially to flow. In the abruptness of a war won, his vivifying sap receded, leaving his throat parched, his hands bloody and his heart ambivalent. Destruction was an easier thing to do than reflect on.

With the momentum of a heavy stone being rolled over a slope, the victors, elated but somewhat torpid, began uncertain cheers that gradually became a raucous, incoherent chorus, as Romans and Massylians sung out the euphoric gratitude of their preservation in a myriad of rasping and formless sonic roars.

Ari found his way to Masinissa's side, to whom he offered his open arms with slightly comical zeal. The embrace was not the intense wrap of lovers but the suffocating squeeze of men who had no better way to express the ardour of their affection for one another than using the muscular power of their chests and arms exuberantly. The thoughts of both of them were firmly in the present, although they were coloured a little by memories of the past, of their premonitions of this day and thoughts of the lost who had paid the greatest price to get there.

"We made it... all the way," Ari commented, becoming a little stupefied as he appeared to contemplate the whole length of their trials in the terse phrase.

Masinissa replied, "All the way and back again. We're back to stay now. We're done. I can start thinking about real things now. I can let everything that's been stored up inside me have a chance. It will be a new life for me and for mine, whoever they turn out to be." Ari smiled.

"Yeah, let's be optimistic again; spark some life back into ourselves; take a look at this blue, blue sky; and forget about all that red, red earth that has been bled on underneath it."

"You got it, kid. It's onwards and upwards for us now" Masinissa grinned back, giving him an affectionate endearment that ought to be completely incongruous and ill-fitting for the weary survivor before him who had lost any traces of innocence long ago, but which was a description that somehow still seemed apt, at least between the two of them. Maybe some parts of who they had been and what they had lost could be reconstituted, and their cheerfulness and allusion to their more youthful days reflected that. Some parts of their souls could be healed, like the curling, browning fronds of pygmy palms that had been neglected too long in their arid soils by careless owners who saw no need to tend such apparently stoic bushes, but which, with just a little water, gave back some of their vibrant lushness.

Ari gave him another squeeze, a little more awkwardly as the first had sufficed, and dug in a little deeper into the mutual illusion of his recovered callowness. "It's time to play with our toys again," he said with a beaming smile, like one a five-year-old might offer guilelessly to a grateful parent, and he rattled the curious little wooden doll that he still wore around his midriff, which had caught Masinissa's bewildered attention the very first time they had met.

"Find some paint and a partner for that now, Ar!" Masinissa returned in kind.

Ari laughed, turned and started to skip in the direction of Do-it Boy and Capuca, like a gazelle that knows the lion is taking his lunch somewhere else, yelling back as a final, delayed riposte, "*You can count on that one Mas! I'm definitely gonna find myself a partner for this thing, for me too with any luck!*" Then he frolicked merrily towards the others, turning his back, it seemed, not just on his commander, but on the war, the vanquished being humiliated in the near distance and, Masinissa hoped, some of the darker shadows of his past.

THE LIES WE TELL OURSELVES

The assessment of the battle was, as is often the case, a stratified affair that gained greater detail with time, at least for the victors for whom communicating news of their own deceased to loved ones remained a solemn duty. Counting the slaughtered and signalling a moratorium on hostilities that would allow time for the detailed terms of submission to be gleefully composed was only the first stage in the oppressive endgame in which the Romans could kick their metaphorical heels right into the prone heads of the Carthaginians. It was clear, just from a view of the battlefield, that the losses were far from equitably distributed between the combatants, and that unevenness had been exacerbated at the end when the Romans settled more than their share of scores on enemies who had neither wanted nor needed to die.

The full calculations of the number of dead were delivered by an emissary of Laelius, who puffed up with almost repellent pride as if the figures were somehow partly his achievement. These calculations were the usual approximations, there being no need for exactitude at the point when you could reduce men to statistics. One more here, one more there – who could be bothered to make such figures precise? Even rounded up, the Carthaginian losses were devastating, and almost evenly divided between the slain and enslaved. Each curse had claimed about 20,000 of them.

There were many fewer Roman and Numidian losses. Scipio had lost only about 1,500 of his own, and Capuca had informed Masinissa that the losses his own cavalry had suffered were only in the low three figures, although there were many more who were nursing injuries that were uncertain in their longevity and impact. Many of them would be fit only for the shade of a tree at that point, Capuca notified him; this was a distinctly kindly reference – which conjured an image of his men in reflective, safe repose – that brought a smile to Masinissa's face. All of those who had ridden with him deserved a little serenity at the edge of a peaceful glade somewhere to do what pleased them: to mourn, make merry or just stare into the void until it went away.

As with many battles on this scale, the main defeated actors had a habit of being elusive, and Hannibal had been no different. Living to fight another day was still his prerogative. Whether he feared death or capture, or just felt that, as leader of the Carthaginian military, he had a duty to escape, he had managed to flee the battle and make his way to his camp at Hadrumentum, abandoning his wrecked troops to their sordid fates.

Nevertheless, the defeat was abject and total, and both Scipio and Carthage knew it. A later emissary, via Capuca, summarised the extent of the reparations, which were severe. Patently, Roman prisoners and deserters had to be returned to the legions to be bestowed with obverse welcomes: one to be saluted and the other savaged. The salient and strongest weapon of war for Hannibal, his elephants, were also all to be confiscated, which seemed to Masinissa a little like military castration. It would be the same as if his men were forced to surrender their horses. They might as well be farmers or cooks for what good they would do serving as infantrymen.

The Carthaginian fleet, another source of pride, was stripped back to ten triremes, and all its overseas territories were surrendered to the Roman suzerain.

At the point when this particular item of the terms was mentioned, Capuca added archly, "Scipio wants to see you about that."

It was clear there was a territorial gift about to be donated. Scipio was honourable and grateful to Masinissa, and his donation to a united Numidian kingdom would no doubt be quite munificent.

*

The appointment for the collection of that particular bounty was a little delayed, as Scipio had other preoccupations to attend to, but, when the time came and the summons was received, Masinissa rode with his closest retinue. As Masinissa's blood kin, Massiva had to go, as did Pun, who was to take over the routine command of the army in the dawning peace. Ari couldn't be dismissed, and Capuca had sniffed out a free meal and a chance to be present at a landmark moment. Conon and Tigerman made up a total of seven, with the latter two serving as reservoirs of distinct types of wisdom and knowledge, both of which Masinissa might need to call upon.

There was a degree of fanfare, as well as a few conspicuous wagons, laden with sacks of gold and other tributes, at the entrance to the Roman camp. Scipio, in as paternalistic a mood as Masinissa had ever known, greeted the seven there, made an earnest play of his indebtedness and asked them to dismount. They were then feted with a little prepared choreography, as the Roman legionaries, almost all in full formal regalia, stood to attention and provided an honour guard through the central avenue of the camp. Many who cheered them were well known and had even become friends. Not wanting to be distracted by each other and show rudeness to their hosts, each of the seven gave the crowd the sort of devotion they would give a new lover by waving, grinning and showing their thankfulness exuberantly for the acclaim they were being showered with so lavishly. It was a sweet moment for all of them, who had known such bitter trials between them.

At the end of the row of purple-scarfed soldiers, Scipio's own headquarters were located, and he ushered them all into the most impressive tent in the inner grounds of the encampment. Rugs, ornaments and burnished armour adorned the interior space, and it seemed both a cosy refuge and a makeshift cave of authority, with Scipio as the resident prowling bear. A number of attendants brought wine to them, and two of the more physically impressive legionnaires manned the door. Despite their muscular expanses, they served more as symmetry to frame the entrance than as guards ready to interpose themselves between their commander and any threat. Their voices would be more beneficial than their swords in the event any violence erupted. Between such friends as Scipio and Masinissa had become, such an incident was extremely fanciful, but it was good form to not leave such an eminence as Scipio without some symbolic protection.

When all the men had their cups filled and were waiting their cue to quaff from them, Scipio raised his and declared, "To you and your men, Masinissa. To your country, which it is my pleasure to act as a guarantor for. May it blossom as a civilised nation, and help preserve peace and prosperity on this continent. Before you and your gallant entourage, and in decrees that will be sent and endorsed in the senate in Rome itself, I, as the representative of the Republic of Rome, relinquish our conquests on these shores into your authority. I am grateful to you, Masinissa; Rome is grateful and promises to you its abiding friendship."

Masinissa, whilst expecting Scipio's act of largesse, was nevertheless moved and grateful in turn. This was not merely a transaction or gift of land. This was the facilitation of the creation of a nation, his nation, the merger of two quarrelsome but indistinguishable tribes into one country, the transitional custodian of which he felt keenly as his personal duty.

"Thank you, Consul. It's hard to find words both to convey my gratitude to you as well as to give any kind of conclusion to all this now, as it appears, we have finally reached a cessation of hostilities which always seemed so distant and elusive a dream these long years." He hesitated, grasping at his new reality. "It's hard to adjust to this as a fact of our lives. My preoccupations have to change, and find new addresses and more peaceful residences to inhabit. I'm a lot less lithe in my thoughts than my actions sometimes, it seems. May I ask about how I should delineate our own territories and new boundaries? Is this something I need to negotiate with Carthage and its *suffetes* about? They would see these as their ancestral lands, for sure."

Scipio scoffed, a little in his cup, "In Jupiter's name, Masinissa, you can be too considerate for your own good. The vanquished have lost their entitlements and the properties of their forefathers. Leave them the coasts. Let them fish and trade. Don't threaten Utica or Hadrumentum, and I would suggest you don't go further than Hippo Diarrhytus in the north and Acholla in the south, but, beyond those provinces, slice as deep as you dare or as far as you can before you meet resistance. As for your own adjustments, you should be able to find peace quicker than me. Rome has multiple enemies and a zeal for conquest. Between us, we have neutered Carthage to your east, to your west is a secure boundary with the great mystery of the endless ocean beyond, and your south is not worth having. Leave the sands to the camels and the Troglodytae. There is no civilisation without water. It should be easy for you to be happy in your realm. It's time for you to put your adventures and risks to bed, and guide your people towards an easier life. It's a privileged thing to reach that point in your life where you can let your adventures find a peaceful, contented home exclusively in your imagination, like captive genies in their bottles. I'm sure they're more fun, and a whole lot safer, when you are the solitary author of them." Scipio, satisfied with his own point, looked down, swirled his tightened lips around his teeth and rubbed the back of his neck, all physical indicators of an encroaching awkwardness that Masinissa read easily.

"That's the easy part out of the way," Scipio stated with a little resignation and a hint of sorrow. "You know, Mas, I would grant you these lands simply as a payment of my debt to you, but, regrettably, there is something of a *quid quo pro* about this particular gathering. I must ask something of you, and I must do so privately."

The burly guards held open the flaps of the tent silently and, with a few exchanged and concerned glances, all bar Scipio and Masinissa – the architects of a new geopolitical southern landscape – left the tent. Even the sentinels withdrew, leaving the tent empty and eerie.

Masinissa was the first to speak, nudging Scipio towards his demand. "OK, I'm ready. Whatever it is, I'm braced."

Scipio looked at him with more emotion in his gaze than Masinissa had previously seen. "I wonder if you are, my friend. I have to take something from you that may be more precious to you than your country or your own life." The general, so used to being decisive, wavered in his resolve and in his words. Coughing out his own objections, he continued, "I, Rome and everyone now know of your marriage. I'm sure it is a sincere and loving commitment, but hardly anyone – not even you, Mas – are entitled to possess your heart's desire. In the minds of the senate, your new wife is too dangerous. She has turned one husband into a resolute and unyielding enemy of Rome already, and it is their concern that her manipulations might turn another. In our dealing with Syphax before his marriage, he seemed to retain elements of pragmatism and flexibility. When he got married, he seemed to have blinkers attached to him, and we can only surmise that the influence who came to dominate his actions was his, and now your, wife. She has cost Roman lives, and there is a forfeit for that too. She is to be a tribute who will be taken back and paraded through Rome as part of my triumph, and then, depending on the mercy of our people, a decision will be made. She may escape chains, but the alternative may be worse, and – to be frank with you – that is not likely. The mob's views are binary: us and them, friend and enemy, Rome and Carthage. What mercy that would be shown to the soul is rarely shown to the body, and, by the time she has been dragged around the Circus Maximus, there won't be much left of her beauty to engender much pity." Scipio checked himself, realising he had overstepped himself in his grizzly candour. "I'm so sorry. I should spare you this, but I can't. It has to be. I've seen the abasement of kings and queens, and your princess will be ruined, believe me."

Seeing the devastated shock in his comrade in arms and catching the cruelty of his own words and perhaps using them as a frame for a more merciful intimation, Scipio seemed to shift and soften his insistence on the vindictive protocols attached to Rome's victory and added, "If she crosses the sea, that is."

Masinissa stared at him numbly for a while, his mouth going from open slackness to tense rigidity as he fought to suppress the rising tide of chaotic emotions that welled with fury and impotence up into his throat. His thoughts were overwhelmed, darting like bats seeking moths in the crepuscular dying light, until they condensed into a single preoccupation of denial as his mind attempted to make sense of a new reality, which he tried to reduce into an obstacle he could bypass but couldn't for all he tried.

"If she crosses the sea?" he asked, trying to find a foothold in the sheerness of Sophonisba's doom.

"It's all I can offer you, my friend. It is better to say goodbye to someone you love knowing no more harm can come to them. If you let her go into the darkness alive and captive, I know your imagination would terrorise you. The mercy of a free death is a fate not many are lucky to be granted. You're a learned man. Give your love the same escape the Greeks gave Socrates."

Masinissa pondered this option grimly. After a while, as all his dreams slumped and then poured over his edges in a pitiful deluge that cracked apart the tenaciously nurtured capsule of his hopes, he exhaled the faintest of assents. "All right."

There was nothing more to do or say. An embrace or commiseration would be insulting and awkward, and any further discussion pointless. Masinissa knew better than to attempt to plea for clemency. Sophonisba had been condemned by an authority he had no hope of petitioning. As he roused himself to leave, he exchanged a final glance with Scipio and saw in his eyes pity and guilt, emotions he knew the consul had mastery over for all their sincerity. He left the tent despondently.

The others, perhaps eavesdropping through the canvas or more likely being in possession of the collective intuition of men who knew when one of their own was in the whirls of grief, asked him no questions as he emerged and allowed him to put a shroud of silence over himself, to brood on his obligation and heartbreaking loss. Their instincts were confirmed in the vacancy with which Masinissa rode, as they all went out of the camp. They knew better than to pose direct questions, but, finally, Ari broke ranks, unable any longer to contain his solicitous urges.

"Is there anything we can do?" he asked.

Masinissa shook his head. "No, but there is something I must do. There is one more sacrifice to put on this war's altar, my brother." He gave his thoughtful Libyan companion a tap of farewell, offered a desultory, broken wave to the group, and kicked his mount ahead, not able to suffer company whilst he brooded on his lover's demise and their trampled destiny, which he had so cherished.

*

The ride to Cirta was spent in a cloud. He drank heavily through the days and harder still in the nights to bludgeon some kind of inebriated oblivion into himself. As he spied the remote precincts of the city in the distance, he tossed the wineskins away and let his despair return with his lucidity. For all his fragility, his duty was to show fortitude and resolve, and carry Sophonisba to her rest with the dignity and care she had a right to. She would see the last of this world in the arms of her man, feeling his strength and not his trembles. How do you prepare for such a revelation and such a finality? His role was as a protector, someone who would draw his sword valiantly, and defend her honour and her breath to her last. She would be convinced, of course, given the starkness of the choice, but would she view him as treacherous and recreant to not accompany her into the afterlife? The thought had crossed his mind. They would not be the first tragic lovers to plunge out of existence hand in hand. His secondary duty, though, was to his nation, and to the men who had died and survived in their many altered ways to give birth to it. He had to live, and she had to die. That was the bitter truth.

With painful pragmatism, he took heed of Scipio's hint and found the most reliable apothecary in the city. He received a quizzical glance when he made his request, but left with his mysterious errand undetected and with a generous dose of *Conium maculatum* swinging like a hangman's noose from a pouch at his belt.

As he entered their villa, waiting for his presence to be felt, much of his constrictions, of mind and body returned. It was as if his agony was creating an analogue of his youthful anxieties, and he was back in the days when Sophonisba was a thrill only of his imagination and the nearness of her was as stressful as it was arousing. Oh for the days when the merest contiguity between them made his heart race!

The reanimation of those endless summer days spent chasing after each other in the cool, penumbral lanes of the Byrsa was revived in her sudden pounce onto him, her hands reaching to cover his eyes and preserve her anonymity with all the playful relish of her youthful self. She squeezed harder and flatter over his sockets, depriving him of the corners of light her fingers had overlooked initially, and wrapped her legs with more limpet tightness around his torso, as if urging him to make the hesitant guess at the identity of his captor.

"It's you, sweetheart," he offered, not able to disguise the crushing sadness in his heart.

Hearing the empty dejection in his voice, she released the grip of her hands and legs, and dropped to the ground. With masculine urgency, she spun him around to face her, in a motion that required some force, as the large, reluctant mass of sorrow that was her love had no power of its own to help her, being incapacitated by the horrific news he was forced to bear.

"What is it?" Sophonisba urged, holding Masinissa by his triceps, squeezing hard into the muscles, digging into him for information and perhaps a transfusion of his physical power into her sudden panic, with her fingernails pricking some resolution into him.

His tears held in his eyes, pooling in a forlorn, aqueous membrane over his sclera, like raindrops briefly holding on to their landed integrity, refusing for the moment to breach his ducts and moisten his cheeks. Resisting his urge to smother her and hide himself in her softness, he took her arms with the same firmness she had held him and let the end of them gasp out of him. "I am so sorry, darling; so, so sorry."

Sophonisba's grip hardened, and if she had possessed the power to shake him, she would have. Instead, she just put tremors into herself as her frustrations and anxieties ricocheted back into her. "What?" she asked.

And, after Masinissa had repeated his apology with an abjection and rigidity somewhere between a ragdoll and a statue, her voice modulated into the frenetic extremes of her register. "*What?*" she repeated, clawing at him urgently.

This compelled Masinissa to splutter out her awful sentence. "Scipio has said he must take you, as part of his triumph. The only mercy he will spare you is if you take your life. Otherwise, the mob of Rome will have their way with you. I know cruelty and degradation. I have seen the vilest extremities of war, and I know how mercy turns callous, and how men lose their humanity and treat others like animals to be tormented and abused as if nothing resided in them but the flesh. Darling, have no misapprehension about them. They will tear you apart like hounds, and their pleasure would only amplify with your suffering."

Such a fate was never going to be easy to digest, but Sophonisba passed through the phases of shock, fear, denial, mourning and acceptance in quick, barely acknowledged succession. Her grief for herself passed over her in wavering flickers. She skipped any attempt at bargaining, rebounding her pointless questions numbly back into herself. After a few minutes of internal wrestling, she sank to the ground and sat in an eerie repose, part of her seemingly already vacating her body, perhaps voyaging ahead to make supplications for the rest of her at the gateways of the next world.

Masinissa looked at her, his heart full of pity, helplessness and loss. He sank by her side, searching for condolences and comforts in his mind and body, but finding nothing adequate for the tragedy that had so suddenly befallen her.

He started to cradle her mutely, attempting to allay her terror with a gently soothing motion, as if his wife were a neonate crying out ignorant tears, not a tortured, defeated soul who was all too aware of the preciousness of the world she was soon to be removed from. In one of his tangential thoughts, which were flying off him like volcanic plumes, he wondered if they might make love a final time, but realised quickly that this gentle rocking was the closest approximation to that intimacy that they had left. Lovemaking needed life. How could he arouse himself with Sophonisba just then? For all the love he held for her in his afflicted heart, he couldn't pump his life and his love through himself and up into her then. No seed would find root. She was nearly dust, and it would be the satisfaction of a selfish urge to attempt to arouse someone stumbling through their last moments and trying to make a peace in the turmoil of their last breaths.

It was a misplaced kindness and the desperation of an already castaway passion to even consider attempting to clamber together to an ecstatic final moment, as inapt as laughter at her wake. Masinissa lost all sense of time as he succumbed to emotional exhaustion and the gentle lapping of his own body against Sophonisba's, which – whilst failing to soothe either of them – gave them an interlude of sweetness that would have to suffice as a final parting. He wondered if he could offer her wine and some oblivion, but she didn't ask for it so he thought better of it. He couldn't lead now, only aid her and offer what solace he could.

She turned to him, kissed him with the softness and finality of someone putting their lips to the brow of the recently deceased, foreshadowing his own imminent action, and gave him an almost peaceful, lambent gaze. This gave Masinissa a cocktail of warmth and bitterness, which he drank with the eagerness of a man desiccated by days in the desert or perhaps from the knowledge that such arid wastelands were just ahead of him. Perhaps her anguish made her taciturn, or perhaps she wanted to focus simply on Masinissa, and he on her, as her words would do no more than trace her despair. Like a woman with only her loosening fingers attaching her to the parapet, she merely gazed deep into Masinissa's eyes, letting the muscles of her face and hands provide her with a semblance of eloquence.

With a fond stroke of his cheek, she added another simple question to her earlier one, the answer to which had torn everything from her, "How?" This was said with a sad pragmatism that hinted at her resignation and readiness to go, to leave him at least until his own death promised to reunite them.

With a clumsiness that betrayed his torment, Masinissa reached for his small sack of poison and gave it to her with a ceremony reminiscent of their exchanges during their betrothal, albeit this time with a far bleaker import. "*Conium maculatum*," he declared. As she appeared puzzled by the Latin description, he clarified, "Hemlock."

Sophonisba took the pouch, turned it in her hand in a play of idleness that was more paralysis and said with heart-breaking resignation, "The creeping Greek poison. I suppose there are worse ways to move between the worlds. It was Socrates's ticket after all. What do we do, darling? What do you do now? No, let's don't dwell on such matters. You will be safe, and I will wait for you. We have made it back to each other, and the gods will accept us as the pair they created us to be. One of us was always going to bury the other. If you mourn inconsolably like an old dog and cease your own breaths tomorrow, or live deep into the years ahead, it won't matter to me. It will be the same. Just hold me until I go, forgive my body any of its final betrayals and my mouth of any bitter last words as the curtain falls over my eyes and heart, and my fears scratch some asperity from my spirit. Maybe I'll be lucky and go like that lame, old dog looking at its master, with all the devotion for which those constant canines are renowned."

As Masinissa reeled and brought his hands to his mouth – half in prayer, half in anguish – Sophonisba intercepted him and tugged his face into the vulnerable part of her neck, between her clavicle and earlobe, as if she were a gazelle inviting the lion to conclude his business at the juncture it always seemed to prefer.

"You always loved my perfumes, didn't you? Take this," she commanded, and she scrunched a small scarf that smelt strongly of her musk into his hand. "And this," she added, and she took a small knife and cut a generous lock of her hair with it. "The scent in the scarf will fade, but wrap this strand of me in it and I will always be there. Always."

Masinissa heaved a sigh in an attempt to exert some control over his collapse. He couldn't manage equanimity, but he showed more love than sorrow in his embrace, and Sophonisba gave him another squeeze.

"Don't worry, sweetheart," she declared, "within the hour I'll be waiting nervously to meet Tanit, I'm sure. Don't mourn me. I'm always here." And she touched him on the ample pectoral that shielded his aching heart, but not from the arrows that assailed it presently.

Perhaps not being able to stretch their agonies any further, and sensing Masinissa's irresolution and helplessness, she took the apothecary's pouch and, in a fluid motion, drank the crypt-cold tea within it. The recoil of her gullet as she swallowed announced her fate more than any lugubrious fanfare the shell of her might receive on the next day, the first without her in this world.

Holding herself still for a moment, almost savouring the unique taste of the poison before it performed it's constrictions on her, her thoughts turned, and she offered a final kindness to Masinissa, exempting him from fidelity to her deactivated womb, which would now grow no life from his seed. "Have children, my love; enjoy the play of sons and daughters, and the comfort of heirs. I cannot deny you what I yearned for us. Please." She gave his desolate face a cupped caress, annulling any of his future indiscretions in her death forfeit. She knew the departed surrender any right to magnanimity or even opinion, but knew her gesture would ease the haunting guilt Masinissa would feel when he took another woman to his bed.

Evacuated of hope, Masinissa strained for a fraction of the power that he rode and killed with, his soul acquiring the emaciated frailty that it would take his body many years to emulate. He kissed his wife on the cheek without the final passion her tenderness deserved, his bewilderment not so extreme that he would risk his own contamination with the same poison that was just starting to intercept the nerve impulses to his beloved's muscles and would swiftly paralyse her.

He prayed she would lose consciousness before the *Conium maculatum* applied it's final stranglehold and deprived her of air. *Let her drown her last, senseless or soporific,* he beseeched the gods helplessly. He wrapped her tighter into him, his arms offering a soft, misleading refuge, like the shawl a mother swaddles an infant in before allowing them to drop. As her respiration began to be more deliberate and shallow, he knew her words and her voice would soon be the first to abandon him.

Recognising the urgency of her farewell, Sophonisba's eyes glazed with sentiment and, oxygen deprived as she was, she managed a soft, philosophical valediction. "My love, so much of our story has been lived in our dreams. We must yearn a while longer."

The words fell on Masinissa hard, but he galvanised all his spirit to give his brave girl a last honour, reeling in his sorrow and pity, even though his eyes could conceal neither. His body mustered enough resilience to ensure that she left the world with his strength still binding her. "It won't be long, sweetheart; we'll have our brighter days, arm in arm, under a beautiful sun," he assured her desperately.

She smiled wanly at his optimism and faith, and gripped his hand hard as her lungs fought for their last inhalation. Her nails dug deep into his flesh, leaving a residue of her life in a transitory irritation. As she fought her final moments, her eyelids closed more peacefully than the movement of her diaphragm subsided, and Masinissa gazed at his lost love mournfully, attentive to the moment when her spirit would rise away. Sensing the absence, he sighed quietly, any rage drowned in his own anguish.

"There is no always," he whispered to the now empty room, allowing his despair its turn.

With an ember of life still clinging on, Sophonisba's eyes blazed wide in apparent affront, and her fingernails stabbed sharper into him, perhaps attempting to rectify his cynicism as they drew pricks of his blood. "Yes," she rasped, "Yes, there is."

It was her last effort and final consolation, a reassurance Masinissa held to as firmly through the rest of his life as he then clutched the lock of her hair in the gossamer scarf she had given him.

Tapash Chakraborty
Pekka Pietiläinen

The Quantum Hall Effects

Integral and Fractional

Second Enlarged and Updated Edition

With 129 Figures

Springer

Professor Tapash Chakraborty
Institute of Mathematical Sciences
Taramani, Madras 600 113, India

Dr. Pekka Pietiläinen
Dept. of Theoretical Physics
University of Oulu
Linnanmaa, FIN 90570 Oulu, Finland

Series Editors:

Professor Dr. Dres. h. c. Manuel Cardona
Professor Dr. Dres. h. c. Peter Fulde
Professor Dr. Dres. h. c. Klaus von Klitzing
Professor Dr. Dres. h. c. Hans-Joachim Queisser
Max-Planck-Institut für Festkörperforschung, Heisenbergstraße 1,
D-70569 Stuttgart, Germany

Managing Editor:

Dr.-Ing. Helmut K. V. Lotsch
Springer-Verlag, Tiergartenstraße 17, D-69121 Heidelberg, Germany

Originally published with the title The Fractional Quantum Hall Effect

ISBN 3-540-58515-X 2nd Ed. Springer-Verlag Berlin Heidelberg New York

ISBN 3-540-53305-2 1st Ed. Springer-Verlag Berlin Heidelberg New York

Library of Congress Cataloging-in-Publication Data
Chakraborty, T. (Tapash), 1950-
The Quantum Hall Effects: Fractional and Integral/
Tapash Chakraborty, Pekka Pietiläinen. - 2nd enl. and updated ed. p. cm.
Includes bibliographical references and index.
ISBN 0-387-58515-X. - - ISBN 3-540-58515-X
1. Quantum Hall Effect. I. Pietiläinen, P. (Pekka), 1946-. II. Title QC612.H3C46 1995

Typesetting: Camera ready by author
SPIN: 10120721 54/3020 - 5 4 3 2 1 0 - Printed on acid-free paper

Foreword

The experimental discovery of the fractional quantum Hall effect (FQHE) at the end of 1981 by Tsui, Störmer and Gossard was absolutely unexpected since, at this time, no theoretical work existed that could predict new structures in the magnetotransport coefficients under conditions representing the extreme quantum limit. It is more than thirty years since investigations of bulk semiconductors in very strong magnetic fields were begun. Under these conditions, only the lowest Landau level is occupied and the theory predicted a monotonic variation of the resistivity with increasing magnetic field, depending sensitively on the scattering mechanism. However, the experimental data could not be analyzed accurately since magnetic freeze-out effects and the transitions from a degenerate to a nondegenerate system complicated the interpretation of the data. For a two-dimensional electron gas, where the positive background charge is well separated from the two-dimensional system, magnetic freeze-out effects are barely visible and an analysis of the data in the extreme quantum limit seems to be easier. First measurements in this magnetic field region on silicon field-effect transistors were not successful because the disorder in these devices was so large that all electrons in the lowest Landau level were localized. Consequently, models of a spin glass and finally of a Wigner solid were developed and much effort was put into developing the technology for improving the quality of semiconductor materials and devices, especially in the field of two-dimensional electron systems.

The formation of a Wigner lattice has been observed for the two-dimensional electron gas at the helium surface with the consequence that all sorts of unexpected results on two-dimensional systems in semiconductors were assigned to some kind of charge-density-wave or Wigner crystallization. First attempts to explain the FQHE were therefore guided by the picture of a Wigner solid with triangular crystal symmetry. However, a critical analysis of the data demonstrated that the idea of the formation of an incompressible quantum fluid introduced by Laughlin seems to be the most likely explanation.

The theoretical work collected in this book demonstrates that the Laughlin wave function forms a very good basis for a discussion of the FQHE. Even though many questions in the field of FQHE remain unanswered, this book offers a valuable source of information and is the first general review of the work of different groups in this field. The intense activity in the field of high-T_c superconductivity also calls for a book about the FQHE since certain similarities seem to be emerging in the theoretical treatment of the quantum Hall effect and that of high-T_c superconductivity.

I hope that this book will inspire scientists to new ideas.

Stuttgart
June 1988

Klaus von Klitzing

On the theoretical side, fractional statistics objects – the *anyons*, have fired the imagination of several researchers investigating the phenomenon of high-temperature superconductivity. Although their relevance in that field has not been proven, anyons gained credibility at a very early stage as the elementary excitations in the fractional quantum Hall state. Recent theoretical studies have indicated that going from electrons to fermions with a Chern-Simons field results in a very useful approach to the understanding of the behavior when the lowest Landau level is half filled by electrons.

All of these issues and more, have been discussed here to make the present edition more up to date. A major addition in the second edition is a *brief* survey of the integer quantum Hall effect which is intended to make the book more self-contained. The emphasis is however, still as in the first edition, to provide a complete, comprehensive review of the exciting field of the fractional quantum Hall effect.

Madras, Oulu, July, 1994

Tapash Chakraborty
Pekka Pietiläinen

Preface

In the field of the fractional quantum Hall effect, we have witnessed tremendous theoretical and experimental developments in recent years. Our intention here is to present a general survey of most of the theoretical work in this area. In doing so, we have also tried to provide the details of formal steps, which, in many cases, are avoided in the literature. Our effort is motivated by the hope that the present compilation of theoretical work will encourage a nonexpert to explore this fascinating field, and at the same time, that it will provide guidelines for further study in this field, in particular on many of the open problems highlighted in this review. Although the focus is on the theoretical investigations, to see these in their right perspective, a brief review of the experimental results on the excitation gap is also presented. This review is of course, by no means complete; the field continues to present new surprises, and more theoretical work is still emerging. However we hope that the compilation in its present form will to some extent satisfy the need of the experts, nonexperts and the curious.

Stuttgart, Oulu, January, 1988

Tapash Chakraborty
Pekka Pietiläinen

* * *

After the first edition of the book was published, there were several interesting developments in the field of fractional quantum Hall effect. Most notably, the experimental evidence of the spin-reversed ground state and quasiparticles which had been predicted earlier in the theoretical studies. Similarly, experimental verification of the fractional charge of the quasiparticles is also a siginificant achievement. Magnetoluminescence experiments are rapidly opening up an entirely new route to study the quantum Hall effect, and the elusive phase transition of the incompressible quantum liquid state to Wigner crystal is becoming more and more transparent in experiments.

Acknowledgments

We wish to express our gratitude to Professor Peter Fulde and Professor Klaus von Klitzing for offering us the opportunity to write this review and for their encouragement and support during the course of this work. We are very much indebted to Professor von Klitzing for writing a foreword for this publication.

One of us (T. C.) would like to thank all his former colleagues at the Max-Planck-Institute, Stuttgart for their invaluable criticism and advice. Among others, he would like to thank particularly T. K. Lee, I. Peschel and G. Stollhoff for critically reading part of the manuscript and offering many suggestions for improvement. He also thanks B. I. Halperin, H. L. Störmer, A. Pinczuk, A. H. MacDonald, F. D. M. Haldane, F. C. Zhang, G. Fano, S. M. Girvin, D. C. Tsui, P. A. Maksym and R. G. Clark for granting permission to reproduce some of the figures from their publications.

The other (P. P.) would like to thank Professor Fulde for arranging a visit to the Max-Planck-Institute, Stuttgart, during the final stage of preparation of the first edition. He also thanks the Department of Theoretical Physics, University of Oulu for support.

The manuscript was typeset by the authors using $\mathcal{AMS}$-$\TeX$. We would like to thank Gabriele Kruljac at the Computer Center of the Max-Planck-Institute, for her assistance in programming. We would also like to thank Dr. A. M. Lahee from Springer-Verlag, whose careful reading of the manuscript and numerous suggestions have greatly improved the presentation.

Last but not the least, we would like to thank our families for their patience and understanding.

In preparing the second edition, T. C. greatfully acknowledges excellent help from Geof Aers at the National Research Council, Ottawa, Canada, who read the entire manuscript and offered numereous suggestions to improve the presentation. T. C. also greatfully acknowledges the kind hospitality of Professor von Klitzing during a visit (July-August, 1994) to the MPI, Stuttgart, where the final touches to the second edition were made. He would also like to express thanks to sveral colleagues at MPI, Stuttgart for their help and encouragement, in particular, Rolf Gerhardts, Rolf Haug and Dieter Weiss, for many helpful discussions.

Contents

1. Quantum Hall Effect: The Basics 1
1.1 Two-Dimensional Electron Gas 1
1.2 Electrons in a Strong Magnetic Field 4

2. Integral Quantum Hall Effect 8
2.1 Experimental Work 8
2.2 Classical Hall Effect 11
2.3 Quantum Mechanical Approach 11
2.4 Integral Quantization: Theoretical Work 12
2.5 Kubo Formula Approach 13
2.6 The Gauge Invariance Approach 15
2.7 The Topological Invariance Approach 17

3. Other Developments 20
3.1 Electron Localization in the Quantum Hall Regime 20
3.2 Renormalization Group Approach 22
3.3 Current-Carrying Edge States 24
3.4 Transport in Edge Channels and Other Topics 26

4. Fractional Quantum Hall Effect: Introduction 32

5. Ground State 39
5.1 Finite-Size Studies: Rectangular Geometry 39
5.2 Laughlin's Theory 45
5.3 Spherical Geometry 53
5.4 Monte Carlo Results 58
5.5 Reversed Spins in the Ground State 61
5.6 Finite Thickness Correction 64
5.7 Liquid-Solid Transition 66
5.8 Magnetoluminescence 71

6. Elementary Excitations 87
6.1 Quasiholes and Quasiparticles 88
6.2 Finite-Size Studies: Rectangular Geometry 97
6.3 Spin-Reversed Quasiparticles 99

6.4 Spherical Geometry 103
6.5 Monte Carlo Results 105
6.6 Experimental Investigations of the Energy Gap 113
6.7 Fractional Statistics and the Anyons 120
6.8 The Hierarchy: Higher Order Fractions 131
6.9 Tilted-Field Effects and Reversed-Spin States 144

7. Collective Modes: Intra-Landau Level 162
7.1 Finite-Size Studies: Spherical Geometry 162
7.2 Rectangular Geometry: Translational Symmetry 163
7.3 Spin Waves 173
7.4 Single Mode Approximation: Magnetorotons 177

8. Collective Modes: Inter-Landau Level 192
8.1 Kohn's Theorem 192
8.2 Filled Landau Level 194
8.3 Fractional Filling: Single Mode Approximation 199
8.4 Fractional Filling: Finite-Size Studies 203

9. Further Topics 208
9.1 Effect of Impurities 208
9.2 Quantization Condition 214
9.3 Higher Landau Levels 221
9.4 Even Denominator Filling Fractions 225
9.5 Multiple Layer Systems 237
9.6 Nature of Long-Range Order in the Laughlin State 240

10. Open Problems and New Directions 247

Appendices
A The Landau Wave Function in the Symmetric Gauge 249
B Kubo Formalism for the Hall Conductivity 253
C The Hypernetted-Chain Primer 257
D Repetition of the Intra-Landau-level Mode in the Inter-Landau-level Mode 267
E Characteristic Scale Values 273

References 274

Subject Index 299

1. Quantum Hall Effect: The Basics

The quantization of the Hall effect discovered by *von Klitzing* et al. [1.1] in 1980 is a remarkable macroscopic quantum phenomenon which occurs in two-dimensional electron systems at low temperatures and strong perpendicular magnetic fields. Under these conditions, the Hall-conductivity exhibits plateaus at integral multiples of e^2/h (a universal constant). The striking result is the accuracy of the quantization (better than a part in ten million) which is totally indifferent to impurities or geometric details of the two-dimensional system. Each plateau is accompanied by a deep minimum in the diagonal resistivity, indicating a dissipationless flow of current. In 1982, there was yet another surprise in this field. Working with much higher mobility samples, *Tsui* et al. [1.2] discovered the fractional quantization of the Hall conductivity. The physical mechanisms responsible for the integer quantum Hall effect (IQHE) and the fractional quantum Hall effect (FQHE) are quite different, despite the apparent similarity of the experimental results. In the former case, the role of the random impurity potential is quite decisive, while in the latter case, electron-electron interaction plays a predominant role resulting in a unique collective phenomenon.

In the following chapters, we shall briefly describe the theoretical and experimental developments in the QHE. It should be mentioned, however, that the QHE has been one of the most active fields of research in condensed matter physics for over a decade. It is therefore, quite impossible to describe here all the details of the major developments. Our aim here is to touch upon the most significant theoretical and experimental work to construct a reasonably consistent picture of the QHE. For more details on the topics discussed, the reader is encouraged to read the original work cited here and some of the reviews available in the literature [1.3–11].

1.1 Two-Dimensional Electron Gas

The major impetus in the studies of the QHE is due to experimental realization of almost ideal two-dimensional electron systems. The electrons are dynamically two-dimensional because they are free to move in only two spatial dimensions. In the third dimension, they have quantized energy levels (in reality, the wave functions have a finite spatial extent in the third dimension [1.12]). In the following, we provide a very brief discussion on the systems where the electron layers are created. For details see the reviews by *Ando* et al. [1.12] and *Störmer* [1.13].

Electron layers have been created in many different systems. Electrons on the surface of liquid helium provides an almost ideal two-dimensional system [1.14,15]. They are trapped on the surface by a combination of an external field and an image potential. The electron concentration in this system is, however, very low ($10^5 - 10^9$ cm^{-2}) and the system behaves classically. The high-density electron systems where the QHE is usually observed are typically created in the Metal-Oxide-Semiconductor Field Effect Transistor (the MOSFET) and in semiconductor heterojunctions.

A schematic picture of an n-channel Si-MOSFET is shown in Fig. 1.1(a). The system consists of a semiconductor (p-Si) which has a plane interface with a thin film of insulator (SiO_2), the opposite side of which carries a metal gate electrode. Application of a voltage (gate voltage V_G) between the gate and the Si/SiO_2 interface results in bending of the electron energy bands. For a strong enough electric field, as the bottom of the conduction band is pushed down below the Fermi energy E_F, electrons accumulate in a two-dimensional quasi-triangular potential well close to the interface [Fig. 1.1(b)]. As the width of the well is small (~ 50Å), electron motion perpendicular to the interface is quantized but the electrons move freely parallel to the interface. In the plane, the energy spectrum is

$$\varepsilon_i(\boldsymbol{k}) = \varepsilon_i^0 + \frac{\hbar^2 k_\parallel^2}{2m^*}$$

where m^* is the effective mass of the electrons, $k_\parallel$ is the two-dimensional wave vector and ε_i^0 is the bottom of the corresponding subband. The system is called an inversion layer because here the charge carriers are the electrons while the semiconductor is p-type.

At low temperatures ($kT \ll \Delta E$, the subband spacing) the electrons are trapped in the lowest subband and the system is purely two-dimensional. The MOSFET is quite useful in the present study because by varying the gate voltage the electron concentration can be varied within a wide range ($n_0 \sim 0 - 10^{13}$cm^{-2}).

Two-dimensional electron layers are also created in semiconductor heterostructures at a nearly perfectly lattice-matched semiconductor/semiconductor interface. One such widely used system is the GaAs/$Al_xGa_{1-x}As$ (0 <

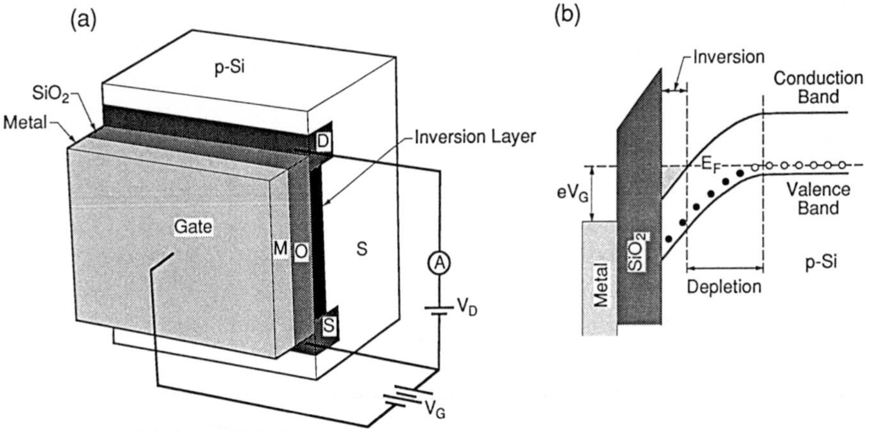

Fig. 1.1. (a) Schematic view of a Si-MOSFET and (b) energy level diagram

$x \leq 1$) heterostructure. The lattice constants of GaAs and $Al_xGa_{1-x}As$ are almost the same so that the interface is nearly free from any disorder. The band gap of the alloy is wider than that of GaAs and it increases with the aluminum concentration x. Carriers in the neighborhood of the hetero-

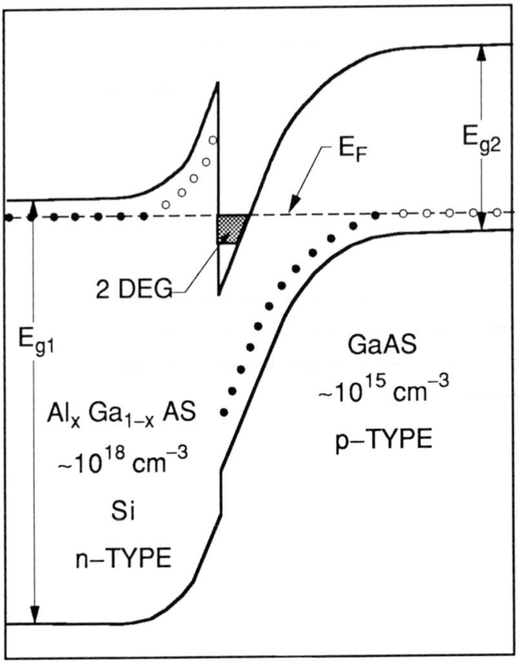

Fig. 1.2. Energy diagram at a GaAs-heterostructure interface

junction transfer from the doped AlGaAs alloy across the interface to the low-lying band edge states of the narrow band gap material (GaAs). The electric field due to the charge transfer bends the energy bands as shown in Fig. 1.2. A quasi-triangular potential well (~ 100Å) formed in the GaAs traps the electrons as two-dimensional carriers.

The mobile carriers are spatially separated from their parent ionized impurities via modulation doping. This leads to very high carrier mobilities and, in fact, the FQHE was discovered in these high-mobility GaAs-heterostructures [1.13]. However, unlike MOSFETs the electron concentration in heterostructures can be varied only within a very narrow range. Carrier densities in these systems typically range from $1 \times 10^{11}\mathrm{cm}^{-2}$ to $1 \times 10^{12}\mathrm{cm}^{-2}$.

1.2 Electrons in a Strong Magnetic Field

Let us begin with the problem of a free electron (with effective mass m^*) in a uniform magnetic field B. The Hamiltonian is then written

$$\mathcal{H}_0 = \left(\Pi_x^2 + \Pi_y^2\right)/2m^* \tag{1.1}$$

where, $\boldsymbol{\Pi} = -\mathrm{i}\hbar\nabla + \frac{e}{c}\boldsymbol{A}$ is the kinetic momentum and $\boldsymbol{A}$ is the vector potential which is related to the magnetic field in the manner, $\boldsymbol{B} = \nabla \times \boldsymbol{A}$. Following *Kubo* et al. [1.16] we introduce the center coordinates of the cyclotron motion (X, Y) as

$$X = x - \xi, \qquad Y = y - \eta \tag{1.2}$$

where

$$\xi = (c/eB)\Pi_y, \qquad \eta = -(c/eB)\Pi_x \tag{1.3}$$

are the relative coordinates. It can be easily seen that (ξ, η) represents a cyclotron motion with frequency

$$\omega_\mathrm{c} = \frac{eB}{m^*c}, \tag{1.4}$$

(cyclotron frequency). Defining the magnetic length

$$\ell_0 \equiv \left(\frac{\hbar c}{eB}\right)^{\frac{1}{2}} \tag{1.5}$$

(cyclotron radius) and from the commutation relation

$$[\xi, \eta] = -\mathrm{i}\ell_0^2$$

it is clear that ξ and η are subject to an uncertainty of order ℓ_0. The Hamiltonian (1.1) is now rewritten in terms of (ξ, η) as

$$\mathcal{H}_0 = \frac{\hbar\omega_c}{2\ell_0^2}\left(\xi^2 + \eta^2\right) \tag{1.6}$$

whose eigenenergies are the discrete *Landau levels* [1.17,18]

$$E_n = \left(n + \tfrac{1}{2}\right)\hbar\omega_c, \qquad n = 0, 1, 2, \ldots \tag{1.7}$$

The Hamiltonian (1.6) does not contain (X, Y) which means that electrons in cyclotron motion with different center coordinates have the same energy. The center coordinates also follow the commutation rule, $[X, Y] = \mathrm{i}\ell_0^2$.

Choosing now the Landau gauge[1] such that the vector potential $\boldsymbol{A}$ has only one nonvanishing component, say, $A_y = Bx$, the Hamiltonian is

$$\mathcal{H}_0 = \frac{1}{2m^*}\left[p_x^2 + \left(p_y + \frac{eB}{c}x\right)^2\right]. \tag{1.8}$$

The variables are easily separable and an eigenfunction is written in the form

$$\phi = \mathrm{e}^{\mathrm{i}k_y y}\chi(x) \tag{1.9}$$

where the usual identification is made, $p_y = -\mathrm{i}\hbar\partial/\partial y \rightarrow \hbar k_y$. The function $\chi(x)$ is the eigenfunction of the time-independent Schrödinger equation

$$-\frac{\hbar^2}{2m^*}\chi'' + \tfrac{1}{2}m^*\omega_c^2\left(x - X\right)^2\chi = E\chi(x) \tag{1.10}$$

where $X = -k_y\ell_0^2$. The above equation is easily recognized as the Schrödinger equation corresponding to a *harmonic oscillator* of spring constant $\hbar\omega_c = \hbar^2/m^*\ell_0^2$, with equilibrium point at X.

The eigenfunction (ignoring the normalization factor) is now written

$$\phi_{nX} = \mathrm{e}^{\mathrm{i}k_y y}\exp\left[-(x - X)^2/2\ell_0^2\right] H_n\left[(x - X)/\ell_0\right] \tag{1.11}$$

with H_n the Hermite polynomial. The functions are extended in y and localized in x. The localization remains unaffected under a gauge transformation. When the system is confined in a rectangular cell with sides L_x

---

[1] The other choice of gauge viz. the symmetric gauge is discussed in Appendix A

and L_y, the degeneracy of each Landau level (number of allowed states) is, in fact, the number of allowed values of k_y, such that the center X lies between 0 and L_x. Using periodic boundary conditions we get, $k_y = 2\pi n_y/L_y$, with n_y an integer. The allowed values of n_y are then determined by the condition

$$X = \frac{2\pi n_y}{L_y}\ell_0^2, \qquad 0 < X < L_x\,. \tag{1.12}$$

The degeneracy N_s can then be expressed in terms of the magnetic length ℓ_0 as

$$N_\mathrm{s} = \frac{L_x L_y}{2\pi\ell_0^2}\,. \tag{1.13}$$

Equation (1.13) can also be reexpressed in terms of the magnetic flux $\boldsymbol{\Phi}$ and the flux quantum $\boldsymbol{\Phi}_0 = hc/e$ as

$$N_\mathrm{s} = \frac{e}{hc}\boldsymbol{\Phi} = \frac{\boldsymbol{\Phi}}{\boldsymbol{\Phi}_0}. \tag{1.14}$$

The Landau level degeneracy is thus the total number of flux quanta in the external magnetic field. One other important quantity is the dimensionless density of the electrons expressed as the *filling factor* of the Landau level

$$\nu = 2\pi\ell_0^2 n_0, \tag{1.15}$$

where n_0 is the electron density in the system.

Thus far, we have ignored the presence of any impurities in the system. In a more general case, the Hamiltonian is written as

$$\mathcal{H} = \mathcal{H}_0 + U(\boldsymbol{r}) \tag{1.16}$$

where $U(\boldsymbol{r})$ is the electron-impurity interaction. Following [1.16] the equation of motion for (X, Y) can be derived as

$$\begin{aligned} \dot{X} &= \frac{\mathrm{i}}{\hbar}[\mathcal{H}, X] = \frac{\mathrm{i}}{\hbar}[U, X] = \frac{\ell_0^2}{\hbar}\frac{\partial U}{\partial y} \\ \dot{Y} &= \frac{\mathrm{i}}{\hbar}[\mathcal{H}, Y] = \frac{\mathrm{i}}{\hbar}[U, Y] = -\frac{\ell_0^2}{\hbar}\frac{\partial U}{\partial x} \end{aligned} \tag{1.17}$$

where we have employed the commutation relation: $[x, \eta] = -[y, \xi] = \mathrm{i}\ell_0^2$. Due to the presence of the impurity potential, the degeneracy of the states with different (X, Y) is lifted and the Landau levels instead of being a series of δ-functions broaden into bands (Fig. 1.3).

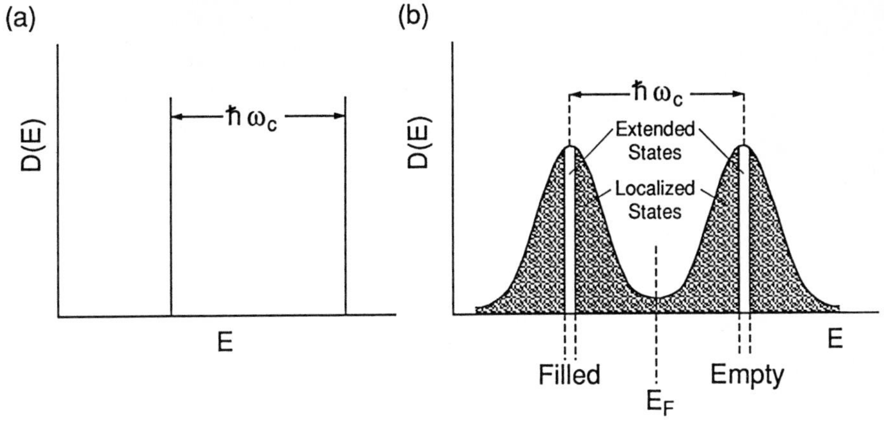

Fig. 1.3. Density of states versus energy in a 2DEG. (a) impurity-free system, $U = 0$. (b) $U \neq 0$, with mobility edges and the localized regions

The density of states $D(E)$ of the two-dimensional electron system is an important quantity for the understanding of the QHE. Several authors have contributed theoretically and experimentally to our present understanding of the density of states (DOS) in the presence of a random potential [1.19–26]. The DOS can be determined by measuring thermodynamic quantities like magnetization [1.27], electron heat capacity [1.28] and quantum oscillations of the chemical potential [1.29], from magnetocapacitance measurements [1.30], from activated conduction [1.31], from the temperature dependence of the slope of the Hall plateau [1.32] or from an analysis of the shape of the Hall plateau [1.33]. A review of the experimental results is available in the literature [1.34]. The results of all these studies can be stated as follows: The DOS between the $D(E)$ peaks is approximately constant and is a significant fraction of the value at zero magnetic field. The width of each peak is $\Gamma \sim B^{\frac{1}{2}}$. It is also established now that there are localized states in the tails of $D(E)$ and extended states which lead to a finite conductivity σ_{xx} and to a contribution to the Hall current in the region of the maximum of $D(E)$. The regions of localized states are known as the *mobility gaps* and their boundaries with the regions of extended states are called the *mobility edges*. For further details on the issue of localization, see Sect. 3.1.

2. Integral Quantum Hall Effect

Before the discovery of the IQHE by *von Klitzing* et al. [2.1] there were experimental indications of the existence of such an effect. The possibility of ρ_{xy} quantization had also been considered theoretically by *Ando* et al. [2.2]. Plateau-like behavior had actually been observed in ρ_{xy} [2.3] and in σ_{xy} [2.4]. However, accurate quantization of the Hall plateau was not achieved in those experiments.

2.1 Experimental Work

In Fig. 2.1, we present the experimental results of *von Klitzing* [2.1,5,6] for a Si-MOSFET inversion layer in a magnetic field of $B = 19$T. The diagonal resistance $R_{xx}(\propto \rho_{xx})$ and the Hall resistance $R_{xy}(= R_{\rm H} = \rho_{xy})$ are plotted as a function of gate voltage $V_{\rm G}$ ($\propto$ electron concentration). The diagonal resistance is seen to vanish at different regions of $V_{\rm G}$, indicating a current flow without any dissipation. In the same regions, R_{xy} develops *plateaus* with $R_{xy} = h/ne^2$ (n integer). The quantization condition on the plateaus are found to be obeyed with *extreme accuracy*. The experimental accuracy so far achieved is better than one part in 10^8 while resistivities as low as $\rho_{xx} < 10^{-10}\Omega/\square$ have been established [2.7]. Another interesting feature of the above findings is that the quantization condition of the conductivity is very insensitive to the details of the sample (geometry, amount of disorder etc.). A comparison between the quantized Hall resistance of a silicon MOSFET with GaAs heterostructures showed no difference within the experimental uncertainty of 4×10^{-10} [2.8]. The quantized Hall resistance is more stable and more reproducible than any wire resistor and from 1 January 1990, the quantized Hall resistance has been used as an international reference resistor. The Hall resistance of a quantized plateau is expressed as $R_{\rm H} = R_{\rm K}/n$ where $R_{\rm K} \approx 25812.807 \pm 0.05\Omega$ is the *von Klitzing constant* which appears to be a universal quantity [2.9,10]. For metrological applications a fixed value of $R_{\rm K-90} = 25812.807\Omega$ is used.

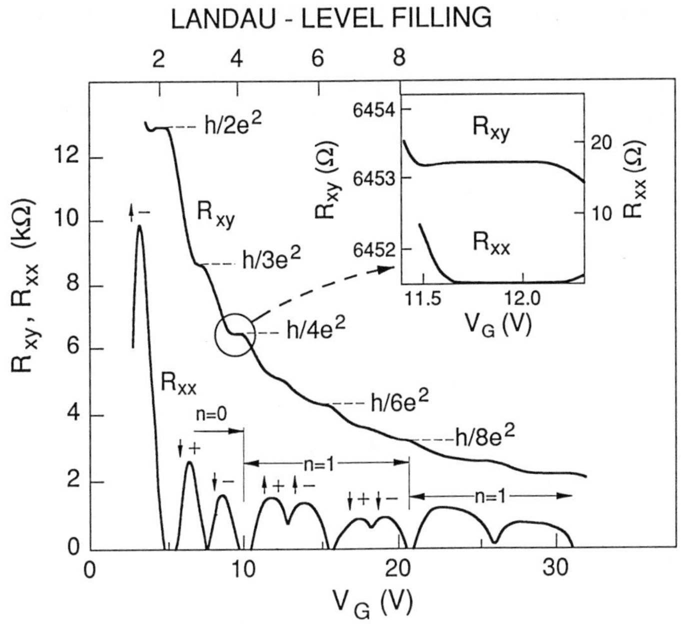

Fig. 2.1. The quantum Hall effect observed in Si(100) MOS inversion layer in a magnetic field of $B = 19\,\mathrm{T}$ at temperature $T = 1.5\,\mathrm{K}$. The diagonal resistance and the Hall resistance are shown as a function of gate voltage ($\propto$ to electron concentration). The oscillations in R_{xx} are labeled by the Landau level index (n), spin ($\uparrow\downarrow$) and the valley ($\pm$). The upper scale indicates the Landau level filling described in the text, and the inset shows the details of a plateau for $B = 13.5\,\mathrm{T}$ [2.6]

The accurate quantization of the Hall resistance can be used to determine the value of the fine-structure constant α [2.1]. This is a quantity of fundamental importance in quantum electrodynamics and is related to the Hall resistance in the manner

$$\alpha = \tfrac{1}{2}\mu_0 c \frac{e^2}{h} = \tfrac{1}{2}\mu_0 c (R_\mathrm{K})^{-1}$$

where both the permeability of the vacuum μ_0 and the velocity of light c are universal constants.

After the initial experiment by von Klitzing et al., there were several other experiments demonstrating integral quantization in a variety of systems. *Tsui* and *Gossard* [2.11] observed the effect in a GaAs-heterostructure. This system was also used by other authors [2.12,13]. Because of the small effective mass m^* of the electrons in GaAs [$m^*(\mathrm{Si})/m^*(\mathrm{GaAs}) > 3$], the Landau level splitting is larger compared to that in Si and the high-quality of the interface results in a high mobility of the two-dimensional electrons

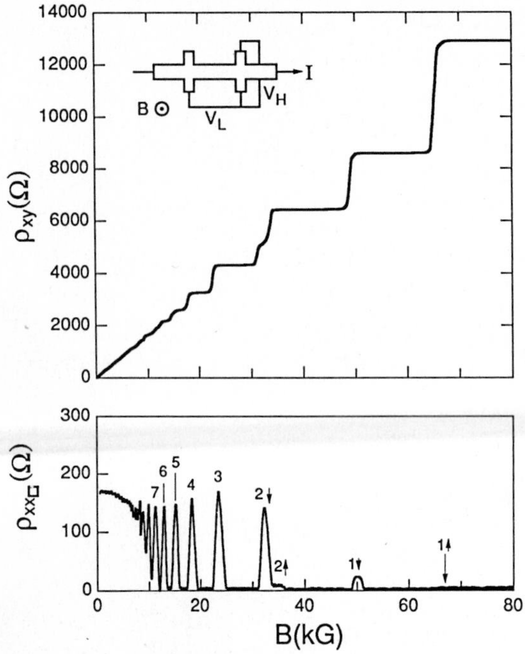

Fig. 2.2. The Hall resistivity ($\rho_{xy} = V_H/I$) and magnetoresistivity ($\rho_{xx} = V_L/I$) of a modulation-doped GaAs-heterostructure. The sample configuration is shown as inset [2.12]

(Fig. 2.2). In addition, the IQHE has been observed in systems like InGaAs/InP [2.14–16], HgTe/CdTe [2.17] and two-dimensional electrons and holes formed in InAs/GaSb heterostructures [2.18], in GaAs heterostructures [2.19], in Si/Ge systems [2.20] and in Si-MOSFETs [2.21].

It is interesting to note that the quantum Hall effect presents a very special situation viz. the conductivity σ_{xx}, describing the current density along the electric field, and resistivity ρ_{xx}, defining the electric field strength along the current path vanish simultaneously. In a two-dimensional system, in the presence of a magnetic field, the current density **j** is related to an electric field **E** in the manner

$$\boldsymbol{j} = \widehat{\sigma}\boldsymbol{E}, \quad \boldsymbol{E} = \widehat{\rho}\boldsymbol{j} \tag{2.1}$$

where $\widehat{\sigma}$ is the conductivity tensor and $\widehat{\rho} = (\widehat{\sigma})^{-1}$ is the resistivity tensor. They are defined as

$$\widehat{\rho} = \begin{pmatrix} \sigma_{xx} & \sigma_{xy} \\ -\sigma_{xy} & \sigma_{xx} \end{pmatrix}^{-1} = \frac{1}{\sigma_{xx}^2 + \sigma_{xy}^2} \begin{pmatrix} \sigma_{xx} & -\sigma_{xy} \\ \sigma_{xy} & \sigma_{xx} \end{pmatrix} \tag{2.2}$$

where we have used the Onsager reciprocity relations [2.22], $\sigma_{xx} = \sigma_{yy}$ and $\sigma_{yx} = -\sigma_{xy}$. Similarly,

$$\widehat{\sigma} = \frac{1}{\rho_{xx}^2 + \rho_{xy}^2} \begin{pmatrix} \rho_{xx} & -\rho_{xy} \\ \rho_{xy} & \rho_{xx} \end{pmatrix} . \tag{2.3}$$

Experimental results show that when a plateau appears, $\rho_{xx} = 0$, which means that, $\sigma_{xx} = \rho_{xx}/(\rho_{xx}^2 + \rho_{xy}^2) = 0$, provided that $\rho_{xy} \neq 0$, and $\sigma_{xy} = -\rho_{xy}/(\rho_{xx}^2 + \rho_{xy}^2) = -1/\rho_{xy}$. In two dimensions, the Hall resistance R_{H} is related to the Hall resistivity ρ_{xy} as $R_{\mathrm{H}} = -\rho_{xy}$, and resistance and resistivity are the same quantity. The dimension of R_{H} is usually expressed as Ω.

2.2 Classical Hall Effect

The motion of an electron moving classically in crossed electric (E_x) and magnetic (B_z) fields is a superposition of a circular motion with frequency ω_{c} and a uniform drift perpendicular to E_x with a velocity $\boldsymbol{v} = (0, v_{\mathrm{D}})$, $v_{\mathrm{D}} = cE_x/B$ [2.23]. The resulting orbit is a *trochoid* and is a consequence of the Lorentz force. The current density is then $\boldsymbol{j} = en_0\boldsymbol{v}$. From our discussion above, we can readily deduce that, $\sigma_{xx} = 0$ and $\sigma_{xy} = -n_0ec/B$. The classical Hall conductivity as a function of electron concentration does not show any quantization. In order to introduce scattering due to random potentials in the system, one adds a term $m\boldsymbol{v}/\tau$, where τ is the scattering relaxation time, to the equation of motion. The resulting diagonal and Hall conductivities are

$$\sigma_{xx} = \frac{n_0e^2\tau}{m}\frac{1}{1+(\omega_{\mathrm{c}}\tau)^2}; \quad \sigma_{xy} = -\frac{n_0ec}{B}\frac{(\omega_{\mathrm{c}}\tau)^2}{1+(\omega_{\mathrm{c}}\tau)^2} = -\frac{n_0ec}{B} + \frac{\sigma_{xx}}{\omega_{\mathrm{c}}\tau}. \tag{2.4}$$

The impurity-free result discussed above is trivially recovered by considering the limit $\omega_{\mathrm{c}}\tau \to \infty$. As we shall see below, this scattering-free situation will occur in very special circumstances.

2.3 Quantum Mechanical Approach

The quantum mechanical results for the dynamics of an electron in a magnetic field are presented in Sect. 1.2. In the case of an electron in crossed electric and magnetic fields, the eigenstates (1.7), (1.9) can be written as [2.24]

$$\begin{aligned} E_{nX} &= (n+\tfrac{1}{2})\hbar\omega_c + eE_x X - \tfrac{1}{2}m^* v_D^2 \\ \phi_{nX} &= e^{ik_y y}\chi(x - X + v_D/\omega_c). \end{aligned} \tag{2.5}$$

These states carry a current in the y-direction. The contribution to the current from an occupied state is

$$\begin{aligned} j_y &= -e\left\langle nX \left| \frac{1}{m^*}\left(p_y + \frac{eBx}{c}\right)\right| nX \right\rangle \\ &= \frac{c}{B}\frac{\partial E_{nX}}{\partial X} = ev_D \end{aligned} \tag{2.6}$$

since, $\dot{\boldsymbol{r}} = \frac{1}{m^*}\left(\boldsymbol{p} - \frac{e}{c}\boldsymbol{A}\right)$. All the electronic states $|nX\rangle$ carry the same Hall current. The total current is then $j_y = n_0 ev_D$ and the Hall conductivity, as discussed above, is readily obtained as $\sigma_{xy} = -n_0 ec/B$. From the definition of the filling factor (1.15), we get the quantization as: $\sigma_{xy} = -\nu e^2/h$. According to the Kubo formula [2.25] (Appendix B), the diagonal term of the conductivity tensor can be expressed entirely in terms of the states at the Fermi surface. The off-diagonal elements of $\widehat{\sigma}$ are, on the other hand, determined by all the states below the Fermi level. Therefore, if the Fermi energy is located inside the mobility gap, $\sigma_{xx} = 0$ (and $\rho_{xx} = 0$) at $T = 0$. For $T \neq 0$, the diagonal conductivity is non-zero, but exponentially small. The non-zero contribution is due to activated excitation of the electrons to the extended states belonging to higher Landau levels, or due to variable-range hopping [2.26]. The Hall-conductivity, σ_H is finite, even at $T = 0$, due to the contribution from extended states below E_F. As the variation of E_F (due to change in n_0 or B) within the mobility gap has no effect on the occupancy of the states (at $T \to 0$), $\sigma_H (= \sigma_{xy})$ remains constant. This accounts for the observation of the plateaus in σ_H as a function of n_0 or B. The accurate quantization of σ_H in the region of a plateau is not, however, explained by the above arguments and is the central issue of several theoretical studies to be discussed below.

2.4 Integral Quantization: Theoretical Work

An explanation of some aspects of the IQHE is possible without introducing the localized states, by invoking the reservoir theory [2.27]. According to this theory, the ionized donors in the heterojunctions serve as a reservoir. The electrons tunnel across a potential barrier to the electron channel. When the density of states in the channel $D(E)$ is a sum of delta functions, thermodynamic equilibrium requires that ν is an integer in certain ranges of B. Then, σ_{H} = constant and so is ν. If the Landau levels (1.7) cross the Fermi energy as the magnetic field is varied, the electron concentration in the layers of the 2DES should change abruptly corresponding to a change in the filling factor by unity. Such a variation is not found experimentally. In addition, the reservoir theory does not properly explain the Si-MOSFET system where the carrier concentration is governed by the gate potential and can not be used in the extreme quantum limit where the lowest Landau level is partially occupied. This theory has not received any experimental support [2.28].

The theoretical approaches discussed below address the most important aspects of the IQHE, viz., the high precision of the QHE and independence of the effects of the sample boundary or the impurities. Also, they shed light on the physical mechanism that is responsible for the occurence of the IQHE.

2.5 Kubo Formula Approach

The Kubo formula [2.22,25] is a general expression for the current, regarded as a linear response to an external field. In this approach the Hall conductivity is written as

$$\sigma_{xy} = -\frac{n_0 ec}{B} + \Delta\sigma_{xy}, \tag{2.7}$$

where $\Delta\sigma_{xy}$ is given by the correlation function of the velocities of the center coordinates X and Y as [2.29–32]

$$\begin{aligned}\Delta\sigma_{xy} = \frac{e^2\hbar}{\mathrm{i}A}\sum_{\alpha}\Big\langle f(E_\alpha)\sum_{\beta}\Re\left(E_\alpha - E_\beta + \mathrm{i}0\right)^{-2} \\ \left[\langle\alpha|\dot{X}|\beta\rangle\langle\beta|\dot{Y}|\alpha\rangle - \langle\alpha|\dot{Y}|\beta\rangle\langle\beta|\dot{X}|\alpha\rangle\right]\Big\rangle,\end{aligned} \tag{2.8}$$

where $f(E)$ is the Fermi distribution function, $|\alpha\rangle$ is the eigenstate of the Hamiltonian (1.16) and A is the area of the system. If $|\alpha\rangle$ is a localized state, then, for any $|\beta\rangle$,

$$\langle\alpha|\dot{X}|\beta\rangle = (\mathrm{i}\hbar)^{-1}\langle\alpha|X|\beta\rangle\left(E_\alpha - E_\beta\right). \tag{2.9}$$

Using (2.8) and (2.9) and the relation, $[X,Y]=\mathrm{i}\ell_0^2$, the contribution from the state $|\alpha\rangle$ to $\Delta\sigma_{xy}$ in (2.9) is, $\Delta\sigma_{xy}^{\alpha}=f(E_\alpha)ec/B$.

From this result, several important observations (at $T=0$) can be made:

(*a*) As long as the Fermi level lies in the energy regime of the localized states, σ_{xy} is constant.

(*b*) If all the states below the Fermi level E_{F} are localized, $\sigma_{xy}=0$ because $\Delta\sigma_{xy}$ exactly cancels[1] $-n_0ec/B$. For the QHE to exist, at least one state per Landau level has to be extended. This shows that the presence of a magnetic field provides a situation different from that predicted by the scaling theory [2.34]. According to that theory, particles moving in a two-dimensional random potential are always localized in the absence of a magnetic field and at $T=0$.

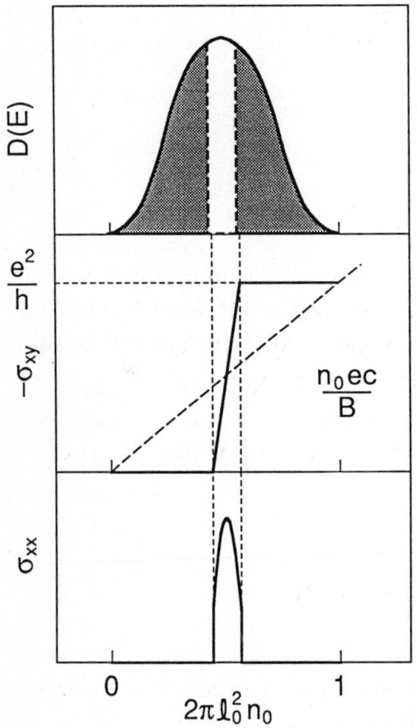

Fig. 2.3. The diagonal conductivity σ_{xx}, the Hall conductivity σ_{xy} and the density of states $D(E)$ as a function of the Landau level filling factor. The dotted diagonal line corresponds to the value n_0ec/B

[1] A similar result was also obtained by *Usov* and *Ulinich* [2.33]

In the case of a strong magnetic field and when E_F lies in a gap between the nth and $(n+1)$th Landau levels, *i.e.*, electrons occupy states up to the nth Landau level such that $\nu = n$, *Aoki* and *Ando* [2.29] showed that $\sigma_{xx} = 0$ and $\sigma_{xy} = -ne^2/h$. The situation is depicted in Fig. 2.3 where, at the onset of the upper plateau, $\sigma_{xy} = -e^2/h$ which is what one expects when *all* the states (including localized states) would carry the Hall current.

Prange [2.35] explained this apparent paradox by studying a model of free electrons interacting with a δ–function impurity. He concluded that the Hall current at the integral quatization is exactly the same as that for free electrons because the loss of Hall current due to the formation of one localized state is exactly compensated by an appropriate increase of the Hall current carried by the remaining extended states.

There are several other important contributions based on the Kubo formula which should also be mentioned. *Thouless* [2.36] has shown that for the integer quantization, the Hall conductivity (as derived from the Kubo formula) is unaffected by a weak variation of the impurity potential. *Streda* [2.37] reformulated the Kubo approach to write the Hall conductivity as

$$\begin{aligned} \sigma_{\mathrm{H}} &= \sigma_{\mathrm{H}}^{\mathrm{I}} + \sigma_{\mathrm{H}}^{\mathrm{II}} \\ \sigma_{\mathrm{H}}^{\mathrm{II}}(E) &= -ec\frac{\partial N(E)}{\partial B}\bigg|_{E=E_{\mathrm{F}}} \end{aligned} \quad . \tag{2.10}$$

Here $N(E)$ is the number of states with energy $\leq E$, and the first term $\sigma_{\mathrm{H}}^{\mathrm{I}}$ depends on the material parameters and impurity potential $U(\boldsymbol{r})$. If, at $T = 0$, the Fermi energy lies in a gap of the energy spectrum of the system, σ_{xx} and $\sigma_{\mathrm{H}}^{\mathrm{I}}$ vanish. If that gap is the n–th Landau gap and the degeneracy of the Landau band is the same as that for free-electron Landau levels, $N(E_{\mathrm{F}}) = neB/hc$ and $\sigma_{\mathrm{H}}^{\mathrm{II}} = -ne^2/h$. The relation (2.10) is thermodynamic.

2.6 The Gauge Invariance Approach

The universal character of the QHE suggests that the effect is due to a fundamental principle. *Laughlin* [2.38] proposed that the effect is due to gauge invariance and the existence of a mobility gap. Following Laughlin, we consider a *gedankenexperiment* involving the *measurement* of the Hall conductivity in the geometry of Fig. 2.4. A two-dimensional electron system is bent into the form of a ribbon. A magnetic field $\boldsymbol{B}$ pierces the ribbon everywhere normal to the surface and a voltage V (Hall voltage) is applied across the edges of the ribbon.

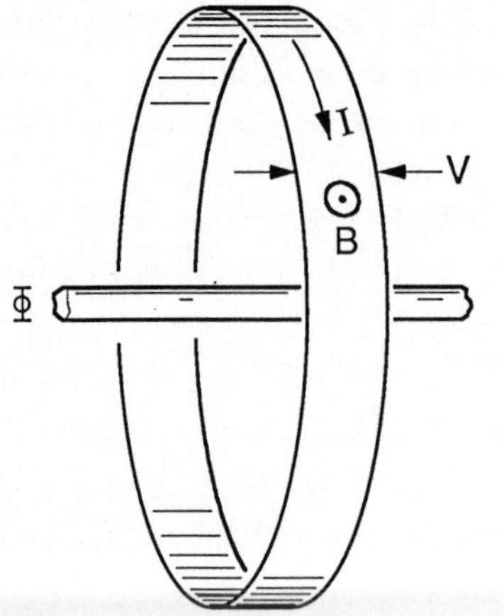

Fig. 2.4. Hall effect in the geometry of Laughlin's gedankenexperiment

Let us now imagine passing a flux $\boldsymbol{\Phi}$ through a solenoid as shown. The current I is then expressed in terms of the total electronic energy of the system U as [2.39,40]

$$I = c\frac{\partial U}{\partial \boldsymbol{\Phi}}. \tag{2.11}$$

Under a gauge transformation $\boldsymbol{A} \to \boldsymbol{A} + \delta A = \boldsymbol{A} + \delta\boldsymbol{\Phi}/L$ where L is the circumference of the loop, the wave function of the electron acquires a phase factor

$$\psi' \to \psi \exp\left(\mathrm{i}\frac{e}{\hbar c}\frac{\delta\boldsymbol{\Phi}}{L}y\right) = \psi \exp\left(2\pi\mathrm{i}\frac{\delta\boldsymbol{\Phi}}{\boldsymbol{\Phi}_0}\frac{y}{L}\right). \tag{2.12}$$

If the electron is localized (*e.g.*, trapped by an impurity), the wave function vanishes outside a localization region which is smaller than L and will not respond to the flux. The energies of localized states are unchanged by the adiabatic process of varying $\boldsymbol{\Phi}$. On the other hand, if the electron is extended, such a transformation is not allowed unless $\delta\boldsymbol{\Phi}/\boldsymbol{\Phi}_0$ is an integer (the wave functions are required to be single-valued). In fact, we have seen earlier that the electrons in Landau levels have extended wave functions and will contribute to the current.

Let us now imagine that the magnetic flux through the loop is increased adiabatically from zero. If the Fermi level lies in a mobility gap (*i.e.*, $\sigma_{xx} = 0$ as discussed above) any localized states which may be present will not *see* the change. The electrons in the extended states will however, respond to the change until the flux reaches $\boldsymbol{\Phi}_0$, when each of these states must map identically into themselves (the transformation is unitary). For free electrons, *Laughlin* [2.38] showed that as the flux is increased adiabatically, each state moves to its neighboring state in the direction of the electric field, as in a shift register [2.41]. When the flux increases by one quantum, the electron distribution must look exactly the same as before. The net result of the adiabatic process is a transfer of charge from one edge of the loop to the other. If n electrons are transferred during a change $\Delta\boldsymbol{\Phi}$ of one flux quantum, the net change in electronic energy is $\Delta U = -neV$, where V is the potential difference between the edges. Writing, $\delta U/\delta\boldsymbol{\Phi} \to \Delta U/\Delta\boldsymbol{\Phi}$, we get, $I = -c\dfrac{neV}{\Delta\boldsymbol{\Phi}} = -n\dfrac{e^2}{h}V$, and $\sigma_{\mathrm{H}} = -ne^2/h$. According to Laughlin's approach, the quantization is so accurate because it is based on two very general conditions: the gauge invariance of the system and the existence of a mobility gap.

Laughlin's work has been extended to the case of a dirty system by *Giuliani* et al. [2.42] and also numerical experiments have been performed [2.43,44] to study the gauge transformation for disordered systems. *Halperin* [2.45] extended the Laughlin approach to include the role of edge states which will be discussed in Sect. 3.3.

2.7 The Topological Invariance Approach

We have thus far, considered only the one-electron system and ignored the many-body interaction. The quantization condition in the presence of a many-body interaction was studied by *Niu* et al. [2.46] (see also [2.47,48]), who showed that the Hall conductance can be expressed in a topologically invariant form. In the following, we briefly discuss the work of Niu et al.

The Hall conductivity of a rectangular plane with sides L_1 and L_2 is written via the Kubo formula as (see Appendix B)

$$\sigma_{\mathrm{H}} = \frac{\mathrm{i}e^2\hbar}{A}\sum_{n>0}\frac{(v_1)_{0n}(v_2)_{n0} - (v_2)_{0n}(v_1)_{n0}}{(E_0 - E_n)^2} \tag{2.13}$$

where $A = L_1L_2$, $|0\rangle$ is the ground state and $|n\rangle$ corresponds to the excited states of the N_{e}-electron Hamiltonian, E_0 and E_n are the corresponding eigenenergies and the velocity operators v_1 and v_2 are defined as

$$\boldsymbol{v} = \sum_{i=1}^{N_{\mathrm{e}}}\frac{1}{m_i^*}\left(-\mathrm{i}\hbar\nabla_i + \frac{e}{c}\boldsymbol{A}_i\right), \quad \boldsymbol{v} = (v_1, v_2). \tag{2.14}$$

Considering the Landau gauge, $\boldsymbol{A} = (0, Bx)$, the wave function ψ for the opposite edges are related by magnetic translations [2.24]

$$\begin{aligned} \psi(x_i + L_1) &= \mathrm{e}^{\mathrm{i}\alpha L_1}\mathrm{e}^{\mathrm{i}y_i L_1/\ell_0^2}\psi(x_i) \\ \psi(y_i + L_2) &= \mathrm{e}^{\mathrm{i}\beta L_2}\psi(y_i) \end{aligned} \tag{2.15}$$

where α and β are phase parameters. Making the unitary transformation

$$\phi_n = \mathrm{e}^{-\mathrm{i}\alpha\sum_{i=1}^{N_e} x_i}\mathrm{e}^{-\mathrm{i}\beta\sum_{i=1}^{N_e} y_i}\psi_n$$

one can write the Hall conductivity as [2.46]

$$\sigma_{\mathrm{H}} = \frac{\mathrm{i}e^2}{\hbar}\left(\left\langle\frac{\partial\phi_0}{\partial\theta}\middle|\frac{\partial\phi_0}{\partial\varphi}\right\rangle - \left\langle\frac{\partial\phi_0}{\partial\varphi}\middle|\frac{\partial\phi_0}{\partial\theta}\right\rangle\right) \tag{2.16}$$

where $\theta = \alpha L_1$ and $\varphi = \beta L_2$.

One major condition for quantization in this approach is that the Hall conductivity is a *local* response function, insensitive to the boundary condition. We can therefore average over all the phases ($0 \le \theta < 2\pi$, $0 < \varphi \le 2\pi$) that specify different boundary conditions

$$\sigma_{\mathrm{H}} = \bar{\sigma} = \frac{e^2}{h}\int_0^{2\pi} d\theta \int_0^{2\pi} \frac{d\varphi}{2\pi\mathrm{i}}\left(\left\langle\frac{\partial\phi_0}{\partial\varphi}\middle|\frac{\partial\phi_0}{\partial\theta}\right\rangle - \left\langle\frac{\partial\phi_0}{\partial\theta}\middle|\frac{\partial\phi_0}{\partial\varphi}\right\rangle\right). \tag{2.17}$$

This can be evaluated as

$$\sigma_{\mathrm{H}} = \frac{e^2}{h}\int_0^{2\pi} d\theta \int_0^{2\pi} \frac{d\varphi}{2\pi\mathrm{i}}\nabla\times\boldsymbol{A} = \frac{e^2}{h}\frac{1}{2\pi\mathrm{i}}\oint d\boldsymbol{l}\cdot\boldsymbol{A}. \tag{2.18}$$

The vector **A** is defined by its components

$$A_\gamma = \frac{1}{2}\left(\left\langle\frac{\partial\phi_0}{\partial\gamma}\middle|\phi_0\right\rangle - \left\langle\phi_0\middle|\frac{\partial\phi_0}{\partial\gamma}\right\rangle\right), \quad \gamma = \theta, \varphi. \tag{2.19}$$

Now, if the ground state is nondegenerate and is separated from the excited states by a gap, the ground state can only change by a phase factor depending on θ and φ. For example, the ground state must go back to itself (up to an overall phase factor) as θ and φ change by 2π. Therefore, $\oint d\boldsymbol{l}\cdot\boldsymbol{A} = 2\pi\mathrm{i}\times$ (integer) and $\sigma_{\mathrm{H}} = \text{integer}\times e^2/h$.

The integral (2.19) is a topological invariant and was originally obtained for noninteracting electrons in a two-dimensional periodic potential [2.49].

An excellent introduction to the connection between the IQHE and the topological idea can be found in [2.50]. Similar arguments for the FQHE have also been put forward by *Niu* et al. [2.46]. A better treatment of the latter case was given, however, by *Tao* and *Haldane* [2.51] and will be discussed briefly in Sect. 9.2.

3. Other Developments

In this chapter, we briefly discuss about the localized states in the quantum Hall regime, various studies on the localization length, and the scaling theory of the IQHE. We have also presented a brief introduction of the edge states and a review of some of the experimental and theoretical studies of transport in the edge channels.

3.1 Electron Localization in the Quantum Hall Regime

We have seen above that the extended and localized states form an integral part of our understanding of the IQHE. Several authors have studied the role of various disorder potentials in the IQHE regime [3.1–6].

For an external potential $U(\boldsymbol{r})$ which varies slowly over length scales of order ℓ_0, and neglecting the inter-Landau-level transition, the motion of an electron reduces to a drift of the center of cyclotron motion along an equipotential line $U(\boldsymbol{r})$ =constant. The state of an electron with energy E (measured from the center of the Landau band) is localized near the line $U(\boldsymbol{r}) = E$, and decreases exponentially from this line. The properties of the equipotential lines for a two-dimensional random potential are fairly well known from the classical percolation model [3.7]. If the potential $U(\boldsymbol{r})$ is symmetric about $E = 0$ (*e.g.*, for equal number of attractive and repulsive scatterers), the equipotentials with $E \neq 0$ are closed curves of finite length, and correspond to localized states. If we call the regions with $U(\boldsymbol{r}) > E$ land and those with $U(\boldsymbol{r}) < E$ water, we get a set of islands for $E > 0$ or a number of lakes for $E < 0$. In that case, we have at least one coast line at $E = 0$. In this picture, all the states in a two-dimensional system subjected to a strong magnetic field are localized, except for the state at the center of the Landau band, which is extended. In an external electric field, analyzing the delocalized drift trajectories, *Iordanski* [3.1] and others [3.2–4] obtained the quantization for σ_{xy}.

The behavior of the localization length in strong magnetic fields has been a very active area of research. Using diagrammatic techniques, *Ono* [3.8] was the first to suggest that only the center of the Landau level is extended while the other states are exponentially localized. *Ando* studied the electron localization by numerically diagonalizing the Hamiltonian matrix for a system with short-range δ-function [3.9] and long-range (Gaussian form) impurities [3.10] which are randomly distributed. The localization length was studied by Ando via the Thouless-number method. The Thouless number $g(L)$ is defined as the ratio of the shifts ΔE of the individual energy levels due to a change in boundary conditions (from periodic to anti-periodic) to the level separation $[L^2D(E)]^{-1}$, where $D(E)$ is the density of states per unit area. For localized states, one can determine the extent of the localized wave functions or the inverse localization length $\alpha(E)$, from

$$g(L) = g(0)\mathrm{e}^{-\alpha(E)L}$$

where L is the sample length [3.11]. The conclusion was that the states are exponentially localized except in the vicinity of the center of each Landau band. The inverse localization length was found to decrease almost linearly with energy when the energy is far from the center of the Landau band, and then smoothly approaches zero with energy. Extremely large localization lengths in the center of the Landau band were also found in numerical studies by other groups [3.12]. Finite-size studies with sample size $\sim$ 50000 times the cyclotron radius [3.13–15] resulted in $\alpha(E) \propto |E - E_n|^s$ near the center E_n, of each Landau level with the critical exponent $s \lesssim 2$ and $s \lesssim 4$ for $n = 0$ and $n = 1$ respectively. From a perturbative calculation *Hikami* [3.16] estimated $s = 1.9 \pm 0.2$. The critical exponent from the classical percolation model is $\frac{4}{3}$ [3.4] and including quantum tunneling one gets $s = \frac{7}{3}$ [3.17]. A percolation model, including quantum tunneling and interference near the percolation threshold [3.18] yielded a one-parameter scaling behavior and a critical exponent $s = 2.5 \pm 0.5$. Recent finite-size scaling studies in the lowest Landau band [3.19,20] revealed a universal one-parameter scaling behavior and a critical exponent $s = 2.34 \pm 0.04$. For more recent results on the finite-size scaling, see the work by *Huo* and *Bhatt* [3.21]. *Koch* et al. [3.22] have investigated the system-size dependence of the width of the transition region between quantized Hall plateaus and deduced a critical exponent $s \sim 2.3$ for the localization length.

3.2 Renormalization Group Approach

This approach is a result of the attempts to unify the weak localization in a two-dimensional electron system [3.23,24] and the quantization of the Hall conductivity. According to the two-parameter scaling theory of the IQHE [3.25–29], σ_{xx} and σ_{xy} (in units of e^2/h) vary with a length scale $\mathcal{L}$, given by the renormalization group equations

$$\frac{d\sigma_{\eta\nu}}{d\xi} = \beta_{\eta\nu}(\sigma_{xx}, \sigma_{xy}), \quad \xi = \ln \mathcal{L} \tag{3.1}$$

where $\beta_{\eta\nu}$ is a periodic function of σ_{xy} with a period of e^2/h. The resulting phase diagram is shown in Fig. 3.1. The beginning of each flow line is selected at a point corresponding to a spatial scale $\xi = 0$, where $\widehat{\sigma}$ can be estimated from the classical formula [2.4]. With increasing system size, all flow lines merge into one of the fixed points at $(\sigma_{xx}, \sigma_{xy}) = (0, -ne^2/h)$ which are the *localization fixed points* and describe localized wave functions of the electrons near the Fermi energy E_{F}. In addition, the system also has unstable fixed points (denoted by $\otimes$) where the flow lines with $\sigma_{xy} = -(n + \frac{1}{2})e^2/h$ terminate. At these points, $\sigma_{xx} > 0$ and describes the singular behavior in the renormalized transport coefficients, corresponding microscopically to the occurrence of a diverging localization length. These *delocalization fixed points* are associated with the extended states at E_{F}. It should be noted that the explicit form of the β-function is not known, only its asymptote is calculated. An approximate calculation of σ_{xx} at the unsta-

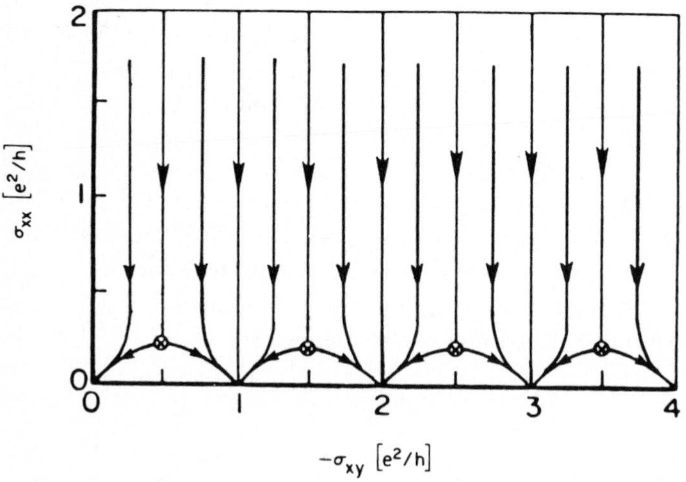

Fig. 3.1. Scaling diagram for the integral quantum Hall effect [3.30]

ble fixed points gives $\sigma_{xx} = (1.4/\pi)e^2/h$ for a white noise random potential [3.30].

The predictions of the two-parameter scaling theory have been tested experimentally [3.31,32]. The study was carried out on the 2DES in InGaAs/InP heterostructures. It was assumed that the effective sample size is governed by inelastic scattering which can be varied via the temperature T, and a phase diagram was constructed (Fig. 3.2) from the measurements of $\sigma_{xx}(T)$ and $\sigma_{xy}(T)$. In this figure, the dashed lines are from the temperature range $4.2 - 10K$, where lowering of T is accompanied by the usual enhancement of the Shubnikov-de Haas oscillations as a result of a change of the Fermi distribution. In the scaling region ($T \sim 0.5 - 4.2K$) the results, presented as full lines, show a tendency (as $T \to 0$) to flow out toward the fixed points $(0, e^2/h), (0, 2e^2/h), (0, 3e^2/h)$ and $(0, 4e^2/h)$. Detailed studies by these authors indicated that there is a remarkable symmetry about the line $\sigma_{xy} = 1\frac{1}{2}$. The data are consistent with the existence of an intermediate coupling, delocalization critical point. A phase diagram for the FQHE based on the scaling hypothesis has also been proposed [3.33]. However, the

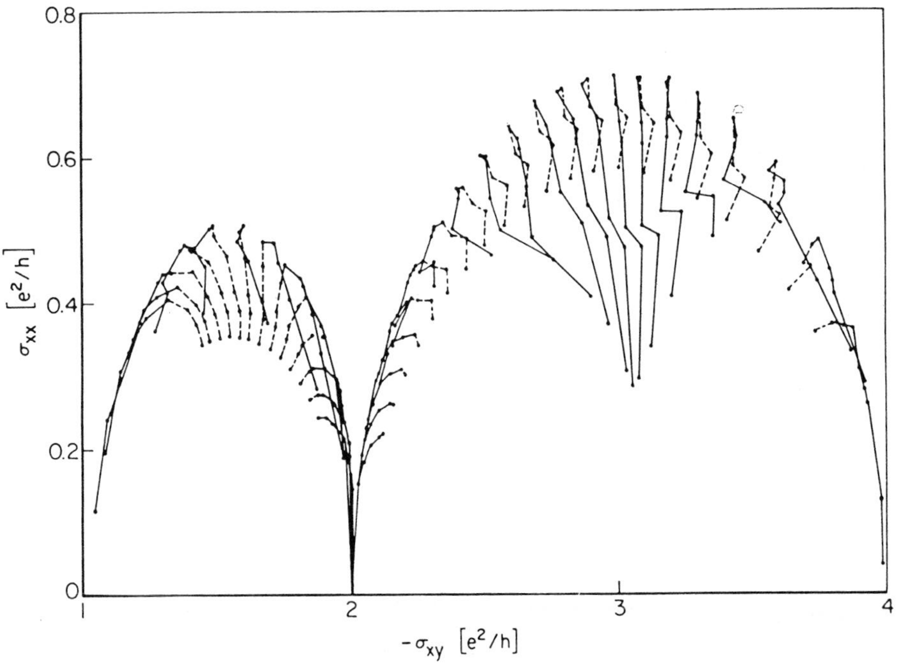

Fig. 3.2. Experimental results for the conductivity plotted as T driven flow lines from $T = 10K$ to $0.5K$. The dashed lines are from 10 to $4.2K$ and the solid lines from 4.2 to 0.5 K [3.30]

theories are still in a state where a fair amount of *guesswork* is required as input.

The two-parameter scaling theory of the IQHE has not received much support from other theoretical work. Finite-size studies of the diagonal and off-diagonal conductivities [3.34] indicate that they are *not* independent but possess single flow lines dependent on the Landau level index which contradicts the scaling theory results discussed above.

3.3 Current-Carrying Edge States

In calculating the Hall current in Sect. 2.3, we assumed that the current is distributed over the entire surface of the two-dimensional layer. Some authors have pointed out that, in fact, the current flows along the one-dimensional channel at the edge of the layer [3.35–37]. *Halperin* [3.35] first obtained this result while exploring the arguments of Laughlin described in Sect. 2.6, for integral quantization of the Hall conductivity. He considered an annulus of two-dimensional conductor bounded by an inner circle of radius r_1 and an outer one of radius r_2. The conductor is in a uniform magnetic field B, and in addition a long solenoid passes through the center of the system, so that the flux in the conductor can be varied without changing the magnetic field. Following arguments very similar to those in Sect. 2.6, Halperin pointed out that localized states do not play any part in the response to a changing flux. If there is a Hall current there must be extended states to respond to the changing flux, and in particular the *edge states* at the Fermi energy must be extended.

Let us consider the noninteracting electrons of Sect. 1.2 but now confined in a potential [3.36]

$$V(x) = \begin{cases} 0, & x \in (-L_x/2, L_x/2) \\ +\infty, & \text{otherwise.} \end{cases} \tag{3.2}$$

Far from the boundary inside the sample, $V(x) \equiv 0$ and the eigenstates are as derived in Sect. 1.2. However, near the boundary, the energy eigenvalues deviate from the Landau energy [1.7] and behave as in Fig. 3.3, as a function of $X = -k\ell_0^2$. For a hard wall potential, the energy of a state is determined by

$$E_{nk} = E(n, \omega_c, X).$$

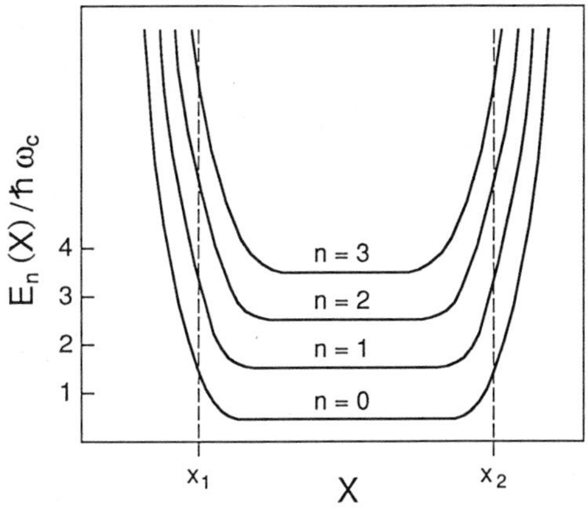

Fig. 3.3. Energy spectrum of a noninteracting electron in an infinite well confining potential, $x_1 = -L_x/2, x_2 = L_x/2$

For a more realistic soft wall potential where the potential changes slowly with the length scale ℓ_0, the energy of a state is just the sum of Landau energy and the electrostatic energy. Carriers in an edge state acquire a longitudinal velocity

$$v_{nk} = \frac{1}{\hbar}\frac{dE_{nk}}{dk} = \frac{1}{\hbar}\frac{dE_{nk}}{dX}\frac{dX}{dk}$$

which is proportional to the slope of the Landau level. At the upper edge X_2, $\frac{dE}{dX}$ is positive and negative at the lower edge X_1. In a strong magnetic field, $\frac{dX}{dk}$ is negative and therefore, the velocity along the upper edge is negative and positive along the lower edge. For n filled Landau levels, one gets n quasi-one-dimensional *edge channels* at the Fermi energy on either side of the sample through which dissipationless current flows. The current in each edge state is [3.36]

$$I_n = \frac{e}{h}\left(\mu^{\mathrm{R}} - \mu^{\mathrm{L}}\right) \tag{3.3}$$

where μ^{R} is the chemical potential at the right (positive- x) edge of the sample and μ^{L} is the chemical potential at the left edge. Edge channels on opposite sides of the sample carry current in opposite directions. A net current is established if there is a difference in the magnitude of these opposite flowing currents. In the equilibrium case ($\mu^{\mathrm{R}} = \mu^{\mathrm{L}}$), there is no current flow – the bulk current which flows in the presence of an electric field (in which case the above result also holds) is exactly cancelled by the surface diamagnetic current. For noninteracting electrons the net current would flow at the edges and the quantized Hall current would be just the difference between the two edge currents. *MacDonald* and *Streda* [3.36] also showed that these results are unaltered by the inclusion of a random potential in the Hamiltonian [3.6]. The role of edge currents has also been studied by *Smrcka* [3.38], who derived the Hall current from the Kubo formula, taking into account the edge states explicitly, and concluded that the IQHE is exclusively due to the edge currents. It has been proposed that the edge currents might be observed from the oscillations in the magnetic susceptibility [3.39]. Several experiments exploring the current-carrying edge states have been reported in the literature [3.40–43].

3.4 Transport in Edge Channels and Other Topics

From the experimental point of view, it is clear that under the quantum Hall conditions the edge states play an important role in transport measurements [3.44]. An electric current can flow through a device only when both the source and drain contacts are connected by a common edge. In Fig. 3.4, we have summarized the different situations where the source and drain contacts are either located at the same edge (quantized two-terminal resistance $R_{\mathrm{SD}} = h/ie^2$) or are connected to different edges [Corbino geometry, Fig. 3.4 (c)]. In the latter case, one obtains $R_{\mathrm{SD}} = \infty$ which can be reduced to the quantized value if a part of the 2DEG is removed as shown in Fig. 3.4 (d).

Experimentally, *Haug et al.* and *Washburn et al.* [3.45] demonstrated the quantization of the diagonal resistance R_{xx} measured across two regions of different filling factors in a series. This result was obtained from the Büttiker-Landauer approach [3.46] where quantization of R_{xx} is obtained simply by counting the number of edge states penetrating the gated region. If the number of edge states in the ungated region is ν and the number of edge states in the gated region is ν_{g}, then R_{xx} is quantized to $(h/e^2)\,(1/\nu_{\mathrm{g}} - 1/\nu)$.

The existence of edge currents can be demonstrated if adjacent edge channels (which originate from different Landau levels) are occupied up to *different* electrochemical potentials. In this case the adjacent edge channels carry different electric currents. Such adiabatic transport is a direct proof for the existence of edge currents. Adiabatic transport is destroyed if the edge channels become equilibrated, *i.e.*, the current is equally distributed among all the edge channels, *e.g.*, via interchannel scattering processes.

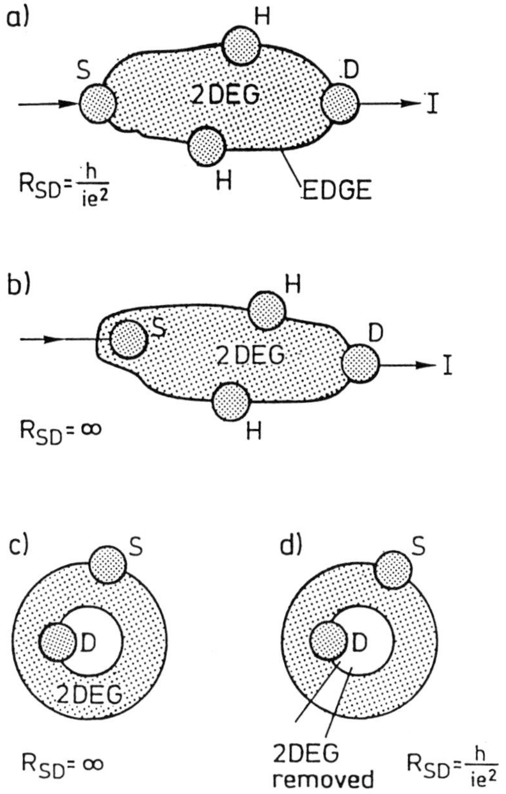

Fig. 3.4. Different arrangements of source (S) and drain (D) contacts which demonstrates the importance of the boundaries of a 2DEG in the quantum Hall effects experiments. (a) Source, drain, and Hall contacts at the same edge (standard Hall geometry). (b) Source contact not at the edge, no current flow in the quantum Hall regime. (c) Source and drain contacts connected to *different* edges of the 2DEG (quasi-Corbino device); infinite source-drain resistance. (d) The quantized value is obtained if a part of the 2DEG is removed in such a way that the contacts are connecetd by the same edge [3.44]

An excellent demonstration of the transition from adiabatic transport to equilibrated transport just by adding a metallic contact at the edge can be found in the experiments on double-barrier systems by *Müller et al.* [3.41].

van Wees et al. [3.40] measured the Hall conductance of a wide 2DEG in a geometry in which two quantum point contacts (constrictions in the 2DEG) form controllable current and voltage probes, separated by less than both the elastic and the inelastic mean free path. In this method, edge states can be selectively populated and detected by these point contacts. These authors found that the value of Hall conductance measured across a bulk 2DEG was determined by the number of edge states reaching the voltage and current probes, rather than by the filling factor in the bulk of the sample.

So far, we have considered a simple one-electron picture: the position of the edge state is determined by the intersection between the Landau-level energy and the Fermi energy. Its width is simply the spatial extent of the wave function at the Landau level, and is of the order of the magnetic length, ℓ_0. To explain most of the experimental observations mentioned above, this simple picture of an edge state is usually enough. However, this picture requires an abrupt change in density within ℓ_0 wherever the Fermi energy intersects a Landau level [Fig. 3.5 (a)-(c)]. In an actual sample, the density decreases gradually near the boundary at $B = 0$. There is, of course, an extra cost of electrostatic energy to deform the gradual density profile at $B = 0$ into a steplike one at $B \neq 0$. On the other hand, a partially filled Landau level at the Fermi energy can accomodate extra charge without changing its energy (perfect screening condition) [3.47]. The system therefore can have a spatially wider region of the Landau level at the Fermi energy and avoid this cost of electrostatic energy. Consequently, each edge state widens into a band of edge states, and the density profile becomes gradual rather than step like. The edge channel, where the Fermi energy aligns with the partially filled Landau level, is compressible – an extra electron can be accomodated without costing any additional energy. The region where the Fermi energy resides in between two Landau levels is at a constant density (or integer filling factor) and is incompressible – adding an extra electron costs finite energy because it has to go to the higher Landau level. Therefore, as we approach the sample boundary, there will be a series of alternating compressible and incompressible regions.

While several authors [3.48] proposed the existence of edge channels with finite-width, as discussed in the preceding paragraph, *Chklovskii et al.* [3.48] (CSG) made a quantitative study of the phase separation near the boundary of the 2DES and analytically calculated the width of the compressible and incompressible regions. They found that these widths scale with the width of the depletion layer l that separates the gate and the boundary of the 2DEG [Fig. 3.5 (d)-(f)] as l (compressible) and as $(a_{\mathrm{B}}l)^{\frac{1}{2}}$ for IQHE (incompressible). Here $a_{\mathrm{B}} = \hbar^2\epsilon/m^*e^2$ is the Bohr radius. As shown in Fig. 3.5 (d)-(f), the incompressible strips are narrower than the adjacent compressible ones, the innermost being the widest. Experimental support for the model describing edge channels as compressible strips separated by incompressible regions has been reported in Ref. [3.49].

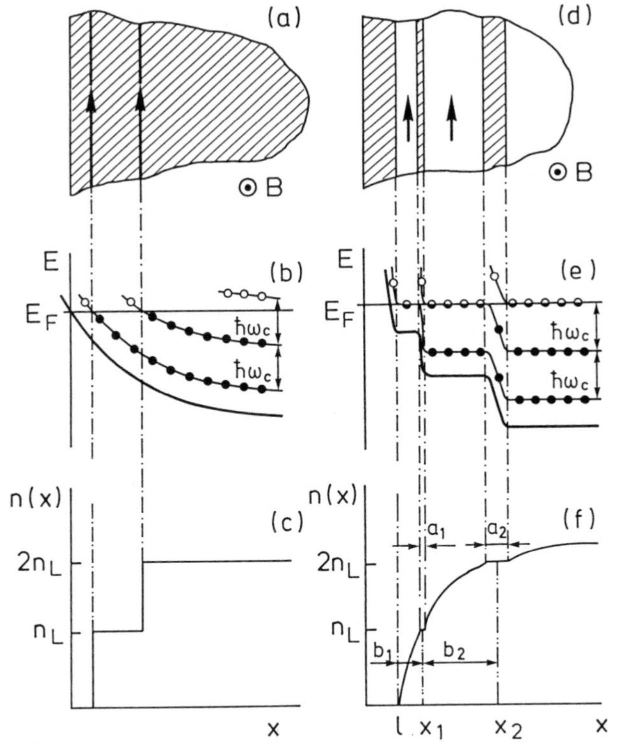

Fig. 3.5. Edge states in the IQHE regime. In the single-electron picture: (a) Top view of the 2DEG near the edge. Arrows indicate the direction of electron flow in the two edge channels. (b) Landau level bending near the edge. Filled circles indicate occupation of the Landau level, and (c) electron density as a function to the boundary. In the self-consistent electrostatic picture: (d) Top view of the 2DEG near the edge with compressible and incompressible regions, (e) bending of the electrostatic potential energy and the Landau level and (f) electron density as a function of distance to the middle of the depletion region. Shaded strips correspond to incompressible regions and the unshaded strips represent compressible regions

The ratio between the edge and bulk currents in the regime of quantum Hall effects was calculated recently by *Hirai* and *Komiyama* [3.50]. For a slowly varying confinement potential, the bulk current was found to dominate in a wide width range of the 2DEG channels. For a steep confining potential, the ratio of edge to total current is higher and can be of the order of unity if one assumes the hard wall confinement potential [3.51].

It should however be pointed out that the quantized Hall resistance is insensitive to the current distribution within the 2DES. For large current densities, one cannot describe the QHE only by the edge currents located within the depletion length at the boundary. The current actually penetrates into the interior of the 2DES as the Hall voltage is increased and behaves more and more like a bulk current. *Dolgopolov et al.* [3.52] have recently demonstrated that the quantized Hall conductivity can be observed in samples of the Corbino geometry [Fig. 3.4 (c)], *i.e.*, without an edge. This implies that the QHE is not exclusively an edge effect but for experiments on Hall devices and small device currents $I_{\rm tot} < 0.1\mu A$ the current flow close to the edge dominates the electronic properties of the system [3.44].

The IQHE breaks down at a critical current density $j_{\rm c}$ (the corresponding critical Hall field $E_{\rm H} = 60$ V/cm at a magnetic field $B = 5$T) where the resistivity increases abruptly by orders of magnitude and the Hall plateau disappears [3.53–55]. A typical result is shown in Fig. 3.6. At a current density of $j_x = j_{\rm c} = 0.5$ A/m, ρ_{xx} at the center of the $\nu = 2$ plateau increases dramatically. A pronounced hysteresis is observed near the breakdown threshold.

There are several mechanisms proposed in the literature as possible causes for the breakdown.

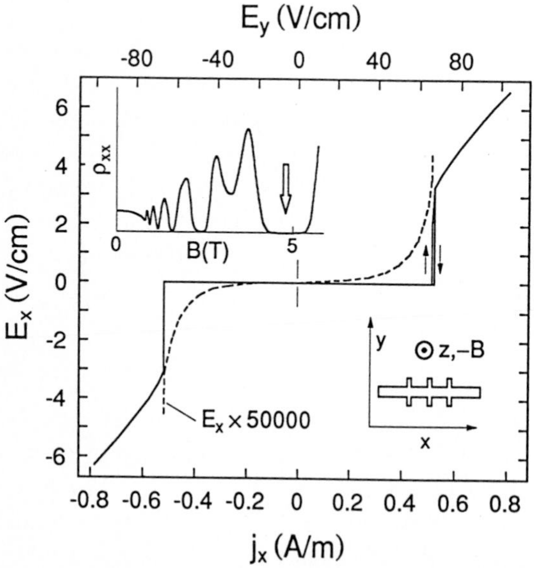

Fig. 3.6. Breakdown of the IQHE under quantum field effect conditions. The current-voltage characteristic of a GaAs-heterostructure at a filling factor $\nu = 2$. The device geometry and the $\rho_{xx}(B)$ curve are shown as insets. (The arrow indicates the field B at which the characteristic is measured)

(*a*) Transition between levels accompanied by the absorption or emission of phonons [3.56]

(*b*) Zener effect: tunneling of the carriers between occupied and empty Landau levels [3.57]

(*c*) Heating instability associated with the breakdown of the balance between the energy gained and released by electrons [3.53,58].

4. Fractional Quantum Hall Effect: Introduction

The FQHE was realized in high-mobility 2DEG in $GaAs/Al_xGa_{1-x}$ As heterostructures [4.1–6] and in high-mobility Si-MOSFETs [4.7]. It is characterized by the fact that the Hall conductance has plateaus quantized to certain simple *fractions* ν of the unit e^2/h and at the same places, the longitudinal resistivity shows an almost dissipationless current flow.

Figure 4.1 shows the effect for a few values of the filling factor ν. For $\nu > 1$, the characteristic features of the integral QHE are clearly visible. However, in the extreme quantum limit, *i.e.*, for $\nu < 1$, and at low temperatures (in this case, $T = 0.48K$), one observes a clear minimum in ρ_{xx} and a quantized Hall plateau at $\nu = \frac{1}{3}$. In later experiments with higher mobility samples the plateau was found to be quantized to better than 3 parts in 10^5 with ρ_{xx} lower than $0.1\Omega/\square$. A weak structure around $\nu = \frac{2}{3}$ is also visible at the lowest temperatures. In subsequent studies [4.8–19] several other fractions were observed, where quantization occurs with very high accuracy.[1] The diagonal resistivity was also found to approach zero (Fig. 4.1) at the magnetic fields where the plateaus were observed, indicating, as in the case of the IQHE, the existence of a gap in the excitation spectrum. The striking feature of the above results is that all fractional fillings appear with *odd* denominators. In Fig. 4.2, we have reproduced the latest results on the FQHE [4.5], where several new (as well as established) fractions have been resolved. It is clear that the Hall resistance is quantized to $\rho_{xy} = h/fe^2$ with f being an exact rational fraction of exclusively odd denominator. The present list of such quantum numbers include:

$$f = \frac{1}{3}, \frac{2}{3}, \frac{4}{3}, \frac{5}{3},$$

$$f = \frac{1}{5}, \frac{2}{5}, \frac{3}{5}, \frac{4}{5}, \frac{7}{5}, \frac{8}{5},$$

$$f = \frac{2}{7}, \frac{3}{7}, \frac{4}{7}, \frac{5}{7}, \frac{10}{7}, \frac{11}{7},$$

[1] We have not attempted to review the experimental work on FQHE by various groups; these can be found *e.g.*, in [4.3,5,6,10].

and several other fractions such as $p/9, p/11, p/13$ and even $p/15$ are observed in ρ_{xx}. These weaker structures are expected to develop into real quantized states in yet higher quality two-dimensional electron systems. Experimentally, several properties of the FQHE states have been established:

(*a*) They are sensitive to disorder. Low-mobility samples do not show a FQHE.

(*b*) The FQHE has a characteristic energy scale of only a few degrees kelvin.

(*c*) There is a tendency for the quantized states with higher denominator to exhibit weaker transport features.

(*d*) Higher magnetic fields promote the observation of the FQHE.

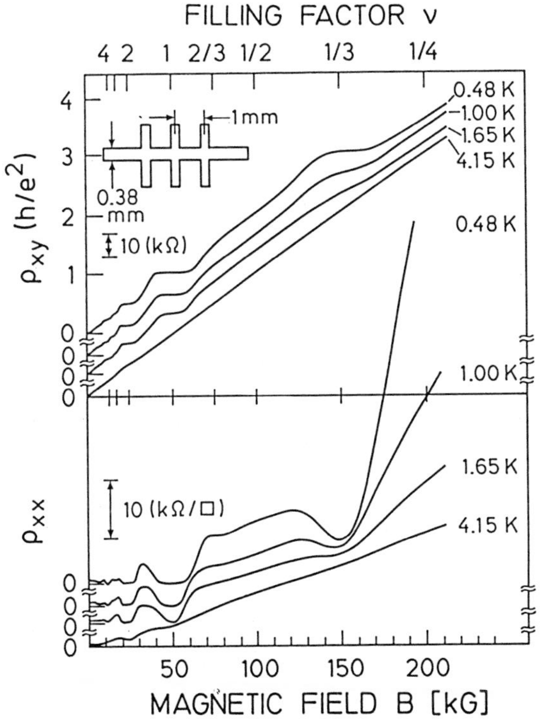

Fig. 4.1. The Hall resistivity ρ_{xy} and the diagonal resistivity ρ_{xx} as a function of magnetic field in a GaAs-heterostructure with electron density $n_0 = 1.23 \times 10^{11}/\mathrm{cm}^2$, where the FQHE was first discovered. The scale on the top shows the *filling factor*, defined in the text [4.1]

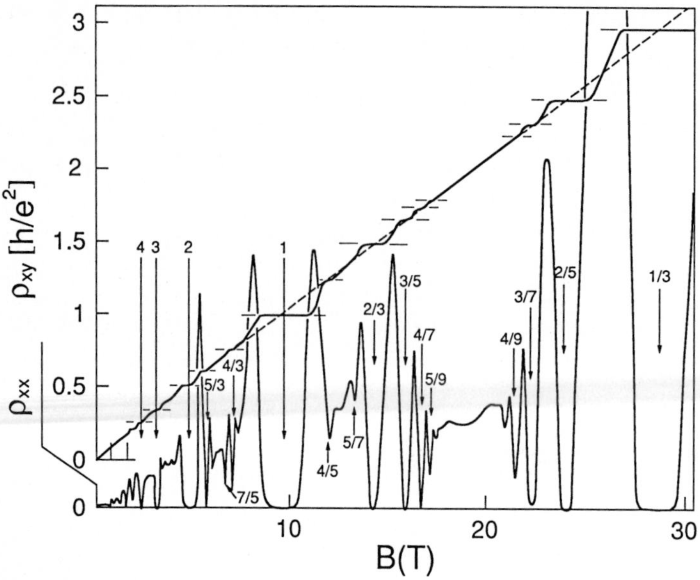

Fig. 4.2. Overview of the observed fractions in the FQHE measurements [4.5]. The Landau level filling factor ν has been defined in the text

The FQHE has also been observed in multiple quantum well heterostructures [4.20] and in an n-type Si/SiGe heterostructures [4.21].

There have also been other surprise in the FQHE. In the second Landau level (n=1), *Clark* et al. [4.11] and *Willett* et al. [4.9] have discovered a fractional Hall plateau at $\rho_{xy} = \left(\frac{h}{e^2}\right)/\frac{5}{2}$, corresponding to an *even* denominator filling $(= 2 + \frac{1}{2})$. This particular finding will be discussed in Sect. 9.4. The influence of reversed spins has been clearly demonstrated in two recent experiments. *Clark et al.* [4.22] observed distinct spin dependent filling fractions. *Eisenstein et al.* [4.19] found a novel transition from the spin-reversed ground state to the fully spin-polarized ground state at $\nu = \frac{8}{5}$. These experimental results lend support to a series of theoretical predictions about the spin-reversed ground state and excitations [4.23-27] and will be discussed in detail in in Sect. 9.4. Finally, following a theoretical prediction about the possibility of observing the FQHE with *even* denominator fractions in multilayer systems [4.28,29], such observations were actually made in a double layer system [4.30] and will be discussed in Sect. 9.5.

In explaining the FQHE, a system of noninteracting electrons is, however, inadequate. According to our present understanding of the FQHE, electron correlations play a major role in this effect, and there have been a variety of theoretical attempts to understand this unique many-electron phenomenon. In the following chapters, we have attempted to survey most of these theoretical approaches, and have tried to present in detail the current state of our understanding of this fascinating effect.

As the fractional Hall steps are observable only in samples of very high mobility, impurity potentials are not expected to be very important in comparison with the electron-electron interactions. The first step in the explanation of the FQHE would therefore be to study the properties of a system of two-dimensional interacting electrons in a uniform positive background with the magnetic field strength such that only the lowest Landau level is partially filled. One could then consider the effect of impurities as a perturbation.

In Chap. 5, we survey various theoretical methods used to study the ground-state properties of a system such as that described above. The unit of potential energy is $\frac{e^2}{\epsilon\ell_0}$, which is taken to be the energy scale throughout. Here, ϵ is the background dielectric constant. For a magnetic field of $B \gtrsim 10\mathrm{T}$, where the FQHE is generally observed, using the values $\epsilon \approx 12.9$ and $m^* \approx 0.067 m_\mathrm{e}$ which are appropriate for GaAs, it is easy to verify that $\frac{e^2}{\epsilon\ell_0} \lesssim \hbar\omega_\mathrm{c}$, the latter being the cyclotron energy (Sect. 1.2). The admixture of states in higher Landau levels can thus be safely ignored as a first approximation.

In the extreme quantum limit (no Landau level mixing), the Hamiltonian describing the two-dimensional electron gas can be written as

$$\mathcal{H} = \frac{1}{2}\sum_q V(q)\left[\bar{\rho}(q)\bar{\rho}(-q) - \rho \mathrm{e}^{-q^2\ell_0^2}\right] \tag{4.1}$$

where $\bar{\rho}(q)$ is the projected density operator (discussed in Sect. 7.4) and ρ is the average particle density in the system. In the absence of kinetic energy, the ground state is expected to be a solid — which means that the Hamiltonian describes a set of interacting classical particles. The operators $\bar{\rho}(q)$ do not commute with one another. However, in the limit $B \to \infty$ [4.31] we get

$$\left[\bar{\rho}_q, \bar{\rho}_{-q}\right] \to \ell_0 \tag{4.2}$$

and one obtains a solid which is presumably triangular in the limit of infinite magnetic field. The earlier attempts to explain the FQHE were mostly centered on crystal state calculations. Such calculations [4.32,33] however, did not find any singularity at $\nu = \frac{1}{3}$. It is also difficult conceptually to understand how the crystal could carry electric current with no resistive loss, since the charge-density wave (CDW) would be pinned by the impurities. Furthermore, if the CDW is not allowed to move with a drift velocity $\boldsymbol{E} \times \boldsymbol{B}c/B^2$, the electron contribution to the Hall conductivity would vanish

[4.11,34]. While there were some claims that a crystal-type trial wave function has a significantly lower energy than that of a liquid state [4.35–37], we believe that a majority of the theoretical work described in this book has clearly established that the ground state of the electron system is a translationally invariant *liquid* state. The major step in arriving at this conclusion was made by *Laughlin* [4.38]. Various other calculations strongly support this conclusion.

In our attempt to explain the fractional Hall steps, we have to understand the exceptionally stable states of the electron system at particular rational values of ν. The pinning of the density at those values of ν would require that the energy versus density curve shows a cusp-type behavior. A cusp would imply a discontinuity of chemical potential, which would in turn, mean that the electron system is, in fact, *incompressible*[2] at those stable states. *Laughlin* introduced a quite radical concept at this point [4.38], proposing that the lowest energy charge excitations in the system are *fractionally* charged quasiparticles and quasiholes. Slight deviations from a stable ν would create those quasiparticles and quasiholes, costing a finite amount of energy. In Chap. 6, we discuss in detail, how these charged excitations are created and the various methods to compute their creation energies. We also review briefly some of the interesting experimental work on the energy gap from thermal activation of the diagonal resistivity, as well as from spectroscopic methods.

Once the lowest energy charged excitations are identified, the next natural step would be to study the lowest lying neutral excitations—the *quasiexcitons*. Finite-size studies have shown that a collective mode exists in the incompressible state with a finite gap and a minimum at a finite wave vector. The mode is also well separated from the continuum. The minimum in the collective excitation spectrum is, in fact, similar to the *roton* minimum in liquid ^{4}He. These topics will be discussed in Chap. 7.

When the Landau levels are completely filled or completely empty the excitations, in the absence of interactions, involve promoting an electron from an occupied state in the nth Landau level to an unoccupied state in the n'th landau level. The corresponding energy is simply the kinetic energy difference between the two levels. In the presence of interactions, one can obtain an expression for the dispersion which is exact to the lowest order in $\frac{e^2}{\epsilon \ell_0}/\hbar\omega_c$. One can also obtain the spin wave spectrum exactly. The dispersion can be studied indirectly through the cyclotron-resonance line shape in the weak-disorder limit. These results are discussed briefly in

[2] The compressibility $\kappa \sim [d^2E/d\nu^2] \to 0$, ($E$ is the energy per particle) at the point where the cusp appears

Chap. 8. In the case where the Landau levels are partially filled, the intra-Landau level mode influences the inter-Landau level mode. This interesting problem has been studied by some authors for infinite systems as well as for finite-size systems, and is also discussed in this chapter.

Chap. 9, surveys various interesting effects, which are very important for our understanding of the FQHE in general, and how they influence the incompressible fluid state. There have been some studies of the effect of impurities on the incompressible fluid state using a Laughlin-type approach, as well as finite-size system calculations. These investigations are far from complete, however. Another interesting problem is the FQHE in higher Landau levels which has been given attention by various authors and is discussed in Chap. 9. Finally, in this chapter, we also discuss recent developments concerning the FQHE for even denominator filling fractions. The theoretical work on these filling fractions is not so exhaustive compared to the vast amount of effort devoted to the odd denominator fractions. The experimental and theoretical results are just emerging. In Sects. 9.4 and 9.5, we have tried to present a brief picture of the present state of our understanding of this phenomenon. The nature of the long-range order in the Laughlin state is discussed in Sect. 9.6.

Finally, in Chap. 10, we present a list of questions related to the FQHE which remain to be studied and discuss the associated problems. We also point out the direction in which the study of low-dimensional electron systems in magnetic fields is heading viz., quantum dots (*artificial atoms*) and antidots (*electron pinball*).

In Appendix A, we present briefly the algebra for the single electron eigenstates in the symmetric gauge, relevant for the Laughlin type of approach. The Kubo formula for the Hall conductivity used in several places of the book is derived in Appendix B. Appendix C contains a brief background on the hypernetted-chain theory, which is essential for understanding the quantitative results for the ground state and elementary excitations in Laughlin's approach. In Appendix D, we present some mathematical details on the magnetoplasmon modes discussed in Chap. 5. A table of numerical values for some of the quantities useful for the study of the QHE is given as Appendix E.

Besides Laughlin's theory for the fractional quantization, there have also been other attempts to describe the effect. *Tao* and *Thouless* [4.39] proposed a method in the Landau gauge in which it was suggested that every third level in the degenerate Landau levels would be occupied in the unperturbed ground state, while the two intervening levels are empty. This could be viewed as a one-dimensional solid in the space of Landau levels. Later, *Thouless* [4.40] noticed that the wave function in their scheme includes long-range correlations. Thouless also found that such a long-range order is absent in Laughlin's wave function. He then argued that, since the odd denominators for fractional quantization come out naturally from Laughlin's theory and since the overlap of the Laughlin wave function with the exact ground state from finite-size calculations are remarkably large, whereas not much could be said in favor of the Tao-Thouless theory, the latter theory should be abandoned. We will not discuss this theory any further in the present review.

Another theoretical approach which will not be elaborated on is the *cooperative ring exchange* mechanism of *Kivelson* et al. [4.41,42]. Using a path integral formalism, these authors found that the important processes are those which involve cyclic exchange of large rings of electrons. While each individual ring makes only a small contribution to the energy, the number of available rings increases exponentially with the length of the ring. For fractional filling of Landau levels with odd denominators, the exchange energies of large rings add coherently and produce a downward cusp in the ground-state energy; for other values of the filling fraction, the rings will contribute incoherently. Recently, *Thouless* and *Li* [4.43] studied this mechanism in a simple model where each ring is confined to a narrow channel. They found that for fractional filling of the Landau level, the exchange energy tends to give an *upward* cusp in the energy, which would imply that the fundamental assumption of the explanation of the FQHE in terms of ring exchange is highly implausible. *Kivelson* et al. have argued [4.44] that the high-magnetic field is essential to obtain the correct results. This theory however needs to be developed further in order to be able to quantitatively compare its predictions with the available results from other theoretical work. In any case, as *Haldane* pointed out [4.45], this alternative approach, in order to be correct, has to be equivalent to Laughlin's theory. Finally, there are also some attempts to develop a so-called Chern-Simon-Landau-Ginzburg theory of the FQHE [4.46], but the topic is beyond the scope of the present book and will not be discussed here.

5. Ground State

As mentioned previously, in the earlier investigations of the FQHE the crucial question was the nature of the ground state. As the GaAs-heterostructures where the FQHE was discovered have very high electron mobility, and because of the subsequent discovery of the FQHE only in high-mobility Si-MOSFETs, the Coulomb interaction between electrons was quite naturally expected to play a dominant role in the FQHE. The earliest numerical calculation of the ground state including Coulomb interactions for various filling fractions was by *Yoshioka* et al. [5.1]. They investigated the eigenstates of an electron system in a periodic rectangular geometry, by numerically diagonalizing the Hamiltonian. Their results, as we shall discuss in the following section, revealed several interesting features; the most important result was, of course, that the ground state had a significantly lower energy than that of a Hartree-Fock (HF) Wigner crystal.

The major breakthrough in this problem was made by *Laughlin* [5.2–4], who proposed a *Jastrow-type* trial wave function for $\nu = \frac{1}{m}$ filling factor with m an *odd* integer. Based on this wave function, he also proposed the low-lying elementary excitations to be quasiparticles and quasiholes of fractional charge. Laughlin's work, as we shall try to demonstrate below, has an enormous influence in this field, and has been a major source of intuition for most of the theoretical studies of the FQHE that followed.

In the following sections, we describe the approaches of Yoshioka et al., and of Laughlin in detail, and compare the results with very accurate Monte Carlo evaluation of the ground-state properties obtained by *Levesque* et al. [5.5] and by *Morf* and *Halperin* [5.6,7]. Finite-size system results in the spherical geometry [5.8,9] are also presented for comparison.

5.1 Finite-Size Studies: Rectangular Geometry

The quantum mechanics for an electron in a strong magnetic field has been described in detail in Sect. 1.2. The single-electron wave function (except for the normalization factor) was found to be

$$\phi = \exp\left[\mathrm{i}Xy/\ell_0^2 - (X - x)^2/2\ell_0^2\right]. \tag{5.1}$$

Let us now follow the work of *Yoshioka* et al. [5.1] and put a finite number of electrons in the cell and introduce interactions among them.

Consider the situation shown in Fig. 5.1, where there are a few electrons in a rectangular cell of sides a and b, and a strong magnetic field perpendicular to the x-y plane. The electrons are considered to be in the lowest Landau level, and are spin polarized. Applying periodic boundary conditions in the y-direction, one obtains, $k_y = X_j/\ell_0^2 = 2\pi j/b$ for an integer j. As for the periodic boundary condition along the x-direction, let us write, for an integer m, $X_m = a$. Clearly, $ab = 2\pi\ell_0^2 m$, and from (1.13), m is the Landau level degeneracy N_s. For N_e electrons in the cell, the filling factor (1.15) is easily calculated as

$$\nu = \frac{2\pi\ell_0^2 N_\mathrm{e}}{ab} = \frac{N_\mathrm{e}}{N_\mathrm{s}}.$$

We thus have m different single-electron states in the cell with wave functions which satisfy the periodic boundary condition

$$\phi_j(\boldsymbol{r}) = \left(\frac{1}{b\sqrt{\pi}\ell_0}\right)^{\frac{1}{2}} \sum_{k=-\infty}^{+\infty} \exp\left[\mathrm{i}\left(X_j + ka\right) y/\ell_0^2 - \left(X_j + ka - x\right)^2/2\ell_0^2\right] \tag{5.2}$$

with $1 \leq j \leq m$. The Coulomb interaction is written in the form

$$V(\boldsymbol{r}) = \frac{1}{ab}\sum_{\boldsymbol{q}} \frac{2\pi e^2}{\epsilon q} \exp(\mathrm{i}\boldsymbol{q}\cdot\boldsymbol{r}) \tag{5.3}$$

where $\boldsymbol{q} = \left(\dfrac{2\pi s}{a}, \dfrac{2\pi t}{b}\right)$ and s and t are integers. The Hamiltonian is now,

$$\mathcal{H} = \sum_j \mathcal{W} a_j^\dagger a_j + \sum_{j_1}\sum_{j_2}\sum_{j_3}\sum_{j_4} \mathcal{A}_{j_1 j_2 j_3 j_4} a_{j_1}^\dagger a_{j_2}^\dagger a_{j_3} a_{j_4} \tag{5.4}$$

where $a_j(a_j^\dagger)$ is the annihilation (creation) operator for the jth state. The single-electron part (interaction between an electron and its image) is a known constant [5.1],

$$\mathcal{W} = -\frac{e^2}{\epsilon\sqrt{ab}}\left[2 - \sum_{l_1 l_2}{}' \varphi_{-\frac{1}{2}}\left\{\pi\left(\lambda l_1^2 + \lambda^{-1} l_2^2\right)\right\}\right] \tag{5.5}$$

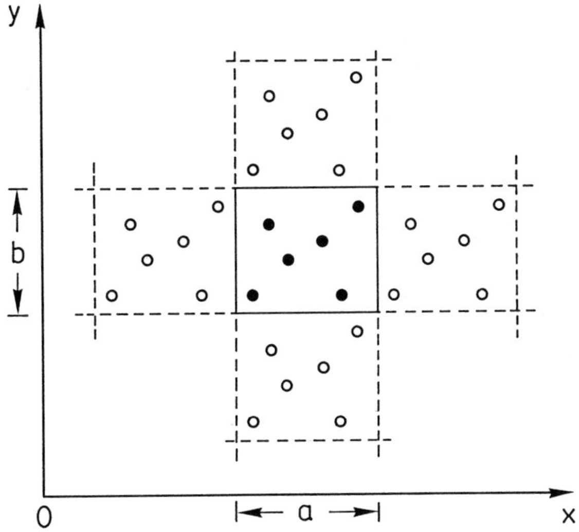

Fig. 5.1. Geometry considered by *Yoshioka* et al. [5.1]. Electrons (drawn as solid circles) are in a rectangular cell in the x-y plane. Because of the periodic boundary conditions, the electrons not only interact among themselves, but also with their images (drawn as open circles)

where λ is the aspect ratio, l_1, l_2 are integers. The prime on the summation indicates that the term with $l_1 = l_2 = 0$ is excluded, and

$$\varphi_n(z) \equiv \int_1^\infty dt\, \mathrm{e}^{-zt}\, t^n .$$

The two-electron part is given by

$$\begin{aligned}\mathcal{A}_{j_1 j_2 j_3 j_4} &= \frac{1}{2}\int d\boldsymbol{r}_1 d\boldsymbol{r}_2 \phi^*_{j_1}(\boldsymbol{r}_1)\phi^*_{j_2}(\boldsymbol{r}_2)V(\boldsymbol{r}_1-\boldsymbol{r}_2)\phi_{j_3}(\boldsymbol{r}_2)\phi_{j_4}(\boldsymbol{r}_1)\\ &= \frac{1}{2ab}\sum_{q}{}^{'}\sum_s\sum_t \delta_{q_x,2\pi s/a}\delta_{q_y,2\pi t/b}\delta'_{j_1-j_4,t}\frac{2\pi e^2}{\epsilon q}\\ &\times \exp\left[-\frac{1}{2}\ell_0^2 q^2 - 2\pi \mathrm{i} s(j_1-j_3)/m\right]\delta'_{j_1+j_2,j_3+j_4} .\end{aligned} \tag{5.6}$$

Here the Kronecker delta with the prime means that the equation is defined modulo N_s (or m), and the summation over q excludes $q_x = q_y = 0$.

The basis is specified by the occupation of the single-electron state: $(j_1, j_2, \cdots, j_{N_\mathrm{e}})$. The total number of bases is given by the number of combinations: $\binom{N_s}{N_e}$. In the absence of Coulomb interaction, all these bases are degenerate. The Coulomb interaction lifts the degeneracy and mixes the bases. Therefore, one needs to diagonalize rather large Hamiltonian matrices.

In order to simplify the calculation, one exploits the symmetry of the system. The total momentum in the y-direction, $J \equiv \sum_{i=1}^{N_e} j_i \pmod{N_s}$, is conserved due to the translational symmetry along the y-axis. For each J, the matrix dimension is $\sim \frac{1}{N_s}\binom{N_s}{N_e}$. Two values of J which differ by a multiple of N_e are equivalent due to translational symmetry along the x-axis. Therefore when N_s and N_e have no common factor, every eigenvalue is at least N_s-fold degenerate. However, if N_s and N_e do have a common

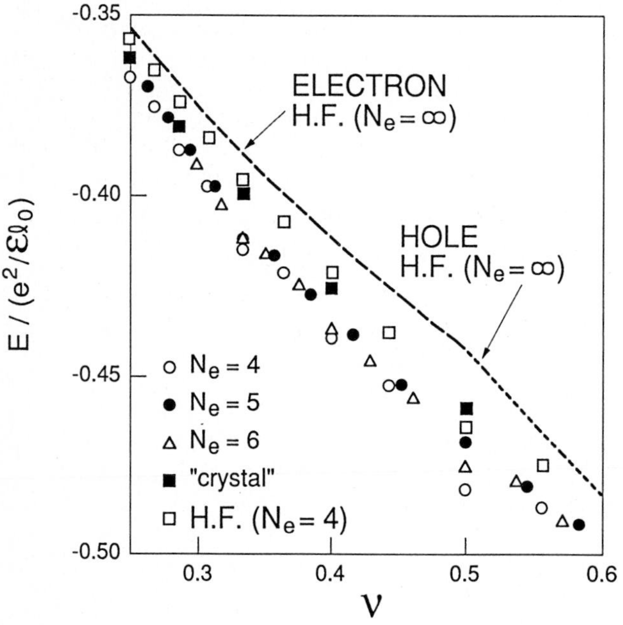

Fig. 5.2. Energies per particle for finite electron systems in a periodic rectangular geometry, as a function of filling factor in the lowest Landau level [5.1]. The dashed and dotted lines are the energy of the electron and hole crystals within the HF approximation for the infinite system. Open circles, closed circles, and triangles are the results for N_e=4, 5 and 6 electrons for $\nu \leq \frac{1}{2}$ and holes for $\nu > \frac{1}{2}$. Closed squares denote the crystal state energies for the N_e=4 system. Open squares show the energy of the crystal state for the N_e=4 system obtained in the HF approximation

factor, the states are less degenerate and the ground state is realized only for certain values of J. As an example, for $N_\mathrm{e} = 4$ and $N_\mathrm{s} = 12$, the three-fold ground state appears for $J = 2, 6$, and 10. Finally, due to the rotational symmetry, the cell with aspect ratio a/b is equivalent to that with aspect ratio b/a.

In Fig. 5.2, we present the numerical results of *Yoshioka* et al. [5.1], for the ground-state energies per particle as a function of filling fraction in the lowest Landau level. There are several interesting features noticeable in the result. Let us first consider the case $\nu = \frac{1}{3}$. The ground-state energy per particle for four-, five- and six-electron systems are (in units of $e^2/\epsilon\ell_0$): $-0.4152, -0.4127$, and -0.4129 respectively, and are extremely insensitive to the system size. As we shall see in the next section, these results are also very close to the infinite system result.

The ground-state energies tend to have downward *cusps* for $\nu = \frac{1}{3}$ and $\frac{2}{5}$. The system size is however too small to realize them more clearly. As discussed in Chap. 4, a cusp at the observed filling fractions is quite naturally required, in order to describe the incompressible fluid state proposed by Laughlin.

In Fig. 5.2, Yoshioka et al. also presented the energy of the crystal state for $N_\mathrm{e} = 4$ system obtained in the exact diagonalization (closed squares) and HF approximation (open squares). The dashed and dotted lines show the energy of the electron and hole crystals resulting from the HF approximation for the infinite system [5.10]. These crystal state results show a smooth behavior at $\nu = \frac{1}{3}$ and are not the lowest energy state.

In order to investigate the eigenstates of the Hamiltonian, *Yoshioka* et al. [5.11,12] calculated the pair distribution function,

$$\begin{aligned} g(\boldsymbol{r}) \equiv & \frac{ab}{N_\mathrm{e}(N_\mathrm{e}-1)} \langle\Psi| \sum_{i \neq j} \delta(\boldsymbol{r}+\boldsymbol{r}_i-\boldsymbol{r}_j) |\Psi\rangle \\ = & \frac{1}{N_\mathrm{e}(N_\mathrm{e}-1)} \sum_{\boldsymbol{q}} \sum_{j_1} \cdots \sum_{j_4} \exp\left[\mathrm{i}\boldsymbol{q}\cdot\boldsymbol{r} - \frac{1}{2}q^2\ell_0^2 - \mathrm{i}(j_1-j_3)\frac{q_x a}{m}\right] \\ & \times \delta'_{j_1-j_4, q_y b/2\pi} \langle\psi| a^\dagger_{j_1} a^\dagger_{j_2} a_{j_3} a_{j_4} |\psi\rangle \end{aligned} \tag{5.7}$$

where $|\Psi\rangle$ is one of the eigenstates. In Fig. 5.3, we reproduce the $g(\boldsymbol{r})$ at $\nu = \frac{1}{3}$ for the four-electron system studied by *Yoshioka* et al. [5.11]. The results are for the ground state and one of the excited states. For the excited state, $g(\boldsymbol{r})$ is almost identical to that of the triangular CDW state obtained from the HF approximation for the infinite system. Therefore these authors identified the state with the CDW state. On the other hand, the ground-state $g(\boldsymbol{r})$ is found to be quite different. It has peaks at $\boldsymbol{r} = (\pm\frac{a}{2}, 0)$

and $\left(0, \pm\frac{b}{2}\right)$, but *not* at $\boldsymbol{r} = \left(\pm\frac{a}{2}, \pm\frac{b}{2}\right)$, where peaks would be expected if the state were a square CDW state. Furthermore, the shape of the peaks is different from the gaussian peak of the CDW state. It was therefore concluded that the ground state is a liquid-like state. The ground-state $g(\boldsymbol{r})$ for higher values of N_e also shows the same structure [5.12].

In the lowest Landau level, there is electron-hole symmetry. The system with N_e electrons in N_s sites is thus equivalent to that with $(N_s - N_e)$ holes in N_s sites. When we choose the products of the single-electron eigenstates as a basis, the off-diagonal matrix elements for $\nu = N_e/N_s$ are the same as those for $\nu = (1 - N_e/N_s)$ for the same J values. The diagonal matrix elements differ only by a constant ΔE given by

$$\Delta E = \sum_{j_1=1}^{N_e} \sum_{j_2=1}^{N_e} (A_{j_1 j_2 j_2 j_1} - A_{j_1 j_2 j_1 j_2}) - \sum_{j_1=1}^{N_s-N_e} \sum_{j_2=1}^{N_s-N_e} (A_{j_1 j_2 j_2 j_1} - A_{j_1 j_2 j_1 j_2}). \quad (5.8)$$

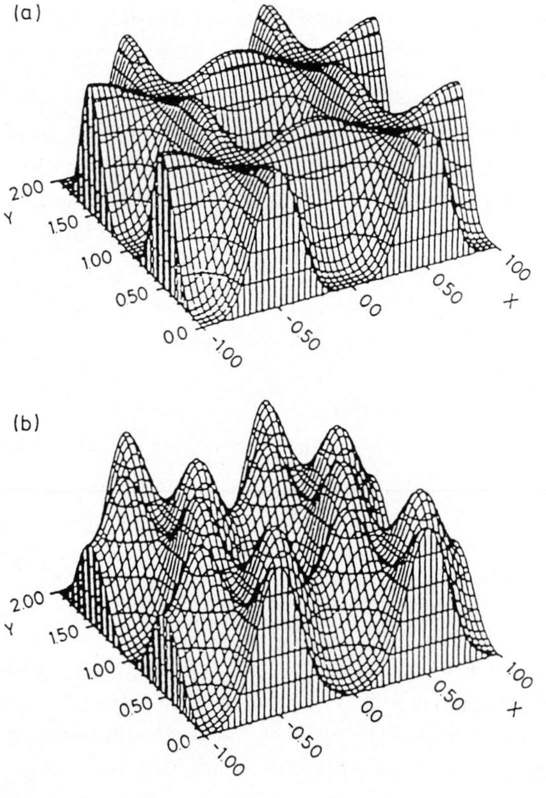

Fig. 5.3. Perspective view of the pair correlation function $g(r)$ obtained in [5.11] for $N_e = 4$ and $N_s = 12$; (a) the ground state (b) an excited state identified as the CDW state. The axes are normalized by the dimension of the cell: $X = x/a$ and $Y = y/b$

The results for $\nu > \frac{1}{2}$, presented in Fig. 5.2 are obtained by the above arguments.

While these numerical results demonstrate that the ground state is not crystalline, as *Halperin* pointed out [5.13], not much insight is gained about the ground-state wave function. The crucial step in obtaining both a ground-state wave function for a translationally invariant liquid state, and the mechanism for stabilizing the system at particular densities, was made by Laughlin, and is described below.

5.2 Laughlin's Theory

The original paper by *Laughlin* [5.2] contains the seminal ideas which have been elaborated since by him [5.3], and by other authors [5.6,13]. The reader is also referred to an article by *Laughlin* [5.4] for an insight on how the theory was orginally conceived. In the following, we discuss briefly the salient points of this theory.

Consider electrons confined in the x-y plane and subjected to a magnetic field perpendicular to the plane. Using the symmetric gauge vector potential, $\boldsymbol{A} = \frac{1}{2}B(x\widehat{y} - y\widehat{x})$, it is convenient to regard the x-y plane as a complex plane. For the lowest Landau level, the single-particle wave functions are eigenfunctions of orbital angular momentum (see Appendix A),

$$\phi_m(z) \equiv |m\rangle = \frac{1}{(2\pi\ell_0^2 2^m m!)^{\frac{1}{2}}} \left(\frac{z}{\ell_0}\right)^m \mathrm{e}^{-|z|^2/4{\ell_0}^2} \tag{5.9}$$

where $z = x - \mathrm{i}y$ is the electron position. The many-electron system is described by the Hamiltonian:

$$\mathcal{H} = \sum_j \left[\frac{1}{2m_\mathrm{e}}|-\mathrm{i}\hbar\nabla_j - \frac{e}{c}\boldsymbol{A}_j|^2 + V(z_j)\right] + \sum_{j<k} \frac{e^2}{|z_j - z_k|} \tag{5.10}$$

where z_j is the location of the jth electron and $V(z)$ is the potential generated by a uniform neutralizing background. It is easy to verify that [5.14],

$$\langle m|r^2|m\rangle = 2(m+1){\ell_0}^2 \tag{5.11}$$

which means that the area covered by a single electron in state $|m\rangle$, moving in its cyclotron orbit, is proportional to m. This result might be considered as an indication of the relation between the interelectron spacing and the angular momentum. From (5.11), it is readily noticeable that the degeneracy of a Landau level N_s, is the upper bound to the quantum number m. This is seen by requiring that,

$$\pi\langle r^2\rangle \leq A \tag{5.12}$$

where A is the area of the system. One then obtains from the above two relations,

$$m \leq N_s - 1 \tag{5.13}$$

where the Landau-level degeneracy N_s is defined in (1.13). From (5.9) and (5.13) we find that the state space of an electron in the lowest Landau level is spanned by $1, z, z^2, \ldots, z^{N_s-1}$ times the exponential factor $e^{-|z|^2/4\ell_0^2}$.

The *Jastrow-type* many-electron wave function proposed by Laughlin for the $\nu = \frac{1}{m}$ state is

$$\psi_m = \prod_{\substack{j,k=1\\ j<k}}^{N_e} (z_j - z_k)^m \prod_{j=1}^{N_e} e^{-|z_j|^2/4\ell_0^2}. \tag{5.14}$$

For m being an odd integer, this wave function obeys Fermi statistics. The wave function is entirely made up out of states in the lowest Landau level. It is also an eigenstate of the angular momentum with eigenvalue $M = \frac{1}{2}N_e(N_e - 1)m$. The total angular momentum M is the degree of the polynomial (conservation of angular momentum). In order to gain more insight about the wave function, let us expand the first product in powers of z_1, keeping all other coordinates fixed. The highest power then would be $m(N_e - 1)$, which must be equal to $N_s - 1$ [see (5.13)]. For large N_e, we then obtain [see (1.13)],

$$m \cong \frac{A}{2\pi\ell_0^2 N_e} = \frac{1}{\nu}. \tag{5.15}$$

The parameter m is thus fixed by the density, and unlike conventional Jastrow theory, we do not have a variational parameter in the trial wave function. For $m = 1$ (filled Landau level), the polynomial $\prod_{j<k}(z_j - z_k)$ is the Vandermonde determinant of order N_e. As $N_e \to \infty$, the particle density in this state tends to $1/(2\pi\ell_0^2)$ [5.15].

For $m > 1$, the wave function vanishes as a high power of the two electron separation, and thus tends to minimize the repulsive interaction energy. The probability distribution of the electron for ψ_m is given by

$$|\psi_m|^2 = e^{-\mathcal{H}_m} \tag{5.16}$$

with

$$\mathcal{H}_m = -2m \sum_{j<k} \ln |z_j - z_k| + \sum_j |z_j|^2/2\ell_0^2. \tag{5.17}$$

For a *charge neutral* two-dimensional classical plasma, the interaction is given [5.16] by

$$V(\boldsymbol{r}) = -e^2 \sum_{j<k} \ln\, r_{jk} + \frac{1}{2}\pi\rho e^2 \sum_j r_j^2 \tag{5.18}$$

where the particles are interacting via a two-dimensional Coulomb (logarithmic) interaction with each other and with a uniform neutralizing background. From (5.17) and (5.18), it is clear that $\mathcal{H}_m$ is the Hamiltonian for a two-dimensional classical plasma with,

$$e^2 = 2m,\ \rho_m = \frac{1}{2\pi\ell_0^2 m}. \tag{5.19}$$

Therefore, in order to achieve charge neutrality, the plasma particles spread out uniformly in a disk with particle density ρ_m, corresponding to a filling factor $\nu = \frac{1}{m}$, where m is an *odd* integer. The classical plasma provides strong support that the Laughlin state is indeed a translationally invariant liquid [5.2,16].

The electrons however, in contrast to the classical plasma particles, interact via the *three-dimensional* Coulomb interaction, and the expectation value of the potential energy in a quantum state is given by

$$\frac{\langle V\rangle}{N_{\mathrm{e}}} = \frac{1}{2}\int v(r)g(r)d\boldsymbol{r}\,, \tag{5.20}$$

where $g(r)$ is the two-particle radial distribution function, which will be calculated below by the classical plasma approach. Introducing the *ion-disk* radius [5.16] $R = \sqrt{2m}\ell_0$ and the dimensionless distance $x = r/R$, the energy per particle is given as

$$\langle E\rangle = \frac{1}{\sqrt{2m}}\frac{e^2}{\epsilon\ell_0}\int_0^\infty [g(x) - 1]\, dx. \tag{5.21}$$

In (5.21), we have included the contribution from the neutralizing background. Because the wave function is for the lowest Landau level, the kinetic energy part is constant. The radial distribution function $g(x)$ was obtained by Laughlin using the hypernetted-chain (HNC)[1] theory, which is a well-established technique for dealing with the classical plasma [5.16,17] and quantum fluids [5.18].

The dimensionless coupling parameter of the plasma $\Gamma = e^2/k_{\mathrm{B}}T$ [5.16, 17], is related to the present problem via, $\Gamma = 2m$. For $m = 1$, the *exact* result is available for the pair correlation function, $g(x) = 1 - \mathrm{e}^{-x^2}$ and the energy, $E = -\sqrt{\pi/8}$ [5.19]. As *Laughlin* pointed out [5.2], $\Gamma = 2$ corresponds to a full Landau level where the total energy equals the HF energy. This correspondence explains the existence of an exact result for $\Gamma = 2$.

The two-dimensional Fourier transform is given by

$$\widetilde{f}(q) = 2\int_0^\infty f(x)J_0(qx)x\,dx \tag{5.22}$$

where $q = kR$, and $J_0(x)$ is the zeroth-order Bessel function. For $m = 3, 5, 7, \ldots$ the distribution function is obtained from the following set of equations [the various functions are defined in Appendix C, see also (C.18)],

$$\begin{aligned} g(x) &\simeq \exp\left[N(x) - u(x)\right] \\ \widetilde{N}(q) &= \left[\widetilde{C}(q)\right]^2 \Big/ \left[1 - \widetilde{C}(q)\right] \\ C(x) &= g(x) - 1 - N(x). \end{aligned} \tag{5.23}$$

with, $u(x) = -2m\ln x$. In order to handle the logarithmic interaction, the standard procedure is to separate the short-range and long-range part of the interactions as [5.17],

$$\begin{aligned} u^{\mathrm{s}}(x) &= 2mK_0(Qx) \\ u^{\mathrm{l}}(x) &= -2m\left[\ln x + K_0(Qx)\right] \end{aligned} \tag{5.24}$$

where K_0 is the modified Bessel function, and Q is a cutoff parameter of order unity. For small x, $u^{\mathrm{s}}(x)$ reduces to the full Coulomb potential in two dimensions, and at large distances it decreases exponentially. Defining the short-range functions [5.20],

$$\begin{aligned} N^{\mathrm{s}}(x) &= N(x) - u^{\mathrm{l}}(x) \\ C^{\mathrm{s}}(x) &= C(x) + u^{\mathrm{l}}(x), \end{aligned} \tag{5.25}$$

[1] An introduction to the HNC method is given in Appendix C.

one obtains the final set of equations

$$
\begin{aligned}
\widetilde{N}^{\mathrm{s}}(q) &= \left\{\widetilde{C}^{\mathrm{s}}(q)\left[\widetilde{C}^{\mathrm{s}}(q) - \widetilde{u}^{\mathrm{l}}(q)\right] - \widetilde{u}^{\mathrm{l}}(q)\right\} \Big/ \left[1 - \widetilde{C}^{\mathrm{s}}(q) + \widetilde{u}^{\mathrm{l}}(q)\right] \\
\widetilde{u}^{\mathrm{l}}(q) &= \frac{4mQ^2}{q^2\left(q^2+Q^2\right)} \\
g(x) &= \exp\left[N^{\mathrm{s}}(x) - u^{\mathrm{s}}(x)\right] \\
C^{\mathrm{s}}(x) &= g(x) - 1 - N^{\mathrm{s}}(x)
\end{aligned}
\qquad (5.26)
$$

which are solved by a straightforward iteration scheme. As explained in Appendix C, the first step in the numerical iteration procedure could be to set, $\widetilde{N}^{\mathrm{s}}(q) = 0$. The pair-correlation function is then trivially obtained with the known function $u^{\mathrm{s}}(x)$. With that $g(x)$ one then obtains $C^{\mathrm{s}}(x)$ and its Fourier transform $\widetilde{C}^{\mathrm{s}}(q)$. The next step is to obtain $\widetilde{N}^{\mathrm{s}}(q)$ from the new $\widetilde{C}^{\mathrm{s}}(q)$ and the inverse Fourier transform $N^{\mathrm{s}}(x)$ then provides the new $g(x)$. The process is repeated until convergence is achieved. The resulting $g(x)$ is plotted in Fig. 5.4 for $m = 3$ as a function of x, and shows characteristics of a *liquid* state. In Fig. 5.4, we also present the radial distribution function for a Wigner crystal state of the form [5.4]

$$
\Psi_{\mathrm{WC}}(z_1, \ldots, z_n) = \sum_{\sigma} \operatorname{sgn}(\sigma)\, \phi_{j_1 k_1}[z_{\sigma(1)}] \cdots \phi_{j_n k_n}[z_{\sigma(n)}],
$$

where σ is a permutation with $\operatorname{sgn}(\sigma)$ the sign and the orbitals are gaussians,

$$
\phi_{jk}[z] = \mathrm{e}^{-\frac{1}{4}\left|z_{jk}^{(0)}\right|^2} \mathrm{e}^{\frac{1}{2} z^* z_{jk}^{(0)}} \mathrm{e}^{\frac{1}{4}|z|^2},
$$

centered at hexagonal lattice sites $z_{jk}^{(0)}$,

$$
z_{jk}^{(0)} = \sqrt{\frac{4\pi m}{\sqrt{3}}}\left[j + \left(\tfrac{1}{2} + \tfrac{1}{2}\mathrm{i}\sqrt{3}\right) k\right].
$$

For small x, $g(x)$ goes to zero as x^2 for the crystal state, while for the Laughlin state, it goes as x^{2m}.

The ground-state energy for the $\nu = \frac{1}{3}$ state, obtained from the HNC $g(x)$ and (5.21) is $E(\nu = \frac{1}{3}) = -0.4056\, e^2/\epsilon\ell_0$. This result is quite close to the exact results obtained for finite electron systems in Sect. 5.1. It should be remarked at this point that Laughlin used a modified HNC version where the so-called *elementary* diagrams (neglected in the above discussion) were approximately summed (the modified HNC approach is briefly discussed in Appendix C) and the result was $-0.4156\, e^2/\epsilon\ell_0$. The ground-state ener-

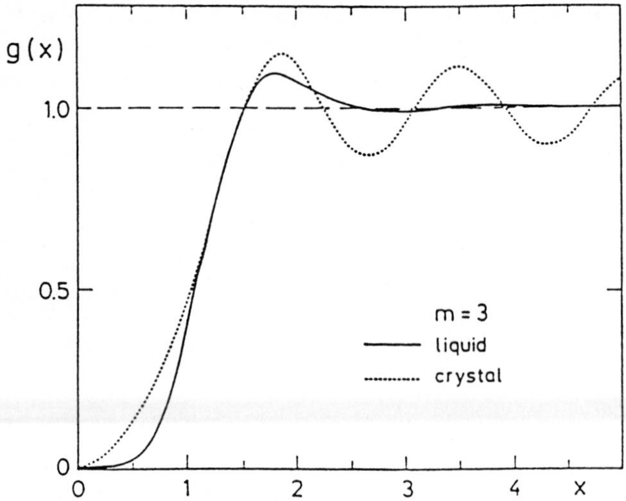

Fig. 5.4. Radial distribution function $g(x)$ as a function of the dimensionless interparticle separation $x = r/\sqrt{2m}\ell_0$, for the Laughlin state at $m = 3$ (solid line) and the WC state in the HF approximation (dashed line) at the same density

gies for various filling fractions can be fitted to the following approximate formula [5.2]:

$$E_{\mathrm{pl}}(m) \cong \frac{-0.814}{\sqrt{m}}\left[1 - \frac{0.230}{m^{0.64}}\right]\left(\frac{e^2}{\epsilon\ell_0}\right) \tag{5.27}$$

which is a smooth function of m.

Several authors have studied the important characteristics of Laughlin's wave function. *Halperin* [5.13] has shown that the m-fold vanishing of the wave function when two electrons come close, helps to minimize the potential energy of the system and also provides exceptional stability of the system at filling factors $\nu = \frac{1}{m}$. To see this point more clearly, we will discuss the zeros of the Laughlin wave function in somewhat more detail [5.21]. Let us imagine freezing the positions of all but the first particle. This leads to an effective wave function $\varphi(z_1)$ parametrized by the positions of the other particles. The function φ is analytic throughout the complex z_1 plane and from a fundamental theorem of algebra, is uniquely defined by the set of its zeros $\{Z_j; j = 1, \ldots, L\}$:

$$\varphi(z_1) = A\prod_{j=1}^{L}(z_1 - Z_j) \tag{5.28}$$

where A is independent of z_1. (In fact, A and the positions of the zeros do depend on $\{z_2, \ldots, z_N\}$.) The probability density for the particle at z_1 is ($\ell_0 \equiv 1$)

$$\rho(z_1) = |\varphi(z_1)|^2 \, \mathrm{e}^{-|z_1|^2/2}. \tag{5.29}$$

From the plasma analogy

$$\begin{aligned} \rho(z_1) &= |A|^2 \, \mathrm{e}^{-\beta\Phi(z_1)}, \quad \beta \equiv \frac{2}{m} \\ \Phi(z_1) &= m \sum_{j=1}^{L} \left[-\ln|z_1 - Z_j| + \tfrac{1}{4}|z_1|^2 \right]. \end{aligned} \tag{5.30}$$

Therefore the zeros of the wave function look like two-dimensional charges which repel the particle (logarithmic interaction). The $|z_1|^2/4$ term corresponds to a uniform background charge of density $\rho_0 = 1/2\pi$. Now if $\rho(z_1)$ is to be roughly uniform and not confined to the origin by the gaussian term, the density of point charges (zeros) must compensate the background. Halperin observed that Laughlin's wave function makes the optimum use of these zeros by placing them directly on the other particles. If m zeros are attached to each particle, they see each other as point Coulomb charges (charge m) and the particle density will be fixed to $\rho = 1/2\pi m$ (the magnetic length is taken to be unity throughout this discussion) by the *charge neutrality* requirement of the plasma.

Haldane and *Rezayi* [5.9] found that for six particles on a sphere, the energy difference between the exact ground state and Laughlin's wave function is smaller than one part in 2000. They have also presented the Laughlin-Jastrow wave function for a geometry which satisfies periodic boundary conditions [5.22]. From this work they concluded that the success of Laughlin's wave function was because of the correct behavior as the particles approach each other and does not depend on the arguments based on the conservation of the angular momentum.

Utilizing the electron-hole symmetry in the lowest Landau level (see Sect. 5.1.), one obtains the Laughlin state for $\nu = 1 - \frac{1}{m}$, [5.3,23]. In the following, we present a brief discussion of the electron-hole symmetry. We follow closely the work of Ref. 5.23. In the symmetric gauge, the many-electron wave function is given by (5.9). As discussed in Appendix A, the exponential factor common to all wave functions can be eliminated by defining a Hilbert space of functions analytic in z with inner product,

$$(\psi, \phi) = \int d\mu(z) \, \psi^*(z)\phi(z) \tag{5.31}$$

with the measure

$$d\mu(z) = \frac{dxdy}{2\pi\ell_0^2} e^{-|z|^2/4\ell_0^2}. \tag{5.32}$$

Invoking particle-hole symmetry, the state with $\nu = 1 - \frac{1}{m}$ must have *holes* described by the state in (5.9).

The properly normalized $(N+1)$-particle state for a filled Landau level is written as

$$\begin{aligned} \boldsymbol{\Phi}_{N+1}(z_1, \ldots, z_{N+1}) &= \frac{1}{Q_{N+1}} \prod_{j<k}^{N+1} (z_j - z_k) \\ Q_{N+1}^2 &= (N+1)! \prod_{j=0}^{N} (2^j j!). \end{aligned} \tag{5.33}$$

For a hole in the single-particle state ϕ_M, we write

$$\theta_M(z_1, \ldots, z_N) = (N+1)^{\frac{1}{2}} \int d\mu(z_{N+1}) \phi_M^*(z_{N+1}) \boldsymbol{\Phi}_{N+1}(z_1, \ldots, z_{N+1}). \tag{5.34}$$

It is to be noted that, $\boldsymbol{\Phi}_{N+1}$ is a single Slater determinant

$$\boldsymbol{\Phi}_{N+1} = \frac{1}{Q_{N+1}} \sum_{\{P\}} (-1)^P \prod_{j=1}^{N+1} z_j^{P_j}. \tag{5.35}$$

In (5.35), P_j is the image of j under a permutation P of $N+1$ points $[0, 1, 2, \ldots, j, \ldots, N]$. From (5.34) and (5.35), one obtains after integration,

$$\theta_M(z_1, \ldots, z_N) = (N+1)^{\frac{1}{2}} \frac{(2^M M!)^{\frac{1}{2}}}{Q_{N+1}} \sum_{\{P\}} (-1)^P \prod_{j=1}^{N} z_j^{P_j} \delta_{M, P_{N+1}}. \tag{5.36}$$

The function θ_M therefore, describes an N-particle Slater determinant with every state ϕ_j occupied for $0 \le j \le N$ except the state ϕ_M, which remains empty. The norm is $(\theta_M, \theta_M) = 1$ as required. Equation (5.34) provides an exact procedure for injecting a hole into any particular state. One can, in fact, readily generalize (5.34) for the case of an arbitary number of holes. For example, the electron wave function,

$$\phi(z_1, \ldots, z_N) = \prod_{k=1}^{M} \int d\mu(z_{N+k}) \prod_{j<k}^{M} (z_{N+j}^* - z_{N+k}^*)^m \boldsymbol{\Phi}_{N+M}(z_1, \ldots, z_{N+M}) \tag{5.37}$$

would correspond to the *hole* wave function as the correlated state ψ_m of (5.9). Therefore, this state has the filling factor $\nu = 1 - \frac{1}{m}$ and for $N \to \infty$ corresponds to the *exact* particle-hole dual of the state with $\nu = \frac{1}{m}$. For a large but finite M we should have: $N + M = mM$ so that the holes cover the same area as the electrons.

Finally, in the case of repulsive interactions of vanishing range, *Trugman* and *Kivelson* [5.24] and independently *Pokrovskii* and *Talapov* [5.25] found that Laughlin's state ψ_m is the exact, nondegenerate ground state for $\nu = \frac{1}{m}$.

5.3 Spherical Geometry

An attractive alternative to the finite-size studies described in Sect. 5.1 is to consider the spherical geometry [5.8]. Here the electrons are confined on the surface of a sphere of radius R with a magnetic monopole at the center. The total magnetic flux, $\boldsymbol{\Phi} = 4\pi R^2 B$ is required to be an integral multiple $N_\mathrm{s} = 2S$ of the elementary flux quantum $\boldsymbol{\Phi}_0$. Therefore, the radius of the sphere is determined as

$$R = S^{\frac{1}{2}}\,\ell_0. \tag{5.38}$$

For an electron of mass m on the surface of the sphere, the kinetic energy is written as

$$\mathcal{K} = |\boldsymbol{\Lambda}|^2/2m = \frac{1}{2}\omega_\mathrm{c}|\boldsymbol{\Lambda}|^2/\hbar S \tag{5.39}$$

where $\boldsymbol{\Lambda} = \boldsymbol{r} \times [-\mathrm{i}\hbar\nabla + e\boldsymbol{A}(\boldsymbol{r})]$ is the kinetic angular momentum; $\nabla \times \boldsymbol{A} = B\widehat{\boldsymbol{\Omega}}$, with $\widehat{\boldsymbol{\Omega}} = \boldsymbol{r}/R$. The angular momentum $\boldsymbol{\Lambda}$ obeys the commutation relations,

$$[\Lambda_\alpha, \Lambda_\beta] = \mathrm{i}\hbar\epsilon_{\alpha\beta\gamma}\left(\Lambda_\gamma - \hbar S\widehat{\Omega}_\gamma\right) \tag{5.40}$$

where $\epsilon_{\alpha\beta\gamma}$ is the antisymmetric rank-three tensor. Let us now define the operators

$$\boldsymbol{L} = \boldsymbol{\Lambda} + \hbar S\widehat{\boldsymbol{\Omega}}, \tag{5.41}$$

which are the generators of rotation with the commutation relations:

$$[L^\alpha, X^\beta] = \mathrm{i}\hbar\epsilon_{\alpha\beta\gamma}X_\gamma \tag{5.42}$$

where $\boldsymbol{X} = \boldsymbol{L}, \widehat{\boldsymbol{\Omega}}$, or $\boldsymbol{\Lambda}$.

As the angular momentum $\boldsymbol{\Lambda}$ has no component normal to the surface, $\boldsymbol{\Lambda} \cdot \widehat{\boldsymbol{\Omega}} = \widehat{\boldsymbol{\Omega}} \cdot \boldsymbol{\Lambda} = 0$, we have, $\boldsymbol{L} \cdot \widehat{\boldsymbol{\Omega}} = \widehat{\boldsymbol{\Omega}} \cdot \boldsymbol{L} = \hbar S$. As a result,

$$|\vec{\Lambda}|^2 = |\boldsymbol{L}|^2 - \hbar^2 S^2 \tag{5.43}$$

and the eigenvalues of $|\boldsymbol{\Lambda}|^2$ are deduced from the usual angular momentum algebra, $|\boldsymbol{\Lambda}|^2 = |\boldsymbol{L}|^2 - \hbar^2 S^2 = \hbar^2 \left\{n(n+1) - S^2\right\}$, n being an integer. The gauge is chosen such that the vector potential is given by $\boldsymbol{A} = \left(\frac{\hbar S}{eR}\right) \widehat{\varphi} \cot\theta$.

For $n = S$, one obtains the lowest landau level with energy $\frac{1}{2}\hbar\omega_{\mathrm{c}}$. The degeneracy of this level is in fact finite: There are $(2S+1)$ independent degenerate eigenfunctions. For complete occupation of these states, the electron density is given by

$$(2S+1)/4\pi R^2 \sim \frac{S}{2\pi R^2} = \frac{1}{2\pi \ell_0^2}$$

for large R, similar to what one obtains in a planar geometry.

In order to find the single-particle eigenstates of the Hamiltonian, *Haldane* [5.8] noted that these are most suitably represented in the space of spinors of rank $2S$. For that purpose he introduced the spinor variables, $u = \cos\left(\frac{1}{2}\theta\right) \mathrm{e}^{\mathrm{i}\varphi/2}$, $v = \sin\left(\frac{1}{2}\theta\right) \mathrm{e}^{-\mathrm{i}\varphi/2}$. The components of the operator $\boldsymbol{L}$ [see (5.41)] can now be written as

$$\begin{aligned} L^+ &= \hbar u \frac{\partial}{\partial v}; \quad L_z = \frac{1}{2}\left(u\frac{\partial}{\partial u} - v\frac{\partial}{\partial v}\right) \\ L^- &= \hbar v \frac{\partial}{\partial u} \end{aligned} \tag{5.44}$$

employing the standard raising and lowering operators $L^{\pm} = L_x \pm \mathrm{i}L_y$. To satisfy, $\boldsymbol{L} \cdot \widehat{\boldsymbol{\Omega}} = \hbar S$ one must have,

$$S = \frac{1}{2}\left(u\frac{\partial}{\partial u} + v\frac{\partial}{\partial v}\right).$$

For any homogeneous polynomial $\psi^{(S)}(u,v)$ of degree $2S$ the following relation holds,

$$|\boldsymbol{L}|^2 \psi^{(S)} = S(S+1)\hbar\psi^{(S)}. \tag{5.45}$$

One can now associate with each unit vector $\widehat{\boldsymbol{\Omega}}(\alpha,\beta)$, a homogeneous polynomial,

$$\psi^{(S)}_{(\alpha,\beta)}(u,v) = (\alpha^* u + \beta^* v)^{2S}, \; |\alpha|^2 + |\beta|^2 = 1$$

which also satisfies the eigenvalue equation

$$\left(\hat{\Omega}(\alpha,\beta) \cdot \boldsymbol{L}\right) \psi^{(S)}_{(\alpha,\beta)} = \hbar S \psi^{(S)}_{(\alpha,\beta)}. \tag{5.46}$$

A single electron may now be represented as a spin S, the orientation of which indicates the point on the sphere about which the state is localized. The analogy between the spin wave functions and the electron wave functions in a magnetic field was first shown by *Peres* [5.26].

Turning our attention to the many-electron states, the Laughlin-type wave function for $\nu = \frac{1}{m}$ is then written as [5.8,9],

$$\psi_m = \prod_{j<k} (u_j v_k - v_j u_k)^m. \tag{5.47}$$

As a function of (u_j, v_j), wave functions are required to be polynomials of degree $2S$. Since the maximum degree in one variable is clearly $m(N_{\rm e} - 1)$ we have $S = \frac{1}{2} m(N_{\rm e} - 1)$. On the other hand, we know that the Landau level is completely filled when all the $(2S + 1)$ single-particle states are occupied. Therefore the product (5.47) corresponds to a filling fraction $\nu = \frac{1}{m}$. As any factor in the product (5.47) describes a pair of particles with total spin zero, one obtains an uniform electron density on the sphere. The wave function also has m-fold zeros when the coordinates of any two particles coincide. The wave function ψ_m is an eigenfunction of $\boldsymbol{L}^2$ with $L = 0$. This implies that $|\psi_m|^2$ is invariant under rotations of the sphere.

The numerical results for finite electron systems in this geometry were first obtained by *Haldane* and *Rezayi* [5.9] and later by *Fano* et al. [5.27]. The exact ground state at flux $2S = 3(N_{\rm e} - 1)$, ($\nu = \frac{1}{3}$), was found to be isotropic with total angular momentum $\boldsymbol{L} = 0$, and separated from the excited states at the same $(N_{\rm e}, S)$ by a gap. Their results for the ground-state energy per particle are plotted in Fig. 5.5 for various values of $N_{\rm e}$. The extrapolated result for $N_{\rm e} \to \infty$ is $-0.415 \pm 0.005\, e^2/\epsilon\ell_0$. The energy values in this geometry are found to be more system-size dependent than those for the rectangular geometry.

Morf et al. [5.28] however noticed that, unlike in the disk geometry the areal electron density is size dependent:

$$\frac{N_{\rm e}}{4\pi R^2} = \frac{N_{\rm e}}{2\pi\ell_0^2} \frac{\nu}{N_{\rm e} - 1}, \tag{5.48}$$

which leads to an energy which reflects this size dependence of the density.

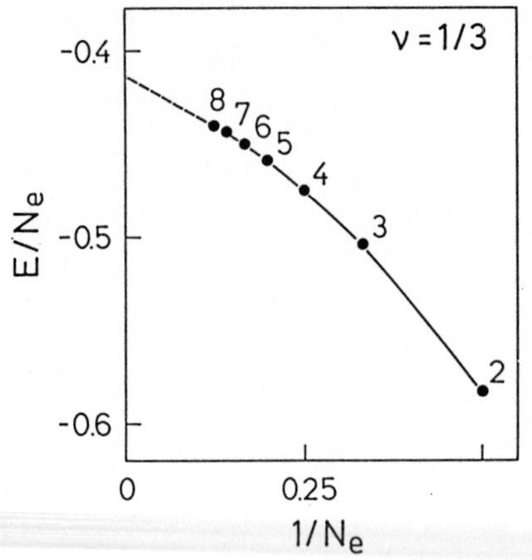

Fig. 5.5. Ground-state energy per particle for finite electron systems in a spherical geometry as a function of electron number N_e [5.9]

This size dependence in the energy can be removed by defining a modified magnetic length,

$$\ell_0' = (2S\nu/N_\mathrm{e})^{\frac{1}{2}}\ell_0 \tag{5.49}$$

such that $\nu/2\pi\ell_0'^2$ is independent of system size. For the interparticle separation, the *chord* distance between electrons i and j was used by *Haldane* and *Rezayi* [5.9]:

$$r(\Theta_{ij}) = 2R\sin\tfrac{1}{2}\Theta_{ij} \tag{5.50}$$

where the angle between position vectors $\boldsymbol{r}_i$ and $\boldsymbol{r}_j$ is written as

$$\Theta_{ij} = 2\arcsin|u_i v_j - v_i u_j|. \tag{5.51}$$

One can alternatively use the *great circle* distance,

$$r(\Theta_{ij}) = R\Theta_{ij}. \tag{5.52}$$

In the limit, $N_\mathrm{e} \to \infty$, however, energies evaluated with these two definitions of distances converge to the same point (see Fig. 5.10).

We mentioned earlier that Haldane and Rezayi have studied the exactness of the Laughlin wave function. The concept of pseudopotentials first introduced in this context by *Haldane* [5.8,9,29] is quite illuminating. The pseudopotential parameters which enter into the interaction Hamiltonian are written

$$V_m = \frac{1}{(2\pi)^2} \int d\boldsymbol{r}\, V(r) \int d\boldsymbol{q}\, \mathrm{e}^{\mathrm{i}\boldsymbol{q}\cdot\boldsymbol{r}} \mathrm{e}^{-(q\ell_0)^2} \left[L_n(\tfrac{1}{2}q^2\ell_0^2)\right]^2 L_m(q^2\ell_0^2) \qquad (5.53)$$

where $V(r)$ is the pair-interaction potential, and $L_n(x)$ is the Laguerre polynomial with Landau index n. These are the energies of pairs of particles with relative angular momentum m. For small m, the parameters V_m describe the short-range part, while V_m with large m describe the long-range part of the interaction. One should note, however, that this description of the interaction is not a local decomposition in real space.

In Fig. 5.6, we reproduce the six-electron results at $\nu = \frac{1}{3}$ [5.9] for the effect of varying V_1 for the lowest Landau level Coulomb system. The other pseudopotential parameters ($V_{m>1}$) are kept at their Coulomb values. In the limit, $V_1 \to +\infty$, the Laughlin state is the only state for which the ground state is independent of V_1, and becomes the exact ground state. The other states have energies which are proportional to V_1 in this limit, and there is a large energy gap. The Laughlin state is the exact ground state of a truncated "hard-core" pseudopotential V^{hc}, where $V^{\mathrm{hc}}_{m'} = V_{m'} \geq 0$

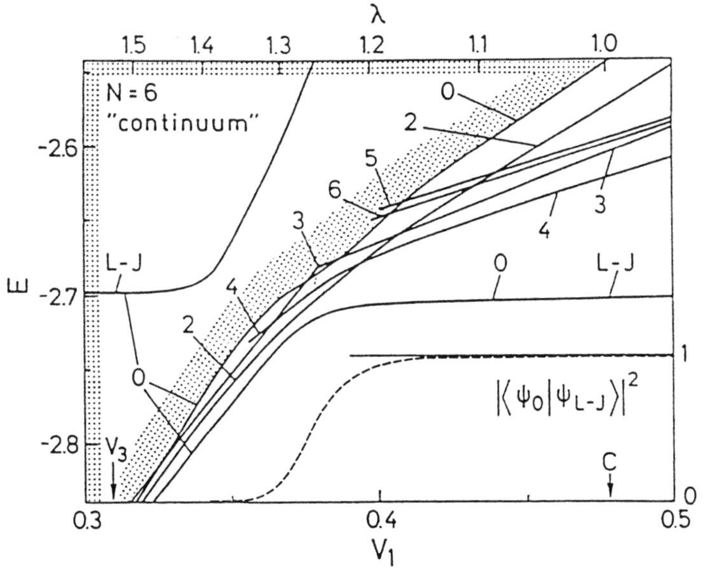

Fig. 5.6. Low-lying states at $\nu = \frac{1}{3}$ ($N_e = 6,\ 2S = 15$) in the lowest Landau level, as V_1 is varied and $V_{m>1}$ are Coulombic. The Coulomb value of V_1 (C) and V_3 are marked. The values of angular momentum quantum number L are indicated in the figure. The projection of the Laughlin state on the ground state is shown. In the gapless regime ($\lambda > 1.25$), the Laughlin-Jastrow (LJ) state is seen to reappear as the *highest* $L = 0$ level [5.9]

for $m' < m$ and 0 otherwise. It is also evident in Fig. 5.6 that the ground state of the potential $V^{\text{hc}} + \lambda(V^{\text{Coul}} - V^{\text{hc}})$ at small but finite values of the perturbation parameter λ is also of Laughlin type. As we lower V_1, the gap persists for $\lambda \leq 1.25$, and in this regime, the Laughlin state has an almost 100% projection on the true ground state. This region also includes the ground state for the pure lowest Landau level Coulomb interaction, which is therefore well described by the Laughlin state. At $\nu = \frac{1}{3}$, the Coulomb potential therefore has the stability limit of $\lambda \approx 1.25$, where there is a first order transition to a gapless state, which was found to be compressible. The Laughlin state is then found as an *excited* state in the gapless regime.

5.4 Monte Carlo Results

As we have seen in the earlier sections, Laughlin's wave function together with the classical plasma theory has provided quite a reliable description of the ground state and is in good agreement with the exact evaluation of the ground-state energies for finite electron systems. There have also been very accurate Monte Carlo studies to confirm these results on quantitative grounds.

Levesque et al., [5.5] obtained the ground-state energy of the Laughlin wave function by evaluating the pair correlation functions for about 256 particles, using the method described by *Caillol* et al. [5.16]. The results for $\nu = \frac{1}{3}$ and $\frac{1}{5}$ are shown in Fig. 5.7. For the ground-state energy they obtained $E(\nu = \frac{1}{3}) = -0.410 \pm 0.0001$ and $E(\nu = \frac{1}{5}) = -0.3277 \pm 0.0002$ (in units of $e^2/\epsilon\ell_0$). A comparison of these almost *exact* results with those obtained via the exact diagonalization for few electron systems and the classical plasma approach described in Sects. 5.1 and 5.2 respectively, should convince the reader of the efficiency of these methods in describing the electron system. This credibility is quite essential, as we proceed to discuss other quantities of interest with these methods in the following chapters.

As a function of filling factor, Levesque et al. obtained the following relation for the energy by fitting their results and the exact result for $m = 1$:

$$E \simeq -0.782133\sqrt{\nu}\left(1 - 0.211\,\nu^{0.74} + 0.012\,\nu^{1.7}\right) . \tag{5.54}$$

In the disk geometry, *Morf* and *Halperin* [5.6] performed a Monte Carlo evaluation of the ground-state energy for up to 144 electrons. The results are shown in Fig. 5.8. The results for the energy (per particle) are fitted

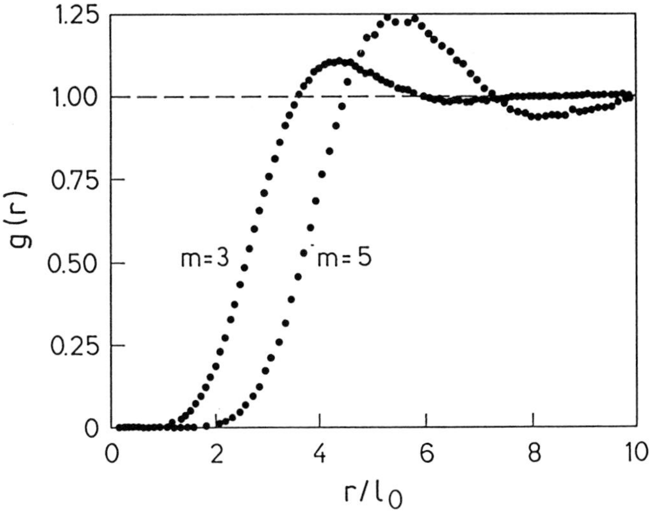

Fig. 5.7. Pair correlation function $g(r)$ for $\nu = \frac{1}{3}$ and $\frac{1}{5}$, obtained from Monte Carlo calculations [5.5]

accurately by the polynomial,

$$E \approx -0.4101 + 0.06006/\sqrt{N_\mathrm{e}} - 0.0423/N_\mathrm{e}. \tag{5.55}$$

Using fits by first-, second-, and third-order polynomials in $N_\mathrm{e}^{-\frac{1}{2}}$ results are obtained for the thermodynamic limit as -0.4092, -0.4101 and -0.4099 (in units of $e^2/\epsilon\ell_0$) respectively. The radial distribution function $g(r)$ obtained from the Monte Carlo calculations of the Laughlin state at $\nu = \frac{1}{3}$ is shown in Fig. 5.9. There is little size dependence seen for small interparticle separation. From the distribution function thus obtained, Morf and Halperin also evaluated the Coulomb energy per particle. The results are, $-0.4096\, e^2/\epsilon\ell_0$ for N_e=42 and 72, and $-0.4097\, e^2/\epsilon\ell_0$ for a system with 144 particles. Their estimate in the thermodynamic limit for the energy per particle $\approx -0.410 \pm 0.001\, e^2/\epsilon\ell_0$ is in good agreement with the results of Levesque et al. described earlier in this section.

Finally, Monte Carlo results for the spherical geometry are also available [5.7] and are shown in Fig. 5.10. A least-squares fit to these results leads to

$$E \approx -0.40973 - 0.0072/N_\mathrm{e} + 0.009/N_\mathrm{e}^2$$

for the chord distance definition of the interparticle separation, and

$$E \approx -0.40975 + 0.012/N_\mathrm{e} + 0.048/N_\mathrm{e}^2$$

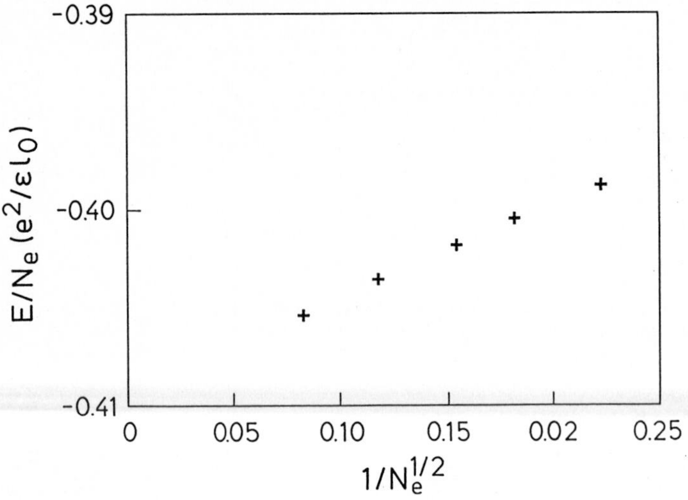

Fig. 5.8. Energy per electron for the $\nu = \frac{1}{3}$ state. Results are obtained for Laughlin's wave function via Monte Carlo calculations in disk geometry and plotted versus $N_e^{-\frac{1}{2}}$ for systems with N_e=20, 30, 42, 72, and 144 electrons. The length of the vertical bars indicates the standard deviation [5.6]

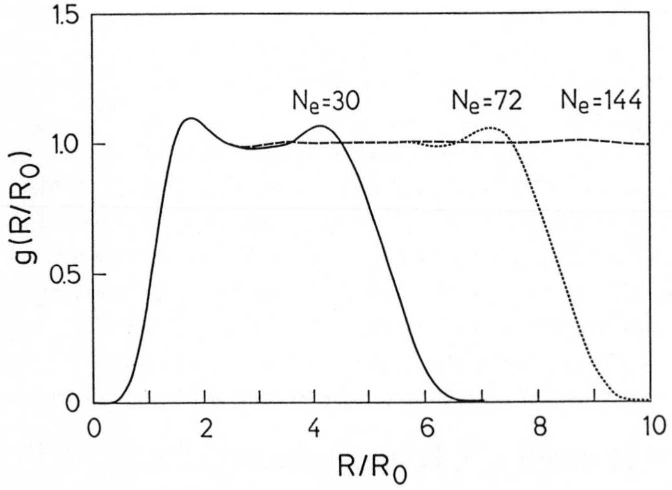

Fig. 5.9. Monte Carlo results for the radial distribution function $g(r)$ for the Laughlin state at $\nu = \frac{1}{3}$. Here R_0 is the ion-disk radius. Results are based on calculations with N_e=30, 72, and 144 electrons [5.6]

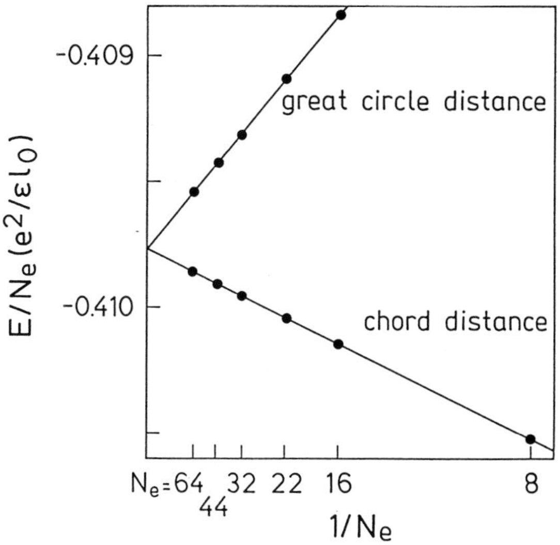

Fig. 5.10. Energy per electron for the $\nu = \frac{1}{3}$ state with Laughlin's wave function in a spherical geometry, as a function of $1/N_e$. The Coulomb energy is evaluated using the *great circle* and *chord* distance definitions [5.7]

for the great circle distance definition. The finite-size corrections are obviously very small.

5.5 Reversed Spins in the Ground State

In our discussions so far, it has been assumed that because of the strong magnetic fields involved, only one spin state is present. *Halperin* first pointed out [5.13] that in GaAs, since the electron g-factor is one-quarter of the free electron value [5.30] and the Zeeman energy is thus approximately sixty times smaller than the cyclotron energy, it might then be possible to have some electrons with *reversed* spins when the magnetic field is not too large. In the case when one half of the electrons have spins antiparallel to the field, Halperin constructed a simple Laughlin-type state of the form

$$\psi = \prod_{i<j} (z_i - z_j)^m \prod_{\alpha<\beta} (z_\alpha - z_\beta)^m \prod_{i,\alpha} (z_i - z_\alpha)^n \prod_i \mathrm{e}^{-|z_i|^2/4\ell_0^2} \prod_\alpha \mathrm{e}^{-|z_\alpha|^2/4\ell_0^2} \tag{5.56}$$

where Roman and Greek indices correspond to spin-up and spin-down electrons respectively. Using the classical plasma approach (5.16–19), the filling factor is given by

$$\nu = \frac{2}{(m+n)}.$$

Halperin suggested the particular case of $m = 2, n = 2$ ($\nu = \frac{2}{5}$). The wave function then has the following desirable properties: (a) all electrons are in the lowest Landau level, so the kinetic energy is an absolute minimum, (b) electrons of the same spin are kept apart very well because the wave function vanishes as the cube of their separation; electrons of opposite spin are kept apart only slightly less well because the wave function vanishes as the square of the separation and (c) the wave function is antisymmetric under interchange of two electrons of the same spin, as required. The wave function can also be shown to give a total spin $S = 0$ state. The ground-state energy for the two-spin state is obtained by considering the spin-up and spin-down electrons as two different species of particles. The total interaction energy is then obtained from

$$E_{\text{int}} = \frac{1}{2\sqrt{m+n}} \frac{e^2}{\epsilon\ell_0} \int_0^\infty \left[g_{11}(x) + g_{12}(x) - 2\right] dx \qquad (5.57)$$

where $g_{\alpha\beta}$ are the partial pair-correlation functions.

For $\nu = \frac{2}{5}$, a generalized two-component HNC approach was employed by *Chakraborty* and *Zhang* [5.31] to obtain $g_{\alpha\beta}$ (for details see Appendix C) and the ground-state energy was obtained as, $E_{\text{unpol}} = -0.434\, e^2/\epsilon\ell_0$. For a spin-polarized state at this filling, a Laughlin-type state does not exist. In order to compare the unpolarized state with a spin polarized state for $\nu = \frac{2}{5}$, the above authors first performed a Laughlin-type calculation for $\nu = \frac{2}{5}$, which was then corrected with Halperin's hierarchical approach described in Sect. 6.8. The resulting energy for the fully spin-polarized state was, $E_{\text{pol}} = -0.429\, e^2/\epsilon\ell_0$. Since then, several different calculations have been reported in the literature [5.6,28] and the result quoted above is close to the Monte Carlo data, $E_{\text{pol}} \approx -0.4303 \pm 0.003\, e^2/\epsilon\ell_0$. Comparing these results, it can be concluded that, in the absence of Zeeman energy, a spin-unpolarized state for $\nu = \frac{2}{5}$ would be energetically favored. The Zeeman energy (per particle) is evaluated from $E_{\text{Zeeman}} = (1-2p)g\mu_{\text{B}}Bs$, where p is the ratio of the number of spins parallel to the field to the total number of spins, $\mu_{\text{B}} = e\hbar/2mc$ the Bohr magneton, and $s = \frac{1}{2}$. For GaAs with all spins parallel to the field, $E_{\text{Zeeman}} = -0.011\, e^2/\epsilon\ell_0$ for a magnetic field of 10 T, the Landé g-factor, $g \simeq 0.52$, and $\epsilon \simeq 13$.

In a later investigation [5.32], a systematic study of spin reversal in various filling fractions was attempted. The finite-size calculations described in Sect. 5.1, are particularly suitable for this purpose, since one need not construct trial wave functions for all the spin states to be studied and comparison is possible for various spin polarizations at different filling factors evaluated with the same numerical accuracy. The method of *Yoshioka* et al., [5.1] can be generalized for various spin polarizations in a straightforward manner. The energy spectrum for the Hamiltonian is classified in terms of the total spin S and its z-component S_z. For a given S, the spectrum is identical for different values of S_z.

Table 5.1. Potential energy (per particle) for the four-electron system at various filling factors with the polarized ($S = 2$), partly polarized ($S = 1$), and the unpolarized ($S = 0$) electron spins, and the partial filling fractions $\nu_\uparrow$ and $\nu_\downarrow$ of the ground states. The Zeeman energy is not included in the energy values. The unit of energy is $e^2/\epsilon\ell_0$.

	Potential energy			Ground state		
ν	$S=2$	$S=1$	$S=0$		$\nu_\uparrow$	$\nu_\downarrow$
$\frac{1}{3}$	−0.4152	−0.4120	−0.4135	Polarized	$\frac{1}{3}$	0
$\frac{2}{7}$	−0.3870	−0.3868	−0.3884	Unpolarized	$\frac{1}{7}$	$\frac{1}{7}$
$\frac{2}{5}$	−0.4403	−0.4410	−0.4464	Unpolarized	$\frac{1}{5}$	$\frac{1}{5}$
$\frac{4}{13}$	−0.3975	−0.3997	−0.3970	Partially polarized	$\frac{3}{13}$	$\frac{1}{13}$
$\frac{4}{11}$	−0.4219	−0.4278	−0.4241	Partially polarized	$\frac{3}{11}$	$\frac{1}{11}$
$\frac{4}{9}$	−0.4528	−0.4600	−0.4554	Partially polarized	$\frac{1}{3}$	$\frac{1}{9}$

In Table 5.1, we present the results for a finite electron system for the case of a polarized state ($S = 2$), a partly polarized state ($S = 1$) and the unpolarized state ($S = 0$). As seen in Table 5.1, except for $\nu = \frac{1}{3}$, the unpolarized states or partly polarized states are energetically favored, as compared to the fully polarized state. In fact, for all the filling fractions considered in this work, the lowest energy is found to correspond to the case where the partial filling factor for each spin state has an *odd* denominator. It is interesting to note that, $\nu = \frac{4}{9}$ has a partial filling factor of $\frac{1}{3}$ for $S = 1$. Based on the fact that the filling factor $\nu = \frac{1}{3}$ is an experimentally observed stable state, it is quite tempting to predict that $\nu = \frac{4}{9}$ should be a stable state with partially polarized electron spins.

Including the Zeeman energy as estimated above, it was found that, except for $\nu = \frac{4}{11}$ and $\frac{4}{9}$, the spin-polarized state was energetically favored for all the other filling fractions considered in this work. For these two filling fractions, even in the presence of Zeeman energy, a partly spin-polarized state was found to have the lowest energy. The fraction $\nu = \frac{4}{9}$ has been observed by *Störmer* and his collaborators [5.33].

One obvious limitation of the above work was the small system size. Inclusion of the spin degree of freedom causes the Hamiltonian matrix size to increase very rapidly. However, for the spin polarized state at $\nu = \frac{4}{9}$, the numerical calculations of *Yoshioka* [5.12] showed that the energy for eight electrons is only ~ 0.002 higher than that for four electrons. If this trend persists even for other spin polarizations, the conclusions would not be severely altered. However, no larger system calculation exists yet, to justify this expectation.

For $\nu = \frac{1}{3}$, the spin state $S = 2$ is found to be energetically favored compared with the other spin states, even in the absence of Zeeman energy. This result is quite supportive of Laughlin's state at $\nu = \frac{1}{3}$, which is fully antisymmetric. For other filling fractions, the possibility exists that the energy could be lowered by introducing the spin degree of freedom. In Sect. 6.3, we shall see that spin reversal plays a more direct role in the elementary excitations. The experimental evidence of the reversed spins discussed in this section, has been obtained from measurements of FQHE in *tilted* magnetic fields [5.34,35]. Details of the experimental results and the theoretical implications are given in Sect. 6.9.

For multivalley semiconductors like Si, it has been predicted [5.36] that there should be spontaneous valley polarization at $\frac{1}{3}$ and $\frac{1}{5}$. The valley degeneracy can be mapped onto the spin systems (without having to add the Zeeman energy) and the results of Table 5.1 have been shown to hold in this case [5.37]. It has been shown that a gapless Goldstone mode exists for the $\frac{1}{3}$ and $\frac{1}{5}$ states. These *valley waves* are analogous to the spin waves described in Sect. 5.3; see also [5.38].

5.6 Finite Thickness Correction

In our discussions of the electron system thus far, we have ignored the finite spread of the electron wave function perpendicular to the two-dimensional plane. In real systems, the wave function of an electron has a finite spread perpendicular to the two-dimensional plane, in the z-direction. It is well known [5.39–42] that inclusion of the finite thickness correction effectively softens the short-range divergence of the bare Coulomb interaction, when the interelectron spacing is comparable with the inversion layer width.

The most common form assumed for the charge distribution normal to the plane is the Fang-Howard variational wave function, first proposed for the inversion layer. It is written as

$$g(z) = \tfrac{1}{2}b^3 z^2 \exp(-bz) \tag{5.58}$$

where the effect of only the lowest subband is considered. The variational parameter is given by

$$b = \left[33\pi m^* e^2 n / 2\epsilon\hbar^2\right]^{\frac{1}{3}} \tag{5.59}$$

where $m^* \sim 0.067m_e$ is the effective mass for GaAs and n is the electron density fixed by the Landau level filling ν. The depletion layer electron density is negligible compared to the electron density and is not included in (5.59). For $n = 10^{11}\text{cm}^{-2}$, one obtains $b^{-1} \simeq 58\text{Å}$. On the other hand, the magnetic length (in Å) can be expressed in terms of the magnetic field as, $\ell_0 = 256.6B^{-\frac{1}{2}}$ with B in Tesla. For $B = 20\text{T}$, $\ell_0 \sim 57\text{Å}$ — the spread of the wave function is expected to have a substantial effect on the physical quantities of interest.

The effective electron-electron interaction is then written as [5.42],

$$V(\boldsymbol{r}) = \frac{e^2}{\epsilon\ell_0}\int dz_1 dz_2\, g(z_1)g(z_2)\left[r^2 + (z_1 - z_2)^2\right]^{-\frac{1}{2}}. \tag{5.60}$$

Using the well-known Fourier transform result

$$F(q) \equiv \frac{q}{2\pi}\int \frac{d\boldsymbol{r}\, \mathrm{e}^{\mathrm{i}\boldsymbol{q}\cdot\boldsymbol{r}}}{\left[(z_1 - z_2)^2 + r^2\right]^{\frac{1}{2}}} = \exp\left[-q|z_1 - z_2|\right] \tag{5.61}$$

and $g(z)$ from (5.58), the interaction term is rewritten as

$$V(\boldsymbol{r}) = \left[\frac{1}{2}b^3\right]^2\left(\frac{e^2}{\epsilon\ell_0}\right)\int_0^\infty dqJ_0(qr)\int dz_1 dz_2\, z_1^2 z_2^2 \mathrm{e}^{-b(z_1+z_2)}\mathrm{e}^{-q|z_1-z_2|}. \tag{5.62}$$

After some algebra the final result is then obtained as

$$V(\boldsymbol{r}) = \left(\frac{e^2}{\epsilon\ell_0}\right)\int_0^\infty dqF(q)J_0(qr) \tag{5.63}$$

with

$$F(q) = \left[1 + \frac{9}{8}\frac{q}{b} + \frac{3}{8}\left(\frac{q}{b}\right)^2\right]\left(1 + \frac{q}{b}\right)^{-3}. \tag{5.64}$$

For large r, one has the usual $1/r$ behavior, and for small r the $\ln r$ behavior is obtained.

In the case of Laughlin's wave function for $\nu = \frac{1}{3}$, *MacDonald* and *Aers* [5.41] and *Chakraborty* [5.43] obtained a substantial reduction of the ground-state energy as a function of $\beta = (b\ell_0)^{-1}$, as shown in Fig. 5.11. The reduction of the energy is a direct consequence of the softening of the Coulomb repulsion. For the excitation energy gap, finite-system calculations were done by *Zhang* and *Das Sarma* [5.42] and *Chakraborty* et al. [5.44,45] and for the Laughlin quasihole by *Chakraborty* [5.43]. These results will be discussed in Chap. 6.

5.7 Liquid-Solid Transition

It is evident from the above discussions that the ground state for $\nu = \frac{1}{m}$ and $1 - \frac{1}{m}$ (and other higher order filling fractions to be described in Sect. 6.8) is the quantum fluid state, and is lower in energy than the crystal state. On the other hand, at low density, *i.e.*, for very small ν, the ground state is expected to be a Wigner crystal. It should be noted that the two-dimensional one-component classical plasma has a crystallization transition which occurs at $\Gamma \simeq 140$, *i.e.*for $m = 70$ [5.16]. Therefore, it would be interesting to estimate the filling factor at which the liquid to solid transition takes place for the present quantum system.

Most computations of the crystal energy have been within the HF approximation [5.1,5,10,46]. Comparing the accurate Monte Carlo results for the Laughlin liquid state (discussed in Sect. 5.4) with the HF crystal energies as a function of filling factor, the critical filling was found to occur at $\nu_c \sim \frac{1}{10}$ [5.5], an estimate similar to that of *Laughlin* [5.2]. In order to improve the calculation for the crystal state, a variational wave function for a *correlated* Wigner crystal was employed *Lam* and *Girvin* [5.47]. After minimizing the energy, a relation valid for $\nu \le \frac{1}{2}$ was obtained:

$$E_{\rm WC}^{\rm c} = -0.782133\,\nu^{\frac{1}{2}} + 0.2410\,\nu^{\frac{3}{2}} + 0.16\,\nu^{\frac{5}{2}}. \tag{5.65}$$

Comparing the energies with the Monte Carlo results of [5.5], the crossover point was estimated to be $\nu_c^{-1} = 6.5 \pm 0.5$. This result is, of course, an

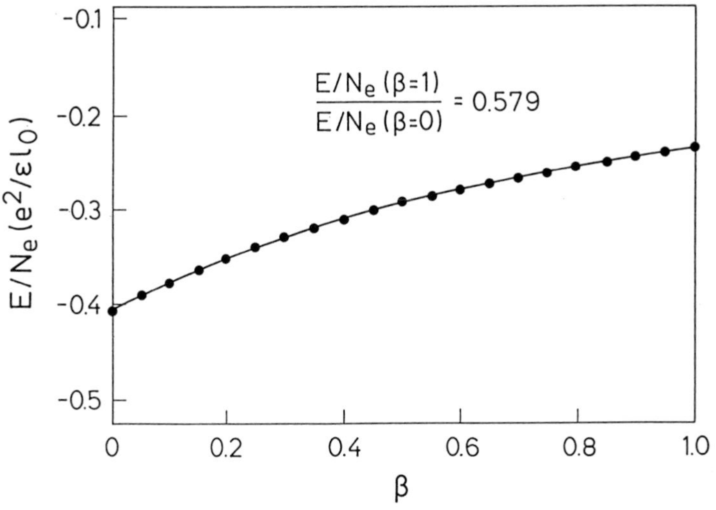

Fig. 5.11. Ground-state energy (per particle) as a function of the dimensionless thickness parameter $\beta = (b\ell_0)^{-1}$ for the Laughlin wave function

estimate for an *ideal* system. In a real system, the finite-thickness correction (Sect. 5.6) and Landau-level mixing would influence this estimate somewhat. Experiments supporting the above prediction have been performed by *Mendez* et al. [5.48], who indicated that ν_c^{-1} may be seven or larger. This conclusion was based on the absence of minima in ρ_{xx} at $\nu = \frac{1}{7}$ and $\frac{1}{9}$ in a low-density sample where a weak structure could still be observed at $\nu = \frac{1}{5}$. *Chang* et al. [5.49] however argued that the weakness of the $\frac{1}{5}$ is most likely a result of localization, and the gap is reduced significantly due to disorder. They argue that a similar reduction in the energy gap also occurs for $\frac{1}{7}$, $\frac{1}{9}$, $\frac{1}{11}$ etc.

A clear indication of the FQHE at $\nu = \frac{1}{5}$ has been observed in the experiments of *Mallett et al.* [5.50], who determined the activation energy of this state [$\Delta \sim 50$mK at 19T] for the first time (see Sect. 6.6 for details on the activation energy). They also reported observation of weak ρ_{xx} minima at $\nu = \frac{2}{9}$, and $\frac{2}{11}$, thereby providing experimental confirmation of the $\frac{1}{5}$ hierarchy, which is different from the sequence of states obtained from $\frac{1}{3}$. Furthermore, the observation of the ρ_{xx} minimum at $\frac{2}{11}$ sets a lower limit to which the FQHE is shown to persist.

The difficulty of performing measurements in the low-ν, low-temperature range was greatly circumvented by *Goldman et al.* [5.51]. In magnetotransport measurements they observed a structure near the filling factor $\nu = \frac{1}{7}$. It was interpreted as evidence for a developing fractional quantum Hall state. The Wigner crystallization is therefore expected to occur for $\nu < \frac{1}{7}$. A structure in ρ_{xy}, indicating the FQHE state at $\nu = \frac{1}{7}$ in a magnetic field up to 18T was also observed by *Wakabayashi et al.* [5.52].

An attempt to observe a magnetic-field-induced liquid-to-solid phase transition for two-dimensional electron system was reported by *Andrei et al.* [5.53]. The experiment was designed to test for the Wigner-solid magnetophonon branch of dispersion, $\omega = c\,(2\pi\mu)^{\frac{1}{2}}\,q^{\frac{3}{2}}/H$ with shear modulus μ. In that experiment, a longitudinal electric wave of wave vector q was generated in the plane of the two-dimensional system. The accessible wave vectors are $q_0 = \frac{2\pi}{16}\mu m^{-1}$ and its harmonics $q = pq_0, p = 2, 3, 4, \cdots$. Frequency-swept sources produce a sequence of resonances at wave vectors $q = pq_0$. From the frequency positions of the resonances, a dispersion relation proportional to $q^{\frac{3}{2}}$ was obtained. The critical filling thereby obtained was $\nu_c = 0.23 \pm 0.04$ and the classical melting temperature, $t = \frac{T}{T_{\rm mc}} = 0.72 \pm 0.1$. *Störmer* and *Willett* [5.54] later pointed out that the data of Andrei et al. appear to be fitted much better to a *linear* relationship between ω and q. They claim that the resonance structure is presumably due to an acoustic lattice mode in the GaAs/AlGaAs host material. *Andrei et al.* however argue that their measurement is insensitive to the surface acoustic waves of the host material [5.55].

In a very interesting paper, *Jiang* et al. [5.56] reported rather unambigiously that in the low-disorder, high-field limit the ground state at $\nu = \frac{1}{5}$ is indeed a Laughlin liquid. They also found that, at filling factors below $\nu = \frac{1}{5}$ as well as in a narrow region above it, ρ_{xx} diverges exponentially as $T \to 0$. This is in clear contrast to the T dependence at any higher ν. These authors suggested that the reentrant behavior is due to a phase transition in the underlying many-particle state. The experimental result of Jiang et al. is reproduced in Fig. 5.12, where R_{xx} is plotted as a function of the magnetic field at $T \approx 90$mK. The most remarkable feature in this result is the sharp resistance spike at $B \approx 20$T ($\nu \approx 0.21$), whose strength vastly exceeds the strength of any feature at lower fields. At fields slightly above the position of the spike R_{xx} drops precipitously, vanishing around $\nu = \frac{1}{5}$ (as expected for a Laughlin liquid) and diverges again at still higher fields.

Jiang et al. then determined the activation energy at $\nu = \frac{1}{5}$ from a standard Arrhenius plot (Fig. 5.13) and obtained $\Delta^5 = 1.1$K (see Sect. 6.6 for details on the activation energy). Besides the predominant $\frac{1}{5}$ minimum in R_{xx} there are other new fractions found in its vicinity. The $\nu = \frac{2}{9}$ minimum is quite strong and appears to be very close to forming a zero-resistance state. The observed transport anomaly for $\frac{2}{9} \gtrsim \nu \gtrsim \frac{1}{5}$ has been interpreted by Jiang et al. as indicative of a pinned solid-like phase in the underlying electronic system and this electronic phase is reentrant in a narrow region above $\nu \sim \frac{1}{5}$. The $\nu = \frac{1}{5}$ liquid phase is therefore embedded within a solid

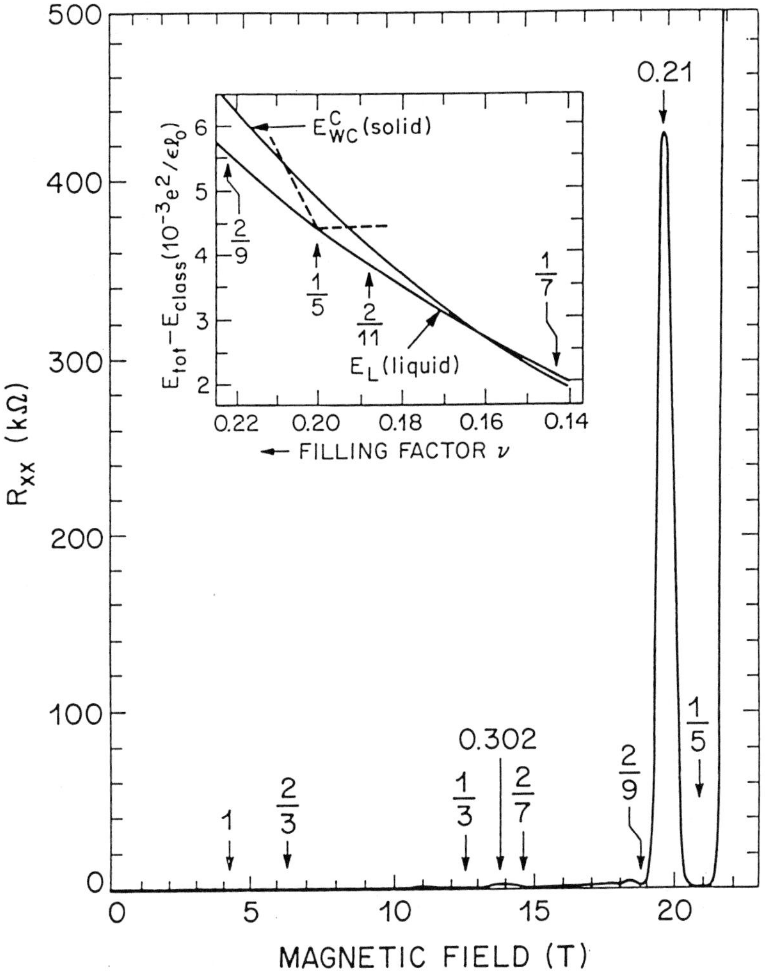

Fig. 5.12. Diagonal resistance R_{xx} versus the magnetic field at $T \approx 90$mK. All FQHE features at low magnetic fields are well developed but practically invisible on this scale. Inset: Result of a calculation for the total energy per flux quantum of the solid (E^{c}_{WC}) and interpolated $\frac{1}{m}$ quantum liquids (E_L) as a function of filling factor [5.45]. A classical energy ($E_{class} = -0.782133\nu^{-\frac{1}{2}}$) is subtracted for clarity. The dashed lines represent the *cusp* in the total energy of the liquid at $\nu = \frac{1}{5}$. Its extrapolation intersects the solid at $\nu \sim 0.21$ and 0.19 suggesting *two* phase transitions from quantum liquid to solid around $\nu = \frac{1}{5}$ [5.56]

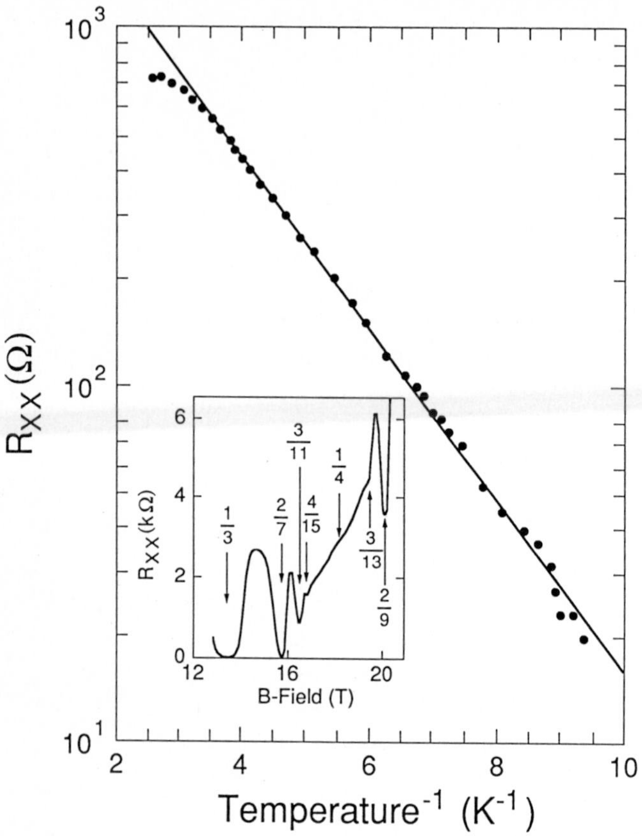

Fig. 5.13. Temperature dependence of R_{xx} at $\nu = \frac{1}{5}$. showing activated behavior [$R_{xx} \propto \exp(-\Delta^5/2T)$] over two orders of magnitude with an energy gap of $\Delta^5 = 1.1$K. Inset: R_{xx} vs the magnetic field at $T \sim 250$mK and at a slightly higher density than in Fig. 5.12 [5.56]

phase. A similar anomaly has also been reported by other groups [5.57]. One other experiment reporting the indication of a liquid-solid transition is the optical recombination process and this will be discussed in the next section.

A two-dimensional electron solid has also been observed in very high-mobility Si-MOSFETs at large filling factors ($\nu > 1$) and low magnetic fields ($B < 5$ T) [5.58,59]. Below a carrier concentration of $\approx 10^{11}$ cm^{-2}, the longitudinal resistance maxima near the filling factors 1.5 and 2.5 increases sharply by more than four orders of magnitude. The magnitude of the resistance maxima is thermally activated below 0.5 K and the activation energy at 8×10^{10} cm^{-2} is about 1K. In the range of concentrations and filling factors where the electron solid is observed, the current-voltage characteristics show a sharp threshold at ≈ 100 mV/cm [5.60].

5.8 Magnetoluminescence

Spectroscopic methods based on radiative recombination of two-dimensional electrons with photoexcited holes have gained considerable interest as an interesting route to study the FQHE. Magneto-optics experiments in the FQHE regime are expected to reveal physics of the many-electron state not accessible in magnetotransport. While transport measurements study the electronic properties close to the Fermi energy, the method of radiative recombination provides information about the whole energy spectrum of the electrons.

Magneto-optical studies in the FQHE regime were first reported in Si-MOSFETs [5.61] and in GaAs-AlGaAs quantum wells [5.62]. The spectral position of the luminescence line is closely related to the chemical potential of the interacting electron. A nonmonotonic dependence of the line position was indeed observed when the filling factor was varied in the region of $\nu = \frac{7}{3}$ (taking the valley degeneracy of Si into account, this filling factor actually describes the $\frac{1}{3}$ state). In the immediate vicinity of $\nu = \frac{7}{3}$, a doublet structure was visible in the luminescence line, which signifies a gap in the energy spectrum of the incompressible quantum fluid.

A similar doublet structure in the luminescence arising from the recombination of holes with the two-dimensional electrons near $\nu = \frac{2}{3}$ was also observed by *Goldberg* et al. [5.62]. The strong temperature dependence of the spectral weights of the two peaks corresponds to the temperature range of the FQHE in these samples, which indicates that the emission doublet is a manifestation of the phenomena underlying the FQHE.

The system of electrons in a GaAs-AlGaAs single heterojunction with holes bound to the acceptors from a δ-layer, located at a certain distance from the interface, is particularly suited to the spectroscopic studies of the FQHE. Fig. 5.14 shows a typical result for free and bound exciton luminescence bands [5.63]. The lines A_1, B_1 and B_0 are due to the recombination of two-dimensional electrons with free holes (A-lines) and holes bound to acceptors (B-lines) (the index corresponds to the number of two-dimensional subbands). In strong magnetic fields each band splits into a series of Landau levels. Fig. 5.15 shows measurements on three different samples where the concentration or the spatial position of the acceptors is changed. The strongest luminescence is observed if the δ-doping is located at $z_0 = 20$nm ($z_0 = 0$ at the GaAs-AlGaAs interface).

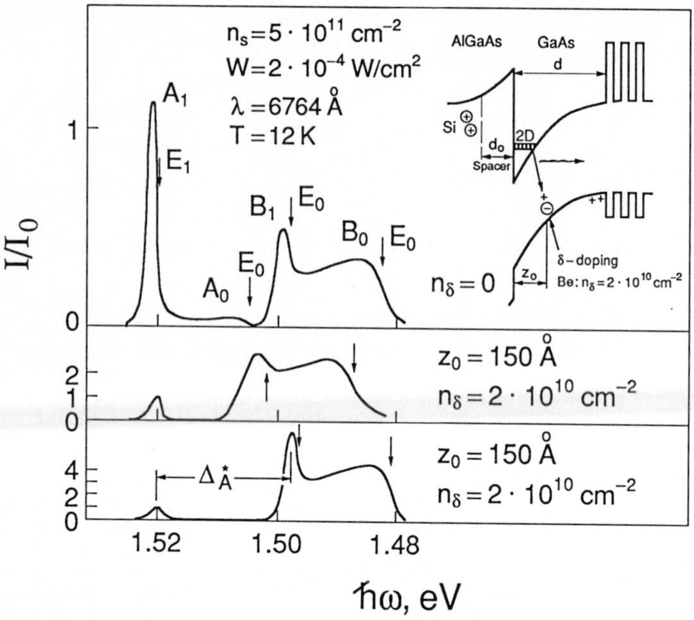

Fig. 5.14. Spectra of the radiative recombination of two-dimensional electrons with photoexcited holes, measured in an acceptor δ-doped single heterojunction [5.63]

Buhmann et al. [5.64] studied the spectra of the radiative recombination of two-dimensional electrons in several GaAs-AlGaAs heterostructures with photoexcited holes localized in a δ-doped monolayer of acceptors (Be atoms) 25 nm away from the interface. Fig. 5.16 shows the observed luminescence spectra at various magnetic fields. The entire energy spectrum below the Fermi energy, as observed at $B = 0$, splits into Landau levels in transverse magnetic fileds. Fig. 5.17(a) shows the peak energies as a function of magnetic field. The peak position appears linear above $\nu = 2$ while in the interval $1 < \nu < 2$, there is a deviation of the behavior of the spectral position of the $N = 0$ Landau level from linear behavior. This deviation is the result of enhancement of the electronic spin splitting. As the magnetic field is further increased additional abrupt changes in the spectral position are observed in the vicinity of $\nu = \frac{4}{5}, \frac{2}{3}, \frac{3}{5}, \frac{2}{5}$, and $\frac{1}{3}$. The amplitude of these jumps is small in comparison with the characteristic cyclotron energy, which sets the basic scale of the changes in the spectral position of an emission line as the magnetic field is varied. Therefore, the same data is replotted in Fig. 5.17(b) but as the energy shift (ΔE) from the line drawn through the low-field data. Also shown in this figure are the plots of ΔE at different temperatures. On raising the temperature to 5K all the jumps associated with odd-denominator ν disappear except that at $\nu = \frac{1}{3}$, which

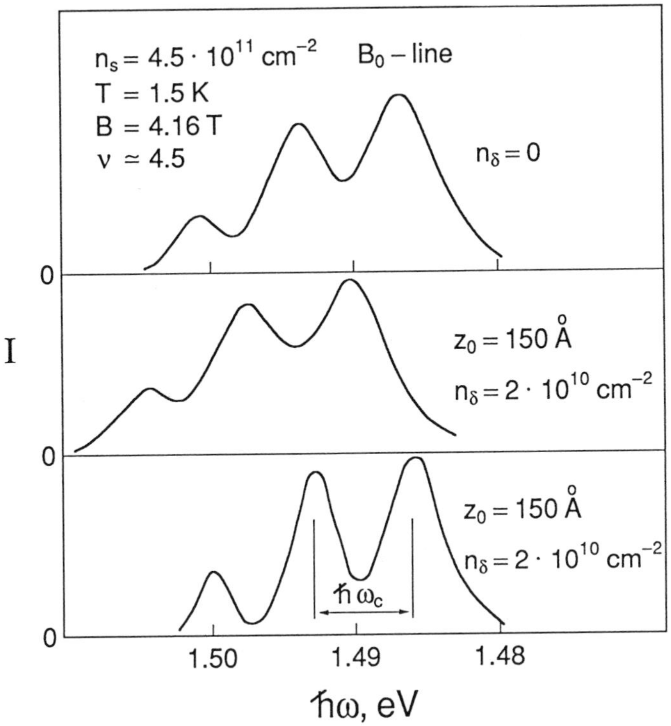

Fig. 5.15. Luminescence spectra at $B = 4.16$ T under different conditions of photoexcitations [5.63]

disappears at $T > 5$K. Also noteworthy is the persistence of a structural feature around $\nu = \frac{1}{2}$ even at 25K. From a series of samples and a range of concentrations Buhmann et al. were able to observe the anomalies at $\nu = \frac{2}{3}, \frac{1}{3}, \frac{1}{5}, \frac{1}{7}$, and $\frac{1}{9}$ [Fig. 5.18(a)]. This is the first observation of the filling factor $\frac{1}{9}$. The temperature dependence of these filling factors are shown in Fig. 5.18(b). A clear observation of $\nu = \frac{1}{9}$ in contrast to the difficulty in observing even $\nu = \frac{1}{7}$ in magnetotransport measurements shows that magneto-optical probes are much less sensitive to the effect of localization due to disorder.

Goldberg et al. also reported an interesting experiment which involved simultaneous measurement of the transport resistivity components and photoluminescnece spectra from one-side-doped GaAs/AlGaAs single quantum wells [5.65]. Their results are reproduced in Fig. 5.19 and Fig. 5.20. The most interesting result was the observation of a sudden shift of the luminescence peak and a minimum in peak intensity at $\nu = \frac{2}{3}$. Precisely at $\nu = \frac{2}{3}$ the peak position was found to shift abruptly to the blue by ~ 0.1 meV.

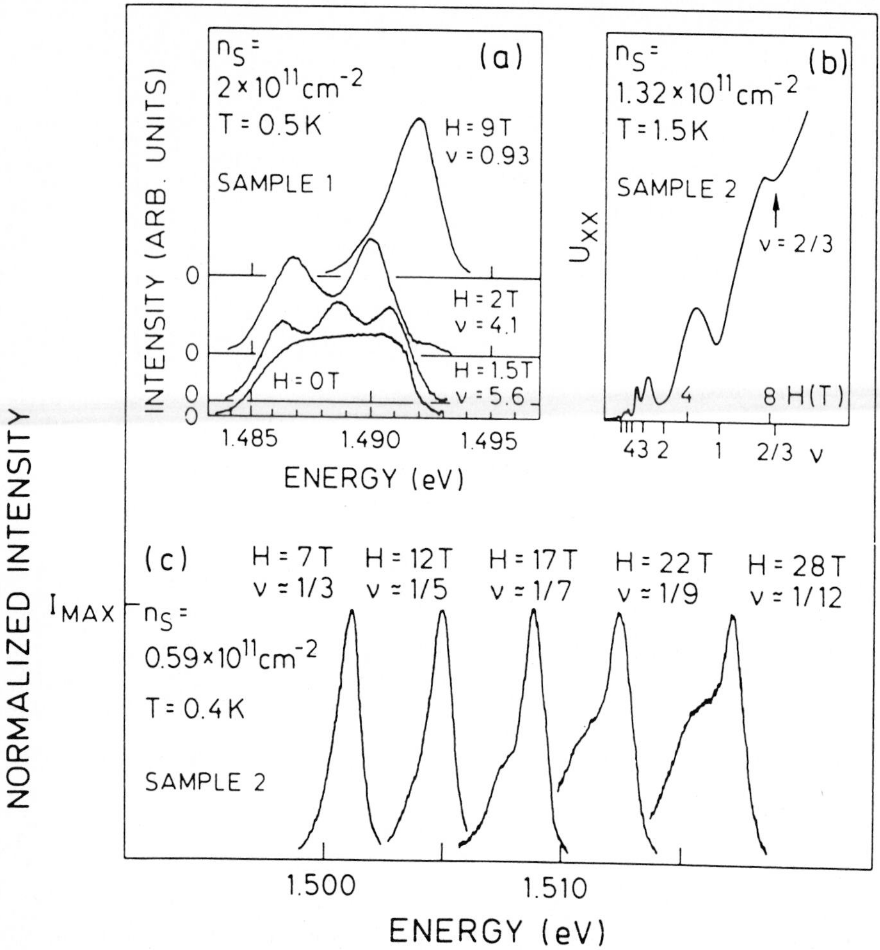

Fig. 5.16. Luminescence spectra (a) at 0.5 K and (c) 0.4 K for two different samples measured at various magnetic fields. (b) The transport Shubnikov-de Haas oscillations [5.64]

In the high-field region about the FQHE states $\nu = \frac{2}{5}$ and $\frac{1}{3}$, Goldberg et al. observed a splitting of the luminescence. The splitting exists only at temperatures low enough for fractional states to be seen and was found to remain unchanged over a significant range of magnetic fields.

Anomalies in the energy of photoluminescence near $\nu = \frac{2}{3}$ were also observed by *Turberfield* et al. [5.66]. They observed a doublet structure at $\nu \approx \frac{2}{3}$ with a separation of 0.16 meV, which is much smaller than the measured energy gap at that filling fraction. A popular account of the three experiments can be found in [5.67]. It has been pointed out by *Goldberg* et

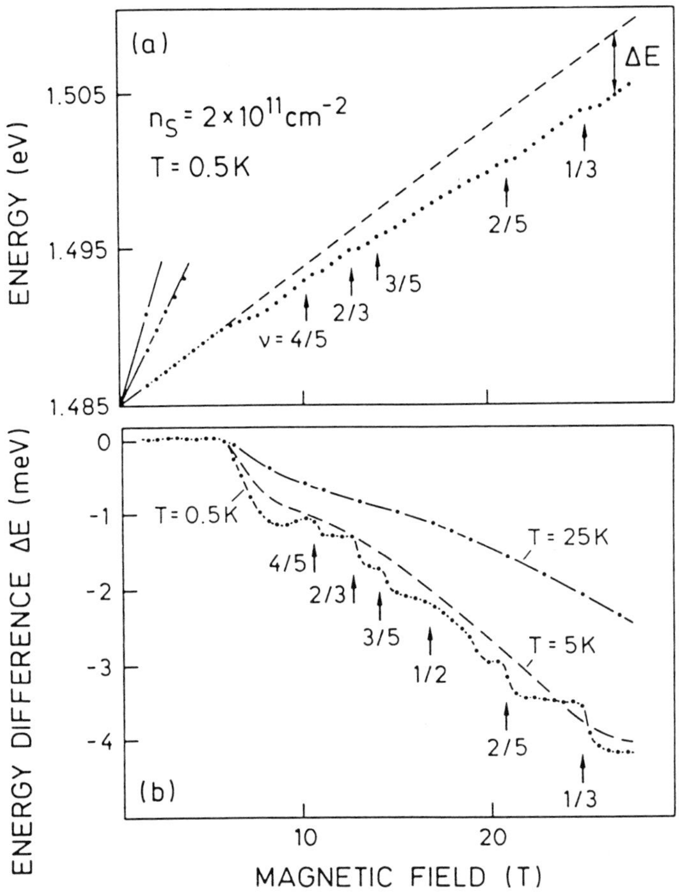

Fig. 5.17. The dependence of the luminescence line peak position on magnetic field. (b) The temperature dependence of ΔE [5.64]

al. [5.68] that the polarization of the luminescence might provide information about the different spin polarizations of the fractionally quantized Hall states.

Theoretical work on the spectroscopy of two-dimensional electron systems in the FQHE regime is not an easy task because the optical transitions involve strongly interacting electrons. In a quantizing magnetic field all the competing energies in the electronic system are comparable in magnitude to the energy of Coulomb interaction. Therefore the intensities of the recombination transitions to the ground state and to electronically excited states are comparable in magnitude. There are several interesting questions which arise in this situation and remain to be answered such as the specific

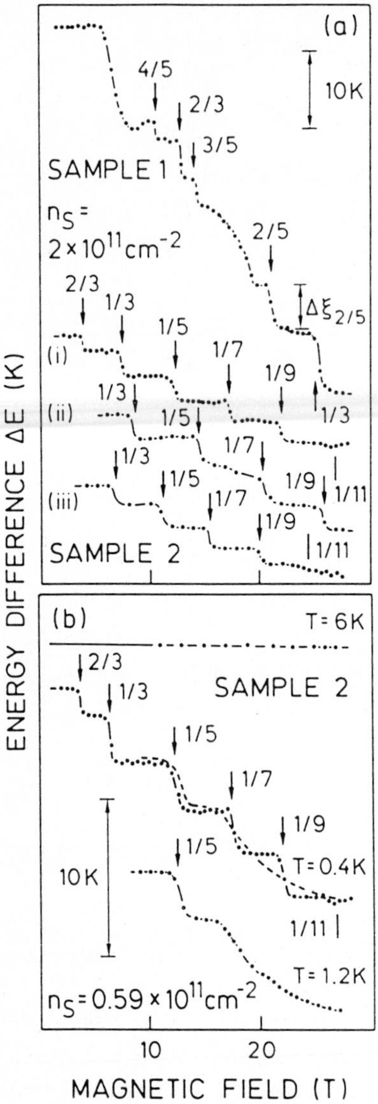

Fig. 5.18. (a) ΔE measured for samples at different concentrations: (i) 0.59×10^{11}, (ii) 0.7×10^{11}, (iii) 0.54×10^{11} cm^{-2}. (b) Temperature dependence of ΔE [5.64]

difference in the emission from spin-polarized (or partially polarized) states, or the dependence of the spectral pattern on the filling factor ν.

Bychkov and *Rashba* [5.69] reported a model calculation for a three-electron cluster where the electrons interact via a short-range pseudopotential such that the wave functions could be obtained analytically. In this

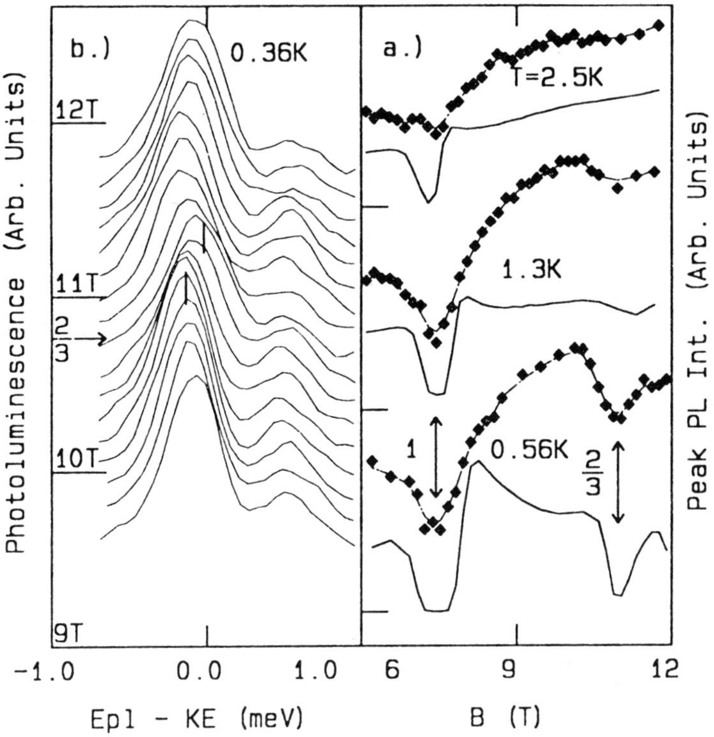

Fig. 5.19. (a) Peak intensity and R_{xx}. (b) Luminescence spectra at fields about $\nu = \frac{2}{3}$. The kinetic energy is subtracted to show the peak shift *just* at $\nu = \frac{2}{3}$ [5.65]

work, the recombination process involves the capture of one of the electrons by a local center which is charge neutral in the initial state and acquires a charge in the final state. The other two electrons then move in the field of that charge. The result was that the intensity distribution depends on the initial spin state of the cluster. For example, if the initial state of the cluster is spin-partially-polarized (total spin $S = \frac{1}{2}$) transitions to the singlet final state will be the most intense. Although the results from this simple model are interesting, due to the short-range model interaction and the absence of any boundary condition, it is difficult to relate them to a realistic situation. The last point is particularly important because, for a three-electron cluster which is a highly inhomogeneous system, the definition of the average density and hence the filling factor is very arbitary. The system is also too small for a comparison of different spin polarizations of the initial state to be useful.

Chakraborty and *Pietiläinen* [5.70,71] found that the spin polarization of the ground state of the electron system has a profound influence on the

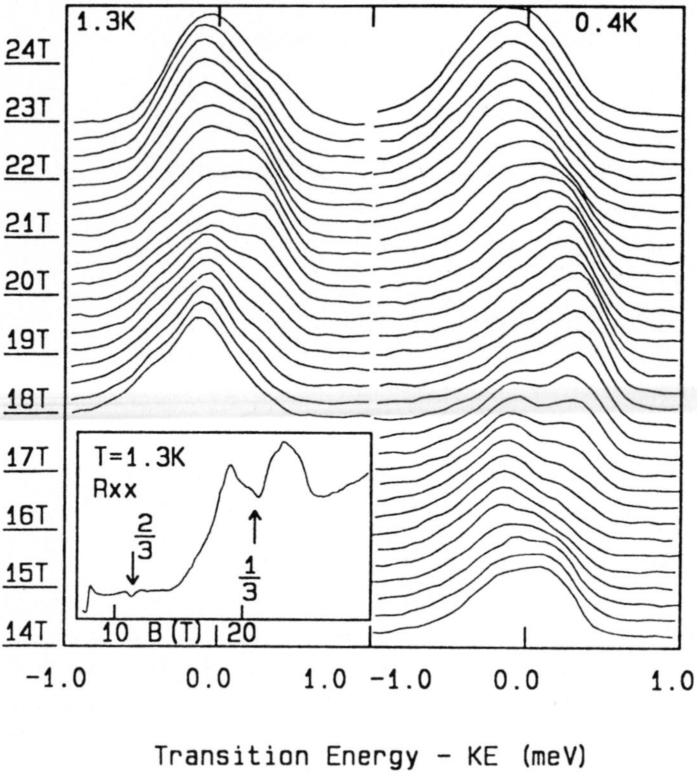

Fig. 5.20. Spectra at $\nu = \frac{2}{5}$ and $\frac{1}{3}$ with $\frac{1}{2}\hbar\omega_c$ subtracted. Inset: R_{xx} vs B taken simultaneously with spectra [5.65]

optical transitions. They used the standard model where the electrons are allowed to move in a cell with periodic boundary conditions and interact via the Coulomb interaction. The initial and final-state wave functions were evaluated exactly by numerical diagonalization of the finite-electron system in a periodic rectangular geometry. In the final state, one electron is missing in the system and the other electrons are moving in the field of a charged impurity. The spatial extent of the impurity center is assumed to be small compared to the magnetic length ℓ_0. The ground state and excitations for a system of four electrons with a charged impurity in the present geometry was studied earlier by *Zhang* et al. [5.72] and is discussed in Sect. 9.1. It should be pointed out that the impurity is assumed to be in the electron plane, while in the actual systems, it is located away from the plane. In order to incorporate this fact in the model, it is assumed that $Z \sim 0.1$, where Ze is the impurity charge. The resulting potential of the defect is thereby weakened.

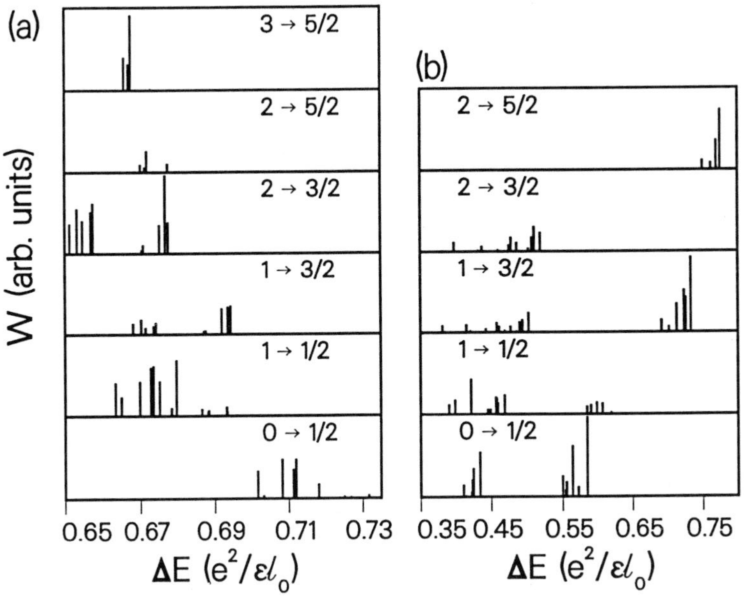

Fig. 5.21. The intensity (in arbitary units) of transitions from (a) an initial state at $\nu = \frac{2}{3}$ with a negative impurity ($Z = 0.1$) in the final state, and (b) a positive impurity ($Z = -0.1$) in the initial state with the final state being at $\nu = \frac{2}{3}$, as a function the interaction energy difference between the initial and final states. All possible spin configurations are considered. The Zeeman energy is not included in these results

The transition probability W is proportional to the square of the overlap of the initial and final states [5.73]. This is evaluated as follows: The initial state is written in occupation representation as (see Sect. 5.1) $|\psi^{\mathrm{i}}\rangle = \sum_{\{j_i\}} c^{\mathrm{i}}_{\{j_i\}} |j_1, j_2, \ldots, j_N\rangle$, where j is the linear momentum in one direction of the rectangular cell. Let us assume that in the final state the impurity is in a cell at position $\boldsymbol{R}$. First the initial state with one electron at position $\boldsymbol{R}$ is written as

$$|\psi^{\mathrm{i}}\rangle = \sum_{\{j_i\}} \sum_{j} \phi_j(\boldsymbol{R}) a_j |j_1, j_2, \ldots, j_N\rangle, \tag{5.66}$$

where $\phi_j(\boldsymbol{r})$ is the single-electron wave function (5.2) and a_j destroys one electron from state j. Then in the final state the electron at position $\boldsymbol{R}$ is replaced by the charged impurity, and the final state is simply

$$|\psi^{\mathrm{f}}\rangle = \sum_{\{j_i\}} c^{\mathrm{f}}_{\{j_i\}} |j_1, j_2, \ldots, j_{N-1}\rangle. \tag{5.67}$$

Stated differently, an *overlap operator* of the type $\mathcal{O} = \sum_j \phi_j(\boldsymbol{R})a_j$ has been introduced into Eq. (5.67). The overlap is then taken over the initial and final states.

Let us first consider the $\nu = \frac{2}{3}$ filling fraction in the initial state. In the periodic rectangular geometry the ground state is multiply degenerate which is known to arise due to the center of mass degeneracy (Sect. 7.2). In the final state this degeneracy is lifted because the impurity interaction mixes the momentum eigenstates. The degeneracy in the initial state poses a special problem because it is well known that in this case there is no unique set of eigenvectors available. Furthermore, the states can not be classified according to their symmetry (in the present case translational symmetry) because it is necessary to compare the degenerate states with the impurity states where there is no translational symmetry. The sum is therefore taken over all the degenerate initial states when evaluating the intensity:

$$W \sim \delta(E - E^{\mathrm{f}} + E^{\mathrm{i}}) \sum_m \left| \langle \psi^{\mathrm{f}} | \psi^{\mathrm{i}}_m \rangle \right|^2, \tag{5.68}$$

for various values of the interaction-energy difference. These authors have studied different spin polarizations ($S = 0 - 3$) in the initial state. The results for the transitions from various spin configurations of the initial state for a six-electron systems are presented in Fig. 5.21(a). The transitions from an initial state with a total spin S to a final state with spin S' is shown in different panels. For a given spin configuration, the intensity line at the lowest energy corresponds to a transition to the lowest energy state and the other lines at that spin state correspond to transitions to higher energy states. It is to be noted that the transitions do not involve spin flip and all possible transitions are shown in the figure. In obtaining these results, the impurity is placed in the middle of the cell for convenience. The effect of varying the impurity position will also be described below.

The interesting result of Fig. 5.21(a) is that only for two particular spin configurations of the initial state, *i.e.*, the spin unpolarized ($S = 0$) and spin-polarized ($S = 3$) states the intensity lines are grouped together. Moreover, the intensities for the $S = 0$ state remain well separated in energy from other spin configurations of the initial state. On the other hand, the intensities for the other spin configurations are seen to be distributed over a wide energy range. These results are notably independent of the system size. This is an important point to establish because in going from the initial state to a final state, the electron number is changed. It should therefore be expected that in actual experiments at low magnetic fields, a broadened luminescence line should exhibit structure due to different spin configurations of the initial state as described above. At low magnetic fields, the ground state for this filling fraction is known to be spin unpolarized ($S = 0$) (Sect. 5.5). This state would presumably manifest itself as a splitting in the luminescence line. An experimentally observed splitting of the peak energy might be related to this calculated *gap* in the intensity distribution (between the lines corresponding to the ground state spin configuration and those with other spin configurations).

It should be emphasized that the results described above do not include the appropriate Zeeman energy contribution for different spin alignments, which increases linearly with the magnetic field. Therefore, with increasing magnetic fields as the fully spin polarized state becomes the favored ground state, the increase in Zeeman energy would shift the spin-polarized state intensities to higher energy. In that case, a sharp peak is expected in the luminescence line [as the lines for the spin-polarized initial state are grouped together in a narrow energy range in Fig. 5.21(a)] which would be *blue shifted* with respect to the main broad luminescence line — a situation reminiscent of the observation by *Goldberg* et al. [5.65].

Chakraborty and Pietiläinen also considered a positive hole in the initial state. The result of that study is presented in Fig. 5.21(b). Just as in the negative impurity case discussed above, the impurity-free state is fixed at the filling fraction $\nu = \frac{2}{3}$ with one electron less than in the initial state. The intensity distribution in this case shows that *only* the spin-polarized state transitions (the $S = 2 \to S = \frac{5}{2}$ lines) are separated from the rest of the transitions and the *gap* is much smaller than that in the negative-impurity case. According to the above discussion, this would mean that one would not expect an appreciable splitting in the luminescence peak but with increasing magnetic fields there will be a blue shift of the spin-polarized state intensities. The shift would be predominant in this case because of the separation of the spin-polarized intensity lines from the rest. The result is again consistent with the observation by Goldberg et al.

In order to compare (or contrast) the above results with another filling factor having a different ground state, similar calculations were performed for a negatively charged impurity at $\nu = \frac{1}{2}$ [5.70,71]. The intensity distribution in this case is shown in Fig. 5.22. This filling factor is particularly interesting because here no FQHE has been observed so far. The ground state is most likely *not* incompressible as it is for the $\frac{2}{3}$ state, but the precise nature of the ground state is also not clear (Sect. 9.4). As expected, the results here are quite different from those of Fig. 5.21. The major difference to note in this case is that none of the transitions from various spin flip ground states are grouped together, but are distributed all over the energy range. Comparing the results for the two different filling factors, it is tempting to conclude that the segregation of the intensity lines for the true ground state (for low magnetic fields) at $\frac{2}{3}$ filling and its absence at

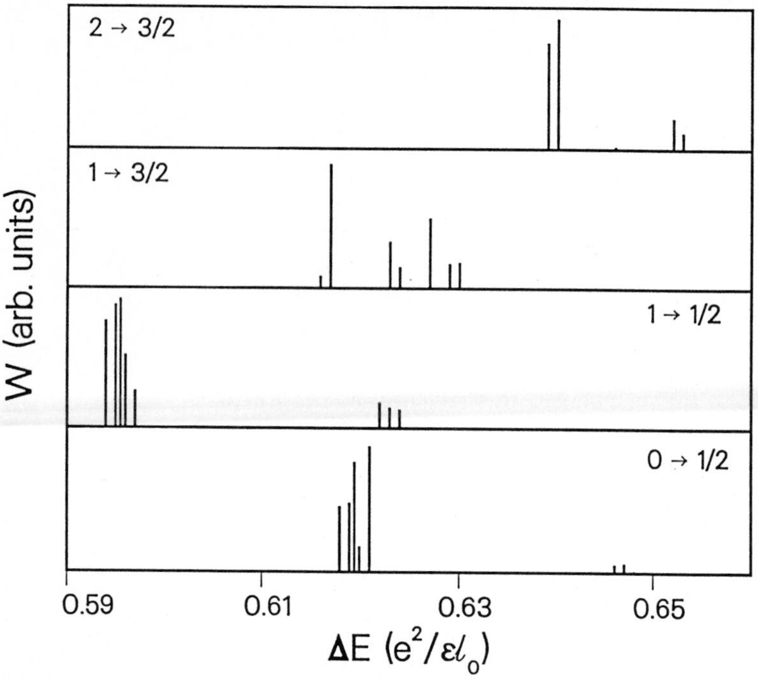

Fig. 5.22. Same as in Fig. 5.21(a) but for $\nu = \frac{1}{2}$ in the initial state

$\nu = \frac{1}{2}$ is a manifestation of the incompressible state for the former filling factor. However, a better understanding of the true nature of the ground state at $\frac{1}{2}$ filling is very much needed to settle that point.

In summary, for the $\frac{2}{3}$ filling of the lowest Landau level and when the spin unpolarized state is energetically stable, the intensity distribution for that spin state is separated from those with different spin polarization and therefore the luminescence line should exhibit a splitting. With increasing magnetic fields such that the initial state is fully spin polarized, the luminescence line should undergo a blue shift due to an increase in Zeeman energy. For a positive impurity in the initial state the splitting is weak at $\nu = \frac{2}{3}$, but the blue shift of the line should be more prominent. For the filling factor $\nu = \frac{1}{2}$ where the ground state is not expected to be incompressible, these features are absent. For a detailed discussion on the spin-reversed FQHE states, see Sects. 5.5,6.2,6.6, and 6.9.

Similar numerical calculations in a spherical geometry were also reported by *Apal'kov* and *Rashba* [5.74,75]. They studied the problem of trapping an electron from the Laughlin liquid by a neutral or attractive Coulomb center

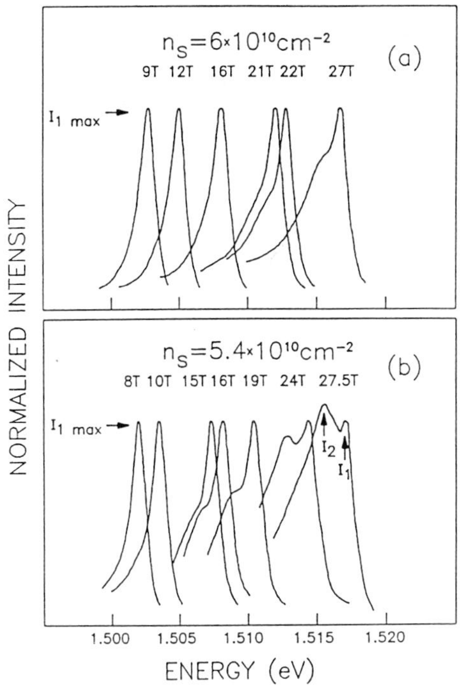

Fig. 5.23. Luminescence spectra at two different concentrations at 0.6 K and at various magnetic fields. I_2 increases nonmonotonically at (a) 22 T ($\nu \simeq \frac{1}{9}$) and (b) 16 T ($\nu \simeq \frac{1}{7}$) [5.77,78]

at an electron density corresponding to a filling factor $\nu = \frac{1}{3}$. In the initial state the system contains six electrons, five in the final state. The spherical geometry and the chord distance (5.51) were employed in the calculation where the continuous rotation group and the associated selection rules were retained. The shape of the emission spectrum is predicted to provide information about the magneto-roton gap. The magnetoroton satellites in the optical absorption spectrum was studied earlier by *Yang* [5.76].

Finally, spectroscopic measurements in the FQHE regime have been able to probe the Wigner crystallization in the strongly interacting electron system at low filling factors. The results obtained for radiative-recombination by *Buhmann* et al. [5.77,78] are shown in Fig. 5.23 at two different concentrations $n_s = 5.4\times10^{10}$ and 6×10^{10} cm^{-2} at various magnetic fields. In both cases above a certain magnetic field (B_c), in addition to the fundamental line I_1, which corresponds to a recombination of electrons from the two-dimensional system discussed above, an additional line (I_2) appears. The line I_2 increases in intensity with increasing magnetic field and at $\nu \simeq 0.1$ it dominates the spectrum. The doublet is shifted in the low-energy direction

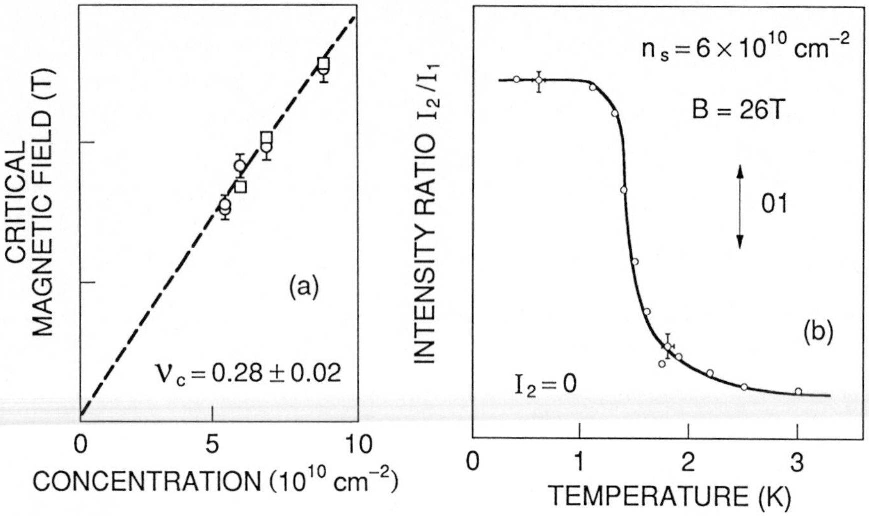

Fig. 5.24. (a) The dependence of (B_c) on n_c. (b) The temperature dependence of the intensity ratio I_2/I_1. T_c has been taken as the temperature at which I_2/I_1 drops to half its maximum value [5.77,78]

with increasing field and the splitting between I_1 and I_2 is ~ 1.4meV. The appearance of the new line is accompanied by a sudden decay of the overall luminescence intensity.

Line I_2 can be characterized by the two critical parameters — ν_c and T_c. Figure 5.24(a) shows that B_c depends linearly on the concentration of two-dimensional electrons. From the slope of B_c vs n_c one obtains $\nu = 0.28 \pm 0.02$. In Fig. 5.24 (b) the temperature dependence of the intensity ratio measured at $B = 26$T ($\nu = 0.09$) is plotted. At this ν and above $T_c = 1.4$K the line I_2 disappears from the spectrum.

Buhmann et al. attributed the appearance of the new line in the radiative-recombination spectra, accompanied by a simultaneous and sharp decrease in the overall luminescence intensity to a crystallization effect in the interacting electron system. In this picture, lines I_2 and I_1 correspond to a radiative recombination of two-dimensional electrons from the crystalline and liquid phases respectively (at $\nu = \frac{1}{5}, \frac{1}{7}$ and $\frac{1}{9}$, the system is an incompressible liquid). The fact that I_2 lies at a lower energy than I_1 means that the ground state of the crystalline phase is the lowest energy state. Also the tendency of I_2 to disappear from the spectra at $\nu = \frac{1}{5}, \frac{1}{7}$ and $\frac{1}{9}$ and the simultaneous enhancement in intensity of I_1 indicate the presence of incompressible fluids at these filling factors. A qualitative phase diagram $T_c(\nu)$ proposed by these authors is shown in Fig. 5.25 where the incompressible

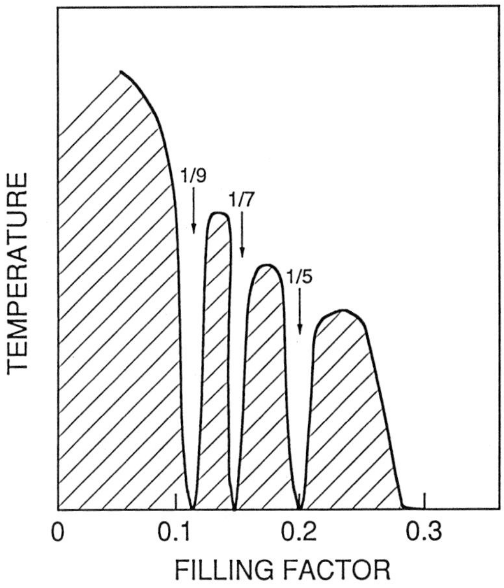

Fig. 5.25. Qualitative form of the phase diagram $T_c(\nu)$ showing FQHE states between reentrant Wigner crystal phases [5.78]

liquid state occurs at as low a density as $\nu = \frac{1}{9}$, but for $\nu < \frac{1}{5}$ all these states are surrounded by the Wigner-crystal-like states (shaded regions). From an analysis of the time-dependent recombination of the electrons in the plane of the 2DEG with the acceptors in the δ-layer, *Kukushkin et al.* [5.79] were able to study in detail the liquid-solid transition and demonstrated that the electrons form a triangular lattice in the WC regime.

There are a few very interesting variational Monte Carlo calculations reported in the literature for the magnetic field induced WC phase in two dimensions. *Zhu* and *Louie* [5.80] made a quantitative analysis of the roles played by exchange, intra-Landau-level correlations and inter-Landau-level mixing in a WC. They found that the effect of Landau-level mixing is quite substantial in the range of carrier density, effective mass, and strength of the magnetic field of experimental interest. *Price, Platzman* and *He* [5.81] reported results of a variational MC calculation of the FQH liquid at finite values of dimensionless density r_s [$r_s = a/a_B, a_B = \epsilon\hbar^2/m^*e^2$ where a is related to the carrier density, $n = 1/\pi a^2$] at the filling factors $\nu = \frac{1}{3}, \frac{1}{5}, \frac{1}{7}$ and $\frac{1}{9}$. They employed a variational wave function ψ_α^ν, which is the Laughlin wave function at ν, multiplied by a Jastrow factor with a single parameter α to calculate the energy. The Jastrow factor is introduced to make the

Laughlin liquid more like a solid. Finite-size calculations were done in a spherical geometry. These authors predict that a phase transition to the solid will take place around $r_s \approx 22$ for $\nu = \frac{1}{3}$ and at an $r_s \approx 15$ at $\nu = \frac{1}{5}$. The study of magnetic field induced Wigner crystallization is one of the most active field of research [5.82-88] at this time.

6. Elementary Excitations

One important result of Laughlin's theory was the observation that the elementary charged excitations in a stable state $\nu = \frac{1}{m}$ are quasiparticles and quasiholes with *fractional* electron charge of $\pm\frac{e}{m}$. If one electron is added to the system, it amounts to adding m elementary excitations and hence, the discontinuity in slope of the energy curve can be written as

$$\left.\frac{\partial E}{\partial N_{\mathrm{e}}}\right|_{\nu_+} - \left.\frac{\partial E}{\partial N_{\mathrm{e}}}\right|_{\nu_-} = m(\widetilde{\varepsilon}_{\mathrm{p}} + \widetilde{\varepsilon}_{\mathrm{h}}) = mE_{\mathrm{g}} \tag{6.1}$$

where E_{g} is the energy required to create one quasiparticle (with energy $\widetilde{\varepsilon}_{\mathrm{p}}$) and one quasihole (with energy $\widetilde{\varepsilon}_{\mathrm{h}}$) well separated from each other.[1] The pinning of the density to $\nu = \frac{1}{3}$ suggests that there will be no low frequency phonon-type of excitations at long wavelengths.

In the *absence* of impurities, there will be no dissipation associated with the flow of current leading to vanishing longitudinal conductivity. In the presence of a weak random potential which does not close up the energy gap, there will still be no dissipation. The uniform electric field $\boldsymbol{E}$ causes the electrons to drift. In a frame of reference moving with the drift velocity $\boldsymbol{v}_{\mathrm{D}} = (\boldsymbol{E} \times \boldsymbol{B})c/B^2$, the electric field is zero and so there is no electric current. The impurities however move relative to the frame with velocity $-\boldsymbol{v}_{\mathrm{D}}$. Because of the energy gap, at low temperatures the time dependent impurity potential will not generate any excitations and hence no dissipation of energy.

When the filling factor ν is slightly shifted from the stable state $\frac{1}{m}$, with m being an odd integer, the ground state of the system is expected to consist of a small density of quasiparticles or quasiholes, with charge $\pm\frac{e}{m}$ and Coulomb interactions. In the presence of impurities, these quasiparticles or quasiholes are expected, for low concentrations, to be trapped in potential fluctuations.

[1] The left-hand side of relation (6.1) is simply $\mu_+ - \mu_-$ where μ is the chemical potential defined in Sect. 6.2.

In the following sections, we describe how the quasiparticle and quasihole states are constructed and various methods are applied to evaluate the energy gap. Several experiments have been reported so far on the energy gap, which is related to the activation energy measured from thermal activation of ρ_{xx}. Finite-size calculations are also useful in obtaining E_{g} and there have been accurate results from Monte Carlo calculations. The following discussion of Laughlin's quasiparticle and quasihole states is based on the articles by *Laughlin* [6.1,2], *Halperin* [6.3–6] and *Chakraborty* [6.7].

6.1 Quasiholes and Quasiparticles

As mentioned earlier, Laughlin's ground-state wave function has m-fold zeros when two particles come close to each other. *Halperin* [6.3] first pointed out that if, in Laughlin's state (5.14), we fix the positions of all electrons except one (say z_1) and move that electron around a closed loop, avoiding other electrons in the system, the phase of the wave function changes by $\Delta\phi \sim 2\pi\frac{\Phi}{\Phi_0}$ for large area A. [In fact, if the test electron goes around say the second electron, we clearly have $(z_1 - z_2)^m = r^m \mathrm{e}^{\mathrm{i}m\theta}$, and when θ is changed by -2π, the phase of the wave function changes by $-2\pi m$.] Recalling that, $\frac{\Phi}{\Phi_0} = N_{\mathrm{e}}m$ [see (1.14) and (5.15)], we see that, for each electron within area A, the wave function must have $N_{\mathrm{e}}m$ zeros as a function of the particle coordinates. This amounts to saying, we have one zero per flux quantum or m zeros per particle. Defining a *vortex* as a point where the wave function is zero in such a way that the phase changes by -2π for counterclockwise rotation, Halperin pointed out that Laughlin's wave function has precisely m vortices at each electron position and no other *wasted* vortices elsewhere in the sample.

Quasiholes: For densities slightly different from $\nu = \frac{1}{m}$, we cannot construct a wave function with exactly m vortices tied to each electron. In order to have electron density slightly *less* than $\frac{1}{m}$, either we add a few extra vortices not tied to electron positions, or have some electrons with more than m vortices. Laughlin considered the first choice, which is easier to realize. His wave function is written as [6.1] (in units where $\ell_0 = 1$)

$$\psi_m^{(-)} = \mathrm{e}^{-\frac{1}{4}\sum_l |z_l|^2} \prod_j (z_j - z_0) \prod_{j<k} (z_j - z_k)^m \tag{6.2}$$

where $z_0 = x_0 - \mathrm{i}y_0$. This wave function has a simple zero at $z_j = z_0$ for any j, as well as m-fold zeros at each point where $z_j = z_k$, for $k \neq j$. Writing

$$|\psi_m^{(-)}|^2 = \mathrm{e}^{-\mathcal{H}_m^{(-)}}, \tag{6.3}$$

we obtain

$$\mathcal{H}_m^{(-)} = \mathcal{H}_m + 2\sum_j \ln|z_j - z_0|, \tag{6.4}$$

which is just the Hamiltonian of a classical one-component plasma in the presence of an extra repulsive *phantom* point charge at point z_0, whose strength is less by a factor $\frac{1}{m}$ than the charges in the plasma. The plasma will neutralize this phantom by a *deficit* of $\frac{1}{m}$ charge near z_0, while elsewhere in the interior of the system, the charge density will not be changed. However, the real three-dimensional electric charge is carried by the electrons and by the uniform positive background, and *not* by the phantom. As the electron charge density cancels the uniform background, a real net charge $-\frac{e}{m}$ is accumulated in the vicinity of z_0. The wave function (6.2) therefore describes a *quasihole* at point z_0.

The quasihole creation energy was calculated by *Chakraborty* [6.7] as follows: The HNC equations for a two-component system are written as [see (5.22–26)][2]

$$\begin{aligned} g_{\alpha\beta}(x) &= \exp\left[N_{\alpha\beta}(x) - u_{\alpha\beta}(x)\right] \\ \widetilde{N}_{\alpha\beta}(q) &= \sum_{\gamma=1,2} \rho_\alpha \widetilde{C}_{\gamma\alpha}(q)\left[\widetilde{C}_{\gamma\beta}(q) + \widetilde{N}_{\gamma\beta}(q)\right] \\ C_{\alpha\beta}(x) &= g_{\alpha\beta}(x) - 1 - N_{\alpha\beta}(x). \end{aligned} \tag{6.5}$$

Here $u_{\alpha\beta}(x) = 2[1-(1-m)\delta_{\alpha\beta}]\ln x$, the indices α, β run over two types of particles, and ρ_α is the number density of species α. A single phantom particle in an otherwise uniform system can be considered as the *impurity limit* of the two-component HNC theory. In this limit, defining $c = \rho_2/\rho$, $\rho = \rho_1 + \rho_2$, one considers the case $c \to 0$. The equations (6.5) then decouple [6.7], and

$$\widetilde{N}_{\alpha\beta}(q) = \rho_\alpha \widetilde{C}_{\alpha\alpha}(q)\widetilde{C}_{\alpha\beta}(q)/\left[1 - \rho_\alpha \widetilde{C}_{\alpha\alpha}(q)\right]. \tag{6.6}$$

The other two functions $g_{\alpha\beta}(x)$ and $C_{\alpha\beta}$ are given as above. Defining the short-range functions as in (5.24), the final form of the HNC equations in the presence of an impurity are

$$\begin{aligned} \widetilde{N}^{\mathrm{s}}_{\alpha\beta}(q) &= \left[\widetilde{C}^{\mathrm{s}}_{\alpha\beta}(q)\widetilde{C}_{\alpha\alpha}(q) - \widetilde{u}^{1}_{\alpha\alpha}(q)\right] \\ C^{\mathrm{s}}_{\alpha\beta}(x) &= g_{\alpha\beta}(x) - 1 - N^{\mathrm{s}}_{\alpha\beta}(x) \\ g_{\alpha\beta}(x) &= \exp\left[N^{\mathrm{s}}_{\alpha\beta}(x) - u^{\mathrm{s}}_{\alpha\beta}(x)\right]. \end{aligned} \tag{6.7}$$

[2] See Appendix C for the explanation of the various functions.

These equations are solved for $g_{11}(x)$ and $g_{12}(x)$ by an iterative scheme. One first solves the equations for the background plasma [thus obtaining $C_{11}(x)$ and $g_{11}(x)$]. The Fourier transform $\widetilde{C}_{11}(q)$ is then used in the impurity equations to solve for $g_{12}(x)$ and $C_{12}(x)$.

The quasihole creation energy is obtained from

$$\widetilde{\varepsilon}_{\mathrm{h}} = \frac{1}{\sqrt{2m}} \int_0^\infty dx\, \delta g_{11}(x) \tag{6.8}$$

where δg_{11} corresponds to the charge in the background function $g_{11}(x)$ due to the presence of the impurity particle. This is calculated [6.7] from

$$\delta g_{11}(x) = \lim_{c \to 0} \frac{dg_{11}(x)}{dc}. \tag{6.9}$$

From (6.7) one can readily obtain the final set of equations:

$$\begin{aligned} &\delta g_{11}(x) = g_{11}(x)\, \delta N_{11}^{\mathrm{s}}(x) \\ &\delta \widetilde{N}_{11}^{\mathrm{s}}(q) = \left\{ \delta \widetilde{C}_{11}^{\mathrm{s}}(q) \left[\widetilde{h}_{11}(q) + \widetilde{C}_{11}(q) \right] + \widetilde{C}_{12}(q) h_{12}(q) \right\} \Big/ [1 - \widetilde{C}_{11}(q)] \\ &\delta C_{11}^{\mathrm{s}}(x) = \delta g_{11}(x) - \delta N_{11}^{\mathrm{s}}(x). \end{aligned} \tag{6.10}$$

In Fig. 6.1, we have plotted $\delta g_{11}(x)$ as a function of x for $m = 3$. The quasihole creation energy is obtained to be $\widetilde{\varepsilon}_{\mathrm{h}} = 0.0276\, e^2/\epsilon \ell_0$ for $m = 3$ and $0.0088\, e^2/\epsilon \ell_0$ for $m = 5$.

Laughlin [6.2] derived the quasihole creation energy in a slightly different way. He started with the two-component HNC equations (6.5). The particle densities are $\rho_1 = 1$ and $\rho_2 = \frac{1}{N_{\mathrm{e}}}$. Using ρ_2 as the small parameter, he then solved the two-component HNC equations perturbatively. To zeroth order, the equations decouple and we get, $g_{11}(x) = g(x)$, which is the ground-state function. More explicitly, one obtains[3]

$$\begin{aligned} \widetilde{h}_{11}(q) &= \widetilde{C}_{11}(q) + 2\widetilde{h}_{11}(q)\widetilde{C}_{11}(q) \\ \widetilde{h}_{12}(q) &= [1 + 2\widetilde{h}_{11}(q)]\widetilde{C}_{12}(q). \end{aligned} \tag{6.11}$$

To first order, one would get the relation

$$h_{11} + \delta h_{11} = C_{11} + \delta C_{11} + 2(h_{11} + \delta C_{11}) + \tfrac{2}{N_{\mathrm{e}}} h_{12} C_{12} + \left[\mathrm{O}\left(\tfrac{1}{N_{\mathrm{e}}}\right)^2 \right]. \tag{6.12}$$

From the above two equations we readily obtain

$$\delta h_{11} = [1 + 2h_{11}]^2 \delta C_{11} + \frac{2}{N_{\mathrm{e}}} h_{12}^2. \tag{6.13}$$

[3] One of us (T. C.) would like to acknowledge very helpful discussions about this derivation with B. I. Halperin and H. Fertig.

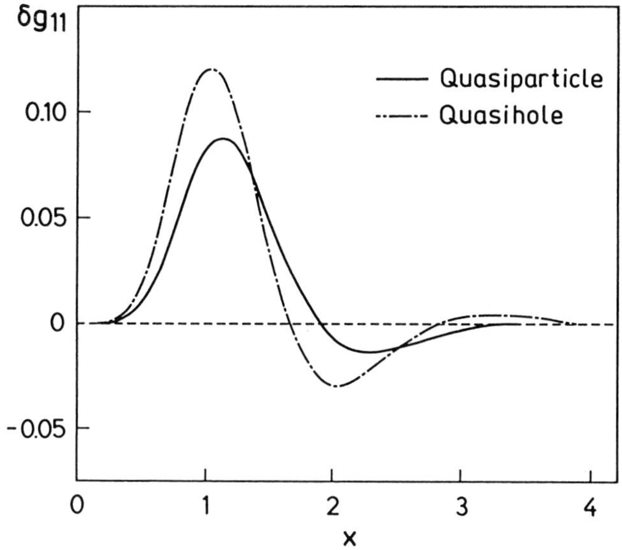

Fig. 6.1. Plot of $\delta g_{11}(x)$ versus x for the quasihole and quasielectron for $m = 3$ [6.7]

The quasihole creation energy is then calculated from,

$$\widetilde{\varepsilon}_{\mathrm{h}} = \frac{N_{\mathrm{e}}}{\sqrt{2m}} \int_0^\infty dx\, \delta h_{11} \tag{6.14}$$

to be $\widetilde{\varepsilon}_{\mathrm{h}} = 0.026\, e^2/\epsilon\ell_0$ for $m = 3$ and $0.008\, e^2/\epsilon\ell_0$ for $m = 5$. Recently, *Fertig* and *Halperin* [6.5] studied a generalization of the HNC approximation and calculated the three-body correlation functions g_{112} for a classical plasma with two particle species. Their result for the quasihole creation energy is $\widetilde{\varepsilon}_{\mathrm{h}} = 0.028\, e^2/\epsilon\ell_0$.

Introducing the finite thickness correction, (see Sect. 5.6), the quasihole creation energy has been calculated by one of us [6.8] and is plotted in Fig. 6.2, as a function of the dimensionless thickness parameter $\beta = (b\ell_0)^{-1}$.

Finally, because the charge accumulated around the phantom is determined by the long-range behavior of the interaction, the *particle excess* can be calculated as [6.4]

$$X = 2 \int_0^\infty \left[g_{12}(x) - 1\right] x\, dx. \tag{6.15}$$

Using the result for $g_{12}(x)$ from the HNC theory (Fig. 6.3) we obtain the expected result [6.8], $X = -0.328$ or $\sim -\frac{1}{3}$.

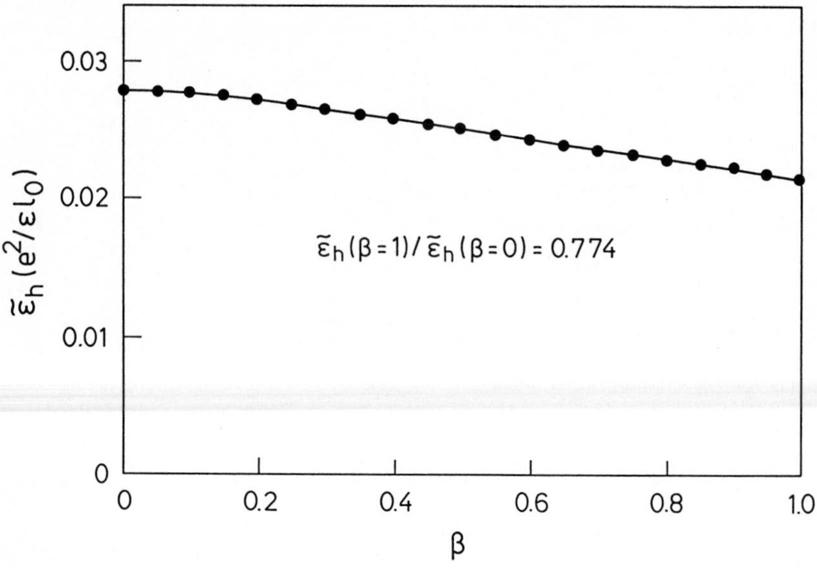

Fig. 6.2. The proper excitation energy for a Laughlin quasihole as a function of the finite thickness parameter β [6.8]

Quasiparticles: In the case when the electron density is slightly *higher* than the stable $\frac{1}{m}$ state, the choice of the wave function is not so clear. In this case, one needs a state with one flux quantum (or equivalently, one zero of the wave function) missing. The wave function proposed by Laughlin for the quasiparticle state is written

$$\psi = \prod_{j=1}^{N_e} \left[e^{-|z_j|^2/4\ell_0^2} \left(2\ell_0^2 \frac{\partial}{\partial z_j} - z_0^* \right) \right] \prod_{l<k} (z_l - z_k)^m . \tag{6.16}$$

In this case, the square of the wave function is not directly interpretable as the distribution in a classical statistical mechanics problem. However, *Laughlin* [6.2] has provided a means to calculate the charge density. In the following discussions, (which closely follow the papers by *Laughlin* [6.2] and *Morf* and *Halperin* [6.4]) we put the phantom particle at the center of the system for convenience.

For any polynomial $P(z)$, the following identity holds:

$$\left| 2\frac{dP}{dz} \right|^2 = \nabla^2 \left| P(z) \right|^2 . \tag{6.17}$$

The one-particle density is then written

$$\langle \rho(\boldsymbol{r}_1) \rangle = \frac{\int |\psi|^2 \, d\boldsymbol{r}_2 \ldots d\boldsymbol{r}_{N_e}}{\int |\psi|^2 \, d\boldsymbol{r}_1 \ldots d\boldsymbol{r}_{N_e}} \tag{6.18}$$

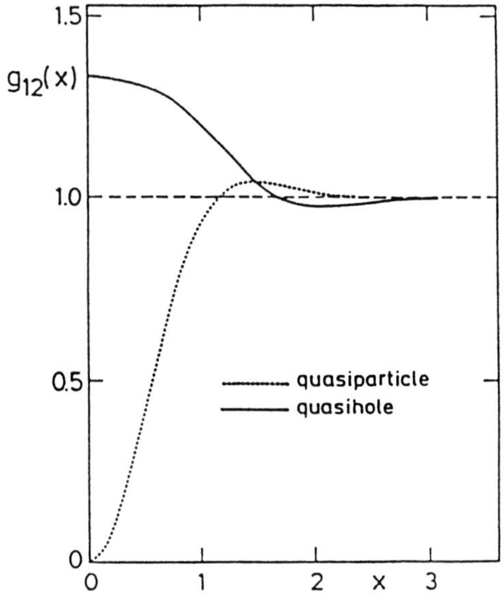

Fig. 6.3. Radial distribution function $g_{12}(x)$ as a function of x for quasiholes and quasiparticles for $m = 3$ [6.7]

with,

$$|\psi|^2 = \prod_{j=1}^{N_e} \left(e^{mr_j^2} \frac{1}{4m^2} \nabla_j^2 \right) \exp\left[2m \sum_{j<k} \ln |\boldsymbol{r}_j - \boldsymbol{r}_k| \right]. \tag{6.19}$$

The denominator of (6.18) is now written as

$$Z \equiv \int |\psi|^2 \, d\boldsymbol{r}_1 \ldots d\boldsymbol{r}_{N_e} = \int \prod_{j=1}^{N_e} d\boldsymbol{r}_j \, e^{-K} \tag{6.20}$$

where,

$$e^{-K} \equiv e^{-\mathcal{H}_m} \prod_{j=1}^{N_e} \left(r_j^2 - \frac{1}{m} \right) \tag{6.21}$$

and $\mathcal{H}_m$ is the one-component plasma Hamiltonian given in (5.17). In (6.20), we have eliminated the Laplacian by performing integration by parts. Similarly,

$$\int |\psi|^2 \, d\boldsymbol{r}_2 \ldots d\boldsymbol{r}_{N_e} = \frac{1}{Z} e^{-mr_1^2} \frac{\nabla^2}{4m^2} \int \prod_{j=2}^{N_e} \left[d\boldsymbol{r}_j \left(r_j^2 - \frac{1}{m} \right) e^{-mr_j^2} \right]$$
$$\times \exp\left(2m \sum_{j<k} \ln |\boldsymbol{r}_j - \boldsymbol{r}_k| \right). \tag{6.22}$$

The final form for the one-particle density is given, after some algebra, by

$$\langle\rho(\boldsymbol{r}_1)\rangle = \left[\frac{1}{4m^2}\nabla^2 + \frac{1}{m}\boldsymbol{r}_1\cdot\nabla_1 + r_1^2 + \frac{1}{m}\right]\frac{\langle\rho^*(\boldsymbol{r}_1)\rangle}{r_1^2 - \frac{1}{m}} \tag{6.23}$$

with the *integrated-by-parts* one-particle density $\langle\rho^*(\boldsymbol{r}_1)\rangle$ given by

$$\langle\rho^*(\boldsymbol{r}_1)\rangle = \int\prod_{j=2}^{N_e} d\boldsymbol{r}_j\,\mathrm{e}^{-K}\bigg/\int\prod_{j=1}^{N_e} d\boldsymbol{r}_j\,\mathrm{e}^{-K}. \tag{6.24}$$

This is again a classical plasma problem where the impurity–plasma interaction is quite unusual (and singular): $v_{12}(r) = -m\ln\left|r^2 - \frac{1}{m}\right|$. The HNC method could still be used to calculate $g_{12}(r)$, since the potential enters the equations only in the form, $\mathrm{e}^{-\beta v_{12}(r)} = r^2 - 1/m$. Laughlin also showed that the charge accumulated around the phantom is as expected, $+\frac{e}{m}$.

Since there is no direct plasma analogy in this case, evaluation of the quasiparticle creation energy via HNC is rather subtle. Laughlin introduced the following approximations: suppose there exists a pseudopotential $v_{12}^{\mathrm{ps}}(r)$ which gives exactly the same $\langle\rho(\boldsymbol{r}_1)\rangle$ as given above. He then writes, $g_{12}(r) = \langle\rho(r)\rangle/\rho$ and uses (6.11–14) to evaluate the quasiparticle creation energy. In this manner, he obtained, $\widetilde{\varepsilon}_{\mathrm{p}} = 0.025\,e^2/\epsilon\ell_0$ for $m = 3$ and $0.006\,e^2/\epsilon\ell_0$ for $m = 5$.

This additional approximation is however *not necessary* if one uses (6.8–10) instead [6.7]. To evaluate $\widetilde{\varepsilon}_{\mathrm{p}}$, we need only $C_{12}^{\mathrm{s}}(x)$ and $\widetilde{u}_{12}^{\mathrm{l}}(q)$ in (6.7). They can be obtained as follows: we write, $u_{12}^{\mathrm{s}}(x) = 2K_0(Qx)$ and invert the HNC-impurity equation (6.7), to obtain,

$$\begin{aligned} C_{12}^{\mathrm{s}}(x) &= [g_{12}(x) - 1] - \ln g_{12}(x) - 2K_0(Qx) \\ N_{12}^{\mathrm{s}}(x) &= \ln g_{12}(x) + 2K_0(Qx) \\ \widetilde{u}_{12}^{\mathrm{l}}(q) &= \widetilde{C}_{12}^{\mathrm{s}}(q)\widetilde{C}_{11}(q) - \widetilde{N}_{12}^{\mathrm{s}}(q)[1 - \widetilde{C}_{11}(q)]. \end{aligned} \tag{6.25}$$

In this manner, the total interaction, $u_{12}(x) = 2K_0(Qx) + u_{12}^{\mathrm{l}}(x)$ would correspond to the $g_{12}(x)$ derived from Eq. (6.23) within the HNC approximation, and no pseudopotential is required. The quasiparticle creation energy was obtained using this method by *Chakraborty* [6.7] with the result, $\widetilde{\varepsilon}_{\mathrm{p}} = 0.025\,e^2/\epsilon\ell_0$ for $m = 3$ and $0.0057\,e^2/\epsilon\ell_0$ for $m = 5$.

In Fig. 6.4, we present $\widetilde{g}_{12}(x)$ [obtained from $\rho^*(x)$ in (6.24)] evaluated via the two-component classical plasma system for $m = 3$ and $m = 5$. These results are similar to those obtained by *Fertig* and *Halperin* [6.5]. The functions $\delta g_{11}(x)$ and $g_{12}(x)$ are plotted for the quasiparticles in Figs. 6.1 and

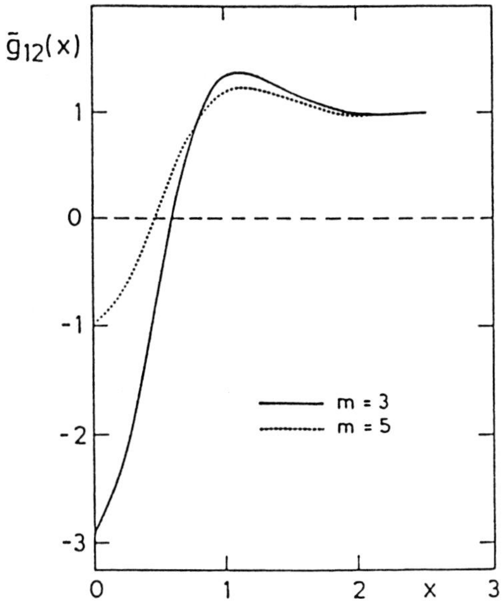

Fig. 6.4. The *integrated-by-parts* $\widetilde{g}_{12}(x)$ as a function of x for $m=3$ and $m=5$ [6.7]

6.3 respectively. As we shall see below, accurate Monte Carlo results based on Laughlin's quasihole wave functions compare quite well with the quasihole energies obtained above. The quasiparticle creation energy obtained via HNC theory, is however, a factor of two *smaller* than the Monte Carlo result. This point will be discussed in detail in Sect. 6.5.

The quasiparticle and quasihole size is the distance over which the one-component plasma screens [6.1]. For a weakly coupled plasma ($\Gamma \leq 2$), this distance is the Debye length [6.9], $\lambda_{\rm D} = \frac{\ell_0}{\sqrt{2}}$. For the strongly coupled plasma relevant to the present case, a better estimate is the ion-disk radius associated with *charge* $\frac{1}{m}$, $R = \sqrt{2}\ell_0$. In this sense, the quasiparticles have the same *size* as electrons in the lowest Landau level. The fractional charge of the quasiparticles and quasiholes, $e^* = \pm\frac{e}{m}$ at $\nu = \frac{1}{m}$, has indeed been confirmed experimentally by *Clark* et al. [6.10] and will be discussed in Sect. 6.6.

Recently, *Bychkov* and *Rashba* [6.11] have presented an interesting geometrical interpretation of the quasihole and quasiparticle creation operators. In the symmetric gauge, the magnetic translation operators are defined as (see Sect. 7.2)

$$T(\boldsymbol{a}) = t(\boldsymbol{a}) \exp\left[\tfrac{1}{2}\mathrm{i}(\widehat{\boldsymbol{z}} \times \boldsymbol{a}) \cdot \boldsymbol{r}\right] , \qquad (6.26)$$

where $t(\boldsymbol{a})$ is the ordinary translation operator and $\widehat{\boldsymbol{z}}$ the unit vector parallel to the magnetic field $\boldsymbol{B}$. We have chosen units in which $\ell_0 = 1$.

For an *infinitesimal* translation, it is possible to write,

$$T(\boldsymbol{a}) \approx 1 + \boldsymbol{a} \cdot \boldsymbol{t} \tag{6.27}$$

where,

$$t = \nabla + \tfrac{1}{2}\mathrm{i}(\widehat{\boldsymbol{z}} \times \boldsymbol{r}). \tag{6.28}$$

The complex operators for infinitesimal translations are then,

$$t_\pm = t_x \pm \mathrm{i}t_y = (\partial_x \pm \mathrm{i}\partial_y) \mp \tfrac{1}{2}(x \pm \mathrm{i}y). \tag{6.29}$$

Applying these operators to the ground-state wave function ψ_m (5.9), we obtain,

$$\begin{aligned} t_+\psi_m &= \mathrm{e}^{-|z|^2/4} z^{m+1} \\ t_-\psi_m &= \mathrm{e}^{-|z|^2/4}\left(2\frac{d}{dz}z^m\right), \end{aligned} \tag{6.30}$$

which, when compared to (6.2) and (6.16), show that the quasihole and quasiparticle operators are in fact generators of infinitesimal magnetic translations.

Fertig and *Halperin* [6.5] pointed out that for small interparticle separation, $\delta h_{11}(r)$ does not have the correct behavior. It is approximately described by $\delta h_{11} \sim r^{2m}$, whereas the correct behavior should be $\sim r^{2m-4}$. In the presence of an infinitesimal density ρ_2 of quasiparticles at random positions, the electron pair correlation function has the form $g_{11}(|\boldsymbol{r}_1 - \boldsymbol{r}_2|) + \rho_2\, \delta h_{11}(|\boldsymbol{r}_1 - \boldsymbol{r}_2|)$, where $g_{11}(r)$ is the ground-state correlation function. Defining the pair correlation function of the electrons in the presence of a quasiparticle at $\boldsymbol{r}_0$ as

$$g_{112}(\boldsymbol{r}_1 - \boldsymbol{r}_0, \boldsymbol{r}_2 - \boldsymbol{r}_0) = \frac{N(N-1)}{\rho^2} \frac{\int |\psi|^2\, d\boldsymbol{r}_3 \ldots d\boldsymbol{r}_{N_\mathrm{e}}}{\int |\psi|^2\, d\boldsymbol{r}_1 \ldots d\boldsymbol{r}_{N_\mathrm{e}}} \tag{6.31}$$

the function δh_{11} is written

$$\delta h_{11}(|\boldsymbol{r}_1 - \boldsymbol{r}_2|) = \int d\boldsymbol{r}_0\, \left[g_{112}(\boldsymbol{r}_1 - \boldsymbol{r}_0, \boldsymbol{r}_2 - \boldsymbol{r}_0) - g_{11}(|\boldsymbol{r}_1 - \boldsymbol{r}_2|)\right]. \tag{6.32}$$

In the limit $|\boldsymbol{r}_1 - \boldsymbol{r}_2| \to 0$ we have $g_{112}(\boldsymbol{r}_1, \boldsymbol{r}_2) \sim |\boldsymbol{r}_1 - \boldsymbol{r}_2|^{2m-4}$. Therefore, $\delta h_{11}(r) \sim r^{2m-4}$. The g_{112} was then obtained by Fertig and Halperin from an inhomogeneous classical plasma model and it was found that, near a quasiparticle, the electron pair correlation function vanishes as $|\boldsymbol{r}_1 - \boldsymbol{r}_2|^2$ for $|\boldsymbol{r}_1 - \boldsymbol{r}_2| \to 0$. However, the quasiparticle creation energy obtained by them was a factor of two *larger* than the Monte Carlo result. Accurate evaluation of the correct quasiparticle energy in the plasma approach is still an open problem.

6.2 Finite-Size Studies: Rectangular Geometry

In Sect. 5.1, we have seen that the ground-state energy per electron in a finite-size calculation [6.12] shows a cusp-like behavior at $\nu = \frac{1}{3}$. As has already been discussed above, the appearance of a cusp means a positive discontinuity in chemical potential. The chemical potential is defined as

$$\begin{aligned} \mu &= E(N_\mathrm{e}+1) - E(N_\mathrm{e}) \\ &= (N_\mathrm{e}+1)E_0(\rho) + \frac{N_\mathrm{e}+1}{A}\frac{dE_0}{d\rho} - N_\mathrm{e}E_0(\rho) \\ &= E_0(\nu) + \nu\frac{dE_0}{d\nu} \end{aligned} \tag{6.33}$$

where E_0 is the energy per particle at $\nu = \frac{1}{3}$ and ρ is the electron density defined in Sect. 1.2. Adding or subtracting a flux quantum at this filling fraction we obtain, $\nu_\pm = N_\mathrm{e}/(N_\mathrm{s} \mp 1)$. Let us define $E_\pm$ to be the ground-state energy per particle at those filling fractions. If we write

$$\mu_\pm \simeq E_0(\nu) + \nu\,[E_\pm - E_0]\,/(\nu_\pm - \nu), \tag{6.34}$$

the quasiparticle-quasihole energy gap is then just the difference between the two chemical potentials [see (6.1)],

$$\begin{aligned} E_\mathrm{g} &= \tfrac{1}{3}(\mu_+ - \mu_-) \\ &\simeq -2N_\mathrm{e}E_0(\nu) + (N_\mathrm{e}+\nu)\,E_0\,(\nu_-) + (N_\mathrm{e}-\nu)\,E_0\,(\nu_+)\,. \end{aligned} \tag{6.35}$$

The factor $\frac{1}{3}$ in (6.35) is introduced because of the fractional electron charge of the quasiparticles and quasiholes. Using this approach for a four-electron system (spin polarized), *Yoshioka* [6.13] obtained the gap, $E_\mathrm{g} \simeq 0.052\,e^2/\epsilon\ell_0$. However, studying somewhat larger systems *Chakraborty* et al. [6.14,15] found that E_g is, in fact, size dependent (see Fig. 6.5) and extrapolation of the results for spin-polarized three- to seven-electron systems (plotted as solid circles) approximately leads to $E_\mathrm{g} \simeq 0.1\,e^2/\epsilon\ell_0$. The

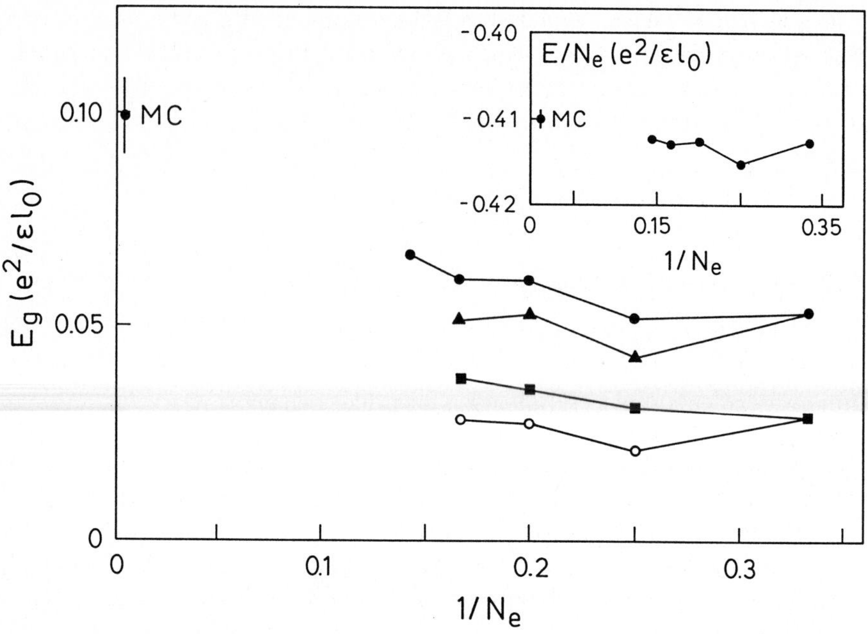

Fig. 6.5. The energy gap for different spin polarization of the quasiparticle (q.p.) and quasihole (q.h.) excitations for three to seven electron systems, in the absence of Zeeman energy [6.14,15]. The Monte Carlo result (MC) is from [6.4] for the spin-aligned q.p. + q.h. (●). The other three cases are: spin-aligned q.p. + spin-reversed q.h. (▲); spin-reversed q.p. + spin-aligned q.h. (■); and spin-reversed q.p. + q.h. (○). The ground-state energy values at $\nu = \frac{1}{3}$ [6.4,12] are given in the inset for comparison

energy gap can also be estimated from the collective excitation spectrum to be discussed in Chap. 7, and provides essentially the same result. In the case of spin-reversed quasiparticles to be described below, the Zeeman contribution to the energy gap is to be calculated from the above expression, by adding the Zeeman energy to the different ground-state energies.

The above discussion of the energy gap is for the $\frac{1}{3}$ filling fraction. For an arbitary filling fraction of $\nu = \frac{p}{q}$, the lowest energy excitations are quasiparticles of charge $\pm\frac{e}{q}$. The energy required to create a pair of these quasiparticles of opposite charge well separated from each other is obtained by modifying (6.35) as

$$E_{\mathrm{g}} \simeq -2\frac{N_{\mathrm{e}}}{p}E_0(\nu) + \left(\frac{N_{\mathrm{e}}}{p} - \frac{1}{q}\right) E_0\left(\nu_+\right) + \left(\frac{N_{\mathrm{e}}}{p} + \frac{1}{q}\right) E_0\left(\nu_-\right) . \qquad (6.36)$$

The energy gap for higher order filling fractions and the Zeeman contribution to the gap to be described later are evaluated from this expression.

6.3 Spin-Reversed Quasiparticles

The finite-size calculations discussed above can be readily generalized to the case where the spin of one of the electrons is *reversed* relative to all the others. The spin reversal in the ground state has already been discussed in Sect. 5.5. The same technique will follow through and, in the present case, we will concern ourselves with the two cases, (a) $S = S_z = \frac{1}{2}N_e$, which corresponds to the fully spin polarized ground state, and (b) $S = S_z = \frac{1}{2}N_e - 1$, which is the spin-reversed excitation we are considering below. Here S and the S_z correspond to the total spin and the z-component of the of the total spin respectively. The spin-reversed quasiparticle and quasihole excitation energy gaps are obtained by evaluating $E_\pm$ in a system where one of the electrons has reversed spin. The ground-state energy at $\nu = \frac{1}{3}$ [denoted by $E_0(\nu)$ in (6.33–36)] is however calculated for the spin-polarized case.

The major bottleneck of a numerical diagonalization scheme, such as the one described in this section and in the preceding section, is the size of the Hamiltonian matrix; this grows very rapidly with the electron number and at a certain point exceeds the storage capacity of a computer. In the case of one reversed spin, the situation is even worse since the electrons can now occupy states with the same momentum. The matrix dimension in this case is increased approximately by a factor $\sim (1 + N_e)$ compared with that for the fully spin-polarized state. For $N_e > 4$, the dimension of the Hamiltonian matrix is more than 11000, and clearly a straightforward diagonalization is not possible. Furthermore, for the one-spin-reversed problem we are dealing with, the numbers of electrons and flux quanta are such that they have no common divisor greater than unity. Therefore, the symmetries based on the magnetic translation group (Sect. 7.2) cannot be employed to reduce the matrix size.

Fortunately, there are some simple ways to work with these huge matrices [6.15]. Firstly, the two-body operator of the Hamiltonian (5.14) can connect only those states which differ by at most two indices labeling the occupied single-particle states. The majority of the matrix elements are therefore zero. Moreover, the coefficients of the two-body operator depend only on the difference between the indices and hence there are only a few ($\sim$ number of flux quanta squared) different matrix elements. When the matrix is stored in the computer by rows keeping only non-zero elements, and these are represented as offsets to the array containing the different elements together with the corresponding column indices, only four bytes of storage per non-zero element is required. Since the matrix is symmetric, only the upper or lower triangle need be stored.

The lowest eigenvalue and the corresponding eigenvector are obtained by minimizing the Rayleigh quotient

$$\lambda(x) = \frac{x^{\mathrm{T}}\mathcal{H}x}{x^{\mathrm{T}}x},$$

where x represents the column vector of the coefficients in the superposition of the basis states. Similarly, the next lowest eigenvalue can then be found by working in the subspace orthogonal to this eigenvector. The required number of eigenvalues and eigenvectors can thus be extracted by repeating the procedure. The minimization of the Rayleigh quotient is done by the conjugate gradient method in which the quotient is approximated by a quadratic function and the minimum in each iteration step is searched for in the plane spanned by the gradient and the search direction of the previous iteration step [6.15].

In Fig. 6.5, the energy gap is plotted for different spin polarizations of the quasiparticles and quasiholes. The spin-polarized quasiparticle–quasihole case has been discussed earlier in Sect. 6.2. The other three cases are: (a) spin-polarized quasiparticle and spin-reversed quasihole gap (plotted as ▲), (b) spin-reversed quasiparticle and spin-polarized quasihole (plotted as ■) and (c) spin-reversed quasiparticle and quasihole (plotted as ○). Obviously at $\nu = \frac{1}{3}$, the lowest energy excitations *in the absence of Zeeman energy* involve spin reversal. The origin of this could perhaps be traced to the results in Sect. 5.5. There it was seen that, for any state other than $\frac{1}{m}$ with m an odd integer (which is spin polarized, in agreement with the Laughlin state), the electron-electron interaction decreases the tendency to spin polarization, resulting in lower energies for the spin reversed cases considered here. The spin reversal is in fact, found to cost somewhat less energy for E_+ (reduction of a flux quantum) than that for E_- (addition of a flux quantum). In any case, in the absence of Zeeman energy, the lowest energy excitations correspond to the case where E_+ and E_- are evaluated for spin-reversed systems.

In Fig. 6.6, we present the energy gap E_{g} as a function of the dimensionless parameter $\beta = (b\ell_0)^{-1}$ (see Sect. 5.6) for four- and six-electron systems at $\nu = \frac{1}{3}$. For the spin-polarized quasiparticle–quasihole case (filled points), five- and six-electron system results are indistingushable in the figure. The interesting point, however, is the fact that there is a substantial reduction

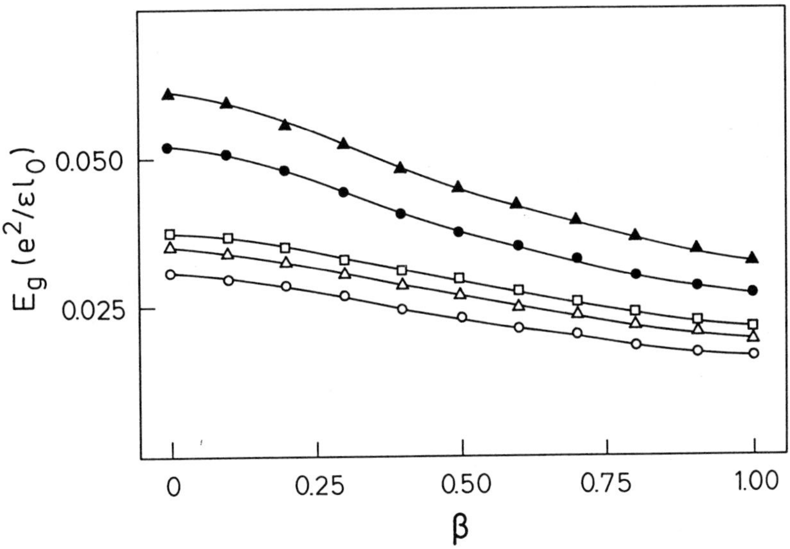

Fig. 6.6. Energy gap $E_{\rm g}$ as a function of the dimensionless parameter $\beta = (b\ell_0)^{-1}$ for four (● and ○), five (▲ and △) and six (□) electron systems. The filled circles are for spin-polarized q.p. + q.h. case, while the open circles are for the spin-reversed q.p. + spin polarized q.h. case. The five and six electron results in the former case are not distingushable in the figure

of the gap in the range $\beta = 0.5$–1.0, compared to the ideal case of $\beta = 0$. In fact, the ratio $E_{\rm g}(\beta = 1)/E_{\rm g}(\beta = 0)$ is 0.53 and 0.52 for the four- (●) and five-electron (▲) systems respectively. In the case of spin-reversed quasiparticle and spin-polarized quasihole (empty points), the reduction is slightly less: 0.55, 0.56 and 0.57 for four- (○), five- (△) and six-electron (□) systems respectively [6.14,15]. A similar reduction of the energy gap was also calculated by *Zhang* and *Das Sarma* [6.16] for finite-size systems. The cases (a) and (c) are not shown in Fig. 6.6, since, as we shall see in Sect. 6.6, they are not energetically favored when the Zeeman energy is added to these results and when compared with the experimental results. In fact, it will be seen in Sect. 6.6 that for small magnetic fields, the spin-reversed quasiparticles are clearly favored energetically.

For an infinite system, *Morf* and *Halperin* [6.4] proposed the following trial wave function for spin-reversed quasiparticles

$$\psi = \prod_{j=2}^{N_{\rm e}} (z_j - z_1)^{-1}\,\psi_m. \tag{6.37}$$

Bringing in the plasma analogy by writing the probability density as

$$|\psi|^2 = \mathrm{e}^{-\mathcal{H}},$$

the plasma Hamiltonian can now be written as

$$\mathcal{H} = -2m\left(1-\tfrac{1}{m}\right)\sum_{j=2}^{N_\mathrm{e}} \ln|z_j - z_1| - 2m \sum_{\substack{j<k\\ j>1}}^{N_\mathrm{e}} \ln|z_j - z_k| + \sum_{j=1}^{N_\mathrm{e}} |z_j|^2/2\ell_0^2. \quad (6.38)$$

In this case, $|\psi|^2$ is the distribution function for a two-dimensional plasma in which particle 1 has its charge *reduced* by a factor $(1-\frac{1}{m})$ in its repulsive interaction with the other particles. The particle 1 has, however, the same attractive interaction with the background as the other particles. Particle 1 will therefore be attracted to the center of the disk, while a two-dimensional *bubble* will be formed near the origin of size $(1-\frac{1}{m})$. As a result, there will be an extra negative charge $\frac{e}{m}$ near the origin. Furthermore, when (6.37) is considered to be a function of the position of any electron other than the singled-out electron 1, there will be one less zero of the wave function than in the case of the ground-state ψ_m.

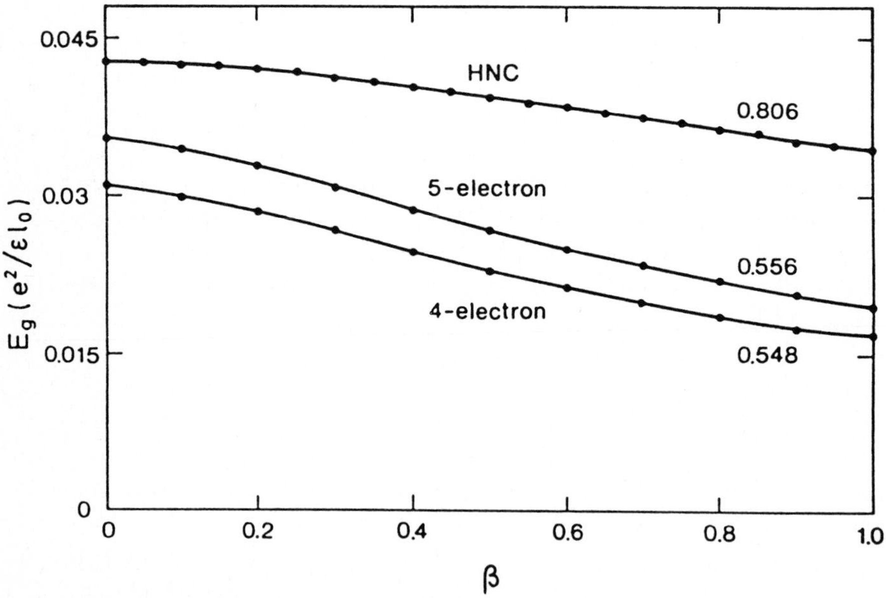

Fig. 6.7. The energy gap E_g (in units of $e^2/\epsilon\ell_0$) for the case of spin-polarized quasihole and spin-reversed quasiparticle as a function of β in the HNC approximation. The four- and five-electron system results are from [6.14]. The number attached to each curve indicates the ratio $E_\mathrm{g}(\beta=1)/E_\mathrm{g}(\beta=0)$

The HNC calculation for the wave function defined above was performed by *Chakraborty* [6.8]. In Fig. 6.7, we present the results for the energy gap for the spin-reversed quasiparticle and spin-polarized quasihole and compare these with the corresponding cases for finite-size systems discussed above. Both types of calculation provide qualitatively similar results.

6.4 Spherical Geometry

In Sect. 5.3, we discussed the ground-state calculations by *Haldane* and *Rezayi* [6.17] in a spherical geometry. These authors also computed the energy gap in three- to seven-electron systems at $\nu = \frac{1}{3}$. Later, *Fano* et al. [6.18] performed similar calculations for larger systems at $\nu = \frac{1}{3}$ and $\frac{1}{5}$. The quasiparticle and quasihole wave functions on the sphere are written

$$\psi_{\mathrm{p}} = \prod_i \frac{\partial}{\partial v_i} \psi_m \tag{6.39}$$

$$\psi_{\mathrm{h}} = \prod_i v_i \psi_m , \tag{6.40}$$

respectively, where ψ_m is the ground-state wave function ($L = 0$). These states have total angular momentum $L = \frac{1}{2} N_{\mathrm{e}}$, and azimuthal angular momentum $M = \pm L$.

Table 6.1. Quasiparticle and quasihole creation energies and the energy gap for finite electron systems in a spherical geometry. HR represents results of [6.17]. The other results are from [6.18]. The unit of energy is $e^2/\epsilon\ell_0$.

N_{e}	$\nu = \frac{1}{3}$				$\nu = \frac{1}{5}$		
	$\widetilde{\varepsilon}_{\mathrm{h}}$	$\widetilde{\varepsilon}_{\mathrm{p}}$	E_{g}	E_{g}(HR)	$\widetilde{\varepsilon}_{\mathrm{h}}$	$\widetilde{\varepsilon}_{\mathrm{p}}$	E_{g}
3	0.04270	0.11968	0.16238	0.13849	0.01269	0.02787	0.04057
4	0.03782	0.10469	0.14251	0.13093	0.01055	0.02337	0.03392
5	0.03549	0.09896	0.13445	0.12543	0.01034	0.02257	0.03290
6	0.03362	0.09363	0.12726	0.12045	0.00849	0.01970	0.02819
7	0.03257	0.09101	0.12359	0.11816	0.00907	0.02019	0.02925
8	0.03172	0.08877	0.12049	—	—	—	—
9	0.03103	0.08700	0.11803	—	—	—	—
∞	0.02640	0.07720	0.10360	0.105±0.005	0.00710	0.01730	0.02440

The numerical results by Haldane and Rezayi for the quasiparticle–quasihole gap for three- to seven-electron systems are shown in Fig. 6.8. Their estimate for the infinite system is $E_g \approx 0.105 \pm 0.005\, e^2/\epsilon\ell_0$. The charge density profiles of the quasiparticle and quasihole obtained for a

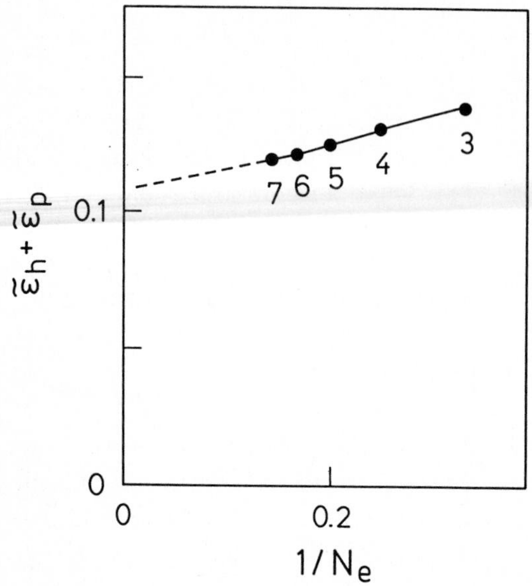

Fig. 6.8. The energy required to create a quasihole plus quasiparticle pair at infinite separation, evaluated in the spherical geometry [6.17]

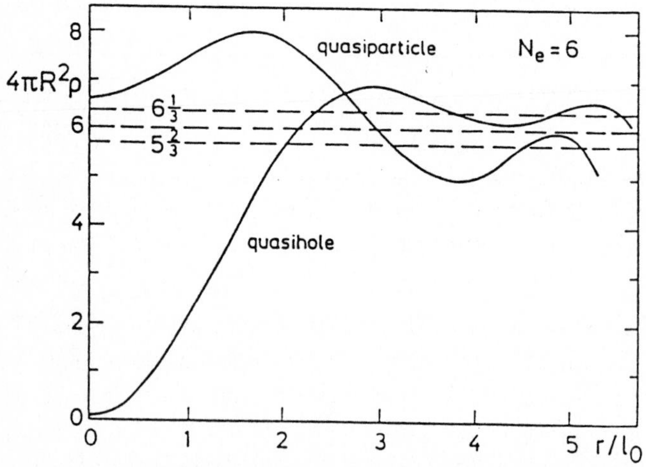

Fig. 6.9. Charge density profiles of a quasiparticle and quasihole [6.17]

six-electron system is shown in Fig. 6.9. As discussed earlier, creation of quasiparticles and quasiholes at fixed total charge would imply that the charge of the background condensate must be decreased or increased by $\frac{e}{m}$, because of the fractional electron charge of the quasiparticles and quasiholes (see Sect. 6.1). The asymptotic charge densities in Fig. 6.9 seem to approach the value $4\pi R^2\rho \approx N \mp \frac{1}{3}$.

Fano et al. [6.18] have performed a similar calculation for somewhat larger systems and claimed to have improved on the results of Haldane and Rezayi. In Table 6.1, we present their results for the quasihole and quasiparticle creation energies and the energy gap for $\nu = \frac{1}{3}$ and $\frac{1}{5}$.

6.5 Monte Carlo Results

For the quasihole and quasiparticle excitation energies, extensive Monte Carlo calculations have been performed by *Morf* and *Halperin* [6.4,6,19]. Let us begin with the results for the quasihole. The results for the electron density $\langle\rho(r)\rangle$ generated via the Monte Carlo simulation of the plasma Hamiltonian (5.4) with a quasihole at the origin ($z_0 = 0$) are shown in Fig. 6.10 for $\nu = \frac{1}{3}$. This density, and the ones that will follow correspond to a system where the change in the occupied area due to the presence of a quasihole or a quasiparticle is not compensated. For small interparticle separation, the results are essentially independent of particle number and are similar to those of Fig. 6.3 for the HNC approximation. The particle excess

$$X(r) = 2\pi \int [\rho(r) - \rho_m]\, r\, dr, \tag{6.41}$$

where $\rho_m = (2\pi\ell_0^2 m)^{-1}$, is evaluated to be, -0.34, -0.326, and -0.327 at system radius $R = 2.5$ [distances are measured in this section in units of the ion-disk radius R_0 (Sect. 5.2)] for the 30-, 42-, and 72-particle systems respectively.

The quasihole creation energy is computed for 20-, 30-, 42-, and 72-electron systems and is plotted in Fig. 6.11. The standard deviation is indicated by the length of the vertical bars in the figure. Due to large statistical errors, reliable extrapolation to the thermodynamic limit is difficult. The result for the 72-electron system, $\widetilde{\varepsilon}_{\rm h} = 0.0268 \pm 0.0033\, e^2/\epsilon\ell_0$ is already close to the HNC result.

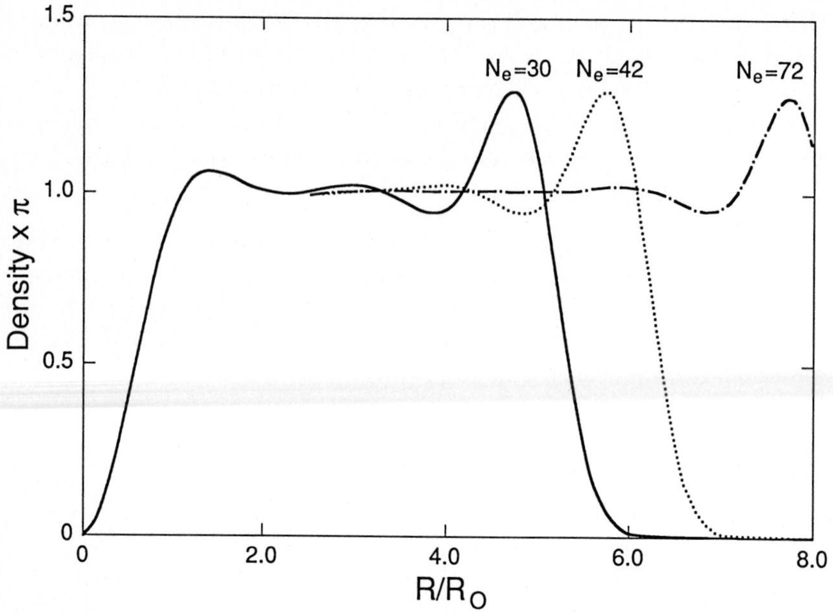

Fig. 6.10. Electron density $\langle \rho(\boldsymbol{r}) \rangle$ for Laughlin's quasihole state at $\nu = \frac{1}{3}$ for N_e=30, 42 and 72 electrons [6.4]

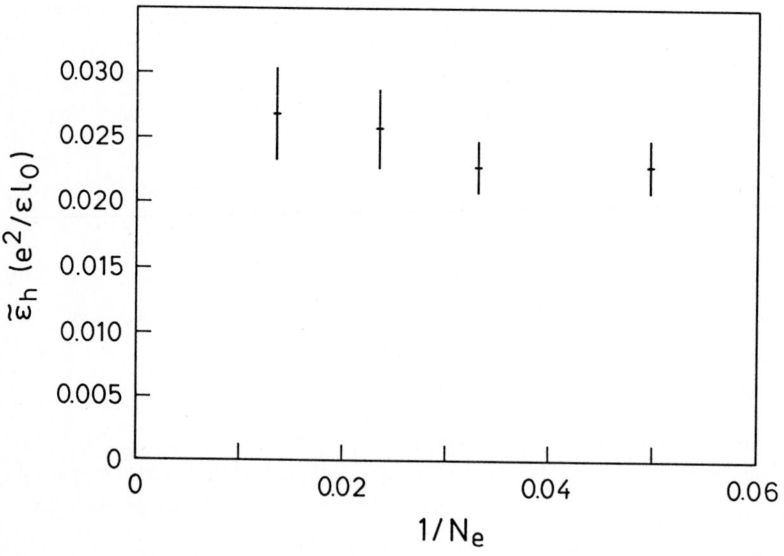

Fig. 6.11. The quasihole creation energy, $\widetilde{\varepsilon}_h$ for $\nu = \frac{1}{3}$ with Laughlin's quasihole wave function [6.4]

For Laughlin's quasiparticle wave function, we have mentioned earlier that a direct plasma analogy is not possible. A plasma analogy exists however for the *integrated-by-parts* one-particle density $\langle \rho^*(\boldsymbol{r}_1) \rangle$ [see (6.24)] for the Hamiltonian K in (6.21). In Fig. 6.12, we show a plot of $\rho^*(\boldsymbol{r}) = (r^2 - \frac{1}{m})\widetilde{f}(r)$, where the solid line is an interpolation of the Monte Carlo results for 30 electrons (dots), using a Padé approximation,

$$\widetilde{f}(r) \simeq (a_0 + a_1 r^2 + a_2 r^4)/(1 + b_1 r^2)\,,$$

and a third-order spline polynomial for $r > 1.2$. The Padé coefficients are $a_0 = 4.05112, a_1 = -2.08448, a_2 = 0.38863$ and $b_1 = 0.42435$. Using this fit for $\widetilde{f}(r)$ in (6.23), *Morf* and *Halperin* [6.4] obtained the final result for the density $\langle \rho(r) \rangle$ as shown in Fig. 6.13.

It is obvious in Fig. 6.13 that the excess charge is located inside a circle of radius $R \approx 2$. There is a pronounced dip at the origin, which is not seen in the plasma approach (Fig. 6.3). A dip is also present in the quasiparticle charge density evaluated on the sphere (Fig. 6.9). For the 72-particle system, the particle excess is evaluated as 0.207, 0.408, and 0.33 at R=1, 2, and 3 respectively. For $3 < R < 6$, $X(R)$ oscillates around $\frac{1}{3}$, as required.

The quasiparticle creation energies obtained for 20, 30, 42, and 72 particle systems with Laughlin's wave function are shown in Fig. 6.14. For

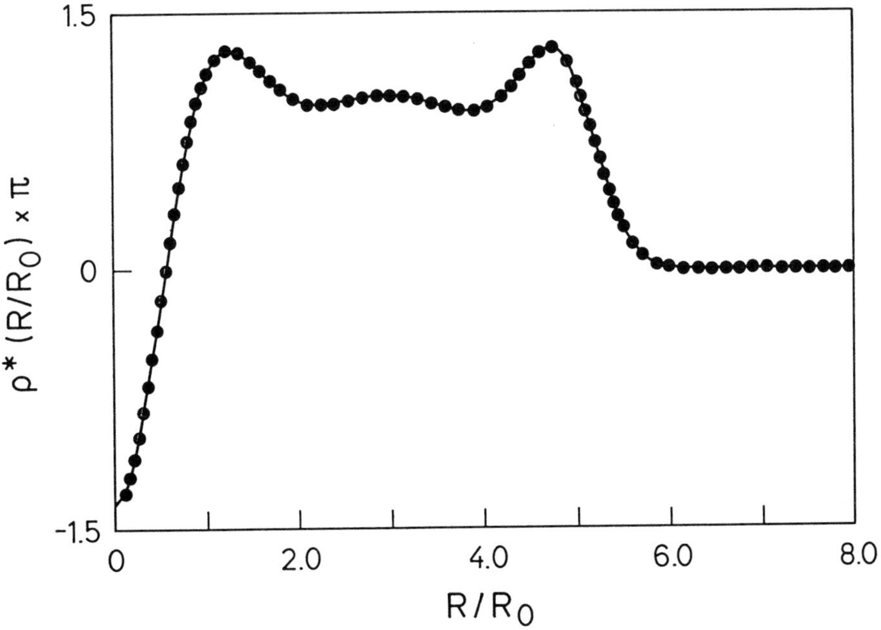

Fig. 6.12. Density $\rho^*(\boldsymbol{r})$ for the Hamiltonian K [see (6.21)] for Laughlin's quasiparticle state at $\nu = \frac{1}{3}$ [6.4]

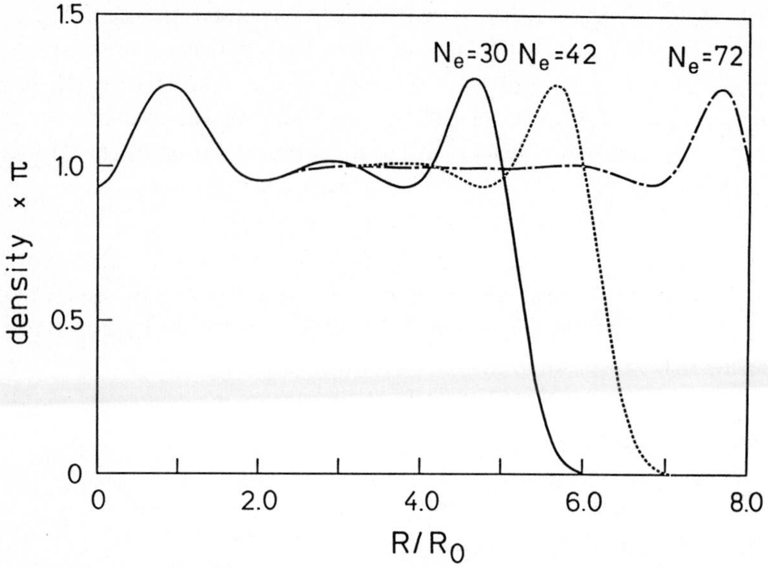

Fig. 6.13. Electron density $\langle \rho(\boldsymbol{r}) \rangle$ for Laughlin's quasiparticle state at $\nu = \frac{1}{3}$ [6.4]

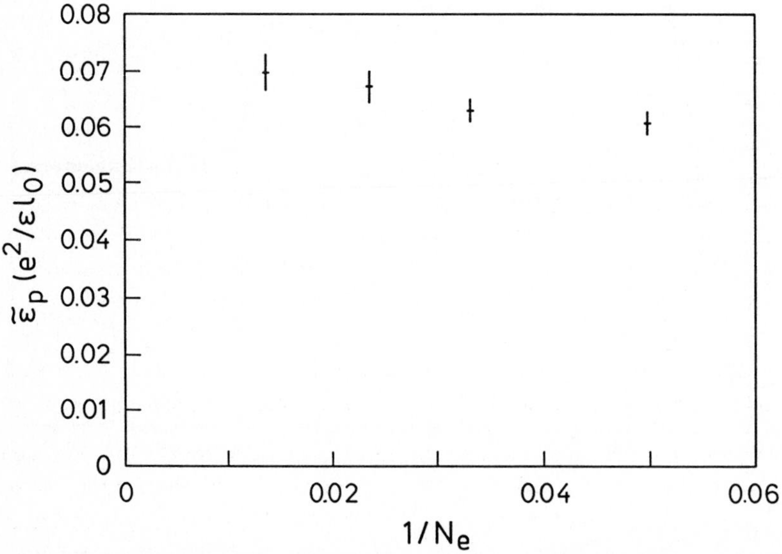

Fig. 6.14. Quasiparticle creation energy $\tilde{\varepsilon}_{\mathrm{p}}$ for the Laughlin wave function at $\nu = \frac{1}{3}$ [6.4]

the 72-electron system, *Morf* and *Halperin* [6.4] obtained the result $\tilde{\varepsilon}_p = 0.0698 \pm 0.0033\, e^2/\epsilon\ell_0$. Reliable extrapolation of the results in Fig. 6.14 to the thermodynamic limit is difficult. However these authors made a plausible estimate of $\tilde{\varepsilon}_p \approx 0.073 \pm 0.008\, e^2/\epsilon\ell_0$. The result is significantly higher than the estimate from the plasma calculation (see Sect. 6.1). The energy gap to create a quasiparticle–quasihole pair far apart from each other is then $E_g \approx 0.099 \pm 0.009\, e^2/\epsilon\ell_0$ in the thermodynamic limit.

An alternative trial wave function for the quasiparticles, which is more directly motivated by a classical statistical-mechanics problem, has been proposed by *Halperin* [6.3]. The Monte Carlo evaluation of the quasiparticle energy and of the correlation function using this wave function has been reported by *Morf* and *Halperin* [6.4,19]. Placing the quasiparticle at the origin, the wave function is written

$$
\begin{aligned}
\psi_0^{(+)}\{z_k\} &= \mathcal{A}\widetilde{\psi}_0^{(+)}\{z_k\} \\
\widetilde{\psi}_0^{(+)}\{z_k\} &= \left[\frac{1}{z_1 - z_2}\right]^2 \prod_{j=3}^{N_e} \frac{z_j - \frac{1}{2}(z_1 + z_2)}{(z_1 - z_j)(z_2 - z_j)}\psi_m \ ,
\end{aligned}
\tag{6.42}
$$

$\mathcal{A}$ being the antisymmetrization operator. It is readily noted that, $\widetilde{\psi}_0^{(+)}$ has the form of a polynomial in $\{z_k\}$, multiplied by a gaussian factor, and therefore describes a collection of particles in the lowest Landau level, for $m > 1$. The plasma analogy in this case results in the following Hamiltonian:

$$
|\widetilde{\psi}_0^{(+)}|^2 = \mathrm{e}^{-\widetilde{\mathcal{H}}}
$$

$$
\begin{aligned}
\widetilde{\mathcal{H}} = \mathcal{H}_m + 4\ln|\boldsymbol{r}_1 - \boldsymbol{r}_2| + 2\sum_{j=1}^{N_e}\Big(&\ln|\boldsymbol{r}_j - \boldsymbol{r}_1| + \ln|\boldsymbol{r}_j - \boldsymbol{r}_2| \\
&- \ln\left|\boldsymbol{r}_j - \tfrac{1}{2}(\boldsymbol{r}_1 + \boldsymbol{r}_2)\right|\Big) .
\end{aligned}
\tag{6.43}
$$

where $\mathcal{H}_m$ is the one-component plasma Hamiltonian (5.27). We thus have an extra logarithmic attraction between particles 1 and 2, resulting in a bound pair. The other particles experience a logarithmic repulsive interaction with the center of gravity of the bound pair, and a logarithmic attraction to the two members of the pair. As a result, an electron somewhat away from the pair, would see a net charge of $(2m - 1)$ on the pair, in units where an unpaired electron has charge m. Therefore, we have a hole of size $(2 - \frac{1}{m})$ about the pair. Including the pair, there will be a net charge of $\frac{e}{m}$.

The wave function $\widetilde{\psi}_0^{(+)}$ is antisymmetric with respect to interchange of particles j and k with $j > 2$ and $k > 2$. It is also antisymmetric with respect to particles 1 and 2. It does not, however, change sign under a permutation, for example P_{13}, that interchanges positions of particles 1 and 3. If the pair of particles 1 and 2 were very tightly bound relative to the separation between pairs, and had no overlap in space with the region occupied by particle 3, $P_{13}\widetilde{\psi}_0^{(+)}$ would have no overlap with $\widetilde{\psi}_0^{(+)}$. There would be no contribution of $\langle\widetilde{\psi}_0^{(+)}|P_{13}\widetilde{\psi}_0^{(+)}\rangle$ to the normalization of $\widetilde{\psi}_0^{(+)}$ and no contribution from $\langle\widetilde{\psi}_0^{(+)}|V|P_{13}\widetilde{\psi}_0^{(+)}\rangle$ to the expectation value of the potential energy. As, $P_{13}^2 = 1$, and P_{13} commutes with V, it is clearly seen that the following relations hold,

$$\langle\widetilde{\psi}_0^{(+)}|P_{13}VP_{13}|\widetilde{\psi}_0^{(+)}\rangle = \langle\widetilde{\psi}_0^{(+)}|V|\widetilde{\psi}_0^{(+)}\rangle$$
$$\langle\widetilde{\psi}_0^{(+)}|P_{13}P_{13}|\widetilde{\psi}_0^{(+)}\rangle = \langle\widetilde{\psi}_0^{(+)}|\widetilde{\psi}_0^{(+)}\rangle$$

and hence the expectation value of the potential energy would be unaffected. In actual practice however, we do not expect a zero overlap of the pair (z_1, z_2) with other other electrons in the system. We can hope that the antisymmetrizer $\mathcal{A}$ has only a modest effect on the energy and correlation functions for the quasiparticle state.

The mean density, $\langle\widetilde{\psi}_0^{(+)}|\rho(\boldsymbol{r})|\widetilde{\psi}_0^{(+)}\rangle$, obtained by Monte Carlo simulation, of a system described by the Hamiltonian $\widetilde{\mathcal{H}}$ (6.42) is shown in Fig. 6.15 for 20, 30, and 42 particles. The quasiparticle energy for a fully antisymmetrized pair wave function $\widetilde{\psi}_0^{(+)}$ obtained for 42 electrons is $0.066 \pm 0.006\, e^2/\epsilon\ell_0$. This result is almost identical (within the statistical uncertainty) to the 42-particle system result from Laughlin's wave function.

Monte Carlo computations of the quantities described above, were also performed for the spherical geometry by *Morf* and *Halperin* [6.19]. For the quasihole state (6.40), energies were evaluated for the two different definitions of distance. For the chord distance, they obtained

$$\widetilde{\varepsilon}_{\rm h} \approx 0.0219(25) - 0.055(30)/N_{\rm e} \tag{6.44}$$

and for the great circle distance

$$\widetilde{\varepsilon}_{\rm h} \approx 0.0229(21) - 0.078(24)/N_{\rm e}. \tag{6.45}$$

For the bulk limit, their best estimate is, $\widetilde{\varepsilon}_{\rm h} \approx 0.0224 \pm 0.0016\, e^2/\epsilon\ell_0$.

In the case of the quasiparticle state (6.39), methods similar to those described in Sect. 6.1 were used. The quasiparticle energy $\widetilde{\varepsilon}_{\rm p}$ at $\nu = \frac{1}{3}$ is displayed in Fig. 6.16 for various values of system size. The *pair* wave function discussed above for the disk geometry, is written for the spherical geometry as

$$\psi^{(+)} = \mathcal{A}\widetilde{\psi}^{(+)}, \tag{6.46}$$

with

$$\widetilde{\psi}^{(+)} = \frac{u_1u_2}{(u_1v_2 - v_1u_2)^2}\psi_m \prod_{j=3}^{N_{\rm e}} \frac{2v_ju_1u_2 + u_j(u_1v_2 + v_1u_2)}{(u_1v_j - v_1u_j)(u_2v_j - v_2u_j)}, \tag{6.47}$$

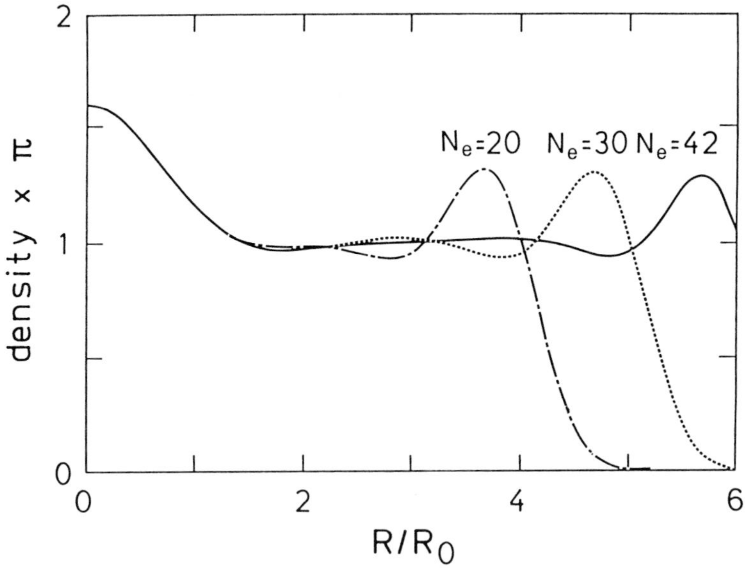

Fig. 6.15. The mean density $\langle\rho(\boldsymbol{r})\rangle$ in the state with quasiparticle excitation at $\nu = \frac{1}{3}$. The Monte Carlo result is obtained for the *non*antisymmetrized pair wave function $\widetilde{\psi}_0^{(+)}$ [6.4]

where u_j, v_j are, as usual, the spinor coordinates of the jth electron. The quasiparticle energy for the fully antisymmetrized pair wave function is also presented in Fig. 6.16. The energies in this case are 4-6% lower than those for the Laughlin state. In the thermodynamic limit, the best estimate is [6.19] $\widetilde{\varepsilon}_{\rm p} \approx 0.070 \pm 0.003\, e^2/\epsilon\ell_0$ for the pair wave function, and $\widetilde{\varepsilon}_{\rm p} \approx 0.075 \pm 0.005\, e^2/\epsilon\ell_0$ for the Laughlin wave function. The energy gap in the spherical geometry at $\nu = \frac{1}{3}$ is $E_{\rm g} \approx 0.092{\pm}0.004\, e^2/\epsilon\ell_0$. Including the finite thickness correction (see Sect. 5.6) the excitation energies as a function of the dimensionless thickness parameter β are as plotted in Fig. 6.17.

The density in the quasiparticle state is shown in Fig. 6.18 for the two wave functions as a function of the great circle distance from the north pole ($r = R/R_0$), for a 32-electron system. For the fully antisymmetrized pair wave function (open circles) and for the Laughlin wave function (solid line), there is a strong dip at the origin. For the nonantisymmetrized wave function (dashed line) $\rho(r)$ has its maximum at the origin.

MacDonald and *Girvin* [6.20,21] proposed a somewhat different approach to calculate the density and energy for the quasiparticle and quasihole state. Their results for the energies at $\nu = \frac{1}{3}$ are, $\widetilde{\varepsilon}_{\rm h} = 0.0287\, e^2/\epsilon\ell_0$ for the quasihole and $\widetilde{\varepsilon}_{\rm p} = 0.085\, e^2/\epsilon\ell_0$ for the quasiparticles. Their quasiparticle density did not show any dip at the origin. These authors also calculated

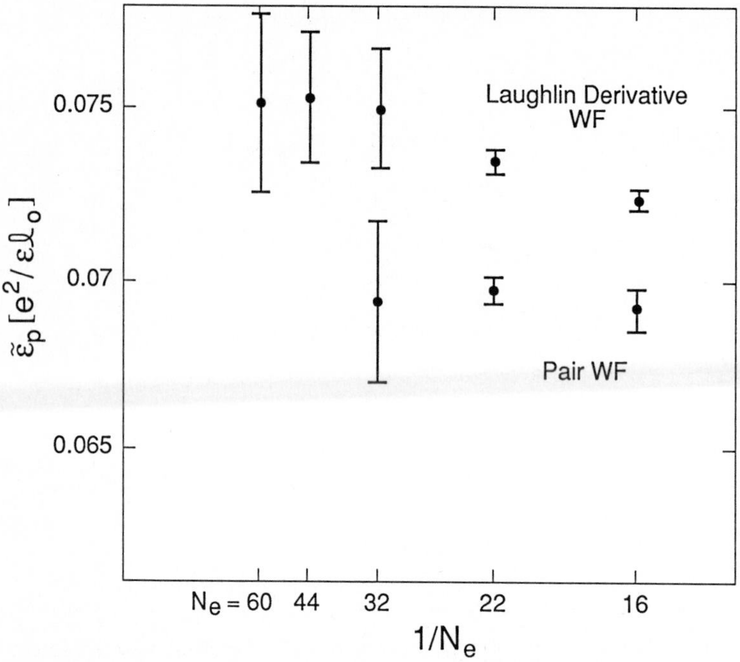

Fig. 6.16. Quasiparticle energy $\widetilde{\varepsilon}_\mathrm{p}$ at $\nu = \frac{1}{3}$ for the Laughlin wave function (full circles) and the fully antisymmetrized pair wave function (diamonds) as a function of $\frac{1}{N_\mathrm{e}}$ [6.19]

the above quantities in the second Landau level, which will be discussed in Sect. 9.3.

In the spherical geometry, *Morf* and *Halperin* also calculated the energy and density for the *spin-reversed* quasiparticle state at $\nu = \frac{1}{3}$ [6.19]. In this case, the wave function (6.37) is written as

$$\psi = \psi_m u_1^{-1} \prod_{j=2}^{N_\mathrm{e}} \left(\frac{u_1}{u_1 v_j - v_1 u_j} \right). \tag{6.48}$$

The energy gap for a spin-reversed quasiparticle and a spin-polarized quasihole was estimated to be, $E_\mathrm{g}' \approx 0.063 \pm 0.005\, e^2/\epsilon\ell_0$, significantly larger than the exact result $E_\mathrm{g}' = 0.037\, e^2/\epsilon\ell_0$ for a six-electron system by *Chakraborty* et al., [6.14,15] (see Sect. 6.3). The density $\rho(r)$ in the spin-reversed quasiparticle state at $\nu = \frac{1}{3}$ could be fitted approximately by:

$$\rho(r) \approx \frac{1}{\pi} \left[1 + 0.46\, \mathrm{e}^{-(r/0.851)^2} \right]. \tag{6.49}$$

No dip at the origin and no local minimum were found in these results.

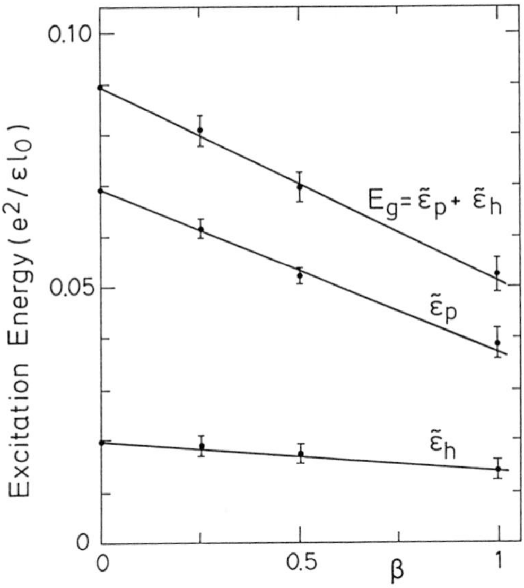

Fig. 6.17. Excitation energies at $\nu = \frac{1}{3}$ versus the dimensionless thickness parameter $\beta = (b\ell_0)^{-1}$. The quasihole results are for the Laughlin wave function, while the quasiparticle results are for the fully antisymmetrized pair wave function. The results in this figure are for a 22 electron system [6.19]. The unit of energy is $e^2/\epsilon\ell_0$

To summarize this section, although the calculated quasihole creation energy is very similar for three different approaches (plasma; Monte Carlo, disk; Monte Carlo, sphere), there is a big discrepancy between the classical plasma result and the Monte Carlo results in the case of the quasiparticle energy. The Monte Carlo results for the disk geometry and the spherical geometry are however consistent. The quasiparticle creation energy is larger than the quasihole creation energy by a factor of three. The energy gap for a quasiparticle and quasihole pair at infinite separation appears from all Monte Carlo estimates to be $E_{\rm g} \approx 0.1\, e^2/\epsilon\ell_0$, which is close to the estimates from finite system calculations. The numerical results for the density also suggest that there is a strong dip at the origin; this is missing in the plasma approach.

6.6 Experimental Investigations of the Energy Gap

After reviewing the theoretical work on the quasiparticle–quasihole gap $E_{\rm g}$ in the FQHE state, we would like to present in this section, a brief review of the experimental investigations of the energy gap. As mentioned in the

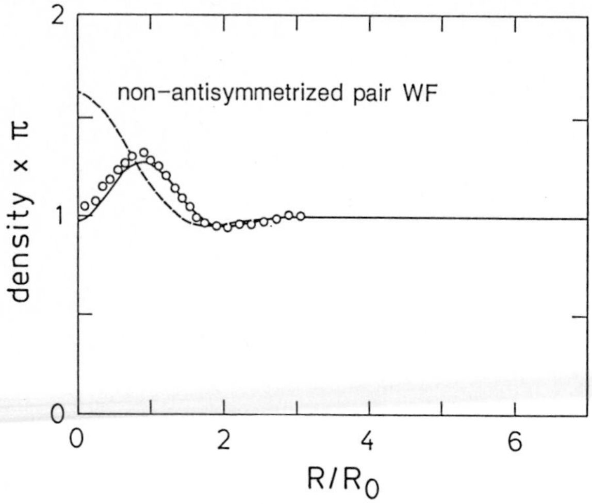

Fig. 6.18. Density $\rho(r)$ in the quasiparticle state at $\nu = \frac{1}{3}$. The solid line corresponds to the Laughlin wave function, while the open circles denote results for the fully antisymmetrized pair wave function. The dashed line is for the pair wave function without the antisymmetrizer. The results are for a 32-electron system [6.19]

introduction, in both the integer and fractional QHE, the vanishing of the diagonal resistivity implies a gap in the excitation spectrum. In the case of the integer QHE, the gap is in the single-particle density of states, whereas in the FQHE, the gap lies in the excitation spectrum of the correlated many-electron ground state. The energy gap is usually obtained from the temperature dependence of the magnetoconductivity, σ_{xx} [or ρ_{xx} since near the ρ_{xx} minima, $\rho_{xx} \ll \rho_{xy}$, and $\sigma_{xx} = \rho_{xx}/(\rho_{xx}^2 + \rho_{xy}^2) \sim \rho_{xx}/\rho_{xy}^2$], as $\sigma_{xx} \propto \rho_{xx} \propto \exp(-W/k_B T)$, where $W = \frac{1}{2}E_g$ is the activation energy, and k_B is Boltzmann's constant. In the case of the integer QHE, *Tausendfreund* and *von Klitzing* found the energy gap obtained from the activation energy measurements to be close to the cyclotron energy (usually smaller because of spin splitting and a finite linewidth of the extended states) [6.22]. For the FQHE, similar measurements for the energy gap have been undertaken by several experimental groups.

The first such work was by *Chang* et al. [6.23] whose results for $\nu = \frac{2}{3}$ indicated that the energy gap does not have a $B^{\frac{1}{2}}$ behavior and also suggested the existence of a mobility threshold below which the $\frac{2}{3}$ effect will not occur. In the theoretical calculations, the energy gap scales with the natural unit of energy $e^2/\epsilon\ell_0$, and hence should have a magnetic field dependence of $B^{\frac{1}{2}}$. This behavior is however changed, as we shall see below, when the finite thickness correction is included in the calculations. A mobility threshold for $\nu = \frac{4}{3}$ was also observed in Si-MOSFETs by *Kukushkin* and *Timofeev* [6.24,25].

A systematic study of the energy gap for the filling fractions, $\nu = \frac{1}{3}, \frac{2}{3}, \frac{4}{3}$, and $\frac{5}{3}$ was reported by *Boebinger* et al. [6.26,27]. The study was performed in four specimens of modulation-doped GaAs-heterostructure with typical mobilities of μ=5 000 000–850 000 cm^2/V.s and electron densities, $\rho_0 = (1.5 - 2.3) \times 10^{11}\text{cm}^{-2}$. The value of ρ_{xx} or σ_{xx} at the minimum corresponding to a particular filling fraction was determined as a function of temperature in the range of 120 mK to 1.4 K. Figure 6.19 shows the activated conduction in the case of $\nu = \frac{2}{3}$ for different values of the magnetic field. At high temperatures, ρ_{xx} deviates from a simple activated dependence. For magnetic fields between 6 and $\sim$ 10 T, simple activated behavior was observed. Data for $B \geq 10$ T showed deviation from simple activated behavior even at low temperatures. Most of the high-field data behaved as shown in Fig. 6.19(b), where the deviation is curved and smooth. Over the entire temperature range, activation plus various models for hopping conduction was found to fit the data very well. One of the samples showed the behavior depicted in Fig. 6.19(c), where the deviation from a simple activation is a sharp break to a second linear region. A similar case was observed by *Kawaji* et al. [6.28,29], who interpreted the results as the existence of two different activation energies. Boebinger et al., however, explained the result as an artifact caused by a nonequilibrium configuration of the electronic state within the sample.

The activation energies for the filling factors $\nu = \frac{1}{3}, \frac{2}{3}, \frac{4}{3}$, and $\frac{5}{3}$ are presented in Fig. 6.20. The following features are noteworthy in the result: (i) No apparent sample dependence was observed. (ii) The data for $\nu = \frac{1}{3}$ and $\frac{2}{3}$ overlap at $B \sim 20$ T. At similar magnetic fields, the data for $\nu = \frac{4}{3}$ and $\frac{5}{3}$ are consistent with the data for $\nu = \frac{2}{3}$. Collectively, the results therefore suggest a *single* activation energy $^3\Delta$, for all the filling fractions mentioned above. A curve for $^3\Delta = Ce^2/\epsilon\ell_0$ with $C = 0.03$ is plotted in Fig. 6.20 for comparison. (iii) The observed activation energies are much *smaller* than the theoretical predictions discussed in the earlier sections. (iv) As mentioned above, $^3\Delta$ does not follow the expected $B^{\frac{1}{2}}$ dependence. For $B \lesssim 5.5$ T, $^3\Delta$ is vanishingly small. For higher magnetic fields, there is a roughly *linear* increase in $^3\Delta$ up to $\sim$ 12 T.

In Sect. 6.2, we reviewed the results for the energy gap, E_g, from finite-size calculations in a periodic rectangular geometry and noticed that spin-reversal for the quasiparticles costs less energy (in the absence of Zeeman energy) compared to fully spin-polarized quasiparticles and quasiholes. In the following, we would like to compare those results with the observed values of $^3\Delta$. At $\nu = \frac{1}{3}$, the magnetic field dependence of the finite-thickness parameter β (Sect. 5.6) is $\beta = 0.525B^{\frac{1}{6}}$. The Zeeman energy contribution (per

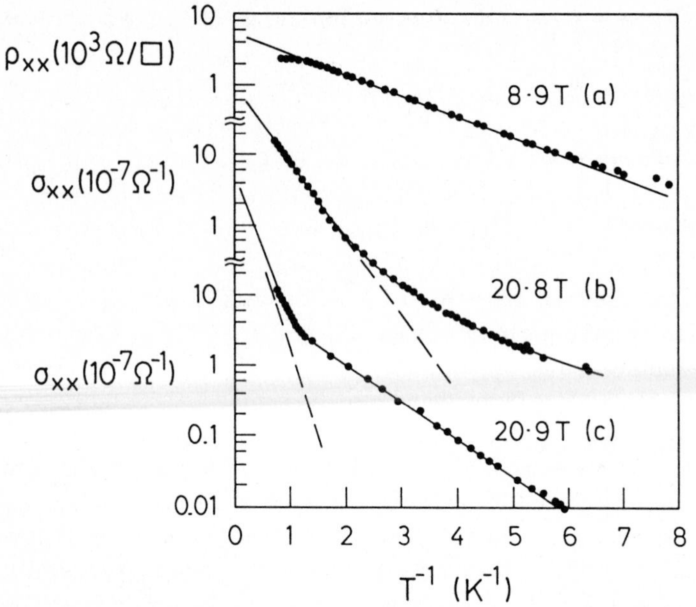

Fig. 6.19. Temperature dependence of $\sigma_{xx}(10^{-7}\Omega^{-1})$ and $\rho_{xx}(10^3\Omega/\square)$ at the minimum for $\nu = \frac{2}{3}$ at (a) B=8.9 T, (b) B=20.8 T, and (c) B=20.9 T [6.26]

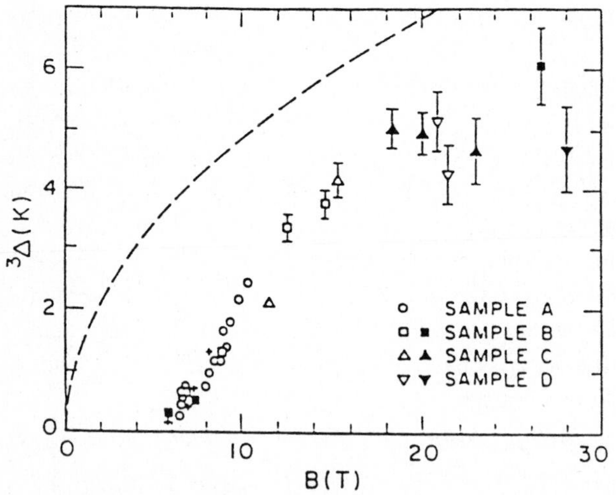

Fig. 6.20. Activation energies for the thirds (in units of K) [6.26,27] as a function of magnetic field. Open symbols are the data for $\nu = \frac{2}{3}$. Filled symbols are for $\nu = \frac{1}{3}$, except for two filled squares at 5.9T and 7.4T, which are for $\nu = \frac{5}{3}$ and $\frac{4}{3}$. The four data points shown as (+) are from [6.30] and [6.31]. The dashed line is explained in the text

particle) to the energy gap for the cases considered in Sect. 6.2 is (a) zero for the fully spin-polarized quasiparticle–quasihole case, (b) $\left(1+\frac{1}{3N_e}\right)\varepsilon_z$ for the spin-reversed quasihole and spin-polarized quasiparticle case, (c) $\left(1-\frac{1}{3N_e}\right)\varepsilon_z$ for the spin-reversed quasiparticle and spin-polarized quasihole case, (d) $2\varepsilon_z$ for the spin-reversed quasiparticle and quasihole case. Here $\varepsilon_z = g\mu_B B$ (Sect. 5.5), with μ_B the Bohr magneton and the Landé g-factor, $g \simeq 0.52$ for GaAs. With B given in Tesla, we obtain $\varepsilon_z = 0.355B$ in Kelvin.

The magnetic field dependence of the energy gap E_g for a five-electron system is shown in Fig. 6.21, where we have presented only the lowest energy results.[4] For low magnetic fields, the curve for the lowest energy excitations rises *linearly* as a result of the *spin-reversed quasiparticles* [case (c) above], which include the dominant contribution from the Zeeman energy, itself linear in magnetic field. Recent experiments which clearly indicate the existence of the spin-reversed quasiparticles and the spin-unpolarized ground states are discussed in detail in Sect. 6.9. As the magnetic field is increased, a crossover point is reached, beyond which the $B^{\frac{1}{2}}$ dependence (modified by the magnetic field dependence of B) is then obtained due to the spin-polarized quasiparticles and quasiholes [6.14,15]. While these theoretical results are open to improvement, the point should be made that, for low magnetic fields, the spin-reversed quasiparticles do play an important role in the elementary excitations in the FQHE. The observation of a threshold field of ~ 5.5 T is not explained, however, by these theories. The activation energy for $p/3$ states has also been measured by *Willett* et al [6.33] in an ultrahigh-mobility ($\mu = 5\times10^6$ cm^2/V sec) quasi-two-dimensional electron system in GaAs-AlGaAs, for which the finite thickness of the carrier system is accurately known. The data is in remarkably good agreement with the theoretical results for the energy gap where Landau level mixing and the finite-thickness effect are taken into account.

A systematic study of the influence of disorder on the activation gap has been made by *Kukushkin* and *Timofeev* [6.24,25]. Their study was based on Si-MOSFETs with a high mobility two-dimensional electron system in the inversion layer. In this case, it is possible to determine the activation energy within the same structure for different filling factors, while the other parameters (*e.g.*, the electron mobility μ_e) and the magnetic field are fixed. For different MOS structures, they found that the activation gaps for $\nu = \frac{1}{3}, \frac{2}{3}, \frac{4}{3}$ and $\frac{4}{5}$ increase as $B^{\frac{1}{2}}$ in the region B=10–20 T (see Fig. 6.22).

[4] In this figure the experimental results contain some additional data not present in Fig. 6.20 (G. S. Boebinger, private communications, and [6.32]).

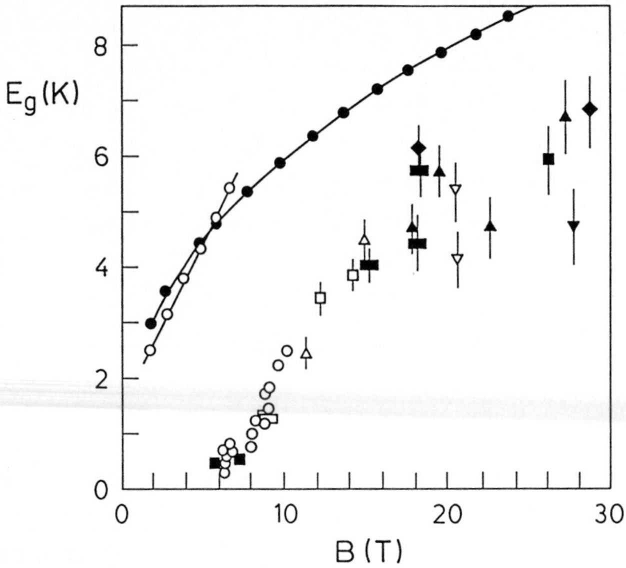

Fig. 6.21. Calculated energy gap $E_{\rm g}$ (in units of K) vs magnetic field B (given in Tesla) for a five-electron system [6.14,15]. The empty points in the theoretical curves are for spin reversed quasiparticles and spin polarized quasiholes, while the filled points are for the fully spin polarized case. The experimental results are from [6.32]

The magnitude of activation gaps, as mentioned earlier, also depend on the mobility. For a given magnetic field, the gaps increase with mobility. The gap W, as a function of mobility can be expressed as (see Fig. 6.23),

$$W_\nu = G_\nu^\infty\left(1-\frac{\mu_0}{\mu_{\rm e}}\right)\frac{e^2}{\epsilon\ell_0}$$

where, G_ν^∞ is the activation gap when $\mu_{\rm e}\to\infty$, and μ_0 is the minimal mobility when the activation energy vanishes (for $W_\nu\to 0$, the FQHE is not observed). Experimentally, it is found that μ_0 does not depend on the magnetic field.

The effect of disorder on the activation gap has been studied theoretically by *MacDonald* et al. [6.34]. In particular, they examined the contribution of remote ionized impurities on the disorder potential. The influence of impurities on the conductivity was treated in the lowest order perturbation theory via a memory function approach. Associating the experimentally observed activation energy with the minimum energy of the disordered band of magnetoroton excitations, they obtained a fit to the experimental results of [6.26], with a qualitatively correct behavior for the disorder threshold.

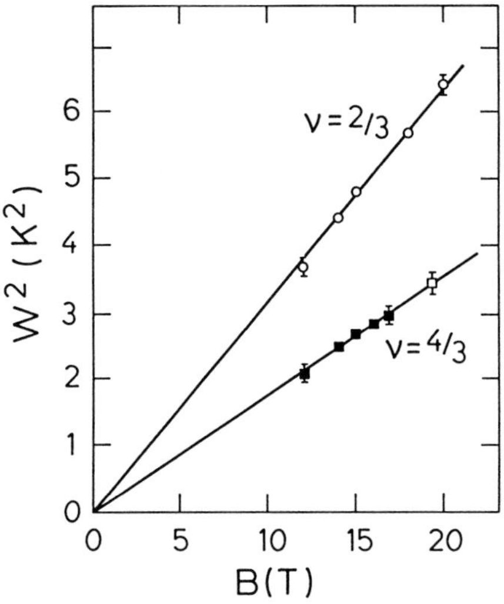

Fig. 6.22. Activation gap W as a function of magnetic field at $\nu = \frac{2}{3}$ and $\frac{4}{3}$ measured for two Si-MOSFETs (closed and open points) with mobility $\mu_e = (3.5 \pm 0.1) \times 10^4 \text{cm}^2/\text{V.s}$ (circles) and $\mu_e = (2.7 \pm 0.1) \times 10^4 \text{cm}^2/\text{V.s}$ (squares) [6.25]

It is not clear however, how the magnetoroton[5] — an electrically neutral object—would explain the magnetotransport measurements. The effect of disorder on the activation energy gap has also been studied by *Gold* [6.35]. Both of these theoretical approaches, however, contain adjustable parameters in order to fit the experimental results by *Boebinger* et al. [6.26,27]. The interesting outcome of these two theoretical studies is the observation of a magnetic threshold, also observed in the experiment. The closing of the gap by disorder has also been studied by *Laughlin* [6.36,37] in a scaling theory (see Sect. 3.2).

There have been other interesting measurements of the activation gaps: *Boebinger* et al. measured the gaps for $\nu = \frac{2}{5}$ and $\frac{3}{5}$ and have extended their work to other samples of different mobilities [6.32]. *Mendez* [6.38] has measured the activation energy at $\frac{1}{3}$ and $\frac{2}{3}$ for two-dimensional holes. *Guldner* et al. [6.39] reported microwave photoresistivity measurements in low density GaAs-heterojunctions and hinted that there might be a nonzero activation energy for $B \lesssim 5\text{T}$, where *Boebinger* et al. observed a threshold. *Jiang* et al. [6.40] reported a very accurate measurement of the activation energy ${}^5\Delta = 1.1\text{K}$ at $\nu = \frac{1}{5}$.

Finally, from the measurement of the activation energy, *Clark* et al. [6.10] made a very important observation. They reported a systematic study

[5] A detailed discussion of magnetorotons is given in Sect. 7.4.

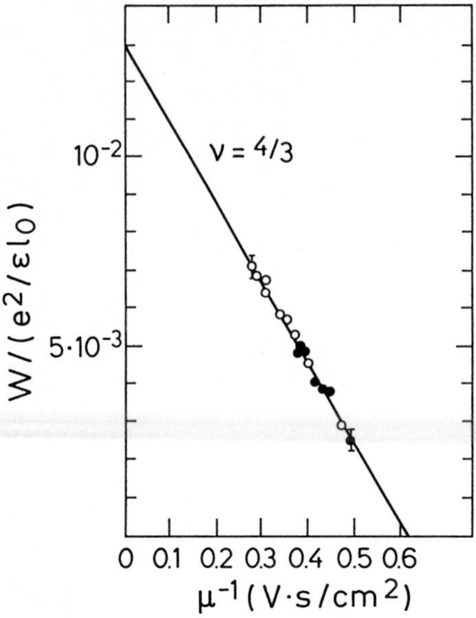

Fig. 6.23. The activation energy as a function of the reciprocal electron mobility at $\nu = \frac{4}{3}$. The filled and empty points are for two different Si-MOSFETs [6.25]

of $\sigma_{xx}^{c} = \sigma_{xx}(1/T = 0)$:

$$\sigma_{xx}^{c} = \frac{\rho_{xx}^{c}}{(\rho_{xx}^{c})^2 + \rho_{xy}^2} = \frac{\rho_{xx}^{c}}{(\rho_{xx}^{c})^2 + \left[\left(\frac{q}{p}\right)\frac{h}{e^2}\right]^2}$$

which is valid at $\nu = p/q$ and ρ_{xx}^{c} is defined by $\rho_{xx} = \rho_{xx}^{c}\mathrm{e}^{-\Delta/kT}$, where Δ is the quasiparticle–quasihole gap discussed above. Clark et al. found that within experimental errors, σ_{xx}^{c} is constant for p/q fractions of the same q. In Fig. 6.24, the conductivity data σ_{xx} are plotted as a function of T^{-1} at both integer and fractional ν. Straight-line fits to the linear region, which corresponds to thermal activation of the quasiparticles and quasiholes across the energy gap, are shown and extrapolated to $T^{-1} = 0$. The extrapolated σ_{xx} intercept is close to e^2/h for the IQHE, whereas for $\nu = p/q$, $\sigma_{xx}^{c} \simeq \frac{1}{h}\left(\frac{e}{q}\right)^2 = e^{*2}/h$ which is consistent with Laughlin's prediction of the fractional charge of the quasiparticles and quasiholes discussed in Sect. 6.1.

6.7 Fractional Statistics and the Anyons

We have learned in Sect. 6.1, that the elementary excitations, *i.e.* quasiholes and quasiparticles, carry the fractional charge $\pm e^* = \pm e/m$ at the

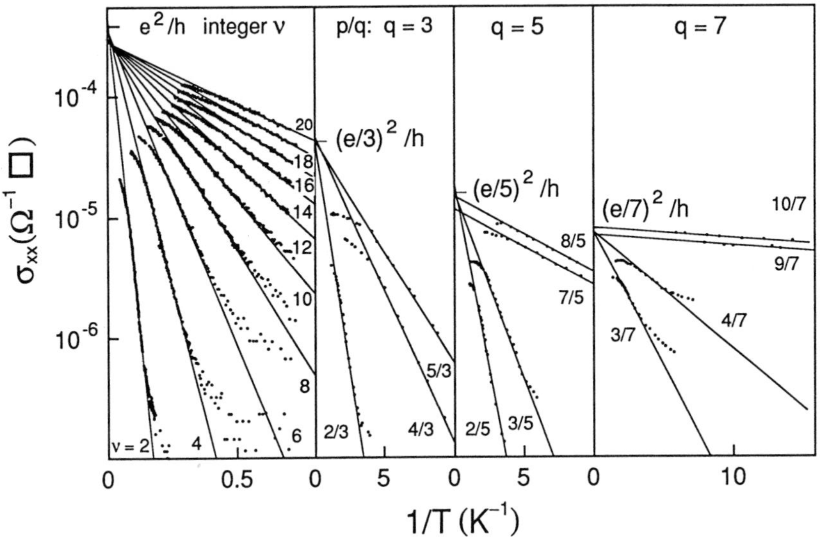

Fig. 6.24. Conductivity σ_{xx} vs T^{-1} results which give the quasiparticle charge $e^* = e/q$ at the integer and fractional filling factors $\nu = p/q$ [6.11]

filling fraction $\nu = 1/m$. We arrived at this conclusion by mapping the excited system to the analogous two dimensional classical plasma. It is instructive, however, to apply a direct method developed by *Arovas* et al. [6.41] for determining the charge of the excitations of the Laughlin state. As a byproduct this approach will also reveal interesting features about the statistics of the quasiparticles and holes. For simplicity we will consider only the quasiholes. The quasiparticles can be treated in a similar fashion.

Let us recall that the Laughlin wave function for the quasihole located at the position z_0 is written as

$$\psi_m^{(-)} = N_- \prod_i (z_i - z_0)\psi_m. \tag{6.50}$$

Here ψ_m is the ground state wave function (3.24) and N_- is the normalization constant. If this quasihole of charge e^* is carried around a loop enclosing the flux $\boldsymbol{\Phi}$ it will gain a change of phase

$$\gamma = \frac{e^*}{\hbar c}\oint \boldsymbol{A}\cdot d\boldsymbol{l} = 2\pi\frac{e^*}{e}\frac{\boldsymbol{\Phi}}{\boldsymbol{\Phi}_0}. \tag{6.51}$$

On the other hand, if we let the position z_0 move adiabatically around this loop, the rate of this change can be expressed as

$$\frac{d\gamma(t)}{dt} = \mathrm{i}\left\langle \psi_m^{(-)} \middle| \frac{d\psi_m^{(-)}}{dt} \right\rangle .$$

When we now substitute the time derivative

$$\frac{d\psi_m^{(-)}}{dt} = \sum_i \frac{d}{dt} \ln[z_i - z_0(t)]\psi_m^{(-)} \tag{6.52}$$

from the explicit wave function (6.50) we get

$$\frac{d\gamma}{dt} = \mathrm{i}\left\langle \psi_m^{(-)} \middle| \frac{d}{dt}\sum_i \ln(z_i - z_0) \middle| \psi_m^{(-)} \right\rangle . \tag{6.53}$$

With the help of the one-particle density

$$\rho^{(-)}(z) = \left\langle \psi_m^{(-)} \middle| \sum_i \delta(z_i - z) \middle| \psi_m^{(-)} \right\rangle \tag{6.54}$$

of the quasihole state this can be written as

$$\frac{d\gamma}{dt} = \mathrm{i}\int dx\, dy\, \rho^{(-)}(z) \frac{d}{dt} \ln[z - z_0(t)], \tag{6.55}$$

where $z = x + iy$. We now expand $\rho^{(-)}(z)$ around the uniform density $\rho_0 = \nu\Phi/\Phi_0$ of the ground state, *i.e.* we write $\rho^{(-)}(z) = \rho_0 + \delta\rho^{(-)}(z)$. Let us first consider the ρ_0 term. When we integrate z_0 around a circle of radius R the total variation of $\ln[z - z_0(t)]$ will be $2\pi\mathrm{i}$ if $|z| < R$ and zero if $|z| > R$. Thus the corresponding change of phase is given by

$$\begin{aligned} \gamma_0 &= \mathrm{i} \int\limits_{|r|<R} dx\, dy\, \rho_0 2\pi\mathrm{i} \\ &= -2\pi\langle n\rangle_R = -2\pi\nu\frac{\Phi}{\Phi_0}, \end{aligned} \tag{6.56}$$

where $\langle n\rangle_R$ is the mean number of electrons in a disk of radius R. The correction $\delta\rho^{(-)}(z)$ is localized in the vicinity of z_0, so its contribution to the change of phase is of the order of size of the quasihole, that is, of the order of ℓ_0^2. In comparison with the constant term contribution, which is of the order R^2, this can be clearly neglected. From equations (6.51) and (6.56) we can now deduce the charge of the quasihole as

$$e^* = -\nu e, \tag{6.57}$$

in agreement with Laughlin's theory in Sect. 6.1.

Let us now consider two quasiholes located at z_a and z_b a distance $|z_a - z_b| = R$ apart. When we carry the hole z_b adiabatically around the circle of radius R centered at the hole z_a the analysis presented above is still valid provided the mean electron number $\langle n \rangle_R$ in the disk is counted correctly. We found out that the quasihole at z_a has a charge $-\nu e$ which we can interpret that exactly ν electrons are removed from the disk, so we must substitute $\langle n \rangle_R - \nu$ for the mean electron number. Hence an extra phase of amount

$$\Delta\gamma = 2\pi\nu \tag{6.58}$$

is gained in the process. The interchange of two quasiparticles can be achieved by letting each of them to make a turn of π around the other. From the treatment above it is obvious that the accumulation of this extra phase is continuous and therefore the total change of phase will be $\nu\pi$. For $\nu = 1$ the quasiholes behave like fermions. For fractional fillings we, however, reach the striking conclusion that the quasiholes (and quasiparticles as well) obey neither Bose nor Fermi statistics. According to *Wilczek* [6.42] particles of this nature are called *anyons* because the interchange of any two of them can result in *any* phase change.

In standard quantum mechanics textbooks it is customary to postulate that the state vectors describing a system of undistinguishable particles are either symmetric or antisymmetric under the interchange of any two of the particles. This symmetry principle has very profound consequences on the physical nature of the system, all of which seem to be in good agreement with the experimental facts. The elementary excitations at the FQHE states seem to be in an apparent contradiction with the experimentally well established symmetry postulate. However, we should bear in mind that until very recently practically all physical systems subjected to experimental observations were three dimensional whereas the quasiholes and quasiparticles are excitations in a two dimensional system. This suggests that the dimensionality of the configuration space might have something to do with the many body statistics. As a further argument in this direction consider the spin — an internal degree of freedom — of a particle. The famous spin-statistics theorem tells us that the spin and the statistical nature of a particle system are deeply connected: particles with integer spins are bosons while those with half integer spins are fermions. Now the spin angular momentum is a realization of the rotational symmetry of the three dimensional space, a consequence of the fact that rotations around different axes do not necessarily commute. In two dimensional space there is only one possible axis of rotation and all rotations necessarily commute so the internal angular momentum can have any value. The spin-statistics connection must therefore be reformulated in two dimensions.

Let us recall how we performed the interchange of the two quasiholes: it involved an actual physical process of dragging particles around each other. We specified concrete trajectories which particles had to follow in the course of the interchange. It is obvious that the detailed shape of these paths is not essential. Only the general characteristics of the paths, e.g. how they twist around each other, matter. Otherwise we can freely bend them as we like. These general features depend on the topology of the configuration space. It is to be expected that the topology has profound effects on the many-particle statistics. The first systematic study along these lines is due to *Leinaas* and *Myrheim* [6.43]. In the following we will discuss their work.

We consider first a *classical* system of N identical particles. Note that the indistinguishability of identical particles is not purely a quantum mechanical phenomenon: it manifests itself, for example, in the famous Gibbs' entropy paradox of mixing of two identical classical fluids. If the one particle coordinate space is denoted by X the possible configurations of the N-particle system are conventionally described in the Cartesian product space X^N. However, this space is much too large since there can be no physical difference between the two points

$$\begin{aligned} \boldsymbol{x} &= (\boldsymbol{x}_1, \boldsymbol{x}_2, \ldots, \boldsymbol{x}_N), \\ \boldsymbol{x}' &= (\boldsymbol{x}_{p(1)}, \boldsymbol{x}_{p(2)}, \ldots, \boldsymbol{x}_{p(N)}), \end{aligned} \tag{6.59}$$

in X^N because $\boldsymbol{x}'$ is obtained from $\boldsymbol{x}$ by permuting its particle indices by p. The true configuration space for the system of N identical particles is therefore the space X^N/S_N which is reduced from the space X^N by identifying the points mapped into each other under the action of the symmetric group S_N. Since S_N is a discrete and finite transformation group the space X^N/S_N is locally isomorphic to X^N, except at its singular points where two or more particles coincide. The difference between these spaces therefore lies in their global nature. Because the dynamics of a classical many-body system is governed only by the local properties of the configuration space it is merely a matter of convenience which one of the spaces is used.

The most common choice for the one-particle space X is the n-dimensional Euclidean space $\mathcal{E}_n$. Since the center of mass coordinate

$$\boldsymbol{X} = \frac{1}{N} \sum_{i=1}^{N} \boldsymbol{x}_i \in \mathcal{E}_n \tag{6.60}$$

is invariant under the action of S_N it is obvious that the N-particle configuration space can be written as the direct product

$$\mathcal{E}_n^N / S_N = \mathcal{E}_n \times r(n, N) \tag{6.61}$$

of the center of mass space and a space $r(n,N)$ representing the $nN-n$ degrees of freedom of the relative motion of the particles. It is obtained from the space $\mathcal{E}_{nN-n}$ by identifying the points connected by S_N.

For simplicity, we limit our considerations to two particle systems, i.e. we set $N=2$. Identification of points $\boldsymbol{x}=\boldsymbol{x}_1-\boldsymbol{x}_2$ and $-\boldsymbol{x}=\boldsymbol{x}_2-\boldsymbol{x}_1$ in the space $\mathcal{E}_n$ will give the space $r(n,2)$. This space has one singular point, $\boldsymbol{x}=0$, where the particles overlap. In practice, the most important cases are $n=2$ and $n=3$. Let us first consider two particles moving in the two-dimensional Euclidean space $\mathcal{E}_2$. The configuration space is

$$\mathcal{E}_2^2/S_2=\mathcal{E}_2\times r(2,2). \tag{6.62}$$

The relative space $r(2,2)$ is obtained from the plane $\mathcal{E}_2$ by identification of points $\boldsymbol{x}$ and $-\boldsymbol{x}$. As shown in Fig. 6.25 this space is the circular cone of half angle 30°. It is now easy to see that there are two kinds of closed curves on this surface. The paths that do not circulate the singular point, i.e. the tip of the cone, can be continuously transformed to a point. On the other hand the paths circulating the tip, no matter how many times, can no way be contracted continuously to a point without passing through the singular

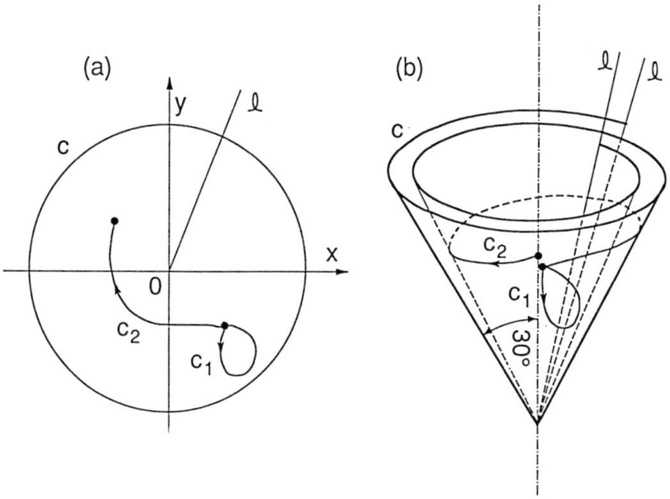

Fig. 6.25. The relative space $r(2,2)$ of two particles moving in the two dimensional Euclidean space $\mathcal{E}_2$ is obtained from the plane at left by identifying the points $\boldsymbol{x}$ and $-\boldsymbol{x}$. This can be effected by cutting the plane along a line l and then folding it twice into a circular cone shown at right. The loop in $r(2,2)$ corresponding to the closed path C_1 in $\mathcal{E}_2$ can be continuously contracted to a point without passing the tip of the cone. However, to interchange the particles we have to follow a path like C_2 connecting the points $\boldsymbol{x}$ and $-\boldsymbol{x}$, which in $r(2,2)$ maps to a loop encircling the singular point

point. Therefore we say that the space $r(2,2)$ excluding the singular point is infinitely connected.

The most illustrative way to depict the three dimensional relative space is to write it as the direct product

$$r(3,2) - \{\mathbf{o}\} = (0, \infty) \times \mathcal{P}_2, \tag{6.63}$$

where the projective plane $\mathcal{P}_2$ is the surface of a 3-dimensional northern hemisphere with diametrically opposite points on the equator identified, Fig. 6.26. Again it easy two see that the curves that do not encircle the singular point $\boldsymbol{x} = \mathbf{o}$ can be continuously contracted to a point whereas the curves circulating *once* the origin cannot. However, the paths encircling the singular point *twice* can be transformed to a point, as illustrated in Fig. 6.26. The relative space $r(3,2)$ excluding the singular point is therefore doubly connected.

We now turn our attention to the quantization of the theory. The formal method of the quantization in a curved space, like $\mathcal{E}_n^N / S_N$, is to introduce a one dimensional Hilbert space, a *fibre*, $h_{\boldsymbol{x}}$ for each point $\boldsymbol{x}$ of the configuration space. The physical state of the system is described by a continuum of vectors $\Psi(\boldsymbol{x}) \in h_{\boldsymbol{x}}$. In each space $h_{\boldsymbol{x}}$ we can specify a normed basis vector $\chi_{\boldsymbol{x}}$ so that the complex wave function $\psi(\boldsymbol{x})$ is the coordinate of the vector $\Psi(\boldsymbol{x})$ relative to that basis, *i.e.*

$$\Psi(\boldsymbol{x}) = \psi(\boldsymbol{x})\chi_{\boldsymbol{x}}. \tag{6.64}$$

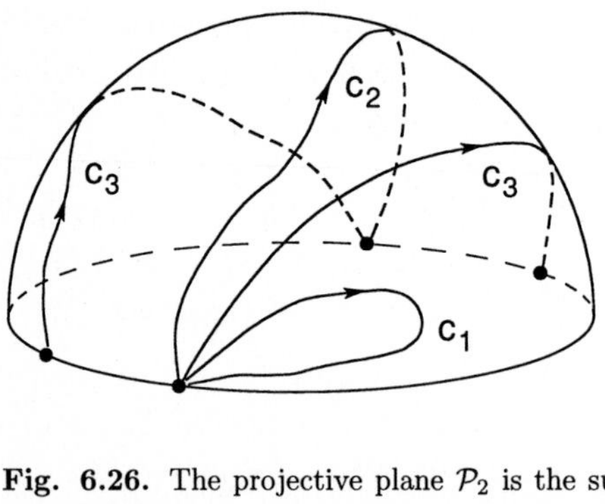

Fig. 6.26. The projective plane $\mathcal{P}_2$ is the surface of the three dimensional sphere with diametrically opposed points identified. Equivalently, as shown here, $\mathcal{P}_2$ is the northern hemisphere with opposite points on the equator identified. C_1 is a closed curve which can be continuously deformed into a point whereas the closed curve C_2 cannot. If C_2 is passed twice we get a curve C_2^2 which can be contracted into a point. The curve C_3 is one possible intermediate stage in this continuous process

We see that the wave function $\psi(\boldsymbol{x})$ depends on the set of basis vectors, the gauge $\{\chi_{\boldsymbol{x}}\}$. Because the vectors $\chi_{\boldsymbol{x}}$ are one dimensional the change of the basis will result in a gauge transformation

$$\psi(\boldsymbol{x}) \to \psi'(\boldsymbol{x}) = \mathrm{e}^{\mathrm{i}\phi(\boldsymbol{x})}\psi(\boldsymbol{x}) \tag{6.65}$$

in the wave function. We have to express the derivatives appearing in the Hamiltonian of the system in a gauge independent way. For that purpose we introduce the linear unitary operator $P(\boldsymbol{x}', \boldsymbol{x})$ which transports vectors from $h_{\boldsymbol{x}}$ displaced (retaining the vector orientation) to $h_{\boldsymbol{x}'}$. We assume that it is possible to choose the gauge $\{\chi_{\boldsymbol{x}}\}$ in such a way that in a neighborhood of the point $\boldsymbol{x}$ we can write

$$P(\boldsymbol{x} + d\boldsymbol{x}, \boldsymbol{x})\chi_{\boldsymbol{x}} = (1 + \mathrm{i}b_k(\boldsymbol{x})d\boldsymbol{x}^k)\chi_{\boldsymbol{x}+d\boldsymbol{x}}. \tag{6.66}$$

It is a straightforward matter to verify that in this particular gauge the differentiation operator

$$D_k = \frac{\partial}{\partial x_k} - \mathrm{i}b_k(\boldsymbol{x}) \tag{6.67}$$

is gauge invariant. It is also easy to see that the commutator

$$f_{kl} = \mathrm{i}[D_k, D_l] = \frac{\partial b_l}{\partial x_k} - \frac{\partial b_k}{\partial x_l} \tag{6.68}$$

is independent of the gauge. It measures the noncommutativity of the components of the gauge invariant differentiation. When we insert the operators (6.67) into the Hamiltonian we are effectively intoducing a vector potential $\boldsymbol{b}(\boldsymbol{x})$. The associated force field is the antisymmetric tensor f_{kl}. We do not want it to describe any real physical force, so we must assume that $f_{kl}(\boldsymbol{x}) = 0$ except at the singular points of the configuration space. Therefore any vector $\Psi(\boldsymbol{x}) \in h_{\boldsymbol{x}}$ displaced along a closed curve which does not encircle the singular point will remain unchanged. If, however, the path circulates once around the singularity the vector $\Psi \in h_{\boldsymbol{x}}$ is mapped to another vector $\Psi' = P_{\boldsymbol{x}}\Psi \in h_{\boldsymbol{x}}$ where $P_{\boldsymbol{x}}$ is a linear unitary operator acting in $h_{\boldsymbol{x}}$. Since this space is one dimensional the operator $P_{\boldsymbol{x}}$ is just a phase factor

$$P_{\boldsymbol{x}} = \mathrm{e}^{\mathrm{i}\xi}. \tag{6.69}$$

The value of the parameter ξ is independent of the point $\boldsymbol{x}$ since

$$P_{\boldsymbol{x}'} = P(\boldsymbol{x}', \boldsymbol{x})P_{\boldsymbol{x}}P(\boldsymbol{x}', \boldsymbol{x})^{-1}, \tag{6.70}$$

and therefore characteristic of the specific two particle system. Recall that this latter path corresponds to a curve joining the points $\boldsymbol{x} = (\boldsymbol{x}_1, \boldsymbol{x}_2)$ and

$-\boldsymbol{x} = (\boldsymbol{x}_2, \boldsymbol{x}_1)$ in the two particle space $\mathcal{E}_n^2$, so the operator $P_{\boldsymbol{x}}$ describes the effect of exchanging the positions of the two particles. Thus for the bosons $\xi = 0$ and for the fermions $\xi = \pi$.

Although no force results from the vector field $\boldsymbol{b}(\boldsymbol{x})$ there are dynamical effects through the differentiation operators D_k. It is possible to eliminate these dynamics by an appropriate selection of the gauge: fix the basis vector $\chi_{\boldsymbol{x}}$ at some arbitrary point $\boldsymbol{x}$ and let $\chi_{\boldsymbol{x}'}$ at any other point $\boldsymbol{x}'$ be the vector $\chi_{\boldsymbol{x}}$ displaced to this point. In this gauge the field $\boldsymbol{b}(\boldsymbol{x})$ clearly vanishes. However, there is an additional cost because all the basis vectors $\chi_{\boldsymbol{x}}, \exp(\pm\mathrm{i}\xi)\chi_{\boldsymbol{x}}, \exp(\pm2\mathrm{i}\xi)\chi_{\boldsymbol{x}}, \ldots$ are generated by transport of $\chi_{\boldsymbol{x}}$ around different closed curves. In other words, this approach transfers the dynamical effects of the singularity in the two particle configuration space to the multivalue character of the wave function $\psi(\boldsymbol{x})$.

To illustrate the two approaches let us consider two free particles in the two-dimensional flat space. The relative part of the free-particle Hamiltonian in polar coordinates is given by

$$\mathcal{H} = -\frac{\hbar^2}{m}\left(\frac{\partial^2}{\partial r^2} + \frac{1}{r}\frac{\partial}{\partial r} + \frac{4}{r^2}\frac{\partial^2}{\partial \phi^2}\right), \tag{6.71}$$

and the wave function $\psi(r, \phi)$ satisfies the condition

$$\psi(r, \phi + 2\pi) = \mathrm{e}^{\mathrm{i}\xi}\psi(r, \phi). \tag{6.72}$$

The parameter ξ describes the many-body character of the particles. As noted above, for bosons we have $\xi = 0$ and for fermions $\xi = \pi$. In the two-dimensional configuration space, however, nothing tells us to restrict the allowed values of ξ to those two. Instead we can have a continuum connecting bosons and fermions.

In the former approach we transfer the multivaluedness of the wave function to the dynamics by defining the single valued wave function as

$$\psi'(r, \phi) = \mathrm{e}^{-\mathrm{i}\frac{\xi}{2\pi}\phi}\psi(r, \phi). \tag{6.73}$$

The Hamiltonian is then transformed to

$$\mathcal{H}' = \mathrm{e}^{-\mathrm{i}\frac{\xi}{2\pi}\phi} H \mathrm{e}^{\mathrm{i}\frac{\xi}{2\pi}\phi} = -\frac{\hbar^2}{m}\left(\frac{\partial^2}{\partial r^2} + \frac{1}{r}\frac{\partial}{\partial r} + \frac{4}{r^2}\left(\frac{\partial}{\partial \phi} + \mathrm{i}\frac{\xi}{2\pi}\right)^2\right). \tag{6.74}$$

To see the effect of the parameter ξ we let the particles interact via the harmonic oscillator potential

$$V(r) = \tfrac{1}{4} m\omega^2 r^2. \tag{6.75}$$

When we separate the coordinates in the Hamiltonian $H' + V(r)$ the wave function can be written as

$$\psi'(r, \phi) = \mathrm{e}^{il\phi} R(r), \tag{6.76}$$

where, due to the single valuedness, the quantum number l can take the values $0, \pm 1, \pm 2, \ldots$. The radial wave function $R(r)$ must then satisfy the equation

$$\left(\frac{d^2}{dr^2} + \frac{1}{r}\frac{d}{dr} - \frac{4}{r^2}\left(l + \frac{\xi}{2\pi} \right)^2 - \frac{1}{4}\frac{m^2\omega^2}{\hbar^2} r^2 + \frac{mE}{\hbar^2} \right) R = 0. \tag{6.77}$$

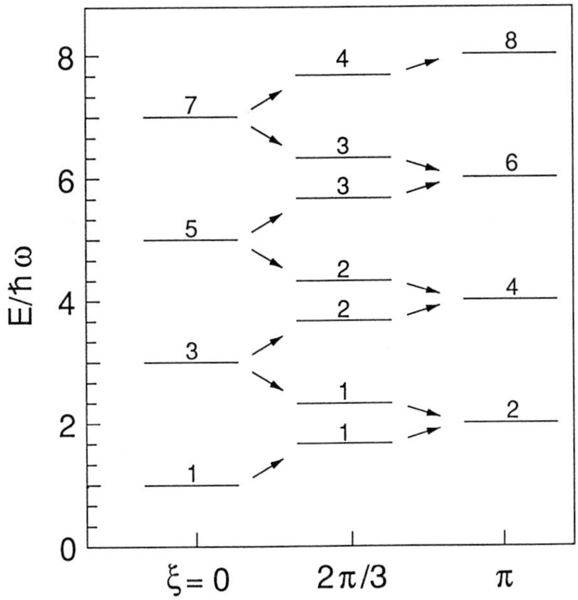

Fig. 6.27. The energy spectrum of a two particle two dimensional system interacting via a harmonic potential. The degeneracies of the energy levels are also given. The value $\xi = 0$ corresponds to bosons and the value $\xi = \pi$ to fermions. There is a continuous transition from the boson case to the fermion case. One particular intermediate value, $\xi = 2\pi/3$, is shown in the figure

This is easily solved following the guidelines of the ordinary two-dimensional harmonic oscillator. The energy spectrum turns out to be

$$E = 2\hbar\omega \left(n + \left| l + \frac{\xi}{2\pi} \right| + \frac{1}{2} \right), \quad n = 0, 1, 2, \ldots , \tag{6.78}$$

which is shown in Fig. 6.27 for the boson case $\xi = 0$, for the fermion case $\xi = \pi$ and for one intermediate value.

We have learned that, in two dimensions, identical particles can in fact obey any statistics, *i.e.*, they can be anyons. In three dimensions there is, however, an additional restriction. We noted that any closed curve encircling the singular point twice can be continuosly transferred to a point. Therefore the operator $P_{\boldsymbol{x}}$ must satisfy the condition

$$P_{\boldsymbol{x}}^2 = 1, \tag{6.79}$$

which implies that $P_{\boldsymbol{x}} = \pm 1$, or that only the values $\xi = 0$, bosons, and $\xi = \pi$, fermions, are allowed. To determine which one of these two values is actually realized the formalism must be generalized to the case where particles can have the spin degree of freedom. The spin-statistics theorem can then be applied to distinguish the cases (for more details, see [6.43]).

Let us now return to the specific case of the quasiparticles in the FQHE state. We saw that the wave function gains an extra phase $\Delta\gamma = 2\pi\nu$ when a quasiparticle at the point z_a encircles a quasiparticle at z_b. According to the previous discussion we can transfer this phase to the dynamics of the system by adding to the actual vector potential $\boldsymbol{A}$ a fictitious vector potential

$$\boldsymbol{b}(\boldsymbol{r}) = \frac{e^*}{\hbar c} \boldsymbol{A}_\phi(\boldsymbol{r}) \tag{6.80}$$

in such a way that

$$\oint \boldsymbol{b}(\boldsymbol{r}) \cdot d\boldsymbol{l} = 2\pi\nu, \tag{6.81}$$

and that the corresponding force field $\nabla \times \boldsymbol{b}$ vanishes. It is easy to see that the potential

$$\boldsymbol{A}_\phi(\boldsymbol{r} - \boldsymbol{r}_b) = \frac{\boldsymbol{\Phi}_0}{2\pi} \hat{\boldsymbol{z}} \times \frac{\boldsymbol{r} - \boldsymbol{r}_b}{|\boldsymbol{r} - \boldsymbol{r}_b|^2} \tag{6.82}$$

satisfies these conditions. The elementary excitations of the FQHE state can therefore be interpreted as quasiparticles (holes) with charge $e^* = \nu e$ $(-\nu e)$ carrying a unit flux tube with them.

Thus far we have considered only two particle systems. *Wu* [6.44] (see also *Arovas* et al. [6.45]) has generalized the formalism to the many particle case. It turns out that the quasiparticle-quasiparticle potential is equivalent to that of the charge e^* acting twice with the flux tube associated with one quasiparticle. The Hamiltonian describing the system of n quasiparticles of mass m^* takes now the form

$$\mathcal{H}' = \sum_{i=1}^{n} \frac{1}{2m^*} \left[\boldsymbol{p}_i - 2\frac{e^*}{\hbar c} \sum_{j \neq i} \boldsymbol{A}_\phi(\boldsymbol{r}_i - \boldsymbol{r}_j) \right]^2 . \tag{6.83}$$

The corresponding wave function $\psi'(\boldsymbol{r}_1, \boldsymbol{r}_2, \ldots, \boldsymbol{r}_n)$ is then symmetric (or antisymmetric if the quasiparticles are treated as fermions) under the interchange of any two of them. Once again it is possible to cast the fictitious dynamics to the multivaluedness of the wave function. The transformation

$$\psi(\boldsymbol{r}_1, \boldsymbol{r}_2, \ldots, \boldsymbol{r}_n) = \prod_{i<j} \mathrm{e}^{\mathrm{i}\frac{\nu}{\pi}\phi_{ij}} \psi'(\boldsymbol{r}_1, \boldsymbol{r}_2, \ldots, \boldsymbol{r}_n), \tag{6.84}$$

where ϕ_{ij} is the azimuthal angle of the relative vector $\boldsymbol{r}_i - \boldsymbol{r}_j$, eliminates the long range vector potential $\boldsymbol{A}_\phi$ from the Hamiltonian (6.83). Consider now two clusters of each of them containing p quasiparticles. When the two clusters are interchanged the wave function (6.84) will gain the statistical phase

$$\theta = p^2 \nu. \tag{6.85}$$

As pointed out by *Thouless* and *Wu* [6.46] this may have some importance for the FQHE. At fillings $\nu = 1/p$ the creation of p quasiparticles, as we have seen, corresponds to adding one electron. This means that the interchange of two clusters of p quasiparticles should obey Fermi statistics, i.e. the phase θ should be an odd integer, which is clearly impossible if p is even. This might be an explanation why only odd denominator filling fractions are observed. However, this is by no means a very rigorous argument, because it seems to be possible to modify the many anyon wave function (6.84) so that the phase $\nu = 1/p$ is replaced by the phase $1/p^2$.

6.8 The Hierarchy: Higher Order Fractions

The theory of Laughlin for the ground state and elementary excitations, is quite successful in describing the filling factors $\nu = \frac{1}{m}$ and $(1 - \frac{1}{m})$ with m an odd integer. However, experimental results for the FQHE of filling factors such as, $\frac{2}{5}, \frac{2}{7}, \frac{3}{7}, \frac{4}{5}$ and the others described in the introduction clearly indicate that a nontrivial extension of Laughlin's theory is required to describe these states. The major efforts in this direction have been made using the hierarchical approach proposed by *Laughlin* [6.2,47], *Haldane* [6.48] and *Halperin* [6.49], where condensation of a finite density of quasiparticles is supposed to form the higher order states in the hierarchy. Another approach to the higher order filling fractions, based on microscopic trial wave functions, has been carried out by Halperin and his collaborators.

According to *Laughlin* [6.47] the quasiparticle[6] motion can be understood by analogy with the electron motion. The quasiparticles behave much like electrons in the sense that their separations are quantized because of angular momentum conservation, but they are different from electrons in that the quantized separations are compatible with the *fractional statistics* as proposed by *Halperin* [6.49].

Following *Laughlin* [6.50], let us define the quasiparticle creation operators in the manner

$$S_{z_A}|m\rangle = \mathrm{e}^{-\frac{1}{4}\sum_j |z_j|^2} \prod_i (z_i - z_A) \prod_{j<k} (z_j - z_k)^m \tag{6.86}$$

and

$$S^\dagger_{z_B}|m\rangle = \mathrm{e}^{-\frac{1}{4}\sum_j |z_j|^2} \prod_i \left(2\frac{\partial}{\partial z_i} - z_B^*\right) \prod_{j<k} (z_j - z_k)^m \tag{6.87}$$

for a quasihole and a quasielectron respectively. In order to determine the two-quasiparticle eigenstates, Laughlin projected the Hamiltonian (5.10) of the many-electron system onto the set of states of the form $S_{z_A}S_{z_B}|m\rangle$ and diagonalized the projected Hamiltonian. The normalization integral is now given by

$$\begin{aligned}\langle m|S^\dagger_{z_B}S^\dagger_{z_A}S_{z_A}S_{z_B}|m\rangle &= \int \cdots \int d^2z_1 \ldots d^2z_N \prod_{j<k} |z_j - z_k|^{2m} \prod_i |z_i - z_A|^2 \\ &\quad \times |z_i - z_B|^2\, \mathrm{e}^{-\frac{1}{2}\sum_l |z_l|^2}.\end{aligned} \tag{6.88}$$

The integrand is readily recognized as the probability distribution of a classical plasma, $\mathrm{e}^{-\mathcal{H}'_m}$ with the corresponding plasma Hamiltonian

$$\begin{aligned}\mathcal{H}'_m = -2m \sum_{j<k} \ln|z_j - z_k| + \frac{1}{2}\sum_l |z_l|^2 \\ - 2\sum_i \left[\ln|z_i - z_A| + \ln|z_i - z_B|\right].\end{aligned} \tag{6.89}$$

In this case, (6.88) could be interpreted as the probability (to within a constant) of finding the *charge*-1 particles at z_A and z_B, if they are allowed

[6] In this section, *quasiholes* and *quasielectrons* are collectively called the *quasiparticles*.

to move around in the plasma. We therefore write

$$\begin{aligned}\langle m|S^{\dagger}_{z_B}S^{\dagger}_{z_A}S_{z_A}S_{z_B}|m\rangle &= \frac{C}{|z_A - z_B|^{\frac{2}{m}}}\,\mathrm{e}^{\frac{1}{2m}(|z_A|^2+|z_B|^2)}\,g_{22}(|z_A - z_B|)\\ &= C\mathrm{e}^{\frac{1}{2m}(|z_A|^2+|z_B|^2)}\,F\left[|z_A - z_B|^2\right]\end{aligned} \tag{6.90}$$

where C is a constant and g_{22} is the radial distribution function for particles of *charge*-1. Laughlin found an approximate fit for F of the form

$$F\left[|z|^2\right] \simeq \frac{1}{4\pi m}\int d^2z'\,\frac{1}{|z'|^{\frac{2}{3}}}\mathrm{e}^{-\frac{1}{4}|z-z'|^2}. \tag{6.91}$$

Let us now choose the basis states

$$|z_A, z_B\rangle = \mathrm{e}^{-\frac{1}{4m}(|z_A|^2+|z_B|^2)}S_{z_A}S_{z_B}|m\rangle. \tag{6.92}$$

The overlap matrix $\langle z_{A'}, z_{B'}|z_A, z_B\rangle$ is analytic in the variables $z_A, z_B, z^*_{A'}$ and $z^*_{B'}$. One could therefore analytically continue the normalization integral in the manner

$$\begin{aligned}\langle z_{A'}, z_{B'}|z_A, z_B\rangle &= C\mathrm{e}^{-\frac{1}{4m}(|z_A|^2+|z_B|^2+|z_{A'}|^2+|z_{B'}|^2)}\\ &\times \mathrm{e}^{\frac{1}{2m}(z^*_{A'}z_A+z^*_{B'}z_B)}\,F\left[(z_A - z_B)(z^*_{A'} - z^*_{B'})\right].\end{aligned} \tag{6.93}$$

The matrix elements of energy can be written similarly:

$$\begin{aligned}\langle z_{A'}, z_{B'}|\mathcal{H}|z_A, z_B\rangle &= C\,\mathrm{e}^{-\frac{1}{4m}(|z_A|^2+|z_B|^2+|z_{A'}|^2+|z_{B'}|^2)}\\ &\times \mathrm{e}^{\frac{1}{2m}(z^*_{A'}z_A+z^*_{B'}z_B)}E\left[(z_A - z_B)(z^*_{A'} - z^*_{B'})\right],\end{aligned} \tag{6.94}$$

where E is fitted by the formula [6.48],

$$E\left[|z|^2\right] \simeq \frac{1}{4\pi m}\int d^2z'\frac{1}{|z'|^{\frac{2}{m}}}\,\mathrm{e}^{-\frac{1}{4m}|z-z'|^2}\left[\frac{(e/m)^2}{|z'|}\right] \tag{6.95}$$

with the ground-state energy taken to be zero.

These matrices are diagonalized by the states,

$$|n\rangle = \int\!\!\int d^2z_A\,d^2z_B\,\mathrm{e}^{-\frac{1}{4m}(|z_A|^2+|z_B|^2)}(z^*_A - z^*_B)^n|z_A, z_B\rangle \tag{6.96}$$

where n is an *even* integer, since the *Bose* representations for the quasiparticles are used. For the *Fermi* representation the basis states are to be chosen as $(z_A - z_B)|z_A, z_B\rangle$ and then n would be odd. The state $(z_A - z_B)|z_A, z_B\rangle$ is the electron-hole conjugate of the two-electron wave function for $m = 1$:

$$\psi(z_1, z_2) = \varphi_{z_A}(z_1)\varphi_{z_B}(z_2) - \varphi_{z_B}(z_1)\varphi_{z_A}(z_2) \tag{6.97}$$

with

$$\varphi_{z_A}(z) = \mathrm{e}^{-\frac{1}{4}|z|^2}\,\mathrm{e}^{\frac{1}{2}zz_A^*}\,\mathrm{e}^{-\frac{1}{4}|z_A|^2}. \tag{6.98}$$

In the Fermi representation, the overlap matrix is,

$$\begin{aligned}\langle z_{A'}, z_{B'}|(z_{A'}^* - z_{B'}^*)(z_A - z_B)|z_A, z_B\rangle &= C\mathrm{e}^{-\frac{1}{4m}(|z_A|^2+|z_B|^2+|z_{A'}|^2+|z_{B'}|^2)} \\ &\times \mathrm{e}^{\frac{1}{2m}(z_{A'}^* z_A + z_{B'}^* z_B)}\, F^{\mathrm{f}}\left[(z_A - z_B)(z_{A'}^* - z_{B'}^*)\right]\end{aligned} \tag{6.99}$$

where

$$F^f\left[|z|^2\right] = |z|^2\, F\left[|z|^2\right]. \tag{6.100}$$

This is diagonalized by the wave function

$$|n+1\rangle = \int\!\!\int d^2z_A d^2z_B\, \mathrm{e}^{-\frac{1}{4m}(|z_A|^2+|z_B|^2)}(z_A^* - z_B^*)^{n+1}(z_A - z_B)|z_A, z_B\rangle \tag{6.101}$$

where $n+1$ is *odd.* Laughlin then showed that this state is same as $|n\rangle$. Like the two-electron state in the lowest Landau level, the two-quasiparticle state does not depend on the repulsive potential between quasiparticles. It is also independent of the choice of basis. For more than two quasiparticles, *Laughlin* [6.50] found the fractional statistics representation of Halperin to be the most convenient one. This treatment of the quasiparticles will be discussed below.

According to *Haldane* [6.48,51], there is a hierarchical system in which q/p states with $1 < p < q$ are formed from a new generation of elementary excitations in the same manner as the Laughlin state is formed by the electrons. Each new generation of elementary excitations appears against a *vacuum* formed by the preceding generation. In this picture, the elementary excitations are supposed to obey Bose statistics, unlike the electrons which obey the Fermi statistics. The chain of equations are

$$n_{\mathrm{s}} = mN_{\mathrm{L}} + \alpha_1 N^{(1)}, \tag{6.102a}$$

$$N_{\mathrm{L}} = p_1 N^{(1)} + \alpha_2 N^{(2)}, \tag{6.102b}$$

$$N^{(1)} = p_2 N^{(2)} + \alpha_3 N^{(3)}, \tag{6.102c}$$

$$\cdots \quad \cdots \quad \cdots \quad \cdots$$

$$N^{(k-1)} = p_k N^{(k)}; \tag{6.102d}$$

where $m \geq 1$ is odd if all $p_j \neq 0$ are even and $\alpha_j = \pm 1$. The above equations are understood as follows: in the first equation the imbalance between the electron density $N_{\rm L}$ and the density of the incompressible state $n_{\rm s}/m$ is compensated by the $N^{(1)}$ particles ($\alpha_1 = -1$) or holes ($\alpha_1 = +1$) ($n_{\rm s} = 1/2\pi\ell_0^2$ is the degeneracy per unit area of the lowest Landau level). The next equation is the same except that it describes the next generation with m replaced by an even quantity p_1. The solution of (6.102) gives the continued fraction for $\nu = N_{\rm L}/n_{\rm s}$:

$$\nu = \cfrac{1}{m + \cfrac{\alpha_1}{p_1 - \cfrac{\alpha_2}{p_2 - \cfrac{\alpha_3}{p_3 - \dots}}}} \qquad (\nu < 1). \tag{6.103}$$

A new liquid $[m, \alpha_1 p_1, \cdots, \alpha_j p_j]$ does not form before the appearance of the preceding liquid $[m, \alpha_1 p_1, \cdots, \alpha_{j-1} p_{j-1}]$. The iterative equations for the filling fractions in this hierarchical scheme are similar to those in the scheme of Halperin and are described later.

The excitation energy of the new fluid state is equivalent to that of a system consisting of $N_{\rm q}$ quasiparticles with fractional charge $e_{\rm q}$ obeying Bose statistics on the sphere of radius R and in a radial magnetic field $B_{\rm q} = \hbar c S_{\rm q}/e_{\rm q} R^2$. The magnetic length for the quasiparticle state is $\ell_{\rm q} = (\hbar c/e_{\rm q} B_{\rm q})^{\frac{1}{2}}$. *Zhang* [6.52] showed how the excitation energy at any hierarchy level can be approximately related to the excitation energy for the $\frac{1}{m}$ state. Considering the Coulomb interaction between point particles of charge $e_{\rm q}$, the excitation energy of the quasiparticles at any level of hierarchy is written as

$$E(\nu) = \left(\frac{e^2}{\epsilon \ell_0}\right) \frac{1}{Q_n^2 - 1} \left(\frac{p_n + 1}{Q_n}\right)^{\frac{1}{2}} f_F(p_n + 1) \tag{6.104}$$

where $f_F(m)$ is the excitation energy of the elementary Laughlin state for the electron system, and Q_n, Q_{n-1} are the denominators of the rational fillings of the new state and the parent state respectively. The above relation also preserves the electron-hole symmetry. The hierarchical scheme has been extended to the case of a system containing impurities.

The hierarchical scheme of *Halperin* [6.49] is very much in the spirit of Laughlin's theory. In this scheme, the quasiparticles, as mentioned above, are required to obey the fractional statistics discussed in the preceding section. If ν_t is a stable filling factor obtained at level t of the hierarchy, the low-lying energy states for filling factors near to ν_t can be described by the addition of a small density of quasiparticle excitations to the ground state at ν_t. There are two types of elementary excitations: p-excitations (particle like) and h-excitations (hole like), with charges $q_t e$ and $-q_t e$ respectively. Halperin then constructed a *pseudo* wave function (where the coordinates are for quasiparticles):

$$\psi\left(Z_1, \ldots, Z_{N_t}\right) = P[Z_j]\, Q[Z_j] \exp\left(-\frac{|q_t|}{4\ell_0^2} \sum_{j=1}^{N_t} |Z_j|^2\right) \tag{6.105}$$

where Z_j is the complex coordinate of the quasiparticle j and N_t is the number of quasiparticles. The polynomial $P[Z_j]$ is chosen to be *symmetric*:

$$P[Z_j] = \prod_{i<j} (Z_i - Z_j)^{2p_{t+1}} \tag{6.106}$$

where p_{t+1} is a positive integer, whose variational properties are known from Laughlin's theory. The function $Q[Z_j]$ determines the symmetry properties of ψ under the interchange of quasiparticles. Now, introducing the concept of fractional statistics discussed in the preceding section, the many-body wave function (6.84) of N_t identical anyons is [6.42]

$$\psi(\boldsymbol{r}_1, \ldots, \boldsymbol{r}_{N_t}) = \prod_{i<j} \exp\left(\mathrm{i}\frac{\xi}{\pi}\varphi_{ij}\right) \psi'(\boldsymbol{r}_1, \ldots, \boldsymbol{r}_{N_t}). \tag{6.107}$$

In (6.107), φ_{ij} is the azimuthal angle of the relative vector $(\boldsymbol{r}_i - \boldsymbol{r}_j)$ and $\psi'(\boldsymbol{r}_1, \ldots, \boldsymbol{r}_N)$ is a single-valued wave function. According to (6.107), a permutation of any two anyons $(\Delta\varphi_{ij} = \pi)$ multiplies ψ by the phase factor $\mathrm{e}^{\mathrm{i}\xi}$. Therefore, when $\eta \equiv \xi/2\pi = q\boldsymbol{\Phi}/2\boldsymbol{\Phi}_0$ is an integer, the anyons are bosons and when η is an half-integer, they are fermions. Here $\boldsymbol{\Phi}$ is the usual magnetic flux.

In terms of the complex coordinates Z_j and Z_j^*, the multivalued wave function (6.107) takes the form

$$\psi = \prod_{i<j} (Z_i - Z_j)^{\frac{\xi}{\pi}} f(Z_i, Z_j^*) \tag{6.108}$$

where $f(Z_i, Z_j^*) = (r_{ij})^{-\xi/\pi}\psi'(Z_j, Z_j^*)$, is a single-valued function of the coordinates.

Let us now consider the first step of the hierarchy when the anyon quasiparticles are derived from electrons. The phase change $\Delta\gamma$ of the wave function of a quasiparticle in a closed adiabatic path around another quasiparticle is $\Delta\gamma = 2\pi q$ and for $\nu = \frac{1}{m}$, $|\Delta\gamma| = 2\pi/m$. Therefore the change of phase that accompanies the interchange of quasiparticles is $\Delta\gamma/2 = \pi\nu = \xi$ (see the preceding section and [6.53]). According to the general structure of (6.108), the factor $Q[Z_j]$ is now

$$Q[Z_j] = \prod_{i<j} (Z_i - Z_j)^{-\alpha/m_t}. \tag{6.109}$$

In Eq. (6.109), $\alpha = \pm 1$, according to whether one is dealing with particle- or hole-type excitations, and m_t is a rational number ≥ 1, to be specified by an iterative equation below.

As in Laughlin's theory for the ground state, the plasma analogy (5.16–19) is applied to the wave function (6.105) which yields

$$m_{t+1} = 2p_{t+1} - \frac{\alpha_{t+1}}{m_t}\,. \tag{6.110}$$

The charge neutrality condition fixes the density of the plasma. A relation similar to (5.19) for the pseudo wave function (6.105) shows that the number of quasiparticles in an area $2\pi\ell_0^2$ is $n_t = |q_t|/m_{t+1}$. Each quasiparticle has charge $\alpha_{t+1}q_t$ so that calculating the *electron* density in the new stable state, the filling factor is obtained from the following relation

$$\nu_{t+1} = \nu_t + \alpha_{t+1}\, q_t|q_t|/m_{t+1}\,. \tag{6.111}$$

Multiplying the pseudo wave function by the factor $\prod_k z_k$, $(k = 1, \dots, N_t)$, we find a *deficit* of $1/m_{t+1}$ quasiparticles at level t near the origin (see Sect. 6.1). This is a hole excitation at level $t+1$. In a similar manner, one can construct a p-excitation where one has an *excess* of $1/m_{t+1}$ quasiparticles at the origin. The iterative equation for q_t is then

$$q_{t+1} = \alpha_{t+1}\, q_t/m_{t+1}\,. \tag{6.112}$$

The starting values for the iterative equations, (6.110–112) are set to, $q_0 = m_0 = \alpha_1 = 1$. Then for any choice of the sequence $\{\alpha_t, p_t\}$, the iterative equations would provide a sequence of rational filling factors ν_t. The allowed values of ν_t may also be expressed as continued fractions in terms of the finite sequence $\{\alpha_t, p_t\}$.

As discussed by Halperin, quantized Hall steps will not, however, be observed for every rational ν. In fact, there exists a maximum value m_c such that, if at any stage of the hierarchy, the calculated m_t is greater than m_c, the quasiparticle density n_t will form a Wigner crystal (see Sect. 5.7), and it would be meaningless to continue from the corresponding electron density further in the hierarchy.

Assuming that at any stage of the hierarchy, the quasiparticles or quasi-holes can be treated as point particles with pairwise Coulomb interactions, an estimate for the potential energy can be obtained as

$$E(\nu_{t+1}) \simeq E(\nu_t) + n_t\,\varepsilon_t^{\pm}(\nu_t) + n_t\,|q_t|^{\frac{5}{2}}\,E_{\rm pl}(m_{t+1})\,, \tag{6.113}$$

where $E(\nu)$ is the energy per quantum of magnetic flux, $\varepsilon_t^{\pm}(\nu_t)$ is the energy required to add one p-excitation or h-excitation (gross energy[7]), and E_{pl} is the interpolation formula given in (5.27) [or (5.54)]. The factor $|q_t|^{\frac{5}{2}}$ reflects the smaller charge and larger magnetic length of the quasiparticles.

Let us consider the $\nu = \frac{2}{5}$ state. In this case, the parent state is $\nu = \frac{1}{3}$, and accurate Monte carlo results are available for the excitation energies at $\nu = \frac{1}{3}$. With $t = 1, p_1 = 2, \alpha_1 = 1$, the state $\frac{1}{3}$ is obtained. For the state $\nu = \frac{2}{5}$ we have $t = 2, p_2 = 1$ and $\alpha_2 = 1$. The iterative equation then yields, $m_1 = 3, q_1 = \frac{1}{3}, m_2 = \frac{5}{3}$, and $n_1 = \frac{1}{5}$. Making use of the result, $E(\frac{1}{3}) \simeq \frac{1}{3} E_{\text{pl}}(3)$, we get the following relation for the energy

$$E\left(\frac{2}{5}\right) \simeq \frac{1}{5}\varepsilon_+\left(\frac{1}{3}\right) + \frac{1}{3}E_{\text{pl}}(3) + \frac{1}{5}\left(\frac{1}{3}\right)^{\frac{5}{2}} E_{\text{pl}}\left(\frac{5}{3}\right). \tag{6.114}$$

The relation between ε_+ and the quasiparticle creation energy $\widetilde{\varepsilon}_{\text{p}}$ (Sect. 6.1) is given in [6.4,49] as

$$\varepsilon_+\left(\frac{1}{3}\right) = \widetilde{\varepsilon}_{\text{p}}\left(\frac{1}{3}\right) + \frac{1}{2}E_{\text{pl}}(3). \tag{6.115}$$

Dividing both sides of (6.115) by $\nu = \frac{2}{5}$, the energy per particle is written

$$(E/N) \approx \frac{13}{12}E_{\text{pl}}(3) + \frac{1}{2}\left(\frac{1}{3}\right)^{\frac{5}{2}} E_{\text{pl}}\left(\frac{5}{3}\right) + \frac{1}{2}\widetilde{\varepsilon}_{\text{p}}\left(\frac{1}{3}\right). \tag{6.116}$$

Using the Monte Carlo estimate, $\widetilde{\varepsilon}_{\text{p}}(\frac{1}{3}) \approx 0.073\, e^2/\epsilon\ell_0$, the energy per particle is estimated to be $\sim -0.424\, e^2/\epsilon\ell_0$, which is quite close to the result $\sim -0.435\, e^2/\epsilon\ell_0$, obtained by *Yoshioka* et al. [6.13] by finite-size calculations in a periodic rectangular geometry.

Using a suitable iterative formula for the quasiparticle energies in Eq. (6.113), the energy versus density curve generated by Halperin for various filling fractions is shown in Fig. 6.28. In the figure, the stable fractions appear with downward pointing cusps. As *Laughlin* remarked [6.50], this curve has the interesting *fractal* property of being everywhere continuous but nowhere differentiable, with slope discontinuity at any point, which reflects the energy gap of the nearest allowed fraction.

MacDonald et al. [6.54] proposed trial wave functions in terms of electron coordinates in each level of the hierarchy. Using an exact sum rule which is valid for any isotropic state in the lowest Landau level, they estimated the pair distribution functions and the energy of a hierarchy state

[7] A detailed discussion of $\varepsilon_t^{\pm}$ is given by *Morf* and *Halperin* [6.4].

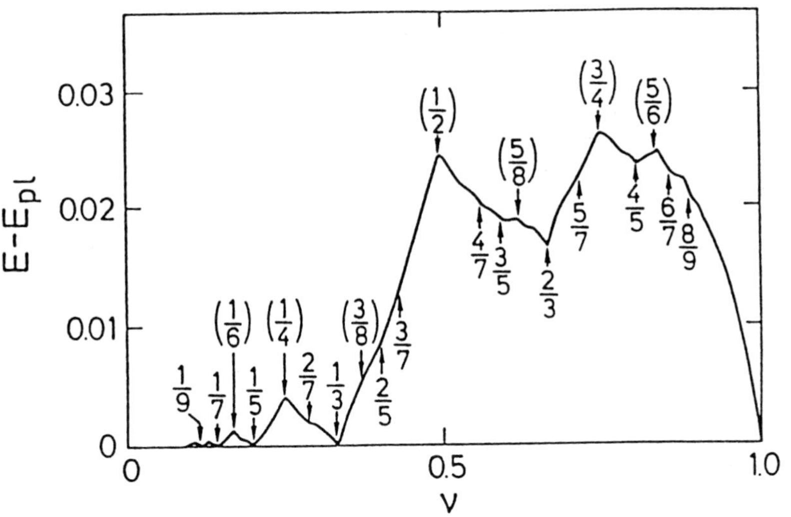

Fig. 6.28. Potential energy $E(\nu)$ per quantum of magnetic flux (in units of $e^2/\epsilon\ell_0$) vs the filling factor ν of the lowest Landau level. The smooth function $E_{\rm pl} = \nu\, E_{\rm pl}(m)$ has been subtracted from the result [6.45]

by constructing a corresponding hierarchy of liquid structure functions. In Fig. 6.29, we present their results for the energies at various hierarchy states, together with the corresponding plasma energies [see (5.54)] and the CDW state energies in the HF approximation [6.55,56]. The essential difference between their results and those of Fig. 6.28 is, as these authors pointed out, that the difference between the hierarchy state energy and the reference plasma energy tends to be larger when a condensate occurs in the quasielectrons rather than the quasiholes. Following this line of approach, *MacDonald* and *Murray* [6.57] constructed trial wave functions for up to eight electrons and obtained the ground-state and excitation energies for states associated with $\nu = \frac{1}{3}, \frac{2}{7}$, and $\frac{2}{5}$.

Finally, the hierarchical scheme described above has been employed by *Zhang* and *Chakraborty* [6.58] to study the condensation of the spin-reversed quasiparticles. According to the hierarchy theory, the spin-1 quasiparticles may form a new Laughlin-type liquid state. The construction of the daughter states is analogous to those for spin-0 quasiparticles. Since the spin-1 quasiparticle has lower energy (see Sect. 6.3), we may argue in the hierarchical consideration that the daughter state formed with spin-1 quasiparticles has lower energy than the corresponding daughter state formed with spin-0 quasiparticles, and the spin polarization of the daughter state at that filling is given by the hierarchical equations. The filling factor of a daughter state $[m; \alpha, p]$ (we consider the first step in a hierarchy), whose parent state filling

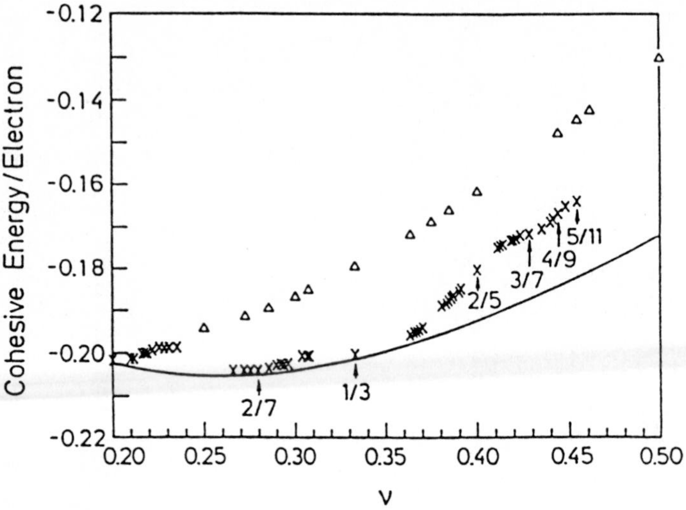

Fig. 6.29. Cohesive energy per electron ($E/N_e - \nu\sqrt{\pi/8}$) as a function of filling factor. The triangles are the CDW energies for a hexagonal lattice, the crosses are obtained using the hierarchy state pair-correlation function. The solid line is the interpolation formula for the plasma energy [6.52]

is $\frac{1}{m}$ is given by

$$\nu(m;\alpha,p) = \frac{1}{m - \frac{\alpha}{p}}, \tag{6.117}$$

where p is an even integer, and $\alpha = +1(-1)$ corresponds to a particle- (hole-) type excitation. The number of the excitations N_q, and the number of electrons N_e is related by $N_q = N_e/p$. For a system with spin-1 quasiparticles, the total spin of the system is reduced by 1 in creating each quasiparticle. The total spin of the daughter state formed with spin-1 quasiparticles is then

$$S = \tfrac{1}{2}N_e - N_q = N_e\left(\frac{1}{2} - \frac{1}{p}\right). \tag{6.118}$$

It is now convenient to define a spin-polarization parameter $Y = 2S/N_e$, which is the ratio of the electron number difference between parallel and antiparallel spins to the total number of spins. The case of $Y = 1$ corresponds to the spin-polarized state, and the case of $Y = 0$ to the unpolarized state. We then have, for a daughter state formed from spin-1 quasiparticles

$$Y = 1 - \frac{2}{p}. \tag{6.119}$$

It follows from (6.119) that the states at $\nu = 2/(2m-1)$ are spin-unpolarized ($p = 2$) and the state at $\nu = 4/(4m-1)$ are partially-spin-polarized with $Y = \frac{1}{2}$. Among these fillings, $\nu = \frac{2}{5}$ and $\frac{4}{11}$ have been studied by us in Sect. 5.5, and the energy for the spin-polarization state given by (6.117) is lower than the energy for the fully spin-polarized state, in agreement with the above hierarchical argument.

The trial wave function for the quasiparticle excitations of the $\nu = \frac{1}{m}$ states with one spin-reversed electron is given in (6.37). For a number n_t of spin-1 quasiparticles in the Laughlin state at $\nu = \frac{1}{m}$, the trial wave function is written

$$\psi(z_1, \dots, z_{N_e}) = \prod_{i<j}^{N_e} \left(z_i - z_j \right)^{m-1+\delta_{\sigma_i \cdot \sigma_j}} \exp\left[-\frac{1}{4\ell_0^2} \sum_{i=1}^{N_e} |z_i|^2 \right], \tag{6.120}$$

where $\sigma_i = -1$ for $i = 1, \dots, N_t$, and $\sigma_i = 1$ for $i = N_t + 1, \dots, N_e$, z_i is, as usual, the complex coordinate of the ith electron. Let us consider the following two cases, (a) $n_t = 1$ and (b) $n_t = \frac{1}{2} N_e$. In the former case, we have the one spin-1 quasiparticle state, and (6.120) reduces to the state (6.37). In case (b), we have the spin unpolarized state at $\nu = 2/(2m-1)$, and (6.120) reduces to the state (5.56) discussed in Sect. 5.5.

Let us now discuss the electron-hole symmetry in the presence of spin degeneracy. With spin degeneracy a state with N_e holes or $2N_s - N_e$ electrons is the conjugate of a state with N_e electrons. As in the spin-polarized case [Sect. 5.1], the off-diagonal matrix elements of the Hamiltonian are the same for hole and for electron systems with the same values of the total spin. The diagonal matrix elements differ only by an overall constant value

$$\Delta E = 2\left(N_s - N_e\right) \left[\mathcal{W} + \sum_{j=1}^{N_s} \left(2A_{j00j} - A_{j0j0}\right) \right], \tag{6.121}$$

where $\mathcal{W}$ and A are defined in (5.5) and (5.6) respectively. As a consequence of this symmetry, the spin polarization of the ground state at electron filling $2 - \nu$ is related to that at ν as,

$$\nu Y(2-\nu) = (2-\nu) Y(\nu). \tag{6.122}$$

We now come to the microscopic trial wave function approach. Several trial wave functions for higher order filling factors were suggested by *Halperin* [6.3]. The most extensive numerical calculations reported so far, are for $\nu = \frac{2}{5}$. There are also results for $\frac{2}{7}$, $\frac{2}{9}$ and for $\frac{2}{3}$. The trial wave function used in these studies is written as [6.6]

$$\psi = \mathcal{A}\widetilde{\psi}$$

$$\widetilde{\psi} = \left[\prod_k \mathrm{e}^{-|z_k|^2/4\ell_0^2}\right]\left[\prod_{k<l}(z_k - z_l)^s\right]\left[\prod_i (z_{2i-1} - z_{2i})^t\right]\left[\prod_{i<j}(Z_i - Z_j)^{2u}\right] \tag{6.123}$$

where s, t and u are required to be integers with $s > 0, u \geq 0, s - t > 0$, and $s - t$ odd. Furthermore, u or t or both are required to be > 0. In (6.123), k and l run from 1 to N_e, while i and j run from 1 to $\frac{1}{2}N_\mathrm{e}$ and $Z_i = \frac{1}{2}(z_{2i}+z_{2i-1})$ is the center of gravity of the ith pair. The corresponding filling factor is given by $\nu = 2/(2s+u)$. The motivation behind constructing such a trial wave function has been discussed by *Halperin* [6.3].

For the $\frac{2}{5}$ state ($s = 2, u = t = 1$), the Monte Carlo results for a disk geometry give an estimate of potential energy per electron of $-0.414 \pm 0.002\, e^2/\epsilon\ell_0$. This energy is much higher than the value of $\sim -0.435\, e^2/\epsilon\ell_0$ obtained from exact diagonalization of systems with up to eight electrons in a periodic rectangular geometry. The trial wave function for $\frac{2}{5}$ is therefore not a good approximation for the true ground state.

For the $\frac{2}{7}$ state ($s = 3, t = 0, u = 1$), a reasonably good result was obtained, $E/N_\mathrm{e} \approx -0.377\, e^2/\epsilon\ell_0$, as compared to $E/N_\mathrm{e} \approx -0.385\, e^2/\epsilon\ell_0$ for a four-electron system in a periodic rectangular geometry. However, in this case the accuracy required for the calculations to be useful is not achieved [6.4].

For the $\frac{2}{3}$ state ($s = u = 1, t = 0$), the trial wave function provides the result $E/N_\mathrm{e} \approx -0.509\, e^2/\epsilon\ell_0$. The $\frac{2}{3}$ state energy can also be computed from Laughlin's $\frac{1}{3}$ state via the electron-hole symmetry relation (Sects. 5.1,2):

$$\nu\, u(\nu) = (1-\nu)\, u(1-\nu) + \sqrt{\frac{\pi}{8}}\frac{e^2}{\epsilon\ell_0}(1-2\nu) \tag{6.124}$$

where $u(\nu)$ is the potential energy per electron in the state. One then obtains $E(\frac{2}{3})/N_\mathrm{e} \approx -0.518\, e^2/\epsilon\ell_0$ which is lower than the trial wave function result.

An alternative wave function has been explored in the spherical geometry for the $\frac{2}{5}$ and $\frac{2}{7}$ state [6.19,59] and for the $\frac{2}{9}$ state [6.18]. The estimate for the $\frac{2}{5}$ state in the thermodynamic limit is given by $E/N_\mathrm{e} \approx -0.4303 \pm 0.0030\, e^2/\epsilon\ell_0$ [6.19].

There has also been an attempt to explain the higher-order filling fractions without introducing the hierarchical approaches described above [6.60]. This approach is basically a rearrangement of the Laughlin-type theory described in Chap. 5. The prime motivation of introducing this approach was, according to the author, to provide a unified description of the integer and fractional QHE. In this approach, the FQHE of electrons is considered to be a manifestation of the IQHE of so-called *composite fermions.* These are electrons with *even* number of flux quanta attached to them. Incompressibility of a state is achieved when the composite fermions simply "occupy an incompressible state" [6.60]. Based on this picture, trial wave functions were constructed for various filling fractions. For example, for filling factors $p = 1/(2m+1)$, the Laughlin state (5.14) can be rewritten as

$$\begin{aligned}\chi_p &= D^m \Phi_1 \\ D &= \prod_{j<k} (z_j - z_k)^2 \\ \Phi_1 &= \prod_{j<k} (z_j - z_k) \exp\left(-\frac{1}{4}\sum_i |z_i|^2\right) .\end{aligned}$$

Therefore, the Laughlin state can be obtained from the $\nu = 1$ IQHE state Φ_1 by multiplying it by D^m, where m is an integer. Similarly, for any other IQHE states Φ_n, one can write

$$\chi_p = D^m \Phi_n$$

and an incompressible state at filling factor p is generated. Accordingly, the trial state at $p = n/(2mn+1)$ is equivalent to the $\nu = n$ IQHE state of composite fermions in the sense that it is identical to the $\nu = n$ IQHE state except that each electron has $2m$ flux quanta attached. Important insights on why this approach works have recently been provided by the Chern-Simons effective field theory developed by *Halperin*, *Lee* and *Read* [6.61] and discussed in Sect. 9.4.

Experimentally, there are indications that the FQHE occurs in multiple series p/q, with fractions of odd denominators [6.62]. Furthermore, at a given temperature, the $\frac{1}{3}$ effect is always the best developed, followed by $\frac{2}{5}$, $\frac{3}{7}$, and $\frac{4}{9}$. The $\frac{2}{3}$ sequence ($\frac{3}{5}, \frac{4}{7}, \frac{5}{9}$) shows a similar behavior. As the magnetic field strength varies by only $\approx 25\%$ within each sequence, the difference in field strength is probably not the reason for the decrease in strength of the effects within a sequence. The hierarchy of the FQHE states has also been investigated by time-resolved magnetoluminescence [6.63]. The chemical potential discontinuity was found to have a linear magnetic field dependence starting from $\nu = \frac{1}{2}, \frac{1}{4}$ or $\frac{1}{6}$ for different families of the FQHE states. Further work on the hierarchical models discussed in this section is required to provide a better explanation of these experimental findings.

6.9 Tilted-Field Effects and Reversed-Spin States

When a strong electric field is applied perpendicular to the two-dimensional electron system, the electron motion in that direction is quantized and the two-dimensional electronic subbands are formed. A magnetic field in the same direction splits each subband into Landau levels. The case where the magnetic field is parallel to the electric field is very special because only in that case can the Hamiltonian be separated into an electric part leading to subbands and a magnetic part leading to Landau levels. For any other orientation of the magnetic filed, the Hamiltonian can not be separated in this manner and one obtains the mixing of Landau levels originating from different subbands. A theoretical study of this mixing was reported in the single electron system by *Maan* [6.64] and was studied experimentally by various groups [6.65,66].

In the following, we present a brief description of Landau levels in a parabolic well in tilted magnetic fields following Maan. We consider a situation where an electron is confined to the xy-plane by a parabolic potential well $V(z) = \mathcal{A}z^2$ and the magnetic field is applied in the $x - z$ plane. We choose the gauge such that the vector potential is $\boldsymbol{A} = (0, xB_z - zB_x, 0)$, where $B_x = B\sin\theta$, $B_z = B\cos\theta$, and θ is the tilt angle from the direction perpendicular to the electron plane. The Schrödinger equation is then written

$$\left[-\frac{\hbar^2}{2m^*}\left(\frac{\partial^2}{\partial x'^2}+\frac{\partial^2}{\partial z^2}\right)+\frac{e^2}{2m^*}\left(x'B_z - zB_x\right)^2 + \mathcal{A}z^2\right] \mathrm{e}^{\mathrm{i}k_y y}\,\psi(x,z) = E\,\mathrm{e}^{\mathrm{i}k_y y}\,\psi(x,z) \tag{6.125}$$

where $x' = x - \hbar k_y/eB_z$. Defining the new coordinates:

$$\xi = x'\cos\phi - z\sin\phi; \qquad x' = \xi\cos\phi + \zeta\sin\phi$$
$$\zeta = x'\sin\phi + z\cos\phi; \qquad z = -\xi\sin\phi + \zeta\cos\phi$$

the Schrödinger equation is rewritten after some algebra as

$$\left[-\frac{\hbar^2}{2m^*}\left(\frac{\partial^2}{\partial \xi^2}+\frac{\partial^2}{\partial \zeta^2}\right)+\xi^2\alpha+\zeta^2\beta\right]\mathrm{e}^{\mathrm{i}k_y y}\chi(\xi,\zeta) = E\,\mathrm{e}^{\mathrm{i}k_y y}\chi(\xi,\zeta) \tag{6.126}$$

where α and β depend on $\mathcal{A}$, B_z and B_x in a complex manner and the angle of rotation of the coordinates is:

$$\phi = \tfrac{1}{2}\arctan\left[\frac{\sin(2\theta)}{\cos(2\theta)-\mathcal{A}\frac{2m^*}{e^2}}\right].$$

The eigenvalues are then those of two harmonic oscillators $(N_1 + \frac{1}{2})\hbar\omega_1$ and $(N_2 + \frac{1}{2})\hbar\omega_2$ with frequencies

$$\omega_{1,2} = \left[\frac{1}{2}\left(\omega_c^2 + \omega_0^2\right) \pm \left\{\omega_c^4 + \omega_0^4 + 2\omega_0^2\left(\omega_x^2 - \omega_z^2\right)\right\}^{\frac{1}{2}} \right]^{\frac{1}{2}} . \qquad (6.127)$$

In Eq. (6.127), $\omega_c = eB/m^*$, $\omega_0 = (2\mathcal{A}/m^*)^{\frac{1}{2}}$, $\omega_z = \omega_c \sin\theta$, $\omega_z = \omega_c \cos\theta$, and m^* is the effective mass. It should be pointed out that the Landau level degeneracy depends *only* on the component of the magnetic field normal to the confinement plane.

The magnetic field dependence of $E = \hbar\omega_{1,2}$ is shown in Fig. 6.30 for different values of the tilt angle. For $\theta = 0°$, *i.e.*, the magnetic field being perpendicular, every subband splits into Landau levels as discussed above. For the magnetic field at any other angle, subband separation depends on the magnetic field and also the Landau level separation depends on the tilt angle.

The dependence of the FQHE on a tilted magnetic field was first studied experimentally by *Haug* et al. [6.67]. In that experiment, the activation energy determined from the measured temperature dependence of the diagonal resistivity was found to *decrease* slightly when the tilt angle was increased

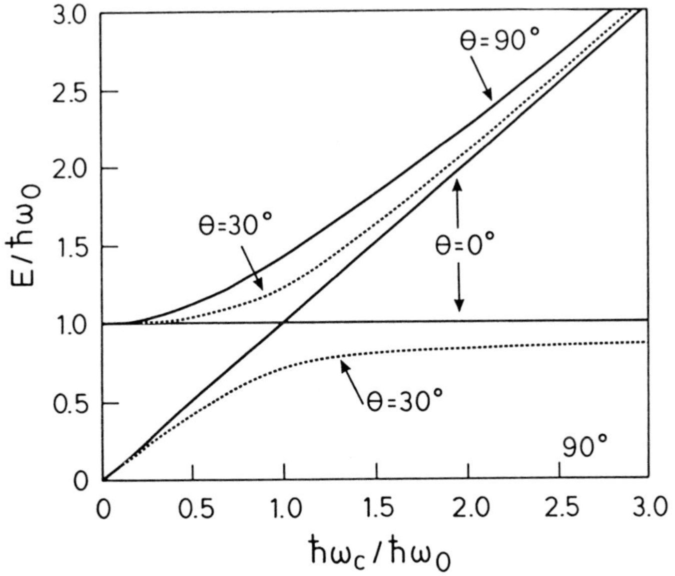

Fig. 6.30. The eigenfrequencies of the Landau levels for an electron in a parabolic potential well for different values of magnetic field and tilt angle θ [6.64]

at $\nu = \frac{1}{3}$ filling factor (the activation energy was $W = 1.67$ K at $\theta = 0°$ and $W = 1.52$ K at $\theta = 63.7°$). However, for the $\frac{2}{3}$ filling, the activation energy showed a rapid *increase* with increasing tilt angle. As discussed in the preceeding section, allowing spin reversal in the ground state, these two filling fractions are no longer electron-hole symmetric. The magnetic field range in the work of Haug et al. is, however, quite large. Therefore, breaking of the electron-hole symmetry might have some other origin in this particular case.

A simple effect of the tilted-field is to influence the wave function perpendicular to the electron plane. To see how that happens let us consider the Landau gauge vector potential, $\boldsymbol{A} = (B_y z, B_z x, 0)$. The magnetic field is therefore in the $y - z$ plane and $B_y = B\sin\theta$, $B_z = B\cos\theta$, θ is the tilt angle and B is total magnetic field. The single-particle Hamiltonian is then written in terms of the perpendicular and parallel components of the total Hamiltonian

$$\mathcal{H} = \mathcal{H}_\perp + \mathcal{H}_\parallel + \mathcal{H}', \tag{6.128}$$

where the various components are

$$\begin{aligned}
\mathcal{H}_\perp &= \frac{p_z^2}{2m^*} + V(z) + \frac{\hbar^2 z^2}{2m^* \ell_\parallel^4}, \\
\mathcal{H}_\parallel &= \frac{1}{2m^*}\left[p_x^2 + \frac{\hbar^2}{\ell_\perp^4}(x+X)^2\right], \\
\mathcal{H}' &= \frac{\hbar}{m^* \ell_\parallel^2} z p_x.
\end{aligned} \tag{6.129}$$

In Eq.(6.129), $\ell_\parallel^2 = \hbar c/eB_y$, $\ell_\perp^2 = \hbar c/eB_z$ are the two components of the total magnetic length ℓ_0, and $X \equiv k_y \ell_\perp^2$ is the center coordinate of the cyclotron motion. The potential energy $V(z)$ in the z direction, which gives rise to the subbands, is given explicitly in [6.68]. In the following discussions we consider only the lowest subband.

Unlike the situation where the parallel component of the field is zero, the variables are not separable in the present case, without specifying the nature of the potential $V(z)$. Following *Ando* [6.69], we consider a simple choice of the basis as

$$\psi_{n,X}(x,y,z) = \exp\left[-\mathrm{i}\frac{X}{\ell_\perp^2}y - \mathrm{i}\frac{\langle z\rangle}{\ell_\parallel^2}(x-X)\right]\chi_n(x-X)\zeta(z) \tag{6.130}$$

where n is the Landau level index, $\chi_n(x)$ is the usual Landau wave function (ignoring the normalization constant)

$$\chi_n(x) = H_n\left[\frac{x}{\ell_\perp}\right]\exp\left[-\frac{x^2}{2\ell_\perp^2}\right], \tag{6.131}$$

$H_n(x)$ is the Hermite polynomial, and

$$\langle z\rangle = \int_0^\infty dz|\zeta(z)|^2 z. \tag{6.132}$$

The function $\zeta(z)$ is chosen to be real and satisfies the following equation:

$$\mathcal{H}_\perp\zeta(z) = E_0(B_y)\zeta(z).$$

If we consider only the lowest subband and neglect couplings between different subbands, the Hamiltonian is diagonal with respect to the motion in the $x-y$ plane for our choice of the basis in (6.130).

For $\zeta(z)$, one can consider the Fang-Howard variational wave function for the lowest subband (5.58)

$$\zeta^2 = \tfrac{1}{2}b^3z^2\mathrm{e}^{-bz}, \tag{6.133}$$

where b is a variational parameter which has to be obtained by minimizing the energy corresponding to the Hamiltonian in (6.128). Following [6.68] for determining b, we arrive at the following equation:

$$\left[\frac{b}{b_0}\right]^4 - \frac{b}{b_0} = \frac{48}{(b_0\ell_\parallel)^4}, \tag{6.134}$$

where b_0 is the value of b when $B_y = 0$ and given in (5.59). There are now several ways to obtain the parameter b. Up to second order in B_y, we can write [6.70]

$$b\ell_\perp = b_0\ell_\perp + \frac{(4\tan\theta)^2}{(b_0\ell_\perp)^3},$$

thereby obtaining b for a given θ and $B_\perp$. *Chakraborty* and *Pietiläinen* [6.71] opted for a numerical solution of (6.134) to obtain b for a given magnetic field and tilt angle. The interesting point to note is that calculation of the energy gap in the presence of a tilted field is now reduced to calculating the energy gap for various values of the finite-thickness parameter b obtained from (6.134).

We have shown in Sect. 5.6 that a finite spread of the wave function perpendicular to the plane effectively softens the short-range divergence of the bare Coulomb interaction when the interelectron spacing is comparable with the inversion layer width. Consequently, the ground-state energy and the excitation energies are quite drastically reduced. At a fixed $B_\perp$, increasing θ means increasing b and a decrease in the dimensionless parameter $\beta = (b\ell_\perp)^{-1}$. As a result, the gap increases with increasing tilt angle. This would mean that the tilt angle squeezes the wave function in the z direction thereby making the electron system more two-dimensional. This simple approach of *Chakraborty* and *Pietiläinen* [6.71] offered a qualitative agreement with the increase of the gap at $\nu = \frac{2}{3}$, but failed to explain the electron-hole symmetry breaking.

Halonen et al. [6.72] studied the effect of subband-Landau level coupling discussed above, in the FQHE regime using finite-size systems in a periodic rectangular geometry (see Sect. 5.1). The appropriate single-particle states are

$$\begin{aligned}\Phi_j(\boldsymbol{r}) = \left[\frac{1}{b'\ell_1\ell_2\pi}\right]^{\frac{1}{2}} \sum_{k=-\infty}^{\infty} \exp\Big\{ \mathrm{i}\left(X_j + ka'\right) y/\ell_0^2 - \left[(X_j + ka' - x\right) \cos\phi \\ + z\sin\phi]^2/2\ell_1^2 - \left[(X_j + ka - x)\sin\phi - z\cos\phi\right]^2/2\ell_2^2 \Big\}\end{aligned} \tag{6.135}$$

where a' and b' are the two sides of the rectangular cell (see Fig. 5.1). The magnetic length is $\ell_0 = (\hbar/m^*\omega_z)^{\frac{1}{2}}$, and $\ell_1 = (\hbar/m^*\omega_1)^{\frac{1}{2}}$, $\ell_2 = (\hbar/m^*\omega_2)^{\frac{1}{2}}$. Index j which describes the linear momentum in y direction, can have values $1 < j \le m$, where m is the Landau-level degeneracy. The two-electron part of the Hamiltonian which includes the Coulomb interaction [see (5.6)] is now written [6.72]

$$\begin{aligned}\mathcal{A}_{j_1,j_2,j_3,j_4} &= \tfrac{1}{2}\int d\boldsymbol{r}_1 \int d\boldsymbol{r}_2\, \Phi^*_{j_1}(\boldsymbol{r}_1)\Phi^*_{j_2}(\boldsymbol{r}_2) v(\boldsymbol{r}_1 - \boldsymbol{r}_2)\Phi_{j_3}(\boldsymbol{r}_2)\Phi_{j_4}(\boldsymbol{r}_1) \\ &= \frac{1}{2ab}\sum_{\boldsymbol{q}}\sum_{s,t} \delta_{q_x,2\pi s/a}\,\delta_{q_y,2\pi t/b}\,\delta'_{j_1-j_4,t}\,\frac{2\pi e^2}{\epsilon q} \\ &\times \exp\left[2\pi\mathrm{i}s(j_1 - j_3)/m - \pi(s^2 + \lambda^2\Omega_1^2 t^2)/(m\lambda\Omega_1)\right] \\ &\times \frac{2}{\sqrt{\pi}} I(s,t)\,\delta'_{j_1+j_2,j_3+j_4}\end{aligned} \tag{6.136}$$

where $v(r)$ is the Coulomb interaction in the periodic rectangular geometry, the Kronecker δ with prime means that the equality is defined modulo m, the summation over q excludes $q_x = q_y = 0$. The last term in (6.136) is written explicitly as follows

$$I(s,t) = \int_0^\infty \exp\left[-z^2 - 2\left\{\frac{\pi}{m\lambda}\frac{s^2+\lambda^2 t^2}{\Omega_3 - \Omega_2^2/\Omega_1}\right\}^{\frac{1}{2}} z\right] \times \cos\left[2\left\{\frac{\pi}{m\lambda}\frac{1}{\Omega_3 - \Omega_2^2/\Omega_1}\right\}^{\frac{1}{2}} \frac{\Omega_2}{\Omega_1} sz\right] dz \quad (6.137)$$

where

$$\Omega_1 = \frac{\omega_1}{\omega_z}\cos^2\phi + \frac{\omega_2}{\omega_z}\sin^2\phi$$

$$\Omega_2 = \left[\frac{\omega_2}{\omega_z} - \frac{\omega_1}{\omega_z}\right]\sin\phi\cos\phi$$

$$\Omega_3 = \frac{\omega_1}{\omega_z}\sin^2\phi + \frac{\omega_2}{\omega_z}\cos^2\phi.$$

The aspect ratio a/b is denoted by λ. As a check, it is easy to verify that when the tilt angle $\theta = 0$ and the strength of the potential $V(z)$ goes to infinity, *i.e.*, $\omega_0 \to \infty$, we obtain $\phi = 0, \Omega_1 \to 1, \Omega_2 \to 0$, and $\Omega_3 \to \infty$.

In the case of the magnetic field perpendicular to the electron plane there is electron-hole symmetry in the lowest Landau level as discussed in Sects. 5.1,2. In that case, the Hamiltonian does not have any explicit dependence on the magnetic field, the properties of $\frac{1}{3}$ and $\frac{2}{3}$ filling factors are always the same. In the present case such an ideal situation, however, does not exist and in order to study the angular dependence of the energy gap for these two filling fractions we need to consider the different frequencies appearing in (6.137) for the two filling fractions. This is obviously a direct consequence of the tilted magnetic field.

We consider the electrons to be in the lowest Landau level and also in the lowest subband. The parameters of the parabolic confinement potential are adjusted such that they correspond to the subband energy of a triangular potential with the Fang-Howard choice of trial wave function. We have considered a six-electron system for the filling factor $\nu = \frac{1}{3}$ and an eight-electron system for $\nu = \frac{2}{3}$. The electrons are considered to be fully spin polarized. For $\frac{1}{3}$ filling, spin reversal in the ground state is not important. But, as explained later in this section, for $\frac{2}{3}$ filling at low magnetic fields, the ground state is known from theory and experiments to be spin unpolarized (total spin, $S = 0$). Therefore, the present work is valid only at high magnetic fields. The energy gap is calculated following the proceedure discussed in Sect. 6.2.

The results for the energy gap (in Kelvin) at $\frac{2}{3}$ filling of the lowest Landau level are shown in Fig. 6.31 as a function of the *total* magnetic field.

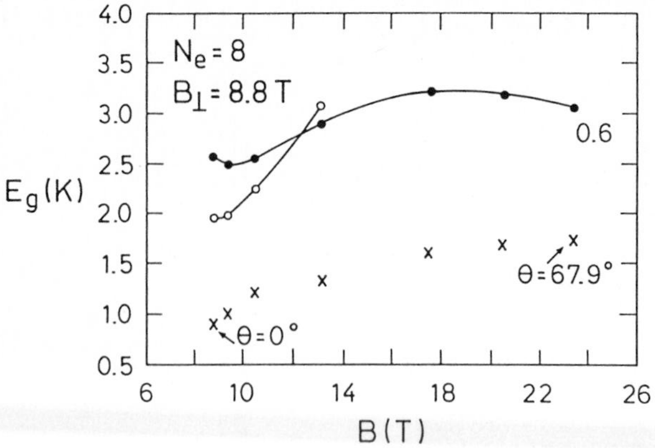

Fig. 6.31. Energy gap E_g (in K) for $\frac{2}{3}$ filling factor as a function of total magnetic field (in Tesla) for $\omega_0/\omega_z = 0.6$. The experimental results (denoted as $\times$) are from [6.67]. The open (closed) points correspond to spin-reversed (spin-polarized) excitations [6.72]

The experimental results of *Haug* et al. [6.67] are also shown for comparison. The angular dependence of the energy gap for large values of the tilt angle is qualitatively the same as found in the experiment. For small tilt angles (*i.e.*, for small values of the total magnetic field), the energy gap shows an unexpected bend upward. This behavior presumably does not have any physical significance since here the fully spin polarized excitations do not have the lowest energy. The excitation energy in this region can in fact be reduced by introducing spin-reversed quasiparticles (see Sect. 6.3). These are plotted in Fig. 6.31 where the Zeeman energy is already included. The angular dependence of the resulting gap is now in good agreement with the experimentally observed behavior. Experimental results for $\nu = \frac{2}{3}$ by *Furneaux* et al. [6.73] are also consistent with these theoretical results.

The results for $\frac{1}{3}$ filling are presented in Fig. 6.32. Although the gap does not decrease with increasing tilt angle as observed by Haug et al., the energy gap as a function of magnetic field is rather flat and its angular dependence is *different* from that of $\frac{2}{3}$ filling. In Fig. 6.33 we have presented the gap ratio for $\frac{1}{3}$ and $\frac{2}{3}$ filling fractions from the experimental data [6.67] and compared with the theoretical results by *Halonen* et al. [6.72]. In order to see the magnetic field dependence of this ratio, we have fitted the calculated value with the experimental result at the lowest magnetic field considered ($\sim$ 10T). Except in the high magnetic field region the calculated magnetic field dependence is found to agree qualitatively with the experimentally observed behavior.

We should mention that even in the case of zero-tilt angle, the magnetic field dependence of the gap is still not clear (see Sect. 6.6). With very

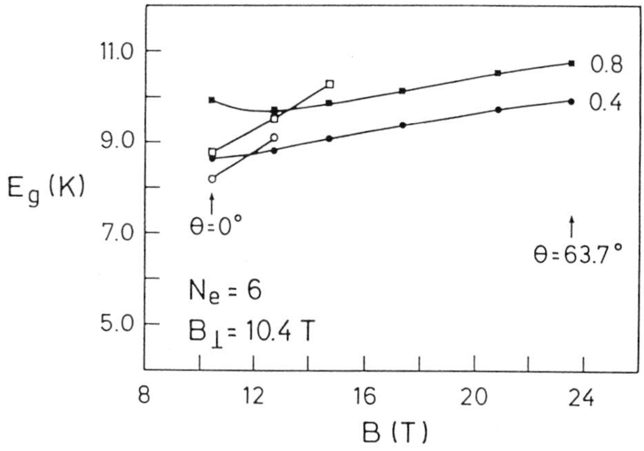

Fig. 6.32. Same as in Fig. 6.31. but for $\frac{1}{3}$ filling of the lowest Landau level [6.72]

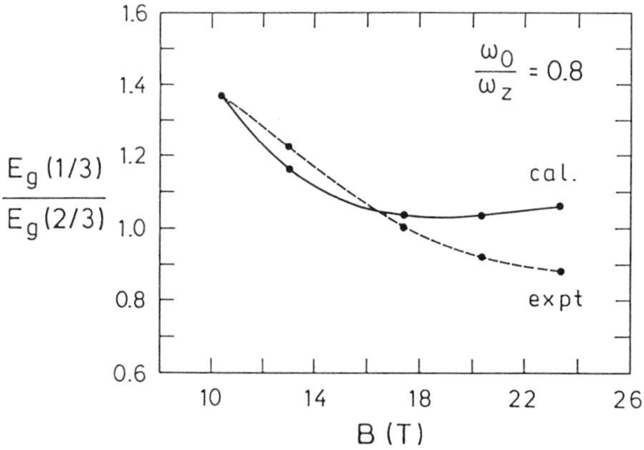

Fig. 6.33. The ratio of the energy gap at $\frac{1}{3}$ and $\frac{2}{3}$ filling fractions. The calculated energy gaps are for $\omega_0/\omega_z = 0.8$ [6.72]

high quality samples, a better quantitative agreement between theoretical and experimental data has been achieved [6.33]. The experimental data for $\nu = \frac{1}{3}$ in [6.67] are of course not from samples of quality similar to those of [6.33]. Moreover, there are only two data points available for $\nu = \frac{1}{3}$. Therefore, unlike the $\frac{2}{3}$ filling, the trend is not clear. The discrepancy in the high-magnetic field region of Fig. 6.33 may be in part due to this experimental uncertainty. More experiments with better quality samples are undoubtedly needed for this filling fraction.

Reversed-Spin States: The first clear-cut evidence for the existence of spin-unpolarized states in the ground state of several filling factors was from the tilted-field experiments by the Oxford group (*Clark* et al. [6.74]). They found that, with increasing tilt-angle, dramatic changes occur in the ρ_{xx} minima of various filling factors. In Fig. 6.34 we present some of the experimental results of ρ_{xx} vs θ by Clark et al. Clearly, the 4/3 state is first destroyed, followed by a reemergence as θ and hence the magnetic field is increased. The same effect was also observed for $\nu = \frac{2}{3}$ [6.75]. In contrast, the ρ_{xx} minima for 5/3 and 1/3 remain essentially unaltered with increasing tilt angle. In fact, the theoretical predictions in Sect. 6.5 and the ground-

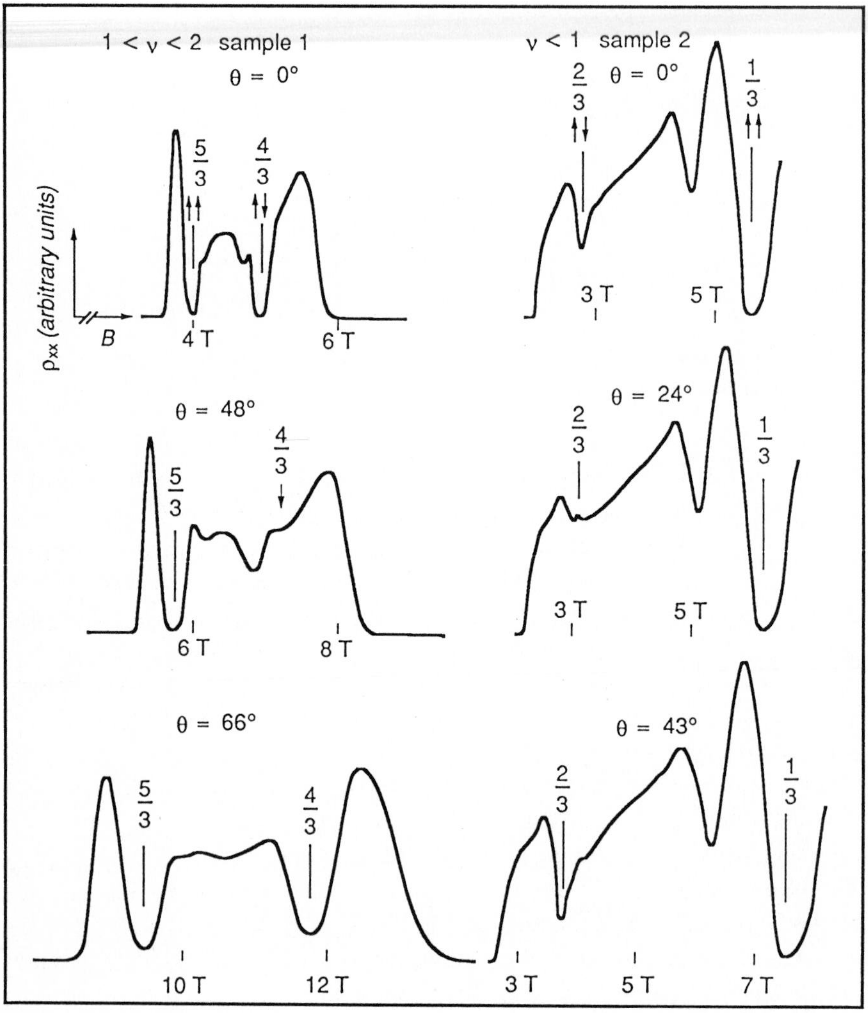

Fig. 6.34. Diagonal resistivity ρ_{xx} for various filling factors vs the titled magnetic field [6.75]

state energy calculations by *Maksym* [6.76] show that at low fields, the 2/3 and 4/3 states should be spin-unpolarized ($S = 0$) (see Table. 6.2) [6.77].

An important clue to understand the experimental results by Clark et al. is the fact that, allowing for the spin degrees of freedom, the electron-hole symmetry is between ν and $2 - \nu$ [6.58]. Therefore, the 1/3 and 5/3 filling factors which are the spin-polarized states even at low magnetic fields, as predicted theoretically (Sect. 5.5), remain unaffected by the tilted-field. For the 2/3 and 4/3 states, the increasing magnetic fields destroy the reversed-spin states and eventually, they reemerge as fully spin polarized states.

Table 6.2. Potential energy (per particle) for the six-electron system at filling factors $\nu = \frac{2}{3}$ and $\nu = \frac{3}{5}$ for various values of spin polarization. The Zeeman energy is not included in the energy values. The unit of energy is $e^2/\epsilon\ell_0$.

	Potential energy				Ground state
ν	$S = 0$	$S = 1$	$S = 2$	$S = 3$	
$\frac{2}{3}$	−0.5331	−0.5291	−0.5257	−0.5232	Unpolarized
$\frac{3}{5}$	−0.5074	−0.5096	−0.5044	−0.50104	Partially polarized

To check that the tilted-field is *not* affecting the wave function in the z-direction, as discussed above, Clark et al. moved the fractional states $\nu = p/q$ to higher $B_\perp$ at $\theta = 0°$ by increasing the electron concentration using persistent photoexcitation techniques. They observed identical effects [6.74], which indicates that increasing the field simply influences the spin states of different filling factors. The experimental work by Clark et al. is an important part of our understanding of the FQHE because it established the theoretical predictions of spin-reversed states discussed in Sect. 5.5, on a firm footing.

Recently the Cambridge group (Davies et al. [6.78]) reported very interesting FQHE experiments in high-quality p-type heterojunctions with tilted magnetic field. They found the same magnetic-field dependent behavior for $\nu = \frac{4}{3}$ as observed in n-type heterojunctions by Clark et al. They also noted that for the two-dimensional hole system one requires a smaller magnetic field to destroy and return the $\frac{4}{3}$ state which suggests that the Zeeman splitting is larger for the present system.

The other important tilted-field experiment indicative of spin-reversed states was by *Eisenstein* et al. [6.79] who discovered a transition between two distinct FQHE states at the same filling factor $\nu = \frac{8}{5}$. The transition is driven by tilting the magnetic field and, as discussed below, the data quite consistently indicate a change from a spin-unpolarized fluid to a polarized fluid. They used a very high-quality sample (two-dimensional carrier concentration of $n = 2.3 \times 10^{11}$ cm^{-2} and mobility of about 7×10^6 cm^2/Vs) to study the $\nu = \frac{8}{5}$ state (Fig. 6.35). As the magnetic field was tilted from the direction perpendicular to the electron plane, an interesting reentrant behavior was observed. Increasing the tilt angle from zero, the $\frac{8}{5}$ state was seen to weaken gradually, and at $\theta \sim 30°$ the ρ_{xx} minimum splits into two weak minima of about equal strength whose field position straddle the location of the $\frac{8}{5}$ filling factor. Increasing the tilt angle further the trend is seen to reverse and at $\theta \sim 37°$ a single, well-developed $\frac{8}{5}$ minimum dominates (Fig. 6.36). Further increase in the tilt angle simply strengthens the minimum. In both the low and high-angle regions the Hall resistance exhibits the expected plateau $\rho_{xy} = 5h/8e^2$.

Eisenstein et al. then measured the activation energy Δ (see Sect. 6.6) versus the tilt angle. For $\theta < 25°$ and $\theta > 40°$ the ρ_{xx} data display activated behavior over almost two decades in resistivity. On the other hand, around $\theta = 30°$ where the $\frac{8}{5}$ minimum split, the temperature dependence is complicated. Figure 6.37 depicts the angular dependence of the observed

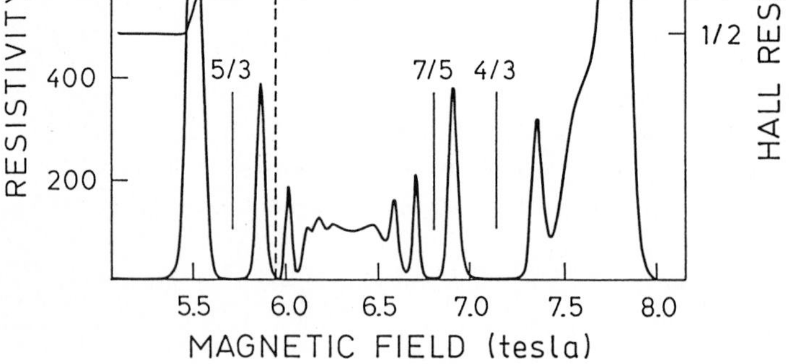

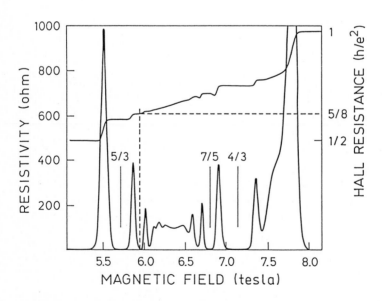

Fig. 6.35. Diagonal resistivity ρ_{xx} and Hall resistance ρ_{xy} at 25 mK, with the magnetic field perpendicular to the two-dimensional plane [6.79]

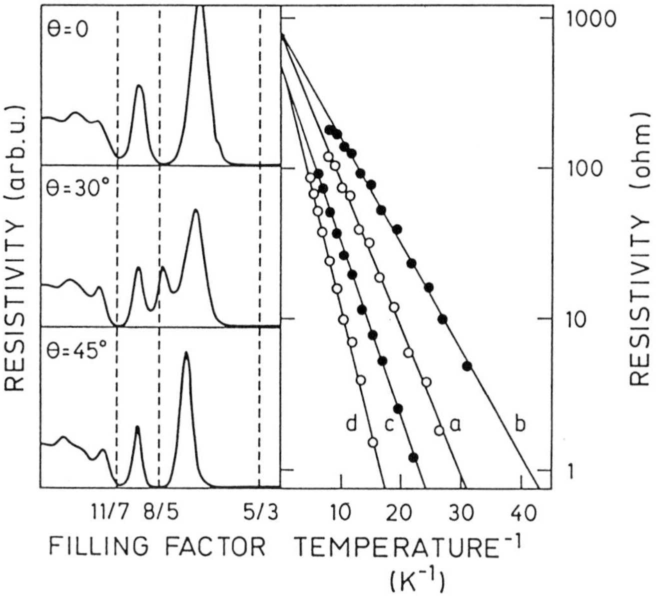

Fig. 6.36. Left panels show the expanded view of ρ_{xx} versus the filling factor in a narrow range around $\nu = \frac{8}{5}$. The right panel shows the arrhenius plots for the $\frac{8}{5}$ minimum at various angles. Plot $a : \theta = 0°; b : \theta = 18.6°; c : \theta = 42.4°$; and $d : \theta = 49.5°$ [6.79]

activation energy, which is the most interesting result as far as the spin-reversed quasiparticles are concerned.

The results presented in Fig. 6.37 are all obtained at a fixed filling factor $\nu = \frac{8}{5}$ and hence a fixed perpendicular magnetic field $B_\perp \sim 5.95$ T. They are plotted against *total* magnetic field, $B_{\text{total}} = B_\perp / \cos\theta$. As θ increases from zero, Δ *decreases* linearly. Beyond about 30°, Δ begins to rise again eventually exceeding its value at $\theta = 0°$. For small angle (*i.e.*, low magnetic field) the ground state is expected to be analogous to the two-spin $\frac{2}{5}$ state (see Sect. 5.5). From the slope $d\Delta/dB_{\text{tot}}$ at small angles in Fig. 6.37, it was found that the g-factor is $g \sim 0.4$ in remarkable agreement with the spin-resonance measurements [6.80] on two-dimensional electrons in GaAs.

At low magnetic fields, the ground state of $\nu = \frac{8}{5}$ is expected to be spin-unpolarized and presumably the low-lying excitations involve spin-reversed quasiparticles. This could explain the linear decrease of the activation energy as the tilt-angle (or the magnetic field) is increased (see below). As the Zeeman energy at $\nu = \frac{8}{5}$ is increased by tilting the magnetic field, the polarized state is energetically favored and eventually it becomes the new ground

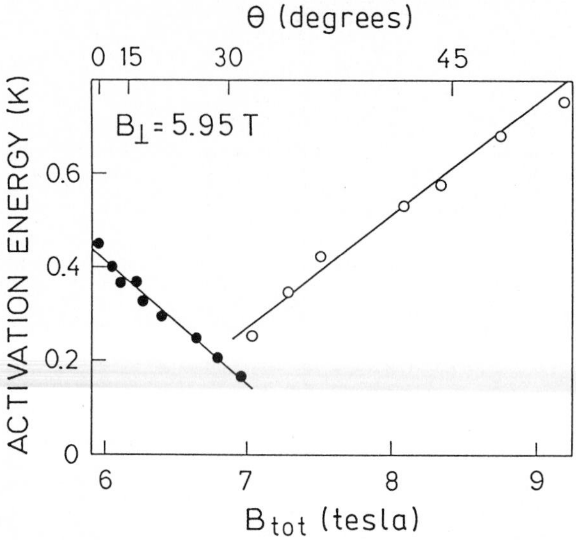

Fig. 6.37. Activation energy of the FQHE state at $\nu = \frac{8}{5}$ versus B_{tot}. Solid and open symbols refer to low-field and high-field components respectively [6.79]

state. The low-lying excitations might still involve spin-reversed quasiparticles. That could explain the linear increase of the activation energy. Further increase of the magnetic field would lead to a fully spin-polarized ground state with Laughlin-type quasiparticle-quasihole excitations and we would expect the usual $B^{\frac{1}{2}}$ behavior of the activation energy (Coulomb gap) seen in Fig. 6.20. The exchange and correlation contributions to the ground-state energy depend to first approximation on $B_\perp$ alone and this is constant at fixed ν.

To summarize the qualitative understanding of the experimental results: at low magnetic fields, the ground states at $\nu = \frac{2}{3}, \frac{4}{3}, \frac{2}{5}$ and $\frac{8}{5}$ are spin unpolarized for low magnetic fields, as expected, and the excitations are also spin reversed. The linear behavior of the activation energy, predicted to be associated with the spin-reversed excitations by *Chakraborty* et al. [6.14,15] (see Sect. 6.3) was indeed observed experimentally. As the magnetic field is further increased the ground state becomes fully polarized but the excitations are still spin-reversed thus explaining the change in the slope of the activation energy curve.

In Fig. 6.38, we present the results for the ground-state energy (per particle) for a four-electron system in a periodic rectangular geometry (see Sect. 5.1 for details) at the filling fractions (a) $\nu = \frac{2}{5}$ and (b) $\nu = \frac{2}{3}$ versus the magnetic field where the Zeeman energy ($g = 0.4$) contributions are included [6.77]. In both cases, we observe a crossover point in the magnetic field below

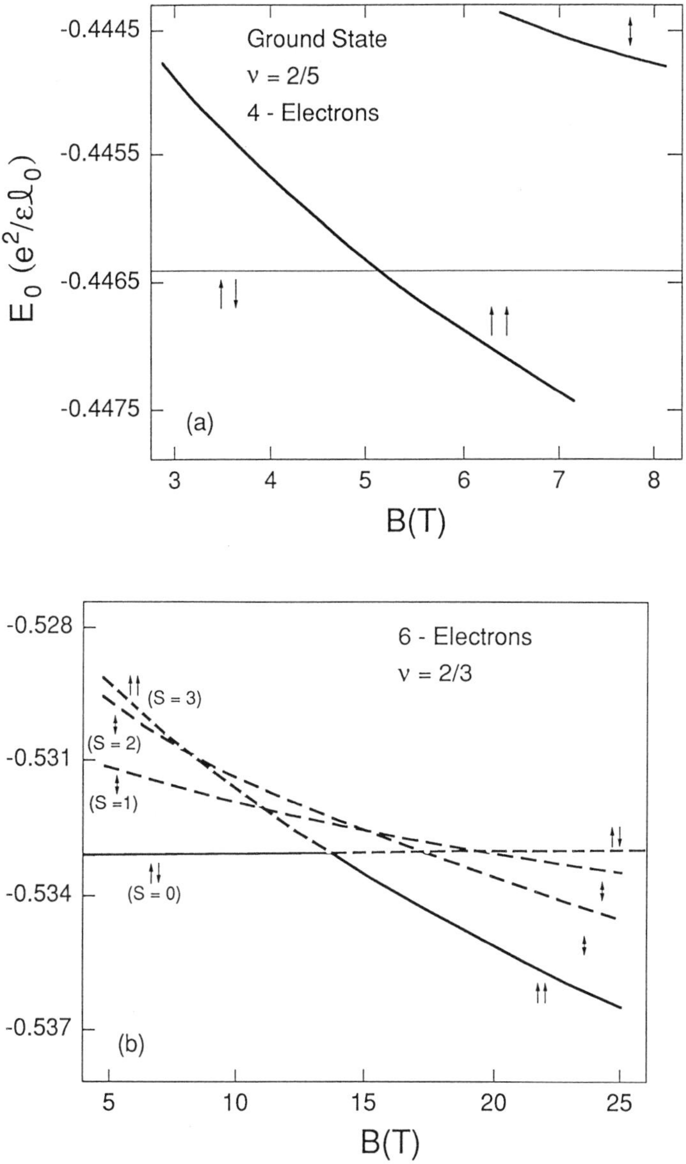

Fig. 6.38. Ground-state energy per particle $(e^2/\epsilon\ell_0)$ vs B (Tesla) for (a) $\nu = \frac{2}{5}$ and (b) $\nu = \frac{2}{3}$ for different spin polarizations [6.78]

which the spin-unpolarized state ($S = 0$) is energetically favored. The fully spin-polarized state ($S = N_e/2, N_e$ is the electron number) is favored for magnetic fields beyond the crossover point. As discussed in Sect. 5.1 the ground-state energies at $\frac{1}{3}$ and $\frac{2}{5}$ filling factors are remarkably insensitive to the system size. Therefore, a similar situation is expected in the present case. From these results it is clear that when we study the quasiparticle (QP)-quasihole (QH) gap (Sect. 6.2), we should consider the two different ground states for two regions of the magnetic field. As discussed in Sect. 6.2, a positive discontinuity of the chemical potential at a certain filling factor signifies a QP-QH excitation energy gap at that filling factor.

The spin-reversed QP-QH gaps for two different ground states (spin-unpolarized and fully spin-polarized) at $\nu = \frac{2}{5}$ are depicted in Fig. 6.39(a). They are the lowest energy excitations in the presence of Zeeman energy. The results are qualitatively similar to the observed behavior at $\nu = \frac{8}{5}$ discussed above. From these calculations *Chakraborty* [6.77] identified the excitations as the spin-reversed QP-QH pair.

The results for the QP-QH gap for $\nu = \frac{2}{3}$ are depicted in Fig. 6.39(b). Just as in Fig. 6.39(a), we plot only the lowest energy excitations as a function of the magnetic field, with the Zeeman energy included. In this case, the situation is clearly different from that of $\nu = \frac{2}{5}$. Below the crossover point the preferred ground state is spin-unpolarized. The lowest energy excitations in this state involve a spin-polarized QP-spin-reversed QH pair. The energy gap decreases rapidly and vanishes before the crossover point is reached. From this point onward the discontinuity in the chemical potential is in fact negative, indicating that FQHE is unstable in this region of magnetic field. Beyond the crossover point, the spin-unpolarized state is no longer the ground state and the energy gap is to be calculated from the fully spin-polarized ground state. In this case spin-reversed QP-spin-polarized QH pair-excitations have the lowest energy and the energy gap steadily increases with the magnetic field. Therefore, between the two ground states exhibiting FQHE there is a *gapless domain* where the FQHE state is not stable. Such a gapless domain is not present at $\nu = \frac{2}{5}$. A somewhat similar situation has indeed been experimentally observed for the filling factor $\nu = \frac{4}{3}$ (electron-hole symmetric to $\frac{2}{3}$) by *Clark* et al. [6.74]. The activation energy for this filling fraction is found to decrease rapidly with increasing magnetic fields. The gap then vanishes for a small region of magnetic field. The gap reappears with increasing magnetic fields. Two recent experiments on $\nu = \frac{2}{3}$ [6.81,82] have failed to observe any gapless domain so far.

The theoretical work on the spin polarization described above leads to a very interesting result for $\nu = \frac{3}{5}$ as shown by *Chakraborty* and *Pietiläinen* [6.83]. In Fig. 6.40 are presented the results for the ground-state energy per particle for $\nu = \frac{3}{5}$ vs the magnetic field where the Zeeman energy ($g = 0.5$) is also included. The results are shown for three values of the total spin ($S = 1, 2$, and 3). Only two states (spin polarized ($\uparrow\uparrow, S = 3$) and partially polarized ($\updownarrow$), with $S = 1$) are found to provide the lowest energy with increasing magnetic fields. The spin-unpolarized state ($S = 0$) is much

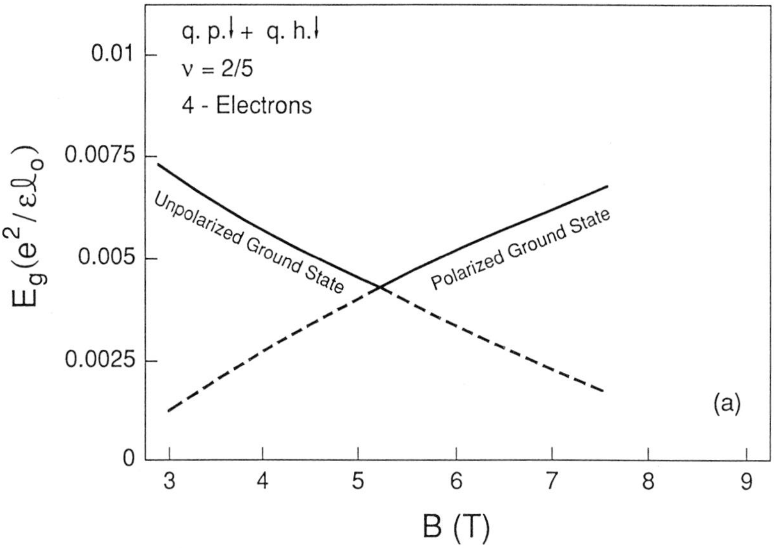

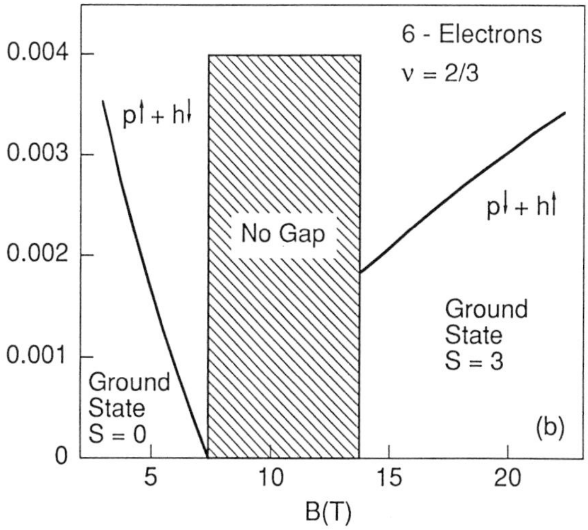

Fig. 6.39. Lowest energy quasiparticle-quasihole gap $(e^2/\epsilon\ell_0)$ vs the magnetic field B (in Tesla) for (a) $\nu = \frac{2}{5}$ and (b) $\nu = \frac{2}{3}$. Above and below the crossover point, two different ground states from Fig. 6.38 are considered. The gap is nonexistent in the shaded region as discussed in the text [6.78]

higher in energy compared to the other two states and is not included in the figure. As for the $\frac{2}{5}$ state, we observe a crossover point in the magnetic field below which the partially polarized spin state is energetically favored. The fully polarized spin state is favored for magnetic fields beyond the crossover point.

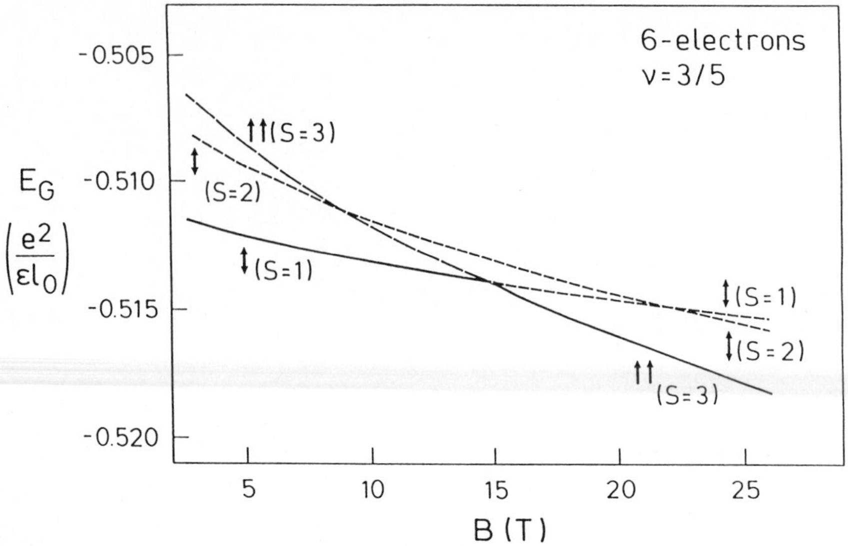

Fig. 6.40. Ground-state energy per particle ($e^2/\epsilon\ell_0$) vs B (Tesla) at $\nu = \frac{3}{5}$ for various spin polarizations; the fully polarized ($\uparrow\uparrow, S = 3$ and partially polarized $\updownarrow, S = 1, 2$) spin states. The dashed lines in all the curves correspond to the energetically unfavored regions [6.84]

The results for the QP-QH gap (in units of $e^2/\epsilon\ell_0$) vs the magnetic field are presented in Fig. 6.41. The Zeeman energy contribution has been included in these results. At low magnetic fields (up to $\sim$ 7.5 T), the spin-reversed-QP–spin-polarized-QH gap is found to have the lowest energy (region I). With increasing magnetic fields, for a short range of magnetic fields (up to $\sim$ 9.5 T) the spin-reversed QH – the spin-polarized QP gap is favored energetically (region II). For a further increase of magnetic fields up to the crossover point (region III), a spin-reversed QP-QH gap is found to have the lowest energy. In the region of magnetic field beyond the crossover point, the spin-partially-polarized state is no longer the ground state and the energy gap is to be calculated from the fully spin-polarized ground state. In this state for $15 \lesssim B \lesssim 21$ T, the gap is, in fact, first *negative* for a few values of B and then vanishingly small, indicating that the FQHE is no longer observable here. The energy gap is however, found to reappear beyond 21 T (region IV), first with the spin-reversed QH – spin-polarized QP gap and eventually, for $B \gtrsim 25$ T (region V), a fully spin-polarized QP-QH gap appears to have the lowest energy. The fully spin-polarized gap is quite expected given the very high magnetic fields in this region. But the existence of spin-reversed excitations prior to this region is quite surprising.

In regions I-III, considering the different Zeeman energy contributions for different spin polarizations of QP's and QH's, the novel transitions

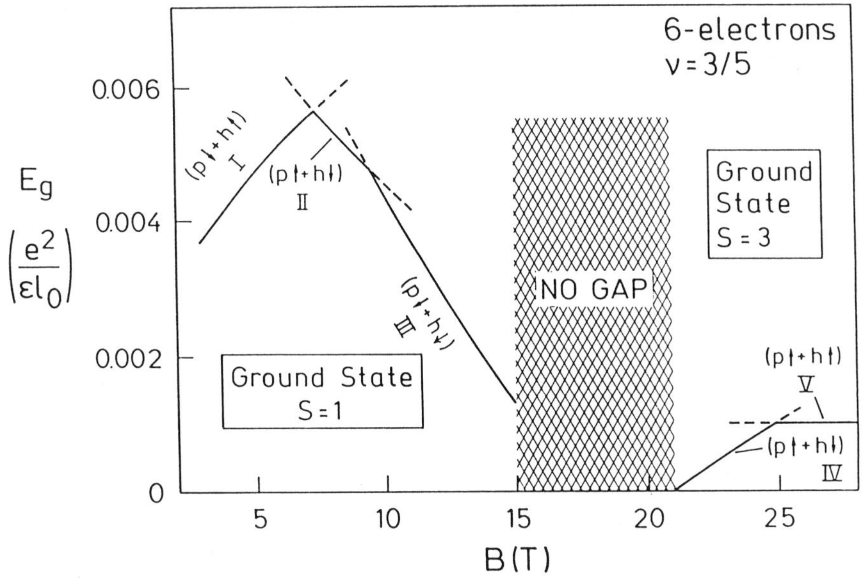

Fig. 6.41. Quasiparticle-quasihole gap $(e^2/\epsilon\ell_0)$ vs the magnetic field B (Tesla) at $\nu = \frac{3}{5}$ for various spin polarizations in two different ground states. The gap is nonexistent in the shaded region, as discussed in the text. The regions I-V are also explained in the text [6.84]

should be observable. The activation energy is expected to be linear in all three states, but the slopes will be different because of the different Zeeman energies. The activation energy in region IV will also be linear while that in the region V does not have a Zeeman contribution and hence a $B^{\frac{1}{2}}$ behavior is expected. An experimental investigation of the activation energy at this filling fraction would be very interesting. If the activation-energy measurements confirm the above predictions for the spin assignments in the energy gap, it would be possible to distinguish the spin-reversed QP state from the spin-reversed QH state. *Sachrajda* et al. [6.84,85] and *Engel* et al. [6.86] have explored some of the filling factors described above in tilted fields. More theoretical and experimental work will be needed to get a satisfactory understanding of the spin-reversed states at filling fractions other than $\nu = \frac{4}{3}$ and $\nu = \frac{5}{3}$.

To summarize this section: The theoretical work on the reversed-spin states in the fractional Hall states has received strong support from recent experiments. At low magnetic fields, the ground state and elementary excitations may not be simply Coulomb induced, but, depending on the filling factor, may be related to reversed spins. The topic is certainly expected to retain much interest for a long time to come.

7. Collective Modes: Intra-Landau Level

In this chapter, we discuss the intra-Landau level collective excitations occurring when the lowest Landau level is fractionally filled. The calculations are mostly focused on the filling factor $\frac{1}{3}$. A few results are available for $\frac{2}{5}$ and are also discussed. Finite-size studies (in the spherical geometry [7.1] as well as in the periodic rectangular geometry [7.2]) are very effective in determining the low-lying collective modes. A Laughlin-type approach with the HNC scheme has not been very successful so far because of the inability of the HNC approach to obtain the correct quasiparticle excitation energy (see preceding chapter, and also [7.3]). The single-mode approximation, which is based on the Feynman's theory of collective excitations for liquid ^{4}He, has been quite successful in bringing out a physical picture for the collective mode. These topics are discussed in detail below. The collective excitations for the FQHE in a superlattice are also described below where in addition to the single-mode approximation for the intra-layer correlations a mean-field theory was introduced to handle the inter-layer correlations.

7.1 Finite-Size Studies: Spherical Geometry

The calculation of the low-lying excitation spectrum for the incompressible fluid state at $\nu = \frac{1}{3}$ in finite-size systems was initiated by *Haldane* and *Rezayi* [7.1,2]. We have discussed earlier their results for the ground state and the quasiparticle-quasihole states obtained in a spherical geometry. In this geometry, the full energy-level spectrum for a seven-electron system at $\nu = \frac{1}{3}$ in the lowest Landau level is shown in Fig. 7.1. The figure contains several interesting features. The ground state appears to be non-degenerate with angular momentum $L = 0$, and is well separated from the other energy levels. The set of low-lying excitations for increasing value of L may be identified as a branch of neutral elementary excitations.

In the spherical geometry, the states of a neutral particle are described by spherical harmonic wave functions. The spectrum for neutral excitations

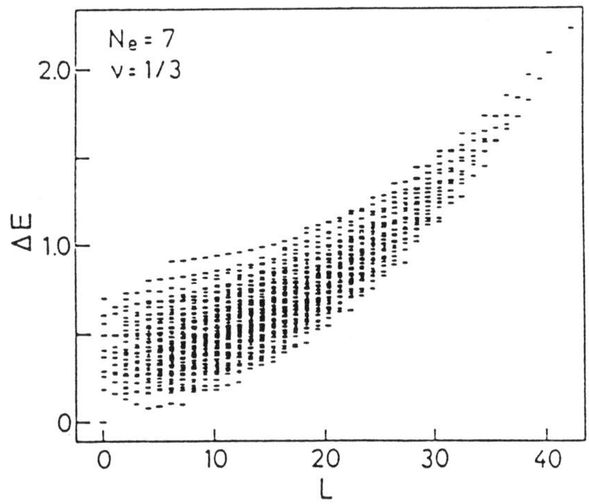

Fig. 7.1. Complete excitation spectrum of 1656 multiplets (50388 states) of a seven-electron system at $\nu = \frac{1}{3}$ in a spherical geometry with the lowest Landau level Coulomb interaction [7.1]

is plotted in Fig. 7.2, as a function of the effective wave number $k = L/R$, where L is the total angular momentum and R is the radius of the sphere. The lowest energy excitations clearly show a collective behavior, well separated from the higher energy states. The excitation gap has a minimum at $k\ell_0 \approx 1.4$. The large L (large k) limit is identified as a well separated quasiparticle-quasihole pair. The mean square separation (chord distance) is given as $2RL/N = k\ell_0^2/\nu$. At large k, the excitation energy of the *quasiexciton* must approach the value of E_g as discussed in the preceding chapter. Numerical calculations for the collective excitation spectrum in the spherical geometry have also been performed by *Fano* et al. [7.4] at $\nu = \frac{1}{3}$ for a nine-electron system and at $\nu = \frac{1}{5}$ for a seven-electron system. Their results for the lowest energy excitations are shown in Fig. 7.3.

7.2 Rectangular Geometry: Translational Symmetry

In the case of a periodic rectangular geometry, the major contribution to calculating the collective excitation spectrum was also by *Haldane* [7.2]. The earlier works by *Su* [7.5,6] on the excitation spectrum in a periodic rectangular geometry were based on the formalism developed by Yoshioka et al. (Sect. 7.1), which gives a q-fold degenerate ground state at $\nu = p/q$.

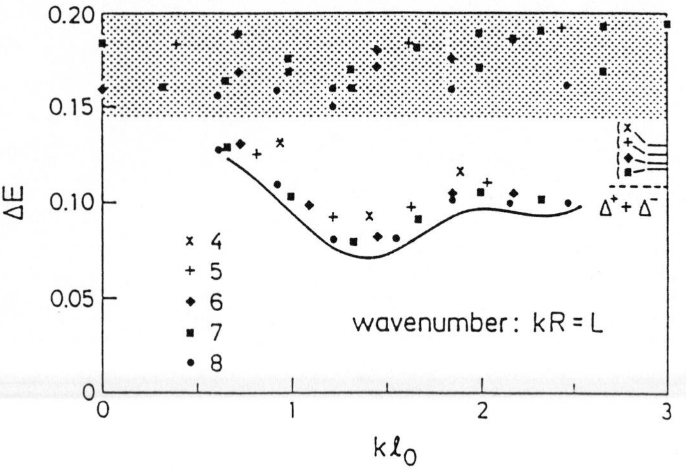

Fig. 7.2. Low-lying excitations at $\nu = \frac{1}{3}$ for four- to eight-electron systems in a spherical geometry. The full line is a guide to the eye. The estimate of $E_g = \Delta^+ + \Delta^-$ for various system size are also given [7.1]

In Laughlin's theory, as well as in the spherical geometry results, the ground state, however, is nondegenerate. This q-fold ground-state degeneracy was considered by many authors as an intrinsic feature to the FQHE [7.7–9]. In his work, Haldane pointed out that the formalism described in Sect. 5.1 employs essentially one-particle symmetry analysis. Introducing translational symmetry into the system, Haldane then found that the q-fold ground-state degeneracy could be identified as a center-of-mass degeneracy common to all states and is without any physical significance. It is present, irrespective of whether the system is an incompressible fluid state or not.

The most interesting outcome of Haldane's analysis was that, at rational values of ν, the states could be characterized by a two-dimensional wave vector $\boldsymbol{k}$, and hence the collective excitation spectrum could be calculated in the periodic rectangular geometry. In the following, we describe in detail the translational symmetry analysis of a two-dimensional many-electron system in a magnetic field.

As we recall, in Sect. 5.1 the finite-size studies were carried out in an infinite lattice with a rectangular geometry. The electrons in one cell of the lattice have identical mirror images in all other cells. This infinite repetition will introduce a symmetry which can be employed to classify the eigenstates of the Hamiltonian. This classification has a further advantange that the size of the matrix to be numerically diagonalized is reduced.

In the absence of a magnetic field, the symmetry analysis would be simple: we would have a translational group in the periodic lattice and the

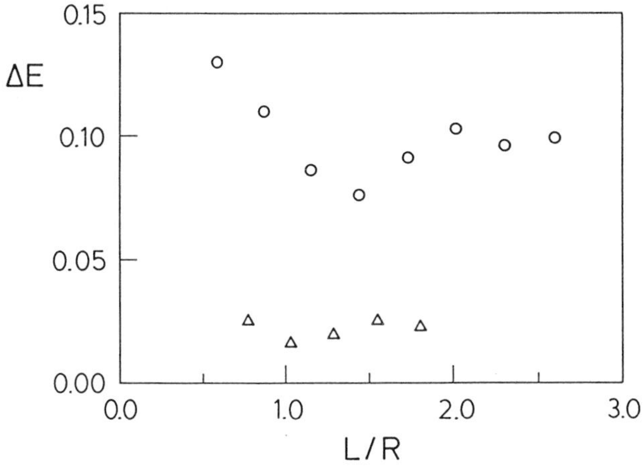

Fig. 7.3. Collective mode at $\nu = \frac{1}{3}$ (for $N_e = 9$, plotted as circles) and at $\nu = \frac{1}{5}$ (for $N_e = 7$, plotted as triangles) [7.4]

eigenstates could be labeled by the wave vectors in the inverse lattice. The physical interpretation of these quantum numbers would of course be the momentum. The presence of the magnetic field, however, slightly complicates the classification scheme. To proceed we could apply the well-known apparatus of group theory which would lead us to the so called *ray representation* of the magnetic translation group [7.2,10–12]. The reason why we do not obtain an ordinary representation is that the symmetry operations of the group obey a non-commutative algebra where the product of operators is an operator of the same group only to within a phase factor. We will take a more direct approach, however. Our aim is to find a complete set of operators which commute with the Hamiltonian and can therefore be simultaneously diagonalized with it. To this end we will closely follow the work of *Haldane* [7.2].

We start with the Hamiltonian operator in configuration space

$$\mathcal{H} = \frac{1}{2m^*} \sum_j \boldsymbol{\Pi}_j^2 + \frac{1}{2} \sum_{i \neq j} V(\boldsymbol{r}_i - \boldsymbol{r}_j) \tag{7.1}$$

where the momentum in the presence of the vector potential $\boldsymbol{A}$ is given by

$$\boldsymbol{\Pi}_j = -\mathrm{i}\hbar \nabla_j - e\boldsymbol{A}(\boldsymbol{r}_j). \tag{7.2}$$

Since we are working in rectangular geometry the most natural choice for the vector potential is to use the Landau gauge. We therefore consider the case, $\boldsymbol{A} = Bx\widehat{\boldsymbol{y}}$. The magnetic field $\boldsymbol{B}$ is then perpendicular to our two-dimensional configuration space. The first step is to find an operator which commutes with the Hamiltonian. It is easy to verify that the quantity

$$\boldsymbol{K}_j = -\boldsymbol{p}_j - eBy_j\widehat{\boldsymbol{x}} \tag{7.3}$$

is such an operator. We now want an operator which corresponds to the translation operator in the non-magnetic field case and can thus be used to construct the momentum eigenstates of the system. We therefore proceed as in the normal system and define the *magnetic translation operator*

$$T(\boldsymbol{L}) = \exp\left\{-\frac{\mathrm{i}}{\hbar}\boldsymbol{L}\cdot\boldsymbol{K}\right\}. \tag{7.4}$$

When we make use of the operator relation

$$\mathrm{e}^A\mathrm{e}^B = \mathrm{e}^{\frac{1}{2}[A,B]}\,\mathrm{e}^{A+B}\,,$$

provided that $[A,[A,B]] = [B,[A,B]] = 0$, the operator T can be split into two parts

$$T_j(\boldsymbol{L}) = \exp\left\{\frac{\mathrm{i}}{\ell_0^2}(L_x y_j - \frac{1}{2}L_x L_y)\right\}\, t_j(\boldsymbol{L}) \tag{7.5}$$

where t_j is the ordinary translation operator.[1] Using this relation it is easy to show that the magnetic translation operators obey the algebra given by

$$T_j(\boldsymbol{L}_1)T_j(\boldsymbol{L}_2) = \exp\left\{\frac{\mathrm{i}}{2\ell_0^2}\widehat{\boldsymbol{z}}\cdot\boldsymbol{L}_1\times\boldsymbol{L}_2\right\}T_j(\boldsymbol{L}_1+\boldsymbol{L}_2)\,, \tag{7.6}$$

which is a gauge independent result. From (7.6) it follows that,

$$T_j(\boldsymbol{L}_1)T_j(\boldsymbol{L}_2) = \exp\left\{\frac{\mathrm{i}}{\ell_0^2}\widehat{\boldsymbol{z}}\cdot\boldsymbol{L}_1\times\boldsymbol{L}_2\right\}T_j(\boldsymbol{L}_2)T_j(\boldsymbol{L}_1). \tag{7.7}$$

It is therefore impossible to remove the phase factor by redefinition of the magnetic operators. The magnetic translations thus form a ray representation of the translation group and cannot be transformed into a vector representation. As a special application of (7.6), we get the quantization

[1] In the case of the symmetric gauge vector potential, $\boldsymbol{A} = \frac{1}{2}\boldsymbol{B}\times\boldsymbol{r}$, the magnetic translation operator can easily be evaluated to be,

$$T_j(\boldsymbol{L}) = \exp\left\{\frac{\mathrm{i}}{2\ell_0^2}\left(\widehat{\boldsymbol{z}}\times\boldsymbol{L}\right)\cdot\boldsymbol{r}_j\right\}\, t_j(\boldsymbol{L}).$$

rule for the number N_{s} of magnetic flux quanta passing through a unit cell as

$$L_x L_y = 2\pi \ell_0^2 N_{\mathrm{s}}, \tag{7.8}$$

when we let the translation vectors $\boldsymbol{L}_1$ and $\boldsymbol{L}_2$ be the unit vectors of the lattice and require that circling the unit cell gives us the identity operator, *i.e.*

$$T_j(L_x\widehat{\boldsymbol{x}})T_j(L_y\widehat{\boldsymbol{y}})T_j(-L_x\widehat{\boldsymbol{x}})T_j(-L_y\widehat{\boldsymbol{y}}) = 1. \tag{7.9}$$

From (7.9) we obtain,

$$\frac{1}{\ell_0^2}\widehat{\boldsymbol{z}} \cdot \boldsymbol{L}_1 \times \boldsymbol{L}_2 = 2\pi N_{\mathrm{s}}. \tag{7.10}$$

The phase factor in (7.6) is thus related to the number of flux quanta passing through the cell. Due to the periodic structure of the configuration space the physical quantities must be invariant under magnetic translations by the amount of any lattice vector. Thus the physical states must be constructed from the eigenstates of these operators and the physical operators from the gauge invariant products of these same eigenstates. By applying a translation which does not correspond to a lattice vector we merely move the representation of our system to another Hilbert space.

Thus far we have treated only single particle operators. To proceed to the many-body system it is useful to define quantities p and q such that the number of electrons N_{e} and flux quanta N_{s} in the unit cell can be expressed in the forms $N_{\mathrm{e}} = pN$ and $N_{\mathrm{s}} = qN$ respectively. Here N is the highest common divisor of N_{e} and N_{s}. The filling factor ν in terms of these quantities is $\nu = p/q$. The center of mass (CM) translation operator $\bar{T}$ which moves every particle by the same vector $\boldsymbol{a}$ is clearly given by

$$\bar{T}(\boldsymbol{a}) = \prod_i T_i(\boldsymbol{a}). \tag{7.11}$$

We now require that the CM translation will not affect the single particle states which are labeled by the eigenvalues of the operators T_i. The most general translation satisfying this requirement is found to be of the form [7.2],

$$\boldsymbol{a} = \frac{1}{N_{\mathrm{s}}}\boldsymbol{L}_{mn} \tag{7.12}$$

where $\boldsymbol{L}_{mn}$ is a lattice vector $[mL_x\widehat{\boldsymbol{x}} + nL_y\widehat{\boldsymbol{y}}]$. Other forms of translation will change the Hilbert space of the system.

Physically, the the overall motion of the system is not very interesting. We therefore split the translation of the particle i into two parts: the CM motion and the relative motion. We define the *relative translation operator* $\widetilde{T}_i$ acting on particle i in such a way that the motion of that particle is compensated by the movement of all the other particles in the opposite direction thus leaving the CM of the system untouched. We then have,

$$\widetilde{T}_i(\boldsymbol{a}) = \prod_j T_i(\boldsymbol{a}/N_\mathrm{e})T_j(\boldsymbol{a}/N_\mathrm{e}). \tag{7.13}$$

Using the algebra (7.6) it is straightforward to verify that the system is invariant under the application of this operator to all the particles, *i.e.*

$$\prod_i \widetilde{T}_i(\boldsymbol{a}) = 1. \tag{7.14}$$

The decomposition of the single particle translation into the CM and relative parts can easily be found to be

$$T_i(\boldsymbol{a}) = T(\boldsymbol{a}/N_\mathrm{e})\widetilde{T}_i(\boldsymbol{a}). \tag{7.15}$$

The relative translation operators will be our fundamental operators providing the quantum numbers we are seeking for the classification of the states of the system. It is thus important to find all operators which leave the Hilbert space invariant and commute with each other. These operators can therefore be simultaneously diagonalized—together with the Hamiltonian. The eigenvalues of the operators of this set will give us a complete set for labeling the many-particle states. In other words our task is to find a maximum set $\mathcal{M}$ of translation vectors for which the commutation relation

$$\left[\widetilde{T}_i(\boldsymbol{a}), \widetilde{T}_j(\boldsymbol{b})\right] = 0 \tag{7.16}$$

holds for any particle i and j and for all vectors $\boldsymbol{a}, \boldsymbol{b} \in \mathcal{M}$. To satisfy the requirement for the invariance of the Hilbert space, these operators must also commute with the operators $T_k(\boldsymbol{L}_{mn})$. Explicit calculations show that this maximum set is given by

$$\mathcal{M} = \{p\boldsymbol{L}_{mn}\}. \tag{7.17}$$

Having now a suitable set of operators at our disposal we still have to give a physical interpretation to their eigenvalues. To this end, we write the eigenvalues of the operator $\widetilde{T}_i(\boldsymbol{a})$ in the form $\mathrm{e}^{\mathrm{i}\boldsymbol{k}\cdot\boldsymbol{a}}$ in analogy with the normal translation operators. We now make the physically plausible statement that the application of the normal momentum operator $\sum_i \mathrm{e}^{\mathrm{i}\boldsymbol{Q}\cdot\boldsymbol{r}_i}$ to a many-particle state will increase its momentum by an amount $\boldsymbol{Q}$ provided $\boldsymbol{Q}$ is an allowed wave vector, *i.e.* a vector in the inverse lattice. It is straightforward to verify the relation

$$\widetilde{T}_i(p\boldsymbol{L}_{mn})\Big(\sum_j \mathrm{e}^{\mathrm{i}\boldsymbol{Q}\cdot\boldsymbol{r}_j}\Big) = \mathrm{e}^{\mathrm{i}\boldsymbol{Q}\cdot p\boldsymbol{L}_{mn}/N_\mathrm{e}}\Big(\sum_j \mathrm{e}^{\mathrm{i}\boldsymbol{Q}\cdot\boldsymbol{r}_j}\Big)\widetilde{T}_i(p\boldsymbol{L}_{mn}) \qquad (7.18)$$

from which we can deduce that the eigenvalues of the relative translation operator can be written in the form $\mathrm{e}^{2\pi\mathrm{i}(ms+nt)/N}$ where s and t are integers. As a special case we can take the vector $\boldsymbol{L}_{mn}$ to be $L_x\widehat{\boldsymbol{x}}$ and $L_y\widehat{\boldsymbol{y}}$ in turn and find that the spectrum of $\widetilde{T}_i$ consists of N^2 points in the inverse lattice.[2] From (7.18) we can also find the connection to the true physical momentum:

$$\boldsymbol{k}\ell_0 = \sqrt{\frac{2\pi}{N_\mathrm{s}\lambda}}\left(s - s_0, \lambda(t-t_0)\right) . \qquad (7.19)$$

Here we have denoted by λ the aspect ratio L_x/L_y and by (s_0, t_0) the quantum numbers corresponding to zero momentum. This particular state can be identified by its symmetry properties. In reciprocal space the $\boldsymbol{k} = 0$ state has the highest symmetry and should therefore remain invariant under all symmetry operations. Thus the eigenvalues of the relative translation operator for this particular state must satisfy

$$\widetilde{T}_i(pL_x\widehat{\boldsymbol{x}}) = \widetilde{T}_i(pL_y\widehat{\boldsymbol{y}}) = \widetilde{T}_i(pL_y\widehat{\boldsymbol{y}} - pL_x\widehat{\boldsymbol{x}}). \qquad (7.20)$$

After a little algebra we find that

$$\mathrm{e}^{2\pi\mathrm{i}s_0/N} = \mathrm{e}^{2\pi\mathrm{i}t_0/N} = (-1)^{pq(N_\mathrm{e}-1)}. \qquad (7.21)$$

This relation will uniquely determine the $\boldsymbol{k} = 0$ state in the Brillouin zone of the reciprocal lattice. If for example the number of electrons N_e is odd then the state for which $(s,t) = (0,0)$ also has $\boldsymbol{k} = 0$. For an even number of electrons the analysis is only slightly more involved. The incompressible fluid state is now characterized by the relative part of the Hamiltonian having a nondegenerate ground state at $\boldsymbol{k} = 0$ and a finite gap for all excitations.

Having completed the symmetry analysis we will apply previous results to the construction of basis states suitable for numerical diagonalization of

[2] It is interesting to note that, in the case of *irrational* filling factors which are obtained as the limit of a sequence where N_e and N_s have the common divisor $N = 1$, the two-dimensional reciprocal space cannot be constructed. In this case, the symmetry analysis of Yoshioka et al. in Sect. 5.1 is complete (see [7.2]).

the Hamiltonian matrix. These states are formed from the single particle eigenstates,

$$\begin{aligned}\phi_{Kj}(\boldsymbol{r}) = C_K \sum_k \exp\left[\frac{\mathrm{i}}{\ell_0^2}(X_j + kL_x)y - \frac{1}{2\ell_0^2}(X_j + kL_x - x)^2\right] \\ \times H_K\left[\frac{1}{\ell_0}(X_j + kL_x - x)\right]\end{aligned} \tag{7.22}$$

of the Hamiltonian operator $\mathcal{H} = \frac{1}{2m}\boldsymbol{\Pi}^2$. Here C_K is the normalization constant, $X_j = \dfrac{2\pi\ell_0^2}{L_y}j$, and H_K is the Hermite polynomial. The quantum number K labels the Landau level and the momentum label j takes values $0, 1, \ldots \pmod{N_\mathrm{s}}$. A direct calculation shows that the states (7.22) are also eigenstates of the translation operators $T(\boldsymbol{L}_{mn})$ defined in (7.5) with eigenvalues 1. We denote by $|j_1, j_2, \ldots, j_{N_\mathrm{e}}\rangle$ the state of N_e electrons constructed from the single particle states (7.22). For simplicity we have omitted the Landau level index as well as the spin label of the electrons. Implicitly, however, we assume that these labels are included in the indices j_i. It is a simple matter to show that these product states are eigenstates of a subset of the relative translation operators:

$$\widetilde{T}_i(pnL_y\widehat{\boldsymbol{y}})|j_1, j_2, \ldots, j_{N_\mathrm{e}}\rangle = \exp\left\{2\pi\mathrm{i}\frac{n}{N}t\right\}|j_1, j_2, \ldots, j_{N_\mathrm{e}}\rangle. \tag{7.23}$$

Here t is the sum of the individual momenta of all particles, $t = \sum_i j_i \pmod{N}$. On the other hand translations in the x-direction will not leave these states invariant. They are instead mapped to another state, namely

$$\widetilde{T}_i(pmL_x\widehat{\boldsymbol{x}})|j_1, j_2, \ldots, j_{N_\mathrm{e}}\rangle = |j_1 - qm, j_2 - qm, \ldots, j_{N_\mathrm{e}} - qm\rangle. \tag{7.24}$$

Using this last relation it is straightforward to construct superpositions which are eigenstates of an arbitrary relative translation operator. We denote by $\mathcal{L}$ the minimum set of all states $|j_1, j_2, \ldots, j_{N_\mathrm{e}}\rangle$ for which the total momentum is t and every member $|j_1, j_2, \ldots, j_{N_\mathrm{e}}\rangle$ of the set $\mathcal{L}$ is related to every other member $|j_1', j_2', \ldots, j_{N_\mathrm{e}}'\rangle$ of the same set by

$$|j_1', j_2', \ldots, j_{N_\mathrm{e}}'\rangle = |j_1 - qk, j_2 - qk, \ldots, j_{N_\mathrm{e}} - qk\rangle \tag{7.25}$$

where k is an arbitrary integer. The number of elements $|\mathcal{L}|$, in this set, is at most N since the momenta j_i are defined $\pmod{N_\mathrm{s}}$ and $qN = N_\mathrm{s}$. The above relation can also be viewed as an equivalence relation which divides all states with a given t into equivalence classes $\mathcal{L}$. The number of these classes is roughly the fraction $1/N$ of the total number of the states. It is clear from the construction that all states in a set $\mathcal{L}$ are mapped by (7.24) to states in the same set. The requirement of the minimality of the set $\mathcal{L}$ also guarantees that $\mathcal{L}$ does not contain any proper subset with the same properties. Applying the operator $\widetilde{T}_i(\boldsymbol{L}_{mn})$ to the state

$$|(0,t);\mathcal{L}\rangle = \sum_{k=0}^{|\mathcal{L}|-1} |j_1 - qk, j_2 - qk, \dots, j_{N_\mathrm{e}} - qk\rangle, \quad |j_1, j_2, \dots, j_{N_\mathrm{e}}\rangle \in \mathcal{L} \tag{7.26}$$

reveals that it is indeed an eigenstate of this operator with the eigenvalues $e^{2\pi \mathrm{i} nt/N}$. The remaining eigenstates can be found with the help of the relation (7.18) which we use to create momentum in the x-direction. Thus we finally arrive at the complete set of normalized states

$$|(s,t);\mathcal{L}\rangle = \frac{1}{\sqrt{|\mathcal{L}|}} \sum_{k=0}^{|\mathcal{L}|-1} \exp\left\{\frac{2\pi \mathrm{i} s}{N} k\right\} |j_1 - qk, j_2 - qk, \dots, j_{N_\mathrm{e}} - qk\rangle \tag{7.27}$$

which belong to the relative momentum (7.19) and are appropriate for numerical finite-size studies.

The procedure to construct the basis states is now summarized as follows: Let us start with the filling fraction $\nu = p/q$, where the integers p and q have no common factors other than 1. Let us now select the number of electrons such that $N_\mathrm{e} = pN$ for some integer N. The number of flux quanta would then be, $N_\mathrm{s} = qN$. Next we choose the momentum label t, $0 \le t < N$, in the y-direction and construct the set of all states $|j_1, j_2, \dots, j_{N_\mathrm{e}}\rangle$ for which $\sum j_i = t \pmod{N_\mathrm{s}}$. We then partition this set into equivalence classes in such a way that each member $|j_1, j_2, \dots, j_{N_\mathrm{e}}\rangle$ of an equivalence class $\mathcal{L}$ is related to any other member $|j_1', j_2', \dots, j_{N_\mathrm{e}}'\rangle$ of the same class by (7.25). We now select the momentum label s, $0 \le s < N$, in the x-direction and map each class by (7.27) to a momentum eigenstate corresponding to the total momentum k given by (7.19).

With the basis states constructed as above, the excitation spectrum is now calculated for a system containing a finite number of spin-polarized electrons [7.2,13]. The many-electron Hamiltonian, (5.4–6) is rewritten as

$$\mathcal{H} = \sum_j K\hbar\omega_\mathrm{c}\, a^\dagger_{Kj} a_{Kj} + \sum_{\substack{j_1 j_2 \\ j_3 j_4}} \sum_{\substack{K_1 K_2 \\ K_3 K_4}} \mathcal{A}_{K_1 j_1 K_2 j_2 K_3 j_3 K_4 j_4}\, a^\dagger_{K_1 j_1} a^\dagger_{K_2 j_2} a_{K_3 j_3} a_{K_4 j_4} \tag{7.28}$$

where K is the Landau level index and,

$$\mathcal{A}_{K_1 j_1 K_2 j_2 K_3 j_3 K_4 j_4} = \delta'_{j_1 + j_2, j_3 + j_4} \mathcal{F}_{K_1 K_2 K_3 K_4}(j_1 - j_4, j_2 - j_3), \tag{7.29}$$

$$\mathcal{F}_{K_1K_2K_3K_4}(j_a, j_b) = \frac{1}{2ab} \sum_q{}' \sum_{k_1} \sum_{k_2} \delta_{q_x, 2\pi k_1/a} \delta_{q_y, 2\pi k_2/b} \delta'_{j_a k_2}$$
$$\times \frac{2\pi e^2}{\epsilon q} \left[\frac{8 + 9(q/b') + 3(q/b')^2}{8(1 + q/b')^3} \right] \mathcal{B}_{K_1K_4}(q) \mathcal{B}_{K_2K_3}(-q)$$
$$\times \exp\left(-\tfrac{1}{2} q^2 \ell_0^2 - 2\pi \mathrm{i} k_1 j_b / N_s\right) , \tag{7.30}$$

$$\mathcal{B}_{K_1K_2}(q) = \begin{cases} 1 & K_1 = K_2 = 0 \\ -\dfrac{\mathrm{i}q_x + q_y}{\sqrt{2}} \ell_0 & K_1 = 0,\ K_2 = 1 \\ -\dfrac{\mathrm{i}q_x - q_y}{\sqrt{2}} \ell_0 & K_1 = 1,\ K_2 = 0 \\ \left(1 - \tfrac{1}{2} q^2 \ell_0^2\right) & K_1 = K_2 = 1 \end{cases} . \tag{7.31}$$

In (7.30), the finite-thickness correction is also included, with the Fang-Howard variational parameter b' (see Sect. 5.6). In the following, we consider the pure two-dimensional case ($b' = \infty$) only.

In Fig. 7.4 we present the results for the density wave mode obtained for four- to seven-electron systems in the lowest Landau level. Only the three lowest excitation energies are shown. The spectrum is in fact, a function of the two-dimensional vector $\boldsymbol{k}$. In the figure we consider only the absolute value of k. The ground state is obtained at $\boldsymbol{k} = 0$, as expected. The lowest energy excitations are separated from the ground state by a large gap, which

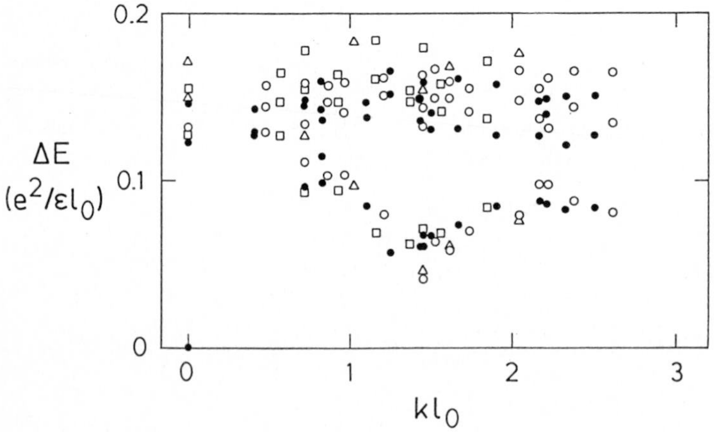

Fig. 7.4. Low-lying excitation energies for four- (△), five- (□), six- (○) and seven-electron (●) systems at $\nu = \frac{1}{3}$

reflects the incompressible nature of the system and they clearly show a collective behavior with a minimum at finite $k\ell_0$ which, as we have seen for the spherical geometry, is a characteristic feature of the excitation spectrum. For small $k\ell_0$, the modes are not very well defined, as they are close to the continuum of the higher energy states. The numerical calculations were done by Yoshioka with an aspect ratio of $N_e/4$, but qualitatively similar results were also obtained earlier by Haldane for a six-electron system in a square geometry. The results are also very similar to the spectrum obtained in the spherical geometry discussed above.

The excitation spectrum as obtained above, can also be used to estimate the quasiparticle–quasihole energy gap, E_g. If we identify the lowest lying excitations as quasiexcitons, E_g would be the asymptotic value of the lowest lying collective dispersion $E(\boldsymbol{k})$ obtained above numerically. As noted by *Kallin* and *Halperin* [7.14], for large values of $k\ell_0$, the quasiexcitons comprise a quasiparticle and a quasihole separated by a large distance, $|\Delta\boldsymbol{r}| = k\ell_0^{*2} = k\ell_0^2 m$, where ℓ_0^* is the effective magnetic length for a particle of charge $e^* = \pm\frac{e}{m}$. For large values of k, we then have

$$E(k) = E_g - \frac{e^{*2}}{\epsilon|\Delta\boldsymbol{r}|} = E_g - \frac{e^2}{m^3\epsilon k\ell_0^2} \tag{7.32}$$

from which the gap is estimated. Using the numerical results for the lowest excitation energy obtained for the maximum value of $k\ell_0$ available in the present numerical work, the gap is estimated to be $E_g \sim 0.1$ [7.13] in agreement with the other theoretical results discussed in Chap. 5. Finally, the effect of mixing of higher Landau levels has been estimated by *Yoshioka* [7.13,15] and found to reduce the energies somewhat.

7.3 Spin Waves

In the earlier sections, we have discussed the role of reversed spins in the ground state and for the quasiparticle-quasihole gap the spin reversed quasiparticles are found to be energetically favorable for low magnetic fields. The collective excitations in the presence of a spin-reversed electron can also be obtained in a similar manner. As discussed in Sect. 6.3, the excited states are classified according to the values of $|\boldsymbol{S}|$ and S_z. In the case of $\nu = \frac{1}{3}$, excited states with $|\boldsymbol{S}| = S_z = \frac{1}{2}N_e$ would correspond to the density wave mode discussed in the preceding section, while for $|\boldsymbol{S}| = S_z = \frac{1}{2}N_e - 1$, the excited state would correspond to the spin-wave excitation.

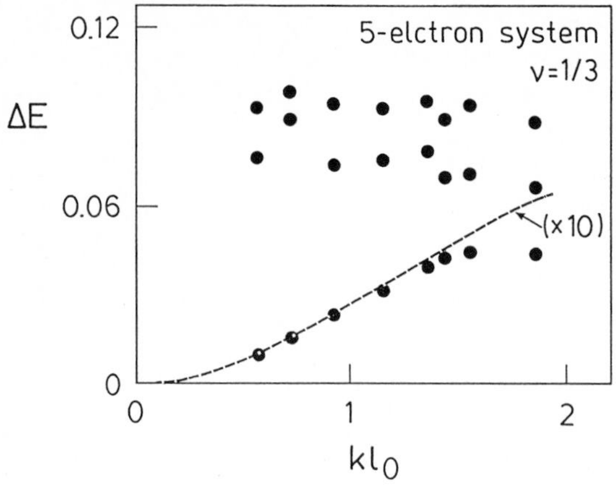

Fig. 7.5. Excitation spectrum for a five-electron system with the spin of one of the electrons reversed relative to the others at $\nu = \frac{1}{3}$. The dashed line is the spin-wave spectrum for $\nu = 1$

In Fig. 7.5, we present the numerical results for the low-lying spectrum in the case of one spin-reversed electron in the system at $\nu = \frac{1}{3}$ in the lowest Landau level. Only the three lowest excitation energies are shown in the figure, as a function of $k\ell_0$. Similar results were obtained by *Yoshioka* [7.16]. For small k, the lowest energy mode has a k^2-dependence similar to that obtained by *Kallin* and *Halperin* [7.14] for a fully filled lowest Landau level (Sect. 8.1). For large $k\ell_0$, the lowest energy mode would be the quasiexcitons with a spin-reversed quasiparticle and a spin-polarized quasihole discussed in Sect. 6.3.

A comparison of the density-wave spectrum and the spin-wave spectrum is given in Fig. 7.6 for a five-electron system. The spin-wave spectrum is clearly seen to be lower for all values of $k\ell_0$. The Zeeman energy will provide a constant shift of the spin-wave curve in the upward direction, and would provide a gap at $\boldsymbol{k} = 0$. Considering the magnitude of the gap for small k, it is clear that the spin-wave spectrum would be favored energetically below the momentum at which the minimum of the density wave occurs.

To illustrate the lowest energy neutral excitation spectrum in the presence of a magnetic field, we have presented below some approximate numerical results based on the exact results of Fig. 7.6. We first make a least squares fit through the two sets of points in Fig. 7.6. Strictly speaking, such a fit is not allowed for a five-electron system, since for a finite number of electrons, we only have a finite number of k-values. However, assuming that the five-electron results for the two collective modes are close to those for an the infinite system, qualitatively, such a fit could be considered. The

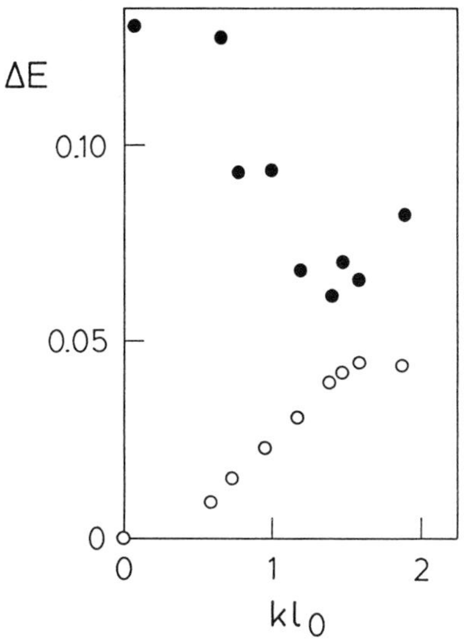

Fig. 7.6. The density-wave spectrum (closed circles) and the spin-wave spectrum (open circles) for a five-electron system at $\nu = \frac{1}{3}$

assumption is drastic, but is reasonable for illustrative purposes. Following the standard procedure of including the finite-thickness correction [see (7.30)], the density-wave mode as a function of magnetic field and $k\ell_0$ is shown in Fig. 7.7.

A similar calculation including the finite-thickness correction is also made for the spin-wave mode, where we have included the Zeeman energy as a function of the magnetic field. The resulting curve is shown in Fig. 7.8, where the linear behavior along the B-axis is due to the dominant Zeeman energy, while the k^2-dependence is clearly noticeable along the $k\ell_0$ axis.

Combining the above two curves and keeping only the *lowest* energy part of the combination, we obtain the result shown in Fig. 7.9. For small $k\ell_0$ the mode is the spin-wave type with the familiar linear behavior with increasing magnetic field, and lower than the density wave mode for all values of magnetic field considered. For $k\ell_0 \sim 1.0$, a crossover line is visible beyond which the density wave mode has the lowest energy, the characteristic minimum of which is discernable in the figure. Note that near the lowest magnetic fields considered here, the spin wave is favored even for large $k\ell_0$. This should lead to the crossover point observed in Fig. 6.21 for infinitely separated spin-reversed quasiparticle and spin-polarized quasihole pair. However, larger systems are needed to study this region in detail.

As mentioned above, these results are for illustrative purposes only. For a many-electron system, the results will certainly be quantitatively dif-

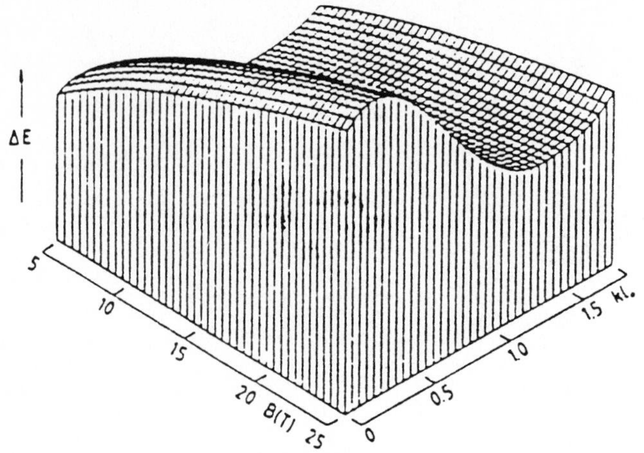

Fig. 7.7. The density-wave mode as a function of $k\ell_0$ and the magnetic field B (in Tesla)

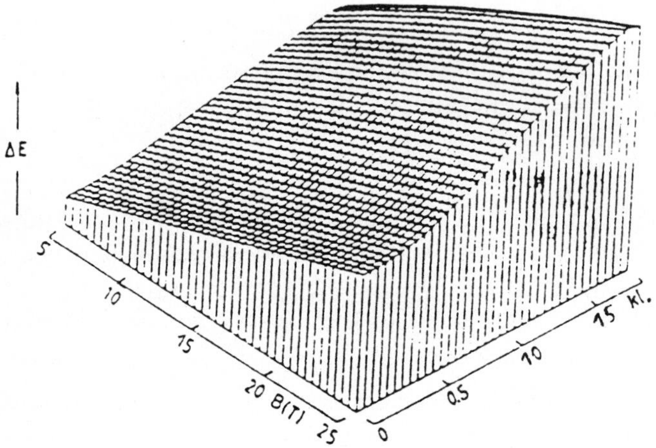

Fig. 7.8. Spin-wave mode as a function of $k\ell_0$ and the magnetic field B (in Tesla)

ferent. However, considering the different momentum dependences of the two modes (density wave and the spin wave), it is conceivable that, such a crossover would exist for a real system. A spin-wave mode has also been obtained in the spherical geometry [7.17]. Finally, considering the valley degeneracy appropriate for Si[110], *Rasolt* and *MacDonald* [7.18] have also studied the these two modes. Their results will be discussed below.

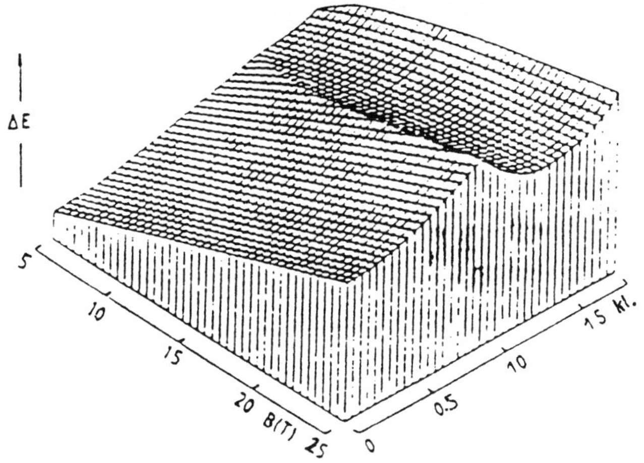

Fig. 7.9. Lowest energy collective mode as a function of $k\ell_0$ and the magnetic field (in Tesla). For values of $k\ell_0$ below the crossover line, the mode is of spin-wave type, while above the line, the mode is of density-wave type

7.4 Single-Mode Approximation: Magnetorotons

The finite-size calculations discussed above provide quite accurate informations for the collective excitations and the energy gap in the FQHE. However, not much physical insight is gained from these numerical calculations. The theoretical work presented in [7.19], drawing analogies from Feynman's well-known theory of liquid ^{4}He, however fills the gap. A brief description of the theory is given below.

Given the exact ground-state ψ, the density-wave excited state at wave vector $\boldsymbol{k}$ is written as [7.20,21]

$$\phi_{\boldsymbol{k}} = N^{-\frac{1}{2}} \rho_{\boldsymbol{k}} \psi \tag{7.33}$$

with the density operator

$$\rho_{\boldsymbol{k}} \equiv \sum_{j=1}^{N} \mathrm{e}^{-\mathrm{i}\boldsymbol{k}\cdot\boldsymbol{r}_j} \tag{7.34}$$

where N is the number of particles. The excitation energy is then given by

$$\Delta(k) = \frac{f(k)}{s(k)}. \tag{7.35}$$

In (7.35) the numerator is written as

$$f(k) \equiv N^{-1}\langle\psi|\rho_{\boldsymbol{k}}^{\dagger}\,(\mathcal{H}-E_0)\,\rho_{\boldsymbol{k}}|\psi\rangle \tag{7.36}$$

where $\mathcal{H}$ is the Hamiltonian and E_0 is the ground-state energy. The function $s(k)$, defined as

$$s(k) \equiv N^{-1}\langle\psi|\rho_{\boldsymbol{k}}^{\dagger}\rho_{\boldsymbol{k}}|\psi\rangle, \tag{7.37}$$

is the static structure function. The quantity $f(k)$ is the oscillator strength. The final form for the excitation energy is given by the well-known formula:

$$\Delta(k) = \frac{\hbar^2 k^2}{2m^* s(k)}\,. \tag{7.38}$$

The above result can be interpreted as saying that the collective mode energy is the single-particle energy $\hbar^2 k^2/2m^*$ renormalized by the static structure function representing correlations among the particles.

Defining the dynamic structure factor ($\hbar = 1$) as

$$S(k,\omega) = N^{-1}\sum_n \langle 0|\rho_{\boldsymbol{k}}^{\dagger}|n\rangle\delta(\omega - E_n + E_0)\langle n|\rho_{\boldsymbol{k}}|0\rangle\,, \tag{7.39}$$

where the sum is over the complete set of exact eigenstates, and using the relation,

$$s(k) = \int_0^\infty d\omega\, S(k,\omega) \tag{7.40}$$

we obtain for the oscillator strength,

$$f(k) = \int_0^\infty d\omega\,\omega\, S(k,\omega). \tag{7.41}$$

These results, when substituted into (7.35) for $\Delta(k)$ show that the Feynman expression for $\Delta(k)$ is in fact the exact first moment of the dynamic structure factor. The quantity $\Delta(k)$ is therefore the average energy for the excitations which are coupled to the ground state through the density. As is well known for liquid ^{4}He there are no low-lying single-particle excitations and the only low-lying excitations are long-wavelength density oscillations — *phonons.* The excitation energy curve vanishes linearly, its slope corresponding to the velocity of sound. Near $k = 2\text{Å}^{-1}$, the excitation energy shows a *roton minimum*, which arises due to the peak of the static structure function.

In the case of the FQHE, if we insist that the excited state is entirely within the lowest Landau level, the density-wave excited state becomes

$$\phi_{\boldsymbol{k}} = N^{-\frac{1}{2}} \bar{\rho}_{\boldsymbol{k}} \psi \tag{7.42}$$

where $\bar{\rho}_{\boldsymbol{k}}$ is the *projection* of the density operator onto the subspace of the lowest Landau level. Following the projection technique discussed in Ref. 7.22 (see also Appendix A) in the symmetric gauge we have

$$\rho_{\boldsymbol{k}} = \sum_{j=1}^{N} \exp\left[-\frac{1}{2}\mathrm{i}kz_j^* - \frac{1}{2}\mathrm{i}k^* z_j\right]$$

$$\bar{\rho}_{\boldsymbol{k}} = \sum_{j=1}^{N} \exp\left[-\mathrm{i}k\frac{\partial}{\partial z_j}\right] \exp\left[-\frac{1}{2}\mathrm{i}k^* z_j\right], \tag{7.43}$$

where the derivative operates to the left. The potential energy and the projected potential energy are then,

$$V = \frac{1}{2}\int \frac{d\boldsymbol{q}}{(2\pi)^2} v(q) \sum_{i\neq j} \exp\left[\mathrm{i}\boldsymbol{q}\cdot(\boldsymbol{r}_i - \boldsymbol{r}_j)\right],$$

$$\bar{V} = \frac{1}{2}\int \frac{d\boldsymbol{q}}{(2\pi)^2} v(q) \left(\bar{\rho}_{\boldsymbol{q}}\bar{\rho}_{\boldsymbol{q}} - \rho \mathrm{e}^{-q^2/2}\right) \tag{7.44}$$

where $v(q)$ is the interaction potential ($v(q) = 2\pi/q$ in the present case) and $\bar{\rho}_q^\dagger = \bar{\rho}_{-q}$. Also, the projected oscillator strength is,

$$\bar{f}(k) = N^{-1}\langle 0|\bar{\rho}_{\boldsymbol{k}}^\dagger[\bar{\mathcal{H}}, \bar{\rho}_{\boldsymbol{k}}]|0\rangle \tag{7.45}$$

where $|0\rangle$ is the ground state. Since the kinetic energy is constant, one can write for $\mathcal{H}$ merely the potential energy,

$$\bar{f}(k) = N^{-1}\langle 0|\bar{\rho}_{\boldsymbol{k}}^\dagger[\bar{V}, \bar{\rho}_{\boldsymbol{k}}]|0\rangle. \tag{7.46}$$

With the help of the commutation relation for the projected density operators,

$$[\bar{\rho}_{\boldsymbol{k}}, \bar{\rho}_{\boldsymbol{q}}] = \left(\mathrm{e}^{k^*q/2} - \mathrm{e}^{kq^*/2}\right) \bar{\rho}_{\boldsymbol{k}+\boldsymbol{q}}, \tag{7.47}$$

the projected oscillator strength is then

$$\begin{aligned}\bar{f}(k) = \frac{1}{2}\sum_{\boldsymbol{q}} v(q) \left(\mathrm{e}^{q^*k/2} - \mathrm{e}^{qk^*/2}\right) \Big[\bar{s}(q)\mathrm{e}^{-k^2/2} \left(\mathrm{e}^{-k^*q/2} - \mathrm{e}^{-kq^*/2}\right) \\ + \bar{s}(k+q) \left(\mathrm{e}^{k^*q/2} - \mathrm{e}^{kq^*/2}\right)\Big].\end{aligned} \tag{7.48}$$

In (7.48) the projected static structure factor $\bar{s}(q)$ is defined as

$$\bar{s}(q) = N^{-1}\langle 0|\bar{\rho}_{\boldsymbol{q}}^{\dagger}\bar{\rho}_{\boldsymbol{q}}|0\rangle. \tag{7.49}$$

In terms of the ordinary static structure factor, the projected structure function can be written as

$$\bar{s}(q) = s(q) - \left(1 - \mathrm{e}^{-|q|^2/2}\right). \tag{7.50}$$

In the single mode approximation (SMA) (so named because of the assumption that the density-wave alone saturates the full projected oscillator strength sum), the excitation energy is,

$$\Delta(k) = \frac{\bar{f}(k)}{\bar{s}(k)}. \tag{7.51}$$

For small k, $\bar{f}(k)$ vanishes like $|k|^4$ and then for a gap to exist, $\bar{s}(k)$ must vanish as $\sim |k|^4$ [7.19]. It is to be noted that the static structure function $s(k)$ is related to the radial distribution function for the ground-state $g(r)$ by

$$s(k) = 1 + \rho \int d\boldsymbol{r} \exp(-\mathrm{i}\boldsymbol{k}\cdot\boldsymbol{r})\,[g(\boldsymbol{r}) - 1] + (2\pi)^2\rho\delta^2(k) \tag{7.52}$$

where ρ is the average density. Expanding (7.52) for small k and, using (7.50), one finds that $\bar{s}(k) \sim |k|^4$, if, and only if, $M_0 = M_1 = -1$ where

$$M_n \equiv \rho \int d\boldsymbol{r}\,\left(\tfrac{1}{2}r^2\right)^n [g(r) - 1]. \tag{7.53}$$

The two-body correlation function was then expressed [7.19] in terms of the occupation of the single-particle angular momentum eigenstates of (5.9) as:

$$g(r) = \frac{1}{\rho^2}\sum_{\alpha\beta\gamma\delta} \phi_\alpha(0)\phi_\beta(r)\phi_\gamma^*(r)\phi_\delta^*(0)\langle c_\alpha^\dagger c_\beta^\dagger c_\gamma c_\delta\rangle, \tag{7.54}$$

where $c_\alpha^\dagger$ is the creation operator for the state α. From the conservation of angular momentum and (5.9), one obtains

$$\rho\,[g(r) - 1] = \frac{1}{2\pi\nu}\sum_{m=0}^{\infty}\frac{1}{m!}\left(\tfrac{1}{2}r^2\right)^m \mathrm{e}^{-\frac{1}{2}r^2}\left(\langle n_m n_0\rangle - \langle n_m\rangle\langle n_0\rangle - \nu\delta_{m0}\right) \tag{7.55}$$

with $n_m = c_m^\dagger c_m$ being the occupation number for state m. Inserting (7.55) into (7.53), we obtain the result

$$M_0 = \frac{1}{\nu}\left(\langle N n_0\rangle - \langle N\rangle\langle n_0\rangle\right) - 1$$
$$M_1 = \frac{1}{\nu}\left[\langle (L+N) n_0\rangle - \langle L+N\rangle\langle n_0\rangle\right] - 1 \tag{7.56}$$

where $N \equiv \sum_{m=0}^{\infty} n_m$ is the total particle number and $L \equiv \sum_{m=0}^{\infty} m n_m$ is the total angular momentum. As L and N are constants of the motion, their fluctuations vanish and finally one obtains the expected result, $M_0 = M_1 = -1$. The implication is that, in the lowest Landau level, any liquid ground state will have $\bar{s}(k) \sim |k|^4$. If one interprets $\bar{s}(k)$ as the mean-square density fluctuation at wave vector k, the gap condition is then a statement of the incompressibility of the system. The gapless excitations within the SMA can occur only as Goldstone modes with broken translational symmetry.

Using the Laughlin wave function for the ground state, the structure factor and the function $\bar{f}(k)$ can be computed numerically from the above relations. The resulting excitation energy obtained in Ref. 7.19 is presented in Fig. 7.10 for $\nu = \frac{1}{3}, \frac{1}{5}$ and $\frac{1}{7}$. The low-lying excitation energy curve reveals several interesting features. The first thing to note is that, unlike ^{4}He, the collective mode has a finite gap at $k = 0$, *i.e.*, the mode is *not* a massless Goldstone mode. It should be pointed out, however, that this gap is *not* due to the charged particles, since the Coulomb force is not sufficiently long-ranged to provide a finite plasma frequency in two dimensions (the plasma

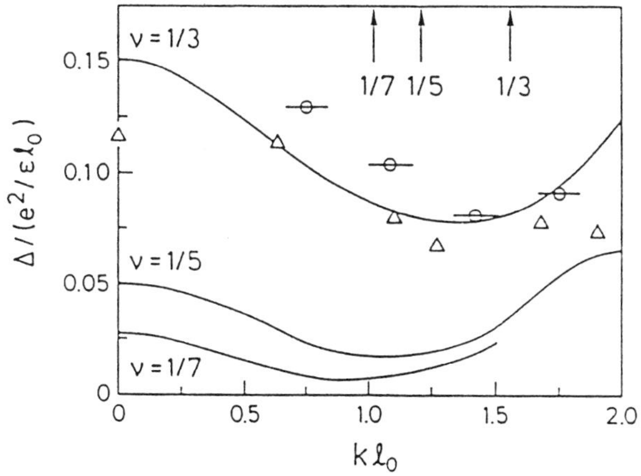

Fig. 7.10. Collective excitation curve in the SMA approximation for $\nu = \frac{1}{3}, \frac{1}{5}$ and $\frac{1}{7}$ filling fractions [7.19]. Arrows at the top indicate magnitude of primitive reciprocal-lattice vector of corresponding Wigner crystal. The circles are from the finite-size calculations of [7.1]. Horizontal error bars are the uncertainties in converting angular momentum on the sphere to linear momentum. Triangles are for $N = 6$ periodic boundary condition calculations with a hexagonal unit cell

frequency goes to zero with a square root dependence on the wave vector). The finite gap originates from the incompressible nature of the electron system at some particular filling fractions.

The collective mode also shows a minimum at a finite k. This minimum is due to the peak in $\bar{s}(k)$ and is thus analogous to the *roton* minimum in liquid ^{4}He. The deepening of the minimum in going from $\nu = \frac{1}{3}$ to $\nu = \frac{1}{7}$ was interpreted in Ref. 7.19 to be a precursor of the collapse of the gap which would occur at the critical filling ν_c (see Sect. 5.7). The magnitude of the primitive reciprocal-lattice vector of the Wigner crystal, shown by arrows in Fig. 7.10, appears close to the position of the magnetoroton minimum. The collective excitation curve, when compared with the finite system results discussed in earlier sections, shows very good agreement.

Feynman's prediction of the roton energy in ^{4}He was about a factor of two larger than the experimental results [7.20,21]. Later *Feynman* and *Cohen* [7.23] noted that a roton wave packet made up of the trial wave functions violates the continuity condition:

$$\nabla \cdot \langle \boldsymbol{J} \rangle = 0. \tag{7.57}$$

Let us consider a wave packet,

$$\Phi(r_1, \ldots, r_N) = \int d\boldsymbol{k}\, \xi(k) \rho_{\boldsymbol{k}} \psi(r_1, \ldots, r_N) \tag{7.58}$$

where $\xi(k)$ is a function (*e.g.*, a Gaussian) which is sharply peaked at a wave vector k located in the roton minimum. As the roton group velocity $d\Delta/dk$ vanishes at the roton minimum, the wave packet is quasistationary. Evaluating the current density, one obtains the result shown schematically in Fig. 7.11(a). The current has a fixed direction and is nonzero only in the region localized around the wave packet. The continuity equation is violated because the density is approximately time independent for the quasistationary packet. The modified variational wave function of Feynman and Cohen includes the backflow shown in Fig. 7.11(b). The discrepancy with the experimental roton energy was thereby reduced considerably.

In the case of the FQHE, the situation is somewhat different. The current density operator is now

$$\begin{aligned} J(\boldsymbol{R}) = \frac{1}{2m^*} \sum_j \Big[\delta^2(\boldsymbol{R} - \boldsymbol{r}_j) \left(\boldsymbol{p}_j + \frac{e}{c} \boldsymbol{A}(\boldsymbol{r}_j) \right) \\ + \left(\boldsymbol{p}_j + \frac{e}{c} \boldsymbol{A}(\boldsymbol{r}_j) \right) \delta^2(\boldsymbol{R} - \boldsymbol{r}_j) \Big]. \end{aligned} \tag{7.59}$$

If we take $\boldsymbol{\Phi}$ and $\boldsymbol{\Psi}$ to be any two members of the lowest Landau level,

$$\langle \boldsymbol{\Phi} | \boldsymbol{J}(\boldsymbol{R}) | \boldsymbol{\Psi} \rangle = -\frac{1}{2} \nabla \times \langle \boldsymbol{\Phi} | \rho(\boldsymbol{R}) \hat{\boldsymbol{z}} | \boldsymbol{\Psi} \rangle \tag{7.60}$$

where $\rho(\boldsymbol{R})$ is the density and $\hat{\boldsymbol{z}}$ is the unit vector normal to the plane. From (7.60), it readily follows that

$$\nabla \cdot \langle \boldsymbol{J}(\boldsymbol{R}) \rangle = 0 \tag{7.61}$$

for any state in the lowest Landau level. Therefore, in the FQHE, the backflow condition is automatically satisfied. The current flow for the magnetoroton wave packet is illustrated in Fig. 7.11(c).

Equation (7.61) implies that $\partial \rho / \partial t = 0$ for every state in the lowest Landau level. This is due to the fact that the kinetic energy has been quenched and perturbations can cause the particles to move by (virtual) transitions to higher Landau levels. One should note however that there are, in fact, two different current operators to be considered: The first is the ordinary (instantaneous) current as discussed above. The second one is

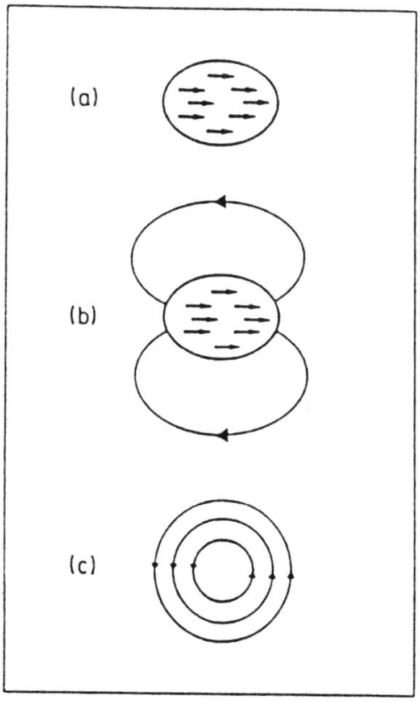

Fig. 7.11 The current distribution in a roton wave packet (schematic): (a) liquid helium with no backflow corrections, (b) helium with backflow corrections, and (c) lowest-Landau-level case [7.19]

the slow (time-averaged) $\boldsymbol{E} \times \boldsymbol{B}$ drift of the particles in the magnetic field. If we restrict the Hilbert space to the lowest Landau level, the fast degrees of freedom associated with the cyclotron motion are eliminated, but the slow (drift) one is retained.

For the magnetoroton wave packet, the excess particle density is circularly symmetric. Therefore the (mean) electric field is radial and particle drift is circular [Fig. 7.11(c)]. This is the reason why the continuity condition is automatically satisfied and the SMA works so well in the region of the magnetoroton spectrum. Similar results were also obtained by *Saarela* [7.24] using Jastrow theory for inhomogeneous fluids.

In the limit of very large wave vectors ($k\ell_0 \gg 1$), the SMA breaks down. We have seen in earlier sections that in the large k limit, the excitation consists of a quasiparticle-quasihole pair. Therefore for wavelengths much shorter than the interparticle spacing, the density wave is no longer a suitable excitation.

Experimental verification of the dispersion of the magnetoroton modes is difficult in part due to the small number of electrons present within a single layer of the two-dimensional electron gas. Recently, *Oji* et al. [7.25] have performed calculations of magnetoroton dispersion in a superlattice composed of electron layers separated by barrier layers. The method is essentially a combination of the SMA for a single layer and a mean-field treatment [7.26] of interlayer coupling. Their essential result is that, for typical fields and layer spacings, the modes broaden into bands. For sufficiently small layer separation, the energy gap vanishes, and they argue that the gap vanishing is to be associated with an instability toward the Wigner crystal state in each layer. A brief description of their work is given below. For a background on the mean-field treatment of the collective-excitation spectrum in a superlattice as used here, see the work of *Das Sarma* and *Quinn* [7.26].

In the lth layer, the induced electron density can be written

$$\delta n_l(\boldsymbol{q},\omega) = \chi_l(\boldsymbol{q},\omega)\left[\phi_l^{\mathrm{ext}}(\boldsymbol{q},\omega) + \sum_{l'\neq l} V_{l'l}(q)\,\delta n_{l'}(\boldsymbol{q},\omega)\right], \tag{7.62}$$

with $\boldsymbol{q}$ as the in-plane wave vector, $\phi_l^{\mathrm{ext}}(\boldsymbol{q},\omega)$ is the frequency dependent external potential in the lth layer, $\chi(q,\omega)$ is the density response function of an isolated layer. The interlayer interaction is given by

$$V_{ll'}(q) = \frac{2\pi \mathrm{e}^2}{\epsilon q}\int dz\,dz'\mathrm{e}^{-q|z-z'|}|\zeta(z-lc)|^2\,|\zeta(z-l'c)|^2 \tag{7.63}$$

where c is the layer spacing, ϵ is the background dielectric constant, and $\zeta(z)$ is the envelope function. Tunneling of electrons between two layers is forbidden and so there is no interlayer exchange term in (7.62). Multiple scattering between electrons in different layers is expected to be small and is neglected.

One can also rewrite (7.62) in a more convenient form

$$\sum_{l'} \left[\Pi^{-1}(q,\omega)\delta_{ll'} - V_{ll'}(q)\right] \delta n_{l'}(q,\omega) = \phi_l^{\text{ext}}(q,\omega) \tag{7.64}$$

with

$$\chi^{-1}(q,\omega) = \Pi^{-1}(q,\omega) - V(q). \tag{7.65}$$

Here $\Pi(q,\omega)$ is the proper polarizability of a single layer and $V(q) \equiv V_{ll}(q)$ is the intralayer interaction.

The collective-mode frequencies are then obtained by requiring

$$\left|\Pi^{-1}(q,\omega)\delta_{ll'} - V_{ll'}(q)\right| = 0. \tag{7.66}$$

In order to study the collective excitation spectrum, it is convenient for zero external potential to use (7.64)

$$\delta n_l(q,\omega) - \Pi(q,\omega)\sum_{l'} V_{ll'}(q)\delta n_{l'}(q,\omega) = 0. \tag{7.67}$$

For a superlattice which is completely periodic in the z direction with periodicity c we can use the following ansatz

$$\delta n_l(q,\omega) = \delta n(q,\omega)\exp(\mathrm{i}k_z lc)$$

where k_z is the *wave number* in the z direction (restricted to the first Brillouin zone of the superlattice). Assuming zero-thickness of electron layers, *i.e.*, $|\zeta(z)|^2 = \delta(z)$ and $V_{ll'} = (2\pi e^2/\epsilon q)\exp(-qc|l-l'|)$, we obtain from (7.67):

$$1 - \frac{2\pi e^2}{\epsilon q}\Pi(q,\omega)\sum_{l'} \exp[-q|l-l'|c - \mathrm{i}k_z(l-l')c] = 0. \tag{7.68}$$

Defining the structure factors $S_\pm$ in the manner

$$1 + S_\pm(\boldsymbol{q},k_z) = \frac{1}{1 - e^{-qc}e^{\pm \mathrm{i}k_z c}}$$

and the structure factor

$$\begin{aligned} S(q,k_z) &= 1 + S_+(\boldsymbol{q},k_z) + S_-(\boldsymbol{q},k_z) \\ &= \frac{\sinh(qc)}{[\cosh(qc) - \cos(k_z c)]} \end{aligned} \tag{7.69}$$

the collective excitation spectrum is finally obtained from (7.69) as

$$1 = \frac{2\pi e^2}{\epsilon q} \Pi(q,\omega) S(q,k_z). \tag{7.70}$$

For strong fields and $\omega \ll \omega_c$, the response function $\chi(q,\omega)$ can be written within the SMA scheme as

$$\chi(q,\omega) = \nu \bar{s}(q)\Delta(q)/\hbar\pi\ell_0^2[\omega^2 - \Delta^2(q)] \tag{7.71}$$

where $\Delta(q)$ is the single layer magnetoroton dispersion, ν is the filling factor, and $\bar{s}(q)$ is the projected static structure factor defined already in (7.49,50). Substituting (7.71) in (7.70), we can write the final form of the expression for the collective excitation spectrum within the SMA

$$\omega(q) = \left[\Delta^2(q) + \left(\frac{e^2}{\epsilon\ell_0\hbar}\right) 2\nu\bar{s}(q)\Delta(q)\left[S(q,k_z) - 1\right]/q\ell_0\right]^{\frac{1}{2}}. \tag{7.72}$$

In Fig. 7.12, the extrema of the magnetoroton band are presented as a function of $q\ell_0$ for c=1.5ℓ_0, $\nu = \frac{1}{3}$ and for $c = 3.5\ell_0, \nu = \frac{1}{5}$. For $qc \gg 1$ (weak coupling limit), $S(q,k_z) \to 1$ and $\omega(q) = \Delta(q)$ and the interlayer coupling vanishes. A similar situation also occurs for $q \to 0$. Near the magnetoroton minimum ($q\ell_0 \sim 1$), $\bar{s}(q)$ reaches a maximum with a substantial effect from interlayer coupling.

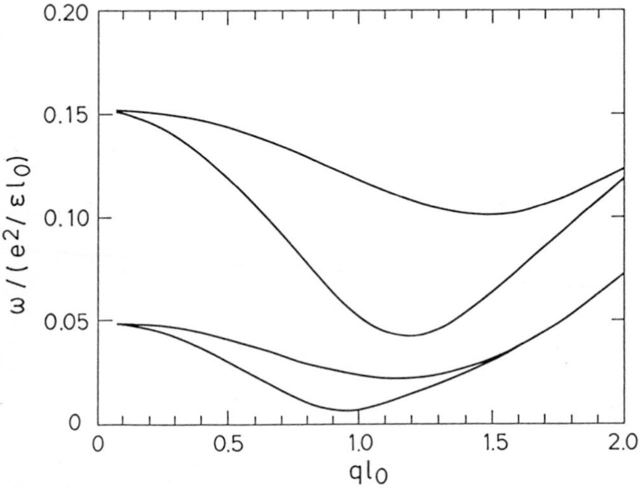

Fig. 7.12. Magnetoroton band dispersion in a superlattice. The higher energy curves are for $\nu = \frac{1}{3}$ and $c = 1.5\ell_0$ while the lower energy curves are for $\nu = \frac{1}{5}$ and $c = 3.5\ell_0$. The maximum and minimum of the band as a function of $q\ell_0$ correspond to $k_z = 0$ and $k_z = \pi/c$ respectively [7.25]

For a given value of $q\ell_0$, the magnetoroton modes are stiffest when the layers are oscillating in phase ($k_z = 0$) and softest when the layers are oscillating out of phase ($k_z = \pi/a$). The minimum excitation energy as a function of c/ℓ_0 is plotted for $\nu = \frac{1}{3}$ and $\nu = \frac{1}{5}$ in Fig. 7.13. At $\nu = \frac{1}{3}$, an instability is found to occur when $c/\ell_0 \lesssim 1.5$ and at $\nu = \frac{1}{5}$ for $c/\ell_0 \lesssim 3.35$. *Oji* et al. [7.25] have concluded that the in-plane and k_z wave vectors for the excitations shown in Fig. 7.13 correspond to the fundamental periods of the Wigner crystal states in the superlattice.

The formalism described above can easily be generalized to study the collective modes in an alternating-density superlattice, *i.e.*, a superlattice where the alternating layers have different electron densities. In the mean-field approach, such a system was refered to earlier [7.26,27] as a type-II superlattice. However, within that approach, the system can have only one type of charge carrier (but with different densities or different masses). In order to consider a system with different types of charge carriers, one needs to treat the interlayer correlations beyond the mean-field approach. *Chakraborty* studied the intra-Landau-level collective modes in a superlattice where the alternating layers have densities corresponding to $\frac{1}{3}$ and $\frac{1}{5}$ filling fractions [7.28]. The dispersion of the mixed modes revealed several distinctive features as compared to that of the individual magnetoroton band dispersion for $\frac{1}{3}$ and $\frac{1}{5}$ filling factors of the lowest Landau level.

Experimentally, the FQHE has been observed in multiple quantum well systems by *Shayegan* et al. [7.29]. The filling factors $\nu = \frac{4}{3}, \frac{2}{3}$ and $\frac{1}{3}$ were

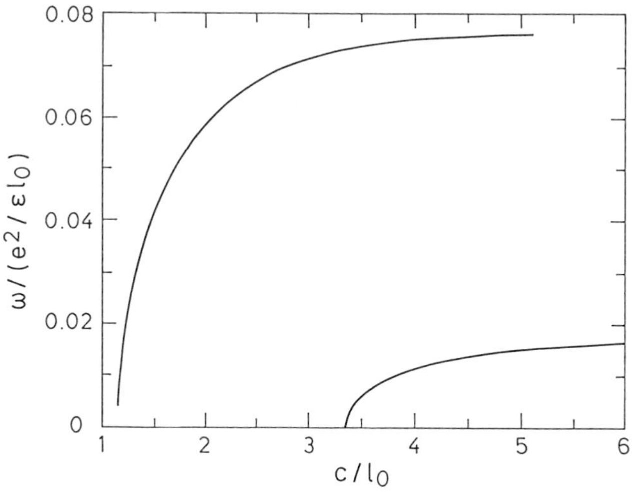

Fig. 7.13. Minimum excitation energy of the superlattice as a function of c/ℓ_0 at $k_z = \pi/c$ for $\nu = \frac{1}{3}$, $q\ell_0 = 1.2$ (upper curve) and $\nu = \frac{1}{5}$, $q\ell_0 = 0.96$ (lower curve) [7.25]

observed in those magnetotransport measurements. The activation energy reported at $\nu = \frac{1}{3}$ was $\Delta \simeq 2$ K, much larger than that reported in other measurements.

As mentioned earlier, within the HF approximation, the ground state of the one-component system is a charge-density wave state with the periodicity of a Wigner lattice. For the two-component (spin or valley) system, *Rasolt* and *MacDonald* [7.18] noticed that the exchange interaction, occurring only between parallel spins, is expected to favor a fully spin-polarized state for $\nu < 1$ and therefore the same energy per electron as for the one-component system. In Table 7.1, we have reproduced their results for the HF energies of fully polarized and unpolarized CDW states for a series of filling factors. The lowest energy HF state for the unpolarized system is, in fact, an antiferromagnetic state where the reduction in exchange energy is compensated by the displacement of the positions of up-spin and down-spin charge — thereby reducing the Coulomb energy. As seen in Table 7.1, for small filling factors, these antiferromagnetic states have energies quite close to those of the CDW state, where they may be regarded as antiferromagnetic and ferromagnetic Wigner lattice states respectively. For larger filling factors, the exchange energy dominates and as a result, the polarized CDW state is strongly preferred at $\nu = 1$. Rasolt and MacDonald have also calculated the spin-wave dispersion as well as density-wave mode dispersion for various filling factors. Making use of the two-component Laughlin-type state (5.56), their results for the two modes at $\nu = \frac{2}{5}$ are shown in Fig. 7.14.

Table 7.1. The energy per electron in the HF approximation for the density wave states for a two-dimensional electron gas at various filling fractions [7.18]. The unit of energy is $e^2/\epsilon\ell_0$

ν	Polarized CDW	Unpolarized CDW	Polarized SDW
$\frac{1}{5}$	−0.3220	−0.1636	−0.3195
$\frac{1}{3}$	−0.3885	−0.2204	−0.3823
$\frac{2}{5}$	−0.4123	−0.2491	−0.4013
$\frac{3}{5}$	−0.4838	−0.3162	−0.4332
$\frac{2}{3}$	−0.5076	−0.3354	−0.4393
$\frac{4}{5}$	−0.5505	−0.3526	−0.4798
1	−0.6267	−0.4154	−0.4693

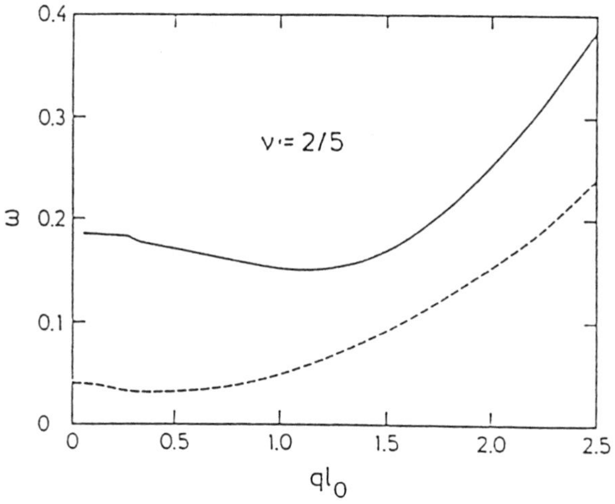

Fig. 7.14 Spin-wave (dashed curve) and density-wave (solid curve) mode dispersion as a function of $q\ell_0$ for the filling factor $\nu = \frac{2}{5}$ [7.18]

Su and *Wu* [7.30] have reported the excitation spectrum for $\nu = \frac{2}{5}$ calculated in a finite-size system. They found that, in contrast to the $\frac{1}{3}$ case, the collective excitation shows two minima, one at $k\ell_0 \sim 0.08$ and the other one at $k\ell_0 \sim 1.6$. The spectrum calculated from the SMA was found to be inadequate to describe this spectrum.

The specific heat in the case of the FQHE ground state has been calculated by *Yoshioka* [7.31]. The calculations were done in a spherical geometry. Numerical diagonalization of the Hamiltonian generates the many-particle energy levels E_i of the system. With these energy levels, the partition function and the specific heat are calculated from

$$
\begin{aligned}
Z &= \sum_i \mathrm{e}^{-\beta E_i} \\
C &= k_\mathrm{B} \sum_i \left[\frac{1}{Z}(\beta E_i)^2 \mathrm{e}^{-\beta E_i}\right] - k_\mathrm{B}\left[\sum_i \frac{1}{Z}\beta E_i \mathrm{e}^{-\beta E_i}\right]^2
\end{aligned}
\tag{7.73}
$$

with $\beta = 1/k_\mathrm{B}T$. The temperature is measured in units of $e^2/\epsilon\ell_0'$, with the modified magnetic length defined by $\ell_0' = (\nu N_\mathrm{s}/N_\mathrm{e})^{\frac{1}{2}}\ell_0$ [see (5.49)].

The numerical results for the specific heat evaluated in the spherical geometry for finite-size systems shows a peak around $T = 0.02\, e^2/\epsilon\ell_0'$. The peak is highest at $\nu = \frac{1}{3}$. When ν deviates from $\frac{1}{3}$, the specific heat gets larger at the lower temperature side of the peak and smaller additional peaks appear. The behavior of the specific heat curve has been explained by Yoshioka as due to the presence of a collective mode with a finite energy gap, which gives rise to a Schottky-like peak in the specific heat. There have been some measurements on the specific heat of two-dimensional electrons in GaAs-GaAlAs multilayer structures [7.32]. However, in these experiments, the effect of impurities is quite dominant.

MacDonald et al. [7.33] studied the thermodynamic properties of a two-dimensional electron system in a strong magnetic field within the HF approximation. At $T = 0$, the ground-state energy of the electron system has a downward-pointing cusp at integer filling factors. Therefore the magnetization

$$M = \left[-\frac{\partial E}{\partial B} \right]_{N_\mathrm{e}}$$

has a discontinuity as a function of B, which is directly related to the discontinuity in the chemical potential. In fact, we have

$$\frac{M_+ - M_-}{N_\mathrm{e}\mu_\mathrm{B}^*} = \frac{(\mu_+ - \mu_-)}{B\mu_\mathrm{B}^*} = \frac{2(\mu_+ - \mu_-)}{\hbar\omega_\mathrm{c}}$$

i.e., the discontinuity in the magnetization per electron in units of effective Bohr magneton ($\mu_\mathrm{B}^* = e\hbar/2m^*c$) is twice the discontinuity of the chemical potential in units of $\hbar\omega_\mathrm{c}$.

In the FQHE regime ($\nu < 1$), MacDonald et al. calculated M using the approximate expression given by *Halperin* [7.34] for the ground-state energies at various filling factors, $E = N_\mathrm{e}\left[e^2 f(\nu)\ell_0 + \frac{1}{2}\hbar\omega_\mathrm{c}\right]$ which results in

$$\frac{M}{N_\mathrm{e}\mu_\mathrm{B}^*} = -1 + \frac{e^2/\ell_0}{\hbar\omega_\mathrm{c}}\left[2\nu f'(\nu) - f(\nu)\right].$$

In the HF approximation, $f(\nu) = (-\nu/2)\sqrt{\pi/2}$ which gives

$$\frac{M^\mathrm{HF}}{N_\mathrm{e}\mu_\mathrm{B}^*} = -1 - \frac{(e^2/\ell_0)\nu}{2\hbar\omega_\mathrm{c}}\left(\frac{\pi}{2}\right)^{\frac{1}{2}}.$$

A more accurate evaluation of M using the finite-size systems would be very interesting. Magnetization measurements on a 2DES in GaAs/AlGaAs single-layer and multilayer heterostructures have been reported by *Störmer* et al. [7.35]. No results in the FQHE regime have been reported yet.

To summarize this chapter, from the theoretical work on finite and infinite systems, the nature of the low-lying collective modes have been well understood. The density-wave mode has been the most thoroughly studied so far. It has a number of characteristic features: For small k, the mode is well separated from the ground state with a large gap. It has a minimum at finite k, which has been found to be analogous to the *roton* minimum present in liquid ^{4}He. The spin-wave spectrum is also quite interesting and needs to be studied further. Unlike the case of the quasiparticle-quasihole gap, no experimental attempt to detect the collective modes has been reported so far. The collective modes are certainly an interesting outcome of the theories initially developed for the stability of the electron system at the experimentally observed filling factors. Experimental verification of these predictions would be an important step in our efforts to understand the FQHE.

8. Collective Modes: Inter-Landau Level

In this chapter, we review some of the theoretical work on the magnetoplasmon dispersion in the 2DES. The effect of electron correlations on this mode has been studied in detail by *Kallin* and *Halperin* [8.1,2], for the case of completely filled Landau levels. There has been a considerable amount of experimental work done on the cyclotron resonance in two-dimensional electron systems. The effect of electron correlations on the magnetoplasmon modes might be useful in understanding the anomalous structure in the cyclotron resonance line shape observed in Si-MOSFET's and in GaAs-heterostructures [8.3–7]. For example, experimental observation of cyclotron resonance linewidth broadening and splitting at certain electron densities [8.6] has been attributed to coupling between the cyclotron mode and finite-wavelength magnetoplasmons. A full review of the experimental and theoretical work on this topic will take us beyond the scope of this book.[1]

8.1 Kohn's Theorem

In a system with translational symmetry the electron-electron interactions cannot affect the cyclotron resonance. To see how that happens let us follow the original work of *Kohn* [8.8] and restrict ourselves to the case of a short range electron-electron interaction. In a uniform magnetic field $B = -|B|\widehat{z}$, the Hamiltonian is

$$\mathcal{H} = \frac{1}{2m^*} \sum_{i=1}^{N} \boldsymbol{P}_i^2 + \sum_{i,j} u(\boldsymbol{r}_i - \boldsymbol{r}_j) \tag{8.1}$$

where,

$$\boldsymbol{P}_i = \left(p_{i,x},\, p_{i,y} + \frac{eB}{c} x_i,\, p_{i,z} \right). \tag{8.2}$$

[1] See the papers by Kallin and Halperin for earlier references.

If we define the kinetic energy of the entire system as, $\boldsymbol{P} \equiv \sum_i \boldsymbol{P}_i$, then

$$\frac{d\boldsymbol{P}}{dt} = \frac{\mathrm{i}}{\hbar}[\mathcal{H}, \boldsymbol{P}] = -\frac{e}{m^*c}\boldsymbol{P} \times \boldsymbol{B} \tag{8.3}$$

which is the Lorentz equation for the entire system. Kohn then defined the operators: $P_\pm \equiv P_x \pm \mathrm{i}P_y$,

$$[\mathcal{H}, P_\pm] = \pm\hbar\omega_\mathrm{c}P_\pm \tag{8.4}$$

where ω_c is the cyclotron frequency (1.4). Let ψ_0 be the true ground state of the system with energy E_0. Then from (8.4)

$$\mathcal{H}P_+\psi_0 - E_0P_+\psi_0 = \hbar\omega_\mathrm{c}\psi_0. \tag{8.5}$$

If we define $\psi_1 \equiv P_+\psi_0$, then ψ_1 is an exact eigenstate of $\mathcal{H}$ with energy $E_1 = E_0 + \hbar\omega_\mathrm{c}$. Now if the system is placed in an *homogeneous* field, we must add to the Hamiltonian the perturbation

$$\mathcal{H}' = -\frac{e}{\mathrm{i}\omega m^*}\mathcal{E}_-P_+\mathrm{e}^{-\mathrm{i}\omega t}. \tag{8.6}$$

The perturbation (8.6) connects the state ψ_0 *only* with the state ψ_1, so that a sharp absorption results at the frequency $\omega = \omega_\mathrm{c}$. The cyclotron resonance is not affected by the interaction because the external field moves each electron in exactly the same manner and the interaction, which is momentum conserving does not affect that motion. In fact, the cyclotron resonance is a transition between Landau levels of the *center-of-mass* (CM) of the many-electron system [8.9].

It is interesting to note that for $\nu = 1$ (filled Landau level), the radial distribution function is known exactly (see Sect. 5.2) to be $g(r) = 1 - \exp(-r^2/2\ell_0^2)$ and the corresponding static structure function, $s(k) = 1 - \exp(-k^2\ell_0^2/2)$. Using these in Feynman's result for the excitation energy (7.38), we get

$$\Delta(k) = \frac{\hbar^2k^2}{2m^*[1 - \exp(-k^2\ell_0^2/2)]}.$$

Since, $\hbar^2/m^*\ell_0^2 = \hbar\omega_\mathrm{c}$, we obtain

$$\Delta(k) = \hbar\omega_\mathrm{c}\frac{(k\ell_0)^2/2}{1 - \exp(-k^2\ell_0^2/2)},$$

which has the correct limit $\Delta(0) = \hbar\omega_\mathrm{c}$ [8.10]. It should be pointed out that in the above derivation, the Landau-level mixing was neglected. However

Kohn's theorem requires that the same result be obtained (for $k \to 0$) for the exact ground state. The arguments leading to Kohn's theorem can therefore be restated as: in the long-wavelength limit an external perturbation couples only to the CM motion. The CM degree of freedom has the excitation spectrum of a single particle in the magnetic field and is unaffected by the correlations and interactions among the individual particles.

Kohn's theorem applies to a system where there is translational symmetry. Kallin and Halperin first pointed out that the presence of impurities allows coupling to magnetoplasmon modes at nonzero wave vector, where correlations are important. A direct measurement of the excitation energies is possible in principle [8.11]. The range of wave vectors accessible at present is, however, not wide enough to test the theoretical predictions described below. In the following, we present a brief review of the studies of a filled Landau level and compare the results with the case where the lowest Landau level is only *fractionally* filled. In the latter case, the magnetoplasmon mode is strongly influenced by the presence of the intra-Landau level mode discussed in the earlier chapter.

8.2 Filled Landau Level

Here we consider the two-dimensional electron system with no impurity scattering, subjected to a strong perpendicular magnetic field B, and with a density such that an integral number of Landau levels are fully occupied. The elementary neutral excitations near ω_c may then be described as magnetoplasmon modes or *magnetic excitons*, which would correspond to the energy required to promote an electron from an occupied Landau level to unoccupied Landau levels. We consider the strong field limit where the cyclotron energy is large compared to the Coulomb energy. In the absence of electron-electron interactions, the excitation energy would be the kinetic energy difference between the two Landau levels (plus the Zeeman energy difference, if the excitation also involves a spin flip). Inclusion of interaction would shift that energy by an amount of order $e^2/\epsilon\ell_0$.

Neglecting the spin degree of freedom, the wave function for an exciton consisting of an electron in the nth Landau level and a hole in the $(n-1)$th Landau level is calculated (in the Landau gauge) as

$$\psi_{\boldsymbol{k}n}(\boldsymbol{R}, \Delta\boldsymbol{r}) = \frac{1}{2\pi} \mathrm{e}^{\mathrm{i}\boldsymbol{k}\cdot\boldsymbol{R}} \mathrm{e}^{\mathrm{i}X\Delta y/\ell_0^2} \phi_n(\Delta\boldsymbol{r} - \ell_0^2\boldsymbol{k} \times \widehat{\boldsymbol{z}}) \tag{8.7}$$

$$\phi_n(\boldsymbol{r}) \equiv \frac{1}{(2n\ell_0^2)^{\frac{1}{2}}} \mathrm{e}^{-r^2/4\ell_0^2} \left(\frac{x+\mathrm{i}y}{\ell_0}\right) L_{n-1}^1\left(r^2/2\ell_0^2\right). \tag{8.8}$$

In (8.7) and (8.8) L_n^α is a Laguerre polynomial, $\boldsymbol{R} \equiv \frac{1}{2}(\boldsymbol{r}_1 + \boldsymbol{r}_2) = (X, Y)$ and $\Delta\boldsymbol{r} \equiv \boldsymbol{r}_1 - \boldsymbol{r}_2 = (\Delta x, \Delta y)$ with $\boldsymbol{r}_1$ and $\boldsymbol{r}_2$ being the electron and hole positions respectively. The vector $\boldsymbol{k}$ plays the role of the total momentum of the particles.

The exciton wave function (8.7) is the direct product (except for a gauge independent phase factor) of a plane wave in the center of mass coordinates $\boldsymbol{R}$ and a function of the relative coordinates $\phi_n(\boldsymbol{r})(\Delta\boldsymbol{r} - \ell_0^2\boldsymbol{k} \times \widehat{\boldsymbol{z}})$, whose magnitude is spherically symmetric about the point $\Delta\boldsymbol{r} = \ell_0^2\boldsymbol{k} \times \widehat{\boldsymbol{z}}$. The dipole moment of the exciton can then be defined as

$$e\langle\psi_{\boldsymbol{k}n}|\Delta\boldsymbol{r}|\psi_{\boldsymbol{k}n}\rangle = e\ell_0^2\boldsymbol{k} \times \widehat{\boldsymbol{z}} \tag{8.9}$$

which is perpendicular to $\boldsymbol{k}$, proportional to k and independent of n. Classically this is what one expects as two particles of opposite charge in a magnetic field move parallel to one another (in contrast to *electrons* in a magnetic field, which orbit one another) with a constant linear velocity perpendicular to their separation. The exciton momentum increases with increasing separation between the particles, even though the velocity decreases.

With the exciton wave function (8.7), Kallin and Halperin have calculated the exciton dispersion relation. The result is *exact* to lowest order in $(e^2/\epsilon\ell_0/\hbar\omega_c)$, where the contributions from the particle-hole ring and ladder diagrams have been included self-consistently. In the case where one spin state is occupied in the lowest Landau level, the exciton energy is given explicitly as

$$\begin{aligned} E(\boldsymbol{k}) = \omega_c + \frac{e^2}{2\epsilon\ell_0}\Bigg[(\pi/2)^{\frac{1}{2}}\Bigg\{1 - \mathrm{e}^{-k^2\ell_0^2/4}\Bigg(\left(1 + \frac{1}{2}k^2\ell_0^2\right) \\ \times I_0\left(\frac{1}{4}k^2\ell_0^2\right) - \frac{1}{2}k^2\ell_0^2\, I_1\left(\frac{1}{4}k^2\ell_0^2\right)\Bigg)\Bigg\} + \nu k\ell_0\mathrm{e}^{-k^2\ell_0^2/2}\Bigg] \end{aligned} \tag{8.10}$$

where I_n is a modified Bessel function. The resulting curve is plotted in Fig. 8.1. The exciton dispersion curve has a maximum at $k\ell_0 \sim 0.9$ and a minimum at $k\ell_0 \sim 2$. The energy shift goes to zero as $k\ell_0 \to 0$, in accordance with Kohn's theorem. For $k\ell_0 \ll 1$, the spectrum is seen to increase *linearly* from the origin as $\Delta E(k) = E(\boldsymbol{k}) - \omega_c = \frac{1}{2}k\ell_0$. Kallin and Halperin also calculated the dispersion within the random phase approximation (RPA), which is seen to be clearly inadequate to describe the mode for large $k\ell_0$ (Fig. 8.1).

MacDonald [8.12] performed a similar calculation where he also included a higher interaction strength within the HF approximation. The net effect

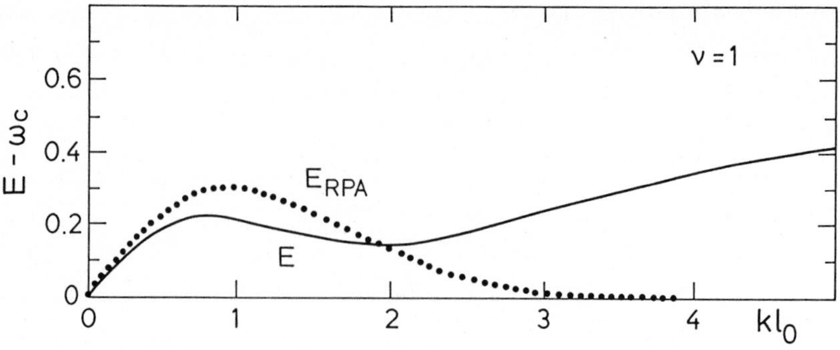

Fig. 8.1. Exciton dispersion curve near ω_c for $\nu = 1$ (spin polarized). The dotted curve is obtained within the random phase approximation (RPA) [8.1]

was found to shift the dispersion curve down from that of the leading order result.

In the case of one spin component occupied in the lowest Landau level, one can also calculate the spin wave spectrum. The dispersion relation for this case was obtained by Kallin and Halperin to be,

$$E(\boldsymbol{k}) - \left|g\mu_{\mathrm{B}}B\right| = \frac{e^2}{\epsilon\ell_0}\left(\tfrac{1}{2}\pi\right)^{\frac{1}{2}}\left[1 - \mathrm{e}^{-k^2\ell_0^2/4} I_0(k^2\ell_0^2/4)\right] , \qquad (8.11)$$

where the second term on the left hand side is the usual Zeeman energy. The result is plotted in Fig. 8.2. The energy shift approaches zero in the limit $k \to 0$. Similar results were also derived by *Bychkov* et al. [8.13].

There have been a couple of interesting experiments done to observe the magnetoplasmon dispersion predicted in the theories described above. *Batke* and *Wu* measured the high-frequency conductivity with far-infrared trans-

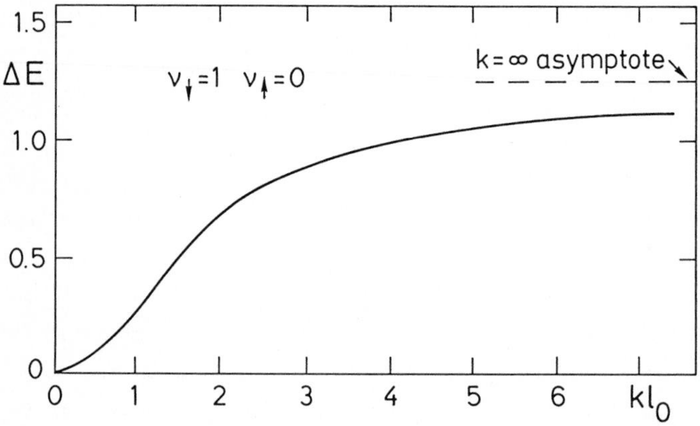

Fig. 8.2. Spin wave spectrum for $\nu = 1$. The Zeeman energy is not included [8.1]

mission spectroscopy and observed new resonance structures with energies close to the cyclotron frequency [8.14]. These were attributed to excitation of magnetic excitons. A more convincing detection of the dispersion of the magnetic excitons were reported by *Pinczuk* et al. [8.15]. They observed the roton-type minimum in the magnetoplasmon dispersion, as predicted by Kallin and Halperin, by resonant inelastic light scattering. Figure 8.3 depicts their results at $\nu = 2$. The spectra have an onset at $1meV$ below $\hbar\omega_c$ (for electron effective mass $m^* = 0.0695$) and a cutoff at an energy that lies well below the onset of intersubband excitations at $28meV$. The spectra overlap with the calculated dispersion as shown in Fig. 8.3(b). The agreement is indicative that these are magnetoplasmons and spin-density

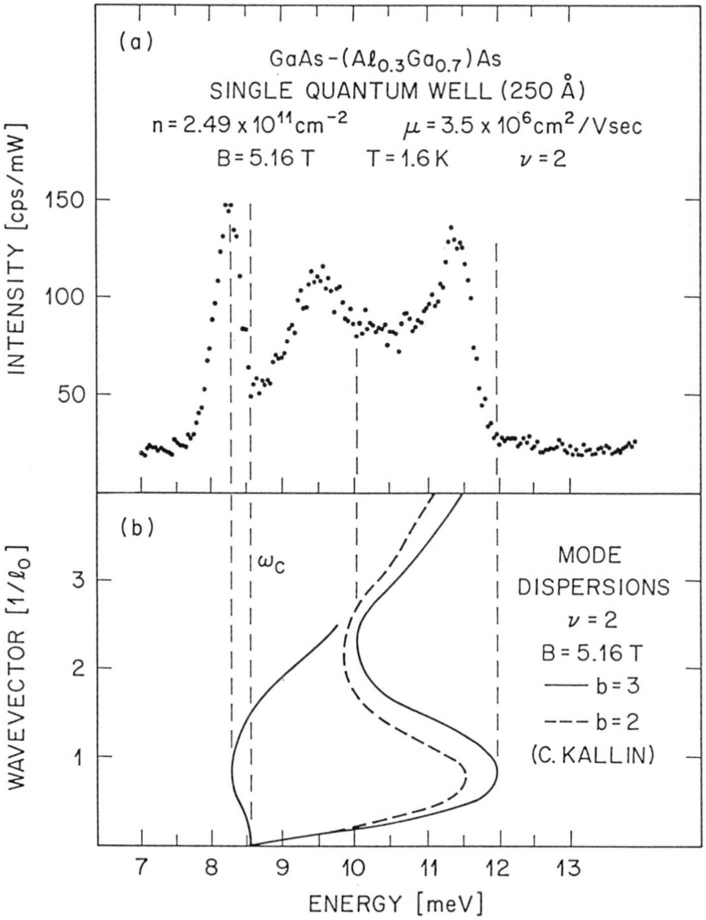

Fig. 8.3. (a) Inelastic light-scattering spectra at three values of the incident photon energy $\hbar\omega_L$. (b) calculated dispersion at $\nu = 2$ (see Sect. 8.1). The magnetoplasmons are presented by a full line and the dotted line is for spin-density excitations [8.15]

excitations at large wave vectors $q \gtrsim q_0 = 1/\ell_0 = 1.1 \times 10^6 cm^{-1}$. These authors also observed excitations associated with higher Landau-level transitions $m\hbar\omega_c$. At $\nu \gtrsim 10$, they observed the modes for $m \leq 5$. Figure 8.4(a) shows the spectra at $\nu = 1$. The scattering in the range $12 \leq \hbar\omega \leq 16meV$ also agrees with the calculated large wave-vector magnetoplasmons shown in Fig. 8.4(b).

The experiment of Pinczuk et al. is an important step forward in our understanding of the role of electron correlations in the inter-Landau level excitations. Similar studies within the intra-Landau level, if possible, would provide a rare glimpse at the collective modes (magnetoroton) discussed in the preceding chapter.

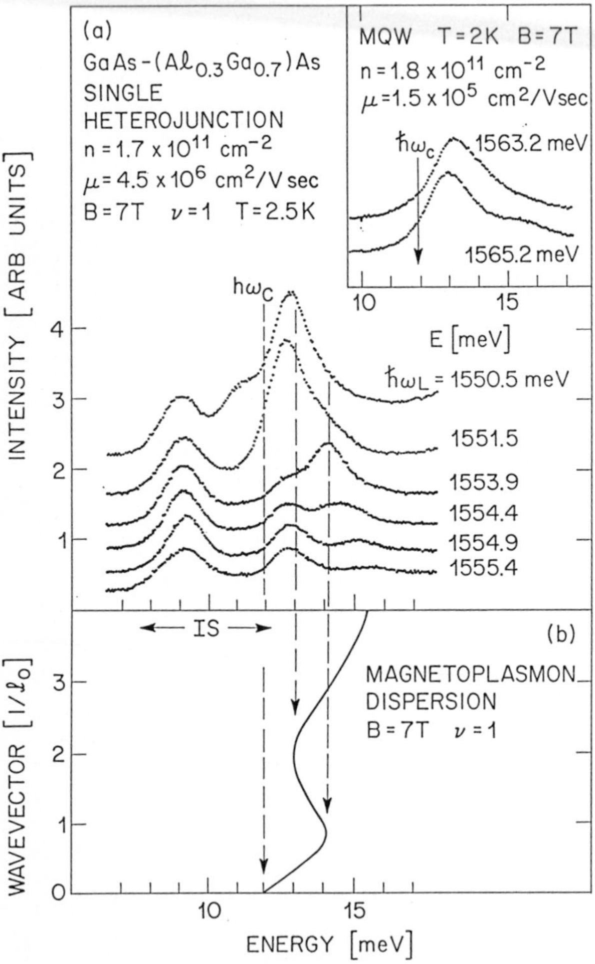

Fig. 8.4. (a) Resonant inelastic light-scattering spectra for different values of $\hbar\omega_L$. (b) calculated mode dispersion at $\nu = 1$ (see Sect. 8.1) [8.15]

8.3 Fractional Filling: Single Mode Approximation

The single mode approximation was discussed in Sect. 7.4 in the context of intra-Landau level collective excitations of fractional quantum Hall states. This approach has been extended by *MacDonald* et al. [8.16] to the present problem of inter-Landau level excitations. Their work is primarily concerned with the magnetoplasmon excitations in the extreme quantum limit where the ground state $|\Psi_0\rangle$ is strictly within the lowest Landau level. In the following we shall present a brief description of their approach.

Let us consider the symmetric gauge where the single particle eigenfunctions are given by (see Appendix A)

$$\Psi_{nm}(z_i, z_i^*) = \frac{1}{(2\pi)^{\frac{1}{2}}} \frac{(a_i^\dagger)^n (b_i^\dagger)^m}{(n!m!)^{\frac{1}{2}}} \, \mathrm{e}^{\frac{1}{4} z_i z_i^*}. \tag{8.12}$$

They are eigenfunctions of the kinetic energy operator

$$\begin{aligned} \mathcal{K}_i \Psi_{nm}(z_i, z_i^*) &= \hbar\omega_c \left(a_i^\dagger a_i + \tfrac{1}{2} \right) \Psi_{nm}(z_i, z_i^*) \\ &= \hbar\omega_c \left(n + \tfrac{1}{2} \right) \Psi_{nm}(z_i, z_i^*). \end{aligned} \tag{8.13}$$

Here, (as discussed in Appendix A) $a_i^\dagger$ and $b_i^\dagger$ are inter-Landau level and intra-Landau level ladder operators respectively. The intra-Landau level collective excitations were created by the projected density operator $\bar{\rho}$. In the present case, however, we must also include other levels. To proceed in an analogous way we therefore decompose the full density operator ρ_k into a sum over Landau levels

$$\rho_k = \sum_{n'n} \rho_k^{n'n} \tag{8.14}$$

where the operator

$$\rho_k^{n'n} = \sum_i A_i^{n'n}(k) B_i(k) \tag{8.15}$$

transfers particles from level n to level n'. The operator $B_i(k)$ is an intra-Landau level operator and is defined in Appendix D. The inter-Landau level operator $A_i^{n'n}$ (also given in Appendix D) can further be written in the form

$$\begin{aligned} A_i^{n'n}(k) &= \exp\left(-\frac{\mathrm{i}}{\sqrt{2}} k a_i^\dagger \right) \exp\left(-\frac{\mathrm{i}}{\sqrt{2}} k^* a_i \right) \\ &= |n'\rangle_i \, {}_i\langle n| G^{n'n}(k) \end{aligned} \tag{8.16}$$

is responsible for the transfer of the particle i from the level n to the level n'. The notation $|n\rangle_i$ describes the state where the particle i is promoted to the level n while all the other particles remain in their original level. The coefficient in the last form is given by

$$G^{n'n}(k) = \sqrt{\frac{n!}{n'!}}\left(-\frac{ik}{\sqrt{2}}\right)^{n'-n} L_n^{n'-n}(\tfrac{1}{2}k^2). \tag{8.17}$$

The wave functions of the excited states of momentum k are expanded in terms of the states $\rho_k^{n'n}|\boldsymbol{\Psi}_0\rangle$

$$|\boldsymbol{\Psi}_k\rangle = \sum_{n',n} \alpha_{n'n}(k)\rho_k^{n'n}|\boldsymbol{\Psi}_0\rangle, \tag{8.18}$$

thereby generalizing the SMA for the intra-Landau level excitations. The diagonalization of the Hamiltonian in the space of these functions leads to the secular equation

$$\sum_{n',n}\left[E_{\text{pl}}(m',m;n',n:k) - \Delta(k)S(m',m;n',n:k)\right]\alpha_{n'n}(k) = 0. \tag{8.19}$$

Here E_{pl} is the matrix element of the Hamiltonian, minus the ground-state energy, between the states in the sum (8.18)

$$E_{\text{pl}}(m',m;n',n:k) = \langle\boldsymbol{\Psi}_0|\rho_{-k}^{mm'}[\mathcal{H},\rho_k^{n'n}]|\boldsymbol{\Psi}_0\rangle. \tag{8.20}$$

The scalar products of these states are denoted by

$$S(m',m;n',n:k) = \langle\boldsymbol{\Psi}_0|\rho_{-k}^{m'm}\rho_k^{n'n}|\boldsymbol{\Psi}_0\rangle \tag{8.21}$$

and are straightforward generalizations of the projected structure function $\bar{s}$ defined by (7.49). The part containing the kinetic energy operator in the commutator appearing in (8.20) is easily evaluated to be

$$[\mathcal{K},\rho_k^{n'n}] = \hbar\omega_{\text{c}}(n'-n)\rho_k^{n'n}. \tag{8.22}$$

Substituting this and the Fourier transform for the potential energy into (8.20), one can rewrite E_{pl} as

$$\begin{aligned} E_{\text{pl}}(m',m;n',n:k) =& \hbar\omega_{\text{c}}(n'-n)S(m',m;n',n:k) \\ &+ \frac{1}{2}\int\frac{d^2q}{(2\pi)^2}V(q)\langle\boldsymbol{\Psi}_0|\rho_k^{mm'}[\rho_{-q}\rho_q,\rho_k^{n'n}]|\boldsymbol{\Psi}_0\rangle. \end{aligned} \tag{8.23}$$

As an application of the formalism, two limiting cases are considered. The first one is the extreme quantum limit case where all excitations are restricted to the lowest Landau level. The secular equation (8.19) then reduces to

$$\Delta(k) = \frac{E_{\mathrm{pl}}(0,0;0,0:k)}{S(0,0;0,0:k)} \tag{8.24}$$

which is clearly equivalent to the expression (7.51) for intra-Landau level excitations. The second case corresponds to the coherent promotion of an electron from the lowest level to nth Landau level. In the extreme quantum limit when there is no Landau level mixing, the secular equation again reduces to

$$\Delta(k) = \frac{E_{\mathrm{pl}}(n,0;n,0:k)}{S(n,0;n,0:k)}. \tag{8.25}$$

In this special case the function S takes a particularly simple form

$$S(n,0;n,0:k) = \langle \Psi_0 | \rho_k^{0n} \rho_k^{n0} | \Psi_0 \rangle = N_{\mathrm{e}} \left| G^{n0}(k) \right|^2 \mathrm{e}^{-\frac{|k|^2}{2}} \tag{8.26}$$

as can be seen by applying the algebra obeyed by the operators $B_i(k)$

$$B_i(k_1) B_i(k_2) = \mathrm{e}^{\frac{1}{2} k_1^* k_2} B_i(k_1 + k_2) \tag{8.27}$$

and using the fact that

$${}_i\langle n| \cdot |n\rangle_j = \delta_{ij}. \tag{8.28}$$

Let us now introduce the notation

$$\begin{aligned} h(q) &= S(q) - 1 \\ \widetilde{h}(q) &= \mathrm{e}^{\frac{1}{2}|q|^2} h(q) \end{aligned} \tag{8.29}$$

and make use of the identities

$$\begin{aligned} \sum_{r \neq s} \langle \Psi_0 | B_r(-k) B_s(k) | \Psi_0 \rangle &= N_{\mathrm{e}} [h(k) + 2\pi\nu\delta^2(k)] \\ \sum_l G^{nl}(k_1) G^{lm}(k_2) &= \mathrm{e}^{-\frac{1}{2} k_1^* k_2} G^{nm}(k_1 + k_2). \end{aligned} \tag{8.30}$$

We obtain the final form for E_{pl} (8.23):

$$\begin{aligned} E_{\mathrm{pl}}(n,0;n,0:k) = S(n,0;n,0:k) \Bigg(& \int \frac{d^2 q}{(2\pi)^2} \mathrm{e}^{-\frac{1}{2}|q|^2} V(q) \\ & \times \left\{ \widetilde{h}(q) \left[G^{nn}(q) \mathrm{e}^{\frac{1}{2}(k^* q - k q^*)} - 1 \right] + \widetilde{h}(k - q) |G^{n0}(q)|^2 \right\} \\ & + n\hbar\omega_{\mathrm{c}} + \frac{\nu e^2}{k} |G^{n0}(k)|^2 \mathrm{e}^{-\frac{1}{2}|k|^2} \Bigg) \end{aligned} \tag{8.31}$$

where the factor inside the big parentheses is the SMA result for $\Delta(k)$. By considering the projected f sum rule it can be shown that for the strong field limit this is an exact result provided that a single mode exhausts all of the projected oscillator strength.

The SMA result (8.31) can be compared, for example, with the summation of the self-consistent Hartree-Fock ladder diagrams performed by *Oji* and *MacDonald* [8.17]

$$\Delta(k) = n\hbar\omega_{\mathrm{c}} + H^n(k) + X^n(k). \tag{8.32}$$

The Hartree term

$$H^n(k) = \frac{\nu e^2}{k}|G^{n0}(k)|^2 e^{-\frac{1}{2}|k|^2} \tag{8.33}$$

is equal to the last term in the SMA. The random phase approximation, which neglects all of the many-body corrections, is obtained by including the cyclotron energy and the Hartree term. It thus corresponds to the last two terms in (8.31). Many-body corrections due to exchange effects are taken into account by the Fock term

$$X^n(k) = -\nu\int\frac{d^2q}{(2\pi)^2}\mathrm{e}^{-\frac{1}{2}|q|^2}V(q)\left\{G^{nn}(q)\mathrm{e}^{\frac{1}{2}(k^*q-kq^*)} - 1 + |G^{n0}(q)|^2\right\}. \tag{8.34}$$

We can see that the SMA reduces to the Hartree-Fock expression when the function $\widetilde{h}(q)$ is replaced by its uncorrelated value, $-\nu$. The SMA is then expected to be an excellent approximation since its takes into account the many-body effects including electron-electron correlations via the function $\widetilde{h}(q)$ which is plotted in Fig. 8.5 for various values of the filling fraction ν. The calculations of $\widetilde{h}(q)$ are based on Laughlin's ground-state wave functions and therefore introduce an approximation to the otherwise exact result (8.31). Nevertheless these wave functions are known to be extremely accurate. The excitation energies for the special case where an electron is promoted from the lowest level to the next level are presented in Fig. 8.6 for the values $\nu = 1, \frac{1}{3}, \frac{1}{5}$ and $\frac{1}{7}$. Compared with the Hartree-Fock results there is a tendency to make the magnetoplasmon mode stiffer which is consistent with the observed narrowness of the cyclotron resonance line found by *Wilson* et al. [8.3,4]. Later measurements however have revealed that there is a broadening or splitting of this line at certain values of the perpendicular magnetic field [8.6,7]. It is expected that the softening of the magnetoplasmon modes at some higher values of the wave vector is responsible for this observed behavior. One way to improve the SMA scheme would be to couple the modes to the intra-Landau level modes which would cause a broadening of the magnetoplasmon excitations.

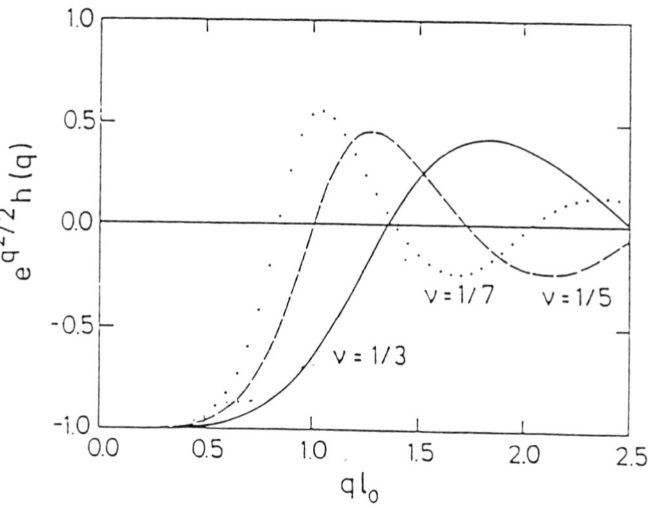

Fig. 8.5. Projected correlation function $\widetilde{h}(q) = e^{|q|^2} h(q)$ for the fractional Hall states at $\nu = \frac{1}{3}$ (solid line), $\nu = \frac{1}{5}$ (dashed line) and $\nu = \frac{1}{7}$ (dotted line) [8.16]

In addition to the coherent excitations described by the SMA there are also incoherent excitations. They are somewhat analogous to the particle-hole excitations in an ordinary Fermi liquid in the sense that the particle promoted to a higher Landau level leaves a hole behind it. In this case, however, the momentum of the hole is exactly opposite to the momentum of the particle. Therefore the total momentum of the excitation is determined by the state from which the electron was removed. In Appendix D we show that the energy of this incoherent excitation mode is an exact repetition, when shifted by $\hbar\omega_c$, of the intra-Landau level mode. Comparing the dispersion curves presented in Figs. 7.10 and 8.6 it can be seen that the incoherent mode is energetically more favorable at values of the wave vector $q\ell_0 \gtrsim 0.7$. The incoherent mode is still well above the $\hbar\omega_c$-level and hence cannot be accounted for the splitting of the cyclotron resonance line. In the presence of impurities these two modes might couple, which would bring one of them near the cyclotron energy.

8.4 Fractional Filling: Finite-Size Studies

Let us now consider the inter-Landau level excitations in a system with a finite number of electrons under exactly the same geometrical conditions as discussed in Sect. 7.2. The symmetry analysis described there can straight-

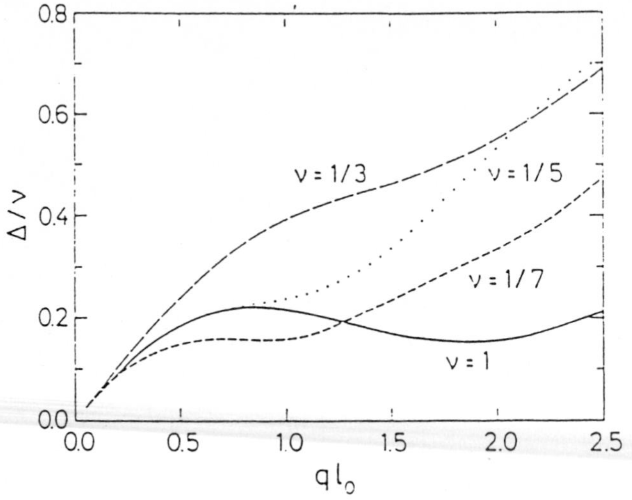

Fig. 8.6. Magnetoplasmon excitation energies measured from $\hbar\omega_c$ (in units of $\nu e^2/\ell_0$) for $\nu = 1$ (solid line), $\nu = \frac{1}{3}$ (long-dashed line), $\nu = \frac{1}{5}$ (dotted line) and $\nu = \frac{1}{7}$ (short-dashed line) [8.16]

forwardly be extended to cover the system where electrons are allowed to occupy arbitrary Landau levels. However, as more particles are distributed among Landau levels, this extra degree of freedom will extremely rapidly increase the number of state vectors needed to describe the system. Therefore, in practice, one can study only those systems where only one of the electrons is promoted from the lowest level and the effects of Landau level mixing are ignored.

As a special case we consider the system of N_e electrons where one electron is elevated to Landau level 1 with the remaining $N_e - 1$ electrons in the lowest level. As before, we work in occupation number space. The N_e-electron state is described by the state vector (see Appendix D for more details)

$$|L;k\rangle = |j_1 0, j_2 0, \ldots, j_k 1, \ldots, j_{N_e} 0\rangle \tag{8.35}$$

which can be interpreted as the state where the electron k lies in the level 1. The complete set of states (8.35) can now be divided into equivalence classes, just as we did in Sect. 7.2, but with the equivalence relation (7.25) replaced by

$$\begin{aligned} &|j_1' K_1', j_2' K_2', \ldots, j_{N_e}' K_{N_e}'\rangle \\ &\qquad = |j_1 - qk\, K_1, j_2 - qk\, K_2, \ldots, j_{N_e} - qk\, K_{N_e}\rangle \end{aligned} \tag{8.36}$$

in order to incorporate the Landau level labeling. From the state (8.35) a momentum eigenstate is constructed according to formula (7.27)

$$|(s,t);\mathcal{L}\rangle$$
$$= \frac{1}{\sqrt{|\mathcal{L}|}} \sum_{k=0}^{|\mathcal{L}|-1} \exp\left\{\frac{2\pi \mathrm{i} s}{N} k\right\} |j_1 - qk\,K_1, j_2 - qk\,K_2, \ldots, j_{N_\mathrm{e}} - qk\,K_{N_\mathrm{e}}\rangle. \tag{8.37}$$

It should be noted that compared with the intra-Landau level system the number of equivalence classes $\mathcal{L}$, and accordingly the number of relative momentum eigenstates $|(s,t);\mathcal{L}\rangle$, are now more than N_e times greater. Firstly, any one of the N_e electrons can be promoted to the next level, with each one of the choices creating a new class. Secondly, it is now possible to doubly occupy a given single-particle state labeled by the quantum number j.

The Hamiltonian, which is diagonalized in the space spanned by the states (8.37), is given in (7.28–31). The kinetic energy part of the Hamiltonian (7.28) is of course already diagonal contributing the constant $\hbar\omega_\mathrm{c}$ to the total energy and could therefore be omitted. On the other hand it represents the *total* kinetic energy and from the treatment presented in Sect. 7.2 we know that the physically relevant quantities are *relative*. The kinetic energy $\mathcal{K}$ is therefore split into two parts, $\mathcal{K} = \mathcal{K}^{\mathrm{CM}} + \mathcal{K}^{\mathrm{R}}$. The physical state must be an eigenstate of the relative kinetic energy operator

$$\mathcal{K}^{\mathrm{R}} = \frac{1}{2mN_\mathrm{e}} \sum_{l<k} (\boldsymbol{\Pi}_l - \boldsymbol{\Pi}_k)^2 \tag{8.38}$$

or, since the states are, by construction, eigenstates of $\mathcal{K}$, an eigenstate of the center of mass operator $\mathcal{K}^{\mathrm{CM}}$.

A numerical calculation based on the formalism presented above was carried out by *Pietiläinen* and *Chakraborty* [8.18]. The results are presented in Fig. 8.7 for the filling fraction $\nu = \frac{1}{3}$, where only the lowest excitation energies are presented. The most striking feature of these results is that they exactly repeat the roton spectrum in the lowest Landau level. In Appendix D, we have presented a proof (see also [8.19]) that among the inter-Landau level excitations there are points which exactly reproduce the intra-Landau excitations when shifted by $\hbar\omega_\mathrm{c}$. The numerical studies show that these repeated points are energetically the lowest modes. This is clearly in contradiction with the SMA results. One should note however that, in practice, it is not possible in a finite system to study the behavior of the dispersion curve at small values of the wave vector where the SMA is supposed to be at its best.

The qualitative features of the finite system results are in agreement with the spectrum where the lower Landau level is fully occupied [8.1,2]. A minimum at a finite wave vector is conspicuously present. The energy shift is smaller than in the $\nu = 1$ case, which is again expected on general

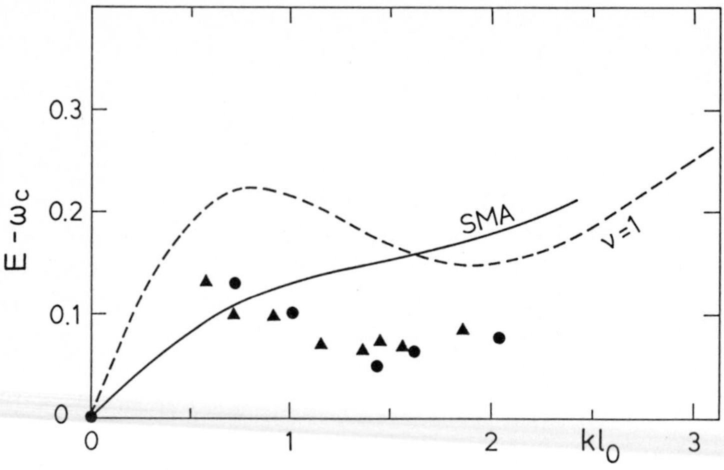

Fig. 8.7. Shift of the lowest energy mode from $\hbar\omega_c$ obtained for $\frac{1}{3}$ filling of the lowest Landau level (Spin polarized). Only the lowest excitation energies are shown for each $k\ell_0$, for four (●) and five-electron (▲) systems. The dashed curve is from [8.1]. The SMA curve is for $\nu = \frac{1}{3}$ from [8.18]

grounds [8.1]. The minimum at finite wave vector can soften and move into resonance with the cyclotron mode, if we introduce the standard procedure of finite-thickness corrections. In Fig. 8.8, we have plotted the spectrum for two values of the dimensionless thickness parameter $\beta = (b\ell_0)^{-1}$ (see

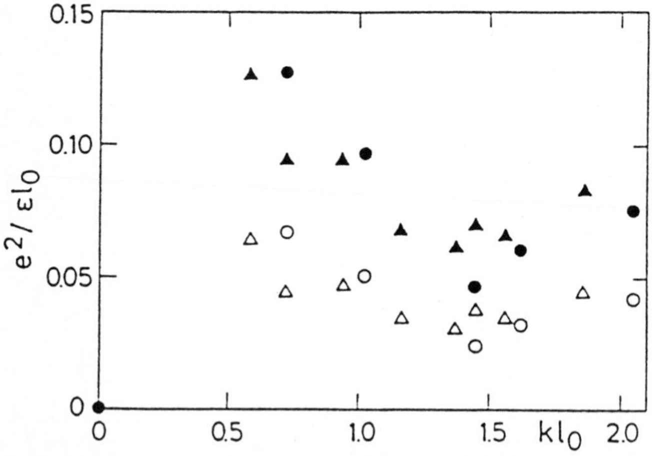

Fig. 8.8. The finite electron system result of Fig.8.7 as function of the dimensionless thickness parameter $\beta = (b\ell_0)^{-1}$. The filled and empty points are for $\beta = 0$ and $\beta = 1$ respectively

Sect. 5.6). The magnetic fields employed so far in the QHE experiments should lie between those values of β.

In Fig. 8.9, we have presented the four- and five-electron results for $\nu = \frac{1}{5}$. This filling factor is interesting since in this case, the SMA result shows a shallow minimum developing around $k\ell_0 \sim 1$, in contrast to the almost monotonic increase of the $\nu = \frac{1}{3}$ spectrum in the SMA (see Fig. 8.6). The change in shape of the spectrum for $\frac{1}{5}$ filling, as explained by *MacDonald* et al. [8.16], is directly related to the structure factor and hence to the correlations which are ν-dependent. Qualitatively, no difference between $\frac{1}{3}$ and $\frac{1}{5}$ fillings in the finite-size calculations is seen in Fig. 8.9.

As pointed out in the previous section and proved in Appendix D, the repetition of intra-Landau-level excitations in inter-Landau-level excitations is not a property of a finite-size system but manifests itself also in a many particle system. From the above studies of the magnetoplasmon spectrum with fractional filling of the lower Landau level the following picture therefore emerges: At small values of the wave vector, $k\ell_0 \lesssim 0.7$, judging from Figs. 7.10, 8.6 and 8.7, the coherent magnetoplasmon mode (8.24) is energetically preferable while at larger values the incoherent mode takes over thus exhibiting the repetition of the magnetoroton mode.

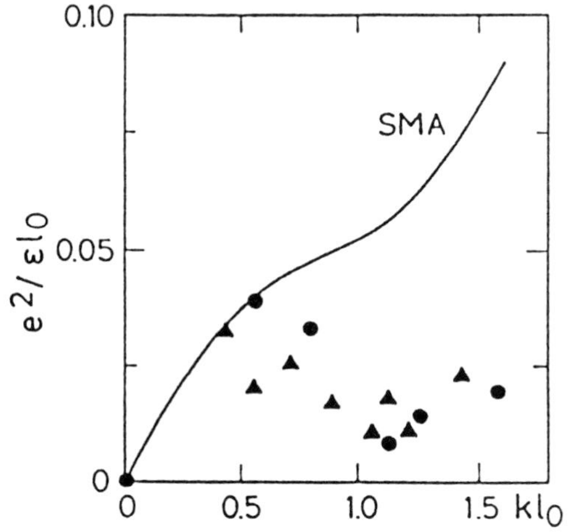

Fig. 8.9. Same as in Fig.8.7 but for $\nu = \frac{1}{5}$ for four-(●) and five-electron (▲) systems and the SMA result is from [8.18]

9. Further Topics

In this chapter, we present a mixed bag of interesting results which are of importance for our understanding of the FQHE. Much of the work described below needs further development and our aim in this chapter is simply to emphasize the important aspects of the presently available results.

9.1 Effect of Impurities

The effect of impurities on the Laughlin ground state has been investigated by *Pokrovskii* and *Talapov* [9.1,2]. They considered a delta-function form for the impurity interaction:

$$V_{\rm i}(r) = V_{\rm i}\,\delta(\boldsymbol{r}). \tag{9.1}$$

Recall that for $\nu = \frac{1}{m}$, Laughlin's state is nondegenerate. For $\nu < \frac{1}{m}$, the ground state is multiply degenerate, and the wave function is written

$$\psi = \psi_m\,Q(z_1, \dots, z_{N_{\rm e}}) \tag{9.2}$$

where Q is a symmetric polynomial of order $s \leq N_{\rm s} - m(N_{\rm e} - 1)$ in each variable [see (5.15)]. The impurities lift the degeneracy. Since $V_{\rm i}$ is positive, the wave function should vanish at points where the impurities are located. We then have

$$\psi = \prod_{\substack{i \leq j \leq N_{\rm e} \\ 1 \leq k \leq N_{\rm i}}} (z_j - \eta_k)\,\psi_m(z_1, \dots, z_{N_{\rm e}}) \tag{9.3}$$

where η_k is a complex coordinate of the kth impurity, and $N_{\rm i}$ is the number of impurities. Such a state can be realized only if $N_{\rm i} \leq s$. Comparing this state with (6.2), one can interpret the state (9.3) as the one in which a Laughlin quasihole of charge $+\frac{|e|}{3}$ is trapped at each impurity.

For $N_\mathrm{i} > s$, we cannot distribute the quasiholes among all the impurities. The ground state in this case would be written as

$$\psi = \prod_{\substack{1 \le j \le N_\mathrm{e} \\ 1 \le k \le s}} (z_j - \eta_k)\, \psi_m(z_1, \ldots, z_{N_\mathrm{e}}) \tag{9.4}$$

where the s impurities are chosen from N_i impurities such that the energy is a minimum. The ground-state energy is

$$E_0 = V_\mathrm{i} \sum_{s<k\le N_\mathrm{i}} \rho(\eta_k) \tag{9.5}$$

where $\rho(\eta)$ is the electron density at position η. Far from the holes one must have $\rho(\eta) \approx N_\mathrm{e}/N_\mathrm{s}$. The above authors have also studied the case of a strong impurity potential and its effect on the Hall steps [9.2].

In a detailed study of the effect of a charged impurity in the FQHE, *Zhang* et al. [9.3] performed finite-size system calculations in different geometries. They considered the electron-impurity interaction term in the Hamiltonian

$$\mathcal{H}_\mathrm{i} = -\sum_j \frac{Ze^2}{\epsilon|\boldsymbol{R}_\mathrm{i} - \boldsymbol{r}_j|} + E_\mathrm{i-b} \tag{9.6}$$

where Ze is the impurity charge, ϵ is the background dielectric constant, $\boldsymbol{R}_\mathrm{i}$ is the impurity position, $\boldsymbol{r}_j$ is the position of the jth electron, and $E_\mathrm{i-b}$ is the constant impurity-background interaction energy. Only the spin-polarized state was considered. The electron Hamiltonian with the additional term $\mathcal{H}_\mathrm{i}$ is then diagonalized numerically for few-electron systems ($N_\mathrm{e} = 3$ to 6).

In the spherical geometry, as we recall, the ground state occurs for the total angular momentum $\boldsymbol{L} = 0$. The presence of an impurity breaks the spherical symmetry. However, the azimuthal symmetry is still preserved and the states could be classified according to L_z. The ground state is at $L_z = 0$ and the excited states, which are degenerate, split because of level mixing by the impurity potential. In Fig. 9.1(a), we present the results of Zhang et al. for the excitation gap in the spherical geometry (defined as the difference between the ground state and the lowest excited state), as a function of the impurity strength Z for N_e=5 and 6. A significant reduction of the gap with increasing Z is noticeable in the result. The screening charge density for different impurity strengths is plotted in Fig. 9.2(a) in the spherical geometry. The screening charge accumulates at the impurity and oscillates away from the impurity with a characteristic length scale of ℓ_0. For fixed Z, the charge density is plotted in Fig. 9.3 for N_e=4, 5 and 6. The screening is quite independent of the system size.

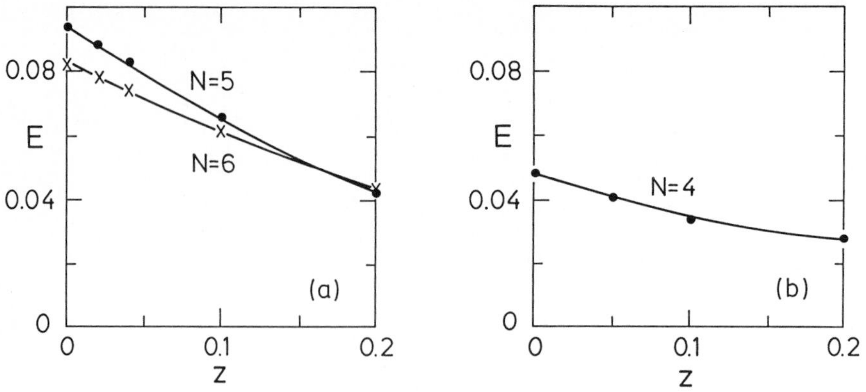

Fig. 9.1. Excitation energy gap (in units of potential energy) at $\nu = \frac{1}{3}$ as a function of the impurity strength Z for (a) spherical, and (b) rectangular geometry for a finite number of electrons [9.3]

Zhang et al. performed similar calculations for other geometries. In a periodic rectangular geometry, the impurity-free ground state is triply degenerate at $\nu = \frac{1}{3}$. The degeneracy is lifted by the impurity potential which mixes the momentum eigenstates. Again defining the excitation gap as the energy difference between the *lowest* ground state and the *lowest* excited state levels, the gap is plotted in Fig. 9.1(b) for N_e=4. The screening behavior for the rectangular geometry is presented in Fig. 9.2(b). These results are qualitatively similar to those for the spherical geometry.

In the disk geometry, there is no downward cusp in the ground state energy, which might be related to the open boundary condition (edge effect). The electronic charge density in the disk geometry both with and without the impurity (placed at the center of the disk), is shown in Fig. 9.2(c). For the impurity-free case, the charge density is *nonuniform*, in contrast to the other two geometries considered, and this is due to the finite-size effect. In the presence of the impurity, the screening behavior is very similar to that of the other two geometries.

The screening oscillation is not related to Friedel oscillation, which arise due to the existence of a sharp Fermi surface, but as these authors pointed out, is a consequence of the incompressiblity of the system. Similar calculations have been reported by *Rezayi* and *Haldane* [9.4] for a spherical geometry.

Rezayi and Haldane studied the effect of a short-range or delta-function impurity potential. Any potential, whose range is much less than the magnetic length could effectively be considered as a delta function with binding energy,

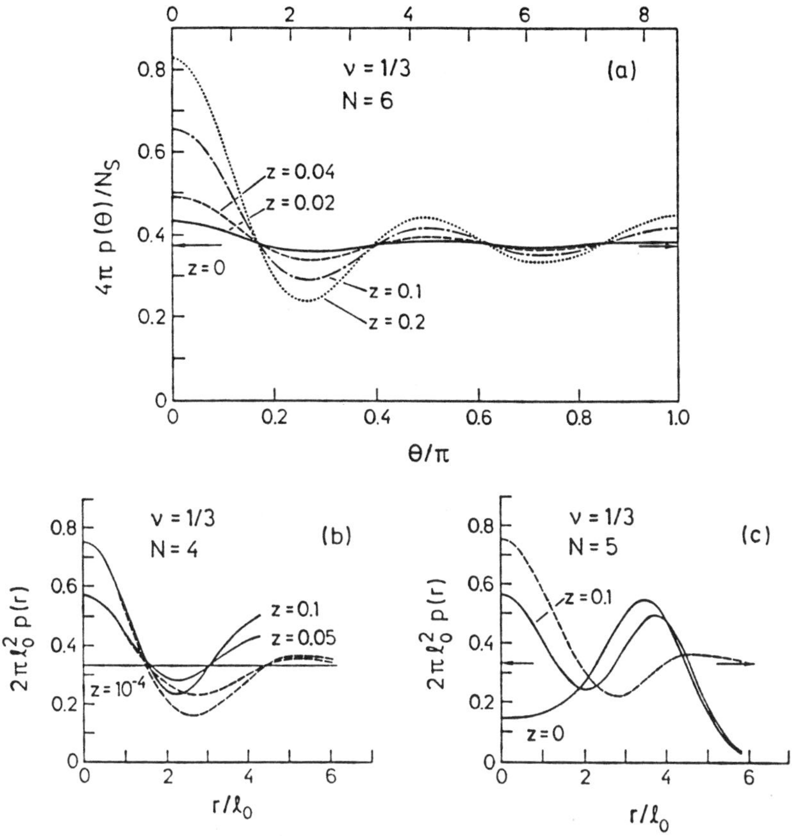

Fig. 9.2. The screening density ρ for different impurity strengths as a function of spatial separation in (a) spherical [$\rho(\theta)$ is the density per unit solid angle], (b) rectangular, and (c) disk geometries. In the rectangular geometry, the rotational symmetry is absent; the solid curves show the charge density in the (0,1) direction and the dashed curve is that in the (1,1) direction. In (c) the dashed curve gives the screening charge density. The arrows indicate the average normalized charge density in the disk at $\nu = \frac{1}{3}$ [9.3]

$$g = \frac{1}{\pi \ell_0^2} \int d\boldsymbol{r}\, V(\boldsymbol{r})\, \mathrm{e}^{-(r/\ell_0)^2}$$

for particles in the lowest Landau level. In fact, the real-space form of the linear response function in the ground state is defined by the charge density response to a weak delta function impurity potential. For a six-electron system in a spherical geometry, it was found that, at the position of the impurity, the charge density increases from zero to the maximum value as the impurity strength varies from $-\infty$ to $+\infty$. In the neighborhood of the impurity, there is a local oscillatory polarization of the charge density. The

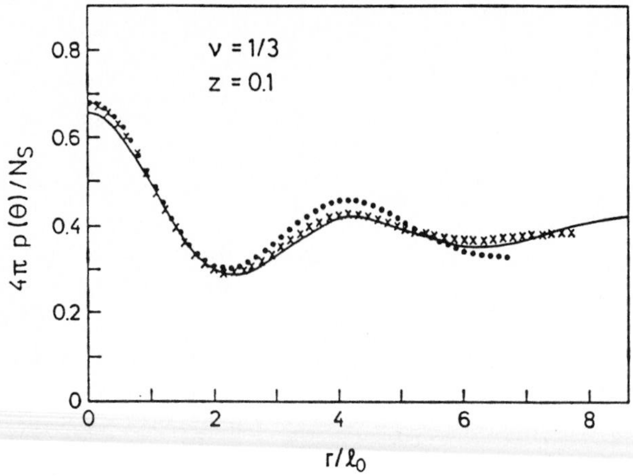

Fig. 9.3. The screening charge in the spherical geometry for a fixed charge $Z = 0.1$ as a function of the interparticle separation for different system sizes: $N_e = 6$ (solid curve), $N_e = 5$ (crosses), and $N_e = 4$ (dots) [9.3]

period of this oscillation is governed by the linear response of the Laughlin state and remains essentially unchanged even well outside the linear response regime.

The above authors also studied the effects of Coulomb impurity potentials for the six-electron system at $\nu = \frac{1}{3}$. The calculations are similar to those by *Zhang* et al. [9.3], described above. The only difference is that, in the calculations of *Rezayi* and *Haldane* [9.4], the charge of the impurity was varied from $+0.5e$ to $-0.5e$. They noticed that, in contrast to short-range impurities, the incompressible state was unstable if the charge of the impurity exceeded a certain critical value. For the six-electron system the critical charges were found to be $+0.38e$ and $-0.30e$.

An interesting upshot of the above studies is the result for the linear response [9.5]. The dynamic structure function in the SMA is given by

$$S(q,\omega) = \bar{s}(q)\,\delta\Big(\omega - \Delta(q)\Big). \tag{9.7}$$

The static susceptibility to an external perturbation is defined as

$$\begin{aligned} \chi(q) &= -2\int_0^\infty \frac{d\omega}{\omega}\, S(q,\omega) \\ &= -\frac{2\bar{s}(q)}{\Delta(q)}. \end{aligned} \tag{9.8}$$

The quantity $\alpha(q) \equiv \bar{s}(q)/\Delta(q)$ is plotted in Fig. 9.4.

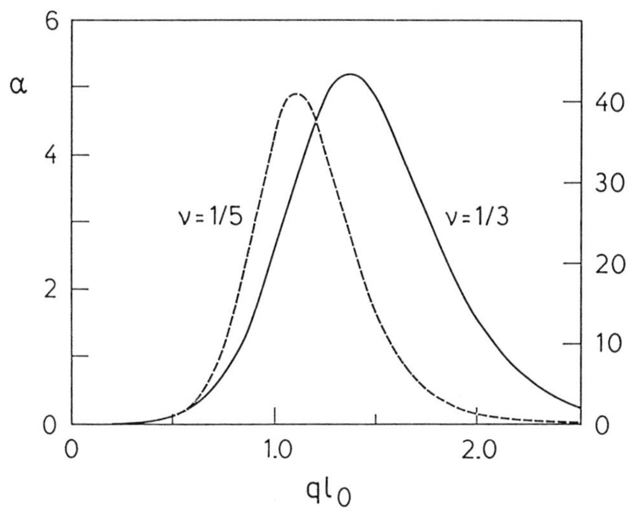

Fig. 9.4. Susceptibility $\alpha = -\frac{1}{2}\chi(q)$ for $\nu = \frac{1}{3}$ (scale on left) and $\frac{1}{5}$ (scale on right) [9.5]

Within linear response theory we have

$$\langle \delta \bar{\rho}_q \rangle = \rho v(q) \chi(q) \tag{9.9}$$

where $v(q) = 2\pi Z e^2/\epsilon q$ is the Fourier transformed Coulomb interaction and the mean density $\rho = e\nu/2\pi\ell_0^2$. The space charge distribution is

$$\frac{\langle \rho(r) \rangle}{\rho} = 1 + Z \int_0^\infty dq\, \chi(q) J_0(qr) \tag{9.10}$$

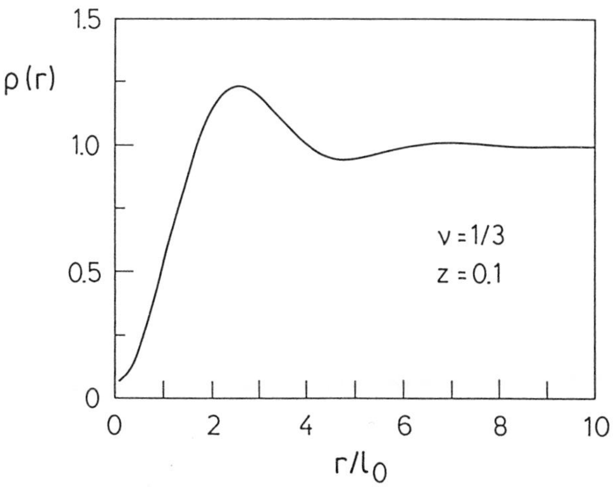

Fig. 9.5. Normalized charge distribution near a repulsive Coulomb impurity with $Z = 0.1$ [9.5]

and is shown in Fig. 9.5. As $\chi(q)$ is sharply peaked at the roton wave vector, the spatial distribution of the charge is oscillatory. This is the simple physical explanation provided in Ref. 9.5, for the charge oscillation observed by *Zhang* et al. [9.3], discussed above (Fig. 9.3). The impurity relaxation energy in linear response is given by

$$\Delta E = \frac{1}{2}\int \frac{d\boldsymbol{q}}{(2\pi)} v(q)\langle \delta\bar{\rho}_q\rangle \,. \tag{9.11}$$

For $\nu = \frac{1}{3}$, one obtains $\Delta E = -1.15Z^2$ [9.5]. For a five-electron system, the result is $\Delta E = -1.2Z^2$ [9.3].

9.2 Quantization condition

Our aim now is to derive the quantization condition for the FQH state, *i.e.* to show that the Hall conductivity is just equal to the filling factor ν in units of e^2/h. For simplicity we will discuss only the case $\nu < 1$. Our treatment, which is based on the work by *Tao* and *Haldane* [9.6], can be easily generalized also to handle higher Landau levels.[1]

We have seen that most of the interesting properties of the FQHE follow from the fact that there is an energy gap between the ground state and the excited states of the system. We have also learned (see Sect. 7.2) that this gap is due to the relative motion of the electrons. For this reason the CM motion has mostly played only a side role in our discussions. In particular, in Sect. 7.2, where we considered the translational symmetries of the two-dimensional electron system in a magnetic field, our emphasis was in relative translational operators. The conductivity, however, is a transport phenomenon where all the electrons move in one direction carrying the CM with them. Let us, therefore, return back to the formalism developed in Sect. 7.2 and look more closely at the CM translation operator (7.11)

$$\bar{T}(\boldsymbol{a}) = \prod_i T_i(\boldsymbol{a}), \tag{9.12}$$

where the magnetic translation operator (7.4)

$$T(\boldsymbol{a}) = \exp\left\{-\frac{\mathrm{i}}{\hbar}\boldsymbol{a}\cdot\boldsymbol{K}\right\}$$

are the operators translating single particles by the vector $\boldsymbol{a}$. Recall that

[1] For the quantization condition in the IQHE regime, see Sect. 2.7 and [9.7]

the most general translation vectors were of the form

$$\boldsymbol{a} = \frac{1}{N_\mathrm{s}}[mL_x\widehat{\boldsymbol{x}} + nL_y\widehat{\boldsymbol{y}}], \tag{9.13}$$

when we required the CM translation operators to commute with single particle operators. Let us, therefore, define the elementary CM translation operators as

$$\begin{aligned} \bar{T}_x &= \exp\left[\frac{\mathrm{i}}{N_\mathrm{s}\hbar}L_x K_x^\mathrm{c}\right] \\ \bar{T}_y &= \exp\left[\frac{\mathrm{i}}{N_\mathrm{s}\hbar}L_y K_y^\mathrm{c}\right]. \end{aligned} \tag{9.14}$$

Here K_x^c and K_y^c are the x and y components of the operator

$$\boldsymbol{K}^\mathrm{c} = \sum_j \boldsymbol{K}_j, \tag{9.15}$$

where the operators $\boldsymbol{K}_j$ in turn were defined as

$$\boldsymbol{K}_j = \mathrm{i}\hbar\nabla_j - eBy_j\widehat{\boldsymbol{x}}. \tag{9.16}$$

It is a simple matter to verify that the translations $\bar{T}_\mu$ satisfy the relation

$$\bar{T}_x\bar{T}_y = \bar{T}_y\bar{T}_x \mathrm{e}^{-2\mathrm{i}\pi p/q}, \tag{9.17}$$

when the number of electrons is $N_\mathrm{e} = pN$, the nuber of flux quanta is $N_\mathrm{s} = qN$ and N is the highest common divisor of N_e and N_s.

To facilitate the calculation of the Hall conductivity we now make a slight modification in the scheme of Sect. 7.2: we let the sample be traversed by magnetic fluxes $\alpha_x\hbar/e$ and $\alpha_y\hbar/e$ of two perpendicular solenoids. The effect of this is to replace the momentum $\boldsymbol{\Pi}_j$ in Eq. (7.2) by

$$\boldsymbol{\Pi}_j + \boldsymbol{b} = -\mathrm{i}\hbar\nabla_j - e\boldsymbol{A}(\boldsymbol{r}_j) + \boldsymbol{b}, \tag{9.18}$$

where $\boldsymbol{b}$ is the vector

$$\boldsymbol{b} = \hbar\left(\frac{\alpha_x}{L_x}, \frac{\alpha_y}{L_y}\right). \tag{9.19}$$

It is easy to see that this addition has no effects to the translation operators we have been discussing thus far. The Hamiltonian $\mathcal{H}$, however, is now changed to

$$\mathcal{H} = \frac{1}{2m^*}\sum_j (\boldsymbol{\Pi}_j + \boldsymbol{b})^2 + \frac{1}{2}\sum_{i\neq j} V(\boldsymbol{r}_i - \boldsymbol{r}_j). \tag{9.20}$$

We split this into the CM and relative parts like

$$\mathcal{H} = \mathcal{H}_{\mathrm{c}} + \mathcal{H}_{\mathrm{r}}, \tag{9.21}$$

where the CM part is given as

$$\mathcal{H}_{\mathrm{c}} = \frac{1}{2m^* N_{\mathrm{e}}} \left(\boldsymbol{\Pi}^{\mathrm{c}} + N_{\mathrm{e}}\boldsymbol{b}\right)^2 \tag{9.22}$$

and the relative part as

$$\mathcal{H}_{\mathrm{r}} = \frac{1}{2m^* N_{\mathrm{e}}} \sum_{i<j} \left[(\boldsymbol{\Pi}_i - \boldsymbol{\Pi}_j) + V(\boldsymbol{r}_i - \boldsymbol{r}_j)\right]. \tag{9.23}$$

The operator $\boldsymbol{\Pi}^{\mathrm{c}}$ in $\mathcal{H}_{\mathrm{c}}$ is the total momentum

$$\boldsymbol{\Pi}^{\mathrm{c}} = \sum_j \boldsymbol{\Pi}_j. \tag{9.24}$$

Since the Hamiltonian of the relative motion does not depend on our artificial fluxes α_x and α_y, we can write the ground state Ψ_0 of $\mathcal{H}$ as the product

$$\Psi_0(\alpha_x, \alpha_y) = \Psi_0^{\mathrm{c}}(\alpha_x, \alpha_y)\Psi_0^{\mathrm{r}}, \tag{9.25}$$

where $\Psi_0^{\mathrm{c}}(\alpha_x, \alpha_y)$ and Ψ_0^{r} are the ground states of $\mathcal{H}_{\mathrm{c}}$ and $\mathcal{H}_{\mathrm{r}}$, respectively.

By construction, the CM translations $\bar{T}_x$ and $\bar{T}_y$ commute with the Hamiltonian $\mathcal{H}$ and with the single-particle operators $T_j(L_x\widehat{\boldsymbol{x}})$ and $T_j(L_y\widehat{\boldsymbol{y}})$. However, due to the relation (9.17) we can only diagonalize $\bar{T}_x^q$, $\bar{T}_y$, $T_j(L_x\widehat{\boldsymbol{x}})$, $T_j(L_y\widehat{\boldsymbol{y}})$ and $\mathcal{H}$ simultaneosly. Therefore, if Ψ_0^0 is a ground state of $\mathcal{H}$ then

$$\Psi_0^0, \bar{T}_x\Psi_0^0, (\bar{T}_x)^2\Psi_0^0, \ldots, (\bar{T}_x)^{q-1}\Psi_0^0 \tag{9.26}$$

form the set of q-fold degenerate ground states of $\mathcal{H}$. Since the operators $\bar{T}_x$ and $\bar{T}_y$ move only the CM of the system and have no effect on the relative motions we see that this degeneracy is actually due to $\mathcal{H}_{\mathrm{c}}$. Therefore, we can write these degenerate ground states in the form

$$\Psi_0^s(\alpha_x, \alpha_y) = \Psi_0^c(s; \alpha_x, \alpha_y)\Psi_0^{\mathrm{r}}, \tag{9.27}$$

where s can take the values $0, 1, 2, \ldots, q-1$. As noted above the state Ψ_0^0 is a simultaneous eigenstate of the operators $\bar{T}_x^q$ and $\bar{T}_y$. Let us suppose that the corresponding eigenvalues are $\exp(\mathrm{i}q\theta_x)$ and $\exp(\mathrm{i}\theta_y)$, respectively. From the relations (9.17) and (9.27) we can deduce that

$$\begin{aligned} \bar{T}_x^q \Psi_0^{\mathrm{c}}(s;\alpha_x,\alpha_y) &= \mathrm{e}^{\mathrm{i}\theta_x}\Psi_0^{\mathrm{c}}(s;\alpha_x,\alpha_y) \\ \bar{T}_y \Psi_0^{\mathrm{c}}(s;\alpha_x,\alpha_y) &= \mathrm{e}^{\mathrm{i}(\theta_y+2\pi ps/q)}\Psi_0^{\mathrm{c}}(s;\alpha_x,\alpha_y). \end{aligned} \tag{9.28}$$

The Hamiltonian $\mathcal{H}_{\mathrm{c}}$ describes the motion of a single particle with the mass $N_{\mathrm{e}}m^*$ and with the location at $\boldsymbol{r}_{\mathrm{c}} = 1/N_{\mathrm{e}}\sum_j \boldsymbol{r}_j$ in the magnetic field. Its eigenstates are then formed exactly like we did in Sect. 7.2. If we take the conditions (9.28) explicitly into account we arrive at

$$\begin{aligned} \Psi_0^{\mathrm{c}}(s;\alpha_x,\alpha_y) = C_0\sum_k \exp\Bigg[&\mathrm{i}q\theta_x k - \mathrm{i}N_{\mathrm{e}}\left(-2\pi s - \theta_y\frac{q}{p} + 2\pi qk\right)\frac{y_{\mathrm{c}}}{L_y} \\ &- \mathrm{i}N_{\mathrm{e}}\left(\xi_s - 2\pi qk\frac{\ell_0^2}{L_y}\right)\frac{\alpha_x}{L_x} \\ &- N_{\mathrm{e}}\left(\xi_s - 2\pi qk\frac{\ell_0^2}{L_y}\right)^2\frac{1}{2\ell_0^2}\Bigg], \end{aligned} \tag{9.29}$$

where C_0 is the normalization constant and

$$\xi_s = x_{\mathrm{c}} + (\alpha_y + 2\pi s + \theta_y\frac{q}{p})\frac{\ell_0^2}{L_y}. \tag{9.30}$$

Let us now examine how the system moves from one ground state to another when we change the fluxes α_x and α_y adiabatically. Due to the energy gap the relative motion of the system remains in this process in its original state Ψ_0^{r}. We can therefore restrict our attention to the CM part $\Psi_0^{\mathrm{c}}(\alpha_x,\alpha_y)$ of the ground state. Let us suppose that originally this state is the superposition

$$\Psi_0^{\mathrm{c}}(\alpha_x,\alpha_y) = \sum_s c_s\Psi_0^{\mathrm{c}}(s;\alpha_x,\alpha_y) \tag{9.31}$$

of the eigenstates of $\mathcal{H}_{\mathrm{c}}$. Using the explicit representation (9.29) it is a straightforward matter to verify that this state transforms to

$$\begin{aligned} \Psi_0^{\mathrm{c}}(\alpha_x+2\pi,\alpha_y) =& \exp\left[-\mathrm{i}2\pi\sum_j\frac{x_j}{L_x} - \mathrm{i}\theta_y - \mathrm{i}\alpha_y\frac{p}{q}\right] \\ &\times\sum_s c_s\exp\left[-\mathrm{i}2\pi s\frac{p}{q}\right]\Psi_0^{\mathrm{c}}(s;\alpha_x,\alpha_y), \end{aligned} \tag{9.32}$$

when α_x is increased by 2π. We see that due to the different phase factors for the states $\Psi_0^c(s;\alpha_x,\alpha_y)$ it is impossible to transform this back to the original one by a gauge transformation. However, if α_x is increased by $2\pi q$ we end up to

$$\Psi_0^c(\alpha_x+2\pi q,\alpha_y)=\exp\left[-\mathrm{i}2\pi q\sum_j\frac{x_j}{L_x}-\mathrm{i}\alpha_y p\right]\Psi_0^c(\alpha_x,\alpha_y), \tag{9.33}$$

which can be transformed to $\Psi_0^c(\alpha_x,\alpha_y)$ by a gauge transformation.

Let us now look at what happens when we let α_y increase by 2π. A straightforward calculation shows that the new state is given as

$$\Psi_0^c(\alpha_x,\alpha_y+2\pi)=\exp\left[-\mathrm{i}2\pi\sum_j\frac{y_j}{L_y}\right]\sum_s c_s\Psi_0^c(s+1;\alpha_x,\alpha_y). \tag{9.34}$$

Again, it is necessary to increase α_y by $2\pi q$ to get a state like

$$\Psi_0^c(\alpha_x,\alpha_y+2\pi q)=\exp\left[-\mathrm{i}q\theta_x+\mathrm{i}2\pi q\sum_j\frac{y_j}{L_y}\right]\Psi_0^c(\alpha_x,\alpha_y), \tag{9.35}$$

which can be transformed back to the original one by a gauge transformation. Therefore, all points of the form $(\alpha_x+2m_xq\pi,\alpha_y+2m_yq\pi)$, where m_x and m_y are integers, are physically equivalent in the $\alpha_x\alpha_y$-space. The whole $\alpha_x\alpha_y$-space is a torus formed from the unit cell $0\le\alpha_x\le 2\pi q$ and $0\le\alpha_y\le 2\pi q$.

We are now in the position to calculate the Hall conductivity. According to Eq. (B.29), at temperatures low enough, the Hall conductivity is given by

$$\sigma_\mathrm{H}=\frac{\mathrm{i}e^2\hbar}{L_xL_y}\sum_{n=1}\frac{\langle\Psi_0|v_x|\Psi_n\rangle\langle\Psi_n|v_y|\Psi_0\rangle-\langle\Psi_0|v_y|\Psi_n\rangle\langle\Psi_n|v_x|\Psi_0\rangle}{(E_n-E_0)^2}. \tag{9.36}$$

In our particular case the velocity operators are

$$\begin{aligned}v_x&=\frac{1}{m^*}\left(\boldsymbol{\Pi}_x^c+N_e\hbar\frac{\alpha_x}{L_x}\right)\\ v_y&=\frac{1}{m^*}\left(\boldsymbol{\Pi}_y^c+N_e\hbar\frac{\alpha_y}{L_y}\right).\end{aligned} \tag{9.37}$$

It is easy to see that they can also be expressed as

$$\begin{aligned} v_x &= \frac{L_x}{\hbar}\frac{\partial \mathcal{H}}{\partial \alpha_x} \\ v_y &= \frac{L_y}{\hbar}\frac{\partial \mathcal{H}}{\partial \alpha_y}. \end{aligned} \tag{9.38}$$

Since the states Ψ_n are orthonormalized eigenstates of the Hamiltonian it is a simple matter to show that

$$\begin{aligned} 0 &= \frac{\partial}{\partial \alpha_\mu}\langle \Psi_0|\mathcal{H}|\Psi_n\rangle \\ &= E_n\left\langle \frac{\partial \Psi_0}{\partial \alpha_\mu}\middle|\Psi_n\right\rangle + \left\langle \Psi_0\middle|\frac{\partial \mathcal{H}}{\partial \alpha_\mu}\middle|\Psi_n\right\rangle + E_0\left\langle \Psi_0\middle|\frac{\partial \Psi_n}{\partial \alpha_\mu}\right\rangle. \end{aligned} \tag{9.39}$$

Similar treatment gives the relation

$$\left\langle \Psi_0\middle|\frac{\partial \Psi_n}{\partial \alpha_\mu}\right\rangle = -\left\langle \frac{\partial \Psi_0}{\partial \alpha_\mu}\middle|\Psi_n\right\rangle. \tag{9.40}$$

We now substitute the velocity operators in the form of Eq. (9.38) into the expression (9.36), employ these last two formulas and note that in the resulting sum it is possible to include the term with $n = 0$ without any effects. After these manipulations the Hall conductivity turns out to be

$$\sigma_{\mathrm{H}} = \frac{\mathrm{i}e^2}{\hbar}\left[\left\langle \frac{\partial \Psi_0}{\partial \alpha_x}\middle|\frac{\partial \Psi_0}{\partial \alpha_y}\right\rangle - \left\langle \frac{\partial \Psi_0}{\partial \alpha_y}\middle|\frac{\partial \Psi_0}{\partial \alpha_x}\right\rangle\right]. \tag{9.41}$$

Since the relative motion part Ψ^{r} does not depend on the parameters α_x and α_y we can replace the total wave function Ψ_0 by its CM part $\Psi_0^{\mathrm{c}}(\alpha_x, \alpha_y)$ in the formula above to get

$$\sigma_{\mathrm{H}} = \frac{\mathrm{i}e^2}{\hbar}\left[\frac{\partial J_y}{\partial \alpha_x} - \frac{\partial J_x}{\partial \alpha_y}\right], \tag{9.42}$$

where the current operator is defined as

$$J_\mu = \left\langle \Psi_0^{\mathrm{c}}(\alpha_x, \alpha_y)\middle|\frac{\partial}{\partial \alpha_\mu}\middle|\Psi_0^{\mathrm{c}}(\alpha_x, \alpha_y)\right\rangle. \tag{9.43}$$

We now probe our system by increasing adiabatically the strength α_x of the first solenoid by $2\pi q$ and after that increasing α_y by the same amount. After these changes the system falls back to its original state. We repeat this basic process continuosly. The Hall conductivity is then the average over one basic cycle, *i.e.*

$$\sigma_{\mathrm{H}} = \frac{\mathrm{i}e^2}{2\pi h q^2} \int_0^{2\pi q} d\alpha_x \int_0^{2\pi q} d\alpha_y \left[\frac{\partial J_y}{\partial \alpha_x} - \frac{\partial J_x}{\partial \alpha_y} \right]. \tag{9.44}$$

Performing one of the integrals we get

$$\begin{aligned} \sigma_{\mathrm{H}} = \frac{\mathrm{i}e^2}{2\pi h q^2} \Bigg[& \int_0^{2\pi q} [J_x(\alpha_x, 0) - J_x(\alpha_x, 2\pi q)] d\alpha_x \\ & + \int_0^{2\pi q} [J_y(2\pi q, \alpha_y) - J_y(0, \alpha_y)] d\alpha_y \Bigg]. \end{aligned} \tag{9.45}$$

Using the transformation properties (9.33) and (9.35) we can easily verify that

$$\begin{aligned} J_x(\alpha_x, \alpha_y + 2\pi q) &= \left\langle \Psi_0^{\mathrm{c}}(\alpha_x, \alpha_y + 2\pi q) \middle| \frac{\partial \Psi_0^{\mathrm{c}}(\alpha_x, \alpha_y + 2\pi q)}{\partial \alpha_x} \right\rangle \\ &= \left\langle \Psi_0^{\mathrm{c}}(\alpha_x, \alpha_y) \middle| \frac{\partial \Psi_0^{\mathrm{c}}(\alpha_x, \alpha_y)}{\partial \alpha_x} \right\rangle \\ &= J_x(\alpha_x, \alpha_y), \end{aligned} \tag{9.46}$$

while

$$\begin{aligned} J_y(\alpha_x + 2\pi q, \alpha_y) &= \left\langle \Psi_0^{\mathrm{c}}(\alpha_x + 2\pi q, \alpha_y) \middle| \frac{\partial \Psi_0^{\mathrm{c}}(\alpha_x + 2\pi q, \alpha_y)}{\partial \alpha_y} \right\rangle \\ &= -\mathrm{i}p + \left\langle \Psi_0^{\mathrm{c}}(\alpha_x, \alpha_y) \middle| \frac{\partial \Psi_0^{\mathrm{c}}(\alpha_x, \alpha_y)}{\partial \alpha_y} \right\rangle \\ &= -\mathrm{i}p + J_y(\alpha_x, \alpha_y). \end{aligned} \tag{9.47}$$

Hence the first integral gives no contribution while the second one evaluates to $-\mathrm{i}2\pi pq$ and the Hall conductivity will be

$$\sigma_{\mathrm{H}} = \frac{p}{q} \frac{e^2}{h}. \tag{9.48}$$

which is the required quantization condition.

9.3 Higher Landau Levels

In this section, we discuss the FQHE states where higher Landau levels are partially occupied. The earliest study of this problem was by *MacDonald* [9.8]. The higher Landau-level generalization of the Laughlin state is given by

$$|\psi_0^n\rangle = \prod_{i=1}^{N_e} \frac{(a_i^\dagger)^n}{\sqrt{n!}} |\psi_0^0\rangle \tag{9.49}$$

where $|\psi_0^0\rangle$ is the ground state for $\nu = \frac{1}{m}$, n is the Landau-level index, and a_i is the inter-Landau level ladder operator (see Sect. 8.3). The nth Landau level radial distribution function was calculated by MacDonald using the plasma analogy and is shown in Fig. 9.6.

In calculating the ground-state energy, *MacDonald* and *Girvin* [9.9] noticed that, the relation between pair-correlation functions in different Landau levels is much simpler in reciprocal space. The procedure is as follows: a plane wave function of any electron coordinate can be written as

$$\mathrm{e}^{-\mathrm{i}\boldsymbol{k}\cdot\boldsymbol{r}_i} = \exp\left(-\frac{1}{\sqrt{2}}k a_i^\dagger\right)\exp\left(-\frac{1}{\sqrt{2}}k^* a_i\right)\exp\left(-\frac{1}{\sqrt{2}}\mathrm{i}k b_i\right)\exp\left(-\frac{1}{\sqrt{2}}\mathrm{i}k^* b_i^\dagger\right) \tag{9.50}$$

where $a_i, a_i^\dagger$ and $b_i, b_i^\dagger$ are inter-Landau level and intra-Landau level ladder operators respectively, and k is a complex number representation of the

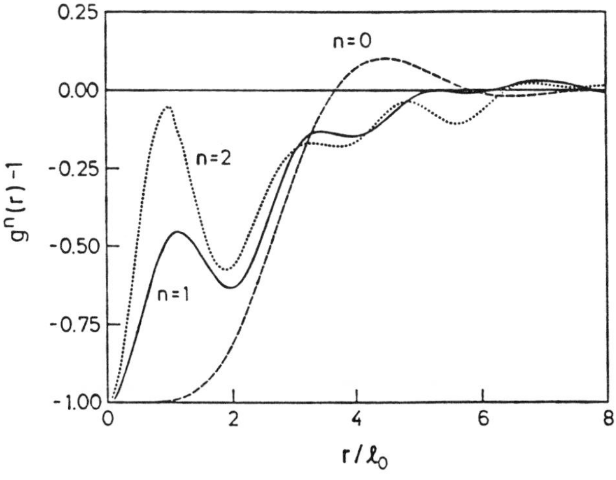

Fig. 9.6. Pair-correlation function for the Laughlin state $g^n(r)$ at $\nu = \frac{1}{3}$ in the case of $n = 0, 1$ and 2 Landau levels [9.8]

wave vector. Recalling the procedure for projection of the density operator onto the nth Landau level (see Sect. 8.3), we have

$$\begin{aligned}\langle\psi_0^n|\rho_{-k}^{nn}\rho_k^{nn}|\psi_0^n\rangle &= \left[L_n\left(\tfrac{1}{2}|k|^2\right)\right]^2\langle\psi_0^n|\bar{\rho}_{-k}\bar{\rho}_k|\psi_0^n\rangle \\ &= N_\mathrm{e}\left[L_n\left(\tfrac{1}{2}|k|^2\right)\right]^2\bar{s}(k)\end{aligned} \tag{9.51}$$

where,

$$\bar{\rho}_k \equiv \sum_i \exp\left[-\frac{\mathrm{i}}{\sqrt{2}}kb_i\right]\exp\left[-\frac{\mathrm{i}}{\sqrt{2}}k^*b_i^\dagger\right] \tag{9.52}$$

and $L_n(x)$ is the Laguerre polynomial. For the higher Landau level Laughlin states, it then follows that [9.9]

$$\begin{aligned}h^n(k) &= \rho_0\int d\boldsymbol{r}\,\mathrm{e}^{-\mathrm{i}\boldsymbol{k}\cdot\boldsymbol{r}_i}[g^n(r)-1] \\ &= \left[L_n\left(\tfrac{1}{2}|k|^2\right)\right]^2 h^0(k).\end{aligned} \tag{9.53}$$

In (9.53) ρ_0 is the areal density of electrons. The evaluation of the energy for the state $|\psi_0^n\rangle$ is then

$$\begin{aligned}N_\mathrm{e}^{-1}\langle\psi_0^n|\mathcal{H}|\psi_0^n\rangle &= \frac{1}{2}e^2\rho_0\int d\boldsymbol{r}\,r^{-1}\,h^n(r) \\ &= \frac{1}{2}e^2\int_0^\infty dq\,\left[L_n\left(\tfrac{1}{2}q^2\right)\right]^2 h^0(q).\end{aligned} \tag{9.54}$$

Using Laughlin's trial wave function (5.14), the ground-state energies for $\nu^{-1} = 3, 5, 7$, and 9 for $n = 0, 1$, and 2 are presented in Table 9.1. The results for the CDW state energies are also given in this Table. They were obtained self-consistently in the HF approximation by MacDonald and Girvin.

Table 9.1. Energy per particle for the Laughlin state and the CDW state in the nth Landau level. The energies are in units of $e^2/\epsilon\ell_0$.

m	$n=0$		$n=1$		$n=2$	
	Laughlin	CDW	Laughlin	CDW	Laughlin	CDW
1	−0.627	−0.627	−0.470	−0.470	−0.401	−0.401
3	−0.409	−0.388	−0.325	−0.316	−0.265	−0.256
5	−0.327	−0.322	−0.294	−0.289	−0.247	−0.250
7	−0.280	−0.279	−0.264	−0.261	−0.252	−0.240
9	−0.250	−0.250	−0.244	−0.238	−0.233	−0.225

From these results, these authors concluded that, (a) the transition to a Wigner crystal ground state occurs at smaller filling factors in higher Landau levels, (b) the incompressible fluid ground state is only marginally stable, if not unstable, in the case where $\nu^{-1} \geq 3 + 2n$ is not satisfied.

These authors have also studied the collective excitations in the higher Landau levels by writing the approximate many-body states as

$$|\psi_k^n\rangle = \frac{\rho_k^{nn}|\psi_0^n\rangle}{\left[\langle\psi_0^n|\rho_{-k}^{nn}\rho_k^{nn}|\psi_0^n\rangle\right]^{\frac{1}{2}}}. \tag{9.55}$$

The collective excitation is then obtained from

$$\langle\psi_{\boldsymbol{k}}^n|\mathcal{H}|\psi_{\boldsymbol{k}}^n\rangle = \langle\psi_0^n|\mathcal{H}|\psi_0^n\rangle + \Delta^n(k), \tag{9.56}$$

where,

$$\Delta^n(k) = \frac{\langle\psi_0^n|\left[\rho_{-k}^{nn}, \left[\mathcal{H}, \rho_k^{nn}\right]\right]|\psi_0^n\rangle}{\langle\psi_0^n|\rho_{-k}^{nn}\rho_k^{nn}|\psi_0^n\rangle}. \tag{9.57}$$

Within the subspace associated with the nth Landau level

$$[\mathcal{H}, \rho_k^{nn}] = \frac{1}{2}\int \frac{d\boldsymbol{q}}{(2\pi)^2}\, v(q) \left[L_n\left(\tfrac{1}{2}|q|^2\right)\right]^2 \left[\bar{\rho}_{-\boldsymbol{q}}\bar{\rho}_{\boldsymbol{q}}, \bar{\rho}_{\boldsymbol{k}}\right]. \tag{9.58}$$

Using (9.58) and (7.47) in (9.59) one obtains,

$$\begin{aligned}\Delta^n(k) = \int \frac{d\boldsymbol{q}}{(2\pi)^2}\, v(q) \left[L_n\left(\tfrac{1}{2}|q|^2\right)\right]^2 \Big[\Big(\mathrm{e}^{(q^*k-k^*q)/2} - 1\Big) \\ \times\, \bar{s}(q)\,\mathrm{e}^{-\frac{1}{2}|k|^2} + \Big(\mathrm{e}^{\boldsymbol{k}\cdot\boldsymbol{q}} - \mathrm{e}^{\boldsymbol{k}^*\boldsymbol{q}}\Big)\, \bar{s}(k+q)\Big]\Big/\bar{s}(k).\end{aligned} \tag{9.59}$$

The collective excitations obtained from (9.59) for $\nu = \frac{1}{3}$ and $\nu = \frac{1}{5}$ are plotted in Figs. 9.7 and 9.8 respectively. Let us first consider the results for $\nu = \frac{1}{3}$. In fact, the curve for $n = 1$, when spin degeneracy and particle-hole symmetry are taken into account, describes the *total* filling fractions $\nu^* = \frac{7}{3}, \frac{8}{3}, \frac{10}{3}$ and $\frac{11}{3}$ in the strong-field limit. The dispersion has lower energy than that for $n = 0$. The result at $\nu = \frac{1}{5}$ for $n = 1$ is, however, quite the opposite presumably indicating that at $\frac{1}{5}$ the system is far from the crystallization transition for the higher Landau level.

Haldane [9.10] has performed a numerical diagonalization of a six-electron Hamiltonian with periodic boundary conditions on a hexagonal cell. He obtained a *gapless* ground state at $\nu = \frac{1}{3}$ for $n = 1$. Finite system calculations have also been performed by *d'Ambrumenil* and *Reynolds* [9.11]. Their conclusion is that the FQHE is likely to occur at $\nu = \frac{1}{5}$ for $n = 1$.

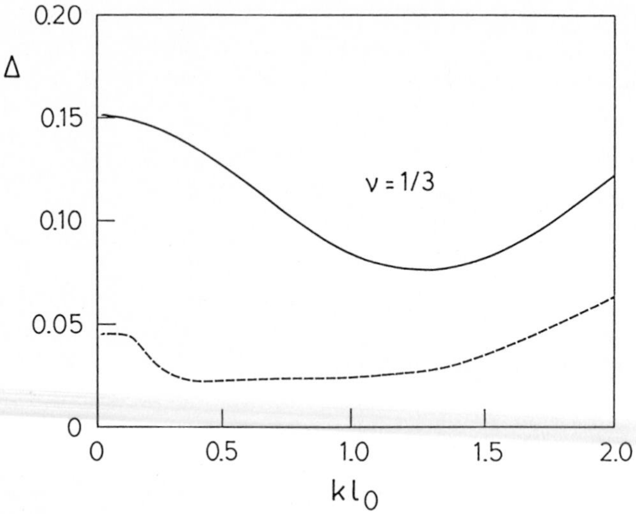

Fig. 9.7. Collective modes at $\nu = \frac{1}{3}$ for the $n = 0$ Landau level (solid line) and the $n = 1$ Landau level (dashed line) [9.9]

However, at $\nu = \frac{1}{3}$, the Laughlin wave function is not a good candidate for the ground state. A small gap is predicted for this filling.

Experimentally, some tendency to form plateaus at $\nu = \frac{19}{7}$ and $\frac{8}{3}$ has been reported [9.12]. More experimental and theoretical work is needed to clarify the situation.

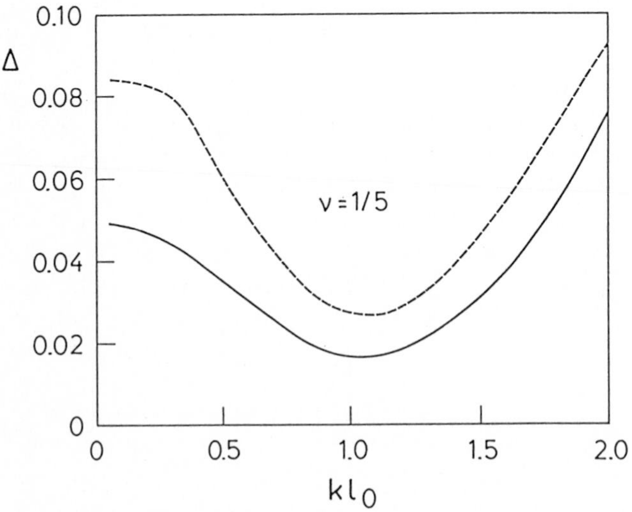

Fig. 9.8. Same as in Fig. 9.7, but for $\nu = \frac{1}{5}$ [9.9]

Finally, estimates for the quasiparticle and quasihole energies for higher Landau levels are also provided by *MacDonald* and *Girvin* [9.13]. The quasiparticle-quasihole energy gap is reported as $E_g(n = 1) = 0.059$ for $\nu = \frac{1}{3}$ and 0.043 for $\nu = \frac{1}{5}$ (in units of $e^2/\epsilon\ell_0$).

9.4 Even Denominator Filling Fractions

In our discussion of the theoretical work so far, we have only described the filling fractions with *odd* denominators. The fact that all investigations focused their attention mostly on these fractions is hardly surprising, because the experimental results clearly demonstrated that for the FQHE to occur, the odd denominators are favored exclusively. As we recall, Laughlin's approach *explains* such a fact by the requirement of antisymmetry under interchange of particles and in the hierarchical scheme, such filling factors are taken as the starting point in developing the higher-order filling factors with odd denominators. The possibility of observing the FQHE for *even* denominator filling factors is not excluded, however, in these theories.

The simplest filling factor with even denominator is $\nu = \frac{1}{2}$. In this case, the Laughlin-type wave function would describe a system of particles obeying *Bose* statistics.[2] However, one can group the electrons into bound *pairs*, and the pairs can then transform as bosons under interchange of their positions [9.15], and a Laughlin-type wave function could still be used. For a finite-size system calculations in a periodic rectangular geometry (Sect. 5.1), with particles obeying *Bose* statistics, a *cusp* at $\nu = \frac{1}{2}$ was in fact found by *Yoshioka* [9.16]. In this geometry, collective modes of the type described in Sect. 7.2, were also calculated by *Haldane* [9.17].

The ground-state energy (per electron) at $\nu = \frac{1}{2}$, calculated for four- to ten-electron systems in a periodic rectangular geometry is shown in Fig. 9.9. In contrast to the case of $\nu = \frac{1}{3}$, the results in this case show strong dependence on the electron number. The extrapolation of the results in the thermodynamic limit leads to the energy $\approx -0.472\, e^2/\epsilon\ell_0$. The results are of course, lower compared to the crystal energy in the HF limit: The energy difference is ≈ 0.028, while for $\nu = \frac{1}{3}$, the corresponding energy difference is ≈ 0.025. However, the energy difference is much smaller (~ 0.01) for the crystal energies obtained for the four-electron system by Yoshioka et al. (see Fig. 5.2). Given such a small difference, it is not possible to entirely rule out the crystal state at $\nu = \frac{1}{2}$. In particular, the absence of the FQHE in the

[2] Interestingly, *Kalmayer* and *Laughlin* have shown that such a wave function would also describe the ground state of a two-dimensional Heisenberg antiferromagnet on a triangular lattice [9.14].

experimental results makes this possibility even more plausible. Improved crystal state calculations are urgently required to settle this interesting issue. The Laughlin state energy at $\nu = \frac{1}{2}$, which corresponds to the boson system, is also given in Fig. 9.9.

The low-lying excitations for several finite-size systems in the periodic rectangular geometry are presented in Fig. 9.10. When we compare these results with the spectrum for an incompressible fluid state (Fig. 7.4), no clear trend is visible in the present spectra. The first difference to note is that, while at $\nu = \frac{1}{3}$, the ground state appears at $\boldsymbol{k} = 0$, in the present case of $\nu = \frac{1}{2}$, the ground state appears at a finite $\boldsymbol{k}$ and varies strongly with the particle number and geometry of the cell (the aspect ratio in these calculations is taken to be $N_e/4$). The whole spectrum is, in fact, particle-number and geometry dependent. The spectrum for an odd number of electrons seems to be somewhat different from that with an even number, presumably indicating the importance of the electron-pair state proposed by *Halperin* [9.15]. However, no general conclusion can be drawn from the present numerical results. Although the lowest energy excitations are separated from the higher energy states (more clearly seen for the odd-electron systems) no clear-cut gap structure is apparent.

For the half-filled lowest Landau level, *Kuramoto* and *Gerhardts* noticed that, within the HF approximation, the ground state is a square CDW with

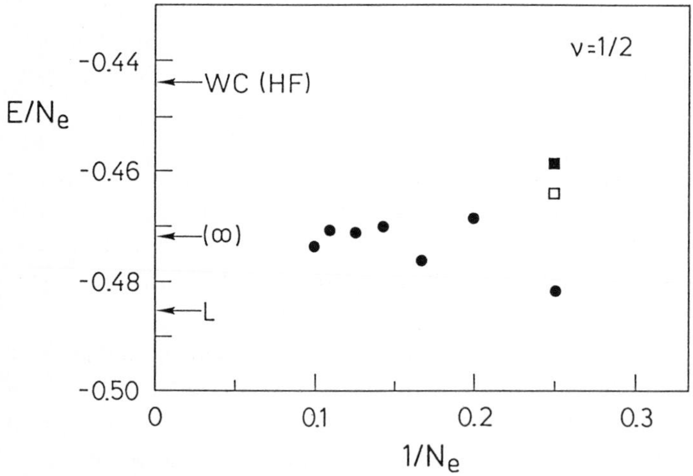

Fig. 9.9. Ground state energy per electron at $\nu = \frac{1}{2}$ (in units of $e^2/\epsilon\ell_0$) as a function of electron number in a periodic rectangular geometry. The closed and open squares correspond to the crystal energies of Fig. 5.2, and the HF energy is given for comparison. The energy of the Laughlin state (depicted as L) and the extrapolation of the finite system results to the thermodynamic limit [depicted as (∞)] are also given

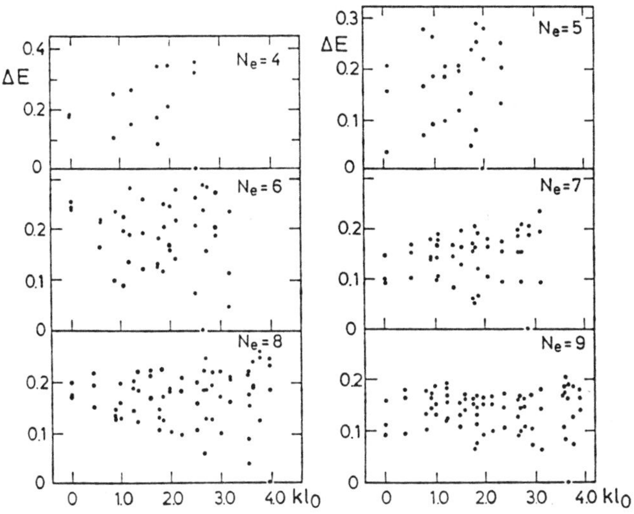

Fig. 9.10. Low-lying excitations at $\nu = \frac{1}{2}$ for finite-size systems in a periodic rectangular geometry as a function of $k\ell_0$

the electron-hole symmetry spontaneously broken [9.18]. The ground state has an energy gap, $\Delta E = 0.330\, e^2/\epsilon\ell_0$. The density profile was, however, found to be very similar to the self-dual square CDW.

In Fig. 9.11(a), we present the pair-correlation function $g(\boldsymbol{r})$ [Eq. (5.17)] of the ground state for a seven-electron system at $\nu = \frac{1}{2}$ in the lowest Landau level. The function has very little structure and is obviously not isotropic. Qualitatively similar results were obtained for other system sizes [9.19]. In Fig. 9.11(b), we present the correlation function for the same system as in Fig. 9.11(a), but at $\boldsymbol{k} = 0$. The function is isotropic (within the rectangular geometry) and has a liquid-like behavior. From these results, we conclude [9.19] that the half-filled lowest Landau level is *not* a stable state. The translationally invariant liquid state appears as an excited state of the system.

Fano et al. [9.20] have done extensive numerical calculations for $\nu = \frac{1}{2}$ in a spherical geometry for up to twelve electrons. They found that, for an even number of electrons, the ground state occurs at $L = 0$ only for $N_\mathrm{e} = 6$ and 12. While for other values of N_e, the ground state occurs at: $N_\mathrm{e} = 4; L = 2, N_\mathrm{e} = 8, 10; L = 4$. For odd numbers of electrons, the ground state has half-integer L. Extrapolating the results to an infinite system, they obtained the ground state energy (per particle) to be, -0.469 ± 0.005.

The excitation spectrum obtained by Fano et al. showed many irregular features, which distinguishes them from the spectrum one gets for an incom-

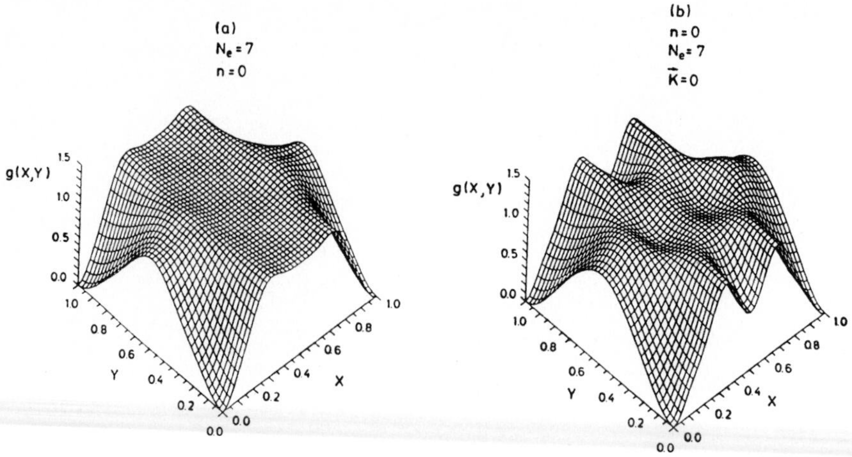

Fig. 9.11. Perspective view of the pair-correlation function $g(\boldsymbol{r})$ for a seven-electron system at $\nu = \frac{1}{2}$ in the lowest Landau level (a) for the ground state and (b) at $\boldsymbol{k} = 0$, which is an excited state of the system. The axes are normalized as $X = x/a$ and $Y = y/b$

pressible state at $\nu = \frac{1}{3}$ (see Chap. 7). In Fig. 9.12, we present the lowest energy spectrum for $N_e = 8$ and 10, and in Fig. 9.13, the lowest energy spectrum for $N_e = 6$ and 12. Only in the latter cases are the ground states obtained at $\boldsymbol{L} = 0$, however, no clear picture has emerged from these spectra. Interesting model calculations at half filling have also been performed by *Greiter* et al. [9.21].

Experimentally, the possibility of observing the FQHE at even denominator filling factors was indicated by several groups. A minimum in ρ_{xx} at $\nu = \frac{3}{4}$ was first observed by *Ebert* et al. [9.22] in the lowest Landau level. Recently, *Clark* et al. [9.12,23] observed minima in the diagonal resistivity in the second Landau level at $\nu = \frac{9}{4}, \frac{5}{2}$ and $\frac{11}{4}$. Correct quantization of ρ_{xy} to these fractional values was not achieved however.

A thorough analysis of these filling factors has been performed by *Willett* et al. [9.24]. Their results for $\nu < 1$ (Fig. 3.3) do not show any sign of the FQHE for even denominator fillings. While some features in ρ_{xx} were seen at $\nu = \frac{3}{4}$, two higher order odd denominator filling factors $\nu = \frac{4}{5}$ and $\nu = \frac{5}{7}$ seem to converge toward this even denominator filling factor. For $\nu = \frac{1}{2}$, ρ_{xy} follows the classical straight line, while the broad minimum in ρ_{xx} is thought to be caused by as yet unresolved higher order odd denominator filling factors.

For $3 > \nu > 2$ (the Landau level index $n = 1$), however, the situation is entirely different. This region of filling factors in Fig. 4.2 is presented in more detail [9.24] in Fig. 9.14. The ρ_{xy} curve shows a plateau at the magnetic

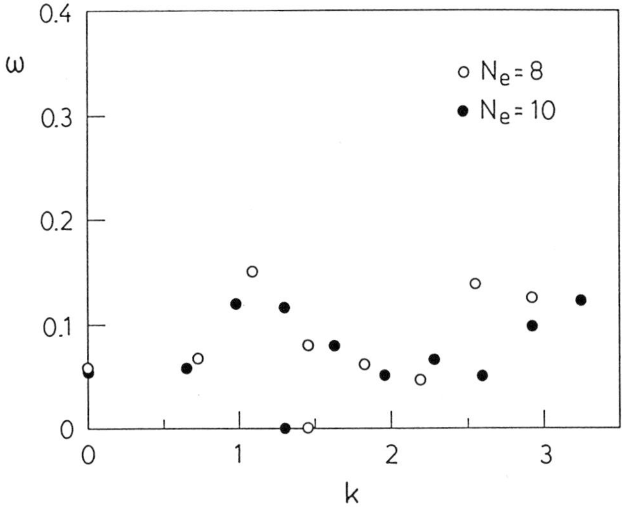

Fig. 9.12. Lowest-lying excitation energies for $N_e = 8$ and 10 as a function of $k = L/R$ in a spherical geometry [9.20]

field which corresponds to $\nu = \frac{5}{2}$, which is centered at $\rho_{xy} = (h/e^2)/\frac{5}{2}$ to within 0.5%. In the same region of magnetic field, a deep minimum is observed in ρ_{xx}. The nearest odd-denominator fillings $\frac{32}{13}$ and $\frac{33}{13}$ $(\frac{5}{2} \pm 1.5\%)$ do not show any indication that the plateau at $\frac{5}{2}$ is caused by the blending of two higher order odd denominators. There are also broad minima near

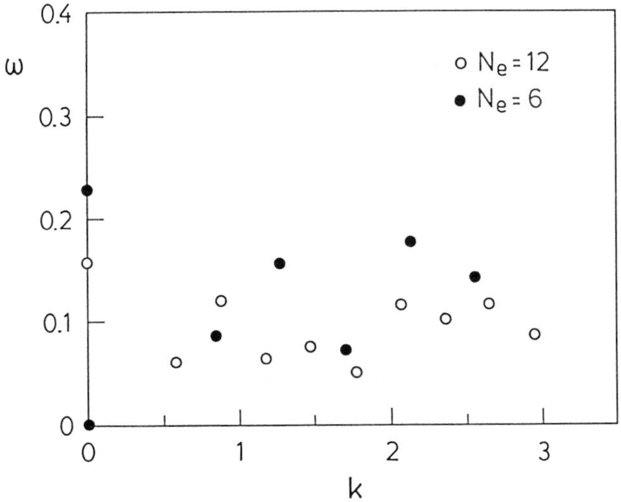

Fig. 9.13. Same as in Fig. 9.12, but for $N_e = 6$ and 12 [9.20]

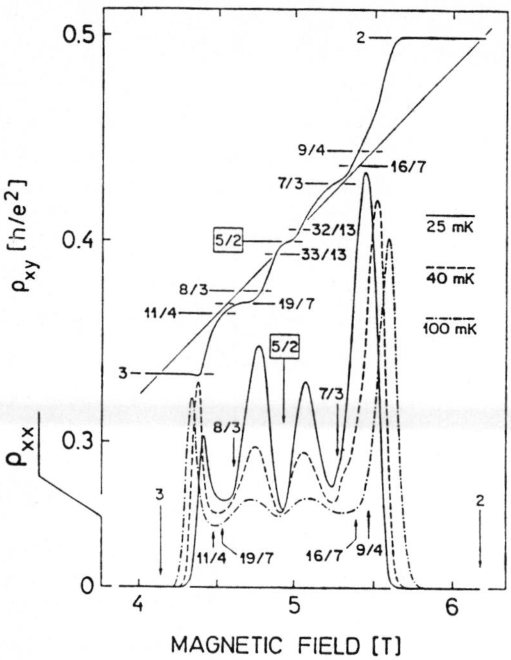

Fig. 9.14. The region of filling factors $3 > \nu > 2$ of Fig. 4.2 shown in detail for temperatures T=25 to 100 mK [9.24]

$\nu = \frac{9}{4}$ and $\frac{11}{4}$ which shift considerably with temperature and, at the lowest temperature considered in these experiments move to $\frac{19}{7}$ and $\frac{7}{3}$. Therefore, the only even-denominator fraction so far unambigiously found is $\nu = \frac{5}{2}$. However, there are indications that other even denominator filling factors exist within the range $4 > \nu > 3$.

Table 9.2. Ground-state energies (in units of $e^2/\epsilon\ell_0$) for four- and six-electron systems at $\nu = \frac{5}{2}$ for various values of the total spin S. The Zeeman energy is not included in the energy values.

N_e	$S = 0$	$S = 1$	$S = 2$	$S = 3$
4	−0.3644	−0.3655	−0.3849	–
6	−0.3782	−0.3783	−0.3785	−0.3797

There have been a few theoretical attempts to explain the experimental finding discussed above. *Haldane* and *Rezayi* [9.25] have proposed a spin-singlet wave function for an incompressible state which occurs at $\nu = \frac{1}{2}$.

From small-system calculations (six electrons) and with model pseudopotentials, they concluded that such a state might be responsible for the $\frac{5}{2}$ effect. For the Coulomb interaction, which is a physically realistic interaction, numerical calculations were performed by *Chakraborty* and *Pietiläinen* [9.19]. The calculations were also based on finite-size systems (up to six electrons in a periodic rectangular geometry), but do not support the conclusions of Haldane and Rezayi. In Table 9.2, we present the ground-state energies for four- and six-electron systems at $\nu = \frac{1}{2}$ in the second Landau level for different spin polarizations. The system has a fully spin-polarized ground state even in the absence of Zeeman energy. The energy difference between the various spin states is very small. However, for a spin-reversed system to be energetically favored, the energy of this state must be larger than that of the spin-polarized state by at least the Zeeman energy contribution. Such a situation might occur for larger systems than the ones considered here, as the even-denominator system results are known to be very much system-size dependent.

MacDonald et al. [9.26] examined the viability of the model interaction of Haldane and Rezayi for the $\frac{5}{2}$ state in a finite-size system calculation. They found that for the $\frac{5}{2}$ case, the Coulomb model is quite far from the models of Haldane and Rezayi which show the FQHE. For the case relevant to the $\frac{5}{2}$ experiment, the Coulombic ground state is fully spin polarized even without a Zeeman term, in agreement with the result of *Chakraborty* and *Pietiläinen* [9.19]. Therefore, if the FQHE at $\frac{5}{2}$ is based on the model state of Haldane and Rezayi, there must be substantial corrections to the Coulomb model. The precise origin and the nature of the corrections are still unclear.

In a tilted field measurement on the $\frac{5}{2}$ state, *Eisenstein et al.* [9.27] observed that the FQHE collapses rapidly at this filling factor. This indicates that the spin degree of freedom is playing a role. However, from the above discussions, it is fair to conclude that finite-size calculations performed so far are unable to provide a suitable explanation of the FQHE at this interesting filling factor.

Some recent experiments have unearthed several puzzling facts about the filling factors $\nu = \frac{1}{2}$ and $\frac{3}{2}$ whose origins are not yet clear. *Jiang* et al. [9.28] observed deep low-temperature minima in ρ_{xx} at these filling fractions. Although their strength exceeds the strength of neighboring FQHE states, there are no plateaus nor any discernible indication of plateau developments visible in ρ_{xy}. Also, there is no discernible temperature dependence at low temperatures as demonstrated in Fig. 9.15 for $\nu = \frac{1}{2}$. The minima do not approach $\rho_{xx} = 0$ but saturate at nonzero values. At the other end of the temperature spectrum, the minima surprisingly persist up to $T \sim 10\text{K}$ at which all features of the FQHE have completely disappeared and

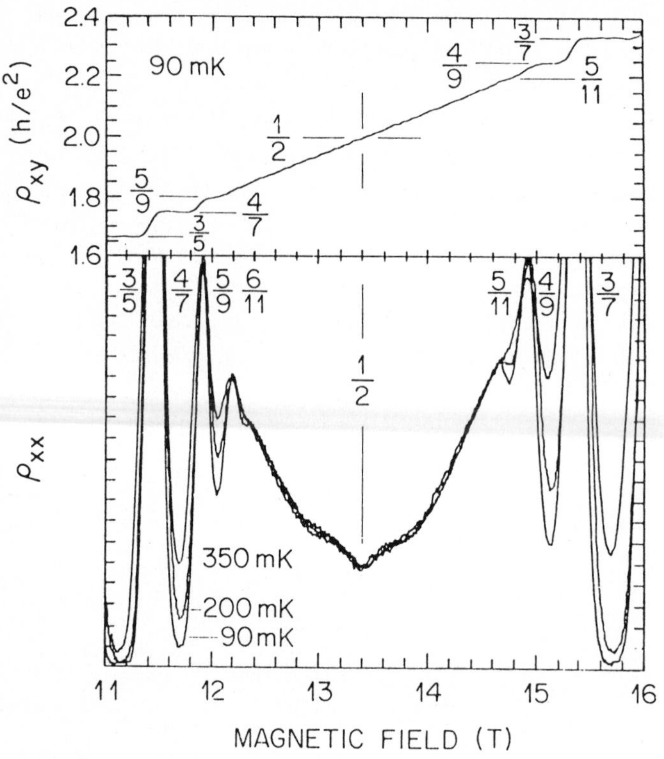

Fig. 9.15. Temperature dependence of ρ_{xx} in the vicinity of filling factor $\nu = \frac{1}{2}$ and the Hall resistance ρ_{xy} at $T = 90$mK [9.28]

only structures of the IQHE remain. The strength of the $\nu = \frac{1}{2}$ minimum was found to vary approximately *linearly* with temperature, and so differs greatly from the exponential dependence of the FQHE features. Because of the unusual T-dependence in ρ_{xx} and the lack of plateaus in ρ_{xy} it is clear that the states at half-filling are distinctly different from the FQHE states. Transport measurements in tilted magnetic fields seem not to alter the above features.

The situation at the even-denominator filling fractions has recently taken a dramatic turn with the surface acoustic wave (SAW) measurements by *Willett et al.* [9.29,30]. The prime motivation of these authors was to study the correlation effects in a 2DEG using a method that will not adversely perturb the system and yet allows measurement of conductivity at small length scales. The technique involves propagating SAW on the heterostructures, thereby generating a spatially and time-varying electric field (due to piezoelectric coupling in GaAs) at the surface which penetrates to the 2DEG layer. The interaction of the SAW electric field with the 2D electrons affects the sound velocity and attenuation. This is therefore a way of measuring (albeit indirectly) the dynamical conductivity $\sigma_{xx}(\boldsymbol{q}, \omega)$ at high frequencies and finite wave vectors $\boldsymbol{q}$. Earlier investigations by Willett et al. [9.29] have revealed that the SAW technique is good for measuring the FQHE as well as IQHE conductivity in a contactless method with a result of $\sigma_{xx}(\boldsymbol{q}, \omega) \approx \sigma_{xx}(DC)$ for IQHE and FQHE states. The surprising result of their recent work is that at $\nu = \frac{1}{2}$ and several other even-denominator filling fractions, the conductivity is found to be *enhanced* and is more robust than the FQHE [*i.e.*, this enhanced $\sigma_{xx}(\boldsymbol{q}, \omega)$ persists to high temperatures at which even the most robust state ($\nu = \frac{1}{3}$) does not exist in their samples]. Both $\sigma_{xx}(q)$ and the width of the effect increase linearly with the SAW wave vector. Willett et al. proposed that the robustness and occurrence of these $\sigma_{xx}(q)$ peaks at multiple even-denominator fractions suggest the presence of a *series* of states, which are complimentary to the series of FQHE states but support gapless excitations.

In a seminal paper, *Halperin, Lee* and *Read* (HLR) have recently proposed a detailed theory of the half-filled Landau level [9.31] which seems to capture the essential physics of this enigmatic filling factor.[3] This theory predicts an anomaly in the SAW propagation which agrees qualitatively with the observation discussed above. The starting point of this approach is the statistical transmutation from electrons to composite fermions [9.32]. Here one employs a singular gauge transformation [Sects. 6.7,8] to convert the electrons to a system of particles interacting with a Chern-Simons gauge field. In this description, a flux tube containing an integer number $\widetilde{\phi}$ of quanta of the Chern-Simons magnetic field is attached to each particle. [Here $\widetilde{\phi}$ denote the strength of the flux tube, in units of the flux quantum $2\pi\hbar$. The fictitious charge of each particle which interacts with the fictitious gauge field has been chosen to have unit strength.] We have already discussed in Sects. 6.7,8, that under a singular gauge transformation one obtains the following form of the wave function for the transformed particles

$$\Psi(z_1, \dots, z_N) = \left[\prod_{j<k}^{N} \frac{(z_j - z_k)^{\widetilde{\phi}}}{|z_j - z_k|^{\widetilde{\phi}}}\right] \Phi(z_1, \dots, z_n)$$

where $\Phi(z_1, \dots, z_N)$ is the electron wave function. As discussed in Sects. 6.7,8, if two of these particles are interchanged in a clockwise manner around

[3] In the following paragraphs we present a brief description of the approach. Readers are urged to consult the original paper which is very informative and contains a detailed discussion of the theory.

a curve which encloses no other particles, then the wave function must change by a phase factor [9.32] $e^{i\theta}$, where

$$\theta = \pi(\widetilde{\phi} + 1) \qquad (\mathrm{mod} 2\pi).$$

If $\widetilde{\phi}$ is chosen to be an even integer, the particles obey Fermi statistics.

The Hamiltonian now contains, in addition to the vector potential due to the external magnetic field, the "Chern-Simons vector potential"

$$\boldsymbol{a}_j(\boldsymbol{r}_j) \equiv \widetilde{\phi} \sum_{k \neq j} \frac{\widehat{z} \times \boldsymbol{r}_{jk}}{|\boldsymbol{r}_{jk}|^2}, \qquad \boldsymbol{r}_{jk} = (\boldsymbol{r}_j - \boldsymbol{r}_k).$$

The fictitious magnetic field arising from the flux tubes is

$$\boldsymbol{b}_j(\boldsymbol{r}) \equiv \nabla \times \boldsymbol{a}_j(\boldsymbol{r}) = 2\pi\widetilde{\phi}\rho(\boldsymbol{r})$$

where $\rho(r)$ is the electron density at $\boldsymbol{r}$, excluding electron j.

In a mean-field approximation [9.31] (no interaction among the particles) the fictitious magnetic field b_i is replaced by its average value (on the assumption that the particles form a state of uniform density)

$$b_i \to \langle b \rangle = 2\pi\widetilde{\phi}n_{\mathrm{e}}$$

where n_{e} is the average electron density. This corresponds to the case of *free* fermions in an effective magnetic field

$$\Delta B = B - 2\pi\widetilde{\phi}n_{\mathrm{e}}.$$

The filling factor of the original electron system ν is then related to the "effective filling factor" ν_{eff} such that

$$\nu^{-1} = \nu_{\mathrm{eff}}^{-1} + \widetilde{\phi}.$$

For $\widetilde{\phi} = 2$, and if ν_{eff} is chosen to be an integer p, we have $\nu = p/(2p+1)$, in which case the mean-field ground state of the transformed system is a collection of non-interacting fermions in an "effective" field whose strength is such that precisely $|p|$ Landau levels are filled. This provides an explanation for the stable states at these filling fractions. The energy gaps for these states of course simply correspond to the cyclotron energy in an effective magnetic field ΔB. It is clear that, at the mean-field level, the fermion Chern-Simons description is essentially equivalent to the composite fermion construction [9.33] of the incompressible quantized Hall states.

In an external magnetic field B such that there are two flux quanta per electron ($\nu = \frac{1}{2}$), one finds that $\Delta B = 0$. This is an extremely interesting result and means that, within the mean-field approximation $\nu = \frac{1}{2}$ corresponds to a system of *free fermions in zero magnetic field.* The ground state of such a system is a filled Fermi sea with Fermi wave vector $k_{\mathrm{F}} = (4\pi n_{\mathrm{e}})^{\frac{1}{2}} = 1/\ell_0$, where ℓ_0 is the magnetic length. Therefore, one of the major results of the HLR theory is that, for an ideal sample with no impurity scattering, there exists at $T = 0$ a sharp Fermi surface at $\nu = \frac{1}{2}$ filling fraction.

If there exists a Fermi surface for $\nu = \frac{1}{2}$, then if the magnetic field deviates slightly from $B_{\frac{1}{2}} = 4\pi n_e$, *i.e.*, the magnetic field at which the Landau level is precisely half full, the behavior of the composite fermion system should resemble the behavior of a noninteracting electron system near $B = 0$. In particular, one would expect to find an energy gap in the excitation spectrum when $e\Delta B = 2\pi n_e/p$, $e\Delta B \equiv eB - 4\pi n_e$. This condition, as discussed above, corresponds to the condition $\nu = p/(2p + 1)$, which characterizes the most prominant sequence of odd-denominator quantized Hall states, tending toward $\nu = \frac{1}{2}$ from above or below as $p \to +\infty$ or $-\infty$. In fact this sequence includes the most prominent fractional Hall plateaus that are observed experimentally in the lowest Landau level. In the mean-field approximation, one can also define an effective cyclotron energy $\Delta\omega_{\mathrm{c}}^* \equiv e|\Delta B|/m^*$ and from that derive the energy gap at $\nu = p/(2p+1)$ to be $E_{\mathrm{g}} \simeq 2\pi n_e/m^*|p|$.

HLR also studied the density and current response functions within the random phase approximation. Here the transformed fermions are treated as free particles which respond to the self-consistent Chern-Simons electric and magnetic field $\langle e(\boldsymbol{r},t)\rangle$ and $\langle b(\boldsymbol{r},t)\rangle$, as well as to the external electromagnetic field and the self-consistent Coulomb potential of the particles. The equations for the "magnetic field" and the "electric field" are

$$\langle b(\boldsymbol{r},t)\rangle = 2\pi\widetilde{\phi}\langle\rho(\boldsymbol{r},t)\rangle$$
$$\langle \boldsymbol{e}(\boldsymbol{r},t)\rangle = -2\pi\widetilde{\phi}\widehat{z} \times \langle \boldsymbol{j}(\boldsymbol{r},t)\rangle$$

where $\langle\rho\rangle$ and $\langle \boldsymbol{j}\rangle$ are the particle density and current, respectively, and $\widetilde{\phi} = 2$. One of the major results of this approach is that, for a system free of any impurities the longitudinal conductivity is [9.31]

$$\sigma_{xx}(q) = \frac{e^2}{8\pi\hbar}\frac{q}{k_{\mathrm{F}}}.$$

If impurity scattering is taken into account, their result is

$$\begin{aligned}\sigma_{xx}(q) &= \frac{e^2}{8\pi\hbar}\frac{q}{k_{\mathrm{F}}}, \qquad q \gg 2/l\\ &= \frac{e^2}{4\pi\hbar}\frac{1}{k_{\mathrm{F}}l}, \qquad q < 2/l\end{aligned}$$

where l is the transport mean free path at $\nu = \frac{1}{2}$. The linear dependence of $\sigma_{xx}(q)$ on q for $q \gg 1/l$ is what is needed to explain the SAW results of *Willett et al.* [9.30]. The absolute value of $\sigma_{xx}(q)$ obtained from the above relation is however, about a factor of two smaller than that obtained in the experiment. We should also mention that a similar but independent work at $\nu = \frac{1}{2}$ was reported by Kalmeyer and Zhang [9.34], who also suggested a metallic phase at this filling factor.

Motivated by the predictions of HLR, several interesting experiments have been reported in the literature. *Du et al.* [9.35] have reported a measurement of the energy gaps for a series of fractional quantum Hall states with $\nu = p/(2p+1)$ and find that they show a linear dependence on $\Delta B = B - B_{\frac{1}{2}}$.

In order to observe the Fermi surface effects at $\nu = \frac{1}{2}$, HLR proposed the observation of magnetoresistance oscillations in a modulated system. In earlier studies of such systems where a 2DEG was modulated by a 1D superlattice potential with period a, oscillatory structures were observed in the magnetoresistance [9.36,37]. The observed oscillations correspond to the condition that the classical cyclotron diameter $2R_c$ is a multiple of a. If there exists a Fermi surface at $\nu = \frac{1}{2}$, then one should see oscillations in magnetoresistance in a modulated sample near $\nu = \frac{1}{2}$. In the absence of any impurity scattering, the quasiparticles should move in a circular orbit with a radius, $R_c^* = \hbar k_F/\Delta B$. Therefore, one expects maxima or minima in the resistivity when $2R_c^*$ is a multiple of a.

Recently, *Kang et al.* [9.38] reported observation of the FQHE in antidot arrays [9.39] where they find indications of the composite fermions. Indications for the existence of composite fermions were also reported in magnetic focusing experiments [9.40]. In addition, new SAW results [9.41] also provide support for the existence of the gauge-transformed fermions at $\nu = \frac{1}{2}$.

Although the theory of HLR provides a very convincing (and yet simple) picture of the FQHE, it is not clear if it is essential to leave the lowest Landau level (even temporarily) to explain the the lowest Landau-level physics [9.42]. A recent finite-size calculation by *Yang* and *Su* [9.43] found that the Hilbert space spanned by the quasiparticle wave functions in the hierarchy theory either include or are exactly the same as the space spanned by the wave functions based on the composite fermion picture as promoted in [9.33]. These authors also provide a strong argument that hierarchy theory and the composite fermion approach are formally equivalent.

9.5 Multiple Layer Systems

In the preceding section, we have reviewed the theoretical and experimental work on the collective excitations for $\nu = \frac{1}{2}$ in a single layer of electrons. In this section, we present the theoretical and experimental work on the FQHE in a *layered* electron system [9.44,45]. Some work on double quantum-well systems in the FQHE regime will also be discussed. Multilayer electron systems have been studied quite extensively as an anisotropic model for an electron gas [9.46–48]. Let us consider a model where two layers with equal density of electrons are embedded in an infinite dielectric. We consider a delta-function-localized electron density in each plane. The electrons move freely in each plane and the interaction of electrons in different planes is considered to be Coulombic. Tunneling of electrons between the two planes is not allowed. The electrons are also considered to be in their lowest subband. This model is often referred to in the literature as the Visscher-Falicov model [9.49]. Experimental systems that can be described reasonably well by this model have been obtained in GaAs-heterostructures by different experimental groups [9.50,51].

The Coulomb potential energy between two electrons situated in planes i and j can be written

$$V(\boldsymbol{r}-\boldsymbol{r}';i,j) = \frac{e^2}{\epsilon}\left[(\boldsymbol{r}-\boldsymbol{r}')^2 + (i-j)^2 C^2\right]^{-\frac{1}{2}} \tag{9.60}$$

where $\boldsymbol{r}$ is a two-vector (x,y), ϵ is the background dielectric constant, and C is the interlayer separation. The Fourier transform of the above expression with respect to $\boldsymbol{r}-\boldsymbol{r}'$ is

$$v(\boldsymbol{k};i,j) = \frac{2\pi e^2}{\epsilon k}\,\mathrm{e}^{-k|i-j|C}, \tag{9.61}$$

where $\boldsymbol{k}$ is a two-dimensional in-plane wave vector. The effect of interlayer interaction is to lift the two-fold degeneracy which would otherwise be present.

The excitation spectrum for a finite electron system was obtained by generalizing the method of Haldane (see Sect. 7.2) for a two layer system. We consider a rectangular cell consisting of two layers each containing an equal number of electrons N_e. For simplicity, we ignore Landau level mixing and impose periodic boundary conditions such that the cell contains an integer number N_s of flux quanta. Furthermore, we consider the electrons to be spin-polarized and take the strong-field limit where the electrons are in the lowest Landau level. The filling fraction is therefore $\frac{1}{2}$ in both the layers.

The Hamiltonian now conserves the *total* momentum as well as the number of electrons in each layer. One can, therefore, diagonalize the Hamiltonian for the set of states, $|\boldsymbol{k}_1; L_1\rangle|\boldsymbol{k} - \boldsymbol{k}_1; L_2\rangle$, where $|\boldsymbol{k}_1; L_1\rangle$ is the momentum eigenstate for N_e electrons in a single layer i belonging to the eigenvalue $\boldsymbol{k}_i$. Here, $L_i = |j_1, \dots, j_{N_e}\rangle$ labels a Slater determinant of Landau orbitals with momentum $\boldsymbol{k}_i$.

In Figs. 9.16 and 9.17, are presented the excitation spectra for a system with four electrons per layer, for two different values of aspect ratio, $\lambda = 1$ (square) and $\lambda = 1.25$ (rectangular), respectively. The first important result is that the ground state is obtained uniquely at $\boldsymbol{k} = 0$ and it remains so for two different aspect ratios. The ground-state energy is, in fact, slightly *lower* for the rectangular geometry. The energy difference between the two geometries is very small however ($\sim 0.005e^2/\epsilon\ell_0$). The other interesting result is that a gap structure in the spectrum is obtained with a characteristic minimum at a finite $k\ell_0$, similar to that of the magnetoroton minimum, discussed in Sect. 7.4. For the square geometry, a few energy levels lie very close, but are separated from the continuum by a large gap (Fig. 9.16). These close-lying energy states can be further separated by moving away from the square geometry (Fig. 9.17). This is due to the fact that the square geometry, as noted by *Maksym* [9.52], has higher degeneracies as compared to the rectangular geometry.

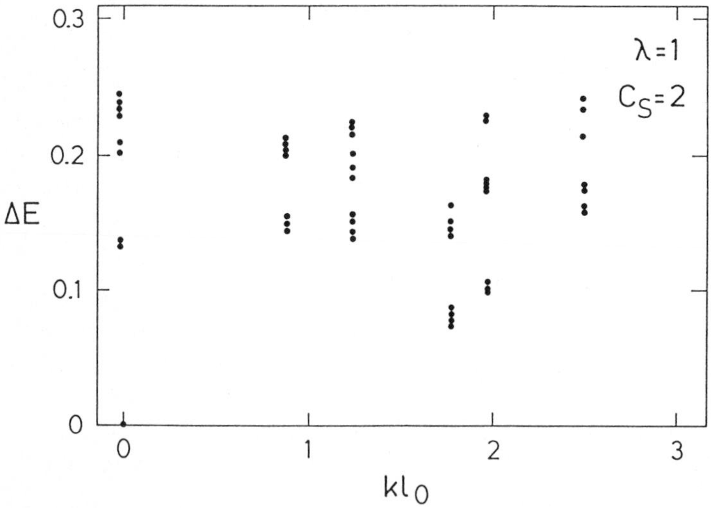

Fig. 9.16. Excitation spectrum of the eight-electron system in a two layer geometry at $\nu = \frac{1}{2}$ for a dimensionless layer separation parameter $C_s = C/\ell_0 = 2.0$ and aspect ratio, $\lambda = 1$ (square cell)

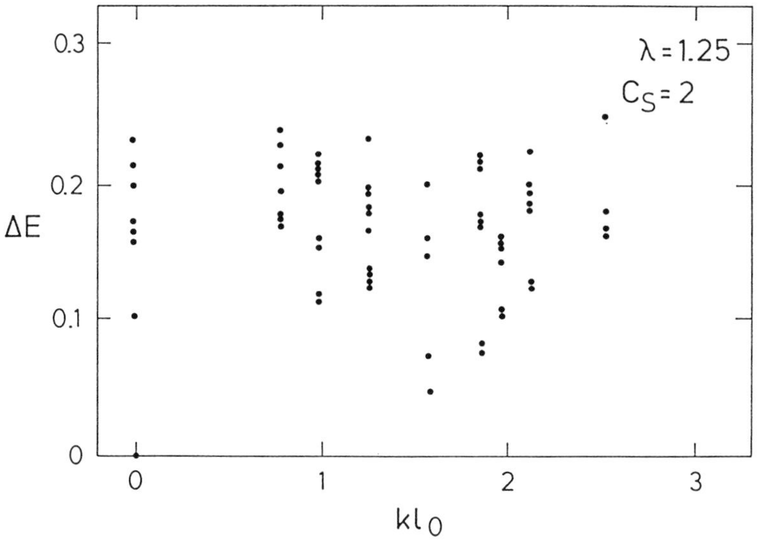

Fig. 9.17. Same as in Fig. 9.16, but for the aspect ratio $\lambda = 1.25$ (rectangular cell)

In Fig. 9.17, the lowest two excitation energies, which are clearly separated from the higher energy states for most values of $k\ell_0$, could presumably be interpreted as the two eigenmodes in a system of two charge layers. They arise due to the electron correlations in the two layers. Such a spectrum at $\nu = \frac{1}{3}$ has been obtained in the SMA [9.53] and discussed in Sect. 7.4.

Comparing the layered system results with those of the single layer, discussed in the preceding section, we notice that the introduction of an interacting electron layer has helped to reorganize the excitation energies of the system, particularly the $\boldsymbol{k} = 0$ state. The observation of the roton-type minimum is also quite interesting. The results indicate the possibility of the occurrence of an incompressible fluid state at $\nu = \frac{1}{2}$ in a multiple layer system. For a better understanding of the layered system results, we need to obtain spectra for larger systems.

Experimental attempts to explore the FQHE in two-layer systems have also been reported. *Lindelof* et al. have reported [9.54] an interesting observation of $\nu = \frac{1}{2}$ in each of the two parallel layers of a selectively doped double heterostructure. Other experimental results with that sample indicate that the system indeed consists of two parallel and independent two-dimensional electron layers. Experimental work by *Eisenstein* et al. [9.55] also support the theoretical work discussed above.

There have been a few other calculations on the two-layer systems. *Yoshioka et al.* [9.56] obtained the ground-state wave functions for finite-size systems on a sphere and compared them with the Jastrow-type wave functions at filling factors $\nu = 1, \frac{1}{2}, \frac{2}{5}$, and $\frac{1}{3}$. Halperin's two-spin state wave function (5.56) was employed. That wave function however, does not contain any parameter characterizing the layer separation. Therefore, the pair-correlation functions obtained with that wave function are independent of the layer separation.

Fertig [9.57] investigated the excitation spectrum of two- and three-layer systems with filling factors $\nu = \frac{1}{2}$ and $\nu = \frac{1}{3}$ respectively, in each layer. The excitation spectra were calculated from the *valley* density response functions in a self-consistent approximation discussed by *Kallin* and *Halperin* [9.58], and the poles of the response functions correspond to the excitation energies of the system. The accuracy of the results are, however, difficult to estimate in the present case, since there is no small expansion parameter. For small $k\ell_0$, the qualitative features of the excitation spectra have the form expected for multivalley semiconductors. For large $k\ell_0$, the spectra indicate the excitonic nature of the excited states. For $C \sim \ell_0$, the dispersion relations develop a dip around $k\ell_0 \sim 1$. These become soft modes when $C > 1.21\ell_0$ for the two-layer system, $C_1 > 0.92\ell_0, C_2 > 1.51\ell_0$ for the three-layer system. This indicates that the system undergoes a phase transition as the layer spacing is increased through these critical separations.

Boebinger et al. [9.59] have reported magnetotransport studies in double-quantum-well structures. They observed a high-magnetic-field regime in which quantum Hall states at odd-integer filling factors are missing. With increasing barrier thickness between the two wells, these authors observed that the odd filling factors are systematically destroyed. Finally, in a theoretical work, *Yoshioka* and *MacDonald* [9.60] have presented a phase diagram of a double quantum well electron-hole system in a strong magnetic field. Finally, *Murphy et al.* [9.61] have presented a series of interesting new results in bilayer 2D electron systems. The $\nu = 1$ QHE was found to continuously evolve from a regime dominated by single-electron tunneling into one where interlayer Coulomb interaction stabilize the state, as described above. This many-body state exhibits a phase transition to a compressible state at large layer separation. In a tilted field, these authors find a second transition to a new incompressible state. It is fair to conclude that a lot more theoretical work will be needed to understand the physics of the FQHE in bilayer electron systems.

9.6 Natur of Long-Range Order in the Laughlin State

The analogy of the FQHE state with liquid ^{4}He has been quite apparent in the study of collective excitations discussed in Sect. 6.1, in particular, the presence of magnetorotons in the excitation spectrum. It is therefore quite natural to look for some other interesting properties in the FQHE state which are known to exist in ^{4}He, notably among them the so-called off-diagonal long-range order (ODLRO) in the density matrices. Extensive literature exists on ODLRO in liquid ^{4}He. There are accurate calculations within the HNC scheme [9.62]. Several very accurate Monte Carlo calcuations of up to 512 particles have also been reported [9.63]. An experimental estimate of the condensate fraction in liquid ^{4}He (the fraction of He-atoms in the zero-momentum state) n_c is also available [9.64] and the various theoretical estimates of this quantity are in reasonable agreement with the experimental result. The Monte Carlo scheme has been applied to two-dimensional [9.65] liquid ^{4}He, where a rather large value of n_c was reported.

In the case of the QHE, the off-diagonal elements of the one-body density matrix in real space exhibit Gaussian decay as first shown by *MacDonald* and *Girvin* [9.66]. The m-body density matrix for a system of N electrons is defined as

$$\begin{aligned}\rho_m\left(\boldsymbol{r}_1, \boldsymbol{r}_2, \ldots, \boldsymbol{r}_m; \boldsymbol{r}_1', \boldsymbol{r}_2', \ldots, \boldsymbol{r}_m'\right) &= N(N-1)\cdots(N-m+1) \\ \times \int d\boldsymbol{r}_{m+1} \cdots \int d\boldsymbol{r}_N \, \psi_0^*\left(\boldsymbol{r}_1, \boldsymbol{r}_2, \ldots, \boldsymbol{r}_m, \boldsymbol{r}_{m+1}, \ldots, \boldsymbol{r}_n\right) \\ \times \, \psi_0\left(\boldsymbol{r}_1', \boldsymbol{r}_2', \ldots, \boldsymbol{r}_m', \boldsymbol{r}_{m+1}, \ldots, \boldsymbol{r}_N\right)\end{aligned} \tag{9.62}$$

where $\psi_0(\boldsymbol{r})$ is the N-electron ground-state wave function. The diagonal elements of $\rho_m(\boldsymbol{r}; \boldsymbol{r}')$ give the m-body distribution function

$$n_m(\boldsymbol{r}) = \rho_m(\boldsymbol{r}, \boldsymbol{r}). \tag{9.63}$$

In the lowest Landau level the wave function is [9.67]

$$\psi_0(\boldsymbol{r}) = f_0(z) \exp\left(-\tfrac{1}{4} \sum_k |z_k|^2\right) \tag{9.64}$$

where $z_k = x_k - iy_k$ and $f(z)$ is analytic in each of the z_k's. Using (9.64) in (9.62) we get

$$\rho_m(\boldsymbol{r}, \boldsymbol{r}') = \prod_{k=1}^{m} \exp\left(-\tfrac{1}{4}|z_k|^2\right) \exp\left(-\tfrac{1}{4}|z_k'|^2\right) F_m(z^*, z') \tag{9.65}$$

and

$$n_m(\boldsymbol{r}) = \sum_{k=1}^{m} \exp\left(-\tfrac{1}{2}|z_k|^2\right) F_m(z^*, z). \tag{9.66}$$

where $F_m(s,t)$ is a function analytic in each s_k and t_k and is uniquely determined by (9.66) if only the diagonal elements of $\rho_m(\boldsymbol{r},\boldsymbol{r})$ are known. If we substitute $\frac{1}{2}(z_k+z_k^*)$ for x_k and $\frac{1}{2i}(z_k^*-z_k)$ for y_k, we obtain

$$n_m(\boldsymbol{r}) = G_m(z^*, z) \tag{9.67}$$

where $G_m(z^*,z)$ is also an analytic function of each z_k and z_k^*. It follows that

$$F_m(z^*, z) = \prod_{k=1}^{m} \exp\left(\tfrac{1}{2} z_k^* z_k\right) G_m(z^*, z) \tag{9.68}$$

and therefore

$$\rho_m(\boldsymbol{r},\boldsymbol{r}') = \prod_{k=1}^{m} \exp\left(\frac{-|z_k|^2}{4} \frac{-|z_k'|^2}{4} + \frac{1}{2} z_k^* z_k'\right) G_m(z^*, z'). \tag{9.69}$$

In the case of uniform electron density, $n(\boldsymbol{r}) = \nu/2\pi$ and

$$\rho_1(\boldsymbol{r},\boldsymbol{r}') = \frac{\nu}{2\pi} \mathrm{e}^{-\frac{1}{4}|z-z'|^2} \mathrm{e}^{(z^* z' - z z'^*)/4}. \tag{9.70}$$

Therefore no ODLRO exists in the one-body density matrix of the 2DES in a magnetic field.

To exhibit ODLRO, a fermionic system has to at least form pairs. This is the case in the BCS theory of traditional superconductivity where the two-body density matrix has extensive eigenvalues [9.68]. Some years ago *Thouless* [9.69] investigated the corresponding density matrix in the context of the FQHE

$$\rho_{m_1,m_2}(n) = \langle a^\dagger_{n+m_1} a^\dagger_{n-m_1} a_{n-m_2} a_{n+m_2} \rangle, \tag{9.71}$$

where, for fixed n, the eigenvalues were determined for finite electron systems in a spherical geometry, as well as for the Laughlin wave function on a square with periodic boundary condition in one direction. The existence of Cooper pairs with *wave number* $2n$ is expected to be indicated by a large eigenvalue of $\rho(n)$. The largest eigenvalues in those calculations, however, were found to *decrease* rather than increase with the number of electrons. The results therefore indicate that there is no sign of any long-range order in the two-body density matrix for the FQHE.

Although the electrons in a strong magnetic field do not exhibit ODLRO, it seems likely that there might be some order hidden in the space of those quantum states. In the pursuit of such an order *Girvin* and *MacDonald* [9.70] considered a singular gauge field $\mathcal{A}_j$ used in the study of *anyons* (see

Sect. 6.7)

$$\mathcal{A}_j(z_j) = \frac{\lambda \Phi_0}{2\pi} \sum_{i \neq j} \nabla_j \Im \ln(z_j - z_i) \tag{9.72}$$

where Φ_0 is the flux quantum and λ is a constant. It corresponds to a vector potential that would be included in the Hamiltonian if each particle had attached to itself a solenoid carrying $\lambda/2$ flux quanta. It should be noted that adding this vector potential to the Hamiltonian we do not make a true gauge transformation since a flux tube is attached to each particle. However if $\lambda = m$, an integer, the net effect is to change the phase of the wave function:

$$\psi_{\text{new}} = \exp\left[-im \sum_{i<j} \Im \ln(z_i - z_j)\right] \psi_{\text{old}} . \tag{9.73}$$

If ψ_{old} is the Laughlin wave function (5.14) we get the transformed state

$$\widetilde{\psi}(z_1, \ldots, z_N) = \prod_{i<j} |z_i - z_j|^m \exp\left(-\tfrac{1}{4} \sum_k |z_k|^2\right) \tag{9.74}$$

which is purely real and is symmetric under particle exchange for both even and odd m. It is truly a remarkable result that both fermion and boson systems map into bosons in this singular gauge.

Making use of the plasma analogy discussed in Sect. 5.2, *Girvin* and *MacDonald* found that [9.70]

$$\widetilde{\rho}(z, z') = \left(\frac{\nu}{2\pi}\right) \exp\left[-\beta \Delta f(z, z')\right] |z - z'|^{-m/2} \tag{9.75}$$

where the inverse temperature $\beta \equiv 2/m$ and $\Delta f(z, z')$ is the difference in free energy between two impurities of charge $m/2$ (located at z and z') and a single impurity of charge m (with arbitary location). The asymptotic value of Δf can be computed using thermodynamic integration of the screening charge density. For $m = 1$ this can be done exactly and one obtains $\beta \Delta f = -0.3942$. For general values of m the screening charge distribution can be found using the ion-disk approximation [9.70] or linear response based on the known static structure factor of the plasma [9.5]. As the plasma screens the impurities completely, the free energy difference $\Delta f(z, z')$ rapidly approaches a constant (Fig. 9.18) as the separation $|z - z'| \to \infty$. The one-body density matrix therefore shows a power-law decay in the long-range. This implies that there is no ODLRO even in the transformed Laughlin state. It should be remembered that in the *ground state* the density matrix should attain a finite value for infinite separation if the ODLRO exists in that system *even in two dimensions* [9.71].

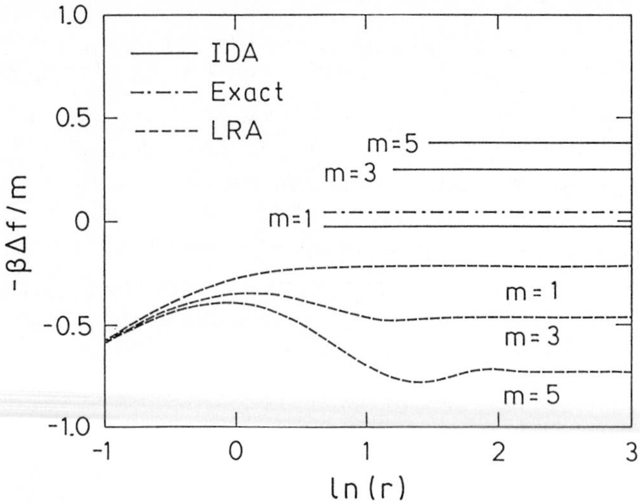

Fig. 9.18. Plot of $-\beta\Delta f(z,z')/m$ vs $r \equiv |z-z'|$ for filling factor $\nu = \frac{1}{m}$. LRA is linear response approximation. IDA is ion-disk approximation (shown only for radii exceeding the sum of the ion-disk radii). Because the plasma is strongly coupled, the IDA is quite accurate at $m = 1$ (*cf.* the exact result) and improves further with increasing m. The LRA is less accurate at $m = 1$ and worsens with increasing m [9.70]

A physical interpretation of the power-law decay of the one-body density matrix for the transformed Laughlin state has been provided by *Chakraborty* and *von der Linden* [9.72]. In determining the one-body density matrix for the modified Laughlin wave function for N electrons, one can map the wave function onto a classical plasma with $N-1$ plasma particles and two additional *phantom* particles residing at sites z and z'. These particles have charges half as large as the original plasma particles and experience an interaction with the plasma particles but not with each other. The one-body density matrix can then be related to the difference in free energy $\Delta F(z,z')$ between this system and the N-particle classical plasma, with inverse temperature $\beta = 1/m$,

$$\rho(z,z') = \rho_0 \mathrm{e}^{\beta\Delta F(z,z')} \tag{9.76}$$

where $\rho_0 = 1/(2\pi m)$ is the plasma density. In the two-component HNC scheme discussed in Sect 6.1 and Appendix C, the one-body density matrix is related to the pair-correlation function of the phantom particles in the zero-concentration limit

$$\rho(z,z') = \lim_{\rho_\gamma \to 0} \left\{ [g_{\gamma\gamma}(0,0)]^{-1} g_{\gamma\gamma}(z,z') \right\}$$

where γ stands for the phantom particles. For systems like ^{4}He, with interactions vanishing at large distances, the asymptotic value of $g(z,z')$ is unity, and therefore the asymptotic value of $\rho(z,z')$ is given by the inverse of the pair-correlation function at the origin. This is not true for systems with *increasing* interactions like the classical plasma in two dimensions as we will see below. The one-body density matrix is written

$$\rho(z,z') = \rho_0 \frac{\int \prod_{1\le j\le N-1} d^2 z_j \exp\left\{-\beta\left[\mathcal{H}_0^{N-1} + \mathcal{H}_1^{N-1}(z,z')\right]\right\}}{\int \prod_{1\le j\le N} d^2 z_j \mathrm{e}^{-\beta\mathcal{H}_0^N}} \tag{9.77}$$

where

$$\begin{aligned}\mathcal{H}_0^N &= -\,q^2 \sum_{1\le j<k\le N} \ln|z_j - z_k| + \tfrac{1}{2}\pi q^2 \rho_0 \sum_{1\le k\le N} |z_k|^2, \\ \mathcal{H}_1^N(z,z') &= -\,qq' \sum_{j=1}^{N} \left(\ln|z_j - z| + \ln|z_j - z'|\right) + \tfrac{1}{2}\pi\rho_0 qq' \left(|z|^2 + |z'|^2\right).\end{aligned} \tag{9.78}$$

The charges of the plasma particles are $q = \sqrt{2m}$ and those of the *phantom* particles $q' = m/\sqrt{2}$. This classical plasma is known to be in the fluid phase for temperatures corresponding to $m \ge 70$, which certainly is the case for the filling factors considered here. Therefore the charges at z and z', entering the free energy in (9.77) will be perfectly screened by the plasma particles on a length scale of the magnetic length ℓ_0. The (z,z') dependence is caused by the induced charges, which asymptotically (z and z' well separated) are point charges. Thus the (z,z') dependent part in the free energy ΔF stems from the interaction of the induced charges among each other and with the *phantom* charges leading to

$$\Delta F = -q^2 \ln\left(|z - z'|\right) + \Delta f_\infty. \tag{9.79}$$

Therefore the asymptotic behavior of the one-body density matrix is expected to be

$$\widetilde{\rho}(z,z') = \rho_0 \mathrm{e}^{-\beta\Delta f_\infty} |z - z'|^{-m/2}, \tag{9.80}$$

where Δf_∞ is independent of z and z' and is determined by, among other factors, the actual shape of the induced charges. *Girvin* and *MacDonald*, who first argued for this power-law decay, calculated this quantity in various approximations [9.70]. The algebraic ODLRO therefore arises due to the logarithmically *increasing* interaction between the particles involved in the state (9.74).

To prove the qualitatively obvious argument leading to (9.75) and to test the efficacy of the HNC scheme, which for ^{4}He has proven to be very

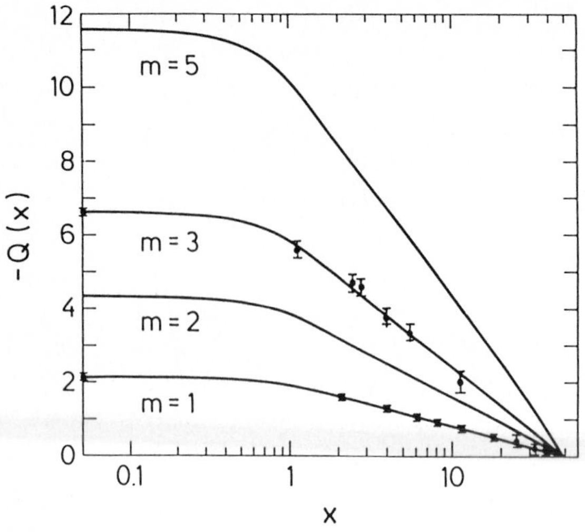

Fig. 9.19. Plot of $-Q(x)$ vs x (defined in the text), measured in units of the mean electronic separation $r_0 = \sqrt{2m}\ell_0$. The HNC results (solid lines) are compared with the Monte Carlo data (solid circles) [9.72]

accurate, *Chakraborty* and *von der Linden* [9.72] performed both HNC calculations and Monte Carlo calculations for up to 1000 particles, in the case of logarithmically increasing interactions. The Monte Carlo scheme was based on Metropolis importance sampling [9.73].

The numerical results of the HNC and Monte Carlo studies are plotted in Fig. 9.19, where we have used the conventional definition of the density matrix in the HNC scheme:

$$\rho(z, z') = n_c \, e^{-Q(|z-z'|)},$$

where $n_c = g_{\gamma\gamma}(0, 0)^{-1}$ is the conventional condensate fraction. The interparticle separation in these calculations is large enough that the asymptotic behavior of $\widetilde{\rho}$ for various m can be extracted very accurately. From this plot we readily obtain the power $(-m/2)$ in agreement with (9.75). The values for $-\beta\Delta f_\infty/m$ are 0.02 for $m = 1$ and 0.24 for $m = 3$ and are in fairly good agreement with those of *Girvin* and *MacDonald* [9.70]. The screening length is of order $\sqrt{2m}\ell_0$. The values of n_c obtained in the HNC scheme are 0.121 for $m = 1$, 0.014 for $m = 2$, 0.0015 for $m = 3$, and $< 10^{-5}$ for $m = 5$.

The comparison of the density matrix results via HNC with the corresponding Monte Carlo data show once more that HNC is a highly accurate approximation scheme, even in the case of increasing interactions.

10. Open Problems and New Directions

Before we close this review of the QHE, a brief recapitulation of some of the open problems in this field is perhaps in order. Despite the fact that the Laughlin-type approaches, as discussed in this book, are quite successful in describing many important aspects of the FQHE, the physical origin of the correlations that are described by the present approaches is not completely clear. Independent approaches, like the cooperative-ring-exchange mechanism might be helpful in providing an answer to that problem. From our point of view, the latter approach should first be used to generate some quantitative results which are comparable to the theoretical results already established by various approaches and described in this book.

On a more practical level, the important problem of finding the critical filling factor at which the liquid to solid transition occurs demands further study. This would require improved calculations for the crystal state, as well as further experimental investigations at low densities.

In the case of elementary excitations, our understanding is still far from complete. Much theoretical work is needed to get the quasiparticle energy in the Laughlin-type approach to match with the energy gap obtained via finite-size calculations, as well as the Monte Carlo estimates. This would be a very important step for calculation of the collective excitation spectrum in Laughlin's theory. Further theoretical work is also needed to remove the discrepancy between the theoretical and experimental results for the energy gap. Influence of disorder on the energy gap is a very important problem to be addressed theoretically. Attempts should also be made to observe the collective modes experimentally. While the theoretical work on the collective excitation spectrum at $\nu = \frac{1}{3}$ is quite exhaustive, there have only been a few attempts to study the higher order filling fractions. Similarly, the inter-Landau level collective mode in the case of fractional filling of the lower Landau level, and the possible role of impurities on this mode need to be studied further.

While Laughlin's wave function is very successful in providing a quantitatively correct picture for $\frac{1}{m}$ (odd m) filling factors (and $1 - \frac{1}{m}$ with particle-hole symmetry), we have not reached such a stage with the higher order fillings. Further theoretical investigations of the experimentally observed higher order filling factors are very much needed. Attempts have to be made to obtain quantitatively accurate results for these states, both in the hierarchical scheme as well as in the trial wave function approach.

Perhaps the most interesting *test* of Laughlin's wave function will be in the case of *even*-denominator filling factors. Whether the experimentally observed $\frac{5}{2}$ fraction describes a different state or is still a Laughlin-type state remains to be investigated further. The ground state and the excitations for the even-denominators, as we have tried to demonstrate in Sect. 9.4, are still unclear. The numerical diagonalization scheme described in Sect. 9.4, has shown that the state is not an incompressible fluid. The experimental finding of one of the even denominators has made the problem quite pressing for the theorists. An interesting approach to the half-filled Landau level based on effective Chern-Simons gauge fields has generated a whole lot of theoretical and experimental activities. Rapid developments in our understanding of the FQHE for other filling fractions along these lines are expected in near future. Layered system results, as discussed in Sect. 9.5, perhaps provide a new opportunity to observe the even denominator fractions.

Recently, the compressibility of a 2DEG at both zero and high magnetic field was measured by *Eisenstein et al.* [10.1]. In the FQHE regime, the results provided useful information about the quasiparticle interactions. This type of thermodynamic probe of the FQHE is expected to help to determine the quasiparticle charge from the jump in chemical potential. Also, these studies might be very useful near the Wigner crystal transition. Studies of edge states in the FQHE regime are expected to be very active direction of research in near future. In the Wigner crystal regime, the electronic structure is expected to provide some important clue about the nature of the insulating state near $\nu = \frac{1}{5}$ [10.2]. More theoretical and experimental work is needed to settle these important issues.

Whither the FQHE? One obvious direction is to go down further in dimensions [10.3]. The present review has dealt mostly with two-dimensional electron systems subjected to a strong perpendicular magnetic field. Restricting the motion of the electrons in one direction of the plane will result in *one-dimensional* or more accurately, quasi-one-dimensional systems, where the magnetic properties of one-dimensional plasmons have already been observed [10.4]. Going down one step further, *i.e.*, confining the electron motion from all directions, we arrive at quasi-*zero-dimensional* systems or *quantum dots* where the experimental results in a magnetic field [10.5] and their theoretical understanding [10.6] are just emerging. One hopes that *dots* (artificial atoms) [10.7] and *antidots* (electron pinballs) [10.8] will provide the same level of surprise as have two-dimensional electron systems in a strong magnetic field.

Appendices

Appendix A The Landau Wave Function in the Symmetric Gauge

In this appendix, we derive the eigenstates of a single electron in the presence of a uniform magnetic field in the *symmetric* gauge [A.1,2]. This choice of vector potential was adopted by Laughlin for his theory described in Sect. 5.2. The magnetic field is directed along the z-axis and we choose the vector potential $\boldsymbol{A} = \frac{1}{2}(-By, Bx, 0)$, so that the Hamiltonian takes the form (here the electron charge is written as $e = -|e|$)

$$\begin{aligned}\mathcal{H} &= \frac{1}{2m^*}\left(\boldsymbol{p} - \frac{e}{c}\boldsymbol{A}\right)^2 \\ &= \frac{\boldsymbol{p}^2}{2m^*} + \frac{1}{2m^*}\frac{eB}{c}\left(xp_y - yp_x\right) + \frac{1}{8}\frac{e^2B^2}{m^*c^2}(x^2+y^2) \\ &= \frac{\boldsymbol{p}^2}{2m^*} + \frac{1}{2}\omega_{\mathrm{c}}p_\phi + \frac{1}{8}m^*\omega_{\mathrm{c}}^2r^2\end{aligned}$$

where p_ϕ is the angular momentum of the electron about the z-axis, and r is its radial separation from the axis.

In cylindrical polar coordinates, the Schrödinger equation is

$$\begin{aligned}-\frac{\hbar^2}{2m^*}\left[\frac{1}{r}\frac{\partial}{\partial r}\left(r\frac{\partial\psi}{\partial r}\right) + \frac{1}{r^2}\frac{\partial^2\psi}{\partial\phi^2} + \frac{\partial^2\psi}{\partial z^2}\right] - \frac{1}{2}\mathrm{i}\hbar\omega_{\mathrm{c}}\frac{\partial\psi}{\partial\phi}& \\ + \left(\frac{1}{8}m^*\omega_{\mathrm{c}}^2r^2 - E\right)\psi = 0.&\end{aligned} \tag{A.1}$$

We now seek a solution of the form

$$\psi = \frac{1}{\sqrt{2\pi}}f(r)\mathrm{e}^{-\mathrm{i}m\phi}\mathrm{e}^{\mathrm{i}k_z z} \tag{A.2}$$

Eq. (A.1) is then written as

$$\frac{\hbar^2}{2m^*}\left(f'' + \frac{f'}{r} - \frac{m^2f}{r^2}\right) + \left[E - \frac{p_z^2}{2m^*} - \frac{1}{8}m^*\omega_{\mathrm{c}}^2r^2 + \tfrac{1}{2}\hbar\omega_{\mathrm{c}}m\right]f = 0. \tag{A.3}$$

Introducing

$$x = \left(\frac{m^*\omega_c}{2\hbar}\right) r^2$$
$$\beta = \frac{1}{\hbar\omega_c}\left(E - \frac{p_z^2}{2m^*}\right) + \tfrac{1}{2}m \tag{A.4}$$

Eq. (A.3) transforms into

$$xf'' + f' + \left(-\frac{1}{4}x + \beta - \frac{m^2}{4x}\right) f = 0. \tag{A.5}$$

Let $f = x^{-\frac{1}{2}}R$, then

$$R'' + \left(-\frac{1}{4} + \frac{\beta}{x} + \frac{(1-m^2)}{4x^2}\right) R = 0. \tag{A.6}$$

This is Whittaker's equation [A.3] and the solutions are $W_{\beta,\frac{1}{2}m}(x)$ and $W_{-\beta,\frac{1}{2}m}(-x)$. Substituting $R(x) = \mathrm{e}^{-x/2}x^{|m|/2}w(x)$ we obtain for $w(x)$ the differential equation

$$xw'' + (|m| + 1 - x)w' + \left(\beta - \frac{|m|+1}{2}\right) w = 0, \tag{A.7}$$

the solution of which is the confluent hypergeometric function,

$$w = F\left[-\left(\beta - \frac{|m|+1}{2}\right), |m|+1, x\right]. \tag{A.8}$$

If the wave function is everywhere finite, $\beta - \left(\frac{|m|+1}{2}\right)$ is a positive integer n. The energy levels are then

$$E = \hbar\omega_c\left(n + \tfrac{1}{2}|m| - \tfrac{1}{2}m + \tfrac{1}{2}\right) + \frac{p_z^2}{2m^*}. \tag{A.9}$$

The corresponding wave functions are

$$R_{n,m}(r) = \frac{1}{\ell_0^{|m|+1}|m|!}\left[\frac{(|m|+n)!}{2^{|m|}n!}\right]^{\frac{1}{2}} \exp\left(-\frac{r^2}{4\ell_0^2}\right) r^{|m|} F\left(-n, |m|+1, \frac{r^2}{2\ell_0^2}\right) \tag{A.10}$$

with

$$F\left(-n, |m|+1, \frac{r^2}{2\ell_0^2}\right) = \frac{\Gamma(n+1)\Gamma(|m|+1)}{\Gamma(n+|m|+1)} L_n^{|m|}\left(\frac{r^2}{2\ell_0^2}\right)$$
$$= \frac{n!m!}{(n+|m|)!} L_n^{|m|}\left(\frac{r^2}{2\ell_0^2}\right).$$

The wave function is then written

$$\psi_{n,m}(r) = \left[\frac{n!}{2\pi\ell_0^2 2^m (n+|m|)!}\right]^{\frac{1}{2}} \exp\left(-im\phi - \frac{r^2}{4\ell_0^2}\right)\left(\frac{r}{\ell_0}\right)^{|m|} L_n^{|m|}\left(\frac{r^2}{2\ell_0^2}\right). \tag{A.11}$$

In the lowest Landau level ($n = 0$)

$$\psi_m(r) = \left[\frac{1}{2\pi\ell_0^2 2^m m!}\right]^{\frac{1}{2}} \left(\frac{r}{\ell_0}\right)^m \exp\left(-im\phi - \frac{r^2}{4\ell_0^2}\right). \tag{A.12}$$

Considering a complex plane: $z = x - iy = re^{-i\theta}$, and noting that only *positive* values of m gives the lowest energy states [choosing $e^{im\phi}$ in (A.2) we can get the lowest energies for *negative* values of m; in that case one should write $-|m|$ for m in (A.9)] the lowest Landau level wave function is written in the final form

$$\psi_m(z) = \left[\frac{1}{2\pi\ell_0^2 2^m m!}\right]^{\frac{1}{2}} \left(\frac{z}{\ell_0}\right)^m \exp\left(-\frac{|z|^2}{4\ell_0^2}\right).$$

As an interesting exercise, following the derivation given above, the single-electron energy spectrum can be calculated for a harmonic confinement in the $x - y$ plane: $V(x,y) = \frac{1}{2}m^*\omega_0^2(x^2 + y^2)$. The energies in this case were derived by *Fock* [A.4] and *Darwin* [A.5]:

$$E_{n,m} = (2n + |m| + 1)\hbar\left[\left(\tfrac{1}{2}\omega_c\right)^2 + \omega_0^2\right]^{\frac{1}{2}} - \tfrac{1}{2}m\hbar\omega_c.$$

This energy spectrum reveals a very interesting feature. At low magnetic fields such that the magnetic length is larger than or comparable to the size of the confining potential, the levels resulting from the spatial confinement and the Landau levels are hybridized. For magnetic length much smaller than the confinement, the effects of spatial quantization become negligible and one recovers free-electron behavior (Landau levels). The effect of electron-electron interaction in this confinement potential has been studied by *Maksym* and *Chakraborty* [A.6].

Let us write the lowest Landau level eigenfunction obtained above as (in units where $\ell_0^{-2} = eB/\hbar c = 1$):

$$\psi[z] = f[z]\, e^{-\frac{1}{4}\sum_i |z_i|^2} \tag{A.13}$$

where $[z] \equiv (z_1, \ldots, z_N)$ and f is a polynomial in the N variables. The exponential factor in (A.13) is common to all wave functions, and is removed by defining a suitable Hilbert space of analytic functions [A.7-9] as described below.

Following [A.7,8], let us now consider a set of entire functions of N complex variables, $\Theta \equiv \{f\}$. These functions are analytic in each of their arguments in the complex plane. For example, for $N = 1$, the function $f(z) = z^3$ is an element of Θ, but the function $f(z) = z^*$ is *not* analytic, (as z^* cannot be expressed as a power series in z), and is excluded from Θ.

Let us now define an inner product on Θ as

$$(f, g) = \int d\mu[z] f^*[z] g[z], \tag{A.14}$$

with the measure

$$d\mu[z] = \prod_{i=1}^{N} \frac{1}{2\pi} e^{-|z_i|^2/2} dx_i dy_i. \tag{A.15}$$

Only those functions with finite norm $(f, f) < \infty$ are included in Θ. The Hilbert space as defined above, is realized by the wave functions of the lowest Landau level as they may always be written in the form of (A.13) with f being a member of Θ. The inner product on Θ is defined in such a manner that

$$\langle \psi' | \psi \rangle = (f', f). \tag{A.16}$$

This definition of the Hilbert space allows one in (A.13) to work only with f, which is analytic, while ψ is not.

Let us now define the orthonormal basis functions,

$$f_n(z) = \frac{z^n}{(2^n n!)^{\frac{1}{2}}}, \tag{A.17}$$

where the following relations can easily be verified:

$$\begin{aligned} z\, f_m &= \sqrt{2}\sqrt{m+1}\, f_{m+1} \\ \frac{d}{dz} f_m &= \sqrt{\frac{m}{2}} f_{m-1}. \end{aligned} \tag{A.18}$$

Therefore one can define the boson ladder operators [A.7,8] as:

$$\begin{aligned} a^\dagger &\equiv \frac{1}{\sqrt{2}} z \\ a &\equiv \sqrt{2} \frac{d}{dz} \end{aligned} \tag{A.19}$$

which are mutually adjoint with respect to the inner product defined in Θ.

It is interesting to observe that the adjoint of z is not the same as the Hermitian conjugate of z. From the definition of the inner product, it is clear that

$$(f_n, z_k^* f_m) = (z_k f_n, f_m) \tag{A.20}$$

as z_k^* is the Hermitian conjugate of z_k. However, from (A.18), the adjoint of z_k is

$$z_k^\dagger = 2\frac{\partial}{\partial z_k} \tag{A.21}$$

so that

$$(f_n, z_k^* f_m) = \left(f_n, 2\frac{\partial}{\partial z_k} f_m\right). \tag{A.22}$$

Therefore, z_k^* and $2\partial/\partial z_k$ have the same matrix elements within the space $\boldsymbol{\Theta}$. However the two operators are not completely equivalent since z_k^* commutes with z_k but $\partial/\partial z_k$ does not. As an example,

$$(f, z_k z_k^* g) = (f, z_k^* z_k g) \tag{A.23}$$

but

$$\left(f, z_k 2\frac{\partial}{\partial z_k} g\right) \neq \left(f, 2\frac{\partial}{\partial z_k} z_k g\right). \tag{A.24}$$

It is clear that only the right-hand side of (A.24) agrees with (A.23). In other words, z^* makes sense only when operating to the left. These observations were useful in obtaining the projection of various operators discussed in Sect. 7.4.

Appendix B Kubo Formalism for the Hall Conductivity

In this Appendix, we shall derive the Kubo formula for the conductivity within the framework of the linear response theory. In so doing, we shall closely follow the treatment by *Morandi* [B.1] (see also the original articles by *Kubo* [B.2,3]). Accordingly, the total many-body Hamiltonian $\mathcal{H}$ is split into the unperturbed part $\mathcal{H}_0$ and into the perturbation $V(t)$:

$$\mathcal{H} = \mathcal{H}_0 + V(t). \tag{B.1}$$

The density matrix ρ is similarly decomposed as

$$\rho = \rho_0 + \Delta\rho(t). \tag{B.2}$$

In the grand canonical ensemble, which is our present choice, the unperturbed density matrix ρ_0 takes the form

$$\rho_0 = \frac{1}{Z} e^{-\beta(\mathcal{H}_0 - \mu\widehat{N})}, \tag{B.3}$$

where $\widehat{N}$ is the particle number operator and Z the grand canonical partition sum

$$Z = \mathrm{Tr}\, e^{-\beta(\mathcal{H}_0 - \mu\widehat{N})}. \tag{B.4}$$

To derive the equation of motion for the fluctuation $\Delta\rho$ we first note that the denstity matrix obeys the Liouville equation

$$i\hbar \frac{d\rho}{dt} = [\mathcal{H}, \rho]. \tag{B.5}$$

We now switch to the interaction picture. For example, the density matrix then transforms to

$$\rho^{\mathrm{I}}(t) = e^{\frac{i}{\hbar}\mathcal{H}_0 t} \rho\, e^{-\frac{i}{\hbar}\mathcal{H}_0 t}. \tag{B.6}$$

Substituting this into Eq. (B.5) and keeping only the terms linear in the perturbation $V(t)$ we end up with the equation

$$i\hbar \frac{d}{dt} \Delta\rho^{\mathrm{I}}(t) = [V^{\mathrm{I}}(t), \rho_0]. \tag{B.7}$$

If we now make the standard asumption that the perturbation is switched on adiabatically in the far past, *i.e.*

$$\lim_{t \to -\infty} \Delta\rho(t) = 0, \tag{B.8}$$

we can integrate the equation of motion:

$$\Delta\rho^{\mathrm{I}}(t) = -\frac{i}{\hbar} \int_{-\infty}^{t} dt' \, [V^{\mathrm{I}}(t'), \rho_0]. \tag{B.9}$$

Let us consider any observable B. Its expectation value is given by

$$\langle B(t) \rangle = \mathrm{Tr}\{B\rho(t)\} = \mathrm{Tr}\{B^{\mathrm{I}}(t)\rho^{\mathrm{I}}(t)\}. \tag{B.10}$$

If, for simplicity, we assume that B has zero expectation value in the unperturbed state, we can write

$$\begin{aligned} \langle B(t) \rangle &= \mathrm{Tr}\{B^{\mathrm{I}}(t)\Delta\rho^{\mathrm{I}}(t)\} \\ &= -\frac{i}{\hbar} \int_{-\infty}^{t} dt' \, \mathrm{Tr}\left\{[V^{\mathrm{I}}(t'), \rho_0] B^{\mathrm{I}}(t)\right\} \\ &= -\frac{i}{\hbar} \int_{-\infty}^{t} dt' \, \mathrm{Tr}\left\{\rho_0 [V^{\mathrm{I}}(t'), B^{\mathrm{I}}(t)]\right\}, \end{aligned} \tag{B.11}$$

where we have also made use of the cyclic invariance of the trace.

We now express the perturbation $V(t)$ as a linear superposition of its Fourier components. Due to the linearity of Eq. (B.11) we can treat one component at a time. Let us pick a particular one, say, $A\mathrm{e}^{-\mathrm{i}(\omega+\mathrm{i}\eta)t}$. To guarantee the boundary condition (B.8) we have introduced here the convergence factor $\eta > 0$ which we let to tend to zero at the end of the calculation. The effect of this Fourier component to the expectation value (B.11) is easily evaluated to be

$$\langle B(t)\rangle = \frac{\mathrm{i}}{\hbar}\int_{-\infty}^{t} dt' \,\mathrm{Tr}\left\{\rho_0[A, B^{\mathrm{I}}(t-t')]\right\}\mathrm{e}^{-\mathrm{i}(\omega+\mathrm{i}\eta)t'}. \tag{B.12}$$

The linear response function χ_{BA} is defined via the relation

$$\langle B(t)\rangle = \int_{-\infty}^{+\infty} dt' \,\chi_{BA}(t-t')\,\mathrm{e}^{-\mathrm{i}(\omega+\mathrm{i}\eta)t'}. \tag{B.13}$$

Comparing these two equations we can write

$$\chi_{BA}(t) = \frac{\mathrm{i}}{\hbar}\,\mathrm{Tr}\left\{\rho_0[A, B^{\mathrm{I}}(t)]\right\}\theta(t) = -\frac{\mathrm{i}}{\hbar}\,\mathrm{Tr}\left\{[A, \rho_0]B^{\mathrm{I}}(t)\right\}\theta(t), \tag{B.14}$$

where $\theta(t)$ is the step function.

Let us consider the μ-th component of the electric current density,

$$-eJ_\mu(\boldsymbol{r}) = -\frac{e}{2}\sum_{i=1}^{N}\left\{v_{i\mu}\delta(\boldsymbol{r}-\boldsymbol{r}_i) + \delta(\boldsymbol{r}-\boldsymbol{r}_i)v_{i\mu}\right\}, \tag{B.15}$$

as the observable B. The quantities $\boldsymbol{v}_i$ are the velocity operators acting on the coordinates of the i-th particle. By definition, the conductivity is the linear response to the applied electric field $\boldsymbol{E}$. The perturbing potential is then

$$V(t) = e\sum_\nu X_\nu E_\nu(t), \tag{B.16}$$

where

$$X_\nu = \sum_{i=1}^{N} r_{i\nu}. \tag{B.17}$$

When we set

$$\begin{aligned} A &= eX_\nu \\ B &= -eJ_\mu(\boldsymbol{r}) \end{aligned} \tag{B.18}$$

the formula (B.14) defines the conductivity tensor $\sigma_{\mu\nu}$:

$$\sigma_{\mu\nu}(\boldsymbol{r},t) = -\frac{\mathrm{i}e^2}{\hbar}\theta(t)\,\mathrm{Tr}\left\{\rho_0[X_\nu, J_\mu^{\mathrm{I}}(\boldsymbol{r},t)]\right\}. \tag{B.19}$$

The trace in the above equation is most conveniently evaluated in the base where the Hamiltonian $\mathcal{H}_0$ is diagonal since in this representation the density operator ρ_0 is also diagonal. Let us denote the eigenstates of $\mathcal{H}_0$ by $|n\rangle$, *i.e.*

$$\mathcal{H}_0|n\rangle = E_n|n\rangle;\ n = 0, 1, 2, \dots, \tag{B.20}$$

where $n = 0$ means the ground state. At low enough temperatures the only contribution to the trace in (B.19) comes from the term containing the matrix element $\langle 0|\rho_0|0\rangle \approx 1$. Furthermore, the ground state cannot carry current so that $\langle 0|J_\mu(\boldsymbol{r})|0\rangle = 0$. Writing for $J^{\mathrm{I}}_\mu(\boldsymbol{r}, t)$ its explicit representation in the form $J^{\mathrm{I}}_\mu(\boldsymbol{r}, t) = \mathrm{e}^{\frac{\mathrm{i}}{\hbar}\mathcal{H}_0 t} J_\mu(\boldsymbol{r})\, \mathrm{e}^{-\frac{\mathrm{i}}{\hbar}\mathcal{H}_0 t}$, we find that

$$\begin{aligned}\sigma_{\mu\nu}(\boldsymbol{r}, t) = -\frac{\mathrm{i}e^2}{\hbar}\theta(t)\sum_{n>0}\Big\{&\langle 0|X_\nu|n\rangle\langle n|J_\mu(\boldsymbol{r})|0\rangle\, \mathrm{e}^{\frac{\mathrm{i}}{\hbar}(E_n - E_0)t} \\ &- \langle n|X_\nu|0\rangle\langle 0|J_\mu(\boldsymbol{r})|n\rangle\, \mathrm{e}^{-\frac{\mathrm{i}}{\hbar}(E_n - E_0)t}\Big\}.\end{aligned} \tag{B.21}$$

Since our goal is the static conductivity $\sigma_{\mu\nu}(\boldsymbol{r})$ we integrate over time to obtain

$$\sigma_{\mu\nu}(\boldsymbol{r}) = \lim_{\eta\to 0+}\int_{-\infty}^{+\infty} dt\, \mathrm{e}^{-\eta t}\sigma_{\mu\nu}(\boldsymbol{r}, t), \tag{B.22}$$

where we have introduced the convergence factor $\mathrm{e}^{-\eta t}$ with $\eta > 0$. The quantity we are finally interested in is the sample averaged conductivity, or conductance, $\sigma_{\mu\nu}$:

$$\sigma_{\mu\nu} = \frac{1}{A}\int d\boldsymbol{r}\, \sigma_{\mu\nu}(\boldsymbol{r}), \tag{B.23}$$

where A is the area of the sample. Performing both of these integrations and noting that

$$J_\mu = v_\mu = \int d\boldsymbol{r}\, J_\mu(\boldsymbol{r}) \tag{B.24}$$

is the total particle current operator, or the total velocity, we have for the static conductance tensor

$$\sigma_{\mu\nu} = e^2\sum_{n>0}\frac{\langle 0|X_\nu|n\rangle\langle n|v_\mu|0\rangle + \langle n|X_\nu|0\rangle\langle 0|v_\mu|n\rangle}{E_n - E_0}. \tag{B.25}$$

Also note that the velocity operator

$$v_\mu = \dot{X}_\mu, \tag{B.26}$$

obeys the Heisenberg equation of motion

$$\mathrm{i}\hbar v_\mu = \mathrm{i}\hbar \frac{d}{dt} X_\mu = [X_\mu, \mathcal{H}_0]. \tag{B.27}$$

We can then rewrite the static conductance into the form

$$\sigma_{\mu\nu} = \frac{\mathrm{i}e^2\hbar}{A} \sum_{n>0} \frac{\langle 0|v_\nu|n\rangle\langle n|v_\mu|0\rangle - \langle 0|v_\mu|n\rangle\langle n|v_\nu|0\rangle}{(E_n - E_0)^2}. \tag{B.28}$$

This is clearly an antisymmetric tensor with vanishing diagonal elements. The Hall conductance σ_{H} is the off-diagonal element

$$\sigma_{\mathrm{H}} = \sigma_{yx} = \frac{\mathrm{i}e^2\hbar}{A} \sum_{n>0} \frac{(v_x)_{0n}(v_y)_{n0} - (v_y)_{0n}(v_x)_{n0}}{(E_n - E_0)^2}. \tag{B.29}$$

Appendix C **The Hypernetted–Chain Primer**

The hypernetted-chain (HNC) method is a well-established procedure to calculate the pair-correlation function for an imperfect gas in classical statistical mechanics. The method was originally proposed by *van Leeuwen* et al. [C.1] and independently by *Morita* and *Hiroike* [C.2]. In this appendix, we present a brief discussion of the method following closely the paper by van Leeuwen et al.

The pair-correlation function at temperature $T = (\beta k_{\mathrm{B}})^{-1}$, and density ρ is given by

$$g(r_{12}) = \frac{N(N-1)}{\rho^2} \frac{\int \exp\left[-\beta \sum_{i<j} \varphi(r_{ij})\right] d\boldsymbol{r}_3 \ldots d\boldsymbol{r}_N}{\int \exp\left[-\beta \sum_{i<j} \varphi(r_{ij})\right] d\boldsymbol{r}_1 \ldots d\boldsymbol{r}_N} \tag{C.1}$$

where $\varphi(r_{ij})$ is the interaction between particles i and j. Let us define the functions

$$f(r_{ij}) = \exp\left[-\beta\varphi(r_{ij})\right] - 1 \tag{C.2}$$

$$h(r_{12}) = g(r_{12}) - 1. \tag{C.3}$$

For values of r_{12} much larger than the range of interparticle interaction, the pair-correlation function is rigorously equal to 1 and hence, $h(r_{12})$ is a short range function, $h(r_{12}) \to 0$ for large r.

One can write the correlation function as a series expansion in powers of density

$$h(r_{12}) = \exp\left[-\beta\varphi(r_{12})\right] \cdot \left[1 + C(r_{12})\right] - 1, \tag{C.4}$$

where,

$$\begin{aligned} C(r_{12}) &= \sum_{k=1}^{\infty} \rho^k \gamma_k(r_{12}) \\ &= \sum_{k=1}^{\infty} \frac{\rho^k}{k!} \int \cdots \int \sum_{(\text{sp. irr.})} \prod f(r_{ij})\, d\boldsymbol{r}_3 \ldots d\boldsymbol{r}_{k+2}. \end{aligned} \tag{C.5}$$

The summation inside the integral of (C.5) is over all different products of $f(r_{ij})$ [excluding $f(r_{12})$] corresponding to the *specific* (distinguishable) *irreducible* $1-2$ diagrams to be described below.

Before we proceed with the diagrammatic scheme, let us first explain the terminologies involved. We define the *external* (or *reference*) points as coordinates which are not integration variables (points 1 and 2) and the *internal* (or *field*) points as the coordinates which are integration variables (points $3, \ldots, k+2$). The internal points are connected by a certain number of bonds, each bond corresponding to one of the factors $f(r_{ij})$ in the product of (C.5). An *irreducible* diagram is *linked* or *connected* (not containing a direct bond $1-2$) in the sense that each point is connected to every other point by at least one bond, and has no *articulation points*. An articulation point is a point where the connected diagram may be split into separate connected subdiagrams.[1] The external points can also be articulation points (Fig. C.1).

In (C.5), the contributions to the integral from two specific diagrams which differ only through a permutation of k internal points, are the same. Therefore, one could perform the summation in (C.5) over the different *generic* diagrams or different topological types of diagrams. The total number of specific diagrams which correspond to one particular generic diagram is $k!/s$ where s is the symmetry number denoting the number of permutations that do *not* lead to a new specific diagram. Then (C.5) is rewritten

[1] An $i-j$ *subdiagram* is a part of $1-2$ diagram which is only connected with the rest of the diagram through points i and j.

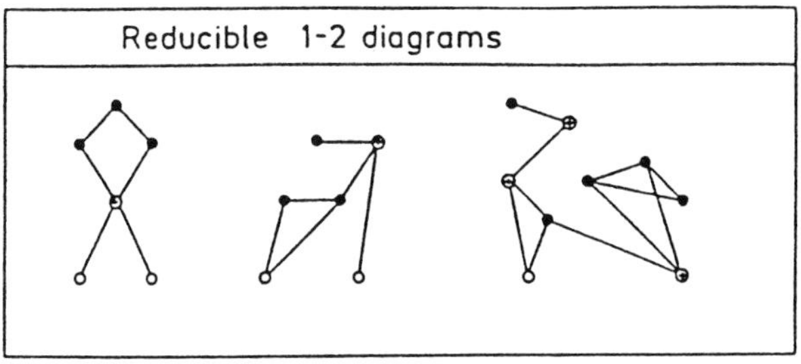

Fig. C.1. Some examples of reducible $1-2$ diagrams. The articulation points are drawn as $\oplus$

as

$$C(r_{12}) = \sum_{k=1}^{\infty} \frac{\rho^k}{k!} \int \cdots \int \sum_{\substack{\kappa \\ \text{(gen. irr.)}}} \frac{1}{s(k,\kappa)} \prod f(r_{ij})\, d\boldsymbol{r}_3 \ldots d\boldsymbol{r}_{k+2} \qquad \text{(C.6)}$$

where the summation runs over all different generic irreducible $1-2$ diagrams κ with k internal points and $s(k,\kappa)$ is the symmetry number corresponding to the generic diagram κ. In (C.6), $C(r_{12})$ is thus a sum of contributions due to all possible generic irreducible $1-2$ diagrams in which the contribution of a particular generic diagram is equal to the product of ρ^k; $1/s(k,\kappa)$ accounts for the symmetry, and the integral $\int \ldots \int d\boldsymbol{r}_3 \cdot d\boldsymbol{r}_{k+2} \prod f(r_{ij})$, corresponding to that diagram.

Parallel connection of diagrams: An irreducible $1-2$ diagram might be composed of two or more $1-2$ *sub*diagrams forming parallel connections between the points 1 and 2. As the points 1 and 2 are not integrated over, the integral corresponding to such a graph is factorizable into products of each $1-2$ subdiagram. A diagram of this type is called a *composite* diagram. If not composite, the irreducible $1-2$ diagram is called *simple.* Examples of simple and composite diagrams are given in Fig. C.2.

The contribution to the integral from all simple irreducible $1-2$ diagrams with l internal points is written as

$$\beta_l(r_{12}) = \frac{1}{l!} \int \cdots \int d\boldsymbol{r}_3 \ldots d\boldsymbol{r}_{l+2} \sum_{\text{(sp. simp.)}} \prod f(r_{ij})$$

or,

$$\beta_l(r_{12}) = \sum_{\substack{\lambda \\ \text{(gen. simp.)}}} \frac{1}{s(l,\lambda)} \int \cdots \int d\boldsymbol{r}_3 \ldots d\boldsymbol{r}_{l+2} \prod f(r_{ij}).$$

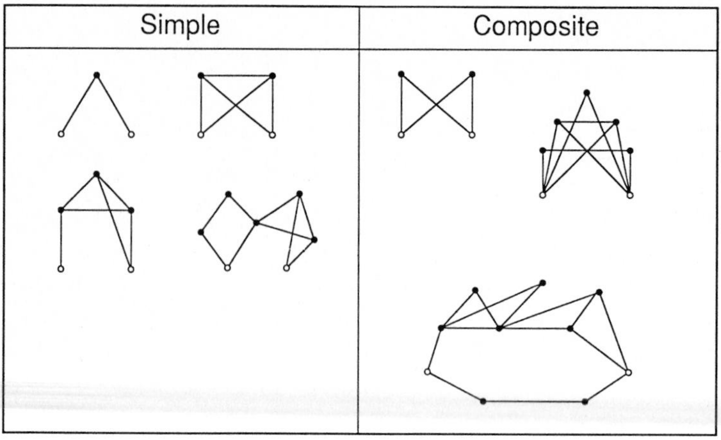

Fig. C.2. Some examples of simple and composite irreducible $1-2$ diagrams (the $\mathcal{C}$-set)

The complete set of all generic composite and simple diagrams of k internal points composed of $\{m_l\} = m_1, m_2, \ldots$ simple subdiagrams of $1, 2, \ldots$ internal points respectively can be obtained as follows: We choose all possible generic simple subdiagrams, one out of each of the $m_1, m_2, \ldots$ complete subset of simple diagrams with $1, 2, \ldots$ internal points. *van Leeuwen* et al. [C.1] then asserted that, in terms of this complete set of simple and composite diagrams, one can write

$$1 + C(r_{12}) = \sum_{\{m_l\}} \prod_l \frac{1}{m_l!} \left[\beta_l(r_{12})\rho^l\right]^{m_l} \tag{C.7}$$

taking proper account of the symmetry factor and correct counting of the subdiagrams. For the $\mathcal{C}$-set of all composite and simple $1-2$ diagrams the following relation is then obtained,

$$C(r_{12}) = \mathrm{e}^{S(r_{12})} - 1 \tag{C.8}$$

with

$$S(r_{12}) = \mathcal{S}f(r) = \sum_{k=1}^{\infty} \beta_k(r_{12})\rho^k \tag{C.9}$$

being the contribution from the $\mathcal{S}$-set of all simple $1-2$ diagrams only. Expanding the exponential we obtain $S(r_{12})$ plus the sum of all composite diagrams with the correct weights. A similar expression was also obtained by *Salpeter* [C.3]. In terms of $C(r_{12})$, the pair correlation function is given by

$$h(r_{12}) = \exp\left[-\beta\varphi(r_{12}) + S(r_{12})\right] - 1. \tag{C.10}$$

Distinguishing in this way between simple and composite diagrams, $C(r_{12})$ can be expressed in terms of the set of simple $1-2$ diagrams.

Series connection of diagrams: The $1-2$ diagram may be either *nodal* or *non-nodal.* A diagram is nodal if it has one or more nodes. A *node* is a point through which all paths from 1 to 2 must go. A composite diagram is by definition non-nodal. Conversely, a nodal (irreducible) $1-2$ diagram is necessarily simple. A simple diagram contributing to $C(r_{12})$ can be either nodal or non-nodal; if non-nodal such a diagram is called *elementary.* Therefore, the contribution $S(r_{12})$ due to all simple $1-2$ diagrams can be divided into contributions $N(r_{12}) = \mathcal{N}f(r)$, due to the $\mathcal{N}$-set of nodal diagrams and $E(r_{12}) = \mathcal{E}f(r)$ due to the $\mathcal{E}$-set of elementary diagrams

$$S(r_{12}) = N(r_{12}) + E(r_{12}), \tag{C.11}$$

and the pair correlation function is rewritten as

$$h(r_{12}) = \exp\left[-\beta\varphi(r_{12}) + E(r_{12}) + N(r_{12})\right] - 1. \tag{C.12}$$

Examples of elementary diagrams are given in Fig. C.3.

In general, any nodal diagram can be built by connecting in series, a number of non-nodal subdiagrams. Our task is to express the contributions due to the nodal diagrams $N(r_{12})$, by series connection of elements of a set of non-nodal diagrams. We are immediately faced with the problem that the set of non-nodal diagram contained in the $\mathcal{C}$-set — considered as $i-j$ subdiagrams rather than $1-2$ diagrams — are simply not sufficient. For example, an essential element for the construction of nodal diagrams by *series* connection is the direct bond, which is not included in the $\mathcal{C}$-set.

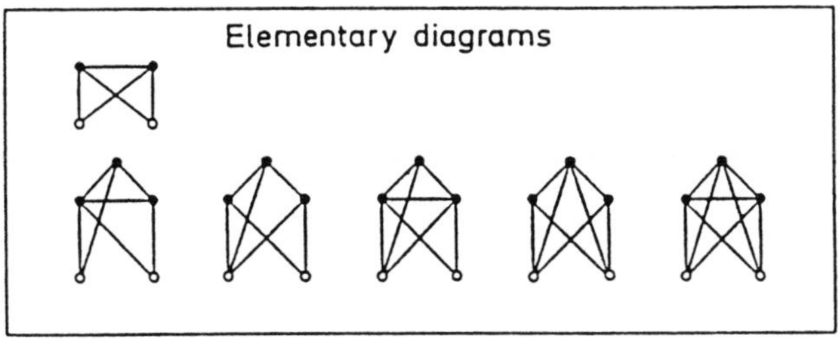

Fig. C.3. Some examples of elementary $1-2$ diagrams (the $\mathcal{E}$-set)

van Leeuwen et al. then introduced an *extended* set of 1 – 2 diagrams, the $\mathcal{G}$-set, which included the original $\mathcal{C}$-set, plus all the diagrams obtained by adding the direct bond corresponding to $f(r_{12})$ to the $\mathcal{C}$-set and the direct bond itself. This set contains all the diagrams corresponding to the different terms in $h(r_{12})$:

$$h(r_{12}) = [1 + f(r_{12})]\, C(r_{12}) + f(r_{12}) = \mathcal{G}(r)f(r). \tag{C.13}$$

The $\mathcal{N}$-set of nodal diagrams, being a subset of the original $\mathcal{C}$-set of (composite and simple) diagrams, is also a subset of the (extended) $\mathcal{G}$-set of diagrams. If $X(r_{12})$ denotes the contributions to the $\mathcal{X}$-set of diagrams (complete set of all possible diagrams to be used as a subdiagram in constructing the nodal diagrams) then,

$$X(r_{12}) = h(r_{12}) - N(r_{12}) = \mathcal{X}(r)f(r). \tag{C.14}$$

Using (C.12), one can then write

$$X(r_{12}) = \exp\left[-\beta\varphi(r_{12}) + N(r_{12}) + E(r_{12})\right] - N(r_{12}) - 1. \tag{C.15}$$

Examples of nodal and non-nodal diagrams of the extended set (the $\mathcal{G}$ set) are given in Fig. C.4.

Following van Leeuwen et al., we now derive an integral equation for the quantity $N(r_{12})$ (corresponding to the nodal diagrams of the $\mathcal{G}$-set) in terms of $X(r_{12})$ (which corresponds to the non-nodal diagrams of the $\mathcal{G}$-set):

$$N(r_{12}) = \rho \int \left[X(r_{13}) + N(r_{13})\right]\, X(r_{32}) d\boldsymbol{r}_3 \tag{C.16}$$

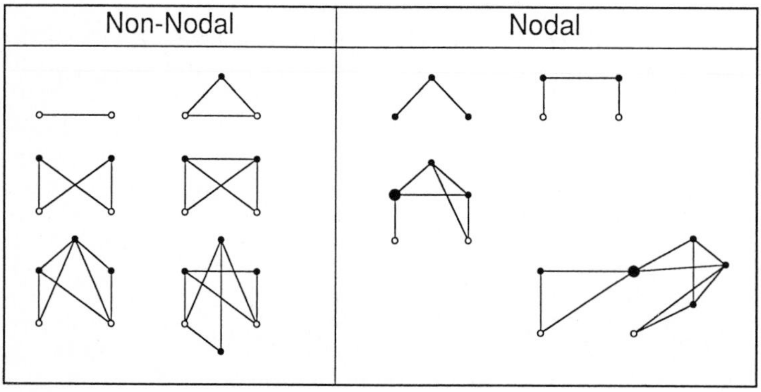

Fig. C.4. Some examples of the nodal and non-nodal diagrams of the extended set (the $\mathcal{G}$-set)

which is completely general and does not involve any approximation. It is easy to check this equation by iteration. As the integration in (C.16) is of a convolution type, going over to the Fourier space, we obtain an algebraic equation,

$$\widetilde{N}(k) = \frac{\rho\left[\widetilde{X}(k)\right]^2}{1-\rho\widetilde{X}(k)}. \tag{C.17}$$

Again, as in (C.8), a massive partial summation has been achieved.

The pair-correlation function is now finally determined within the hyper-netted-chain scheme by solving the following set of coupled equations which are exact,[2]

$$\begin{aligned} X(r_{12}) &= h(r_{12}) - N(r_{12}) \\ \widetilde{N}(k) &= \rho\left[\widetilde{X}(k)\right]^2 \Big/ \left[1-\rho\widetilde{X}(k)\right] \\ g(r_{12}) &= \exp\left[-\beta\varphi(r_{12}) + E(r_{12}) + N(r_{12})\right]. \end{aligned} \tag{C.18}$$

In the actual calculations, however, one faces the problem that the contribution corresponding to all elementary (simple non-nodal) diagrams is not explicitly available as a function of r. As a first approximation, we set $E(r) = 0$. This approximation has been used throughout in the book. To get some feeling about the above equations, we now perform a few iteration steps analytically: In the zeroth order let us put

$$N_0^{(0)} = 0.$$

Then from (C.15) we obtain,

$$X_0^{(0)}(r) = \exp\left[-\beta\varphi(r)\right] - 1 = f(r)$$

(the subscript 0 is to denote the case of $E(r) = 0$). The pair-correlation function is then simply

$$h_0^{(0)}(r_{12}) = f(r_{12}) = \exp\left[\beta\varphi(r_{12})\right] - 1.$$

In the first order, we take the Fourier transform, $X_0^{(0)}(k) = f(k)$ and obtain

$$\widetilde{N}_0^{(1)}(k) = \frac{\rho\left[\widetilde{X}_0^{(0)}(k)\right]^2}{1-\rho\widetilde{X}_0^{(0)}(k)} = \frac{\rho\left[\widetilde{f}(k)\right]^2}{1-\rho\widetilde{f}(k)}$$

[2] In (5.23), we have defined $C(r_{12}) \equiv X(r_{12})$, used the approximation $E(r_{12}) = 0$ and the density ρ has been absorbed in the Fourier transform, (5.22). Also, the interaction potential is $\beta\varphi(r) = u(r)$.

and the inverse Fourier transform provides $N_0^{(1)}(r)$, which corresponds to *all possible* nodal diagrams obtained by connecting in series the single bonds $f(r)$. The improved approximation to $X(r_{12})$ is then,

$$X_0^{(1)}(r) = [1 + f(r)] \exp\left[N_0^{(1)}(r)\right] - N_0^{(1)}(r) - 1$$

which corresponds to all possible diagrams obtained by connecting in parallel all possible nodal diagrams out of the set of diagrams which contribute to $N_0^{(1)}(r)$. The pair correlation function, in this iteration step is

$$h_0^{(1)}(r_{12}) = \exp\left[\beta\varphi(r_{12}) + N_0^{(1)}(r_{12})\right] - 1.$$

In the next step, we take the Fourier transform of $X_0^{(1)}(r)$ and evaluate a better approximation,

$$\widetilde{N}_0^{(2)}(k) = \frac{\rho\left[\widetilde{X}_0^{(1)}\right]^2}{1 - \rho\widetilde{X}_0^{(1)}(k)}.$$

The inverse Fourier transform, $N_0^{(2)}(r)$ now corresponds to all possible nodal diagrams connecting in series all possible diagrams out of the set corresponding to $X_0^{(1)}(r)$.

Repeating this procedure of series and parallel connections, starting with the single bond, we generate a huge class of diagrams. In Fig. C.5, we have sketched the iteration procedure, and in Fig. C.6, we show the type of diagrams that are obtained in the successive steps of the iteration procedure. It should be emphasized here that, in each step of the calculation, an infinite set of diagrams up to *infinite order* (but of a certain type) are taken into account.

In the case of a classical plasma, the contribution from the elementary diagrams has been approximately evaluated by *Caillol* et al. [C.4]. Making use of the exact results for the correlation function in the case of $\Gamma = 2$, the functions corresponding to elementary diagrams are obtained as:

$$\begin{aligned} E_{\Gamma=2}(x) &= \mathrm{e}^{-x^2} + \ln\left[\left(1 - \mathrm{e}^{-x^2}\right)/x^2\right] + C(x) \\ C_{\Gamma=2}(x) &= -2\gamma - \sum_{j=1}^{\infty} \frac{1}{j}\left[\mathrm{e}^{-x^2/j} - 1\right] \end{aligned} \qquad \text{(C.19)}$$

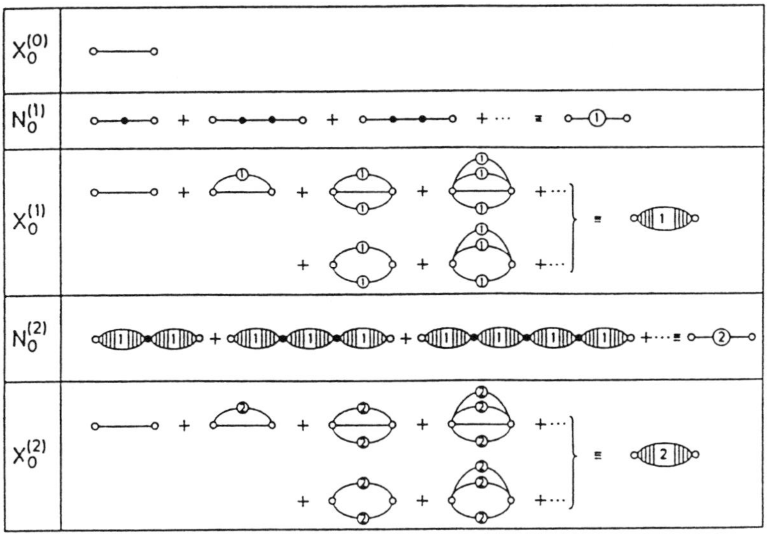

Fig. C.5. The steps of the series-parallel iteration process demonstrated symbolically

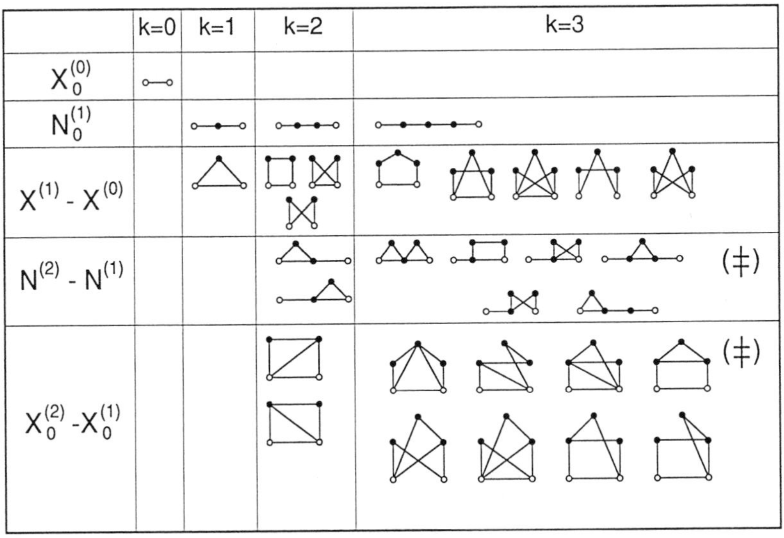

Fig. C.6. Diagrams of the $\mathcal{G}_0$-set obtained in the steps of the series-parallel iteration procedure with 1, 2 and 3 internal points. (‡) The diagrams which one can obtain by an interchange of the external points are omitted

where γ is Euler's constant. The function $E(x)$ is then represented quite accurately by the simple functional form,

$$E_{\Gamma=2}(x) = \mathrm{e}^{-x^2}\left[E_0 + E_2x^2 + E_4x^4 + E_6x^6\right]$$

with the coefficients: $E_0 = 1 - 2\gamma = -0.1544313, E_2 = -0.00949726, E_4 = 0.00835662$ and $E_6 = 0.00108723$. Caillol et al. then assumed that the shape of the function $E(x)$ does not change significantly with Γ, and made the following ansatz:

$$E_\Gamma(x) = \alpha\tfrac{1}{2}\Gamma E_{\Gamma=2}(x). \tag{C.20}$$

The coefficient α is adjusted to achieve thermodynamic consistency.

In the FQHE calculations, our experience is that the pair-correlation functions within the HNC scheme (not including the elementary diagrams) are almost indistinguishable from the very accurate Monte Carlo results. The contribution of the elementary diagrams is noticeable only in the results for energy.

Finally, the two-component HNC method is a straightforward generalization of the single-component HNC procedure discussed above [C.5–7]:

$$\begin{aligned} g_{\alpha\beta}(x) &= \exp\left[N_{\alpha\beta}(x) - u_{\alpha\beta}(x)\right] \\ \widetilde{N}_{\alpha\beta}(q) &= \sum_{\nu=1,2} C_{\nu\alpha}\left[C_{\nu\beta} + N_{\nu\beta}\right] \\ C_{\alpha\beta}(x) &= g_{\alpha\beta}(x) - 1 - N_{\alpha\beta}(x) \end{aligned} \tag{C.21}$$

where $\alpha, \beta = 1, 2$ denotes the two species of particles in the system. The equation for $\widetilde{N}_{\alpha\beta}(q)$ is easily solvable and one obtains,

$$\begin{aligned} \widetilde{N}_{11} &= \left(\widetilde{C}_{11}^2 + \widetilde{C}_{12}^2/D\right)/(1 - \widetilde{C}_{11}) \\ \widetilde{N}_{22} &= \left(\widetilde{C}_{22}^2 + \widetilde{C}_{12}^2/D\right)/(1 - \widetilde{C}_{22}) \\ \widetilde{N}_{12} &= \widetilde{C}_{12}(1 - D)/D \end{aligned} \tag{C.22}$$

with, $D = (1 - \widetilde{C}_{11})(1 - \widetilde{C}_{22}) - \widetilde{C}_{12}^2$. An iteration scheme similar to that used in the single-component case could be used here to obtain $g_{\alpha\beta}(x)$.

Appendix D Repetition of the Intra-Landau-level Mode in the Inter-Landau-level Mode

In the following, we shall consider only those kinds of inter-Landau level excitations where exactly one electron from the lowest level is elevated to the second level. Our aim is to show that, in the spectrum of those excitations, there are points which exactly repeat — when shifted by $\hbar\omega_c$ — the intra-Landau level spectrum of the lowest Landau level. We shall present the proof for the finite-size system and also provide the evidence for the infinite system within the framework of the SMA model described in Sect. 7.4.

We will first concentrate on systems with a finite number of particles. For the time being it is enough if we consider only the potential energy part $\mathcal{V}$ of the total Hamiltonian $\mathcal{H} = \mathcal{K} + \mathcal{V}$ since the kinetic energy $\mathcal{K}$ is diagonal in our representation. In occcupation number space the potential energy part of the Hamiltonian is given by [see (7.28)],

$$\mathcal{V} = \sum_{\{j_i K_i\}} A_{j_1 K_1 j_2 K_2 j_3 K_3 j_4 K_4} a^\dagger_{j_1 K_1} a^\dagger_{j_2 K_2} a_{j_3 K_3} a_{j_4 K_4} . \tag{D.1}$$

To simplify the appearance of the formulae we use the shorthand notation

$$V_{j_1 K_1 j_2 K_2 j_3 K_3 j_4 K_4} = A_{j_1 K_1 j_2 K_2 j_3 K_3 j_4 K_4} a^\dagger_{j_1 K_1} a^\dagger_{j_2 K_2} a_{j_3 K_3} a_{j_4 K_4} \tag{D.2}$$

for the terms of the potential energy. The vector

$$|L\rangle = |j_1 0, j_2 0, \ldots, j_{N_e} 0\rangle \tag{D.3}$$

is used to describe the state where all N_e electrons are in the lowest Landau level and

$$|L; k\rangle = |j_1 0, j_2 0, \ldots, j_k 1, \ldots, j_{N_e} 0\rangle \tag{D.4}$$

the state where exactly one electron is elevated to the next level. The set of corresponding indices $\{j_1, j_2, \ldots, j_{N_e}\}$ is denoted by L. The projections of the Hamiltonian (D.1) onto the subspaces spanned by the vectors (D.3) and (D.4) are denoted by $\mathcal{V}^0$ and $\mathcal{V}^1$, respectively. The shorthand notation (D.2) is applied to the representations of these operators with the obvious usage of superscripts 0 and 1.

To show the existence of the repeated spectrum we choose an arbitrary eigenstate $|\Psi\rangle$ of $\mathcal{V}^0$

$$\mathcal{V}^0 |\Psi\rangle = \varepsilon |\Psi\rangle \tag{D.5}$$

where the state $|\Psi\rangle$ is a superposition

$$|\Psi\rangle = \sum_L c_L |L\rangle \tag{D.6}$$

of state vectors of the lowest level. The operator $\mathcal{V}^0$, being a projection onto the states (D.3), maps those vectors into a superposition of the same vectors

$$\mathcal{V}^0 |L\rangle = \sum_{L'} h_{L'L} |L'\rangle \tag{D.7}$$

where the coefficients are given by

$$h_{L'L} = A_{j_1 0 j_2 0 j_3 0 j_4 0}, \ \{j_1, j_2\} \subset L', \ \{j_3, j_4\} \subset L. \tag{D.8}$$

With this notation the eigenvalue equation (D.5) can be written in the form

$$\sum_{L'} h_{L'L} c_{L'} = \varepsilon c_L. \tag{D.9}$$

As a first step of our proof let us show that the state

$$|L\rangle_{\mathrm{e}} = \sum_{k=1}^{N_{\mathrm{e}}} |L; k\rangle \tag{D.10}$$

behaves under the operation of the partial Hamiltonian V^1 according to the formula

$$\sum_{\substack{K_1 K_2 \\ K_3 K_4}} V^1_{i_1 K_1 i_2 K_2 i_3 K_3 i_4 K_4} |L\rangle_{\mathrm{e}} = h_{L'L} |L'\rangle_{\mathrm{e}}\,. \tag{D.11}$$

Because, by definition, V^1 preserves exactly one electron on the second Landau level, it is easy to see that

$$\begin{aligned}\sum_{\substack{K_1 K_2 \\ K_3 K_4}} V^1_{i_1 K_1 i_2 K_2 i_3 K_3 i_4 K_4} |L\rangle_{\mathrm{e}} = &\sum_{\substack{k \\ j_k \neq i_3 \\ j_k \neq i_4}} V_{i_1 0 i_2 0 i_3 0 i_4 0} |j_1 0, j_2 0, \ldots, j_k 1, \ldots, j_{N_{\mathrm{e}}} 0\rangle \\ &+ V_{i_1 1 i_2 0 i_3 0 i_4 1} |j_1 0, j_2 0, \ldots, i_4 1, \ldots, j_{N_{\mathrm{e}}} 0\rangle \\ &+ V_{i_1 0 i_2 1 i_3 0 i_4 1} |j_1 0, j_2 0, \ldots, i_4 1, \ldots, j_{N_{\mathrm{e}}} 0\rangle \\ &+ V_{i_1 1 i_2 0 i_3 1 i_4 0} |j_1 0, j_2 0, \ldots, i_3 1, \ldots, j_{N_{\mathrm{e}}} 0\rangle \\ &+ V_{i_1 0 i_2 1 i_3 1 i_4 0} |j_1 0, j_2 0, \ldots, i_3 1, \ldots, j_{N_{\mathrm{e}}} 0\rangle .\end{aligned} \tag{D.12}$$

From the definition (D.8), the first term gives

$$h_{L'L}\sum_{\substack{k\\ j'_k\neq i_1\\ j'_k\neq i_2}} |j'_1 0, j'_2 0, \ldots, j'_k 1, \ldots, j'_{N_e} 0\rangle,\ j'_k = j_k. \tag{D.13}$$

The next two terms can be shown to give,

$$h_{L'L}|j'_1 0, j'_2 0, \ldots, i_1 1, \ldots, j'_{N_e} 0\rangle \tag{D.14}$$

and the remaining terms become

$$h_{L'L}|j'_1 0, j'_2 0, \ldots, i_2 1, \ldots, j'_{N_e} 0\rangle, \tag{D.15}$$

if we use the explicit dependence of the coefficients $A_{i_1K_1i_2K_2i_3K_3i_4K_4}$ on the Landau level:

$$A_{i_1K_1i_2K_2i_3K_3i_4K_4} = b(i_1, i_2, i_3, i_4; q)B_{K_1K_4}(q)B_{K_2K_3}(-q). \tag{D.16}$$

The factors $B_{KK'}$ are given by the table:

K	K'	$B_{KK'}$
0	0	1
0	1	$-\frac{1}{\sqrt{2}}\left(\mathrm{i}q_x + q_y\right)\ell_0$
1	0	$-\frac{1}{\sqrt{2}}\left(\mathrm{i}q_x - q_y\right)\ell_0$
1	1	$1 - \frac{1}{2}q^2\ell_0^2$

Our assertion (D.11) is then proved by summing the terms (D.13-15).

When we now sum both sides of (D.11) over the indices i_j we get

$$\mathcal{V}^1|L\rangle_e = \sum_{L'} h_{L'L}|L'\rangle_e \tag{D.17}$$

which, when multiplied by c_L and summed over L, leads to

$$\mathcal{V}^1|\Psi\rangle_e = \varepsilon|\Psi\rangle_e\,. \tag{D.18}$$

The remaining task is to show that the state $|\boldsymbol{\Psi}\rangle_{\mathrm{e}}$ is an eigenstate of the relative kinetic energy operator $\mathcal{K}^{\mathrm{R}} = \frac{1}{2mN_{\mathrm{e}}}\sum_{l<k}(\boldsymbol{\Pi}_l - \boldsymbol{\Pi}_k)^2$. This can be accomplished if we first note that the application of the scalar product of momentum operators yields

$$\begin{aligned}\boldsymbol{\Pi}_1 \cdot \boldsymbol{\Pi}_2 \, |j_1 K_1 j_2 K_2\rangle \\ &= \frac{\hbar^2}{\ell_0^2} C_{K_1} C_{K_2} \left[\frac{K_2}{C_{K_1+1} C_{K_2-1}} |j_1 K_1 + 1 j_2 K_2 - 1\rangle \right. \\ &\qquad \left. + \frac{K_1}{C_{K_1-1} C_{K_2+1}} |j_1 K_1 - 1 j_2 K_2 + 1\rangle \right]\end{aligned} \tag{D.19}$$

using the explicit expressions for the single particle states. Thus the cross terms of the operator $\mathcal{K}^{\mathrm{R}}$ can easily be seen to satisfy

$$\frac{1}{mN_{\mathrm{e}}} \sum_{k<l} \boldsymbol{\Pi}_k \cdot \boldsymbol{\Pi}_l \, |L\rangle_{\mathrm{e}} = \hbar\omega_{\mathrm{c}} \left(1 - \frac{1}{N_{\mathrm{e}}}\right) |L\rangle_{\mathrm{e}} \, . \tag{D.20}$$

This state is of course also an eigenstate of the direct terms of $\mathcal{K}^{\mathrm{R}}$.

Combining this last result with (D.18) completes our proof of the repeated spectrum in the finite-electron system. It should be emphasized, however, as is obvious from the treatment above, that the existence of repetition does *not* depend on any particular number of electrons and a further analysis of the terms $B_{KK'}$ reveals that it does not depend on the form of the interaction either.

Let us now turn our attention to a many-particle system following closely the SMA scheme. Let us suppose that the wave vector $|\boldsymbol{\Psi}_0\rangle$ describes the true ground state of a partially filled lowest Landau level. As before we study excitations where exactly one particle is elevated to the next level. There are several possibilities to raise a particle from the ground state. For example we can excite the particles *coherently* if we give some amount of linear momentum to a particle and at the same time promote it to the next Landau level, or we can excite them *incoherently* if we first give momentum to the particles and then elevate a particle to the higher level. The first alternative leads us to the SMA excitation which is described by the wave function

$$|\boldsymbol{\Psi}_{\mathrm{C}}\rangle = C_{\mathrm{C}} \tilde{\rho}_k^{10} |\boldsymbol{\Psi}_0\rangle \tag{D.21}$$

and the second one by the wave function

$$|\boldsymbol{\Psi}_{\mathrm{I}}\rangle = C_{\mathrm{I}} L_{+} \bar{\rho}_k |\boldsymbol{\Psi}_0\rangle . \tag{D.22}$$

Here $L_+ = \sum_i a_i^\dagger$ is the Landau level raising operator. The coherent excitation operator is given by

$$\tilde{\rho}_k^{10} = \sum_i a_i^\dagger B_i(k). \tag{D.23}$$

The corresponding momentum creation operator on the lowest Landau level is defined by

$$\bar{\rho}_k = \sum_i B_i(k) = \sum_i \exp\left\{-\mathrm{i}pb_i\right\} \exp\left\{-\mathrm{i}p^* b_i^\dagger\right\}. \tag{D.24}$$

The relevant commutation relations for our purposes are

$$[a_i, a_i^\dagger] = 1, \quad [a_i, B_i] = [a_i^\dagger, B_i] = 0. \tag{D.25}$$

A straightforward application of these relations provides us with the normalization coefficients

$$\begin{aligned} C_\mathrm{C} &= \frac{1}{\sqrt{N_\mathrm{e}}} \mathrm{e}^{+\frac{1}{4}|k|^2} \\ C_\mathrm{I} &= \frac{1}{N_\mathrm{e}} \bar{s}^{-\frac{1}{2}} \end{aligned} \tag{D.26}$$

where $\bar{s}$ is the projected static structure function (7.49,50). Similar calculation also reveals that $|\Psi_\mathrm{C}\rangle$ and $|\Psi_\mathrm{I}\rangle$ are indeed independent excitation modes since their scalar product

$$\langle \Psi_\mathrm{C} | \Psi_\mathrm{I} \rangle = \sqrt{\frac{\bar{s}}{N_\mathrm{e}}} \mathrm{e}^{+\frac{1}{4}|k|^2} \tag{D.27}$$

vanishes as the number of particles tends to infinity.

Our next step is to evaluate the energies. From now on we will concentrate solely on the incoherent states (D.22) since the other mode will yield the well-known SMA magnetoplasmon excitation energies (see Sect. 8.3). The state (D.22) is obviously an eigenstate of the kinetic energy operator which, with the help of the level raising operators, can be written in the form $\mathcal{K} = \hbar\omega_\mathrm{c} \sum_i \left(a_i^\dagger a_i + \frac{1}{2}\right)$. The relevant part of the potential energy is given by

$$\mathcal{V} = \int \frac{d^2q}{(2\pi)^2} V(q) \rho_{-q} \rho_q, \tag{D.28}$$

where ρ is the full density operator defined by

$$\rho_q = \sum_i A_i(q) B_i(q) \tag{D.29}$$

where

$$A_i(q) = \exp\left\{-\frac{\mathrm{i}}{\sqrt{2}} q a_i^\dagger\right\} \exp\left\{-\frac{\mathrm{i}}{\sqrt{2}} q^* a_i\right\}. \tag{D.30}$$

The expectation value of the Hamiltonian in the incoherent state can now be written in the form

$$\Delta\epsilon \equiv \langle \Psi_\mathrm{I} | \mathcal{H} | \Psi_\mathrm{I} \rangle - E_0 - \hbar\omega_\mathrm{c} N_\mathrm{e} = C_\mathrm{I}^2 \langle \Psi_0 | L_- \bar{\rho}_{-k} [\mathcal{V}, L_+ \bar{\rho}_k] | \Psi_0 \rangle. \tag{D.31}$$

Here E_0 denotes the ground-state energy. Let us now apply the commutation relation,

$$[\rho_q, L_+] = -\mathrm{i} \frac{q^*}{\sqrt{2}} \rho_q \tag{D.32}$$

where we have used the identity

$$[A_i(q), a_j^\dagger] = -\mathrm{i} \frac{q^*}{\sqrt{2}} \delta_{ij} A_i(q) \tag{D.33}$$

obtained from the commutation rules (D.25) and the definition (D.30). It is now a simple matter to show that the potential energy *commutes* with the Landau level raising operator, *i.e.*,

$$[\mathcal{V}, L_+] = 0\,. \tag{D.34}$$

Substituting this result and the normalization coefficient from (D.26) into (D.31) and introducing the strength factor defined earlier (7.45) as

$$\bar{f}(k) = \frac{1}{N_\mathrm{e}} \langle \Psi_0 | \bar{\rho}_{-k} [\mathcal{V}, \bar{\rho}_k] | \Psi_0 \rangle,$$

we have

$$\Delta\varepsilon = \frac{\bar{f}(k)}{\bar{s}(k)}\,. \tag{D.35}$$

This is clearly the intra-Landau level magnetoroton energy in the SMA scheme [see (7.51)] and thus proves our assertion.

Again it should be emphasized that the validity of the formula (D.35) does not depend on the form of the interaction as long as it can be written according to (D.28), nor does it depend on any particular filling fraction.

The results we have obtained above are summarized in a simple statement: The interaction does not depend on the Landau level. This statement is however not so trivial as it at first sight appears to be. Due to projections applied to various operators it is by no means obvious that the commutation relation (D.34) holds although it is physically reasonable. It is even less obvious in the case of a finite electron system.

Appendix E **Characteristic Scale Values**

In the following, we present the numerical values of some of the quantities which are often used in the study of the QHE. A more general list is available in [E.1,2]. Wherever applicable the numerical values refer to GaAs only [E.3].

Bohr radius (effective)	$a_{\mathrm{B}}^* = \dfrac{\epsilon\hbar^2}{e^2 m^*}$	$9.95[nm]$
Bohr magneton	$\mu_{\mathrm{B}} = \dfrac{e\hbar}{2m_{\mathrm{e}}c}$	$0.0579\,[\mathrm{meV\,T^{-1}}]$
Coulomb energy	$\dfrac{e^2}{\epsilon\ell_0}[\mathrm{K}]$	$51.67\,(B[\mathrm{T}])^{\frac{1}{2}}$
Cyclotron energy	$\hbar\omega_{\mathrm{c}} = \dfrac{\hbar eB}{m^*c}$	$\hbar\omega_{\mathrm{c}}\,[\mathrm{meV}] = 1.728\,B[\mathrm{T}]$
Dielectric constant	ϵ	12.6
Effective mass	m^*	$0.067m_{\mathrm{e}}$
Filling fraction	$\nu = 2\pi\ell_0^2 n_0$	$4.137n_0\,[10^{11}\mathrm{cm^{-2}}]/B[\mathrm{T}]$
Flux quantum	$\Phi_0 = \dfrac{hc}{e}$	$4.136\times 10^{-11}\,\mathrm{Tcm^2}$
Magnetic field	$1\,\mathrm{T}$	$10^4\,\mathrm{G}$
Magnetic length	$\ell_0 = \left(\dfrac{\hbar c}{eB}\right)^{\frac{1}{2}}$	$\ell_0\,[\mathrm{nm}] = 25.65\,(B[\mathrm{T}])^{-\frac{1}{2}}$
Rydberg (effective)	$Ry^* = \dfrac{e^2}{2\epsilon a_{\mathrm{B}}^*}$	$5.74[meV]$
Spin splitting	$g\mu_{\mathrm{B}}B\,[\mathrm{meV}]$	$0.1158\,B[\mathrm{T}]g/2$
von Klitzing constant	$R_{\mathrm{K}} = \dfrac{h}{e^2}$	$25812.807\,[\Omega]$

References

Chapter 1

1.1 K. von Klitzing, G. Dorda, M. Pepper: Phys. Rev. Lett. **45**, 494 (1980)

1.2 D. C. Tsui, H. L. Störmer, A. C. Gossard: Phys. Rev. Lett. **48**, 1559 (1982)

1.3 J. Hajdu, G. Landwehr: In *Strong and Ultrastrong Magnetic Fields and Their Applications*, ed. by F. Herlach (Springer-Verlag, 1985)

1.4 B. I. Halperin: Helv. Phys. Acta **56**, 75 (1983)

1.5 H. Aoki: Rep. Prog. Phys. **50**, 655 (1987)

1.6 A. H. MacDonald: ed. *The Quantum Hall Effect: A Perspective* (Jaca Books, Milano, 1989)

1.7 G. Morandi: *Quantum Hall Effect* (Bibliopolis, Napoli, 1988)

1.8 R. E. Prange, S. M. Girvin: eds., *The Quantum Hall Effect*, (Springer, New York, Berlin, Heidelberg 1989), 2nd Edition

1.9 E. I. Rashba, V. B. Timofeev: Sov. Phys. Semicond. **20**, 617 (1986)

1.10 T. Chakraborty: In *Handbook on Semiconductors*, ed. by P. T. Landsberg (North-Holland, New York, 1992), vol. 1, ch. 17

1.11 M. Janßen, O. Viehweger, U. Fastenrath, J. Hajdu: *Introduction to the Theory of the Integer Quantum Hall Effect* (VCH, Weinheim, 1994)

1.12 T. Ando, A. B. Fowler, F. Stern: Rev. Mod. Phys. **54**, 437 (1982)

1.13 H. L. Störmer: In *Advances in Solid State Physics*, ed. by P. Grosse, (Vieweg, Braunschweig 1984), vol. 24, p. 25

1.14 C. G. Grimes: Surf. Sci. **73**, 379 (1978)

1.15 Y. P. Monarkha, V. Shikin: Sov. J. Low Temp. Phys. **8**, 279 (1982)

1.16 R. Kubo, S. J. Miyake, N. Hashitsume: Solid State Phys. **17**, 269 (1965)

1.17 V. Fock: Z. Phys. **47**, 446 (1928)

1.18 L. Landau: Z. Phys. **64**, 629 (1930)

1.19 L. B. Ioffe, A. I. Larkin: Sov. Phys.–JETP **54**, 556 (1981)

1.20 F. Wegner: Z. Phys. B**51**, 279 (1983)

1.21 E. Brezin, D. J. Gross, C. Itzykson: Nucl. Phys. B**235** [FS 11], 24 (1984)

1.22 T. Ando, Y. Uemura: J. Phys. Soc. Jpn. **39**, 959 (1974)

1.23 T. Ando: J. Phys. Soc. Jpn. **52**, 1740 (1983)

1.24 T. Ando: J. Phys. Soc. Jpn. **53**, 3101, 3126 (1984)

1.25 T. Ando, H. Aoki: J. Phys. Soc. Jpn. **54**, 2238 (1985)

1.26 H. Aoki, T. Ando: Phys. Rev. Lett. **54**, 831 (1985)

1.27 J. P. Eisenstein, H. L. Störmer, V. Narayanamurti, A. Y. Cho, A. C. Gossard, C. W. Tu: Phys. Rev. Lett. **55**, 875 (1985)

1.28 E. Gornik, R. Lassnig, G. Strasser, H. L. Störmer, A. C. Gossard, W. Wiegmann: Phys. Rev. Lett. **54**, 1820 (1985)

1.29 V. M. Pudalov, S. G. Semenchinsky, V. S. Edelman: Sov. Phys. JETP **62**, 1079 (1985)

1.30 T. P. Smith,III, B. B. Goldberg, M. Heiblum, P. J. Stiles: Surf. Sci. **170**, 304 (1986)

1.31 E. Stahl, D. Weiss, G. Weimann, K. von Klitzing, K. Ploog: J. Phys. C**18**, L783 (1985)

1.32 H. P. Wei, A. M. Chang, D. C. Tsui, M. Razeghi: Phys. Rev. B**32**, 7016 (1985)

1.33 V. M. Pudalov, S. G. Semenchinsky: Solid State Commun. **55**, 593 (1985)

1.34 E. Gornik: In *The Physics of The Two-Dimensional Electron Gas*, eds. J. T. Devreese, F. M. Peeters (Plenum, New York, 1987), p. 365

Chapter 2

2.1 K. von Klitzing, G. Dorda, M. Pepper: Phys. Rev. Lett. **45**, 494 (1980)

2.2 T. Ando, Y. Matsumoto, Y. Uemura: J. Phys. Soc. Jpn. **39**, 279 (1975)

2.3 T. Englert, K. von Klitzing: Surf. Sci. **73**, 70 (1978)

2.4 J. Wakabayashi, S. Kawaji: Surf. Sci. **98**, 299 (1980)

2.5 K. von Klitzing: Surf. Sci. **113**, 1 (1982)

2.6 K. von Klitzing: Rev. Mod. Phys. **58**, 519 (1986)

2.7 H. L. Störmer: In *Advances in Solid State Physics*, ed. by P. Grosse, (Vieweg, Braunschweig 1984), vol. 24, p. 25

2.8 A. Hartland: Metrologia **29**, 175 (1992)

2.9 T. Quinn: Metrolgia **26**, 69 (1989)

2.10 B. N. Taylor: Physics Today, **42**, 23 (1989)

2.11 D. C. Tsui, A. C. Gossard: Appl. Phys. Lett. **38**, 550 (1981)

2.12 M. A. Paalanen, D. C. Tsui, A. C. Gossard: Phys. Rev. B**25**, 5566 (1982)

2.13 G. Ebert, K. von Klitzing, C. Probst, K. Ploog: Solid State Commun. **44**, 95 (1982)

2.14 R. J. Nicholas, K. von Klitzing, Th. Englert: Solid State Commun. **34**, 51 (1980)

2.15 Y. Guldner, J. P. Hirtz, J. P. Vieren, P. Voisin, M. Voos, M. Razeghi: J. Physique Lett. **43**, L613 (1982)

2.16 Y. Guldner, J. P. Vieren, M. Voos, F. Delahaye, D. Dominguez, J. P. Hirtz, M. Razeghi: Phys. Rev. B**33**, 3990 (1986)

2.17 W. P. Kirk, P. S. Kobiela, R. A. Schiebel, M. A. Reed: J. Vac. Sci. Tech. A**4**, 2132 (1986)

2.18 E. E. Mendez, L. Esaki, L. L. Chang: Phys. Rev. Lett. **55**, 2216 (1985)

2.19 H. L. Störmer, Z. Schlesinger, A. M. Chang, D. C. Tsui, A. C. Gossard, W. Wiegmann: Phys. Rev. Lett. **51**, 126 (1983)

2.20 F. F. Fang: Surf. Sci. **305**, 301 (1994)

2.21 G. M. Gusev, Z. D. Kvon, I. G. Neizvestnyi, V. N. Ovsyuk, P. A. Cheremnykh: JETP Lett. **39**, 541 (1984)

2.22 R. Kubo: J. Phys. Soc. Jpn. **12**, 570 (1957)

2.23 H. L. Störmer, D. C. Tsui: Science **220**, 1241 (1983)

2.24 E. Brown: Solid State Phys. **22**, 313 (1968)

2.25 R. Kubo, S. J. Miyake, N. Hashitsume: Solid State Phys. **17**, 269 (1965)

2.26 Y. Ono: J. Phys. Soc. Jpn. **51**, 237 (1982)

2.27 G. A. Baraff, D. C. Tsui: Phys. Rev. B**24**, 2274 (1981)

2.28 V. M. Pudalov, S. G. Semenchinsky, V. S. Edelman: JETP Lett. **39**, 576 (1984)

2.29 H. Aoki, T. Ando: Solid State Commun. **38**, 1079 (1981)

2.30 T. Ando: *Anderson Localization*, eds. Y. Nagaoka, H. Fukuyama (Springer-Verlag, 1982), p. 176

2.31 T. Ando: In *Recent Topics in Semiconductor Physics*, eds. H. Kamimura, Y. Toyozawa (World Scientific, Singapore, 1983), p. 72

2.32 H. Aoki: Rep. Prog. Phys. **50**, 655 (1987)

2.33 N. A. Usov, F. R. Ulinich: Sov. Phys.-JETP **56**, 877 (1982)

2.34 E. Abrahams, P. W. Anderson, D. C. Licciardello, T. V. Ramakrishnan: Phys. Rev. Lett. **42**, 673 (1979)

2.35 R. E. Prange: Phys. Rev. B**23**, 4802 (1981)

2.36 D. J. Thouless: J. Phys. C**14**, 3475 (1981)

2.37 P. Streda: J. Phys. C**15**, L717 (1982)

2.38 R. B. Laughlin: Phys. Rev. B**23**, 5632 (1981)

2.39 N. Byers, C. N. Yang: Phys. Rev. Lett. **7**, 46 (1961)

2.40 F. Bloch: Phys. Rev. B**2**, 109 (1970)

2.41 R. B. Laughlin: Springer Series in Solid State Sciences, **53**, eds. G. Bauer, F. Kuchar, H. Heinrich (Springer-Verlag, 1984), p. 272

2.42 G. F. Giuliani, J. J. Quinn, S. C. Ying: Phys. Rev. B**28**, 2969 (1983)

2.43 G. C. Aers, A. H. MacDonald: J. Phys. C**17**, 5491 (1984)

2.44 H. Aoki: J. Phys. C**15**, L1227 (1982)

2.45 B. I. Halperin: Phys. Rev. B**25**, 2185 (1982)

2.46 Q. Niu, D. J. Thouless, Y. S. Wu: Phys. Rev. B**31**, 3372 (1985)

2.47 Y. Avron, R. Seiler: Phys. Rev. Lett. **54**, 259 (1985)

2.48 H. Aoki, T. Ando: Phys. Rev. Lett. **57**, 3093 (1986)

2.49 D. J. Thouless, M. Kohmoto, M. P. Nightingale, M. den Nijs: Phys. Rev. Lett. **49**, 405 (1982)

2.50 G. Morandi: *Quantum Hall Effect* (Bibliopolis, Napoli, 1988)

2.51 R. Tao, F. D M. Haldane: Phys. Rev. B**33**, 3844 (1986)

Chapter 3

3.1 S. V. Iordansky: Solid State Commun. **43**, 1 (1982)

3.2 R. F. Kazarinov, S. Luryi: Phys. Rev. B**25**, 7626 (1982)

3.3 S. Luryi, R. F. Kazarinov: Phys. Rev. B**27**, 1386 (1983)

3.4 S. A. Trugman: Phys. Rev. B**27**, 7539 (1983)

3.5 R. Joynt, R. E. Prange: Phys. Rev. B**29**, 3303 (1984)

3.6 S. M. Apenko, Yu. E. Lozovik: Sov. Phys.-JETP **62**, 328

3.7 R. Zallen, H. Scher: Phys. Rev. B**4**, 4471 (1971)

3.8 Y. Ono: J. Phys. Soc. Jpn. **51**, 237 (1982)

3.9 T. Ando: J. Phys. Soc. Jpn. **52**, 1740 (1983)

3.10 T. Ando: J. Phys. Soc. Jpn. **53**, 3101, 3126 (1984)

3.11 D. C. Licciardello, D. J. Thouless: J. Phys. C**11**, 925 (1978)

3.12 L. Schweitzer, B. Kramer, A. MacKinnon: J. Phys. C**17**, 4111 (1984)

3.13 T. Ando, H. Aoki: J. Phys. Soc. Jpn. **54**, 2238 (1985)

3.14 H. Aoki, T. Ando: Phys. Rev. Lett. **54**, 831 (1985)

3.15 H. Aoki, T. Ando: Surf. Sci. **170**, 249 (1986)

3.16 S. Hikami: Prog. Theor. Phys. **76**, 1210 (1986)

3.17 G. V. Mil'nikov, I. M. Sokolov: JETP Lett. **48**, 536 (1988)

3.18 J. T. Chalker, P. D. Coddington: J. Phys. C**21**, 2665 (1988)

3.19 B. Huckestein: Physica A**167**, 175 (1990)

3.20 B. Huckestein, B. Kramer: Phys. Rev. Lett. **64**, 1437 (1990)

3.21 Y. Huo, R. N. Bhatt: Phys. Rev. Lett. **68**, 1375 (1992)

3.22 S. Koch, R. J. Haug, K. von Klitzing, K. Ploog: Phys. Rev. Lett. **67**, 883 (1991)

3.23 E. Abrahams, P. W. Anderson, D. C. Licciardello, T. V. Ramakrishnan: Phys. Rev. Lett. **42**, 673 (1979)

3.24 L. P. Gorkov, A. I. Larkin, D. E. Khmel'nitzkii: JETP Lett. **30**, 228 (1979)

3.25 A. M. M. Pruisken: Nucl. Phys. **235** [FS11], 277 (1984)

3.26 A. M. M. Pruisken: Phys. Rev. B**32**, 2636 (1985)

3.27 H. Levine, S. B. Libby, A. M. M. Pruisken: Phys. Rev. Lett. **51**, 1915 (1983)

3.28 D. E. Khmel'nitzkii: JETP Lett. **38**, 552 (1983)

3.29 D. E. Khmel'nitzkii: Phys. Lett. A**106**, 182 (1984)

3.30 S. Hikami: Phys. Rev. B**29**, 3726 (1984)

3.31 H. P. Wei, D. C. Tsui, A. M. M. Pruisken: Phys. Rev. B**33**, 1488 (1985)

3.32 H. P. Wei, A. M. Chang, D. C. Tsui, A. M. M. Pruisken, M. Razeghi: Surf. Sci. **170**, 238 (1986)

3.33 R. B. Laughlin, M. L. Cohen, J. M. Kosterlitz, H. Levine, S. B. Libby, A. M. M. Pruisken: Phys. Rev. B**32**, 1311 (1985)

3.34 T. Ando: Surf. Sci. **170**, 243 (1986)

3.35 B. I. Halperin: Phys. Rev. B**25**, 2185 (1982)

3.36 A. H. MacDonald, P. Streda: Phys. Rev. B**29**, 1616 (1984)

3.37 T. Ando: In *Transport Phenomena in Mesoscopic Systems*, eds. H. Fukuyama, T. Ando (Springer-Verlag, 1992), p. 185

3.38 L. Smrcka: J. Phys. C**17**, L63 (1984)

3.39 M. Ya. Azbel: Solid State Commun. **53**, 147 (1985)

3.40 B. J. van Wees, E. M. M. Willems, C. J. P. M. Harmans, C. W. J. Beenakker, H. van Houten, J. G. Williamson, C. T. Foxon, J. J. Harris: Phys. Rev. Lett. **62**, 1181 (1989)

3.41 G. Müller, D. Weiss, S. Koch, K. von Klitzing, H. Nickel, W. Schlapp, R. Lösch: Phys. Rev. B**42**, 7633 (1990); G. Müller, D. Weiss, A. V. Khaetskii, K. von Klitzing, S. Koch, H. Nickel, W. Schlapp, R. Lösch: Phys. Rev. B**45**, 3932 (1992)

3.42 R. J. Haug: Semicond. Sci. Technol. **8**, 131 (1993)

3.43 C. W. J. Beenakker, H. van Houten: Solid State Phys. **44**, 1 (1991)

3.44 K. von Klitzing: Physica B**184**, 1 (1993); Adv. Solid State Phys. **30**, 25 (1990)

3.45 R. J. Haug, A. H. MacDonald, P. Streda, K. von Klitzing: Phys. Rev. Lett. **61**, 2797 (1988); S. Washburn, A. B. Fowler, H. Schmid, D. Kern: Phys. Rev. Lett. **61**, 2801 (1988)

3.46 M. Büttiker: Adv. Solid State Phys. **30**, 41 (1990); Phys. Rev. B**38**, 9375 (1988)

3.47 S. Luryi: In *High Magnetic Fields in Semiconductor Physics*, ed. by G. Landwehr (Springer-Verlag, 1987)

3.48 C. W. J. Beenakker: Phys. Rev. Lett. **64**, 216 (1990); A. M. Chang: Solid State Commun. **74**, 871 (1990); D. B. Chklovskii, B. I. Shklovskii, L. I. Glazman: Phys. Rev. B**46**, 4026 (1992); L. Brey, J. J. Palacios, C. Tejedor: Phys. Rev. B**47**, 13884 (1993); K. Lier, R. R. Gerhardts: Phys. Rev. B**50**, 7757 (1994)

3.49 N. B. Zhitenev, R. J. Haug, K. von Klitzing, K. Eberl: Phys. Rev. Lett. **71**, 2292 (1993); Phys. Rev. B**49**, 7809 (1994); S. W. Hwang, D. C. Tsui, M. Shayegan: Phys. Rev. B**48**, 8161 (1993)

3.50 H. Hirai, S. Komiyama: Phys. Rev. B**49**, 14012 (1994)

3.51 D. J. Thouless: Phys. Rev. Lett. **71**, 1879 (1993)

3.52 V. T. Dolgopolov, A. A. Shashkin, N. B. Zhitenev, S. I. Dorozhkin, K. von Klitzing: Phys. Rev. B**46**, 12560 (1992)

3.53 G. Ebert, K. von Klitzing, K. Ploog, G. Weimann: J. Phys. C**16**, 5441 (1983)

3.54 H. Sakaki, K. Hirakawa, J. Yoshino, S. P. Svensson, Y. Sekiguchi, T. Hotta, S. Nishii: Surf. Sci. **142**, 306 (1984)

3.55 V. M. Pudalov, S. G. Semenchinsky: Solid State Commun. **51**, 19 (1984)

3.56 P. Streda, K. von Klitzing: J. Phys. C**17**, L483 (1984)

3.57 M. E. Cage, R. F. Dziuba, B. F. Field, E. R. Williams, S. Girvin, A. C. Gossard, D. C. Tsui, R. J. Wagner: Phys. Rev. Lett. **51**, 1374 (1983)

3.58 S. Komiyama, T. Takamasu, S. Hiyamizu, S. Sasa: Solid State Commun. **54**, 479 (1985)

Chapter 4

4.1 D. C. Tsui, H. L. Störmer, A. C. Gossard: Phys. Rev. Lett. **48**, 1559 (1982)

4.2 H. L. Störmer, A. M. Chang, D. C. Tsui, J. C. M. Hwang, A. C. Gossard, W. Wiegmann: Phys. Rev. Lett. **50**, 1953 (1983)

4.3 H. L. Störmer: *Advances in Solid State Physics*, ed. by P. Grosse, vol. 24 (Vieweg, Braunschweig 1984), p. 25

4.4 D. C. Tsui, H. L. Störmer: IEEE J. Quantum Electron. QE-**22**, 1711 (1986)

4.5 H. L. Störmer: Physica B**177**, 401 (1992); Phys. Scr. T**45**, 168 (1992)

4.6 R. G. Clark: Phys. Scr. T**39**, 45 (1991)

4.7 V. M. Pudalov, S. G. Semenchinsky: JETP Lett. **39**, 170 (1984); M. G. Gavrilov, Z. D. Kvon, I. V. Kukushkin, V. B. Timofeev: JETP Lett. **39**, 507 (1984)

4.8 A. M. Chang, P. Berglund, D. C. Tsui, H. L. Störmer, J. C. M. Hwang: Phys. Rev. Lett. **53**, 997 (1984)

4.9 R. Willett, J. P. Eisenstein, H. L. Störmer, D. C. Tsui, A. C. Gossard, J. H. English: Phys. Rev. Lett. **59**, 1776 (1987)

4.10 T. Sajoto, Y. W. Suen, L. W. Engel, M. B. Santos, M. Shayegan: Phys. Rev. B**41**, 8449 (1990)

4.11 R. G. Clark, R. J. Nicholas, A. Usher, C. T. Foxon, J. J. Harris: Surf. Sci. **170**, 141 (1986)

4.12 E. E. Mendez, L. L. Chang, M. Heiblum, L. Esaki, M. Naughton, K. Martin, J. Brooks: Phys. Rev. B**30**, 7310 (1984)

4.13 G. Ebert, K. von Klitzing, J. C. Maan, G. Remenyi, C. Probst, G. Weimann, W. Schlapp: J. Phys. C**17**, L775 (1984)

4.14 G. S. Boebinger, A. M. Chang, H. L. Störmer, D. C. Tsui: Phys. Rev. B**32**, 4268 (1985)

4.15 H. W. Jiang, R. L. Willett, H. L. Störmer, D. C. Tsui, L. N. Pfeiffer, K. W. West: Phys. Rev. Lett. **65**, 633 (1990)

4.16 V. J. Goldman, M. Shayegan, D. C. Tsui: Phys. Rev. Lett. **61**, 881 (1988)

4.17 R. L. Willett, H. L. Störmer, D. C. Tsui, A. C. Gossard, J. H. English, K. W. Baldwin: Solid State Commun. **196**, 257 (1988)

4.18 J. R. Mallett, R. G. Clark, R. J. Nicholas, R. Willett, J. J. Harris, C. T. Foxon: Phys. Rev. B**38**, 2200 (1988)

4.19 J. P. Eisenstein, H. L. Störmer, L. Pfeiffer, K. W. West: Phys. Rev. Lett. **62**, 1540 (1989)

4.20 S. F. Nelson, K. Ismail, J. J. Nocera, F. F. Fang, E. E. Mendez, J. O. Chu, B. S. Meyerson: Appl. Phys. Lett. **61**, 64 (1992)

4.21 M. Shayegan, J. K. Wang, M. santos, T. Sajoto, B. B. Goldberg: Appl. Phys. Lett. **54**, 27 (1988)

4.22 R. G. Clark, S. R. Haynes, A. M. Suckling, J. R. Mallett, P. A. Wright, J. J. Harris, C. T. Foxon: Phys. Rev. Lett. **62**, 1536 (1989)

4.23 B. I. Halperin: Helv. Phys. Acta **56**, 75 (1983)

4.24 T. Chakraborty, F. C. Zhang: Phys. Rev. B**29**, 7032 (1984)

4.25 F. C. Zhang, T. Chakraborty: Phys. Rev. B**30**, 7320 (1984)

4.26 T. Chakraborty, P. Pietiläinen, F. C. Zhang: Phys. Rev. Lett. **57**, 130 (1986)

4.27 T. Chakraborty, P. Pietiläinen: Phys. Scr. **T14**, 58 (1986)

4.28 T. Chakraborty, P. Pietiläinen: In *Recent Progress in Many-Body Theories*, eds. A. Kallio, E. Pajane, R. F. Bishop (Plenum, New York 1988), p. 113.

4.29 T. Chakraborty, P. Pietiläinen: Phys. Rev. Lett. **59**, 2784 (1987)

4.30 J. P. Eisenstein, G. S. Boebinger, L. N. Pfeiffer, K. W. West, S. He: Phys. Rev. Lett. **68**, 1383 (1992); S. Q. Murphy, J. P. Eisenstein, G. S. Boebinger, L. N. Pfeiffer, K. W. West: Phys. Rev. Lett. **72**, 728 (1994)

4.31 H. Fukuyama, P. M. Platzman, P. W. Anderson: Phys. Rev. B**19**, 5211 (1979)

4.32 D. Yoshioka, P. A. Lee: Phys. Rev. B**27**, 4986 (1983)

4.33 D. Yoshioka, B. I. Halperin, P. A. Lee: Phys. Rev. Lett. **50**, 1219 (1983)

4.34 R. B. Laughlin: In *The Quantum Hall Effect*, ed. by R. E. Prange, S. M. Girvin (Springer-Verlag, 1987) p. 233

4.35 S. T. Chui: Phys. Rev. B**32**, 1436 (1985)

4.36 S. T. Chui, T. M. Hakim, K. B. Ma: Phys. Rev. B**33**, 7110 (1986)

4.37 F. Claro: Solid State Commun. **53**, 27 (1985)

4.38 R. B. Laughlin: Phys. Rev. Lett. **50**, 1395 (1983)

4.39 R. Tao, D. J. Thouless: Phys. Rev. B**28**, 1142 (1983)

4.40 D. J. Thouless: Phys. Rev. B**31**, 8305 (1985)

4.41 S. Kivelson, C. Kallin, D. Arovas, J. R. Schrieffer: Phys. Rev. Lett. **56**, 873 (1986)

4.42 D. H. Lee, G. Baskaran, S. Kivelson: Phys. Rev. Lett. **59**, 2467 (1987)

4.43 D. J. Thouless, Qin Li: Phys. Rev. B**36**, 4581 (1987)

4.44 S. Kivelson, C. Kallin, D. Arovas, J. R. Schrieffer: Phys. Rev. B**37**, 9085 (1988)

4.45 F. D. M. Haldane: In *The Quantum Hall Effect*, ed. by R. E. Prange, S. M. Girvin (Springer-Verlag, 1987) p.303

4.46 S. C. Zhang: Int. J. Mod. Phys. **6**, 25 (1992)

Chapter 5

5.1 D. Yoshioka, B. I. Halperin, P. A. Lee: Phys. Rev. Lett. **50**, 1219 (1983)

5.2 R. B. Laughlin: Phys. Rev. Lett. **50**, 1395 (1983)

5.3 R. B. Laughlin: Surf. Sci. **142**, 163 (1984)

5.4 R. B. Laughlin: In *The Quantum Hall Effect*, ed. by R. E. Prange, S. M. Girvin (Springer-Verlag, 1987), p. 233

5.5 D. Levesque, J. J. Weis, A. H. MacDonald: Phys. Rev. B**30**, 1056 (1984)

5.6 R. Morf, B. I. Halperin: Phys. Rev. B**33**, 2221 (1986)

5.7 R. Morf, B. I. Halperin: Z. Phys. B**68**, 391 (1987)

5.8 F. D. M. Haldane: Phys. Rev. Lett. **51**, 605 (1983)

5.9 F. D. M. Haldane, E. H. Rezayi: Phys. Rev. Lett. **54**, 237 (1985)

5.10 D. Yoshioka, P. A. Lee: Phys. Rev. B**27**, 4986 (1983)

5.11 D. Yoshioka, B. I. Halperin, P. A. Lee: Surf. Sci. **142**, 155 (1984)

5.12 D. Yoshioka: Phys. Rev. B**29**, 6833 (1984)

5.13 B. I. Halperin: Helv. Phys. Acta **56**, 75 (1983)

5.14 R. B. Laughlin: Phys. Rev. B**27**, 3383 (1983)

5.15 Yu. A. Bychkov, S. V. Iordanskii, G. M. Eliashberg: JETP Lett. **33**, 143 (1981)

5.16 J. M. Caillol, D. Levesque, J. J. Weis, J. P. Hansen: J. Stat. Phys. **28**, 325 (1982)

5.17 J. P. Hansen, D. Levesque: J. Phys. C**14**, L603 (1981)

5.18 J. G. Zabolitzky: Adv. Nucl. Phys. **12**, 1 (1981)

5.19 B. Jancovici: Phys. Rev. Lett. **46**, 386 (1981)

5.20 J. F. Springer, M. A. Pokrant, F. A. Stevens: J. Chem. Phys. **58**, 4863 (1973)

5.21 S. M. Girvin: In *Interfaces, Quantum Wells, and Superlattices*, ed. by C. Richard Leavens, R. Taylor (Plenum, New York, 19887), p. 333

5.22 F. D. M. Haldane, E. H. Rezayi: Phys. Rev. B**31**, 2529 (1985)

5.23 S. M. Girvin: Phys. Rev. B**29**, 6012 (1984)

5.24 S. A. Trugman, S. Kivelson: Phys. Rev. B**31**, 5280 (1985)

5.25 V. L. Pokrovskii, A. L. Talapov: J. Phys. C**18**, L691 (1985)

5.26 A. Peres: Phys. Rev. **167**, 1449 (1968)

5.27 G. Fano, F. Ortolani, E. Colombo: Phys. Rev. B**34**, 2670 (1986)

5.28 R. Morf, N. d'Ambrumenil, B. I. Halperin: Phys. Rev. B**34**, 3037 (1986)

5.29 F. D. M. Haldane: In *The Quantum Hall Effect*, ed. by R. E. Prange, S. M. Girvin (Springer-Verlag, 1987), p.303

5.30 W. Duncan, E. E. Schneider: Phys. Lett. **1**, 23 (1963)

5.31 T. Chakraborty, F. C. Zhang: Phys. Rev. B**29**, 7032 (1984)

5.32 F. C. Zhang, T. Chakraborty: Phys. Rev. B**30**, 7320 (1984)

5.33 H. L. Störmer, A. M. Chang, D. C. Tsui, J. C. M. Hwang, A. C. Gossard, W. Wiegmann: Phys. Rev. Lett. **50**, 1953 (1983)

5.34 R. G. Clark, S. R. Haynes, A. M. Suckling, J. R. Mallett, P. A. Wright, J. J. Harris, C. T. Foxon: Phys. Rev. Lett. **62**, 1536 (1989)

5.35 J. P. Eisenstein, H. L. Störmer, L. Pfeiffer, K. W. West: Phys. Rev. Lett. **62**, 1540 (1989)

5.36 M. Rasolt, F. Perrot, A. H. MacDonald: Phys. Rev. Lett. **55**, 433 (1985)

5.37 M. Rasolt, A. H. MacDonald: Phys. Rev. B**34**, 5530 (1986)

5.38 M. Rasolt, B. I. Halperin, D. Vanderbilt: Phys. Rev. Lett. **57**, 126 (1986)

5.39 T. Ando, A. B. Fowler, F. Stern: Rev. Mod. Phys. **54**, 437 (1982)

5.40 F. F. Fang, W. E. Howard: Phys. Rev. Lett. **16**, 797 (1966)

5.41 A. H. MacDonald, G. C. Aers: Phys. Rev. B**29**, 5976 (1984)

5.42 F. C. Zhang, S. Das Sarma: Phys. Rev. B**33**, 2903 (1986)

5.43 T. Chakraborty: Phys. Rev. B**34**, 2926 (1986)

5.44 T. Chakraborty, P. Pietiläinen, F. C. Zhang: Phys. Rev. Lett. **57**, 130 (1986)

5.45 T. Chakraborty, P. Pietiläinen: Phys. Scr. **T14**, 58 (1986)

5.46 K. Maki, X. Zotos: Phys. Rev. B**28**, 4349 (1983)

5.47 P. K. Lam, S. M. Girvin: Phys. Rev. B**30**, 473 (1984)

5.48 E. Mendez, M. Heiblum, L. L. Chang, L. Esaki: Phys. Rev. B**28**, 4886 (1983)

5.49 A. M. Chang, P. Berglund, D. C. Tsui, H. L. Störmer, J. C. M. Hwang: Phys. Rev. Lett. **53**, 997 (1984)

5.50 J. R. Mallett, R. G. Clark, R. J. Nicholas, R. Willett, J. J. Harris, C. T. Foxon: Phys. Rev. B**38**, 2200 (1988)

5.51 V. J. Goldman, M. Shayegan, D. C. Tsui: Phys. Rev. Lett. **61**, 881 (1988)

5.52 J. Wakabayashi, A. Fukano, S. Kawaji, K. Hirakawa, H. Sakaki, Y. Koike, T. Fukase: J. Phys. Soc. Jpn. **57**, 3678 (1988)

5.53 E. Y. Andrei, G. Deville, D. C. Glattli, F. I. B. Williams, E. Paris, B. Etienne: Phys. Rev. Lett. **60**, 2765 (1988)

5.54 H. L. Störmer, R. L. Willett: Phys. Rev. Lett. **62**, 972(C) (1989)

5.55 E. Y. Andrei, G. Deville, D. C. Glatlli, F. I. B. Williams, E. Paris, B. Etienne: Phys. Rev. Lett. **62**, 973(C), 1926(E) (1989)

5.56 H. W. Jiang, R. L. Willett, H. L. Störmer, D. C. Tsui, L. N. Pfeiffer, K. W. West: Phys. Rev. Lett. **65**, 633 (1990)

5.57 V. J. Goldman, M. Santos, M. Shayegan, J. E. Cunningham: Phys. Rev. Lett. **65**, 2189 (1990); Y. P. Li, T. Sajoto, L. W. Engel, D. C. Tsui, M. Shayegan: Phys. Rev. Lett. **67**, 1630 (1991); M. B. Santos, Y. W. Suen, M. Shayegan, Y. P. Li, L. W. Engel, D. C. Tsui: Phys. Rev. Lett. **68**, 1188 (1992)

5.58 M. D'Iorio, V. M. Pudalov, S. G. Semenchinsky: Phys. Lett. **150**, 422 (1990)

5.59 M. D'Iorio, J. W. Campbell, V. M. Pudalov, S. G. Semenchinsky: Surf. Sci. **263**, 49 (1992)

5.60 S. V. Kravchenko, V. M. Pudalov, J. Campbell, M. D'Iorio: JETP Lett. **54**, 532 (1992)

5.61 I. Kukushkin, V. Timofeev: JETP Lett. **44**, 228 (1986)

5.62 B. B. Goldberg, D. Heiman, A. Pinczuk, C. W. Tu, A. C. Gossard, J. H. English: Surf. Sci. **196**, 209 (1988)

5.63 K. von Klitzing: Physica B**164**, 43 (1990)

5.64 H. Buhmann, W. Joss, K. von Klitzing, I. V. Kukushkin, G. Martinez, A. S. Plaut, K. Ploog, V. B. Timofeev: Phys. Rev. Lett. **65**, 1056 (1990)

5.65 B. B. Goldberg, D. Heiman, A. Pinczuk, L. Pfeiffer, K. West: Phys. Rev. Lett. **65**, 641 (1990)

5.66 A. J. Turberfield, S. R. Haynes, P. A. Wright, R. A. Ford, R. G. Clark, J. F. Ryan, J. J. Harris, C. T. Foxon: Phys. Rev. Lett. **65**, 637 (1990)

5.67 John M. Worlock: Physics World **3**, 26 (November, 1990)

5.68 B. B. Goldberg, D. Heiman, M. Dahl, A. Pinczuk, L. Pfeiffer, K. West: Phys. Rev. B**44**, 4006 (1991)

5.69 Yu. A. Bychkov, E. I. Rashba: Sov. Phys. JETP **69**, 430 (1990)

5.70 T. Chakraborty, P. Pietiläinen: Phys. Rev. B**44**, 13 078 (1991)

5.71 T. Chakraborty, P. Pietiläinen: In *High Magnetic Fields in Semiconductor Physics III*, ed. by G. Landwehr (Springer-Verlag, 1992) p. 199

5.72 F. C. Zhang, V. Z. Vulovic, Y. Guo, S. Das Sarma: Phys. Rev. B**32**, 6920 (1985)

5.73 L. M. Roth, B. Lax, S. Zwerdling: Phys. Rev. **114**, 90 (1959)

5.74 V. M. Apal'kov, E. I. Rashba: JETP Lett. **53**, 49 (1991)

5.75 V. M. Apal'kov, E. I. Rashba: JETP Lett. **53**, 420 (1991)

5.76 S.-R. E. Yang: Phys. Rev. B**40**, 1836 (1989)

5.77 H. Buhmann, W. Joss, I. V. Kukushkin, K. von Klitzing, A. S. Plaut, V. B. Timofeev, JETP Lett. **53**, 426 (1991)

5.78 H. Buhmann, W. Joss, K. von Klitzing, I. V. Kukushkin, A. S. Plaut, G. Martinez, K. Ploog, V. B. Timofeev: Phys. Rev. Lett. **66**, 926 (1991)

5.79 I. V. Kukushkin, R. J. Haug, K. von Klitzing, K. Ploog: Phys. Rev. Lett. **72**, 736 (1994); I. V. Kukushkin, V. I. Fal'ko, R. J. Haug, K. von Klitzing, K. Eberl, K. Tötemayer: Phys. Rev. Lett. **72**, 3594 (1994); I. V. Kukushkin, N. J. Pulsford, K. von Klitzing, R. J. Haug, K. Ploog, V. B. Timofeev: Europhys. Lett. **23**, 211 (1993)

5.80 X. Zhu, S. G. Louie: Phys. Rev. Lett. **70**, 335 (1993)

5.81 R. Price, P. M. Platzman, S. He: Phys. Rev. Lett. **70**, 339 (1993)

5.82 R. Cote, A. H. MacDonald: Phys. Rev. Lett. **65**, 2662 (1990)

5.83 P. A. Maksym: J. Phys.: Condens. Matter **4**, L97 (1992)

5.84 M. Ferconi, G. Vignale: Europhys. Lett. **20**, 457 (1992); G. Vignale: Phys. Rev. B**47**, 10105 (1993)

5.85 M. K. Ellis, M. Hayne, A. Usher, A. Plaut, K. Ploog: Phys. Rev. B**45**, 13765 (1992)

5.86 M. A. Paalanen, R. L. Willett, R. R. Ruel, P. B. Littlewood, K. W. West, L. N. Pfeiffer: Phys. Rev. B**45**, 13784 (1992)

5.87 M. Saitoh (ed.): *Proceedings of the Yamada Conference XXX on Electronic Properties of two-Dimensional Systems*, Surf. Sci. **263** (1992)

5.88 H. W. Jiang, H. L. Störmer, D. C. Tsui, L. N. Pfeiffer, K. W. West: Phys. Rev. B**44**, 8107 (1991)

Chapter 6

6.1 R. B. Laughlin: Phys. Rev. Lett. **50**, 1395 (1983)

6.2 R. B. Laughlin: Surf. Sci. **142**, 163 (1984)

6.3 B. I. Halperin: Helv. Phys. Acta **56**, 75 (1983)

6.4 R. Morf, B. I. Halperin: Phys. Rev. B**33**, 2221 (1986)

6.5 H. Fertig, B. I. Halperin: Phys. Rev. B**36**, 6302 (1987)

6.6 B. I. Halperin: Surf. Sci. **170**, 115 (1986)

6.7 T. Chakraborty: Phys. Rev. B**31**, 4026 (1985)

6.8 T. Chakraborty: Phys. Rev. B**34**, 2926 (1986)

6.9 J. M. Caillol, D. Levesque, J. J. Weis, J. P. Hansen: J. Stat. Phys. **28**, 325 (1982)

6.10 R. G. Clark, J. R. Mallett, S. R. Haynes, J. J. Harris, C. T. Foxon: Phys. Rev. Lett. **60**, 1747 (1988)

6.11 Yu. A. Bychkov, E. I. Rashba: JETP **63**, 200 (1986)

6.12 D. Yoshioka, B. I. Halperin, P. A. Lee: Phys. Rev. Lett. **50**, 1219 (1983)

6.13 D. Yoshioka: J. Phys. Soc. Jpn. **53**, 3740 (1984)

6.14 T. Chakraborty, P. Pietiläinen, F. C. Zhang: Phys. Rev. Lett. **57**, 130 (1986)

6.15 T. Chakraborty, P. Pietiläinen: Phys. Scr. **T14**, 58 (1986)

6.16 F. C. Zhang, S. Das Sarma: Phys. Rev. B**33**, 2903 (1986)

6.17 F. D. M. Haldane, E. H. Rezayi: Phys. Rev. Lett. **54**, 237 (1985)

6.18 G. Fano, F. Ortolani, E. Colombo: Phys. Rev. B**34**, 2670 (1986)

6.19 R. Morf, B. I. Halperin: Z. Phys. B**68**, 391 (1987)

6.20 A. H. MacDonald, S. M. Girvin: Phys. Rev. B**33**, 4414 (1986)

6.21 A. H. MacDonald, S. M. Girvin: Phys. Rev. B**34**, 5639 (1986)

6.22 B. Tausendfreund, K. von Klitzing: Surf. Sci. **142**, 220 (1984)

6.23 A. M. Chang, M. A. Paalanen, D. C. Tsui, H. L. Störmer, J. C. Hwang: Phys. Rev. B**28**, 6133 (1983)

6.24 I. V. Kukushkin, V. B. Timofeev, P. A. Cheremnykh: JETP Lett. **41**, 321 (1985)

6.25 I. V. Kukushkin, V. B. Timofeev: JETP **62**, 976 (1985)

6.26 G. S. Boebinger, A. M. Chang, H. L. Störmer, D. C. Tsui: Phys. Rev. Lett. **55**, 1606 (1985)

6.27 G. S. Boebinger, A. M. Chang, H. L. Störmer, D. C. Tsui, J. C. M. Hwang, A. Cho, C. Tu, G. Weimann: Surf. Sci. **170**, 129 (1986)

6.28 S. Kawaji, J. Wakabayashi, J. Yoshino, H. Sakaki: J. Phys. Soc. Jpn. **53**, 1915 (1984)

6.29 J. Wakabayashi, S. Kawaji, J. Yoshino, H. Sakaki: J. Phys. Soc. Jpn. **55**, 1319 (1986)

6.30 G. E. Ebert, K. von Klitzing, J. C. Maan, G. Remenyi, C. Probst, G. Weimann, W. Schlapp: J. Phys. C**17**, L775 (1984)

6.31 V. M. Pudalov, S. G. Semenchinskii: JETP Lett. **39**, 170 (1984)

6.32 G. S. Boebinger, H. L. Störmer, D. C. Tsui, A. M. Chang, J. C. M. Hwang, A. Y. Cho, C. W. Tu, G. Weimann: Phys. Rev. B**36**, 7919 (1987)

6.33 R. L. Willett, H. L. Störmer, D. C. Tsui, A. C. Gossard, J. H. English: Phys. Rev. B**37**, 8476 (1988)

6.34 A. H. MacDonald, K. L. Liu, S. M. Girvin, P. M. Platzman: Phys. Rev. B**33**, 4014 (1986)

6.35 A. Gold: Europhys. Lett. **1**, 241, 479(E), (1986)

6.36 R. B. Laughlin, M. L. Cohen, J. M. Kosterlitz, H. Levine, S. B. Libby, A. M. M. Pruisken: Phys. Rev. B**32**, 1311 (1985)

6.37 R. B. Laughlin: Surf. Sci. **170**, 167 (1986)

6.38 E. Mendez: Surf. Sci. **170**, 561 (1986)

6.39 Y. Guldner, M. Voos, J. P. Vieren, J. P. Hirtz, M. Heiblum: Phys. Rev. B**36**, 1266 (1987)

6.40 H. W. Jiang, R. L. Willett, H. L. Störmer, D. C. Tsui, L. N. Pfeiffer, K. W. West: Phys. Rev. Lett. **65**, 633 (1990)

6.41 D. Arovas, J. R. Schrieffer, F. Wilczek: Phys. Rev. Lett. **53**, 722 (1984)

6.42 F. Wilczek: Phys. Rev. Lett. **49**, 957 (1982)

6.43 J. M. Leinaas, J. Myrheim: Nuovo Cim. **37**, 1 (1977)

6.44 Y. S. Wu: Phys. Rev. Lett. **52**, 2103 (1984); *ibid.* **53**, 111 (1984)

6.45 D. P. Arovas, R. Schrieffer, F. Wilczek, A. Zee: Nucl. Phys. B**251**, 117 (1985)

6.46 D. J. Thouless, Y. S. Wu: Phys. Rev. B**31**, 1191 (1985)

6.47 R. B. Laughlin: In *Proceedings of the 17 th Int. Conf. on the Physics of Semiconductors*, ed. by D. J. Chadi, W. A. Harrison (Springer-Verlag, 1985) p. 255

6.48 F. D. M. Haldane: Phys. Rev. Lett. **51**, 605 (1983)

6.49 B. I. Halperin: Phys. Rev. Lett. **52**, 1583, 2390(E) (1984)

6.50 R. B. Laughlin: In *The Quantum Hall Effect*, ed. by R. E. Prange, S. M. Girvin (Springer-Verlag, 1987) p. 233

6.51 F. D. M. Haldane: In *The Quantum Hall Effect*, ed. by R. E. Prange, S. M. Girvin (Springer-Verlag, 1987) p. 303

6.52 F. C. Zhang: Phys. Rev. B**34**, 5598 (1986)

6.53 I. V. Krive, A. S. Rozhavskiǐ: Sov. Phys. Usp. **30**, 370 (1987)

6.54 A. H. MacDonald, G. C. Aers, M. W. C. Dharma-wardana: Phys. Rev. B**31**, 5529 (1985)

6.55 D. Yoshioka, P. A. Lee: Phys. Rev. B**27**, 4986 (1983)

6.56 A. H. MacDonald: Phys. Rev. B**30**, 4392 (1984)

6.57 A. H. MacDonald, D. B. Murray: Phys. Rev. B**32**, 2707 (1985)

6.58 F. C. Zhang, T. Chakraborty: Phys. Rev. B**34**, 7076 (1986)

6.59 R. Morf, N. d'Ambrumenil, B. I. Halperin: Phys. Rev. B**34**, 3037 (1986)

6.60 J, K, Jain: Phys. Rev. Lett. **63**, 199 (1989); Phys. Rev. B**40**, 8079 (1989)

6.61 B. I. Halperin, P. A. Lee: Phys. Rev. B**47**, 7312 (1993)

6.62 H. L. Störmer, A. M. Chang, D. C. Tsui, J. C. M. Hwang, A. C. Gossard, W. Wiegmann: Phys. Rev. Lett. **50**, 1953 (1983)

6.63 I. V. Kukushkin, R. J. Haug, K. von Klitzing, K. Ploog: Phys. Rev. Lett. **72**, 736 (1994)

6.64 J. C. Maan: In *Two Dimensional Systems, Heterostructures and Superlattices*, ed. by G. Bauer, F. Kucher, H. Heinrich (Springer-Verlag, 1984) p. 183

6.65 M. A. Brummell, M. A. Hopkins, R. J. Nicholas, J. C. Portal, K. Y. Cheng: J. Phys. C**19**, L107 (1986)

6.66 V. E. Kirpichev, I. V. Kukushkin, V. B. Timofeev, V. I. Fal'ko: JETP Lett. **51**, 436 (1990)

6.67 R. J. Haug, K. von Klitzing, R. J. Nicholas, J. C. Maan, G. Weimann: Phys. Rev. B **36**, 4528 (1987); R. J. Haug: Dissertation, Max-Planck-Institut, Stuttgart (1988)

6.68 T. Ando, A. B. Fowler, F. Stern: Rev. Mod. Phys. **54**, 437 (1982)

6.69 T. Ando: Phys. Rev. B**19**, 2106 (1979)

6.70 Y. Uemura, Y. Matsumoto: J. Jpn. Soc. Appl. Phys. Suppl. **40**, 205 (1971)

6.71 T. Chakraborty, P. Pietiläinen: Phys. Rev. B**39**, 7971 (1989)

6.72 V. Halonen, P. Pietiläinen, T. Chakraborty: Phys. Rev. B**41**, 10 202 (1990)

6.73 J. E. Furneaux, D. A. Syphers, A. G. Swanson: Phys. Rev. Lett. **63**, 1098 (1989)

6.74 R. G. Clark, S. R. Haynes, A. M. Suckling, J. R. Mallett, P. A. Wright, J. J. Harris, C. T. Foxon: Phys. Rev. Lett. **62**, 1536 (1989)

6.75 Robert Clark, Peter Maksym: Physics World **2**, 39 (September, 1989)

6.76 P. A. Maksym: J. Phys.: Condens. Matter **1**, L6299 (1989)

6.77 T. Chakraborty: Surf. Sci. **229**, 16 (1990)

6.78 A. G. Davies, R. Newbury, M. Pepper, J. F. F. Frost, D. A. Ritchie, G. A. C. Jones: Phys. Rev. B**44**, 13 128 (1991)

6.79 J. P. Eisenstein, H. L. Störmer, L. Pfeiffer, K. W. West: Phys. Rev. Lett. **62**, 1540 (1989)

6.80 M. Dobers, K. von Klitzing, G. Weimann: Phys. Rev. B**38**, 5453 (1988)

6.81 R. G. Clark, S. R. Haynes, J. V. Branch, A. M. Suckling, P. A. Wright, P. M. W. Oswald, J. J. Harris, C. T. Foxon: Surf. Sci. **229**, 25 (1990)

6.82 J. P. Eisenstein, H. L. Störmer, L. N. Pfeiffer, K. W. West: Phys. Rev. B**41**, 7910 (1990)

6.83 T. Chakraborty, P. Pietiläinen: Phys. Rev. B**41**, 10 862 (1990)

6.84 A. Sachrajda, R. Boulet, Z. Wasilewski, P. Coleridge, F. Guillon: Solid State Commun. **74**, 1021 (1990)

6.85 A. Buckthought, R. Boulet, A. Sachrajda, Z. Wasilewski, P. Zawadzki, F. Guillon: Solid State Commun. **78**, 191 (1991)

6.86 L. W. Engel, S. W. Hwang, T. Sajoto, D. C. Tsui, M. Shayegan, Phys. Rev. B**45**, 3418 (1992)

Chapter 7

7.1 F. D. M. Haldane, E. H. Rezayi: Phys. Rev. Lett. **54**, 237 (1985)

7.2 F. D. M. Haldane: Phys. Rev. Lett. **55**, 2095 (1985)

7.3 R. B. Laughlin: Physica **126B**, 254 (1984)

7.4 G. Fano, F. Ortolani, E. Colombo: Phys. Rev. B**34**, 2670 (1986)

7.5 W. P. Su: Phys. Rev. B**30**, 1069 (1984)

7.6 W. P. Su: Phys. Rev. B**32**, 2617 (1985)

7.7 D. Yoshioka: Phys. Rev. B**29**, 6833 (1984)

7.8 Q. Niu, D. J. Thouless, Y. S. Wu: Phys. Rev. B**31**, 3372 (1985)

7.9 J. Avron, R. Seiler: Phys. Rev. Lett. **54**, 259 (1985)

7.10 E. Brown: Solid State Phys. **22**, 313 (1968)

7.11 P. Maksym: J. Phys. **C18**, L433 (1985)

7.12 R. Tao, F. D. M. Haldane: Phys. Rev. B**33**, 3844 (1986)

7.13 D. Yoshioka: J. Phys. Soc. Jpn. **55**, 885 (1986)

7.14 C. Kallin, B. I. Halperin: Phys. Rev. B**30**, 5655 (1984)

7.15 D. Yoshioka: J. Phys. Soc. Jpn. **53**, 3740 (1984)

7.16 D. Yoshioka: J. Phys. Soc. Jpn. **55**, 3960 (1986)

7.17 E. H. Rezayi: Phys. Rev. B**36**, 5454 (1987)

7.18 M. Rasolt, A. H. MacDonald: Phys. Rev. B**34**, 5530 (1986)

7.19 S. M. Girvin, A. H. MacDonald, P. M. Platzman: Phys. Rev. Lett. **54**, 581 (1985); Phys. Rev. B**33**, 2481 (1986)

7.20 R. P. Feynman: *Statistical Physics* (Benjamin, Reading Mass. 1972) Chap. 11

7.21 E. Feenberg: *The Theory of Quantum Fluids* (Academic, New York, London, 1969)

7.22 S. M. Girvin, T. Jach: Phys. Rev. B**29**, 5617 (1984)

7.23 R. P. Feynman, M. Cohen: Phys. Rev. **102**, 1189 (1956)

7.24 M. Saarela: Phys. Rev. B**35**, 854 (1987)

7.25 H. C. A. Oji, A. H. MacDonald, S. M. Girvin: Phys. Rev. Lett. **58**, 824 (1987)

7.26 S. Das Sarma, J. J. Quinn: Phys. Rev. B**25**, 7603 (1982); Phys. Rev. B**27**, 6516 (1983)

7.27 A. C. Tselis, J. J. Quinn: Phys. Rev. B**29**, 3318 (1984)

7.28 T. Chakraborty: Phys. Rev. B**41**, 5396 (1990)

7.29 M. Shayegan, J. K. Wang, M. Santos, T. Sajoto, B. B. Goldberg: Appl. Phys. Lett. **54**, 27 (1989)

7.30 W. P. Su, Y. K. Wu: Phys. Rev. B**36**, 7565 (1987)

7.31 D. Yoshioka: J. Phys. Soc. Jpn. **56**, 1301 (1987)

7.32 E. Gornik, R. Lassnig, G. Strasser, H. L. Störmer, A. C. Gossard: W. Wiegmann, Phys. Rev. Lett. **54**, 1820 (1985)

7.33 A. H. MacDonald, H. C. A. Oji, K. L. Liu: Phys. Rev. B**34**, 2681 (1986)

7.34 B. I. Halperin: Phys. Rev. Lett. **52**, 1583, 2390 (E) (1984)

7.35 H. L. Störmer, T. Haavasoja, V. Narayanamurti, A. C. Gossard, W. Wiegmann: J. Vac. Sci. Technol. B**2**, 423 (1983); T. Haavasoja, H. L. Störmer, D. J. Bishop, V. Narayanamurti, A. C. Gossard, W. Wiegmann: Surf. Sci. **142**, 294 (1984); J. P. Eisenstein, H. L. Störmer, V. Narayanamurti, A. Y. Cho, A. C. Gossard, C. W. Tu: Phys. Rev. Lett. **55**, 875 (1985)

Chapter 8

8.1 C. Kallin, B. I. Halperin: Phys. Rev. B**30**, 5655 (1984)

8.2 C. Kallin, B. I. Halperin: Phys. Rev. B**31**, 3635 (1985)

8.3 B. A. Wilson, S. J. Allen, D. C. Tsui: Phys. Rev. Lett. **44**, 479 (1981)

8.4 B. A. Wilson, S. J. Allen, D. C. Tsui: Phys. Rev. B**24**, 5887 (1981)

8.5 G. L. J. A. Rikken, H. W. Myron, P. Wyder, G. Weimann, W. Schlapp, R. E. Horstman, J. Wolter: J. Phys. C**18**, L175 (1985)

8.6 Z. Schlesinger, S. J. Allen, J. C. M. Hwang, P. M. Platzman, N. Tzoar: Phys. Rev. B**30**, 435 (1984)

8.7 Z. Schlesinger, W. I. Wang, A. H. MacDonald: Phys. Rev. Lett. **58**, 73 (1987)

8.8 W. Kohn: Phys. Rev. **123**, 1242 (1961)

8.9 S.-K. Yip: Phys. Rev. B**40**, 3882 (1989)

8.10 S. M. Girvin: In *The Quantum Hall Effect*, ed. by R. E. Prange, S. M. Girvin (Springer-Verlag, 1990) 2nd Ed. p. 401

8.11 E. Batke, D. Heitman, J. P. Kotthaus, K. Ploog: Phys. Rev. Lett. **54**, 2367 (1985)

8.12 A. H. MacDonald: J. Phys. C**18**, 1003 (1985)

8.13 Yu. A. Bychkov, S. V. Iordanskii, G. M. Eliashberg: JETP Lett. **33**, 143 (1981)

8.14 E. Batke, C. W. Tu: Phys. Rev. Lett. **58**, 2474 (1987)

8.15 A. Pinczuk, J. P. Villadares, D. Heiman, A. C. Gossard, J. H. English, C. W. Tu, L. Pfeiffer, K. West: Phys. Rev. Lett. **61**, 2701 (1988); Surf. Sci. **229**, 384 (1990)

8.16 A. H. MacDonald, H. C. A. Oji, S. M. Girvin: Phys. Rev. Lett. **55**, 2208 (1985)

8.17 H. C. A. Oji, A. H. MacDonald: Phys. Rev. B**33**, 3810 (1986)

8.18 P. Pietiläinen, T. Chakraborty: Europhys. Lett. **5**, 157 (1988)

8.19 P. Pietiläinen: Dissertation, University of Oulu (1988); Phys. Rev. B**38**, 4279 (1988)

Chapter 9

9.1 V. L. Pokrovskii, A. L. Talapov: JETP Lett. **42**, 80 (1985)

9.2 V. L. Pokrovskii, A. L. Talapov: JETP **63**, 455 (1986)

9.3 F. C. Zhang, V. Z. Vulovic, Y. Guo, S. Das Sarma: Phys. Rev. B**32**, 6920 (1985)

9.4 E. H. Rezayi, F. D. M. Haldane : Phys. Rev. B**32**, 6924 (1985)

9.5 S. M. Girvin, A. H. MacDonald, P. M. Platzman: Phys. Rev. B**33**, 2481 (1986)

9.6 R. Tao, F. D. M. Haldane: Phys. Rev. B**33**, 3844 (1986)

9.7 Q. Niu, D. J. Thouless, Y. S. Wu: Phys. Rev. B**31**, 3372 (1985)

9.8 A. H. MacDonald: Phys. Rev. B**30**, 3550 (1984)

9.9 A. H. MacDonald, S. M. Girvin: Phys. Rev. B**33**, 4009 (1986)

9.10 F. D. M. Haldane: In *The Quantum Hall Effect*, ed. by R. E. Prange, S. M. Girvin (Springer-Verlag, 1987) p. 303

9.11 N. d'Ambrumenil, A. M. Reynolds: J. Phys. C**21**, 119 (1988)

9.12 R. G. Clark, R. J. Nicholas, A. Usher, C. T. Foxon, J. J. Harris: Surf. Sci. **170**, 141 (1986)

9.13 A. H. MacDonald, S. M. Girvin: Phys. Rev. B**34**, 5639 (1986)

9.14 V. Kalmeyer, R. B. Laughlin: Phys. Rev. Lett. **59**, 2095 (1987); see also, Yu. E. Lozovik, O. I. Notych: JETP Lett. **54**, 91 (1991)

9.15 B. I. Halperin: Helv. Phys. Acta **56**, 75 (1983)

9.16 D. Yoshioka: Phys. Rev. B**29**, 6833 (1984)

9.17 F. D. M. Haldane: Phys. Rev. Lett. **55**, 2095 (1985)

9.18 Y. Kuramoto, R. R. Gerhardts: J. Phys. Soc. Jpn. **51**, 3810 (1982)

9.19 T. Chakraborty, P. Pietiläinen: Phys. Rev. B**38**, 10 097 (1988)

9.20 G. Fano, F. Ortolani, E. Tosatti: Nuovo Cimento **9D**, 1337 (1987)

9.21 M. Greiter, X. G. Wen, F. Wilczek: Nucl. Phys. B**374**, 567 (1992)

9.22 G. E. Ebert, K. von Klitzing, J. C. Maan, G. Remenyi, C. Probst, G. Weimann, W. Schlapp: J. Phys. C**17**, L775 (1984)

9.23 R. G. Clark, R. J. Nicholas, J. R. Mallett, A. M. Suckling, A. Usher, J. J. Harris, C. T. Foxon: In *Proc. of the Eighteenth Int. Conf. on the Phys. of Semicond.*, ed. by O. Engstrom (World Scientific, Singapore 1987) p. 393

9.24 R. Willett, J. P. Eisenstein, H. L. Störmer, D. C. Tsui, A. C. Gossard, J. H. English: Phys. Rev. Lett. **59**, 1776 (1987)

9.25 F. D. M. Haldane, E. H. Rezayi: Phys. Rev. Lett. **60**, 956 (1988)

9.26 A. H. MacDonald, D. Yoshioka, S. M. Girvin: Phys. Rev. B**39**, 8044 (1989)

9.27 J. P. Eisenstein, R. Willett, H. L. Störmer, D. C. Tsui, A. C. Gossard, J. H. English: Phys. Rev. Lett. **61**, 997 (1988)

9.28 H. W. Jiang, H. L. Störmer, D. C. Tsui, L. N. Pfeiffer, K. W. West: Phys. Rev. B**40**, 12 013 (1989)

9.29 R. L. Willett, M. A. Paalanen, R. R. Ruel, K. W. West, L. N. Pfeiffer, D. J. Bishop: Phys. Rev. Lett. **65**, 112 (1990)

9.30 R. L. Willett, R. R. Ruel, M. A. Paalanen, K. W. West, L. N. Pfeiffer: Phys. Rev. B**47**, 7344 (1993)

9.31 B. I. Halperin, P. A. Lee, N. Read: Phys. Rev. B**47**, 7312 (1993)

9.32 F. Wilczek, *Fractional Statistics and Anyon Superconductivity* (World Scientific, Singapore 1990); A. López, E. Fradkin: Phys. Rev. B**44**, 5246 (1991)

9.33 J. K. Jain: Phys. Rev. Lett. **63**, 199 (1989); Phys. Rev. B**40**, 8079 (1989)

9.34 V. Kalmeyer, S. C. Zhang: Phys. Rev. B**46**, 9889 (1992)

9.35 R. R. Du, H. L. Stormer, D. C. Tsui, L. N. Pfeiffer, K. W. West: Phys. Rev. Lett. **70**, 2944 (1993)

9.36 R. R. Gerhardts, D. Weiss, K. von Klitzing: Phys. Rev. Lett. **62**, 1173 (1989); D. Weiss, K. von Klitzing, K. Ploog, G. Weimann: Europhys. Lett. **8**, 179 (1989);

9.37 R. W. Winkler, J. P. Kotthaus, K. Ploog: Phys. Rev. Lett. **62**, 1177 (1989)

9.38 W. Kang, H. L. Stormer, L. N. Pfeiffer, K. W. Baldwin, K. W. West, Phys. Rev. Lett. **71**, 3850 (1993)

9.39 D. Weiss, K. Richter, E. Vasiliadou, G. Lütjering, Surf. Sci. **305**, 408 (1994); D. Weiss, M. L. Roukes, A. Menschig, P. Grambow, K. von Klitzing, G. Weimann: Phys. Rev. Lett. **66**, 2790 (1991)

9.40 V. J. Goldman, B. Su, J. K. Jain: Phys. Rev. Lett. **72**, 2065 (1994)

9.41 R. L. Willett, R. R. Ruel, K. W. West, L. N. Pfeiffer: Phys. Rev. Lett. **71**, 3846 (1993);

9.42 F. D. M. Haldane, unpublished (1994)

9.43 J. Yang, W. P. Su: Phys. Rev. Lett. **70**, 1163 (1993)

9.44 T. Chakraborty, P. Pietiläinen: In *Recent Progress in Many-Body Theories*, eds. A. Kallio, E. Pajane, R. F. Bishop (Plenum, New York 1988), p. 113.

9.45 T. Chakraborty, P. Pietiläinen: Phys. Rev. Lett. **59**, 2784 (1987)

9.46 W. L. Bloss, E. M. Brody: Solid State Commun. **43**, 523 (1982)

9.47 S. Das Sarma, J. J. Quinn: Phys. Rev. B**25**, 7603 (1982); Phys. Rev. B**27**, 6516(E) (1983)

9.48 T. Chakraborty, C. E. Campbell: Phys. Rev. B**29**, 6640 (1984)

9.49 P. B. Visscher, L. M. Falicov: Phys. Rev. B**3**, 2541 (1971)

9.50 G. Fasol, N. Mestres, H. P. Hughes, A. Fischer, K. Ploog: Phys. Rev. Lett. **56**, 2517 (1986)

9.51 A. Pinczuk, M. G. Lamont, A. C. Gossard: Phys. Rev. Lett. **56**, 2092 (1986)

9.52 P. Maksym: J. Phys. C**18**, L433 (1985)

9.53 H. C. A. Oji, A. H. MacDonald, S. M. Girvin: Phys. Rev. Lett. **58**, 824 (1987)

9.54 P. E. Lindelof, H. Bruus, R. Taboryski, C. B. Sørensen: Semicond. Sci. Technolog. **4**, 858 (1989)

9.55 J. P. Eisenstein, G. S. Boebinger, L. N. Pfeiffer, K. W. West, S. He: Phys. Rev. Lett. **68**, 1383 (1992)

9.56 D. Yoshioka, A. H. MacDonald, S. M. Girvin: Phys. Rev. B**39**, 1932 (1989)

9.57 H. Fertig: Phys. Rev. B**40**, 1087 (1989)

9.58 C. Kallin, B. I. Halperin: Phys. Rev. B**30**, 5655 (1984)

9.59 G. S. Boebinger, H. W. Jiang, L. N. Pfeiffer, K. W. West: Phys. Rev. Lett. **64**, 1793 (1990)

9.60 D. Yoshioka, A. H. MacDonald: J. Phys. Soc. Jpn. **59**, 4211 (1990)

9.61 S. Q. Murphy, J. P. Eisenstein, G. S. Boebinger, L. N. Pfeiffer, K. W. West: Phys. Rev. Lett. **72**, 728 (1994)

9.62 T. Chakraborty: Phys. Rev. B**39**, 869 (1989); M. Puoskari, A. Kallio: Phys. Rev. B**30**, 152 (1984); P. M. Lam, M. L. Ristig: Phys. Rev. B**20**, 1960 (1979); S. Fantoni: Nuovo Cimento A**44**, 191 (1978)

9.63 W. L. McMillan: Phys. Rev. **138**, A442 (1965); M. H. Kalos, D. Levesque, L. Verlet: Phys. Rev. A**9**, 2178 (1974); M. H. Kalos, M. A. Lee, P. A. Whitlock, G. V. Chester: Phys. Rev. B**24**, 115 (1981); P. Whitlock, R. M. Panoff: Can. J. Phys. **65**, 1409 (1987)

9.64 V. F. Sears: Can. J. Phys. **63**, 68 (1985)

9.65 P. A. Whitlock, G. V. Chester, M. H. Kalos: Phys. Rev. B**38**, 2418 (1988)

9.66 A. H. MacDonald, S. M. Girvin: Phys. Rev. B**38**, 6295 (1988)

9.67 R. B. Laughlin: Phys. Rev. Lett. **50**, 1395 (1983)

9.68 C. N. Yang: Rev. Mod. Phys. **34**, 694 (1962); O. Penrose: Philos. Mag. **42**, 1373 (1951); O. Penrose, L. Onsager: Phys. Rev. **104**, 576 (1956)

9.69 D. J. Thouless: Phys. Rev. B**31**, 8305 (1985)

9.70 S. M. Girvin, A. H. MacDonald: Phys. Rev. Lett. **58**, 1252 (1987)

9.71 L. Reatto, G. V. Chester: Phys. Rev. **155**, 88 (1967)

9.72 T. Chakraborty, W. von der Linden: Phys. Rev. B**41**, 7872 (1990)

9.73 N. Metropolis, A. W. Rosenbluth, M. N. Rosenbluth, A. M. Teller, E. Teller: J. Chem. Phys. **21**, 1087 (1953)

Chapter 10

10.1 J. P. Eisenstein, L. N. Pfeiffer, K. W. West: Phys. Rev. B**50**, 1760 (1994)

10.2 H. Fertig, R. Cote, A. H. MacDonald, S. Das sarma: Phys. Rev. Lett. **69**, 816 (1992)

10.3 L. J. Challis: Contemp. Phys. **33**, 111 (1992)

10.4 T. Demel, D. Heitmann, P. Grambow, K. Ploog: Phys. Rev. Lett. **66**, 2657 (1991)

10.5 W. Hansen, T. P. Smith III, K. Y. Lee, J. M. Hong, C. M. Knoedler: Appl. Phys. Lett. **56**, 168 (1990); Ch. Sikorski, U. Merkt: Phys. Rev. Lett. **62**, 2164 (1989); T. Demel, D. Heitmann, P. Grambow, K. Ploog: Phys. Rev. Lett. **64**, 788 (1990)

10.6 P. A. Maksym, T. Chakraborty: Phys. Rev. Lett. **65**, 108 (1990); T. Chakraborty: Comm. Cond. Matt. Phys. **16**, 35 (1992)

10.7 B. Meurer, D. Heitmann, K. Ploog: Phys. Rev. Lett. **68**, 1371 (1992)

10.8 K. Kern, D. Heitmann, P. Grambow, Y. H. Zhang, K. Ploog: Phys. Rev. Lett. **66**, 1618 (1991); D. Weiss, M. L. Roukes, A. Menschig, P. Grambow, K. von Klitzing, G. Weimann: Phys. Rev. Lett. **66**, 2790 (1991)

Appendix A

A.1 R. B. Dingle: Proc. Roy. Soc. A**211**, 500 (1952)

A.2 L. D. Landau, E. M. Lifshitz: *Quantum Mechanics*, (Pergamon, Oxford 1977) p. 458

A.3 E. T. Whittaker, G. N. Watson: *A Course of Modern Analysis* (Cambridge University Press, London, 1962), ch. 16

A.4 V. Fock: Z. Physik **47**, 446 (1928)

A.5 C. G. Darwin: Proc. Cambridge Philos. Soc. **27**, 86 (1930)

A.6 P. A. Maksym, T. Chakraborty: Phys. Rev. Lett. **65**, 108 (1990)

A.7 S. M. Girvin, T. Jach: Phys. Rev. B**28**, 4506 (1983)

A.8 S. M. Girvin, T. Jach: Phys. Rev. B**29**, 5617 (1984)

A.9 V. Bergmann: Rev. Mod. Phys. **34**, 829 (1962)

Appendix B

B.1 G. Morandi: *Quantum Hall Effect* (Bibliopolis, Napoli 1988)

B.2 R. Kubo: J. Phys. Soc. Jpn. **12**, 570 (1957)

B.3 R. Kubo, S. J. Miyake, N. Hashitsume: Solid State Physics **17**, 269 (1965)

Appendix C

C.1 J. M. J. van Leeuwen, J. Groeneveld, J. de Boer: Physica **25**, 792 (1959)

C.2 T. Morita, K. Hiroike: Prog. Theor. Phys. **23**, 1003 (1960)

C.3 E. E. Salpeter: Ann. Phys. **5**, 183 (1958)

C.4 J. M. Caillol, D. Levesque, J. J. Weis, J. P. Hansen: J. Stat. Phys. **28**, 325 (1982)

C.5 K. Hiroike: Prog. Theor. Phys. **24**, 317 (1960)

C.6 T. Chakraborty: Phys. Rev. B**26**, 6131 (1982)

C.7 T. Chakraborty, P. Pietiläinen: Phys. Rev. Lett. **49**, 1034 (1982)

Appendix E

E.1 T. Ando, A. B. Fowler, F. Stern: Rev. Mod. Phys. **54**, 437 (1982)

E.2 B. N. Taylor, W. H. Parker, D. N. Langenberg: Rev. Mod. Phys. **41**, 375 (1969)

E.3 S. Adachi: J. Appl. Phys. **58**, R1 (1985)

Subject Index

Activation energy 67–68, 114–119, 145–146, 154–156
Activation gap 117–119
  as a function of mobility 118
  in a tilted magnetic field 155–156
  measurements of the 67–68, 113–120, 155–156
Angular momentum
  azimuthal 103
  conservation of 46, 51, 132, 180
  eigenstate of 46
Alternating-density superlattices 187
Anyons 120–131
  wave function of many 131
Articulation point 258
Aspect ratio 41, 149

Backflow 182–183
Basis states 41–42, 133–134, 169–171
  construction of 41–42, 169–171
Blue shift of the luminescence peak 73, 81–82
Boson ladder operators 252
Boundary conditions
  periodic 6, 40
Breakdown of the quantum Hall effect 30–31

Center-of-mass translation 167
Charge-density-wave 35, 222
Chemical potential 25, 36, 87, 97
  discontinuity 87, 97, 190
Chern-Simons description 233–235
  gauge field 233
  magnetic field 234
  vector potential 234
Classical plasma
  analogy 47–51, 89–90, 94–95
  charge neutrality condition of 47, 51
  crystallization transition 66
  dimensionless parameter of 48
  Hamiltonian 47, 89
  inhomogeneous 96
  ion-disk radius of 47, 95, 105
  one-component 47–51, 264
  two-component 89–95, 266
Collective excitation
  energy 163, 172–176, 178–181, 186–189
  in higher-Landau levels 201, 205–207
  in a mean-field approach 184
Composite fermions 143, 234–236
  mapping to 233–234
Compressible edge channels 28
Conductivity 10–15, 17, 218–220, 257
  diagonal 10–11
  Hall 10–11, 218–220, 257
  tensor 10–11, 255
Condensate fraction 241
Continuity condition 182–184
Correlation function
  pair 47–48, 58–60, 62, 91, 94, 96, 244, 257, 266
  three-body 96
Coulomb interaction
  energy 42, 49, 59
  in finite-size studies 40
Cusp in ground state energy 36, 43, 97, 138, 210, 225
Cyclotron radius 4
Cyclotron energy 5, 35
Cyclotron frequency 4
Cyclotron resonance 192–194, 197–198

Debye length 95
Definition of distance
  chord 56, 110, 163
  great circle 56, 110

Degeneracy
of the ground state 163–164
landau level 6, 40
Density matrix 241–242
Density of states (DOS) 7, 21
Density operator 177
projected 179
Density-wave spectrum 172, 181
Diagrams
composite 259
elementary 261
irreducible 258
linked 258
(non) nodal 261
simple 259
Disorder
effect on the activation gap 117–118
effect in the quantum Hall regime 20–21
Double quantum-well 240
Drift velocity 11, 87, 183–184

Edge channels 25
Edge currents 25–26
Edge states 25–26
Effective cyclotron energy 235
Effective magnetic field 234–235
Effective filling factor 234–235
Electron-hole symmetry 44, 51–53, 141–142
breaking of 146
Energy
approximate formula for 50, 58–59
ground-state 43, 49–50, 55, 58–59
interaction 47, 63
Energy gap 57–58, 97–105, 138, 149–151, 158–161, 163, 172–175, 180–181, 209–210, 235–236, 238–239
experimental results of 114–120, 154–155, 236
Even-denominator filling fractions
experimental results on 34, 228–233
theoretical work on 225–228, 233–236
Exact diagonalization 41–43, 99–100, 169–172, 238
Excitations
coherent 201–202, 267–272
incoherent 202, 267–272
Excitation energy
at any hierarchy level 134–135, 137–138
Excitation spectrum
finite-size studies of 162–163, 172–175, 238–239
in single-mode approximation 181, 186–187
in a superlattice 184–187
Extended states 7, 20–21

Fang-Howard variational function 65
Feynman theory 177-178
Filled Landau level
energy of a 48
pair-correlation function for a 48
Filling factor (fraction) 6, 40, 46, 62
as a continued fraction 135
observed in FQHE experiments 32–33
Finite-thickness correction 64–66
parameter 65
Flux quantum 6
Fractional charge
of quasiholes 89, 91
of quasiparticles 94
experimental results on 119–120
Fractional statistics 123–131
Fundamental theorem of algebra 50

Gapless domain 57–58, 158
Gauge transformation 127, 131, 233, 243
Ground state spin polarization
theoretical results on 61–64
experimental results on 152–153

Hall conductance
as a topological invariant 18
gauge invariance approach to 15–17
Hall conductivity 10-11, 13, 17, 218–220, 257
Harmonic oscillator 5, 129, 145
Hartree-Fock
approximation 43, 190, 202
energy 48, 188
Hierarchy of states 134–140, 143
Higher order filling factors 32, 143
trial wave function approach of 141–142
Hypernetted-chain method
one-component 48–49, 257–264
two-component 62, 89, 94, 266

Impurity interaction 6, 208–209, 211
delta-function (short-range) 21, 208, 211
Impurity limit 89
Impurity-plasma interaction 89, 94
Incompressible edge channels 28
Incompressiblity 36
of the Laughlin state 36, 43, 172–173, 181
Intensity of optical transitions 80, 83–84

Jastrow (-type) wave function 46, 61

von Klitzing constant 8, 273
Kohn's theorem 192–194
Kubo formula 13, 17, 253–257

Landau level 5
degeneracy of 6, 40, 46
Laughlin wave function
for higher Landau levels 221
ground state 46
in spherical geometry 55
quasihole state 88
quasiparticle state 92
two-component 61
Layered electron systems 237
excitation spectrum of 238–239

Magnetic exciton 194
energy 195
wave function of 194
Magnetic length 4, 65
for the quasiparticle state 135
modified 56
Magnetic translation operator 166
Magnetization 190
Magneto-optical transitions 71
Magnetoroton band in a superlattice 186
Magnetoroton mode 182
repetition of 205, 267
Magnetoplasmon mode 194
Mobility edges 7
Mobility gap 7
Mobility threshold 114
Monte Carlo results for
ground state energy 58–60
pair-correlation functions 59–60
quasihole creation energy 105
quasiparticle creation energy 107
Multilayer structure 237–240

Off-diagonal long-range order (ODLRO) 241
One-half filled Landau level
experimental results 231–233
theoretical work on 225–228, 233
One-particle density 92
integrated by parts 94, 107
Oscillator strength 178
projected 179
Overlap operator 80

Partially polarized states 63
Particle excess 91, 105
Particle-hole symmetry 44, 51, 141
Periodic rectangular geometry 39, 163
symmetry analysis 165–169
Pseudopotential parameters 57–58
Phantom point charge 89, 244

Quantization condition 17–18, 214
Quasiexciton 163, 173–174
Quasihole 88
creation energy 89–91
wave function 88
Quasiparticle 92
creation energy 94
spin-reversed 99-101
wave function 92
Quasiparticle and quasihole size 95

Radial distribution function
finite-size systems 43
ground state 49
Radiative recombination 71
Ray representation 166
Resistivity tensor 10
Reversed-spin states 61, 80–82, 99-103, 151–161
Roton minimum 178, 182, 186, 197–198, 238–239

Single-particle eigenstates
in Landau gauge 5
in symmetric gauge 45, 251
Single-mode approximation
breakdown of 184
for inter-Landau level excitations 199
for intra-Landau level excitations 180
singular gauge transformation 233, 243
Specific heat 189

Spherical geometry
ground state energy in 55
quasiparticle and quasihole in 103
Spin-reversed ground states 61
Spin-reversed quasiparticles 99–103
experimental results on 154–156
finite-size studies of 98, 117
in spherical geometry 112
wave function for 101
Spin-unpolarized ground states 63
Spin-wave dispersion 173, 196
Spinor variables 54
Static susceptibility 212
Structure function
dynamic 178
projected static 180
Subband-Landau-level coupling 148

Thouless number 21
Tilted-field effects 144–151
Tilted-field measurements 151–156
evidence of reversed spin in 151–156
phase transition in 155–161
Two-component systems 62, 89, 94, 102, 244, 266
Transition probability 80
Translational symmetry 42, 164
Transmutability of fermions 233

Valley waves 64
Vector potential
Landau gauge 4
symmetric gauge 45
in spherical geometry 54
Visscher-Falicov model 237
Vortex 88

Wigner crystal 49, 66–70, 83–86
correlated 66

Zeeman energy 62, 117
Zeros of the wave function 50–51, 88

Springer Series in Solid-State Sciences

Editors: M. Cardona P. Fulde K. von Klitzing H.-J. Queisser

1 **Principles of Magnetic Resonance** 3rd Edition 2nd Printing By C. P. Slichter
2 **Introduction to Solid-State Theory** 2nd Printing By O. Madelung
3 **Dynamical Scattering of X-Rays in Crystals** By Z. G. Pinsker
4 **Inelastic Electron Tunneling Spectroscopy** Editor: T. Wolfram
5 **Fundamentals of Crystal Growth I** Macroscopic Equilibrium and Transport Concepts 2nd Printing By F. E. Rosenberger
6 **Magnetic Flux Structures in Superconductors** By R. P. Huebener
7 **Green's Functions in Quantum Physics** 2nd Edition 2nd Printing By E. N. Economou
8 **Solitons and Condensed Matter Physics** 2nd Printing Editors: A. R. Bishop and T. Schneider
9 **Photoferroelectrics** By V. M. Fridkin
10 **Phonon Dispersion Relations in Insulators** By H. Bilz and W. Kress
11 **Electron Transport in Compound Semiconductors** By B. R. Nag
12 **The Physics of Elementary Excitations** By S. Nakajima, Y. Toyozawa, and R. Abe
13 **The Physics of Selenium and Tellurium** Editors: E. Gerlach and P. Grosse
14 **Magnetic Bubble Technology** 2nd Edition By A. H. Eschenfelder
15 **Modern Crystallography I** Symmetry of Crystals. Methods of Structural Crystallography 2nd Edition By B. K. Vainshtein
16 **Organic Molecular Crystals** Their Electronic States By E. A. Silinsh
17 **The Theory of Magnetism I** Statics and Dynamics 2nd Printing By D. C. Mattis
18 **Relaxation of Elementary Excitations** Editors: R. Kubo and E. Hanamura
19 **Solitons** Mathematical Methods for Physicists 2nd Printing By. G. Eilenberger
20 **Theory of Nonlinear Lattices** 2nd Edition By M. Toda
21 **Modern Crystallography II** Structure of Crystals 2nd Edition By B. K. Vainshtein, V. L. Indenbom, and V. M. Fridkin
22 **Point Defects in Semiconductors I** Theoretical Aspects By M. Lannoo and J. Bourgoin
23 **Physics in One Dimension** Editors: J. Bernasconi and T. Schneider
24 **Physics in High Magnetics Fields** Editors: S. Chikazumi and N. Miura
25 **Fundamental Physics of Amorphous Semiconductors** Editor: F. Yonezawa
26 **Elastic Media with Microstructure I** One-Dimensional Models By I. A. Kunin
27 **Superconductivity of Transition Metals** Their Alloys and Compounds By S. V. Vonsovsky, Yu. A. Izyumov, and E. Z. Kurmaev
28 **The Structure and Properties of Matter** Editor: T. Matsubara
29 **Electron Correlation and Magnetism in Narrow-Band Systems** Editor: T. Moriya
30 **Statistical Physics I** Equilibrium Statistical Mechanics 2nd Edition By M. Toda, R. Kubo, N. Saito
31 **Statistical Physics II** Nonequilibrium Statistical Mechanics 2nd Edition By R. Kubo, M. Toda, N. Hashitsume
32 **Quantum Theory of Magnetism** 2nd Edition By R. M. White
33 **Mixed Crystals** By A. I. Kitaigorodsky
34 **Phonons: Theory and Experiments I** Lattice Dynamics and Models of Interatomic Forces By P. Brüesch
35 **Point Defects in Semiconductors II** Experimental Aspects By J. Bourgoin and M. Lannoo
36 **Modern Crystallography III** Crystal Growth 2nd Edition By A. A. Chernov
37 **Modern Chrystallography IV** Physical Properties of Crystals Editor: L. A. Shuvalov
38 **Physics of Intercalation Compounds** Editors: L. Pietronero and E. Tosatti
39 **Anderson Localization** Editors: Y. Nagaoka and H. Fukuyama
40 **Semiconductor Physics** An Introduction 5th Edition By K. Seeger
41 **The LMTO Method** Muffin-Tin Orbitals and Electronic Structure By H. L. Skriver
42 **Crystal Optics with Spatial Dispersion, and Excitons** 2nd Edition By V. M. Agranovich and V. L. Ginzburg
43 **Structure Analysis of Point Defects in Solids** An Introduction to Multiple Magnetic Resonance Spectroscopy By J.-M. Spaeth, J. R. Niklas, and R. H. Bartram
44 **Elastic Media with Microstructure II** Three-Dimensional Models By I. A. Kunin
45 **Electronic Properties of Doped Semiconductors** By B. I. Shklovskii and A. L. Efros
46 **Topological Disorder in Condensed Matter** Editors: F. Yonezawa and T. Ninomiya
47 **Statics and Dynamics of Nonlinear Systems** Editors: G. Benedek, H. Bilz, and R. Zeyher

Springer Series in Solid-State Sciences

Editors: M. Cardona P. Fulde K. von Klitzing H.-J. Queisser

48 **Magnetic Phase Transitions**
Editors: M. Ausloos and R. J. Elliott

49 **Organic Molecular Aggregates**
Electronic Excitation and Interaction Processes
Editors: P. Reineker, H. Haken, and H. C. Wolf

50 **Multiple Diffraction of X-Rays in Crystals**
By Shih-Lin Chang

51 **Phonon Scattering in Condensed Matter**
Editors: W. Eisenmenger, K. Laßmann, and S. Döttinger

52 **Superconductivity in Magnetic and Exotic Materials** Editors: T. Matsubara and A. Kotani

53 **Two-Dimensional Systems, Heterostructures, and Superlattices**
Editors: G. Bauer, F. Kuchar, and H. Heinrich

54 **Magnetic Excitations and Fluctuations**
Editors: S. W. Lovesey, U. Balucani, F. Borsa, and V. Tognetti

55 **The Theory of Magnetism II** Thermodynamics and Statistical Mechanics By D. C. Mattis

56 **Spin Fluctuations in Itinerant Electron Magnetism** By T. Moriya

57 **Polycrystalline Semiconductors**
Physical Properties and Applications
Editor: G. Harbeke

58 **The Recursion Method and Its Applications**
Editors: D. G. Pettifor and D. L. Weaire

59 **Dynamical Processes and Ordering on Solid Surfaces** Editors: A. Yoshimori and M. Tsukada

60 **Excitonic Processes in Solids**
By M. Ueta, H. Kanzaki, K. Kobayashi, Y. Toyozawa, and E. Hanamura

61 **Localization, Interaction, and Transport Phenomena** Editors: B. Kramer, G. Bergmann, and Y. Bruynseraede

62 **Theory of Heavy Fermions and Valence Fluctuations** Editors: T. Kasuya and T. Saso

63 **Electronic Properties of Polymers and Related Compounds**
Editors: H. Kuzmany, M. Mehring, and S. Roth

64 **Symmetries in Physics** Group Theory Applied to Physical Problems
By W. Ludwig and C. Falter

65 **Phonons: Theory and Experiments II**
Experiments and Interpretation of Experimental Results By P. Brüesch

66 **Phonons: Theory and Experiments III**
Phenomena Related to Phonons
By P. Brüesch

67 **Two-Dimensional Systems: Physics and New Devices**
Editors: G. Bauer, F. Kuchar, and H. Heinrich

68 **Phonon Scattering in Condensed Matter V**
Editors: A. C. Anderson and J. P. Wolfe

69 **Nonlinearity in Condensed Matter**
Editors: A. R. Bishop, D. K. Campbell, P. Kumar, and S. E. Trullinger

70 **From Hamiltonians to Phase Diagrams**
The Electronic and Statistical-Mechanical Theory of sp-Bonded Metals and Alloys By J. Hafner

71 **High Magnetic Fields in Semiconductor Physics**
Editor: G. Landwehr

72 **One-Dimensional Conductors**
By S. Kagoshima, H. Nagasawa, and T. Sambongi

73 **Quantum Solid-State Physics**
Editors: S. V. Vonsovsky and M. I. Katsnelson

74 **Quantum Monte Carlo Methods in Equilibrium and Nonequilibrium Systems** Editor: M. Suzuki

75 **Electronic Structure and Optical Properties of Semiconductors** 2nd Edition
By M. L. Cohen and J. R. Chelikowsky

76 **Electronic Properties of Conjugated Polymers**
Editors: H. Kuzmany, M. Mehring, and S. Roth

77 **Fermi Surface Effects**
Editors: J. Kondo and A. Yoshimori

78 **Group Theory and Its Applications in Physics**
By T. Inui, Y. Tanabe, and Y. Onodera

79 **Elementary Excitations in Quantum Fluids**
Editors: K. Ohbayashi and M. Watabe

80 **Monte Carlo Simulation in Statistical Physics**
An Introduction 2nd Edition
By K. Binder and D. W. Heermann

81 **Core-Level Spectroscopy in Condensed Systems**
Editors: J. Kanamori and A. Kotani

82 **Photoelectron Spectroscopy**
Principle and Applications
By S. Hüfner

83 **Physics and Technology of Submicron Structures**
Editors: H. Heinrich, G. Bauer, and F. Kuchar

84 **Beyond the Crystalline State** An Emerging Perspective By G. Venkataraman, D. Sahoo, and V. Balakrishnan

85 **The Quantum Hall Effects**
Fractional and Integral 2nd ed.
By T. Chakraborty and P. Pietiläinen

86 **The Quantum Statistics of Dynamic Processes**
By E. Fick and G. Sauermann

87 **High Magnetic Fields in Semiconductor Physics II**
Transport and Optics Editor: G. Landwehr

88 **Organic Superconductors**
By T. Ishiguro and K. Yamaji

89 **Strong Correlation and Superconductivity**
Editors: H. Fukuyama, S. Maekawa, and A. P. Malozemoff

Printing: Mercedesdruck, Berlin
Binding: Buchbinderei Lüderitz & Bauer, Berlin